Reap Justice

By Annie Pearson

Chaos House

RESTORATION RULES SERIES
No One Dies
Reap Justice
Call the Reavers

RAIN CITY INCIDENTS SERIES
The Grrrl of Limberlost
Artemis in the Desert
Nine Volt Heart
The Pirate King

Restoration Rules
Number Two

Reap Justice

Annie Pearson

For JRS, who always wants another story.

Contents

Epigraph — *ix*

Milestones: The Foxes of Marborne Parish — *x*

Day 1, Tuesday: The Heroic Code

1. A Knight Bachelor, at Least — *3*
2. Foxe Kits — *9*
3. Vero, Vero — *18*
4. The Hawkers' Master — *30*
5. A Scholar and a Young Earl — *34*
6. A Spectacle — *46*
7. Cudgels and a Book — *58*
8. Intelligence — *71*
9. Night Tales — *79*
10. A Watcher's Sinecure — *87*
11. A Forger, a Spy, and a Warrior — *94*

Day 2, Wednesday: Mazes

12. A Letter by Lamplight — *105*
13. A London Marvel — *111*
14. A Portraitist — *115*
15. A Hawker and a Peterman — *121*
16. Xanthus House — *126*
17. A Demon — *131*
18. A Barrister — *139*
19. Pocket Pickers — *146*
20. Chancery Lane — *155*
21. Holborn — *167*
22. Knightsbridge — *179*
23. Tidying Up — *189*
24. Lincoln's Inn — *195*
25. St James Place — *207*
26. Pillar to Post — *224*
27. Two Pounds Sterling — *230*
28. Arcadia House — *240*
29. Epiphany — *254*

Day 3, Thursday: Discoveries
30. Polity — *259*
31. Treasures — *266*
32. Commerce — *276*
33. Chalgrove House — *279*
34. Revelation — *294*
35. Confederation — *303*
36. Visitant — *316*
37. Three Weaknesses — *328*
38. Black Tribute — *340*
39. St James Square — *355*
40. Yearning for Home — *367*
41. A Proud Heart Knows — *377*
42. Duties Not Dreamt Of — *385*
43. Regard the Gods — *391*
Day 4, Friday: To Undreamed Shores
44. How to Flee — *403*
45. Sin-concealing Chaos — *441*
46. If the Gods Are Willing — *419*
47. Under the Tower's Shadow — *430*
48. Knights of the Marborne Fens — *441*
49. Fortune's Wheel — *450*
50. No Apologies — *460*
51. Pool of London — *469*
52. The Phoenix — *479*
53. The Zeewolf — *489*
54. Magic and the Sanest Man — *495*
55. A Sure Uncertainty — *505*
56. Littlecote House — *512*
57. A Fête — *522*
58. Calculations — *531*
59. Resolutions — *541*
Day 5, Saturday: Out of This Nettle
60. Let Me Hear Thee Going — *555*
A Casual Glossary for the Curious — *567*
Author's Notes — *576*

Reap Justice

Restoration Defined:
1) The era after the English Civil Wars
when the monarchy was restored.
2) The Foxe family actions to achieve restorative justice
when English law fails.

—

The Foxe Family's Restoration Rules:
No one dies.
Reap justice, shun revenge.
Never trick a woman.
Reave when sins are ripe.
Never bilk a neighbor.
Our allies shall be innocent.

—

Doctor Foxe's Rules for Enlightened People
I keep my promises.
My family obligations are sacred.
I was born to help others.
The world improves from my toil.
I never fool an honest man.

Milestones:
The Foxes of Marborne Parish

1650: Samuel Foxe leads local royalists in Civil War
Commonwealth & Interregnum, 1649–1660

1655: Samuel Foxe is 15th Earl of Marborne
Oliver Cromwell is Lord Protector

1660: Foxe cousins born, 1659–1661
Restoration; Charles II, 1660–1685

1665: Foxe cousins orphaned
London Plague and Great Fire

1670: Foxe cousins at Revelstone House
Test Act, 1673

1675: Ysabel serves Mary Stuart; Rowland in Paris
Mary Stuart marries William of Orange, 1677

1680: Ysabel and Rowland in Amsterdam
Charles II repeatedly dissolves Parliament

1685: Ysabel at home, February; Rowland at home, August
James II, 1685–1688
Duke of Monmouth invades, June
...
James deposed, 1688
Mary II & William III, 1689–1702

Day 1, Tuesday:
The Heroic Code

Fortune, the great commandress of the world,
Hath diverse ways to advance her followers:
To some she gives honour without deserving,
To other some, deserving without honour;
Some wit, some wealth,
and some wit without wealth...
— The Poet Known as Homer, *The Iliad*
(George Chapman, translator)

1

A Knight Bachelor, at Least

⮜❦.❦⮞

— MR. CORNELIUS ROSEWURME —

CHALGROVE HOUSE,
COVENT GARDEN

CORNELIUS ROSEWURME SHRUGGED ON the gold-braided crimson brocade coat his wife had ordered made for him. Its long, Paris-style skirts swishing around his legs reminded him of how he'd last enfolded his dear but now departed wife, which led him to cross his arms in remembrance of that sweet embrace.

Cornelius appeared every bit the man he played in London. Deuce it! He looked like a man who deserved to be Sir Cornelius, given all he'd done for certain English lords. A Knight Bachelor, at least. Yet he still labored at his many hawking ventures, simply because no lord wanted Cornelius's services to be known in the public square.

The newly hired, overly timid footman knocked at Cornelius Rosewurme's bedchamber door. "My lord? I…I beg your pardon. Good…um…good day."

Bless him, the lad had quickly adopted the customs of the house, calling Cornelius "my lord" the way former servants addressed their mistress as "my lady" (but who'd struggled to properly address him when he became master).

"Yes, Frank. What is it?"

"I'm called Farley, my lord."

"Sorry, lad. My mind wandered. The boy before you was called Frank." Cornelius privately vowed to never again make that mistake. He'd heard his own name mangled often enough.

"Once more, my lord, there's a woman on the front steps asking for the master of the house."

"You have your instructions. Inform all visitors that I'm on the Continent. You do not know when I shall return."

"But she asked for a Cornelius Knatchgull, so I—"

"S'welp me, did I not explain the first day you came here? It doesn't matter what name any woman...ah, or man asks."

It was so hard to find servants to take care of their assigned business without sticking their noses in his. Too bad he'd had so little time with his wife that he had no chance to learn from her the skill of managing servants.

"Yes, my lord. You are absent to any inquiring woman." The fellow lingered. "My lord, Cook says six of your elixir bottles broke in the night. It's the heat, Cook says, and none of her fault."

"I shall conduct a review of the circumstances." Cornelius returned to settling his collar and cuffs.

The sun rose over the rooftops of the houses opposite, lighting the tinted diamond window panes and casting jewel-colored shapes on the floor of his late wife's dressing room. Each morning, he sighed in pleasure because that light was a blessing bestowed by his own dear flittermouse. She'd lived in this simple beauty, no crinkum-crankum in this house.

Never one for vanity, Cornelius treasured in the private chambers of his heart that his late wife had insisted that the Creator had endowed Cornelius with a finer countenance than most men. He tipped the looking glass to tie his cravat in his own special way, to hide that his Creator marked the advancing of years only on his neck.

"S'welp me," Cornelius said aloud, "God Himself thrust me into my dear lady's arms."

She'd married him in late spring. Then, like a dying summer rose, she faded and was gone. Under law, she could not leave him her title, but he did possess her house, which was a comfort. In the end, the courts would pass the remainder of her wealth to him, though his barrister never used the word "speedily," however much Cornelius was obliged to offer gratuities and significant sums for expenses.

Odspitikins! Cornelius had paid a bounty to a wizened scribe in Fleet Street for his beloved's will and testament. If chancery required more documents, he'd be forced to spend more silver on that wretched scribbler. Meanwhile, Cornelius must continue the soul-grinding tasks required to assist his patrons. As soon as the courts ruled, he'd resign those alliances and let those lords find new agents to support their endeavors.

Cornelius finished arranging his cravat. Fruits, flowers, birds, and cherubs flowed in a delicate cascade along the frame of the Venetian mirror, in the same way his spirit cascaded with exuberant affection at the thought of his dearworthy wife. Cornelius believed Grinling Gibbons himself had carved the frame, which brought to mind that he needed to invite an agent to assess its value.

Ready for his work in the world, Cornelius passed through the empty kitchen (Cook must be gone to the market) and went to check the still room. The six broken bottles had been swept up, either by Cook or the day-girl.

Assured that no one was near, Cornelius pried up a tile in the farthest corner of the still room. Lifting the box from below the floor, he poured in the farthings his hawkers had earned for him over the last week. The screech of the tile soothed him as he shoved it securely in place.

He removed the cover from the largest of the crockery and determined that the new aqua vitae did well. A premium product. He had the contented sense of having done well with his talents, tending to this part of his livelihood like a country gentleman tends to his cattle. He stirred genever into a new crock of elixir, the smell of juniper berries rushing up his nose.

He began packing the flats of bottles to deliver to his boys, smiling at the thought of how they'd admire the red ink on the new labels for the same old elixir. Today, with Cornelius's clever change to the labels, they'd proclaim Doctor Roseworld's Elixir for the Faltering to be a grand scientific progress.

~

"My lord, I have your messages from the King's Head."

"Very good, Farley," Cornelius said, looking up from where he gently stacked flats of elixir in the still room. "Leave them on that little table in the foyer."

"Yes, my lord. But one has 'urgent' writ on it. And it has a wax seal that's stamped."

"Read it to me. I'm due at a meeting and haven't time for others' business."

Over the clink of elixir bottles he slipped into the flats, he heard Farley prying at the seal. When Cornelius had needed a new footman, Farley was the best found at the wage offered, but it was painful to hear him read aloud. Cornelius preached to all his lads that reading gave a smart boy his way out of the gutter. He must warn Farley to improve his skills. For instance, Farley just then read: "Rosewurme, *mon petit homme*." But he stammered and pronounced it *moon pet-it home*, not knowing what he read.

Yet Cornelius felt a fire spark in his belly not because of the halting reader, but because of the message's author. Such anger had been a stranger to his heart while he lived in this house, guided by the love of his wife. Without her by his side, the old fire of resentment was kindled again.

Farley didn't seem to notice the change in Cornelius's stance and expression. He read on:

> We require your knights of the blade again on Friday mid-day, as we did at Easter week. And Lord W requires an accounting for his pamphlets. Wednesday afternoon at...

"I'm sorry, my lord. The number is difficult to make out. A three, mayhap. Or it could a nine."

"It cannot be a nine," Cornelius said. "Read the rest, Farley."

"Yes, sir. 'Wednesday afternoon at three o'clock, my little man. No later.' Then it is signed D-U-X."

"Thank you, Farley." His hand gripped a bottle of elixir, his knuckles white. He set the bottle down with care, intending to betray nothing to the world of how Sir Duxwold's condescension vexed him. "My lads are waiting on me. Please fetch the news case from the work room. You did pack it last night, I trust."

"Yes, my lord."

Cornelius perched his hat jauntily, the good boiled felt one with the Biscayne-blue ostrich feather, and made sure his cravat remained in place. With the news case slung over one shoulder and the elixir flats under the other arm, he exited his beautiful house by way of the kitchen door and the garden, escaping unseen up the alleyway, regretting that the rough dirt lane made passage so difficult in his good scarlet heels. He increased his speed as soon as his heels met decent cobbles on the main road, where a footman chased away beggars from the corner. As usual when encountering such scenes, he crossed the street to escape the clamor. Once, a long, long time ago, he'd been such a beggar, chased away from nice houses like his.

His lads lolled about at a crossing-way near the King's Head tavern. Cornelius distributed flats to the elixir hawkers, pointing out the new red-ink labels. "Proclaim this elixir as brand new from the scientists at Oxford."

Then he distributed pamphlets to the smaller lads. His heart (and a desire for his wife to smile on him from heaven) made him cautious about which pamphlets to give the youngest mites to flog. Not one of his boys should be lashed for the sake of his patron's religious screed. Those papers went only to the fastest boys.

"Farewell till the morrow!" He sent them on their way.

A dropped pamphlet wafted onto the toe of his shoe. He picked it up, seeing the headline his lordship had insisted on for this new batch of pamphlets: "Prepare to Fight Papal Tyranny Once More." Twenty-five years ago, he'd peddled papers that welcomed the supposedly Protestant king, Charles, back to England. All the turmoil of the war and the interregnum were to be forgotten while every man in England rushed into the Restoration. That's how he'd met the duke, his first mentor. Now, here he was sending boys out to stir men against the Catholic king, James.

Was the world once again turning upside down?

He shouted after his lads as they hurried up the street. "Watch out for each other! And stay away from the militia!"

Cornelius groused that the new king had no business keeping an army on the streets of London when there was no war. No use grumbling out under the hot sun. Best find ale and a pie at a tavern, with company to share his complaints.

2
Foxe Kits

-ᴡᴏ.ᴏ⌒-

—THOMAS CAIUS FOXE—

BENSON'S LODGING HOUSE
COVENT GARDEN

"SHALL WE REVEL IN the bearbaiting today?"

Tom Foxe had spent the last half year in bed, trying not to die. Now, he wanted more. He wanted…whatever came next. Meanwhile, it was taking too long for the troop of Foxe kits and their friends to finish breakfast.

"That is to say," Tom goaded for a response, "if the king hasn't closed the pleasure gardens for fear of rebellion."

"Good stars, in this heat? Your passion overwhelms your good sense." His twin Tamsin, their captain, was a model of brilliance and compassion, who assessed each of their talents and flaws too accurately. Tamsin's dark hair and snub nose could be called charming; the same features were forgettable in Tom. "You and Ned heaved your supper the last time you saw bears baited."

"Nay, only Ned heaved his. I'm sturdier than that." Was. In former days.

Ned, his bone-white hair flashing in a stray sunbeam, didn't look up from pitching pennies with Perry Frake. A devil-drawer, Ned created forged paintings that helped keep them afloat for the past decade. No need for that now, because five days earlier, Tamsin and Rowland Foxe had led a special restoration to destroy the cheat who'd ruined their Uncle Absolom's last days. As a consequence of that gambol, they'd escaped dire poverty, and the king had at last restored the Marborne earldom to their family.

On this Tuesday, as the cousins and their friends dawdled over oat porridge and Spanish oranges, they didn't look like land pirates. Or cavalier thieves, if anyone knew to accuse them of such. But no one outside this hired room had knowledge of their doings, which strictly followed their Restoration Rules.

When the kitchen maid gathered away the empty breakfast trays, the lodging-house footman set down a silver salver bearing two letters. Action at last, however modest!

Tom prepared to break the seal on his letter. Tamsin circled her palm with one finger. Reminded, he passed two farthings to the footman, which might be too much, but surely their large party overstretched the lodging-house staff.

"Bones of me!" Tom protested as he read. "The barber on Henrietta Street promises that Mr. Foxe's periwig has been restored and will be returned to him for a shocking amount of silver. This is your letter, Rollo. It's your wig."

Rowland glanced up from where he flirted with the dark and regal Lizzie Foxe. He was tall, with a decent-enough face for polite society, and had been surprised—no, alarmed!—last Friday to find himself the Earl of Marborne. "It's you, Tom, who wore *my* good Paris wig out in the rain. Hence, the damage must be to your purse." He opened the other letter, glanced at it, then made to tuck it under his breakfast plate.

Lizzie trapped the letter under her hand. "That letter has a Crown seal. In all fairness, you cannot hide it from us." When he yielded, she read it aloud:

> The Crown of England promises a gratuity to the king's intelligencers, Lieutenant Rowland Matthew Foxe and Sergeant Peregrine Frake, for service in discovering the traitor, Danvers Duncombe, and his syndicate which supported the Duke of Monmouth's rebellion.

"Go, miting," Lizzie said. "See your colonel today."

Rowland didn't glance up from peeling an orange. "I abide by the principles Absolom taught us. Such gratuities corrupt the soul. I shan't accept one farthing."

"Not farthings," Tom said, taking the letter from Lizzie. "It's to be the king's gold."

Perry, being taller than most men, reached across Ned, then across the table to snatch the letter from Tom. Among them, only Perry resembled a pirate, with his fiercely-drawn face and straw-colored locks.

"It says, 'And Peregrine Frake,' which is me, my mother's oldest son. I shall accept my part, Rollo. My mother and my five brothers depend on me. And your own relations depend on you now. Will they mind if you forego the sum of…" Reading the amount, Perry whistled. "You canna refuse. I find your bennish principles distressing, my lord."

Leave it to Perry, far more brilliant than the Goliath he appeared to be, to remember to call Rowland "my lord," when his cousins most often forgot.

Tom said, "*Vero, vero,* you must accept what the king offers, Lord Rollo, so as not to offend."

"Thou, Thomas Foxe, dost speak with the wisdom of angels in heaven," Perry said. "But I beg you, no Latin. We are in an English dining salon, not a magistrate's courtroom, where I intend to never be found."

Tamsin next had the letter from Perry. "Good stars! It's far too much to refuse, Rollo. Especially given the paltry wages you had over the last ten years."

"Hear, hear!" Perry said. "Think like an earl, Rollo. Did we ever meet any titled lord who'd turn his back on gold, honestly earned or otherwise?"

Rowland said, "I feel in my bones that outsized gratuities and emoluments open the devil's door to civic corruption. Hence, I have never accepted a gratuity for doing my duty."

"That accounts for your abject poverty," Lizzie said, "during all the years you served on the Continent."

"Emoluments oil the wheels of England's commerce," Tom said. "For shipping from the Pool of London. For the courts that govern law and inheritance. For the king's officers and diplomats. Gratuities like this keep us civilized."

"Yet Uncle Absolom insisted," Rowland said, "that this rotten system of briberies will end as soon as enlightened people refuse to take part."

"Nothing is gained," Tom said, "by your personal refusal. Absolom meant that all the people must refuse at the same time. *Exampli gratia*, as we say in law, by an Act of Parliament."

"Speak me no Latin." Perry wagged a finger, as if offended.

Rowland's eyes darted, as if his resolution might be battered. "I feel that I—"

"Must accept it," Lizzie and Perry said together.

"Especially," Lizzie said, "since the king so kindly restored the Marborne title without requiring us to pay a garnishment."

"It was kind of him not to require such," Tamsin added, rather archly, "for what should always have been ours."

"It's commonly known that the king," Tom imitated his most gaseous tutor from Trinity College, "can command a garnishment for any title in abeyance."

"You all believe 'the better part of valor' is to accept?" Rowland frowned, his one quizzical eyebrow rising far above the other. "Then I shall, but only for the good of the family."

Lizzie had the letter again from Tamsin. "What a fine prize, lambkin! We should go out this morning to buy clothes for when we meet the king." Lizzie, always fit to meet royalty, had appeared at breakfast in a gown of mourning-grey, like a Barbary dove, while the others resembled dusty sparrows.

Tom said, "I'd rather prefer to—"

Lizzie wasn't listening. "Not one of you owns so much as a handkerchief that's fit for the king's court. A morning spent shopping will be invigorating."

"Collecting my gratuity will be invigorating," Perry said. "Come along, Mr. Wijck. We are going to meet our colonel."

Ned went upstairs to fetch his hat and the other two of their party, Tamsin's particular friend, Camilla Candecote, and Tom's physician, Winwood Oakes. For the last half year, Winwood had been dosing Tom with a physick if he so much as lost an eyelash. Then last week, their friend Camilla, the opposite of piratical with her honey-colored curls and lace, took a shot from an ancient pistol, giving Winwood a new body to tend.

"We are walking to Portugal Street, to find the best shops," Lizzie said to Camilla, who embraced the notion, discounting Winwood's admonition to guide her health.

Tom, it seemed, was consigned to the ladies' party, with Winwood's caution to avoid exerting himself. It was, at least, better than no action at all. Besides, it would be their first adventure in buying new clothes, since before now, they'd only ever bought clothes out of pawn.

— YSABEL FLORES FOXE —

LIZZIE, HAPPY AND INVIGORATED, led Tamsin, Camilla, and Tom through six shops in Portugal Street. She chattered, because sometimes the coming change to their lot in life felt overwhelming.

"I wish we could be there," she said, "when the lords recognize the Marborne title on Friday."

"We should have a feast that night," Camilla said. "Rollo will be so happy."

"I'm not sure about that," Tamsin said. "He doesn't yet seem comfortable being earl. Our Lizzie, though, quite likes the notion of becoming the Countess of Marborne."

"Yes, I do not deny that ambition." Especially since Rowland was to be earl, and not Tom. She loved Tom like a brother, which was exactly why a union could never have worked when it was thought that Tom would be the earl.

Tom, she felt sure, would be happier when he finally became a barrister. That led Lizzie to notice that Tom's vitality was severely drained. She led their little party to settle on a shop with an array of both new and pawned finery. Proving what she'd noticed, Tom sank onto a small, hard bench just inside the shop door. He idly fingered the fabric of a suit that hung nearby, a deep Bristol Red linen suit, embroidered in figures of the same rich shade of red and lined with silk taffeta in cane-buff. When the clerk offered help, Tom glanced up to refuse, the smudge under his eyes as dark as coal ash. She'd seen that smudge and his cautious glance each time Tom strove to hide his fatigue from the others. His rouge, which she'd applied before breakfast, no longer covered the splotches from his illness. Half the patches she'd pasted over his pox scars were gone.

However, Lizzie's attention was captured by a silk gown in a bright color that her painter brother Ned called Merry Widow yellow, which gave off its own light, glimmering like gold coins soaked in vinegar and burnished. She didn't need the clerk to tell her the silk was from Italy. Her fingers knew at first touch. The quality of the braid and embroidery was nearly as good as what she'd do with her own needle, though she had no time for that here in London. She'd wear this gown when the Earl of Marborne introduced them at the king's court.

Tamsin's voice drifted to her. "This seems frivolous." She held an overly decorated garnet-colored gown that a dowager must have pawned. If Lizzie could rework the cloth and decor, she'd get two gowns out of it, at least. But that wasn't what provoked Tamsin's comment.

"Whether it is frippery depends on where you are," Lizzie said. "In the king's court, clothes can be power. Or not."

Lizzie felt ready to make up her mind about the gold gown, but when she looked up from that treasure, she found Tamsin and Camilla hesitating among too many choices. Tamsin asked, "Are these the best colors for mourning?"

Camilla held a shimmering blue dress, a color called watchet that Ned used in landscape paintings. "I wonder what Doctor Foxe would advise. Perhaps nothing too shiny?"

They paused over the finery, Tamsin's and Camilla's eyes darting between each other.

Lizzie lost her spark. They all fell into a long moment's sense of loss, even Tom on the settle, where he was busy pretending he wasn't dead with fatigue. Absolom, their great-uncle and caretaker, had died ten days ago, a sharp loss that often rose to burst their bubbling joy over the defeat of their enemy and their escape from poverty.

"You're right, of course," Lizzie said, though she couldn't yet release that shining-gold silk gown.

Camilla shrugged off a thought, then spoke up to justify embroidery. "Not with pearls. Only good needlework. Doctor Foxe always admired my needlework, which was very kind of him, since yours is a marvel, Lizzie."

Tamsin held a pewter-grey gown, quite suitable for sober mourning, but stared elsewhere, her eyes dark, like the day they'd lost Absolom. Their uncle had been a guiding presence throughout their lives. Absolom had one day, a decade earlier, declared all their fates, and now Lizzie could again smell the smoke of his pipe while remembering his words.

Tamsin shall save the parish, Absolom said. She'd worked hard at that, then succeeded the previous week. Tamsin had embraced the fate Absolom named, and was happy, having Camilla at her side every day.

Rowland shall, Absolom claimed, serve the true king. He'd spent ten years in service on the Continent, taken advantage of by the lords and liars that Charles Stuart sent as ambassadors.

Absolom had judged Lizzie's brother Ned as a good soul with talented hands. So true! And now, Ned no longer had to produce forgeries to pay the Marborne mortgage.

Tom's fate, as Absolom declared it, will be to bring the law into service for everyone. During the months when everyone feared for his life, Tom had claimed only to be malingering, dodging his dreary clerkship.

Lizzie must serve a queen, Absolom had said. Rushing into that fate, she'd left home first, serving the Princess Mary for a decade, until she was sent home, instructed by Mary to find a titled husband. Which would be soon! With Rowland! Then she'd be welcomed back to real service, instead of the inconsequential errands she'd been performing for people from Mary's court.

The shoppers remained undecided, lost together in a fog. Tom held out his hand. "Let me hold that gown for you, Lizzie. The gold silk suits you. We won't always be in mourning."

Cradling the gown, Lizzie halted.

Tom said, "I cannot imagine Uncle Absolom objecting to a bit of elegance in the king's court. He had not one puritan bone in his body."

Lizzie nodded, though she didn't know Absolom's ideas about mourning clothes, only that he'd always trusted their judgment. She let Tom hold the gold silk. Then she chose a second gown, embroidered brocade in a shade of dove-grey similar to her walking-dress. Camilla chose a tawney-colored gown with a separate snow-white bodice, its embroidery nearly as complex and fine as Lizzie's own needlework. Tamsin kept her first choice of a simple pewter-grey gown. Lizzie silently promised to add modest art with her needle, knowing not to offend Tamsin with lace and ruffles.

Then Lizzie quickly made selections for the men who'd gone with Rowland to collect the king's gratuity. For Ned, a bottle-green brocade suit, and, for Perry, a whey-colored suit of light wool, both with long, Paris-style coats. She also chose an embroidered scarlet waistcoat for Perry, declaring that Ned would approve since it was a color he loved to paint.

Finally, she chose a rich ultramarine suit for Rowland and a russet one for Tom, both with double rows of brass buttons and deep cuffs, plus wide skirts on the long coats. She prompted Tom to try it on, but he said, "I trust you, queen of all needlewomen, to assess what's best for any man."

Tom then paid for it all and left a gratuity for the clerk, though Lizzie longed to tell him that was not customary. However, the poor clerk had spent considerable time waiting while the Foxe kits chased their tails.

Tom was out the door first, clearly eager to return to their lodgings. Camilla tucked her arm in his elbow—as if Tom had the strength to assist her on the street. When Lizzie glanced back at the shop, Tamsin was making another purchase. A gentleman's sword-stick! Tamsin was telling the clerk, "It's to be a present for my brother."

They walked to their lodgings, with Tamsin admonishing Tom to walk slowly for Camilla's sake. Lizzie felt her vigor rising again, eager to show the others how she'd saved them from a shopping chore they'd avoided since Saturday last.

3

Vero, Vero

ROWLAND TOUCHED THE CORNER of Lizzie's mouth, catching a tiny drop of honey from her taffety tart. He licked his finger and winked at her. Almost made her laugh.

"Lord Marborne, you have a message," the footman said.

Tom tugged at Rowland's coat sleeve, whispering, "Attend, Rollo," which roused him from being so absorbed with Lizzie.

"Bless you, Adam. It's no intrusion." Rowland still didn't hear *Lord Marborne* as his own name.

Adam said, "My uncle's master had a card for the playhouse today. Hearing that we are hosting the new Earl of Marborne, he sent the card here, so you might take your pleasure."

"How very kind," Rowland said. "Is there time enough?"

"It's three o'clock, your lordship. The play begins at four. If they start on time. Which, I'm told, doesn't happen often."

"Please send your uncle's master a bottle of port with my gratitude." He caught Tamsin circling her palm and took her meaning. "Add it to our reckoning, Adam."

He passed two farthings from the coins in his pocket as a gratuity, then studied the theatre pass, a delightful gift. But Lizzie wrinkled her nose as she read the card.

"'A Shakespearean Spectacle.' In this heat? No, thank you, your lordship. It's better if you come with me, Rollo." Bewitching and beloved, Lizzie waved her own invitation for three days with friends of the Princess Mary. She whispered a name from their shared past in Amsterdam, where the princess lived, married to her cousin, William of Orange. "Colonel Kilbuck asked me to meet three lords who claim to be Mary's friends."

"'Meet?' No, thank you. I am no longer a spy. Perry and I resigned from the king's service this morning." After a decade skulking on the Continent as a poverty-stricken Crown intelligencer, Rowland intended to live his own life henceforth.

"Spy is an ugly word," Lizzie said. "We were raised to serve the Crown. I am compelled to help Mary."

"We must work for Marborne. Mary Stuart has others to hold her pearl-stitched skirts. The English royals do not need our help."

"We were raised to serve the Crown," Lizzie repeated.

Am I failing her somehow? "My mistress' eyes are raven black..." *O Dark Lady, be gentle with me.*

Rowland whispered, "Absolom claimed we must endure monarchy until Parliament proves it can rule justly. I serve the Crown for the sake of peace in England, not for any particular royal person." And he did not want royal machinations to divide her from him. "Besides, it's my first chance to see Shakespeare played on a London stage. Please come, Lizzie."

"I shall join you another day, lambkin. Today, I have promises I cannot abandon." She touched his hand with what he hoped was regret, then went up to her room.

Left behind, Rowland clutched the playhouse card in his hand, rose from the table, and glanced around for his hat.

Perry called, "Watch out, Rollo. You heard the rumor today from our colonel. Danvers Duncombe's friends want revenge. Make sure you aren't followed."

~

Rowland stepped out the door, choosing odd turnings and two double-backs and frequently looking over his shoulder on his way to the theatre, all while considering which of the Bard's words best expressed how Lizzie disturbed his soul.

"'There's beggary in the love that can be reckon'd.'" He spoke aloud as he walked to Drury Lane.

That earned glances from a muffin hawker and a band of urchins, as if he were a lunatic loose on the town. No, he was just an ordinary man (with an unlooked-for title hung on him), exhilarated at the prospect of the playhouse. Absolom and Shakespeare had worked as a pair to form Rowland's notion of the world. "'There's beggary...'" He'd seized a good line for this very moment from...what play? Ah, *Antony and Cleopatra*. He spoke the general's answer, too.

"'Then must thou needs find out new heaven, new earth.'"

How to convince Lizzie that they could now walk "a new earth," freed from their former service to Stuart royalty? When he'd resigned from the king's service that morning, he told the colonel that he'd now be too well-known to overhear rumors while gambling with diplomats' sycophants. In truth, before the Marborne title fell on his head, he wanted out of service, appalled at his small role in the king's many executions after the Duke of Monmouth's failed rebellion.

While still wishing Lizzie had come with him, Rowland liked that she hadn't demanded that he trail after her. Her allegiance to Princess Mary was ten years in the making. He would not interfere, but he couldn't join her. He badly needed an afternoon with the Bard, given the duties he now shouldered. That morning, Tamsin posited that the new earl should make a gift to the parish cottagers and freeholders of fifteen cows and thirty sheep. Never in the twenty-five years of his life had Rowland been obliged to buy one cow, much less fifteen of the beasts. Yet he agreed: most of what they'd earned in last week's restoration must be put to work for the parish. How long could they live on what they'd earned? Five years? He'd have to admonish his cousins to live frugally while they searched for new income.

"'The better part of valor...'"

That line from Shakespeare echoed when he'd agreed that he couldn't refuse gratuities from the Crown. To feed villages (and keep his cousins from returning to piracy), he needed to take every possible advantage a peer of the realm might have, while still abiding by Absolom's guidance for enlightened people. He'd accepted the king's gratuity, because his family needed the money. He had to figure how to avoid such corrupting compromises going forward, while finding which of his perverse talents might help keep Marborne out of poverty.

But he didn't want to think about how to finance Marborne. He wanted to think about Lizzie. She'd said she loved him, but he still feared that she didn't mean "love" like the burning punk smoldering in Rowland's heart for the five years he'd served English diplomats in Amsterdam. He'd lived near where Lizzie served the Princess Mary.

But never close enough.

— EDUARD WIJCK —

WHILE THE OTHERS DAWDLED through luncheon, Ned and Perry played Game of Cupid. The footman had loaned them a pasteboard so old it might have come from Spain on the Armada. While they played, Perry didn't take note of half the moves Ned made. After a dozen throws of the dice, Perry cried, "I forfeit! Such a drubbing you've given me, Eduard Wijck."

Ned said, "The Fates have gifted me with luck."

And also, Absolom taught him strategy for games of luck. Ned smiled at the pleasure of that memory. Zooterkins, but he missed his crafty old uncle. He got so caught up thinking about the blessed man, he was surprised when Perry's hands brushed his paint-stained fingers when dropping the dice into their battered leather case. This many days together—eight!—and still Ned's heart skipped at each stray touch.

"Rollo and Miss Foxe have gone their own ways." Perry addressed the others in the salon. "Shall we see more of London?"

Ned agreed, unfolding his boney frame from the table. But then, he had become used to taking up whatever idea Perry had for adventures in London.

Tom said, "I'll come along." As if every single body in the room didn't see that Lizzie had run Tom off his legs earlier.

"I don't want to say…" Tamsin began one of her nags disguised as a suggestion, but then trailed off and didn't finish.

Tom's shoulders rose to his ears, but everyone went along with it when he pretended dismay over Tamsin's concern. "Do you think me feeble? I'll have you know—"

He stood up.

It must have been too fast, because he grasped the table for support, then toppled to the floor. Tamsin leapt up with a cry.

Ned laughed. "Sit down, Tamsin. Any soul can see he's clowning. You know what Tom gets up to."

Perry stood over Tom, who did his best to play the jester while grasping Perry's hand to be hauled off the floor.

"Thou art a merry fool," Perry said. But Ned heard in his voice that he too saw through Tom's ruse.

"Need a physicking?" Winwood said.

"Thou tyrant!" Tom cried. "We agreed yesterday that I am your friend, not a patient."

"It's our fault," Tamsin said. "Lizzie made Tom traipse up and down Portugal Street with us. It's no wonder he fainted."

"It was a jest." Tom quickly lied with passion. He had always been talented that way.

"What are we doing this afternoon?"

Ned begged a return to the earlier question, certain that whatever they chose, Tom would be bullied into staying at the lodging house. Privately, Ned wagered that it'd be either Tamsin or Winwood to do it.

Perry said, "Whatever we do later, I must first stop at my mother's house to unburden myself of the greater part of the king's gratuity. Want to join us, Tom?"

Tom looked dismayed. "Alas, I have suddenly remembered my promise to consult with Camilla about her legal needs. I regret to find just now that I'm not free to visit your mother."

Zooterkins! Ned had lost his own bet so quickly. He should have known that Perry could dissuade Tom from taking on too much without nagging him, unlike what Tamsin tended to do.

The others started the long discussion it took for every venture out of the lodging house, determining who had an errand or a preferred destination, and who never wanted to venture into that part of town. Ned took to his own dodge: studying that wretched engraving of what might be a Stuart king, pasted on a board and hung on the dining salon's south wall. Fortunately, the sun was fading it, so it was more like a dream than a vivid engraving. Add a bit of color, properly done, and it might be able to be rescued from its wretchedness.

Perry said, "What do you want most, Ned?"

"Since I can now forget devil drawing," Ned said, "then of all things, I should like to paint portraits. Like Levy or Velazquez."

"I mean to ask, chucking," Perry said, "what do you want to do this afternoon?"

"Oh, of course. I did want to see if the new St Paul's is far enough along that I might draw it. Then we can walk through Bloomsbury, to see how those sorts of people choose to live." The kind of people who wanted their portraits painted.

"God's teeth, that's hard work for a hot day," Perry said.

"Aye," Ned agreed about the heat and wanted to propose what might please Perry. "We shall, therefore, be called upon to explore the variety of taverns on offer in London."

Tamsin and the others all demurred from that proposal. She looked up when Ned and Perry prepared to depart. "Don't wear your new suits out in the heat and dust. Lizzie wouldn't like to see her efforts undone before you ever meet the king."

"Me in a spanking new suit of the Paris style?" Perry said. "It'd frighten my old mum."

That then was to be Ned's day. Meet Perry's mother. See St Paul's. Tour the taverns between the Tower Hill Hamlets and Covent Garden. Alone with Perry. Ned looked about for his hat.

— THOMASINE ANA FOXE —

TAMSIN STILL WORRIED ABOUT Tom, but resolved to keep her concerns to herself. Meanwhile, Winwood again raised the question of what to do for the afternoon. "I have a letter from a cousin that begs for help with certain difficulties, without telling me more. If Camilla feels up to it, we might go meet my cousin."

"Oh, a mystery!" Camilla always yearned for adventure.

"I'll come too," Tom said. "My vigor has been restored by way of Winwood's elixir, so I can once more pursue joy."

When Tom reached for the jug of mulled wine on the table, Winwood stopped his hand, saying, "Force of will won't speed your healing."

Tom said, "We all abide by Doctor Absolom Foxe's ethical rules for enlightened people. The first rule is, 'Don't lock your litter mates in a cage.'"

Camilla said, "Tom, you simply must abide by Winwood's strictures, as I do." Her foul demon of a husband, Leighton Fairchild, had injured her the previous week; her strength still waxed and waned each day.

"If you feel up to it, I suggest we do as Rowland has done this afternoon," Winwood said. "My cousin performs at that theatre. I didn't speak up when Rollo went on his way, since it was clear he wanted no company but Miss Foxe's."

Camilla said, "We shall need walking clothes again!" She headed for upstairs, her fingers wrapped around Tamsin's wrist.

Though Camilla was excited, Tamsin changed clothes faster, so Tamsin returned to the salon before either Camilla or Winwood came downstairs. When she sank onto a chair near Tom, her skirts billowed. She'd bought the gown out of pawn on Monday, and Lizzie had mended a small tear and embroidered a lily over a stain but was too busy reading poetry and flirting with Rowland to have time to remove the excess lace and ribbon. Tamsin quarreled with her skirts.

Tom cleared his throat. "Did you notice the contretemps between Rollo and Lizzie? Yet they didn't have the good manners to share their debate with the rest of us."

"Let them have their secrets." The starched stiffening of Tamsin's bodice dug into her ribs. "Instead, worry about Rollo's new burdens. As for Lizzie, we can read her like a book. She wants only to return to the Princess Mary's court."

"Read her like a book?" Tom laughed. "She's a closed volume, clasped with a lock. And Rollo doesn't have the key."

"He knows she longs to return to court. Don't worry. Trust them to know how to get on."

"It is I who should admonish you, dear sister." Tom grasped her hand so she couldn't fiddle with the annoying lace. "Stop worrying about Marborne. Enjoy London for a few days."

She wanted to rebel against his advice. She wasn't worrying, only longing to be home, to begin the work to be done there. But instead, she changed the subject.

"How to endure these bindings and fripperies?" To manage Marborne business while Tom lay ill, she'd pretended to be him, feeling free in breeches. "This wretched gown is like prison chains."

"Poor soul! Yet it is I who am caged in this house."

"My soul weeps for your captivity." Tamsin returned the jest, grateful that Tom was well enough to resume his teasing. "You can borrow a gown to hide from Winwood. I warn you, though, you'll be donning another kind of fetters."

"Ah, an escape! I can send the footman out to hire a feminine wig from a barber. I'd be invisible with skirts and locks." He scratched at his head, where his hair was growing back after being shaved for months.

"I'll lend you a guinea for that expense." Tamsin prolonged the mutual foolery, which had been missing for months.

"Miss Foxe?" Adam the footman came in with a packet of letters that proved to have come from Revelstone. She became engrossed in reading while Tom jittered, crossing and uncrossing his legs to distract her.

"My dear Tom," she said. "It's only a message from Mrs. Bell." She held out the first sheet to him. "She sends her best wishes and says they've begun the first harvests."

"*Mirabile dictu!* I weep at what we are missing out." He took the page. "Dear sister, I long to roast in the fiery sun—"

"'While coated in the dust of the ages,' which you proclaim at every harvest. That's the difference between us. I'd rather be coated in field dust than paper dust and ink stain."

"Hurry and finish. I want to read the rest."

Tamsin nodded, reading rapidly through the housekeeper's message, then handed that sheet to Tom. She unfolded another enclosure, a torn scrap.

"My stars!" She jumped up, shivering as if ice flowed over her, then sat again. "This is for you, Tom. I didn't see the address when I opened it. But no matter, it's meant for me."

He read the scrap aloud with ridiculous dramatics.

To the Master of Revelstone: The malicious Viscount Heydon tried to prevent it, but I found a runner to carry two messages. One tells my friend Ducks in London that I have been betrayed and require revenge. This one warns you and Camilla that you shall soon burn in Hades for destroying my family. —L. Fairchild

A quick spark of fear burned through her, then a fierce determination flared. She silently vowed to protect Camilla at all costs. Leighton Fairchild would never again harm her dearest friend.

"Not at all like a gentleman." Tom handed back the scrap. He didn't show more than mild curiosity, saying, "Who might this Ducks fellow be? Leighton never brought anyone called Ducks to visit in Cambridge, I'm sure."

"Perhaps a fellow reprobate?" To sooth her agitation, Tamsin rubbed at the Archangel coin that hung from her neck on a gold chain. "What shall we do?"

"Nothing at all. Did his little huff alarm you?" He caught her hand, the one that fiddled with a strip of lace. "Our friend Heydon removed that hedge-bird from England last week. Forget about the Ducks chap. Except for swans and geese, waterfowl are never ferocious."

"But how shall we protect Camilla?"

"Do as you have planned. Push Camilla's writ of annulment through the chancery court quickly as can be. I'm still of a mind that it's best if Camilla goes to my old cully from Trinity College. Luke Holywell would do whatever is possible."

"Did you not see the threat, Tom? Leighton says he'll have Camilla killed. And me."

"Leighton is a drunken scoundrel with no true friends, much less any who'd undertake murder on his behalf. He has no wherewithal to hire an assassin." Tom still held her hand, as if to comfort her, which was ridiculous. "In point of fact, Leighton mistook you for me ever since I fell ill. In sooth, it's me he wants dead. Your worry shall prove to be for naught."

Though Tom discounted the threat, Tamsin felt an ember of anger, its smoke occluding Tom's assurances. "Are you feigning bravado for my sake? As you did when you were ill?"

"Not pretending, Tamsin." Tom again clutched her hand. "I am fearless, however frail the wide world perceives me."

"Yes, but—"

"Also, if I take up your kind offer of skirts and a new wig, I shall never be found by any assassin. You're already safe."

Camilla appeared before Tamsin could insist that she was not convinced by Tom's teasing.

"My sweet nutting," she said to Camilla, "we deserve the same freedom in London that my cousins enjoy. Let us wear the breeches I packed, so we can walk freely in London."

"We will not!" Camilla exclaimed. "This pink frock was my father's last gift. And it's perfect in this weather. We deserve to be as beautiful upon this occasion as Lizzie always is."

Camilla ignored protests and joined Winwood at the door, beckoning for Tamsin to follow.

Tamsin whispered to Tom, "Do not alarm Camilla with this news. I swear that Leighton shall never again make her afraid."

"Tell her." Tom shook his head, as if dismayed by Tamsin's resolve. "You are making a mistake. I know Camilla. She will not appreciate your project to protect her."

"I wish we weren't going out in frills, unprotected." She still wanted to persuade Camilla about the value of disguise.

"Tamsin, if an assassin comes looking—and I deny that possibility—you'll be mistaken for me if you once again wear my breeches and coat."

"I want to be free to run if I'm pursued."

"Yet I abjure you to not put my breeches in jeopardy. And stop trying to protect us all. If you're worried, ask Perry and Rollo for protection. Don't keep it a secret."

"No. I refuse to alarm Camilla." Resolution settled on her shoulders, like a heavy mantle in winter. "Leighton's threat gives him power over her. I won't allow it."

Waving for Camilla and Winwood to wait, Tamsin ran upstairs and slung over her shoulder the worn leather baldric that held the knife she carried when working in the barns and fields. Then she donned the linen coat she'd last worn to church, covering all that excess lace and ribbon. She buckled one more item onto her baldric: the sword-stick she'd purchased that morning.

— TOM —

AFTER CONSIDERABLE COMMOTION, THE others were all on their way, leaving Tom alone, because they still saw him as pathetically infirm after he'd escaped a Job's quantity of afflictions. In an instant, he was battling his habit of loneliness, though he'd resolved not to indulge that funk.

He snagged a glass and the jug of wine from luncheon, carrying them into the lodging's withdrawing room, which had two high-backed wooden settles, each suitable for only two people and devoid of even a cushion for comfort. From the sole window there, he examined the narrow street below, up to the next horizon, beyond which his dreams tugged at his desires.

His spirits had been pulled down by more than fatigue. While they were shopping, Tamsin had set off a bout of mourning that left him pondering what he owed Absolom. He'd felt like weeping in that shop, because he missed the man so much. He'd spent months, while his world had shrunk to his bedroom, feeling he'd failed his uncle. Life still felt like a too-tight suit of clothes, but he intended to launch his new plan to reach the fate Absolom had declared for him. Soon. A line from Homer flitted through his head, from when Absolom had last read to him from *The Odyssey*.

> If only the gods are willing.
> They rule the vaulting skies.
> They're stronger than I to plan
> and drive things home.

During all the months he'd been ill, his mind fluttered in meditation, often on whether he'd soon discover if anything lay beyond this life. Other times, his heart cringed at knowing he'd created a living hell for his sister and cousins, who worried deeply for him. He fought pain and fever dreams while the weight of his life fell like a stone into the small pond of the Foxe family's life.

Then one day the fever released its siege on his brain, but it wasn't like awakening from deep sleep. It was a haunting: having returned from the edge of his own grave, what did he owe his family? Now, with Absolom's sudden passing, and the equally sudden return of the Marborne title, that haunting had become more acute. What did he owe his cousins—and himself—in this spanking new world?

Time to seize his fate. He hadn't shared his plan with Tamsin. While packing for London, he'd tucked in a letter from his late master that recommended Tom as an excellent clerk with great promise. Come tomorrow, he'd visit his old school friend from Trinity, Luke Holywell, who was now a barrister at the Inns of Court. Tom intended to seek to finish his clerkship there.

The footman called to him. "You have guests, Mr. Foxe."

Surprise shook Tom him from reverie. He hadn't yet written to Luke, so no one knew him to be in London. He hoped it might be an adventure, and not the barber demanding payment for repairing Rowland's overly sumptuous Paris wig.

4

The Hawkers' Master

— C O R N E L I U S —

AFTER SETTING UP HIS lads for their day's hawking, Cornelius walked to Lincoln's Inn to visit the chambers of his barrister.

"Good day! But such a hot one." He greeted the clerk. "It's Elisha, isn't it?"

"Yes, sir. You've just missed my master. He's off for midday dinner. But please come in out of the heat."

"Alas, I regret missing him. I lost time over morning chores."

In fact, Cornelius had taken to visiting the chambers while the barrister was absent at midday, since he'd been made to feel that he importuned with his weekly questions. He carried a burden of resentment for such treatment. One man goes into a tavern and asks for ale, his money is as good as another's. The same man goes into a barrister's chambers, offers his coin, and is treated like a beggar seeking crusts. Cornelius had just reached into his pockets, believing it'd take a few farthings to get answers to his oft-repeated questions, when Elisha surprised him.

"This came for you this today, Mr. Rosewurme. I believe from the covering message that it concerns certain properties you've been enquiring about."

"How unexpected!" Cornelius exclaimed, though he'd been owed an accounting for six months. If it weren't for his dear wife's generous spirit...no, no use thinking of disaster.

"I'll leave you to take a moment to read this." Elisha was retreating into his clerk's mousehole. "If you've a message that must be returned, please call my name."

Inside the parcel he found a portion of his heart's desire: receipts for the delivery of four parcels of land to the deserving widows and orphans he had named. Ah, at last! This was the reward he'd negotiated for the last two years' work, his fond hopes for ensuring the well-being of those who'd been most kind to him in years past. He'd made enormous efforts as a humble servant of certain lords who sought more equitable distribution of land in England, land that would otherwise go to the king.

He closed his eyes, happy with the results of his labors, pleased with his own contribution to making sure that the king's ambition did not result in the control of all land in England.

With a happy sigh, he read the covering letter again, this time to the end. His happiness wafted away into the day's heat.

> Our valuation of rents lost from granting deeds to these properties is greater than your agreement with his lordship for your services. Please also find enclosed his lordship's billing for services owed as your new debt to him.

New debt?

He despised being indebted to those born in the treetops. He'd done more than all the baronets who'd dusted the path for the Stuart scions' return from France. He did better for his patrons, certainly, than the rude Sir Duxwold, who lent himself out as a message boy for better lords. Cornelius could point to the papers he preserved in his study, verifying each act done for certain English lords who preferred that the public know nothing of their private business. He deserved the reward of a title, not new debt, for all he'd done in the past decade.

> Cultivating rough pathways for lords seeking new lands and business opportunities.

> Finding hirelings to undertake work that lords couldn't trust to their own servants.

> Flogging news in the countryside, to guide men's hearts to elect men to the House of Commons, as best suited his patrons. Or, in older days, to secure men's hearts for the king, while the country continued to shirk off dissident Puritanism.

He'd leave off doing all of this as soon as his inheritance was freed by the chancery courts. While waiting, though, he had to cover expenses. He loathed the idea of dipping into the coins he preserved under his still-room floor. And of performing services that a lord demanded in payment for "new debt."

The clerk Elisha's voice stirred him. "Is everything as you wish it to be, Mr. Rosewurme?"

"Yes, s'welp me." He plucked the gratuity he'd planned from his waistcoat pocket. "Any news for me from chancery?"

"Thank you, sir." The clerk made the coins disappear. "No, we've no word on the progress of your case. The master always says that pressuring anyone in the chancery courts is like boiling water without a kettle."

"Ha!" Cornelius pretended to laugh. "No kettle? Clever."

Then why had the barrister taken coin for the very purpose of greasing Cornelius's case in chancery?

He said farewell and fled to the street, lest he betray the resentment boiling in his breast.

He trudged to The Rose off Russell Street where he asked for cool ale and a pie, then looked about for the amanuensis who wrote letters for copper coins.

When he found the little scribbler, he dictated four letters of fond affection and hopes to visit come fall. He had to be clever in how he asked for confirmation that each had received a deed for her cottage and garden. He didn't want to raise hopes if any woman had not yet received a deed. He didn't know how to press a cause with his lordship if no deed had been forthcoming. He needed to ponder that, because if there was any man in England who was likely to cheat those who served him, it was the lord he'd toiled under for the past year.

He couldn't promise to be free, even by Michaelmas, so his letters expressed only vague hopes to visit soon. However, he felt a longing for a progression through Oxford and the south of England once the heat passed. Such a journey to visit those dear women promised days of succor and joy.

After passing coin to the letter-writing fellow, plus directions for where and how each letter was to be sent, Cornelius fell to savoring his mutton pie. To calm the turmoil beneath his ribs, he turned to memories of his dear lost wife, as if her hands might pluck away the thorn of resentment. He had every intention of meeting his beloved in heaven without his soul being muddied by bitterness over his treatment by peers of the realm. Rather, he intended to arrive at heaven's door as a Knight Bachelor.

"Cornelius? You didn't ask for me? You cruel man."

When he turned to answer, his face was suddenly pressed against a soft feminine bosom. He inhaled a dew of rosemary over the human musk of a too-hot summer's day.

"Phebe! It is a good day when you come to say hello."

"Would that I had time for more. I've missed you, my dove."

Phebe, the barmaid, often pretended she didn't recognize him since the inn's owner was now her husband. And lucky for her, since she must be getting on in years. After all, Cornelius had met Phebe when he first came to London.

"The Rose's honorable owner has gone for the afternoon?" he asked, pretending to be shy, because he knew she liked that.

"Ah, my darling fauntkin." Her Yorkshire accent came forth whenever she spoke endearments. "Don't you have a room close by? We cannot play here."

He hesitated for a heartbeat. He didn't need chancery to declare it; he did have a room of his own. An entire house.

5
A Scholar and a Young Earl

-ᏮᏟᎦᎾ.ᏩᏚᏩ-

— T O M —

"MR. FOXE, YOU HAVE guests. I'm to say that the gentleman is the Earl of Cloudesley."

A skittish young man entered, a terrier puppy tucked in one elbow, his other fist clutching the gloved hand of a smaller, veiled companion.

Tom jumped up, delighted.

"Jacob! Welcome, my friend. I am most happy to see you again." He bowed to Jacob's smaller companion. "I am honored, Lady Withersea. Do not wonder at my surprise, seeing you here."

Tom lost two heartbeats while catching his breath, but not because he stood up so fast. He fumbled for what to do. Thankfully, Adam still hovered at the door.

"Refreshments?" Tom asked.

Lady Withersea shook her head, but looked to Jacob, tipping her head. "Perhaps water for Jacob's dog?"

While Adam fetched a bowl of water, Tom said the next obvious thing, still breathless. "Please, have a seat."

Not knowing why she'd come or how to receive her, he didn't dare touch her, even to shake her hand. She'd last left him quite confused years ago, and now inhabited a state far above his.

She slipped onto the other wooden settle gracefully, as if she had no bones, and lifted her veil. She'd become a strikingly handsome woman in the past decade; her face was more marked with character, so she appeared as patrician as the marble statues of the Greek heroes she admired.

34

Jacob, watching his dog at the water bowl and not looking up, tugged her gloved hand as if begging to ask a question.

"It's Tom, Jacob. Remember, we came to find him here."

"Tom? My friend Tom?" Jacob was born tongue tied, in addition to other limitations. He stared for a moment, then smiled broadly. "Dish took your spoon, Tom!"

"Yes, my friend. And you're the man in the moon." Tom repeated the ritual response from when they'd met at Trinity College. He offered his hand, waiting for Jacob to touch him first. "I must now call you 'my lord.' Please accept my condolences on the loss of your father and older brothers, my lord."

"My lord." Jacob echoed Tom. Didn't take his hand.

"Such a good dog you have, Jacob. What's his name?"

"Pip. It's my new Pip. The old one..." Jacob reached for words, then swiped at his eyes. "The old Pip went to heaven."

Lady Withersea said, "You look well, Tom."

"Thank you, my lady." He knew what he looked like: a frayed linen coat hung on his boney frame; cravat and shirt wilted in the heat; close-cropped head bare of a wig; face masked with rouge and patches. "Pray tell me, to what do I owe this surprise?"

In the silence, when Tom didn't receive an answer, Jacob glanced between his sister and Tom, then said, "Come play with Pip. At my house."

"Wait, Jacob." While she stroked Jacob's hand, her words came out disjointed. "Is it true, Tom? That...that you've gained the Marborne title at last?"

Tom's pulse quickened. She'd asked (thousands of nights past): *Come to my father when you are made earl.* Then, she never spoke to him again, and five years ago she'd married a marquess. What happened back then proved confusing, so he remembered only the friendship the three of them once enjoyed. And she now came only under the mistaken notion that he was the new earl.

"Jacob, to my deep regret, I have obligations such that I cannot accept your invitation." He advanced that minor falsehood, not wanting to reveal his enfeebled state. Then, the truth for

Jacob's sister: "My cousin Rowland is the new earl. He's more than welcome to have that duty."

"Oh? I misunderstood the rumors." She paused, glancing at her brother. "I need you to save Jacob."

"How can I help?" Tom spoke with remarkable calm. And since they hadn't clasped hands, he could hide his febrile trembling. Or any other sign of the confused turmoil inside him.

"Please call me—"

"Rory," Jacob said to Tom. "You know Rory."

"Please call me Aurora," the marchioness said. "Jacob, my own dear heartling, show Tom."

"Yes, Jacob. Please sit by me," Tom said. "There's room for you and Pip." He offered as much space for Jacob as possible.

It took a moment, but Jacob scooped up his dog, sat down, and let Pip sniff Tom. Awkwardly shifting Pip in his arms, Jacob dug around in the deep cuff of his coat and produced a worn piece of paper, which he unfolded and offered Pip a peek.

"It's Tom."

Jacob held a drawing of Tom and Tamsin that Ned had dashed off a decade ago.

"Indeed, it is me. With my sister Tamsin." A bolt of regret shot through Tom's heart. Jacob had treated that scrap like a treasure all these years. Why had he let time and titles divide him from that friendship? "When I gave this to you, Jacob, I said we'd always be friends."

"My friend Tom." He again showed it to Pip, then carefully folded the drawing and tucked it into his cuff.

"Jacob," Aurora spoke with even greater gentleness. "Show Tom your arm, like you promised to do."

"Hurts," Jacob said.

"I know, dear heart. Let me roll back your sleeve."

Clutching Pip close in his other arm, Jacob offered his hand. She tugged up his coat cuffs, turned back his sleeve, and unwrapped a bandage, revealing five bright crimson slashes, three so deep that lines of bloody scab had formed.

"God's hooks!" A red-hot anger flashed through Tom's heart and belly. "What rotten cur did this?"

"God's hooks," Jacob echoed.

Aurora began to wrap Jacob's arm again, but Tom stopped her. He fetched a clean table linen from the salon and gave it to Aurora, who then wrapped Jacob's arm and covered it with his shirt and coat again.

"God's hooks," Jacob repeated.

"Don't use such words, lamb," Aurora said. "What can you say instead?"

"Rotten cur! Chittifaced worm!" Jacob again clutched Pip close. "Pip was bad. Wants to bite."

Tom shook his head, while wanting to weep that anyone treated Jacob so cruelly. "No, you and Pip are never bad." He glanced at Aurora, saying only, "How?"

"My husband the marquess has been in a monstrous rage since Saturday," she said. "The king froze significant funds held by his business agent. When the marquess raged again this morning that he couldn't access his own funds for a year, Jacob crossed his path at the wrong moment." She pointed to Jacob's arm.

"What shall I do?"

"Destroy the man who did that." Her voice was icy as winter. "Zeus has transformed him into a wolfish creature. I didn't fully see it until Jacob came to live with me after my father died. Stop that wolf before he devours Jacob."

"I shall," Tom said without hesitation, consumed with fury at the sight of Jacob's wounds. Such a tragic way to revisit the friendship they'd known that winter at Trinity.

TRINITY COLLEGE, CAMBRIDGE
WINTER 1676

"I foresee, Tom Foxe, that you shall one day practice law to protect the weak and innocent." His uncle Absolom, the famed doctor of philosophy, proclaimed this at the start of Tom's last term at Trinity. "You shall also be the best prevaricator of this age."

Tom said, "I surmise you mean that as a compliment."

"*Vero, vero.* However, I must beg you to attend the Trinity master's Greek tutorials this term. His situation requires the assistance of an enlightened person."

Tom protested. "Uncle, I have no use for more Greek."

"Yet we can all use more practice in kindness." Absolom lit his clay pipe and sipped a thoughtful draft. "After a bout of apoplexy last summer, Doctor Madstone is not as swift as he was. Last term his scholars practiced small tortures on him. This term, you shall stop such cruelties."

The next day Tom mounted the stairs to Doctor Madstone's chamber, which smelled of old chamber pot, spilled beer, and unwashed flesh, and sat among four younger scholars. When a sixth scholar slipped in and took the stool closest to the Master, the others swiveled their attention, like iron filings drawn to a magnet. With thick spectacles that magnified sky-grey orbs, the scholar appeared as goggly-eyed as a dragonfly. Mouse-colored locks hung in damp straggles, lost in a nappy wool scarf that must have been knitted by a derelict crone. This scholar had a hairless (and guileless) face, like a cherub minus golden feathered wings.

A protective urge welled up in Tom's core. This chap stood no chance among the other scholars. Then the lad said his name to the Master: Arthur Rôche. This was the new pensioner that rumor had heralded, a visitor whose grand family contributed remarkable sums to the college each year.

The Master called upon Rôche, who recited lines from *The Iliad* in a song-like voice, his soft hands stroking the air with the rhythm of the verse, as if playing an invisible lyre. When Madstone or others recited lines, Rôche mouthed the words silently, brows lifting above spectacles at other scholars' awkward pauses or mispronunciation. One scholar offered a poor explication.

"The Poet glories in war. The Greeks were heroes like our King Harry. The Trojans were brutes, like the French at Agincourt."

Arthur Rôche snorted.

Madstone said, "You disagree, young Rôche?"

Rôche recited the first line of *The Iliad*, begging the Muse to sing of Achilles' wrath, and then said, "Sir, the Poet tells us of the flawed victims of fickle gods striving under their warriors' code of honor. The Poet shows great pathos as the war brings tragedy to both sides."

Tom despaired, his head in his hands. All of England's wealth could not protect this lad from a long winter of torture by these young scholars.

"You don't agree with our new pensioner, Mr. Foxe?" Madstone caught Tom's gesture.

"Sir, the Poet indeed shows these men as striving for greatness by advancing their personal honor." Tom offered his own recitation, a line about always striving to be best, to be distinguished above all others. Then he began an explication. "We can understand the ancients' symbols of honor without—"

"Without," Rôche interrupted, "also believing that one proves one's worth by gaining horses and armor and women in battle." Then, in hacked lines from *The Iliad*: "'Two fates carry me to my day of death. First, if I lay siege to Troy, my glory never dies.'"

"That proved true," Tom said, "since we sit here repeating tales of their glory."

Madstone corrected Rôche's hacked Greek lines, making his own errors. "You've caught the Poet's sprites…I mean, the spirit of the poem, Mr. Rôche. But you have not yet grasped all of the Poet's rhythm and grace."

"Grace?" One of the other scholars whispered. "God bless this food we are about to receive."

Rôche turned. "It means freedom from the tyranny of ignorance, should the gods grant you that possibility."

The new pensioner might as well have volunteered for the pillory on the Cambridge commons.

When the Master dismissed them, Tom followed the cloaked scholar out the lower door. A tall lad sitting by the porter's brazier sprung up from his stool and joined Rôche. The pair walked westward, the lad running ahead, out Nevile's Gate to the frozen path by the River Cam. Rôche called out, and they stood in debate, the tall lad gesturing away from the college while Rôche motioned back toward Trinity.

The icy January air stung Tom's nose and lungs. The other scholars pushed past Tom at the Gate, shoving each other like village boys at a Guy Fawkes bonfire. One lad swung out a leg, forcing Rôche to stumble and lose his spectacles on the snow-covered path. When Rôche bent to retrieve those spectacles, the next scholar knocked Rôche into the River Cam.

The foul-spirited band of scholars sprinted up the path away from the Gate. On the stream bank, Rôche's companion shrieked for help, stepping close to the edge, then lurching back, clearly afraid of the water.

Shedding his cloak and gown, Tom jumped in after Rôche, filled with the protective ideals Absolom taught. A strong swimmer, Tom soon had hold of the sodden coat and got an arm around the plump fellow. Tom hauled Rôche close to the bank just as the boat-porter ran over, offering a pole that first the scholar and then Tom used to climb out of the river.

"Misfortune found me," Rôche said through chattering teeth. "Jacob, I'm fine. Don't fret."

While in the water, Tom had felt through the many layers of sopping wool that swaddled the half-drowned pensioner. With that, plus Jacob's inarticulate pleas, he understood that nothing was as it appeared. He scooped up the fallen spectacles and handed them to the shivering Rôche.

Thus, Tom's prophesized career began, first by prevaricating to protect others.

~

Tom badgered the pair to come to his chamber. He coaxed the younger lad into sitting close by the fire, then peremptorily instructed Rôche to strip.

"Come, Rôche. Out of those wet clothes before you turn to ice." He passed a suit of clothes over the dressing screen. "Wear

these and wrap up in my other cloak," he switched to the Poet's
Greek, "'before blackness covers your eyes.'"

"You are kind," Rôche said, then corrected Tom's Greek.

While Tom changed into dry clothes, he called to Rôche over
the screen. "We shall share a tot of brandy. Our housekeeper sent
it from home in case I ever feel the grippe or quinsy coming on.
Certainly, this is our hour of need."

While they sipped toddies by the fire, Tom made the proposal
he'd decided on before bringing the sopping scholar to his room.

"As you see, I'm alone in my chambers. My friend Luke left
last term to begin a clerkship in London. Then I heard today that
the Rôche heir entered Trinity College as a pensioner."

"Aye." Rôche's voice rose to a higher register. "This is my
brother Jacob. The rest of our family is in Paris. My aunt in London couldn't keep Jacob when I declared my intention to come
to Trinity College. Hence, we are here as a pair."

"How do you do, Jacob? I'm pleased to meet you." Tom offered his hand. Rôche took Jacob's empty toddy cup so he'd be
free to shake hands. But the lad didn't.

"Pleased to meet you." The awkward Jacob was physically
tongue-tied. He proved to be a tall thirteen-year-old. And a natural. He kept a grip on Rôche's sleeve.

"You must call me Tom. We shall all be friends."

"We are Arthur and Jacob." Rôche nudged Jacob. "Remember, brother? Here in Cambridge, I am called Arthur."

"Yes, Rory."

Tom said, "Might you agree to sharing my chambers? There's
room for three of us. I'm here until the end of this term. How
long will you remain at Trinity?"

A long silence. "Jacob and I will accept your kind offer. I came
only for the winter." Another pause. "I cannot pretend to be
modest. I intend to become a translator of the ancient poets and
want to be known as a disciple of Trinity's Doctor Madstone."

"Then today, you saw that will be awkward," Tom said. "You
should have come two years ago."

"I'm here now. We shall all do our best."

The next day, Tom arranged to be free whenever Rory had a tutorial. Jacob came with Tom to Absolom's chambers, where he rested his head on Tom's shoulder while Tom read aloud from Chapman's translation of *The Iliad* (since Tom had no use for more Greek). On some days, Absolom amused Jacob by teaching him string tricks. Privately with Tom, Absolom insisted that Jacob was much brighter than the lad's few words revealed.

Besides carrying out Absolom's request to protect Doctor Madstone in seminar sessions, Tom had his own quest to protect Jacob. He achieved little else that term.

Jacob and Tom quickly built a playful friendship. Jacob teased: "*Cat ate your shoe.*" "*Porter took your cheese.*" "*Rory hid your pens.*" Tom—always looking for his shoes, asking if all the cheese was gone, never finding a pen that didn't need mending—pretended to fall for each jest. Then Jacob would cry, "Dish took your spoon!" After which, Tom had to say, "You're the man in the moon!" And Jacob laughed.

Tom helped hide the stray orange cat Jacob brought into their chambers. Called Pip, the long-haired cat hissed at Tom but calmed Jacob, who rocked and petted it. Tom carried dinner up to their shared chambers, so Jacob needn't venture into the chill air.

Each night, Rory said, "'So, surrender to sleep at last,'" to which Jacob replied, "Good night," and soon began to snore softly. With only the light from the dying fire,

Then Tom would trade lines of Greek and English poetry with Rory, whose hands stroked the air whenever reciting Greek, advancing arguments that indicated a brilliant mind.

"I live by a heroic code," Tom claimed. "My uncle Absolom taught us rules for enlightened people. Hence, kindness serves as my sword in the battle for justice and mercy."

Rory said, "The Poet forgot to add kindness to the heroic code."

At the end of their sixth week together, Tom snuffed the last candle. "You've already said, 'So, surrender to sleep,' so I should say *bonne nuit.*"

Except a silence followed, until Rory whispered, "It's adieu, my friend. My father has returned from the Continent and summoned me home. His carriage will carry us away at dawn."

Jacob stirred but didn't wake. In the dark, the chinks of the firebrands collapsed. Finally, Tom whispered, "How did you think this could ever succeed, you here at Trinity?"

"By writing the correct words on my slate, saying the correct words to the Master." Then a line from Homer in Greek, "'The proud heart feels not terror nor turns to run.'"

"Did you never see that I helped?"

"Yes. You must imagine my gratitude. For how you make us laugh. For your many kindnesses to Jacob."

"I discovered what you are when I fished you from the River Cam. And I kept your secret."

"My secret?" Rory sighed. "You said nothing."

"I treasure our friendship. If you or Jacob should ever need help, I vow to do whatever you ask. But what shall I call you when we meet again? Surely you weren't christened Arthur."

"Call me Aurora." She whispered close by his ear. Then she slipped under the covers with him on his narrow cot.

He hadn't thought of her in that way, but he returned her kisses—awkwardly, because he'd never kissed a woman before. They held each other until the porter knocked on the door at dawn and declared a carriage for Master Rôche.

While putting on his coat, Jacob learned that Pip the cat was not to come with him. His keening echoed Tom's feelings. Aurora could not coax Jacob down the stairs.

"No! Staying with Pip and Tom," Jacob protested.

Tom used the voice to calm Jacob that he'd learned the day they met. "My friend, I'd like you to have this, to remember me." He gave Jacob a drawing his cousin Ned had made at Christmas.

"Two Toms," Jacob said, studying the drawing before taking it from Tom's hand.

"Yes, one is my sister. This one," he pointed, "is me. I shall always be your friend."

"But Pip?" Jacob's voice squeaked the cat's name.

"I'll take care of Pip. You can trust me."

After Tom guided Jacob into the carriage, Aurora said, "Come to my father when you become earl. That way, I'll have a friend instead of a master when I'm forced to marry."

He stood by her shivering, not because he was cold, though he'd left his heavy coat upstairs, but because this head-strong, impulsive young woman had suddenly changed their friendship in a confusing way. The best answer he had at that moment: "I've already vowed to do whatever you ask, if you need help."

In Greek, she said, "May the gods ignore you, if they cannot be bothered to help."

Then the pair was gone, leaving him to sift through his feelings, unmoored by the sudden loss of his friends, while upset and confused by what happened the night before, then by what she'd asked of him at dawn.

The next Sunday, Tom brought Pip home to live in the Revelstone barns. The cat soon had kittens, and the kittens had kittens, down to the orange ratcatchers now in the Revelstone barns.

Tom left Trinity at Easter to begin his clerkship, but in Cambridge, since there wasn't spare coin for Tom to enter a clerkship in London. He spent time wondering about Aurora's long, wild kisses while enduring the tedium of a clerk's work and the cold, dark loneliness of his bed. So very unlike her. He longed to ask her what it meant. Were they to be lovers?

Then a letter came from Kent. He'd unfolded it with excitement, but it proved to be a curt note from her father to convey a guinea for his children's board while living at Trinity College.

No other word came from Aurora, and he learned only by rumor that she'd married. By then, Tom thought of those halcyon weeks at Trinity as puerile foolishness. About the same time, Tamsin declared that she'd never marry. She proceeded to enliven their dreary endeavors to patch Marborne finances by convincing Tom, Ned, and Camilla to undertake meticulously moral highway robberies, to snatch back coin from swindlers.

Ever since Trinity, he'd practiced a private loneliness, while he was saluted for his cunning wit by his relations at home and the others in the barrister's chambers where he clerked.

Like cunning Odysseus, taking an inglorious decade to sail home from Troy.

Now, fever gone, Tom wanted to live, to be more than a boulder dropped in a pond. Further, although Tom had sworn to honor Absolom's principles for enlightened people, he'd failed Jacob as a friend. Amends were owed.

~

There in Benson's withdrawing parlor, Tom said, "I vowed long ago to do whatever you ask if you need help. I keep my promises. Jacob?" When Jacob heard his name, he looked up from his dog. "Do you want my help?"

Jacob offered a broad, mischievous smile, the same as long ago. "Dish took your spoon, Tom."

"And you are the man in the moon, my friend."

6

A Spectacle

PIE HAWKERS AND PAMPHLETEERS plagued the crowd around the playhouse, increasing the noise. Rowland repeatedly dodged hawkers in the jostling crowd. Swerve and duck as he might, he still ended up with several pamphlets in his hands.

Doctor Roseworld's Tonic for the Green Sickness, Faltering Hearts, and Pox Afflictions

Prepare to Fight Papal Tyranny Once More as Romanism Shows a Vile Royal Face

Rowland tried to see who had passed anti-Catholic papers, but found only an old woman with a basket of sad-looking buns and a freckled lad with a tray of swede-and-gammon pies. Rowland did as others, tossing the pamphlets to the ground.

This antipapal pap must rankle our new Catholic king, but why should I care? I'm no longer the king's agent. I'm free!

Entering a long passageway from Bridges Street, intensely excited to be there, Rowland came into the yard where the theatre stood, its three sides open to the sky. When he'd lived in Paris, he'd often enjoyed plays, having read Shakespeare under Absolom's tutoring. He was also pleased by the popular operas, with their moving scenery, dancing, and clever surprises. Whether today's play would be tragedy or comedy, he was eager to enjoy an English play in a London theatre.

People milled about, chattering and laughing. The benches against the wall opposite the stage were covered in green canvas.

He spied people in the risers flashing cards the same color as the pass from Adam the footman. Hence, he mounted the risers and found a seat by a well-dressed older man who endured the afternoon's heat in a linen vest, wide-skirted coat, and periwig. A squad of garrulous gentlewomen went silent upon seeing Rowland. He smiled, bowed, and slid onto the bench, studying the crowd. Several parties of gentlemen were seated on the risers across the way, which was when Rowland recognized he'd mistakenly chosen to sit among parties of ladies, save for the one older man.

A hand waved from the party opposite. Gad, it was Viscount Heydon, who'd been so significant in the previous week's restoration in Cambridge. Rowland raised a hand in greeting. When they'd first met, Rowland mistakenly believed Heydon to be a dangerous antagonist. It seemed, here in London, they must be friends, or at least friendly.

A herald stepped onto a ledge above the stage and blasted a horn. Rowland had heard about that tradition in the London theatres, but hadn't expected the thrill of anticipation it let loose within his breast. His heart beat harder, if not faster, and his attention became fixed on the stage.

A svelte young man in silver satin appeared under the proscenium arch, commanding attention by juggling three balls. The program began with the silver-clad man spouting the welcome lines from *Pericles*.

> To sing a song that old was sung,
> From ashes ancient Gower is come;
> Assuming man's infirmities,
> To glad your ear, and please your eyes.

Instead of continuing that play, three pairs of actors shouted lines from half a dozen different plays, with no united story. Once Rowland shed his bewilderment, he found joy in each brief scene, congratulating himself for knowing the source of each line, laughing with the audience when the actors overplayed the humor, tumbling about the stage.

In the middle of one silly tumble, a wizened man stood at the edge of the stage, emoting over the riotous clowning behind him.

I have lived long enough. My way of life
Is fallen into the sere, the yellow leaf,
And that which should accompany old age,
As honor, love, obedience, troops of friends,
I must not look to have.

While Rowland reached into memory to place the lines, the tumbling actors sent another actor crashing into the arms of an over-painted woman who smothered him in her embrace. Lines from *Macbeth* had mashed into a comical scene where they had no business. He mouthed those lines again: *I have lived long enough. My way of life is fallen into the sere, the yellow leaf.*

Which tumbled him into a memory: sitting at Absolom's study table, asking the meaning of a word he was too young to understand. "You might save that play for a few years," Absolom said, "when it can answer your questions on its own."

Grief welled, the dark grief he'd fought these ten days.

Why hadn't he returned to England a week earlier?

Why had fate kept him from enjoying even one more day with his uncle?

He conquered the need to weep and closed over the hole in his heart, as he had every day, saving it for later, forcing his attention to what played on the stage, since he'd insisted to Lizzie how much he needed Shakespeare that afternoon.

The spectacle concluded with a set of sliced-up scenes from *A Comedy of Errors*, with Dromio escaping beatings, tumbling about, and returning insult for insult. Still wishing that Lizzie was at his side, Rowland mouthed the words as actors cavorted across the stage. *She is a virtuous and a reverend lady. It cannot be that she hath done thee wrong.*

Aye. Of course, Lizzie had not done wrong. They merely hadn't yet found their new way in a changed world.

We came into the world like brother and brother,
And now let's go hand in hand, not one before another.

The Foxe cousins had declared themselves a band of brothers more than a decade before. Just last week, he hadn't dared to wish that Lizzie might join in the passion he felt for her.

"Teach me, dear creature, how to think and speak..."

God's blinding rays! He had so needed these few hours alone, to ponder the future. By the time the actors took their final bows, Rowland felt his inner turmoil stilled by way of the Bard's words. He clapped with enthusiasm, happy to have seen Shakespeare's work played, even hacked into a spectacle.

"Hah! Pithy outrage! My cook makes better hash," said his neighbor, the greying gentleman. "The maestro even let old Cartwright out to croak lines from *Macbeth*." He didn't pause to let Rowland answer. "We must all admit, must we not, that Dromio was droll? It's our good luck that the maestro wanted to try out his new ingénue in a breeches role today."

"Dromio was indeed a shining light," Rowland replied.

The elder gentleman wandered off, so Rowland didn't have to admit that he hadn't noticed that a woman played Dromio. Which made the second time in a week he'd been fooled by that sort of ruse. The first had been his cousin Tamsin, who'd masqueraded as Master of Revelstone while Tom was ill. In skirts again, Tamsin still led the cousins. For example, last Sunday morning: "The lodging-house servants spread the story of the newly found Earl of Marborne. And so, Rollo, you owe a morning in church so our temporary neighborhood can enjoy the sight of you." Unable to say no, Rowland ended up sitting in a humid, crowded church so that people might gawk and whisper about the lost earl, particularly a portly little man in black silk and lace, who licked his lips, as if Rowland might be good to eat.

Among the departing crowd at the theatre, the same whispered questions passed among ladies on the risers in the theatre. *"They say he's the lost earl." "He don't look like an earl." "More like a shopkeeper." "Nay, a clerk for a country lawyer."*

Was Lizzie right? Do clothes make the man? He'd never had coin for more than what kept him warm and dry, or for a pawned suit whenever his duties took him to Mary's court in Amsterdam. He'd have to learn how to look like an earl, but privately, without allowing the entire skulk of Foxe cousins to take pleasure in judging his choices.

Or he could just let Lizzie choose for him, like she had that morning when she purchased his new suit. But then, Perry would be merciless if Rowland let his beloved choose his clothes.

Convinced that he caught sight of Viscount Heydon, Rowland wiggled through the departing knots of ladies, intent on doing the proper thing and saying hello.

— TAMSIN —

TAMSIN FELL BEHIND ON the walk to the theatre. She repeatedly swiveled around to see who followed them down the lane. Tom had said, "I am fearless," after reading Leighton's missive, but Tamsin now found all of London to be threatening. Also, it took a bit of practice to walk comfortably with that sword-stick on the belt slung over her shoulder. Tom was welcome to have such an awkward and pathetic weapon when she returned home to Revelstone House.

At the theatre, Winwood led them through the crowd to a place close to the stage, which meant a lot of squirming and apologizing for knocking knees and elbows while making their way. Tamsin clutched the skirts of Winwood's coat to keep from losing him in the press of people, and she clutched Camilla's sleeve with her other hand as they snaked their way through smelly, sweating, rude people to find a place quite near the front of the stage.

Winwood said, "We're lucky that my cousin sent me a card that lets us stand right by the stage."

"We are grateful," Camilla said. Then she boxed Tamsin's arm and whispered, "You might smile instead of flouncing about like an ill-mannered imp. What put you off the good mood we enjoyed this morning?"

"It's the heat. It's distracted me."

Tamsin offered a falsehood, but she meant only to protect Camilla from Leighton's threats, not to deceive her, which would be wicked.

They stood in the heat for what felt like an hour, endeavoring to make small talk, until at last a horn blew and a slender young man in ragged silver clothes came out to recite a speech, spewing a shower of spittle on Tamsin and her friends, since they stood so near the stage.

"Is that your cousin?" Camilla whispered.

"It shall be my delight to hear your surmises," Winwood said. He shook his head each time Camilla whispered a guess. His teasing thrilled Camilla.

"Is it the one who's tall like you, Winwood? The one who did the speech about 'This happy breed of men'?"

Winwood laughed, soundlessly. Then another actor swung onto the stage and drew Camilla's attention.

In a break from all the business on stage, Camilla said, "It's the one in the brown robe, who had the speech, 'Give every man thy ear, but few thy voice.' Just like you. And he was a doctor."

Pretending to be grave, Winwood said, "He was a fool. Is that how he resembles me?"

For three hours, Camilla exclaimed in fright, then laughed along with the shuffling, smelly crowd around them. While laughing, Camilla, she pressed her hot hand into Tamsin's under the wide-skirted linen coat that Tamsin wore over her gown.

Meanwhile, Tamsin caught the eye of any rogue who glanced their way, ready at each moment to fight off assassins. To put that message from Leighton out of her mind, Tamsin remembered the long letter from Mrs. Bell, with details of the first harvest, which she would join next week. And after harvest, she could bargain with the thatchers and builders over repairs in the burned village. In late winter, after the thaw, she'd organize men in the parish to rebuild the mill on Marborne's stream. The notion of Revelstone House and the parish going on without her left a longing for home, like an illness she couldn't shake off while in London, where she had no real work to turn her hand to.

Camilla stirred, laughing at a hapless but droll actor being beaten on the stage. She clutched Tamsin's hand again under the skirts of Tamsin's linen coat. A comfort. She had Camilla beside her all day, all night, every day. She'd go home on Saturday, ending this too-long holiday spent suffocating in the crush of strangers. She'd resume her real life, doing what Absolom said she was born to: the care of Marborne's parish and woods and fields and great barns. She'd ride her horse and pet her dog.

That was days away, though. What to do? She couldn't fill idle hours with needlework like Camilla and Lizzie always did. Though, as Tamsin repeatedly fiddled with the excess lace on her walking dress, she could take a penknife to all the ribbons and lace on the two gowns she'd purchased in London.

With each stage trick, when the crowd drew a collective breath, Tamsin quit breathing, prepared for calamity to fall. Perspiration beaded and dripped on her neck. When the crowd's gasps gave way to laughter, the crowd's coughing and clacking echoed Leighton Fairchild's threat. *You shall soon burn in Hades...*

During a dull, droning speech by a ragged old man, Tamsin surveyed the crowd, her eyes fixing on a trio in the second tier who watched Camilla. Were these Leighton's assassins, having tracked them to London? Tamsin's heart thumped while a dreadfully painted old woman wiggled and flirted through a speech about love. Should she be afraid? Or did those men stare at Camilla simply because she was beautiful?

"Did you guess that the raggedy old man is my cousin?" Winwood teased Camilla.

"No, you have a lordly bearing," Camilla said. "Your cousin must share that."

When the commotion on the stage increased again, Tamsin studied the audience, spying Rowland among well-dressed ladies in broadbrimmed hats fanning themselves in the heat. He was, of course, immersed in the play. While she stared, hoping to be noticed by him, she again saw that trio of toughs, their eyes now on Rowland, as if they'd followed her attention.

She endeavored to do as Tom warned, not to fret.

And Tom had to be right: that weak, drunken Leighton could not raise any menace, much less hire an assassin. What she needed was to dispose of the fear he'd raised in her.

That dread twitching in her cheek? She smiled, broadly.

The trepidation that bent her neck? She stood tall.

She didn't master her roaming eyes, which kept searching the crowd, seeking possible danger.

The play ended with vigorous bouncing and shouts and insults hurled between the actors and the rowdier parts of the audience. Camilla clapped wildly; Tamsin, however, had no sense of what happened at any point in the play.

"Who is it, Winwood? Which is your cousin?" Camilla begged while they waited for the crowd to thin before walking to the gates. Winwood, grinning, only shook his head. She cried, "Lord save me from Dromio! Tamsin, you make a more convincing man dressed as Tom. You could teach Dromio more than one lesson."

That compliment wafted over Tamsin like a breeze after that hot afternoon in the crowd. She pressed Camilla's hand, then found her own palm too damp for that to be pleasant.

"Are you chiding me?" Camilla whispered.

"For speaking your mind, sweeting? Never." Tamsin rubbed her damp hands in the pockets of her linen coat.

"Leighton squeezed my hand whenever he wanted me to hold my tongue."

"Good stars!" The reprehensible Leighton Fairchild again imposed evil upon the day. "You have a writ of annulment in hand, my love. Also, have I ever chided you?"

"Often. Usually for not running fast enough after one of your infamous restorations."

"Neither famous nor infamous, because no one ever knew it was us."

Can assassins know it's us now? Good stars, stop worrying!

They followed Winwood to the street, ready to be introduced to his cousin. He glanced back for the two women, finding them on his heels. "Miss Candecote, slow down. I beg you. It's less than a week since your injury, and—"

"You've had me immobilized for days. And I just stood stock still for hours. I must move to heal."

"Here's the actors' gate." Tamsin listened to the banter between Winwood and his patient, knowing Camilla didn't like being fussed over. Tamsin yearned to fuss, the same way they'd exhausted themselves with worry over Tom for the past one hundred eighty days. Now that Fate had turned in their favor, Tamsin had to let Camilla and Tom do what they thought best.

— T O M —

IN BENSON'S WITHDRAWING ROOM, Aurora sat still as a merlin on a fence, her grey eyes watching while Tom petted Jacob's puppy.

"Tell me all," Tom said. "Declare the ill-fated hour from which sprung devastation."

She said, "These past years, Jacob has lived happily on my father's estates. The marquess and I never truly united. We worked out ways to live our separate lives." Aurora waved her hands as if leading an invisible choir to tell her tale, in the same way she did while reciting Greek in Madstone's chambers. That wave plucked chords in Tom's heart, replaying their old friendship, up to when she'd confused him that last night at Trinity. "I long to separate my life from that greedy man. However…"

"However, the laws of England do not allow a woman the privilege of making her own choices." He anchored his mind in known fact, like the barrister Absolom wanted him to be.

"Alas, yes," she said. "At Christmas, my father, upon seeing the marquess's true nature, revised the bonds for my marriage settlement and added Lord Kettlebottom as a guardian to protect Jacob and set aside funds to be held for his future."

"Papa died." Jacob sighed, pulled his puppy closer. "And Pip died too. The old Pip."

Tom, his spirit weighted down by how he'd failed Jacob, asked where Pip liked to be scratched, a distraction while Aurora continued a dramatic story worthy of Sophocles.

"Our father and older brothers died in a sailing accident the week before Easter. Then on Easter Monday, Lord Kettlebottom was killed by highwaymen on the Oxford Road. That's when Jacob came to live with me. I thought…"

When she paused for too long, Tom said, "You thought you could manage it, like going to Trinity to study Greek."

"Aye. 'The proud heart feels not terror nor turns to run.' I've managed my aspirations. But now, with Jacob…"

"Your marquess and Jacob do not rub along together."

"That's too mild. Yesterday, out of either greed or malice, the marquess sold Jacob's greatest treasure, our mother's portrait."

"He took Mother." Jacob grasped Tom's sleeve, touching him for the first time. "Her picture. I need it. Or I will forget." He tugged hard at Tom's sleeve. "Can't forget. Must not."

His eyes pierced Tom, like a glass shard thrust in his heart.

"When Jacob protested this morning, the contretemps led to that." She pointed to Jacob's injured arm.

"What shall I do?" Tom broke from Jacob's pleading eyes to ask Aurora.

"Get my picture, Tom." Jacob loosened his grip, but still held Tom's sleeve. "You can do it."

"It's most likely gone, love," Aurora said to her brother. To Tom: "Make sure Withersea never touches Jacob or ever dips into Jacob's wealth and title."

Tom swallowed profound dismay since he had no power of to do anything like that. Lord Withersea was too far above an earl's cousin.

She slipped into Greek. "'Sing, O goddess, the anger of Achilles.'" Then, returning to English: "Greater is my anger. I am consumed with wrath."

Tom couldn't see that anger in her face, which was as calm as he remembered, yet her fingers pressed together, white at the tips. He gestured toward Jacob's injured arm, pretending to be calm while seething inside. "The marquess is despicable."

"I am fiercely angry, and disappointed in myself, that it was only today that I witnessed why Jacob frantically fears the man. I should have seen it and found help sooner. My brother deserves to live in peace."

"And you?" Tom asked.

She touched his hand, but her hand was gloved, and so neither heat nor cold reached him. "I once bragged to you about how the gods gave me great gifts."

"I remember that." The memory left him feeling as if he again peered into a deep well of loneliness.

"I am humbled now," she said, "like Daedalus in grief over his failure. I need your help, to make sure Jacob is safe." She hesitated, looking grave. "Yet, it's not you but your cousin who is the Earl of Marborne?"

"Yes. Fate made Rollo earl, and I rejoice with all my heart."

He now believed that she wouldn't have wanted him even if Tom had become earl. That moment at Trinity was pure foolishness. And this many years later, why did she choose to come to him? He forged on, feigning courage.

"I'm not the earl, but can I help Jacob without a title?"

"The marquess, now Jacob's guardian, wants to confine Jacob on one of his estates near the Scottish border."

"Scotland?" Tom asked, echoing that notion feebly. "But you are his sister and—"

"And I have no power in the matter. The marquess will make a case with the lords' Committee for Privileges and Conduct, that Jacob is unable to hold the Cloudesley title."

"The Committee for…" Tom paused. "Rowland's title is to be approved by the lords' Committee this Friday."

"This Friday is when they will consider Jacob's case," Aurora said. "If the marquess succeeds, the king will hold Jacob's title in abeyance. Then the marquess will pay the king a garnishment and take Jacob's title and land."

"A garnishment. My cousin Rowland calls it a bribe," Tom said. "But is Jacob able take his place in the House of Lords?" He disliked talking about Jacob when he was right there, holding Pip up to see pigeons flying past the window. "Can you do it, Jacob?"

"I'll do what you say, Tom." Jacob rocked on his heels as was his habit, clutching his dog. "Pip will too."

Aurora said, "The House of Lords...doesn't matter. I've met enough dulpickles among them who may have more words than Jacob but not more wit. Please, protect Jacob."

She did not say it: *As you promised long ago.* Instead, she surprised him.

"With my father gone, there isn't another man on this earth that I can ask for help." Her eyes begged him. "And there's no one, Tom, that I can trust in the way I can trust you."

He didn't hide his astonishment, though she'd unpacked a chest of surprises. Or was she opening Pandora's box for him?

"Make Pip safe too. Please. He needs you." Jacob rested his head on Tom's shoulder, the way he used to do when Tom read to him at night. "And find my mother. I lost her picture."

7
Cudgels and a Book

"MARBORNE!" A HIGH-PITCHED VOICE shouted from behind several lines of people leaving the theatre.

It took Rowland a heartbeat to recognize what was now his name before he began to look around, expecting to see Viscount Heydon, then thought he spied a face familiar from Amsterdam. Duck-man? Duckpond? No, that wasn't right, but Rowland couldn't unite a name with that small man and his eagle's beak of a nose. A knight he'd met in Mary's court? When Rowland raised his hand, the man turned away, lost in the milling crowd.

Jostled along with the masses, Rowland emerged on the street. His enthusiasm waned as he faced a long evening and two empty days ahead, while Lizzie did what mattered most to her.

"'Nay, 'tis for me to be patient.'"

He again spoke lines aloud as he stepped into a narrow lane now deserted of hawkers.

"Quick, my lord!" A youth jostled Rowland's elbow. "Where is Miss Ysabel Foxe?"

"Not here. What—"

"Have you steel, sir? They are upon us."

"What?" Even as he repeated the word, Rowland reached for the knife in his boot, not yet seeing a reason to draw it.

"Take my pistol." The youth reached toward Rowland. "Get it in your hand, man, if we're to have a chance together."

It was Dromio, the pantaloon-wearing actress, slim as the swept-hilt rapier she now wielded. Behind her, two figures came up the lane, one swinging a cudgel, the other flashing a Dutch Walloon sword, the sort militia men carry home from the Low Countries. Dromio pressed Rowland up against a brick wall to protect him while passing him a flintlock. She then brandished her steel, advancing on the Walloon bearer while pointing for Rowland to take the man seeking to cudgel Rowland's brain.

Knife in hand, Rowland cast it as he'd been taught, aiming for that whapper's shoulder, but instead striking his forearm. The haft stuck out for several heartbeats while the fellow cursed and struggled to dislodge the blade. Meanwhile, the sound of steel on steel echoed from the brick walls lining the narrow lane. Dromio managed to avoid being touched by the gargantuan attacker swinging the thick Walloon, but hadn't yet drawn blood with her rapier.

And Dromio continued to shout, "The dag! The dag!"

Rowland, holding the pistol in one hand, kicked the cudgel out of reach from his own bleeding attacker and advanced on the second man. When the sound of Rowland cocking the pistol echoed against the walls of the passageway, Dromio's attacker stepped back, hesitating. Rowland stepped forward to force the retreat, but the fellow swung out a leg, taking Rowland down.

"The dag, my lord!"

Prompted, Rowland lifted the pistol and fired into the sky. Ears still ringing, he endured a heavy-booted kick to his ribs, then to his gingamobs.

"Heigh ho! We run now!"

It wasn't Rowland's screams that made the rogue run, only the exhortation of his fellow ruffian, who gushed gore where Dromio (a veritable cacafuego) had slashed the arm Rowland had previously stabbed. The pair took off, hobbledygee, looking back to be sure they weren't followed.

Dromio bent over Rowland, who groaned, wrapped up in pain, lying on the filthy cobbles. Dromio picked up the pistol. "For a soldier, you're no Captain Hackum. But you did keep them from obtaining their keen desire."

When Rowland gathered sufficient breath to speak, he said, "It's not my first meeting with the footpads of London."

"Footpads?" Dromio offered a hand as if to help Rowland up from the cobbles, which Rowland refused since he'd suffered enough humiliation. "Those desperados didn't want your purse. Those assassins sought to send you to the famed Elysian fields."

"Assassins?" Rowland couldn't breathe without pain.

"Indeed. I'd best see you to your door, your lordship."

"I'm called Rollo by my friends."

"I know. I'm Michel Chêne."

Not Dromio. And not an actress. Rather, a young man on the extreme side of slim, like his steel blade. Michel Chêne wore a mouse-colored suit and vest, with a linen shirt and a barely notable neckcloth; a man that, by Rowland's estimation, didn't want to be noticed. Exactly the way Rowland lived in his former life, in mud-colored wool while playing subaltern to spy on Monmouth's militia in Holland.

"I can get home without your aid, Mr. Chêne."

"As you say, my lord. Please take care in London. It's not like Amsterdam."

"How can I thank you?"

"No need. I shall call on you tomorrow. Colonel Kilbuck sent me to protect you. And Miss Foxe, if she should ask for it. It's a pleasure to serve you, your lordship."

The youth Michel was gone in the shadows, leaving nothing but questions behind him.

A man sent to protect him and Lizzie? A guardian, barely old enough to go armed in the streets? And he, Rowland Foxe, had let Lizzie go off on her own to…well, he didn't know where she'd gone, unable to recall the invitation she'd flashed at him.

— TOM —

"WHEN YOU CAME TODAY, I didn't adequately express condolences for the loss of your father," Tom said. "I said the proper words to Jacob, but I didn't know that Jacob lost his protector."

Perched on the carved settle in the withdrawing room, Aurora looked thoughtful. "You never met my father. And you had many harsh words for him when we said goodbye at Trinity College."

"Did I?" Tom didn't remember that.

"Jacob repeated them half way to Kent. It took the entire rest of the journey to make him forget."

"I confess, I believed your father had dashed your dreams by forcing you home from Trinity. That you wouldn't be able to become a translator, as you wished."

"Yet I did advance my work." Aurora fished spectacles from her reticule, put them in place, and again became the goggly-eyed scholar. She took out a small volume, neatly bound in mottled leather, red with a white-and-green sewn headband. She passed it to Tom, offering her familiar wry smile. "Jacob has attained some notoriety as a translator of Greek and Latin."

Hearing his name, Jacob looked over, blinking, but then resumed scratching his dog's ears.

"*Aias Mastigophoros.* Ajax the Whip-Bearer." Tom translated the title stamped in gold on the spine. The binding was smooth and warm to the touch, with gold-flecked endpapers pasted inside. Tom turned to the frontispiece.

Sophocles
Ajax: Aias Mastigophoros
Translated in prose and verse by
Arthur Jacob Rôche

"Magnificent, Aurora. My felicitations."

"I've set that work aside for now. I'm overwhelmed with worry for Jacob. The marquess has suffered losses, and Jacob's wealth presents an attractive means for his recovery. Without more help than I can render, Jacob will be lost to the world."

Jacob made a sound, rather like a plea, but then spoke only to his little dog. "Tom will help."

Yes. Seeing the wicked slashes on Jacob's arm, Tom rededicated his soul to doing as Absolom had taught since the Foxe cousins' early childhood: *I keep my promises.*

"First," Tom said, "I'll ensure there is protection for Jacob."

Jacob tipped his head. "You'll come to my house, Tom?"

"That's not possible." Tom could not explain the fatigue, the elixirs, or his solicitous sister and physician. "Your problems require tasks I can only undertake in London. Another trustworthy man must come to your house, to keep you both safe."

"How can I hire such a man?" Aurora opened her hands, as if grasping without hope.

"I'll send a man I'd trust with my own life." Tom held up her red book. "Does the marquess allow you funds to pursue art?"

"He never denies me trivialities." She wrenched her hands once more.

"Write to Simon Touchstone today." Tom focused on the first tasks to stave off a flood of feelings: fear, uncertainty, the nagging sense that he'd long failed Jacob as a friend. "He deals in paintings and antiquities near the French Church on Threadneedle Street. Request the services of the Dutch portraitist Eduard Wijck." He paused, then dared to commit Ned to this venture. "Mr. Wijck will come tomorrow."

"And me? Can I help, Tom?" Jacob pleaded, though it was impossible for him to do any of what must be done.

"Stay safe. Be careful, like I taught you at Trinity." Tom scratched Pip's ears, then turned to Aurora. "Are you prepared to leave the marquess's protection?"

"I wanted to flee today. But I cannot access the funds our father left us. Can you help with that?"

Tom considered fifty possibilities. "Most likely, you shall have to leave England entirely, which will take time to prepare. Do you have friends on the Continent who can help you?"

"No. I must do it on my own. How shall I free my marriage portion for funds upon which to live?" She touched him again.

Tom twitched at the soft sensation of her gloved hand. She'd once whispered, *Will you come to my father...*, which had confused him for a half decade, until he finally understood that they'd only shared a quixotic friendship.

"Tomorrow, we'll free Jacob from terror, then make a plan for you both to escape England as quickly as the gods allow."

"Will you, like Zeus, strike out against men who have no honor?" She shifted on the settle, fury reddening her face. She next spoke in Greek.

The other gods and the armed warriors on the plain slept soundly, but Zeus was wakeful, thinking how to do honor to Achilles, and destroy many people...

"Are you as resourceful as Odysseus?" She asked in English.

"Rory, no." Tom drew a painful breath, as if a cooper had tightened iron barrel-bands around his chest. "We don't live in your Greek heroes' world. I can help to remove the marquess from your life, but not from this earth."

"Rory, no." Jacob echoed Tom's words.

"Thank you, Jacob." Tom lowered his voice. "I live by the principles my uncle taught. I solemnly swear to pursue justice, while maintaining my family's rules. One rule is no one dies."

"I am not cruel Athena," she said. "I want Jacob to be free of Withersea. I don't want you to murder the man. I am, however, quite uneasy, because the marquess has been in a murderous rage since the king froze his fund last Saturday."

"Since Saturday?" The barrel-bands tightened even harder around Tom's chest. He'd been listening to echoes of his past failure through this entire exchange. He'd missed out earlier, not hearing that distinct word: Saturday. "Aurora, who is the marquess's business agent?"

She shook her head. "I don't know. He keeps the details of his business away from me. I only hear when the marquess boasts of successes or condemns how others failed him."

"What was he planning to do with the frozen funds?"

"Pay the king garnishments. And he placed other men's investments with his. Those funds are frozen too. In his rage, he complained about lost opportunities for true lords in England."

"What does the marquess want that requires paying garnishments to the king?"

"Two titles seized in the Monmouth rebellion. He's done it before, once for a small holding in the marches and another near Scotland. And he often purchases lands where the owner has died without heirs. It's a scheme he's practiced since early in the Restoration. I'm sure he's cheated his way to every piece of land that wasn't inherited from his father."

Tom let her go on while he managed to catch his breath, to keep from raging like Achilles.

"You must know, Aurora." Tom said gently. "The king froze several investors' funds on Saturday because the business agent Mr. Danvers Duncombe was arrested for treason."

"All the more reason Jacob is in danger."

"I shall make sure Jacob is safe. Please be assured." Though he wasn't sure yet how; he'd just make it so.

"Beware, Tom. The marquess always seems to get what he wants. And many men in the chancery courts owe the marquess their sinecures." Aurora rose suddenly from the settle. "We have tarried too long. And Jacob needs his supper. Let's go, Jacob."

"Go?" Jacob rocked on his heels, clutching his dog.

"Sadly, yes," Tom said. "A sister must be obeyed."

Aurora stroked Jacob's hand again, coaxing him downstairs. In the lodging house's vestibule, the porter went to fetch her carriage driver. With the three of them alone, she bid Jacob say goodbye, and Jacob let Tom shake Pip's paw.

She said, "Farewell, Tom. May the gods ignore you, if they cannot be bothered to help." She dropped her voice to a whisper. "Do not trust anyone. You will have to battle as hard as the greatest of Homer's heroes."

Jacob tugged at her arm. Her coachman was at the door. Brother and sister disappeared into the waiting carriage.

That left Tom to wonder how he was to stop one of the most powerful men in England from doing whatever he wanted. Yet how could Tom not do whatever it took to protect Jacob? And at least he wasn't called to wield swords and shields and pikes. The law would be his weapon.

A YOUNG MAN LEANED against the brick wall behind the theatre, sharing a slim claro with an old fellow who must be the porter. Spying Winwood, the younger man gave the burning cigar to the older one and came forward, hand out in greeting.

"Winwood, you are so much taller than I remember."

"Felicity, dear cousin, you are no longer eight years old."

"*Bonne nuit, mon ami.*"

The slender figure, who still held Winwood's hand, proved to be Dromio from the play, the actress Camilla had disparaged as not so convincing a man. Still wearing Dromio's buckskin pantaloons, Felicity had cast off the raggedy jerkin that signaled (on the stage) "servant from the time of Good Queen Bess," and now wore a gentleman's lavender linen coat, its cuffs and collar a bit frayed, with a carelessly tied lacy cravat. She carried a gentleman's walking stick in her left hand.

"We should go," Winwood said. "I ordered supper at our lodging house, and Miss Candecote needs—"

"To be introduced." Camilla had her hand out in greeting. "I am Camilla Candecote, and this is Tamsin Foxe. You gave us a merry afternoon, mademoiselle, seeing you tumble about."

"*Merci beaucoup, mademoiselle. Je m'appelle* Felicity." She took Camilla's hand. "I am of the Paris house of emigres that are called Oakes in England." She drew Camilla closer, lifted her hand to kiss it. "And I hope that you, with your blue eyes and lovely hair like spun honey, are not married. Your manners, Miss Candecote, announce you as *une femme libre d'esprit.*"

Felicity leaned quite close to Camilla, who drew closer to Tamsin, who'd never seen anyone flirt with Camilla. Tamsin couldn't name her feelings when her adventure-seeking friend shrank away from their exuberant new acquaintance. Perhaps because Tamsin had spent so much of the afternoon being afraid, a bit of petty happiness broke free.

"Marriage is behind me," Camilla said. "Tamsin and I both consider ourselves free spirits."

Warmed by Camilla's response, Tamsin said, "Our lodging house is across Covent Garden. Turn left here."

Camilla said, "Winwood says you have troubles we must help mend."

"Winwood!" Felicity slapped the doctor's shoulder, like fellows do with each other. "It is a private family matter."

"In England," Winwood said, "this is my family."

"These are your sisters then?"

"In every way except sharing the same mother."

Winwood's claim gratified Tamsin. The doctor had done so much for Tom, treating him more like a brother than a patient.

Felicity said, "Then you two are also my cousins? In that case—" She cast a glance behind them as they walked in the evening shadows of the narrow lane. "*Ça me fait chier!* My enemies are stalking me again. I swear on the blue heavens, I shall not be cowed by my enemy."

"Who?" Tamsin and Winwood looked back at the same time. A pair—no, a trio of shadows moved on the other side of the lane, gaining on the slower moving quartet. Tamsin stood up straight, intending to be as fearless as Tom.

Winwood said, "What do we do?"

"Pretend you don't notice." Felicity tossed her head and picked up her pace. "It's the blobber-lipped blackguards sent by our aunt's antiquated rotter of a husband. They'll only whisper that I'd best return to Paris if I want to be safe."

"There's more of us than them." Tamsin mustered the same calm as a restoration required.

"And Winwood is tall," Camilla said, sounding casually fearless. "Though he's more of a peacemaker than a fighter."

"Fine. You make me brave." Felicity slipped a narrow sword from her walking stick. "Winwood, protect your sisters while I confront my enemies." She shouted, projecting her stage voice. "Hoy, rogues. Flee now!"

The trio didn't pause.

Reaching inside her coat, Tamsin pulled her knife free of its holster. With her other hand, she drew that new sword-stick from its case, then had to shake loose a tangled strip of that execrable lace. Tamsin whipped the sword around with her left hand. It felt foreign. Yet the blade whirred when she flashed it. She handed it to Winwood, who always went unarmed.

He looked like she'd handed him a live snake.

Camilla held a muff pistol Tamsin had never seen before.

"Stand!" Tamsin assumed the commanding tones she'd mastered when disguised as Tom. "State your business."

Knives in hand, two stalkers advanced on Winwood, likely because he was tall. He stepped in front of Tamsin, who then stepped beside him, thinking she had a better sense of defense than he did. She'd learned the basics of knife-fighting by watching young men battle for prizes at village fairs, and had practiced in the privacy of Revelstone's great barn.

Winwood then stepped in front of Camilla, which seemed like a bad idea, what with the muff pistol in her hand. Tamsin motioned Camilla into the position she always took during Foxe family restorations, to Tamsin's side and back a pace.

God's bones! Couldn't they just run?

Winwood and Felicity both twitched their swords. A soft whir echoed.

The trio of stalkers paused. One, hatless, had a massive jaw and wide jowls below a narrow forehead. A second was as a gangly as a common scarecrow set up to fend off jackdaws, with a painful-looking carbuncle on his forehead. The third, much younger, was merely a bow-legged child with carrot-red hair that stood up as if he'd taken a fright.

"*Allez-vous-en, Monsieur Tête de Poire!*" Felicity shouted like Dromio, calling one Monsieur Pear Head, which must be the big-face fellow. She advanced on the trio.

Which wasn't the action Tamsin would choose, yet they were all now committed.

Tamsin circled to Felicity's right. Camilla moved to her left. They'd practiced such moves for their restorations, but for those actions, they'd had the advantage of surprise and pistols. And breeches rather than ribbon-bedecked skirts.

"Halt, dogs!" Winwood pitched his voice in a battlefield shout that Tamsin hadn't heard from him before that moment.

Felicity somersaulted across the lane, like she had on the stage, and kicked at Mr. Pear Head's groin. He shrieked and fell. Felicity stood over him. Meanwhile, Winwood whipped his thin blade closer and closer to the redheaded stalker's forearm. Tamsin moved on the scarecrow, brandishing her dagger like she'd seen the village boys. Her blade caught a stray sunbeam as she stepped close enough to strike.

"Take flight or fight!" Camilla cried.

"Flee, ruffians!" Winwood shouted, a better choice of commands. He twitched his sword-stick again.

We are the ones who should run!

Tamsin stepped in to the close-hand mêlée. When the scarecrow approached, she sliced his cuff with her knife, then struck hard with the flat of her blade, sending a vibration up her arm.

Cursing, the man grabbed for her, having a much longer reach than hers.

Then Camilla held her miniscule muff pistol high in the air. Instead of firing, she screamed, like only Camilla can scream.

Dogs barked. Window shutters flew open. Heads poked out of doorways. Camilla screamed again, the shrill sound echoing in the narrow street.

The stalkers beat a retreat.

"You are a fine one! Brave and beautiful too. Like a goddess created in the blue heavens." Felicity put one arm around Camilla, the other hand still dangling her narrow sword, which Tamsin saw was a blade with no edge or point. A stage prop.

Felicity had just drawn them into a dangerous public affray while protected only with make-believe.

The actress sheathed her edgeless sword in its case.

Camilla pocketed her unused pistol.

Winwood handed Tamsin that thin sword. She rammed it into its sheath, catching it in a streamer of torn lace, but soon it was once more merely a cane.

"We should run now," Tamsin said, still wishing that's what they'd done when the encounter began.

"But you fine ladies cannot run!" Felicity cried.

Tamsin had hold of Camilla's hand, to force speed on her. The two of them had grown up running the trails in Marborne parish, trails that led away from the fens, which were usually muddy and offered less sure footing than this city lane.

"Wait!" Felicity and Winwood called repeatedly.

Camilla and Tamsin finally slowed on the street by their lodgings. Tamsin took two deep breaths, calming her heart. She raised her hand to brush perspiration from her face, but that stick-sword was still caught on some frippery. She freed it but saw that it left someone's blood on the torn lace, which she tucked into her sleeve. Intending to give the sword-stick to Tom, Tamsin privately vowed to never touch it again, once she had a chance to clean it.

Camilla stood, hands on her hips, more than a little proud of her efforts, though her chest still heaved while she quieted her breath after their scampering run.

"I told you we should wear breeches out on the street," Tamsin said, having caught her breath.

"Much more amusing," Camilla said, "to see those rogues running from women. What will they tell their friends?"

"Miss Tamsin, Miss Camilla," Felicity panted when she caught up. "You must teach me how to run in skirts. I have not yet mastered that on the stage."

Winwood greeted the porter at the lodging house, asking for the room where their supper was to be served. He begged his companions to wait while he checked that the room was ready. In the foyer, the three women shared the looking glass and helped each other wipe away stains from that mêlée. Camilla's face glowed scarlet, even after catching her breath.

"Today was too much." Tamsin slipped her arm in under Camilla's. "To bed with you, my dear?"

"Never in this life," Camilla said. "I must hear Felicity's story. I do not believe that heaven could free me from my husband but then let me die at supper a week later."

Winwood beckoned for them to come upstairs. But before following him in to supper, Tamsin asked the night porter whether her cousins were on the premises.

"His lordship the earl, Mr. Wijck, and Mr. Frake have not yet returned," the porter said. "Miss Ysabel Foxe left a message that she has gone to visit friends in the country. And Mr. Thomas Foxe retired upstairs some time ago."

So, at least she didn't have to worry about Lizzie, who was away visiting her rich friends, or about Tom, who'd stayed safely in the lodgings where no mischief could wear on his delicate health. Then Tamsin touched her Archangel coin, remembering her vow to stop worrying about people when she hadn't been asked to help.

8

Intelligence

THOUGH HE ACHED EVERYWHERE, Rowland stopped at The Rose to eat a meat pie and to nurse his dignity over a pitcher of ale.

The crowd in the tavern included several sharps. Others hunkering over tumblers of ale were toothless and haggard, aged beyond what God usually allows, but still sipping tobacco from clay pipes. The young men wore dusty working-man's clothes. The pie and ale were consoling, and let Rowland delay returning to the lodging house, where he'd be forced to explain to his curious cousins and friends about the many bruises, the ruined coat, and the loss of his best knife.

At the lodging house, Rowland had to knock on the door to gain entry, since the porter always locked it after dinner. Bruised, his groin still aching, Rowland badly wanted to find Perry, since he needed his long-time comrade's counsel.

Which, of course, would be: *I warned you to take care.*

The night porter answering Rowland's knock shifted anxiously from one foot to the other.

"You have company, your lordship. We offered the gentleman refreshments, but he wanted only sherry and biscuits." The porter shuffled again. "We're entertaining his men in the kitchen."

"Thank you. It's Hugh, isn't it? Will you add their refreshments to my reckoning? And share this with those helping in the kitchen." Rowland passed him a significant gratuity, thinking he'd have to reconsider the Foxe family funds if they were forced to entertain other lords and their coteries.

Hugh opened the salon door, revealing the portly gentleman who longed to devour Rowland in church. Last Sunday, it had been too dark to recognize the man, but under the bright candlelight of the salon, he proved to be the Duke of Bagsham, whom Rowland had known in Paris while serving English diplomats, when the duke had been the English ambassador to Louis XIV.

"My lord duke." Rowland bowed, exactly as low as Lord Bagsham had taught him a decade earlier. "It is a pleasure to see you, your grace. And to see you well in body. I hope in spirit, too, after Sunday morning's healing of our souls."

"Yes, yes. It took us a bit to locate you. We tried to catch you after church, surprised to see you in my cousin's congregation."

"I'm sorry to have missed you, your grace." No, that wasn't true. After church, he'd gone with Ned and Perry to bowl ninepins behind a tavern Perry found. If the duke had caught him, that dull morning would have turned into a grueling afternoon.

"Lord Marborne." Lord Bagsham sipped daintily from a crystal glass. "I shall call you that, although the Committee for Privileges and Conduct doesn't meet until…when is that?"

"Friday. In three days." Rowland knew the duke to be the presiding official for the Committee; hence, his grace knew exactly when it was to meet.

"Our good King James suggests that I help you find your way. Though I suspect you aren't often lost."

"A kindness, your grace." Rowland sat when the duke indicated he might—and was reminded of the boot at his groin.

"As our first order, you must learn the Committee's customs. How you shall greet the men, the traditional emoluments to be offered, the toast you shall make to the king, and so on."

"I appreciate your guidance." Rowland had learned long ago to govern his expression when close to power. By good luck, he had that morning gained enough gold from one royal gratuity to pay another to the Committee.

"Truly, Marborne? Your honored uncle always had his back up about our customs."

"Your grace, our family has long served the Crown."

"Yes, yes. However, I could never persuade Doctor Foxe to follow the customs." The duke wrung his small hands. "He refused to part with one farthing in emoluments to the consistory court to advance the Foxe inheritance."

When the duke looked his way, seeking affirmation, Rowland nodded.

"Or to the Committee," the duke continued, "for its help in advancing the Marborne title. Doctor Foxe always brought a country barrister with him, to argue with the king's clerks and bishop's proctors."

"That sounds like my Uncle Absolom, who—"

The duke forged on. "With proper gratuities and promises of future service to the Crown, any barrister from Lincoln's Inn could have achieved the good doctor's goals."

Rowland nodded. An ache closed his throat. He pressed back at an instant sadness, wishing Absolom had lived to see the title returned to the family. No, he simply missed his uncle.

Lord Bagsham didn't notice. He pushed at his spectacles, smashing them up his nose with his whole hand, leaving smudges on the lenses. The duke sighed, shook his head, then resumed his modest tirade.

"To hear Doctor Foxe declaim his beliefs, you'd think he'd been asked to indulge in immoral corruptions of power. You were trained among lords on the Continent. Surely, you did not inherit his unorthodox tendencies, did you, Marborne?"

Yes, I did.

But, to answer the duke's expectant and judgmental expression, Rowland said, "Because I served on the Continent, I didn't know all of Doctor Foxe's forays into philosophy. My own heart is governed by poetry. He did, however, teach us to serve the well-being of England."

And Absolom Foxe listened to his own celestial melodies.

"Excellent. You shall therefore make rapid progress with the peers and bishops, which your uncle never could. Now, to get to our real business." The duke stretched his fingers, as if preparing for physical labor. "Tomorrow when we meet, we shall discuss a new assignment our king has for you, because he so appreciates your talents as intelligencer."

"Thank you, duke." Disappointment coursed through his veins. "However, I have resigned from my military life, and—"

"Military? Ah, no. Other men nose about the business of generals and colonels." The duke brushed crumbs from the knee of his silk pantaloons. "Your king needs you to look for traitors among your own class of people. You shall serve as one of the king's watchers."

The Dutch clock in the hall struck eleven tones. Rowland hid his dismay while waiting for the chimes to finish. The duke had administered the night's second kick to Rowland's groin.

~

Watcher? Rowland knew that to be another word for a spy.

I said yes to Tamsin's cows. Can I say no to a duke? To a king?

"Your grace, the Marborne parish and lands are in disrepair. The people I am responsible for need me to—"

"Your king needs your ability to find what others cannot." Lord Bagsham had a distinct tendency to interrupt, all while rubbing his very small hands.

"Your grace, you are aware of the spiritual tax charged against the souls of intelligencers. To be honest, my past work rubbed my soul raw. I serve the Crown still, but in another—"

"Remember," the duke interrupted, "when we first met in Paris? When I held school for new aides about manners and court protocol? You retained all such knowledge, Marborne?"

"Yes, your grace. You were a masterful teacher."

"Then you know a diplomat considers it unprincipled to be brutal with the truth."

"I hope I'm not—"

"It would be brutal if you forced me to compromise my principles, Lord Marborne."

"I never would, your grace."

"Good. And in return, I'd never reveal that the king's master intelligencer detected pages missing from the traitor's business ledger that you uncovered last week. The master wondered whether that gap indicated you'd spared some guilty men."

"Likely a clerk's error." Rowland doused a flash of anger at this threat and instead donned a simpleton's mask. "More the fool me, not to stay while the colonel's clerks assessed Danvers Duncombe's ledger." He wouldn't reveal a truth that wasn't his to share. A Marborne neighbor, Viscount Heydon, had asked Rowland to omit a page from the ledger that showed his brother's wife to have joined a syndicate supporting Monmouth's rebellion.

The duke rubbed his small fingers, as if they were cold. "It'd be exceedingly unprincipled of me to reveal what my own intelligencers have discovered, that Miss Ysabel Foxe spies on the Crown. I mean that rather brown girl from Mary's court, the one Sir Didlington always called 'señorita' to tease her. She is your cousin, is she not?"

A familiar feeling prickled at Rowland's neck. Years ago, whenever the Foxe kits got up to the kind trouble that warranted penalties, only Rowland was ever snared, being better suited to take punishment than the others.

"Your grace, your intelligencer is mistaken. Miss Foxe cares only about her gowns and her hopes of becoming a countess. I am the Foxe who served as a Crown agent. And I'd never—"

"You didn't know she was Colonel Kilbuck's agent in Amsterdam, the same as you? Dear me. Are you also, like Miss Foxe, working for Mary and William here in England?"

"I'd never…" *Snared, like a fox in a leg-hold trap!* "I'd never ask you to compromise your principles."

"Then tomorrow, as I suggested, we'll explore the details of your new work for the king."

Not intending to signal surrender (or to reveal the heat of his anger), Rowland took a breath and allowed the duke to push that confrontation to tomorrow.

Lord Bagsham mashed his spectacles in place again. "But first, I must advise that you not go about dressed in tatters."

"My apologies, your grace. After leaving the playhouse in Covent Garden this evening—"

"Ah. You obtained a pass? The theatres closed when Charles died, but the king knows the gentry attends private plays. Surely there aren't unwashed crowds. How are you so tossed about?"

"I was set upon by footpads, your grace."

"Tch. Did you acquit yourself, Marborne?" The duke pushed up his spectacles again, apparently concerned only about Rowland's clothes and battle skills, while Rowland still wondered who had attacked him. And why.

"It involved more steel than I am used to, your grace, but I can claim victory."

Which I have not managed in this interview.

"I'll send a man around for lessons on how a gentleman handles steel," the duke said, as if to imply that Rowland possessed the skills of a churl. "Here in London, a gentleman needs steel for protection. It's best to carry a sword-stick, day and night. Unless you keep personal guards, as I do."

"As you say. And—"

"I've a proposition for you, Marborne. I own a house here in Covent Garden that should do for you. It's no good having a peer of the realm living in hired lodgings."

"I cannot afford a house, your grace. It will be some years until we can return wealth to Marborne lands. Our thin pockets demand we take lodgings when in London."

"All of my house becomes yours, as a sinecure for your service to the Crown."

"I pledged my service, upon my honor. There's no need—"

"My men shall help with your removal." Bagsham never really listened.

"No need to bother your men, your grace. I have scant baggage." Rowland understood, as far down as his toes, that he could not refuse this sinecure. He had to protect Lizzie.

The duke again didn't seem to listen. "We shall be happy partners, you and I. My secretary will send a schedule. We shall begin tomorrow afternoon. At three o'clock."

"I need to find an attorney tomorrow, your grace."

"Best that you go to Mr. John Mordaunt, the barrister. His chambers are at Lincoln's Inn. I'll send a note for him to expect you. Shall I say, ten o'clock?" He didn't wait for Rowland's answer. "Mordaunt knows the chancery courts better than the Lord Chancellor himself."

"Thank you, your grace." *But no thanks for dragging me into Crown business again.*

"That is enough for tonight." The duke rose. Rowland must also stand, however much his groin ached at that moment.

"Your grace, I swear on my honor that Miss Ysabel Foxe is loyal to the Crown. She is not spying on England."

The duke, not answering that plea, said instead, "Go to your new house tonight. I'll leave a footman to guide you. The household staff knows to expect you."

Waving away Rowland's subdued expression of gratitude, Lord Bagsham bid him adieu and departed. Which relieved Rowland from hiding his irate and profound resentment.

God blind me! There's no escape!

While the duke's footman waited in the foyer, Rowland went upstairs and packed his satchel.

Absolom had remained above the corruption that Tom claimed greased the workings of England. Only five days after the king fulfilled Absolom's dream of the title returning to the family, and now Rowland was already enmired in the Crown's stealthy ways. He might as well swim in the Thames. In applying old-fashioned black tribute to force Rowland to become the king's watcher, the duke seemed sure of Rowland's obedience. Indeed, he'd been so certain that Rowland would choose to protect Lizzie that the duke had come prepared with an emolument as big as a house to reward Rowland's service.

Another "gratuity" he couldn't refuse.

His groin hurt from being stomped in the street.

His belly churned from an interview that made him ill.

His heart ached because he had to protect Lizzie—and yet never tell anyone.

He scratched a message for Perry to join him at this new house. He'd return to Benson's in the morning to explain to the others, without revealing what he'd got himself stuck in.

Had he learned nothing from Absolom about how to avoid that which corrupts one's soul?

No, it was about honor; Absolom didn't believe in either souls or salvation.

9

Night Tales

THE OLD DUTCH CLOCK in the lodging house struck ten o'clock not long after Tamsin joined her friends in the small salon where Winwood was hosting their supper. Which meant it would be midnight before the evening ended and Camilla could be coaxed into going to bed.

Felicity exclaimed with delight over the feast. "This is better than the fare in the taverns near our theatre."

She attacked her supper while maintaining tidy Continental manners like Lizzie's, speaking rapidly and often slipping into French, then sliding as easily into a London lady's accent. "Ah, a French pottage with lentils. As if I am once more in the world of my childhood."

With soft candlelight, the small parlor where they dined felt elegant. Winwood had ordered an impressive supper.

Pressed tongue with soft, thinly sliced bread.

A pie stuffed with cabbage and greens and potatoes.

Carrots sliced into sticks and heated in butter.

Hot apples with cinnamon and cream.

Felicity began a long recitation of her story, often pausing to exclaim over a new dish passed to her. Camilla was enraptured by Felicity's story; therefore, Tamsin practiced patience, listening to the details of how Felicity entered the theatre in Paris, quarreled with her father, came to live with an aunt in London, and joined the theatre in Covent Garden.

Finally, Tamsin prompted for a speedier story. "Tell us about your jeopardy, Miss Oakes."

"It began," Felicity sipped her punch, "when I joined the troupe's summer tour in the north. I had three supporting parts and played Dromio as you saw me tonight. Aunt Letitia invited a friend to live with her in my absence."

Camilla said, "Bright horizons for you."

"It did seem to promise so, lovely lady." Felicity flashed a smile that Tamsin distrusted. When Felicity touched Camilla's hand, she peeked at Tamsin, as if to assess her reaction. "Alas, it came to tragedy."

"What happened?" Tamsin refrained from showing her impatience with this overly-dramatic young person. Felicity might be an actress, but she was a poor storyteller.

"I came home to find the companion gone and my beloved Aunt Letitia mute and ill. She died in my arms the next day."

"Providence save me!" Winwood said. "I was called to England to assist her last winter, but then she wrote that she was well. If only I'd known, I'd have been here."

"Mayhap," Felicity said. "There wasn't time to summon you, Cousin Winwood."

"I am sorry for your loss," Camilla said.

"I, too." Tamsin rubbed her Archangel coin, thinking of her own Uncle Absolom.

"The worst is to come." Felicity sipped her wine punch. "In my absence, she'd married a clownish dissident preacher who provided my aunt healing draughts. This charlatan claims my aunt left her house and chattel goods to him. But I swear, she'd promised it all to me. He set my baggage by the door on the day of her funeral, insisting I be gone."

"God keep my giddy cat!" Camilla voiced her over-excited dismay, which provoked more dramatics from Felicity.

"You are sweet to care, *ma chère dame*." Felicity messed about with the slice of pie on her plate. "I call daily on the blue heavens for justice."

Winwood said, "Why send rogues after you on the streets?"

"The threats began when I applied to my aunt's lawyer to bring this usurper to the courts. Yet the courts will take forever, because I cannot afford the customary emoluments. And so, Winwood, I need your help."

"I'm a doctor, not a lawyer." A peculiar note of hesitancy in his voice left Tamsin wondering whether Winwood trusted his cousin. "It's the chancery courts where you have challenged this usurper? I haven't funds to help with fees."

Not waiting for Felicity to answer, Camilla said, "Can we commence a restoration?" She clasped Tamsin's hand under the tablecloth and mouthed one word: *Please.*

Hence, Tamsin felt compelled to agree to it.

"What?" Winwood's expression revealed more trepidation than he'd shown while Felicity told her story.

Though reluctant, Tamsin said, "Camilla means that we should help return Felicity's goods to her possession. Of course, we'd do it when that rogue is gone from the premises."

"It should be simple," Camilla said, who had never planned a restoration, only come along for the adventure. However, she revealed her confidence in any plan Tamsin might make.

"You want to break into our aunt's house and steal Felicity's things." Winwood restated Camilla's idea, not asking for clarification. "It's a rather a leap from her problem to your solution."

"It isn't theft," Felicity said. "I have a letter from our aunt which the lawyers believe fully proves her intent."

"Yes, not theft. It's a restoration," Camilla said. She tugged at Tamsin's sleeve under the tablecloth, clearly wanting Tamsin to apply her talents to this restoration.

"We know how to undertake justice where others cannot." Tamsin wondered why Winwood shrank from the restoration.

That Dutch clock in the hallway chimed.

"Oh! Oh no!" Felicity jumped up, startled. "Winwood, with those dogs following me, I must beg you to escort me home tonight. I regret to ask it of you."

Camilla stirred. "Stay with us. Tamsin's cousin Lizzie is gone for the week, so her bed is empty. You'll be safe here."

"I am amazingly grateful." Felicity cheerfully accepted. "I lost all the safety I enjoyed when I abided with my aunt."

"I'm happy to help with a restoration," Tamsin said. "But Winwood, why are you hesitating?"

"It's occurring so rapidly," Winwood said. "But if you plan this restoration, Miss Foxe, then I'm sure we shall succeed."

Tamsin felt heat in her face, thrilled at Winwood's trust in her, then reined in that feeling, since she shouldn't be proud to have a peculiar talent for planning restorative thefts. She said, "To begin, we must watch your aunt's house to know when this man is not at home. Is tomorrow too early?"

"No," Felicity said, delight in her voice like music.

"We shall need a cart," Tamsin said.

"That is beyond my resources." Felicity turned glum.

"We have connections with a man who keeps a stable nearby," Tamsin said. "He can help us to hire a cart."

"My friends from the theatre can assist," Felicity said. "I vow to match your friendship with gratitude as long as I draw breath on this earth."

"We must consult with Perry about your plan. And about those stalkers." Winwood's uncertainty lingered.

"Who is this Perry to be consulted?" Felicity raised her brows, but only to flirt with Camilla.

Camilla said, "He's a Crown intelligencer who is a close comrade of Tamsin's cousin Rowland."

"Crown intelligencers?" Felicity clutched at her throat, alarm in her voice. Tamsin had just endured an hour of the woman's performance and couldn't see why Felicity now feigned shock.

"Formerly an intelligencer," Tamsin said. "He's now the overseer for our lands in Cambridgeshire. He has a good deal of uncommon wisdom."

"I hope to meet him soon." Felicity sounded pleasant, yet Tamsin heard forced words.

"But I don't think we need Perry for this simple task." Yet having recognized Winwood's hesitation, Tamsin should have agreed to involve Perry, just to reassure Winwood. But she'd been planning small-scale restorations for years, which was longer than she'd known either Winwood or Perry.

With plans for the next morning's activities, the women bid good night to Winwood. Tamsin intended to ask again in the morning, privately, about Winwood's hesitation. She suspected he shared the same suspicion she did, that there was more to Felicity's story. Or perhaps it was the seeming illegality of this small restoration. He'd always begged to be innocent of any knowledge about the acts of justice the Foxe cousins undertook on their home ground.

Felicity's case for justice seemed solid, and this small restoration would satisfy Camilla's desire for adventure while they dealt with a tedium of lawyers for the rest of the week. And it satisfied Tamsin's desire to be busy until she was free to return home to Revelstone House.

Upstairs, Tamsin went to close the shutters before they undressed for bed. On the street below, three figures lurked in the doorway of an empty house across the way. The same three stalkers who'd pursued Felicity out of the theatre. Tamsin's cheeks twitched, so she smiled. Nothing to be afraid of.

Come breakfast, she'd ask Perry to find guards, using Felicity's enemies as an excuse, but with protection for Camilla as her own special desire.

— TOM —

AFTER JACOB AND AURORA left him in solitude once more, Tom asked Adam to bring biscuits, claret, and water to his bedchamber. Then he sat in his room and opened the red-leather book with Aurora's Greek translation.

The first thing he learned after reading a few pages of the translation: he and his cousins had got it all wrong in the past year, pursuing first the Earl of Hawksmoor, then Danvers Duncombe as Absolom's nemesis. In fact, the Foxe cousins were the nemesis of his enemies. Surely Tom had introduced that mistaken appellation since he was supposed to be the scholar. He'd paid poor attention in his Greek tutorials, especially those with Aurora.

The one line in Greek he always remembered was Aurora's claim for bravery:

The proud heart feels not terror nor turns to run.

When he flipped a page in the *Ajax* translation, a single sheet covered in familiar handwriting fell to the carpet. He picked it up to find a note in Greek. He mouthed the words while reaching into dusty, disused memory to translate.

> Do not waste time seeking honor among W's confederates, who call themselves Hawkins' Heirs. If they are like W, they are devoid of honor.

Below that warning, she'd scrawled the names of Withersea's business partners. Tom shuddered at the idea that men would choose to call themselves after the despicable Admiral Hawkins, who advanced the slave trade while serving Queen Elizabeth. In the list of ten names, Tom recognized only the Marquess of Withersea's name, the man who sought to destroy Jacob's life.

When he'd first seen those raw wounds on the utterly innocent Jacob, Tom had wanted to wreak the greatest evil. However, he needed only to serve justice. To be a true friend. He had to learn quickly how to ensure Jacob's safety. But he was inclined to look further, to destroy the marquess.

Except, as he tried to press his mind to the work, he could not stop thinking of Aurora. No, not in the way she'd invaded his dreams the night before she left Trinity; he'd accepted long ago that they did not share their deepest hearts, only friendship. But that friendship had not endured after Trinity. She had not written him, and only came now when Jacob needed help.

He thought over what they'd exchanged. He had to know more, especially about the funds the king had frozen. And he needed to consider the coincidence she'd mentioned, though far too briefly. Jacob's father and brothers died in an accident. A week later, Jacob's new guardian was killed in a robbery. Was Aurora too caught up in her grief to notice such outrageous coincidences?

He set *Ajax* aside when the Dutch clock struck one tone, marking the beginning of Wednesday, leaving Tom two days and two nights to advance a plan. He again considered Jacob's situation and the related horror. Each time, his mind roamed over twenty ideas of what could be done, what must be done.

His heart beat hard and fast, as if he'd been running a race since Jacob and Aurora departed. Was he falling ill again? A few delirious, febrile moments before fever and lethargy consumed him once more?

He did what Winwood taught him when intense excitement left his heart thudding: examine what he was feeling, everywhere in his body. It took several moments to name what he felt, because it had become unfamiliar.

He was happy. He'd undertaken tasks he might very well be capable of doing. The aspiration—he felt sure of success—kicked awake something deep inside, as if he'd grown a new organ that was keen to take on the world, to go to battle for Jacob.

All he needed was for Ned and Perry to return. Since Tom had had ample time to form a plan of action, he came down to the salon they'd hired in the lodging house and asked the night porter to bring the fixings for punch.

"Hugh, do you have Jamaican rum in the house? If not, perhaps arrack? May I beg for citrons, rose water, and sugar? And nutmeg, cloves, and mace, if your cook has such."

"Sufficient for your entire party?" Hugh asked.

"No. There'll be only three of us." Tom passed the man what he hoped was the proper gratuity. Then he thought again to add more to the gratuity, to purchase information. He learned that:

Miss Ysabel Foxe had departed after luncheon and entered a hired carriage with a night bag.

Miss Thomasine and her friends, including a new friend from the London theatre, had enjoyed supper in another part of the house (without pausing to find Tom).

After midnight, the doctor had prescribed an ointment for Hugh's sore toe, then retired to bed.

The Earl of Marborne had met with the Duke of Bagsham, who set a meeting for the morrow with a barrister named Mordaunt. The earl then departed with his baggage, leaving an enormous gratuity but no message for Tom.

Hence, without departing from the house, Tom had confirmation of Rowland's claim that servants always hear everything. For Tom's purposes, Mordaunt and Bagsham demanded his immediate attention come morning, since both names appeared on Aurora's list of Hawkins' Heirs.

While stirring the hot punch, Tom heard Perry in the foyer. Tom prepared to voice his plan:

It falls on the three of us as brothers in arms to save a pair of old friends from the straits of Scylla and Charybdis.

And it fell on Tom to do what Absolom predicted: practice law to protect the innocent. Yet few would know how he intended to harness his great talent for prevarication.

10
A Watcher's Sinecure

WHEN THEY'D SERVED ON the Continent, Rowland was frequently scolded by Perry. "You're England's champion at fretting. 'Tis a pity you can't just drink and let a decision creep into your mind when the time is right."

Rowland followed the duke's footman, who was called Isaac, across Covent Garden to the house the duke offered as a sinecure. Because Rowland was to be his spy. A watcher for the king.

For the entire journey, Rowland fretted about how the Duke of Bagsham had enmired him so swiftly. To stave off his vexation, Rowland resumed his meditations on Marborne parish and his cousins. He must now become as principled and methodical a man as Uncle Absolom had been.

They crossed a few streets in Covent Garden, and Rowland hadn't time to sufficiently marshal his thoughts before they stopped at a door in the middle of a row of homes.

"Here is Xanthus House, your lordship," Isaac said. "Though I don't know what the name means. Seems foreign."

"It's named after Achilles' horse." Tom would be delighted to find a horse from the poet Homer in London.

"Was he a general in the last English wars?"

"No, it's from old stories, like Shakespeare, but another poet and another country."

"Foreign then, eh, your lordship?"

"You might say."

The house stood midway along a row of identical brick town-houses built after the Great Fire, spanning what had once been two independent units. The door, painted a deep brown, opened only one step up from the cobbled street, its overhang just wide enough to get out of the rain while opening the door.

Isaac said, "The butler is called Lazarus. You can trust him to know his business."

Then Isaac rapped on the door, which was opened by an austere man who said, "Good evening," in a voice as dry as bones.

"Good evening, Lazarus. This is the Earl of Marborne. I'll leave him in your care, since you have the duke's instructions." Isaac dropped Rowland's bag on the step and was gone.

"Welcome, my lord." The man opened the door wider. "Cook has a late supper for you, to be served in your chamber. We didn't know if you've dined."

Lazarus (such a name must have been a burden in childhood) took possession of Rowland's bag and handed it to a boy to take to his lordship's bedchamber.

"May I show your lordship the house while your midnight supper is being laid?"

Lazarus had stiff manners, like diplomats' servants in Paris and Amsterdam. Such a man must be uncomfortable having a new Dick Whittington (sans cat) thrust upon him. Hence, Rowland expected that, dressed as he was in a seven-shilling suit that had rolled on London cobbles with Rowland inside it, he'd have to do better than his best to earn this man's respect.

"Please be my guide, Mr. Lazarus." Try as Rowland might, he could not catch the man's direct gaze.

"I'm called only Lazarus, my lord. A custom of the house."

"I shall respect all your customs, Lazarus."

"If you so wish."

Up the stairs from the foyer, Rowland was shown a library, a withdrawing room, and an immense dining hall, then enough bedrooms up the next two floors that his cousins and friends should all fit.

The house had all the modern accoutrements, like the handsome, highly polished longcase clock in the hallway near what Lazarus indicated was Rowland's bedchamber. The clock struck the hour just then with a delicate chime.

"This is a superiorly maintained house, Lazarus. The housekeeper must be proud. Please tell her I said so."

"I shall give her your compliments." He still avoided meeting Rowland's gaze.

Forcing a lighter tone, Rowland said, "At home in Cambridgeshire, none of us dare disobey our housekeeper. I hope our Mrs. Bell taught me well enough that you and the staff shall find me an agreeable tenant."

"Tenant, sir? As I understand from his grace, the duke, you are to be master of the house. The staff and the contents of the house are wholly at your disposal."

"Including these closets?" Rowland swept his hand to encompass the array of clothes in the dressing room that adjoined his sleeping chamber.

"Yes, my lord, including the wardrobe. I believe you are about the size of…" Lazarus's voice, dusty and quiet, broke for a heartbeat. "…the previous resident."

"Does the duke keep this house for lost strangers like me?" Rowland wanted a light tone, but Lazarus didn't notice.

"He gave it to Viscount Bravewood, the duke's nephew and heir." Lazarus cleared his throat. "But his lordship the viscount perished in the battle at Sedgemoor this last July. We here at Xanthus House find it…ah, I hope you don't mind me saying so, but we experienced a great sadness. He was a good man and the best master."

"God blind me! That's only a month ago!" Rowland resisted grasping the man's shoulder, the way he'd console a friend. "I am sorry for your loss. And a total stranger is thrust upon you."

"The staff considers your arrival to be a blessing, my lord." Lazarus finally lifted his eyes. "It is good to be busy again. We hope you find yourself comfortable at Xanthus House."

"It is I who must thank you for your welcome, Lazarus." *God smite me, what has the duke thrust me into?* "I beg that you will guide me, so I can best keep your customs."

"If you wish, my lord."

Rowland had visited the houses of diplomats and lords on the Continent but had no such experience in London. He didn't know how to reward the staff or how to offer consolation over the loss of their former master.

"Lazarus, it is a custom from my home in Cambridge that everyone is to have Sunday free and another half day during the week. You can assign who takes which half-day."

"That is perhaps too generous, my lord. But I shall discuss such with the housekeeper come morning."

"How many," Rowland didn't know the proper way to ask, "are on your staff?" He did not ask: Who does the duke expect will pay the staff's wages?

Lazarus answered with his now-familiar remote manner. "We are a small staff. The duke has kept eight of us here in town. Others have returned to the Bravewood estates. But the duke has assured us we shall all remain under his protection."

"I should like to meet everyone in the morning."

"Of course, your lordship." The butler shifted, even more stiffly formal. "After you have enjoyed your supper, may I assist you as groom of the chamber?

Rowland declined, unprepared to be attended so closely.

Lazarus nodded, not showing any surprise. Or any emotion at all. Then he left Rowland in his new chambers, where a cold supper had been laid for him, better than the soggy meat pie he'd dined on at The Rose after leaving the theatre.

~

Rowland sat on a cozy chair and kicked off his shoes, saying aloud, "Now I am to be the dashed duke's damnable creature."

He meant to sound Shakespearean, but it rang out as bitter. Was he to be raised up in society by Lord Bagsham, then forced to be the man's tool ever after? The duke had lost his only heir thirty days ago, then installed Rowland to live in the dead man's house, wear his clothes, command his servants. Did the duke have any human feeling, either for his lost heir or for Rowland? The duke had, though, promised the staff could keep their places. That signaled a degree of goodness.

Hoping Perry might arrive that night to discuss this unexpected upheaval, Rowland stayed up until the longcase clock down the hall chimed two o'clock. He and Perry had much to do and much to discover quickly:

Find out who stalked Rowland with evil intent.

Learn whether Michel Chêne is truly Kilbuck's own spy.

Create a tale to account for pages missing from Duncombe's ledger of traitors who funded Monmouth's invasion.

Take up burdens for Marborne, which Tamsin had carried for too long.

Find Lizzie. Beg her to stop working for Colonel Kilbuck.

He began shivering, first thinking he was cold, then knowing he quivered over his inability to act. He needed to remove Lizzie from jeopardy, for her own sake, not only to escape the duke's command of Rowland's cooperation.

Yet he couldn't ask Lizzie to stop doing what she wanted to do.

He lay down on a bed more comfortable than any barracks in his previous life. And he didn't have to listen to other men snoring and groaning in the night. But it was merely a new kind of barracks, since despite his wishes, Rowland was now a watcher for the king, his life not his own to command. He was so revolted by what the duke forced him into, he felt ill. In his belly, in his heart. He shifted his mind from useless rage to ponder how he might advance Marborne's well-being.

Since he couldn't sleep, Rowland juggled dangerously large numbers, given that he was used to only figuring how much he might spend on tavern food versus subsisting on barracks' fare until the next time the king bothered to pay wages. He began doing sums with scant information, starting with what he'd been earning: thirty pounds a year as a lieutenant. From Tamsin's calculations, the rents at Marborne parish should be worth a hundred pounds each year, but with catastrophes such as fire and bad harvests, she said the rents received were more like thirty pounds, with each family of cottagers living on five pounds a year.

Whenever he'd dreamed of leaving his soldier's poverty behind, while wanting to be admitted to Lizzie's company as a gentleman, he'd calculated that a gentleman needed an impossible one hundred pounds a year. Setting aside any idea of what might be demanded of an earl, Rowland took his guess of a gentleman's hundred pounds and added the entire family and the Revelstone household, plus the parish rector and other dependents. That meant they needed five hundred pounds income a year.

Which meant that, for all they'd earned in the last week's gambol and all Tamsin planned to spend to restore the parish, they had only a year's income left. Rents would sustain them only if the villages miraculously became wealthy in an instant from Rowland's gift of sheep and cows. They'd be attending the king's court in patched suits bought out of pawn. While eating turnips and hoping for cheese from the new sheep.

Whatever way he found to go forward, it was Rowland's turn to serve the parish needs. He did not want his cousins to return to their makeshift ways: Ned's forgeries, Tom's pittance as a barrister's clerk, Tamsin's highwayman methods for serving justice. At their next meeting, he'd ask the duke what a "king's watcher" earned on a regular basis, because he couldn't keep his family (much less Marborne villages) out of poverty with only gratuities or city sinecures like Xanthus House.

He drifted toward sleep, then jerked awake, his arm remembering the retort of that pistol jangling up his arm. Then he drifted again, wondering who'd set out to kill him.

When he next jolted awake, a brilliant idea rose from his deepest recesses. The new earl, master of Marborne villages and woods and farms, needed to become a reaper of justice—and on a scale grander than Tamsin's desperado methods. He must turn his new predicament into a hunt for a guilty and wealthy man who deserved to be plundered by a skulk of foxes in need of a restoration.

How to discover a great sinner in England? Could that name be among those on the page missing from Duncombe's ledger? He tried to remember the names on that page, beyond those that Viscount Heydon had wanted to protect.

In whatever way he proceeded, Rowland must find a way out of Lord Bagsham's snare so that he might live by the principles that Absolom taught. Especially: *My family obligations are sacred.*

11

A Forger, a Spy, and a Warrior

"You'd have to be bog-eyed not to see the threat."

Perry, hands on his hips, upbraided the night porter at Benson's lodging house. He stood in the open doorway, complaining about the ruffians they'd seen on the street.

"I'm here to watch the door, not the street." Hugh got his back up, not liking the scolding.

Ned, a bit in the altitudes, spoke over wine-numbed lips. "It's not a dog worth whistling for. I'm sure Hugh knows his work."

But Perry persisted. "How, Mr. Hugh, am I to apprehend that you know your business?"

"I'm sorry, sir," Hugh said. "What did I miss?"

"We came upon three bram coves in the shadows, cuddling with their cudgels and watching your door. We affrighted them our own selves, though you should never have let them be so content to linger at the steps of your house."

"Bram coves, sir?"

"Rogues. The kind hired for their brawn."

"It won't happen again, sir. I believe Mr. Tom Foxe awaits you in the dining salon."

On the way to the salon, Perry admonished Ned. "I tell you, chucking, your bare hands are never to be offered in a brawl. God gave you a talent. Hence, it is a sin for you, Ned Wijck, to risk your hands going up against berks in an alley."

"Stop playing the martinet, Mr. Frake. What did your mother mean when she insisted that you must take up the reins?"

"You know the kinds of things mothers want and the things they say to get it."

"Alas, I do not," Ned said. "I never did. And until today, I didn't know about your mother's influence in your life."

"Did I invoke sadness for your mother?" Perry said.

"No." Ned wasn't sad about a mother he'd never known; he wanted to understand about Perry's mother and her influence.

They found Tom alone in the salon, which ended that conversation. Tom stood at the head of the table, mixing a punch in a tin-glazed delftware bowl. It wasn't, to Ned's eye, among the finest holland ware sold into England.

Tom pointed to the chairs beside him and held up a pair of copper mugs. "This fillip," he gestured to the punch bowl, "is a real dog's nose, my friends. May I offer you a mug?"

Perry slumped into a chair, surely as worn as Ned from perusing taverns between his mother's cottage in the Tower Hill hamlets and Covent Garden. He tucked stray strands of pale hair behind his ear and held out his hand for a mug.

"Such lavish punch, Tom. Do you agree, chucking?" Perry sang a bit of the song men had been singing in The Rose tavern:

> If these delights thy mind may move,
> Then live with me and be my love.

Ned accepted a mug and took a dram. "Our Tom wants something from us."

"Verily, Tom Foxe?" Perry wrinkled his big Roman nose, ice-blue eyes probing at Tom's soul.

"Yes, gentleman. If you will agree to help me, it falls upon us to plan a gambol to save an old friend from the straits of Scylla and Charybdis."

Perry said, "I know not in what county Charybdis might be found, being gone from England so many years. But if your Charybdis and Scylla be in the Low Countries, I'll find it in a jot."

"Surely an adventure was writ in the stars when Tamsin allowed Tom to come to London." Ned tossed back his own mop of hair, shaking his head in hopes of clearing it.

"We three need a plan," Tom said, not seizing on their jibes, which was unlike him, given Ned's long knowledge of Tom's merry ways. "There's none but us to take the proper action."

"What makes you say so?" Perry became serious.

"Tamsin deserves a rest," Tom said. "She's had a year of working to save us all."

"Aye," Perry said. "No use mithering Miss Thomasine. She can stay a'reight and tight while we perform whatever chores you've invented for us."

Ned said, "You are about to claim, aren't you, Tom, that Fate banged Rollo hard on the head? That he deserves a rest?"

Perry said, "Rollo has been running gambols for the Crown every living day since Twelfth Night. It's what he's best fit for. And yet, his head has been in the clouds since—"

"Since Sunday," Ned said.

"Nay," Perry said. "Since Miss Ysabel Foxe gave him permission to make love to her."

Ned studied the bottom of his copper mug, then handed it back to Tom for another dollop of punch. "Come, Tom. You take too long to say what you want."

"It distresses me also," Perry said. "I'm yearning for my bed, yet Tom has stirred our hearts while saying nowt. Tell us what chaos you plan to let loose."

Tom said, "An old friend I knew at Trinity College visited today. He needs my help to keep the Marquess of Withersea from stealing his inheritance. That lord injured my friend cruelly with a whipping. Then he stole a picture of my friend's mother and sold it, solely to hurt him."

"That's bad business," Ned said.

"Yet can it not wait for the morning?" Perry said. "If this rescue requires lawyers and courts and such, it canna be fixed in the wee hours of today."

"Beyond what my friends need for protection." Tom shifted, a mite shaky to Ned's mind, "Withersea seeks to steal my friend's title. He's a bad man, and we must stop him in his evil."

No one breathed. Or sipped punch. Or shuffled.

Ned sighed, resigned that he must follow Tom into this jumble. "So, what shall we do?"

"Wait! Hold back your war horse a moment," Perry said. "How did your old school crony become involved in Withersea's business, Tom?"

"My friend was a child when I last knew him, not a student at Trinity. He came with his sister, the marquess's wife. She asked me to save him from being disinherited."

"The marquess hurt a child?" Perry sat up, indignant.

"He's grown now," Tom said. "But childlike from birth. He is a friend, and I promised to protect him, both long ago and again today. His rescue is important to me."

Ned frowned. "How do you know this marchioness, Tom? Withersea is far north, nowhere near our part of the country."

"The three of us shared chambers at Trinity College."

Ned sputtered in his copper mug.

Perry guffawed.

"Though not even for a full term," Tom said.

"There's nowt so queer as folk!" Perry slapped Tom's shoulder hard enough to send Tom back to the shire. "Or so my granddam said, and she never met the likes of you, Tom Foxe."

Tom continued. "I promised the marchioness I would —"

"Do armed battle with her enemies?" Perry's voice pitched with delight. "Prepare the marquess for the sexton's spade?"

"No! No one dies!" Tom's face was a portrait of dismay. "We shall only prevent the marquess from spoiling Jacob's life."

"Rather than so much travail," Perry said, "why not simply flee England with your inamorata and her brother? Must you punish that man to win the lady's heart?"

"I seek only protection and justice for her brother Jacob. I am not seeking her heart." Tom showed his empty hands.

Ned always tended to accept Tom's claims and felt too sleepy to judge otherwise. "So, our Restoration Rules abide? No one dies. Reap justice. Shun revenge."

"And retrieve a stolen picture," Perry said, tapping Ned's thumb to add that item. "Perhaps you can do that come morning, my heartling."

"That's the whole of it for this gambol," Tom said. "Now, to proceed, we need a plan."

"Mayhap," Perry said, "there's another dollop of punch while we think on it?"

~

"I shan't claim this new gambol distresses me," Perry said. "Only last week we destroyed an earl, a new-fashioned baron, a tipsy solicitor, and a London man of business. Mayhap, stopping one single marquess from evil is easier work."

Ned said, "I'd be proud if it was our actions that did it all last week, but our neighbor, Viscount Heydon, levied our enemies' total ruin. We are innocent of such deep schemes."

Perry rubbed along the fading paint stains on Ned's fingers. "You are so very, very innocent, Mr. Wijck."

At that touch, Ned felt all his bones straighten and his heart beat with its true strength.

Tom, however, wanted to talk business. "I need your help tonight, Ned. Please adjust this letter from my old barrister, to say that I've finished my apprenticeship."

"Rather than lying in bed for half a year?" Perry prodded Tom with one long finger. "I admire your wit and will, launching your career in the law by way of a forgery."

"Nothing wrong," Ned said, "with forgery for the sake of our family. I'll start in the morning when there's good light."

"Tonight, please," Tom said. "Come morning, I have more tasks for you, while Perry and I go to meet a corrupt lawyer called Mordaunt before he gets his hooks in Rollo."

"Wait!" Perry said. "You began with a tale of an evil marquess." He tapped Tom's index finger. "Then you introduced your inamorata, the marchioness." Second finger tapped.

"She's not my lover." Tom's hands twitched.

Perry shook his head at the disclaimer. "Next, you say we shall pursue a bad lawyer called Mordaunt." Third finger. "I wager you shall ask me to prowl this lawyer," pressing Tom's fourth finger on the table, "for the sake of a gambol that you have yet to describe. And that now seems to include Rollo."

"Yes, you have the nub of it." Tom eased his hand from under Perry's. "Tonight, a duke visited Rollo, sending him to the lawyer Mordaunt for help to move Marborne business through the chancery court. The marchioness gave me of Withersea's business confederates, which included both the duke's and the lawyer's names. And so…"

Perry said, "And so, we must save Rollo from the wolves?"

"That's your work and mine early tomorrow," Tom said. "And Ned must see Simon Touchstone, who will send him to paint portraits of Withersea's family."

Ned breathed heavily into his cup. "But I wanted to return with Perry to Revelstone on Saturday." He balanced the chance to paint a portrait against his desire to go home. With Perry.

"You must live in the marquess's house, to be my eyes and hands, until we launch the gambol," Tom said.

Perry coughed, sputtering mulled wine on the table, which he wiped away with his hand. "Hold thy dog on a strong rope, Tom Foxe. You want Ned to spy on the evil Lord Withersea? Not me?"

"Ned must protect my friend Jacob from the marquess."

Perry dipped his cup in the bowl for more punch. "There's them that say a lob-cock fellow like myself is slow witted, because a thought must travel a long way until it finds voice."

"You are in no way slow witted," Tom said.

"Now, I am to prowl this lawyer called Mordaunt to protect Rollo. Ned is to paint and protect a different lord's kinder."

"You have it!" Tom said. "Jacob's father and guardian have both died, so there's only us to save him."

Perry threw up his hands. "It's now as clear as water in a Dutch canal. And Ned will protect your inamorata with his paintbrush?"

"Not my inamorata," Tom said. "Only an old friend."

"Must I fight the marquess?" Ned said. "I can pretend to be a highwayman for a restoration, but I cannot strike a lord. And don't marquesses have armies of servants? And even real armies with hackbuts and sabers and such?"

"No, you won't fight anyone." Tom held up his hands, as if pleading innocent of that intent. "Your presence in the house will protect Jacob while we prepare a gambol. Tomorrow night, you'll help Perry enter the marquess's mansion, so he can prowl there for letters and writs to help my scheme."

"Odsme! A lawyer in the morning, a marquess at night. That's me done up if I'm caught." Perry begged God to smite him, calling imprecations on the man (now in heaven) whose unpropitious copulation brought his son to this moment, all salted with mild doses of *bloomings* and *flippings*.

When Perry ceased emoting, Ned said, "Am I to alter evil writs to make sure that they cannot be used against your friend?"

"Lo, you perceive my direction," Tom said.

"I'll fetch ink and quills from my room." Ned rose.

"Sit. Finish your punch first," Tom said. "Early tomorrow, Perry and I will seek all the details we can gather in London. I shall be wedded to the barrister's chambers. Perry, you will employ your excellent talents at that man's house. *Vero, vero.*"

"Speak me no Latin," Perry said. "We are in England."

"Will Tamsin let you out to visit the barrister?" Ned asked.

"I'll leave a note that I'm meeting a friend."

"And Rollo? What do we tell him?" Perry said.

Tom hesitated. "That's a bit complicated. You see—"

"Beg pardon, sirs." Hugh the porter knocked, bearing a letter. "Mr. Frake, his lordship the earl asked me to leave a message in your room. I thought you might like to have it now."

Perry read the note in silence. "Rowland wants me to join him at a Covent Garden house the Duke of Bagsham lent him."

"He left the rest of us here at the lodging house?" Ned asked. He didn't mean to sound resentful that Perry was called to do Rowland's bidding, but it leaked out of him.

"What do you suppose he's got up to?" Perry rose.

Ned tugged at Perry's sleeve. "Find out tomorrow, dear heart. We have Tom's task tonight."

Perry stared at Ned, as if waiting to hear more. Then he seemed to perceive Ned's meaning. "We'll ask Rollo in the morning. The note says he has a ten o'clock meeting with the barrister."

Tom said, "You can join him there, Perry, after we begin our morning explorations."

"Hold on to your fine felt hat for a minute. Do I understand it all?" Perry held up a massive paw and began once again to tick items on his fingers. "The Marquess of Withersea is a wicked lord who seeks to steal the title and estates of his brother-in-law."

Tom said, "Yes, the evil against Jacob forces us into action."

Perry tapped each of his fingers, counting off all that Tom had presented for them to do.

"You forgot one thing," Tom said. "Tomorrow night you'll meet Ned at the marquess's house to search there."

"It is delightful," Perry said, "that you shall allow us to be reunited in the middle of your gambol. Ned?"

Not answering, Ned stirred the punchbowl, seeking a dram, finding he nursed a resentment that Rowland had summoned Perry to his new house but had forgotten anyone else.

As if knowing Ned's thoughts, Perry leaned close. "I am quite remorseful, sweeting, that I rose so fast to answer Rollo's message, when it's important to stay and help your work. It's a habit. I shall do better the next time, I swear it on my granddam's head."

Tom ignored them. "On Thursday, we launch the gambol."

"Which you have yet to tell us about," Perry said.

"We can guess," Ned said. "To start, Tom shall want to trade my devil-writing for any original papers you find."

"You have it, Ned!" Tom grabbed Ned's hand to shake it, resulting in spilt punch to be mopped up with a napkin.

"Tell us the end of the scheme." Perry tapped his thumb, which hadn't yet been counted. "How do we keep the marquess from launching any further evil?"

"We won't know," Tom said, "until we prowl through his business. For example, it seems that the king froze funds that Withersea had lodged with an agent."

Perry folded his arms, shaking his head, then declared his thoughts by forming a circle with his hand. "Your plan, as it stands now, has nowt at its end?"

"I shall remain open," Tom said, "to any inspiration and insight you can bring to this gambol."

Perry laughed. He knocked the table with the flat of his tally hand. "I shall endorse your half-done plan, Tom. Rollo's plans always leave me stabbing in the dim and dark. We shall decide tomorrow night how it ends."

"How fast must we act?" Ned asked. "Is the danger near?"

"We have until Friday morning," Tom said. "That's when the Committee for Privileges and Conduct will either stop or approve Withersea's scheme against Jacob's title."

Seeing Perry wince at that short time, Ned said, "At its beginning, this plan gives me what I have wished for. But two days isn't enough time to paint a portrait. Only to sketch and choose my palette colors. Still, it's a beginning."

"My dear Ned," Perry said, "you inspire me. This is my first task as the new Marborne overseer. It's my chance to become one of Doctor Foxe's enlightened people."

Ned entertained the idea that he'd be doing what Uncle Absolom had foreseen, using his hands to do good work. But he'd had too much of Tom's punch. Tears welled up. Absolom wasn't there to know all their successes.

Day 2, Wednesday:
Mazes

———————————

O how falsely men
Accuse us gods as authors of their ill,
When by the bane their own bad lives instill
They suffer all the miseries of their states,
Past our inflictions, and beyond their fates.
— The Poet Known as Homer, *The Odyssey*
(George Chapman, translator)

—

I have heard of your paintings too, well enough;
God has given you one face,
and you make yourselves another.
— William Shakespeare, *Hamlet*

12
A Letter by Lamplight

SHE HAD TO ASK a servant for quill, ink, and paper, there being none in her guest chamber. Then Lizzie wrote quickly, too aware that there'd been more than enough wine at dinner, leaving her giddy. So much to say, yet there was no one in England she felt free to talk with in an unguarded way

> *Carissime,* Dear Lady: I have an unforeseen opportunity for my letter to be carried by a trusted friend. I therefore bend my head and take up this ill-formed pen under the light of a single candle to write to you.

> It is many months since we sat together to unburden our hearts (not to call it gossip). Mayhap it shall be many more months before I see your sweet face again. I may as well have sailed for the New World with tribes of Quakers and Methodists. Or to the Antipodes with rebels who accepted transport to avoid hanging. I feel this separation heartily. It is a strange new world from which I write.

> In my last to you, I wrote from the bucolic green country where I was born. I have, as you know, abided patiently with my unworldly cousins, who have been striving in poverty while on a perpetual quest to reclaim our family's title. That is one surprise I am sending to you. Our family fortunes reversed last week.

How that occurred I shall share with you at another time, for it would take an entire book to relate all the details. In sum, King James has at last agreed that the Foxe family rightfully holds the Marborne title. We rejoice—except it happened just days after my uncle, Doctor Absolom Foxe, departed these earthly realms. You have often graciously allowed me to chatter on about his kindnesses for the pack of wild Foxe cousins he inherited after our fathers and mothers died in the plague. Hence, a thorn remains in our current garden of delight, that he did not live to see our family's own restoration.

Because of your good-heartedness, you will understand my grief. You will also be amused by one complication in the Foxe family's new fortunes. You see, it is not my cousin Thomas Foxe (whom you have never met) that is to be the Earl of Marborne. No, because of a simple trick of Fate (the order in which all our fathers perished), it is Lieutenant Rowland Foxe who is earl. Yes, you know him. Yes, you whispered in my ear a hundred times that he had a secret *tendre* for me, just as you laughed fifty times at his dreadful tendency to quote Shakespeare (though most men have deeper, darker faults).

My dear friend, I am excessively happy for his good luck. Yes, you were correct about what has been in his heart all the while he lived in Amsterdam. It was beyond flattering to hear him speak of such tender feelings. Do not mock me with faux amazement when you hear that I have agreed he should ask the king to allow us to marry, which he shall do quite soon. This Friday, the Committee for Privileges and Conduct shall complete its pro forma approval of his title, based on the confirming documents the king has in hand.

Allow me to confess that, for a single unworthy heartbeat, I accepted Lord Marborne's proposal with a thought only for how quickly I could return to court in Amsterdam. But then, whether due to the heady bubbles of champagne, or my cousins' ebullient celebration of our family's restoration, or because of the man's own true goodness, I saw Rowland in the candlelight, and for the first time truly saw him for what he is.

You will say...have always said, that Rowland Foxe is well-formed, tall, and pleasing enough to look at. That he has gracious court manners. That, despite his quizzical brow, he is kind where most courtiers laugh in their sleeves. You know that about him. You are not too hard-hearted to believe a woman in the first flush of love when she declares that she's given her heart to the best man in Creation.

Well, he isn't the best man.

Rowland tells fantastical falsehoods in an instant and can conjure a crowd to believe every word. Likely, this proved a handy trait when he was under the command of our mutual friend. But this is not, surely, an endearing trait when one wishes to be open-hearted. Know this of My Lord Marborne:

He drinks. Not to excess, but it leads to reciting sonnets by his Bard, who owns a larger portion of his heart than does anyone else. Even me, perhaps.

He gambles, employing the cheating tricks that our uncle taught. But he doesn't cheat to win, the way my naïve little brother cheats. No, Rowland cheats to lose when he seeks to put his fellow gamblers at ease, so they'll speak when they'd otherwise be silent. Again, a useful skill for an intelligencer (which role he declares he has abandoned).

When we disagree, he concedes quickly. Is that a gambler's trick to make me reveal what I sought to keep secret? How am I to know that I've truly won any point of contention? How does such an infuriating man leave me feeling as if I might catch fire and perish when he's too near me?

He has a plan. Rowland Foxe always has a plan, for most everything. But even I, whom he calls most precious of all his cousins, am allowed to see only snippets of his plans, as if these are like a coin trick that can never be revealed to the beholder.

Hold! Know this also: He does coin tricks. Children love it. I do too, as if I am a child—and you know how far my heart has traveled over rocky ground since I left bucolic green Cambridgeshire for the hazards of court life.

And more, he honors the debt our uncle Absolom charged us with: to improve the world, to behave as enlightened people, to keep promises, and to treat family obligations as sacred.

Does all that help you to perceive the jeopardy in which I am caught? And I am caught because I have opened my heart to him. I have never shown my true self to anyone except you, and certainly not to any man. This opening of my heart, however, challenges me to the core. I am forced to revise my long-held understanding of where I belong in the world, and of what I shall be called to do if—when—I become the Countess of Marborne. Formerly, my only wish was to return to the royal court in Amsterdam. Now, I am mourning my uncle, a great man. Each private tear demands that I do the best possible in the world, as he taught us, doing the most with whatever position Fate grants me.

And I see similar demands weighing on Rowland. Yesterday, he refused to come visit with our "friends" when I described a few days' party in the country. He quickly perceived what I've been asked to do. He avows that he'll leave his old service behind, as he must now worry about the sheep and cows and grinding mills at Marborne. We parted with me rushing off to meet these alleged friends. Sadly, the only joy I've had from this party was to find H— here, who solemnly promised to carry this missive to you.

It's now coming close to dawn, so I must finish this letter and give it into H—'s hands. To conclude, besides my fondest wishes for your health and happiness, I have invented a new pattern for lace, as you challenged me in your letter. You have long admired my genius with the needle. I hope this will please you, and I hope you will share it with our mutual friend. —Your own true friend, Y

~

Lizzie slipped a gossamer-thin scrap of paper from inside the endpapers of a book she'd found at a bookseller's stall on Monday, a much-read copy of Dryden's *Essay of Dramatick Poesie*. With a rotten, unmendable quill, she scratched her lace scheme, consulting the key on that thin paper only twice, since she knew the key from much practice.

Sir: At your command, I have met those allies you call The Three Magi (a cruel joke) to assess whether they can be trusted. I looked for Monmouth taint, antipapal ranting, and fear of Louis of France.

Here is my news after an afternoon and a long night among them. I was invited for a few days, but most have departed, leaving me to find my own transport home. Two of your magi are corrupt to the bottom of their souls, more than is typical in London. I suspect they supported the Duke of Monmouth but have not yet confirmed that.

I sat at dinner with several guests, including two magistrates and a bishop from a chancery court. Your Balthazar was one of these; he owes your Melchior his sinecure. He was silent while we were asked to contribute to an antipapal campaign in London and central England, allegedly for the protection of Protestant souls. This is, I know, the opposite of what our mentor would wish in England.

The smallest magi, whom you call Caspar (I'd met him in Amsterdam), arrived much later than the others. He served as tout for the investment syndicate promoted at this event, a scheme he calls Hawkins' Heirs. The syndic, formed last winter, invests in ships carrying what he calls "African cargo" to the New World. Everyone in the room last night understood that he meant enslaved people, not ivory. Never ask me again to meet this muddy-souled creature.

As for your Melchior: He drinks. To excess. And becomes loquacious. He insults his wife in the presence of others. He invited his guests into a mercantile scheme like a trumpeter for a London banker. He put his hands upon me when his wife was away.

Thou shalt not trust this man. You chided me once, that my judgments are naïve. Yet have I ever been wrong about a man who indulges in repulsive actions? As the poet Dryden says, 'Bold knaves thrive without one grain of sense.'
— Your sibyl in Albion

Three times, due to haste while tortured by her pen, she'd had to blot and start a coded line anew. And she had scant faith in this easy-to-decipher code, so kept to aliases. If Colonel Kilbuck wanted more such petty chores from her, he needed to provide easier and more secret ways to send messages. After leaving her letter in the hands of H—, she went to bed, locking the door of her guest chamber, hoping her host had no other key.

She laid her head on the herb-stuffed pillow and closed her eyes. Then she sat up, despairing of her own witlessness.

Why hadn't she asked H— to take her to London with him? She rose and checked her reticule, to relieve her mind, that she had sufficient coin to hire a carriage in the morning. She could not abide another day in this house of corruption.

13
A London Marvel

TAMSIN REMAINED IN BED after dawn for the fifth consecutive morning, solely for the pleasure of listening to Camilla sigh in her sleep. And then…

"Are you kind and magnificent ladies awake? When can we begin our campaign?" Felicity, up from her bed in Lizzie's room and dressed, apologized neither for coming in unannounced nor for waking them.

"In a few moments." Camilla rose, yawning. She shook out a fresh shift and her walking dress from the wardrobe. Once again, Tamsin tried to persuade Camilla that they should go abroad in breeches while scouting for a restoration.

"We aren't playing highwayman in a Cambridgeshire copse," Camilla said.

Tamsin argued that the previous night's attack proved they'd be safer dressed in Tom's old clothes.

"Wear your grey walking gown." Camilla tossed it to her.

Barely allowing them time to dress, the insistent Felicity said, "Can we go now?"

Tamsin sent a message to Winwood and Tom to join them, then learned that Tom had left with Ned and Perry immediately after Winwood made him swallow his medicine and eat a coddled egg. Winwood had departed to visit an apothecary shop. Felicity fidgeted. Camilla begged. Tamsin decided: They'd begin their first exploration without Winwood. But first she looked out a window to confirm that Felicity's stalkers were gone.

That early, before seven o'clock in the morning, no one paid attention as two women in plain clothes emerged with a threadbare dandy from the rear of the lodging house. Yet Tamsin glanced about as they entered each new street and continually looked over her shoulder as the trio walked to the thoroughfare.

It being the second week of August, and far into a long hot spell, the mist from the Thames had burned off, and the streets rendered the summer odors of London. Felicity led the way to her aunt's house on the other side of Covent Garden. She kept rushing ahead, then circled back to instruct Camilla.

"Miss Candecote, you remain too beautiful, too elegant for people to fail to notice what you are. Try what my maestro teaches his ingénues who must play servants when they come on stage."

Felicity took ten steps to demonstrate an exaggerated gait, which Camilla then imitated—to no great achievement, from Tamsin's view. Yet Camilla preened under Felicity's praise, even more like a fine woman in her walking dress. Yet people on the streets were interested only in their own journeys, not the three odd characters dodging carts and barrows across Covent Garden.

"Here we are!" Felicity exclaimed. "Oh, it's a sin against decency that beautiful Chalgrove House came to be in the hands of a scoundrel."

Tamsin had perceived before then that Felicity held strong views about "sinned against" and less concern about "sinning" and no observable concerns for heaven's view of transgressions.

The house had been new-built after the Fire in one of the rows of similar houses around a central garden square. A single stone step, which hadn't been swept for a long age, led up to the shiny black door, its knocker gone, replaced by a small knotted circle of black ribbon. The house stood three stories high, plus a garret at its top. Unlike its neighbors in the row of houses, the stories above the street had large bay windows surrounded by ornate plaster-cast oak leaves, roses, and fanciful animals, mostly dogs. The glass windows were mounted in diamond-shaped lead grids, with colored glass at the top.

"Let us inspect the back first," Felicity said. She pointed to an arched passage. A decade earlier, a narrow passage had opened to the back alley, but as with most all such alleys in London, an ambitious builder had added a narrow structure over the passageway, allowing rear access through what was now an arched tunnel. The trio passed under that arch.

"It's like in a famous story." Camilla's voice echoed on the brick walls.

Just as they emerged into the back alley, a man poked his head from a gate down the way.

"There he is," Felicity whispered.

Of all the marvels Tamsin had witnessed in London, the greatest appeared before her now. The man had a head too large for his reed-thin neck, plus a bush of ruddy hair, much redder than you'd expect for his age and complexion. He possessed an extraordinarily handsome face, even more than that actor at Felicity's theatre who all London proclaimed a beauteous man. Large, long-lashed eyes. Brows sculpted by a master creator. Perfection.

Except.

The large, handsome head was set atop a gangly body, not as tall as Tamsin. His tailor's efforts couldn't hide scrawny bowed legs. His gait wobbled on high, red-heeled shoes, like a child who'd dressed up but not mastered the artifice.

"Behold! Mr. Cornelius Rosewurme!" Felicity called from inside the tunnel, her voice carrying to the alley. Camilla tugged at Felicity, as if to stuff words back inside the actress.

The odd fellow looked around at hearing his name called but didn't spy the trio in the shadows of the tunnel. His over-large head swiveled on his neck twice, then he scuttled off to the other end of the alley, turned a corner, and was gone.

"You see now." Felicity stepped out of the shadows. "My aunt would never have been beguiled by that man unless she had been put out of her mind by his false elixirs."

"It's not yet eight o'clock," Tamsin said. "Is it his habit to leave at this time?"

"Rather at nine o'clock most days," Felicity said.

"How many servants?"

"Only his footman lives in," Felicity said. "The maid and cook come in after dawn. We shall need to remove them from the premises while we work."

"Also, we'll need someone on the street to waylay Mr. Rosewurme if he returns," Tamsin said. "Did the servants work for your aunt?"

"No. He has all new people."

"We'll ask Perry how to deal with the servants," Tamsin said. "Or perhaps we find new positions for them. They are too new to be loyal to your Cornelius Rosewurme."

"He's not mine, Miss Foxe."

When they returned to the main street, a woman stood at Chalgrove House's front entry, hands on her hips as if ready to scold the closed door. When the woman turned, her wide skirts swept the portico and its bannisters, her hems white with dust. A light shawl wrapped the front of a nicely embroidered stomacher, the kind of embroidery that helped merchants' wives wear finer clothes than they might afford from a modiste. The woman had a sturdy figure and a round, sweet face, resembling an aged child. Her eyes set upon the trio studying her from across the street. She drew up her shoulders and headed south, away from them.

Felicity hailed her. "Madam? Do you know Mr. Cornelius?"

The woman paused. "Mr. Cornelius Spittlehame is gone from home to the Continent. His useless footman won't even accept a letter for him. If you've business, send your messages to the King's Head near Chancery Lane. Much good it will do you. He might be lying dead in the king's service in Bruges or Lyons, and we'll never know." The woman scurried away.

Felicity, for a rare moment, lost her words. Then she shook, rather like a greyhound come in from the rain. "Mr. Spittlehame is gone from home? We just saw him in the alley. And the villain's name is Rosewurme."

Tamsin said, "Then now we go to the King's Head."

14
A Portraitist

AT SEVEN O'CLOCK WEDNESDAY morning, the heat already rose from the cobbled pavement on Threadneedle Street. Or, more likely, the stones no longer cooled at night after so many weeks of broiling weather.

Knocking at the door of the warehouse so early wasn't unusual for Ned. His journeys to London over the past five years always began that way. Simon Touchstone commenced work at dawn in his gallery and storehouse, and he was always eager to greet Ned, because they'd soon be lost in the warehouse, looking at new works for which Simon was seeking rich buyers.

Simon's wife, Hildegonda, greeted Ned effusively that morning (because his work brought good prices). And she was always kind enough to never notice that half of what Ned brought his agents were forgeries of dead artists' work.

"A friend claims you have a portrait commission for me," Ned announced.

"I received the request late yesterday, just before we locked up shop." Simon shook Ned's hand vigorously, excited at the news. Ned should be even more excited but mostly felt himself to be on the edge of panic. "A commission at Arcadia House, eh? You are a lucky fellow. And I haven't yet begun to solicit custom for the portraitist Eduard Wijck, as I promised you last week." Simon Touchstone waggled his brow. Ned's art dealer was intrigued to be handing him a note on heavy linen paper that bore the seal of the Marquess of Withersea.

"Mutual friends suggested my name," Ned said, "which is why I heard news this morning of the commission."

Simon said, "I've delivered to that house many times. You shall find your work to be well compensated."

"The house is on the road to Knightsbridge?"

"Aye. It's a bit more than a house, so you can't miss it. It's new-built in the Palladio style, though most rich men stopped building houses like Roman temples after the Puritans chopped off the old king's head. Most new manors out Knightsbridge way are overly fanciful. Baroque they call it. The owners must all claim Sir Christopher Wren as their brother-in-law."

Ned studied the brief letter. "This work requires a large canvas. 'Life size' must mean six feet tall, at least. Do you have any prepared canvases?"

"My lads scraped such a canvas just last week. But you came on foot. You can't lug it through the streets."

"My friend has gone to hire a carriage and a driver for me. While we wait, may I—"

"Browse my warehouse?" Touchstone nodded. "You will appreciate that I have a lovely sketch by Peter Lely and a rather alarming Ribeiro to show you."

"But Lely does portraits," Ned said as he followed Touchstone. "Who would ever sell off his work, even a sketch, instead of hanging it in the family gallery?"

When Touchstone pulled back the canvas flap hung over the portrait, Ned was immediately caught up, studying the Lely.

"A lord learned his wife invested in Monmouth's rebellion. He's divorcing her and sold me Lely's sketch to be rid of her memory. 'Twill be a pity if she's caught as a traitor. I don't know if that's a sister or a daughter in the sketch. Both are pretty."

"Lely has mastered the ways that give the effect of beauty." Ned studied the Lely, thrilled to see how that artist had formed a study for a rich patron. "I say, Mr. Touchstone, I'm in London without my paints and kit. While we tour your warehouse, can you send a lad to fetch brushes and supplies?"

When Touchstone agreed, Ned wrote out the list of what he wanted, for the first time not having to juggle shillings in his pocket to decide which of two pigments he could afford. He detailed the brushes he required, a palette and knife, a dozen basic minerals for color, linseed oil, turpentine, rags, and canvas for a drop cloth.

"Mr. Touchstone, might I rely on you to send more pigments once I establish the palette for this portrait? It's impossible to guess the colors that will suit a lady I've never seen. Oh, here's the carriage come to fetch me to Knightsbridge. I hope the driver won't be impatient while you and I finish inspecting the Lely and the Ribeiro."

~

"The carriage I hired is being loaded in the alley," Perry said. "I'll walk back there with you."

When turning off Threadneedle Street, Ned and Perry passed a pair of militia officers walking together, deep in conversation, their elbows locked against the buffeting of the crowded street. Perry watched them pass, then locked his elbow with Ned as the pair of them surged against the tide of the crowd. For a moment, Perry sang that song he'd enjoyed the night before.

The shepherds' swains shall dance and sing
For thy delight each May morning...

"You have the voice of an angel," Ned said.

"Why, thank you. Now, my heartling," Perry said, "let us discuss what we do next."

Ned said, "I suppose, after Friday, we'll all go back to Revelstone House. Whenever my agent secures portrait work for me, I'll come to London. Will you come to town on such occasions?"

"I do not mean to distress you," Perry said, "but I am asking what we will do now that everything has changed."

"Ah, yes, I see. Because of our successful restoration last week, Tamsin will stop worrying about taxes and the mortgage. Rollo will be the earl. And it seems that Tom will go back to the law now that he's no longer confined to bed."

"That beautiful skull of yours, under such so-white hair, is a wee bit thick, ain't it? Let me ask again. What shall *you and I* do, now that everything is changed for us?"

"Because you are no longer in the king's service? Because I won't have to paint forgeries? It means that each day shall be more pleasant than in our past travails."

"God's teeth, chucking. Let me ask specifically. Shall we live together in Revelstone House? Or build our own cottage? Where we can rise each morning, eat our breakfast, and make the day belong to us." Perry cast a deep, knowing glance at Ned, then looked away again.

"Us." Ned repeated the word, needing two heartbeats to skip over any regret at taking so long to understand. "Yes, a new cottage might be what we do next."

Possible, Ned thought, now that neither of them had burdens of care, like when Ned had to help Tamsin worry about Marborne. Like Perry did, when he worked as an intelligencer. Before everything changed.

As another change, Ned had to accept that Perry felt compelled at times to admonish Ned, who accepted another caution as they traveled toward Knightsbridge.

"Mind you, Mr. Wijck, when you are among such folk, no gawping. Never let rich folk know you're struck down in awe." Perry's deep voice vibrated through Ned's body, since his friend sat so close in the carriage. *For thy delight each May morning...* "And be sure, sweeting, that you are not so overcome as to forget why you're going there."

"I shan't forget. I am to spy on the marquess and ensure his wife and her brother are safe while I paint her. Or paint someone. It is not clear whose portrait I shall be painting."

"Nay, my fine lad. That's your second duty. Most important, discover what manner of fizgig stole Tom Foxe's heart. Then send a message to London to describe her for the rest of us."

"She must be beautiful if she's married to one of the most powerful men in England."

"Or she might be plain as a mouse yet rich enough to entice a marquess. Send word with Daniel or Neriah as soon as you know. Don't make me wait until late tonight when I come to show you how to prowl a lord's house."

Daniel and Neriah, two of Perry's five younger brothers, rode atop the carriage, having been recruited to run messages between Knightsbridge and London. One needed only a brief glance at Perry to see the resemblance, though neither had yet gained Perry's height and heft.

"Ah, sweeting. You shall turn here for Knightsbridge. I must go find Tom, to do his chores."

It was the first time in a week that Ned had been farther away from Perry than the next room, and Ned didn't like the sensation. Rather too much like a punch in the ribs. All along the ride into the countryside, he pondered that unpleasant feeling, an unfamiliar kind of loneliness.

Us.

Before they arrived at Arcadia House, Ned had the driver stop at an inn called World's End, where Ned arranged lodging and board for Daniel and Neriah. Then he asked the driver to pause near his destination, where he let out the boys and admonished them to get the lay of the land, pointing to an immense hedge where he hoped to find them when he needed to send a message.

"Cor!" The driver finally stopped at Ned's destination. "This ain't a house. It's a palace."

Arcadia House was indeed in the Palladio style, its pillared portico soaring overhead as if it were an actual Roman temple. Or rather, what Ned had seen in paintings of Italy in Touchstone's warehouse. As instructed by Perry, he refused to be intimidated. He'd lived his whole life in an earl's country mansion, however dilapidated it had become since Elizabeth was queen.

The driver departed as soon as Ned's kit was dropped on the portico. Ned straightened the wide-skirted coat and waistcoat of the new green brocade suit Lizzie had chosen for him. He stepped onto the portico, confident. Until Tuesday, the only suits Ned had owned were bought from abandoned pawn. He felt himself to be a fine figure. He'd seen his reflection in the window at Touchstone's warehouse: no one would think that person usually dressed in thrice-darned linsey-woolsey. He looked and felt ready for lordly clients, a true professional.

A lad in livery opened the door before Ned knocked. Promising to take care of the baggage, he escorted Ned into a walnut-paneled room, saying softly, "The artist, my lord."

A figure rose from a large, wingback chair near a window that opened onto a side garden. The man who advanced on Ned, about the same height and build as Rowland, wore a periwig of natural chestnut hair.

But there the resemblance ended since this lord was twice Rowland's age. He was sunny-faced with a thin-as-knife-blade nose, a port-colored web across his cheeks, and a slight paunch. A man who liked his wine and food, and padded the shoulders of his coat.

This was the monster they were to destroy.

15

A Hawker and a Peterman

AT THE ROSE TAVERN, Cornelius ordered a hot pie. On this Wednesday morning, the inn's owner was at the bar, watching Phebe jealously. She often pretended not to know Cornelius, save for a wink when her lord and master ducked into the kitchen.

Cornelius paid his reckoning and glanced about. Here at midmorning, the room held its usual collection of older men hiding from their wives (they with the clean linen) and other untidy sorts (this being a better place than wherever such men kip for the night). Many bent over checkered boards, muttering while playing draughts, the click of pieces echoing against the stone walls. Several pairs played at backgammon, two sharps among them, though The Rose had a reputation for chasing out professional gamblers. No darts or other boisterous play, it being too early on a hot day for anyone to make the effort.

"Neely, old boy!"

Only one man in the world called him that. Cornelius spied Nathaniel Merryboy across the room, his bald pate shining even in the dim light from the mullioned windows, the man he'd known since their days as boys in Oxford.

Merryboy shouted and waved as if Cornelius might miss his friend, the man who kept an ever-changing gang ready to work as knights of the post, principally for patrons in need of hirelings who'd do anything for a day's wage. Merryboy made up his crews out of rough men new to London with no trade or those who'd left a ship because sea life didn't suit.

When they were young boys, Cornelius and Merryboy had to find their own bread and a safer place to sleep than with other urchins in abandoned tenements. In those old times, Cornelius hawked other men's elixirs and pamphlets, and Merryboy performed as a peterman and picker of Puritans' pockets, both in thrall to old man Fowlmere, who'd been a fountain of wisdom for how to progress in the world when you began in the gutter.

"Here you go, my love." Phebe slapped several rumpled pamphlets on the table and dropped his pie on top. Cornelius ventured a pat on her soft rump, sure the husband didn't see.

"I've been thinking," Cornelius said after Phebe had gone, "of how Fowlmere taught us."

"Aye, the old man said you'd get out of the gutter if you was willing to do anything. Anything others might not dare."

These days, Cornelius preferred to tell boys like Farley at his house that you'd best learn to read and write if you wanted to rise from a life in rotting doss houses. If he'd known what he knew now, he'd answer as much to old Fowlmere.

Merryboy slapped the table at the reminder of old times. "That was us, running smobble, taking what we might grab and dashing away, until old Fowlmere took us on and showed us the up end of things."

"Then we took a romantical notion," Cornelius said, "and declared us'uns to be brothers of the blade. Fowlmere looked about to foul himself laughing at us."

"Didn't you just luck it, Mr. Spittlehame that was? Your fat duke taking a fancy to you, 'cause of how you hawked his Presbyterian pamphlets and shouted the glory and promise of King Charles's return."

The Duke of Bagsham had indeed helped make Cornelius the man he'd become, serving as a mentor who urged Cornelius to make a bold show, directing people's minds in the right course. Those were good years, taking the duke's coin to help guide elections to the House of Commons, keeping a string of informers for Lord Bagsham's interests. "The man that knows the news first," the duke always said, "knows best." Such sweet work. Cornelius soon had his own hawkers to sell his elixirs along with Bagsham's pamphlets, doubling his profits. The good days, before he met the lord who now ate the heart out of Cornelius's life.

"It wasn't as if," Merryboy said, "you'd ever take to the way of muscle and force that God deigned to be my lot. My way's not suited to the gentle nature God gave you, Neely."

Muscle or not, Cornelius knew even in those early days that his compeer Merryboy was destined to keep a low station. And Cornelius would soar, though who'd ever expect how high he'd flown this year, marrying his dear flittermouse?

"Aye." He slipped a jingling bag from within his waistcoat and tossed it to Merryboy. "That's for the muscle my patron requested Tuesday. He will again require a dozen of your knights of the post this Friday that's coming."

"Twelve men? Mayhap your patron's next task requires the kind of men what don't mind dirtying their hands?"

"S'welp me, I don't know, but it might be like the work you did Easter week."

"Terms?

"Again, similar to last Easter."

"Silver quid?" Merryboy scratched his ear. "Or gold with the French king's face on it?"

"Can't promise the color of the coin until we learn more."

"Remind your patron that it costs more," Merryboy said, "when it's messy. My lads were upset at Easter to find they'd kilt a lord. They'll ask more this time."

"Killed a lord? I didn't know." Like a flash of lightning, Cornelius saw what this work was costing his soul. He'd sworn that when his wife's fortune came to him, he'd never shepherd business for that evil lord again. But he hadn't known till that moment how much his soul had been blackened by that lord. His face must have revealed how his mind raced into dark thoughts.

"Odds bods, Neely! You didn't know?" Merryboy spoke too loudly, slamming his hand on the table, rattling Cornelius's ale cup. "No, that's right, 'twas your other man what paid us and gave the instructions. And here's me thinking it was so kind of you not to take a share of that fine sack of quid." He wagged a teasing finger at Cornelius. "You didn't want to mire your hands, being so lofty now."

"I just didn't know," Cornelius repeated, coughing to hide the quaver in his voice.

"You're safe as a swaddled foundling, Neely." Merryboy gulped ale, winking at Cornelius over his mug. "I'll not breathe your name to the king's men if I'm ever caught."

"I'd never think so." Cornelius grabbed his own ale mug to hide behind. Of course, Merryboy would tell all if he were caught at so much as filching a muffin.

"Best worry about when your friendly murdering lord decides to turn on us both. You and I have seen it before, the type who seeks to wipe his own trail. They got the same evil sort up high in the House of Lords as we who live with down here with the paupers and petermen."

Where Cornelius refused to ever live again. Damp with sweat, Cornelius felt he needed a Saturday-style bath, to wash away the sudden rush of fear, sure that harm was coming from either Merryboy or that evil lord. No bath would wash away the soil in his heart, the sense of sin and horror. Of corruption.

While he finished his pie, Cornelius described this week's work for Merryboy. He had to provide the kind of direction that should not be writ down, and just as well, since Merryboy could never be bothered to learn to read. To steer toward safer waters, Cornelius instead pointed Merryboy to future meetings with Sir Duxwold, wanting to remove himself from any service that might lead to a public hanging.

Phebe came by after Merryboy said his adieus. With one hand, she wadded up the old pamphlets that had been under his serving plate. With the other, she set down a tin of ale.

"Messages for me?" he asked.

"Not yet this morn," she said. "You're early today, my love."

She ran her thumb up his spine before she swished away.

Alack, he'd been a different boy when he came to London. Not innocent, but his soul untrammeled. Just this spring, his dear lady-love had been his salvation. Now she was gone, and a bad lord commanded his services. Who would he be by next season, if he allowed that lord to heap muck on his soul?

16
Xanthus House

WEDNESDAY MORNING, ROWLAND ROSE early, the scents and sounds of Xanthus House rousing him. He was examining the bruises and scrapes from the previous night's mêlée, all of which felt worse than they looked, when Lazarus appeared. He carried hot water, soap, and a razor, and assumed without asking that he'd shave Rowland. Unused to such luxury, yet happy that he didn't need to find a barber, Rowland leaned back and yielded to the man's ministrations, first asking, "Can you help me understand how the house is staffed?"

"Yes, your lordship," Lazarus set to his efficient work, using milled soap that smelled of herbs. "You already know that I serve as your butler and groom of the chamber. The house boy is my son, Peter, who's handy as can be, given his size. The viscount's footman and groomsman left for the Bravewood estates in Kent and took the horses. You may command their return if you have no groomsman of your own."

Rowland held up a hand, to stop the razor while he answered. "It'll take me a few days to know whether I need them."

"As you wish, my lord." Lazarus returned to his task with the razor. "There's Mrs. Boxworth, the housekeeper, and Mrs. Flurry, your cook, and her scullery girl, Eve. And Jane lights fires, carries water, and cleans all but the kitchen. Mrs. Boxworth sends out the laundry. She doesn't keep staff to do laundry on premises, which the viscount wished. That is, he preferred a lean staff."

"Of course," Rowland said, as if he fathomed such business. How will these people cope with him bringing the Foxe hotchpotch to live here? The house would require more servants. And more coin gone from Rowland's pocket.

"We do not keep a gardener," Lazarus continued. "A man and his lad come down from the Bravewood estates every fortnight to tend the back garden. It is only a small terrace and does not, I might well surmise, compare to what you must be used to at your home in Cambridgeshire."

"I did not expect a garden." Rowland hadn't expected a house, a wardrobe, servants, or a library either.

"Whatever you require, my lord, I shall consult with Mrs. Boxworth to find suitable help."

He declined Lazarus's offer to assist with his dress, uncomfortable with another man tugging on clothes for him. After Lazarus departed, Rowland searched through the wardrobe in the dressing room, choosing a severe black suit and a snow-white linen shirt with modest lace cuffs. Using the paper and plumbago pencil he found on a table in the dressing room, he wrote a note to again beg Perry to join him, hoping that Lazarus's son might run the message across to Covent Garden.

When he emerged from the dressing room, the young lad he wanted was carefully setting a tray down on a side table. The tray held a bread roll on a majolica plate, plus a pitcher filled with something steaming hot.

"Hello, Peter. Would you—"

Startled, the lad dropped the pitcher, which by good fortune did not break but did send hot coffee spilling across the floor.

"Pish and pestilence!" Peter exclaimed. He then looked as abashed for the minced oath as for spilling the coffee, freckles emerging as his face paled. He scrambled for toweling from under the washstand. "My lord, I'm so sorry."

"Entirely my fault, Peter. I surprised you." He needed to say more, because the lad looked frantic. "Accidents happen."

"They should not, my lord."

"Anyway, I don't drink coffee in the morning. I should have said as much to Lazarus."

Rowland did not want to be standing over a lad who was on his knees, scrambling to correct a minor problem.

"I'm glad you're here, Peter." He held out his folded message. "Leave off worrying about that. Can you please take this letter to my friend at Benson's lodging house?"

Peter looked up, still surprised, still pushing at spilled coffee with his towel, and...

Blind me! That wall moves when the boy touches it.

"Yes, my lord. One moment."

When Peter rose, Rowland put a hand on the boy's shoulder while explaining exactly how to find Benson's. "I cannot express how grateful I am, Peter. I see that you care to do your work properly."

Rowland had no idea whether it was a done thing, for an earl to praise the boot boy, and he'd have to go on guessing every moment about how to behave. He waved when the lad departed, wishing he could push the boy out the door.

Because Rowland wanted to examine that moving wall.

It took a bit of knocking and pressing at latches and medallions until the wall sprung inward. He stepped into a room similar in size and paneling to the dressing room. It smelled of beeswax and wood polish and lavender. *No, it's rosemary, which Lizzie prefers.* Like the dressing room, it had no window, only a mirror and a lamp on a table, and was as immaculate and extraordinarily organized as the outer chamber.

Except the room held a woman's clothes.

Recalling everything he'd seen in the house when Lazarus guided him, there'd been no indication a woman had been in residence. Conveniences for a mistress? A very tall mistress, from the length of the skirts and sleeves.

Would that mistress be knocking on the door, asking for her clothes back?

He examined the clothes, which didn't look like what a man might choose for a mistress. More stern stuff like the puritan costumes in the other closet, in an array of colors from dove grey to tobacco brown to rust-speckled black. With modest shawls and straw hats. Not a thing in the room that Lizzie would wear unless it was her turn in a gambol to pretend to be a rector's wife.

The most flamboyant gown, a rose-hued garment with a simple embroidered bodice and modest amounts of lace, could perhaps be worn at court. It was better constructed, finely tailored, and nicer materials—brocade and silk—than the gown Rowland had purchased out of pawn to use as a disguise when he and Perry fled the Low Countries. He held up the rusty-black gown, the way he had in the pawn broker's shop when seeking a possible costume in Amsterdam. It was tailored for a person his size like the suits in the other room. Whoever wore the woman's shoes lined up on a shelf had good-sized feet.

Was the departed Viscount Bravewood like Lord S— in Paris, who was Rowland's first guard duty for diplomats? Lord S— proved to be a sybaritic adventurer, leading them into dark parts of Paris where he dressed as a courtesan. Because it helped him relax after the day's diplomatic travails.

But that would require more decorative gowns than this line of rector's wife's clothes. These garments were meant to hide, not shout for attention the way Lord S— preferred.

Lifting the lid of a box on one closet shelf, Rowland sought this mistress's undergarments and secrets. He found not silk or linen, but four throwing knives and two stilettos, in the style popular among certain women he knew in Paris five years ago. One had a silver handle, the other polished ivory.

The clothes hanging beside the mirror were also not those of a mistress. Unless the departed viscount's mistress dressed like the fellows who write letters for a farthing in the Inns of Court. Or like Covent Garden tavern masters.

He tugged on the black lace gloves from the table, which fit tightly, making his hand appear to be smaller, yet he could flex his fingers. Clutching the silver-handled stiletto, Rowland held the rose-colored gown against his torso, gazing in the mirror.

Not a convenient clothes cache for a visiting mistress. Not gowns for flamboyant nights in a private cellar club. Rather, costumes for a watcher.

Lazarus's face peered at Rowland in the mirror.

"My lord, I have your breakfast."

"Thank you, Lazarus. I appreciate it." He returned the gown to its hook and laid the stiletto on the table.

"My lord, if you might permit me to make a recommendation for carrying any of these firearms."

"Please, feel free." So, they were going to speak of firearms and not of the watcher's closet.

"Might I show you this newer style flintlock? The maker designed it for a gentleman's pocket."

When Lazarus offered it, Rowland took up the piece, liking the weight. The lockplate, breech, and trigger plate had come from the maker's forge as a single piece.

"Thank you, Lazarus. I should like to try it. May I borrow it?"

"It belongs to the house, my lord. You can do with it as you please." Lazarus withdrew, discreetly carrying away Rowland's laundry with him, along with the coffee-soaked toweling.

Cogitating on his discovery, Rowland gobbled down breakfast, which indicated that the cook was a genius with sweetened bread. And the house had an excellent brew master. His now-clean and shiny shoes stood by the door, which he hadn't noticed when Peter first appeared. The morning sun burst through the upper banks of windows, casting rainbows on the floor. This far past dawn, Rowland understood that he wasn't the first watcher Lord Bagsham had housed here.

Rowland was merely a replacement.

Was the deceased viscount even the duke's actual nephew?

17
A Demon

— N E D —

"MR. WIJCK? PLEASED YOU could come. I'm Withersea." The marquess extended his big, soft hand, his smile spreading into the side-curls of his periwig.

"My lord, I'm flattered to be invited." Without giving it any consideration, Ned spoke in a Dutch accent like his father's. He compared his new green brocade with the elegant cut of the marquess's coat, a color called The Devil in the Head, bright as emeralds, or what emeralds look like in paintings. But it reminded Ned to strip to his shirtsleeves while painting and to hang his new coat and waistcoat out of the way.

Withersea looked past Ned at the footman. "Gabriel, I believe the housekeeper has Lady Withersea's directions."

When the door closed, the marquess motioned for Ned to take a chair near his own wingback monstrosity, while Ned wondered how to converse with the smiling devil he'd been sent to spy on.

"It's my wife who asked for you," the marquess said. He was busy tucking folded letters into a purple velvet sack. "She has, sadly, lost her father recently, and begged to begin the portrait of her young brother, which she thinks should have been done in her father's lifetime."

"I'm sorry for your loss, my lord." Ned broadened his Dutch accent. He knew well the custom of condolences, since he'd spent the past week hearing condolences from everyone in Marborne parish after Uncle Absolom died. But Ned noticed the marquess

131

had made no mention of his wife's older brothers who'd also departed this earth quite recently.

"Thank you, Mr. Wijck. He was quite elderly. Such was to be expected. Yet one does what one can to console those left behind. Hence, we have you here, now. I suggested she hire Lely, but—"

"I see you have a painting by my father here." Ned, who'd used his talents to help his family survive, pointed to a humble kitchen scene hanging on an opposite wall. The room was stuffed with paintings, carvings, and whatnots, all displayed to prove that Withersea was a connoisseur—of the valuable, if not the beautiful. Ned intended to prove his own mastery.

"That?" Withersea frowned. "It's from Rembrandt's workshop. I acquired it last winter."

"Yes, that's where my father trained. Turn it over, and you will find Jan Wijck's mark. He had his own fame for a time in the Low Countries. Do you favor the homely scenes of those Holland artists? Many now prefer the florid Italians."

"I'm not an expert, except to know what warrants investment. It's my wife who's the prodigy. She's a true Original." The marquess twitched in a way that told Ned he longed to turn over the humble picture to find Jan Wijck's mark. A mark that Ned had drawn when he forged the picture last September, after he'd exercised his usual practices, making his work appear fifty years older.

"Then will it be her ladyship who will express what's desired for the portrait?"

"Ah, um, why certainly. She will…" Withersea fiddled with a carved ivory bottle atop his crowded desk. "I say, Mr. Wijck, will you share a pinch of snuff?"

The marquess held out the bottle in a way that indicated that the "son of Rembrandt's apprentice" improved his view of Ned, though most in Cambridgeshire saw Ned as the bastard son of a Dutch prisoner of war freed from digging drains in the fens.

"You are kind, your lordship. I never learned to indulge."

Ned spoke the words with every modulation of gratitude he'd been taught. Yet he longed to seize what the marquess offered: an entire story carved and painted on a tiny ivory bottle not even a third the size of his hand.

"Do you admire my little flask?" Withersea had caught Ned's flame of longing. He let Ned hold it. "Clever what these oriental fellows do for their emperors, isn't it? England's kings have never commanded such beauty from our artists."

"Is it from China?" Ned kept his voice casual, as if he were used to holding the most beautiful object in the world. Not as if he wanted to run from the room and keep it for himself.

"Yes, Mr. Wijck. Had it from a ship's captain just this week." Withersea smirked while holding his hand out to receive back his bottle. "That old sea-dog tried to swindle four times the price I paid him. Though I estimate he bought this beauty off thieves. All the paysans and pirates in the orient are stealing whatever they can to sell to their new masters."

The port-wine spiderweb that crossed the marquess's cheeks glowed as he expanded on his thoughts. Ned offered nothing but nods and soft yeses, but the marquess didn't need that encouragement, lost in telling of his successes.

"But that's the way the world is now. We send ships and establish factors to reap wealth from failed empires. England will soon be the next empire."

For Ned, those words signified that the Marquess of Withersea was a greedy man who exploited people he scorned. This was the man, Tom claimed, who sought to steal a title and land from his own wife's brother. A despicable human, whom Fate was about to smite, with help from Tom and his friends.

Yet Ned wanted that bottle in his hands again.

~

The door behind Ned opened. The marquess glanced over Ned's shoulder but didn't get up when he spoke.

"Good morning, Lady Withersea. Your artist has arrived."

Ned rose and bowed to the slight figure standing in the doorway. He offered an accented greeting. "Lady Withersea. An honor."

Given the shadows where she stood, he could make out only a small, stiff-postured woman in black silk that made her round face appear pale, even in the shadows. She wore spectacles and blinked repeatedly, as if trying to see Ned clearly.

"Mr. Wijck!" Her voice was melodic. "Mr. Touchstone speaks well of your work. We are delighted to find you available."

"Thank you, my lady. I've been working on a family portrait for the Foxes of Marborne. However, that entire household has removed to London for the coming weeks."

"Foxe of Marborne?" Withersea sparked more alive than he'd been thus far.

"*Ja.*" Ned stayed with his false accent. "The discovery of the new earl left me without employment until Michaelmas, which was why I could answer your request, my lady."

"We are so fortunate to—"

"What's the Marborne estate like?" Withersea spoke over his wife. "In Cambridgeshire, isn't it?"

"About five miles from the university town. The house was built during Elizabeth's reign, they say, but came upon hard times in Cromwell's wars and hasn't been restored since. A fire damaged the village and church badly last year, so the new earl has hard work ahead, to set Marborne to rights."

Withersea wanted to hear more. "What kind of man is this new earl?"

"He wasn't at Revelstone House while I was in residence, my lord." Ned debated whether to paint Rowland as a great man. Instead, he offered a blank canvas. "I cannot say."

"Oh, well." Withersea was disappointed; then he brightened. "Perhaps when you return there in the fall, we might carry you thence. I've a hankering to see Cambridge again. Haven't been there since I was at school, just before the Great Fire."

While the marquess nattered on, Ned harkened back to what his father claimed was the value of sitting in the stone-cold Marborne church. "*Best time to see a family's truth is when they feel their masks to be firmly in place. You're a good painter; you can show both their masks and the truth behind the masks."* Each Sunday after church, Ned drew what he'd observed: The haughty patriarch of too many children, who all resented his harsh authority; the pale, bruised woman who twitched when the rector recited biblical guides to obedience while her husband stared out of the arched church window.

Thinking of that, Ned observed the marquess. Like Midas, Lord Withersea considered his wife one of his valuable collectibles, a *rara avis* like the great auk in a glass case. Or like his extravagant snuff bottle. His lady betrayed no resentment for her husband's careless words. She must have the patience of a saint (one that Cromwell's bullies hadn't crushed into dust).

A bang against the window startled Ned. The marquess ceased speaking. Lady Withersea folded her hands.

"You see, my dear lady." Lord Withersea's voice turned testy. "We must act with a strong hand. No sensible man should be forced to abide in such chaos."

"As you say." The marchioness spoke conciliatory words but didn't appear to be conceding anything. "Mr. Wijck, please allow me to show you how this house will accommodate your work and your daily needs."

"If you please." Ned prepared to follow. "Thank you, your lordship, for your gracious welcome."

Tom wants you to rot, before you go to Hades.

Lord Withersea set aside that glorious snuff bottle and took up another ornately carved piece of ivory. Rather than answering Ned, he said, "My dear, I'm leaving for the City just now and staying until Friday. I have much business with my barrister."

The mask fell from the marchioness's face for a heartbeat, then just as swiftly returned. "But your guests, my lord! You insisted on inviting—"

The marquess waved a hand, the one not holding the ornate ivory. "I'll take Duxwold with me. You will do well on your own with the others who are still here." He set down the ivory carving and took up the purple sack he'd stuffed earlier.

After saying farewell to the marquess, she led Ned through the hallways, chatting the whole while in a light-hearted way, not like a woman who'd come to Tom in desperation. Ned hadn't yet seen what attracted Tom and perhaps wouldn't until he painted her. All this time, he hadn't known Tom to have the same romantic bent as Rowland.

Then sunlight fully illuminated her face.

It was one of the women from the Lely sketch that Touchstone had shown him.

Which meant that the marquess had sold it to Touchstone.

Not noticing that Ned stood thunderstruck, the marchioness pointed down a hall to where he'd find his bedchamber. "You can take meals in the parlor off the kitchen. Withersea's secretary is in London, so you don't have to share with a stranger."

But Touchstone said that the lord who'd sold the sketch did it because his wife invested in Monmouth's rebellion. Surely Tom hadn't sent Ned into a nest of traitors.

They'd entered a room that might seat twenty people on the cushioned divans and velvet chairs, its large north-facing windows casting good light. She looked directly at Ned, revealing ordinary, pale features, with round grey eyes and long lashes magnified by her spectacles. He was distracted from her face by the graceful motions of her hands, eager to touch the velvet fabrics and carved objects on tables as she moved through the room. She paused to lift a shard of pottery from a table that held an aged tome (too large to be called a book), plus a collection of beads and small bowls, all anticks like Uncle Absolom used to collect.

"I know," she spoke in such a low tone that Ned dipped his head to hear, "that Tom lives by a code. Do you?"

"The very same, except we only call them rules. We've sworn to always uphold each other, like brothers in arms."

"I live by a code learned from the poet Homer. 'The proud heart feels not terror nor turns to run.'"

"Our codes are in harmony," he reassured her. Though her code didn't match the soft, warm woman who welcomed him.

Repeatedly brushing that shard of pottery with slim, white fingers, the marchioness gazed out to the garden. A tall, gangly fellow played with a small dog. He tossed two balls, then wrestled over possession of one ball after the little terrier fetched it. The dog held its grip, even as the young man tugged hard enough to lift the dog onto its hind legs.

"Jacob looks to be only a boy, doesn't he?" She hesitated. "That's my brother, the Earl of Cloudesley. He was born special."

"As I was given to understand."

She spoke in a whisper, her eyes darting sideways at Ned. "You know Tom Foxe well?"

"Since the cradle. He is one of my cousins." Ned discarded his false accent. "I am here for Tom's sake."

"Please make friends with Jacob." She gestured into the garden. "We must do whatever it takes to keep him safe."

"My lady, I am as capable as Tom for all help you need. Except I cannot manage the law and courts for you."

Jacob tossed the ball in an ungainly, awkward motion. The ball skittered across the grass, struck the doorstep, bounced past Ned and the marchioness, then rolled into the marquess's study.

A dog scrambled after the ball.

Jacob ran in after his dog, tripping on the step, wind-milling to catch his balance, and not seeing Ned or his sister. He slipped again at the entry to the study and pitched inside.

"Come, Pip!" Jacob coughed the words, mid-stumble.

Withersea's contumely words were more like that of a Billingsgate oyster-wife than what one might expect to hear from a peer of the realm.

"You bird-witted, clod-pated fool," the marquess railed. "You chittifaced worm! You aren't worth the bacon scraps I'm forced to feed you."

"S–Sorry, sir."

"You make me crop sick. You are only your mother's flux filth." If Jacob answered this, his words didn't carry. The marquess raged on. "Make your bed in the servants' jakes, where I cannot see you."

The cringing sound of flesh on flesh echoed into the hall.

"And keep your stinking bugbear out of the house. I won't have cattle roaming my halls. You cow-handed nick-ninny."

The ball flew out the study's door at high velocity, followed by a flying dog, which landed hard on the floor. It scrambled up, whining, and ran into the garden.

Withersea. Every bit the demon Tom had described.

Jacob crept past, never looking at his sister. He returned to the garden with shoulders bent, slinking toward the hedge.

The marchioness was even more pale, looking stricken. She spoke softly. "I am so ashamed that happened in my house. I want to be strong enough to stop it, but I'm failing."

Before Ned could answer to reassure her, a voice called, "I found the blue ball in the herbary."

A woman in a golden morning dress emerged from the shrubbery at the garden's far end. The dog ran to her, rustling in her skirts as if seeking shelter. After a few beckoning gestures, urging Jacob to join her, she tossed the blue ball for Pip to chase, her gown a streak of gold with the motion. She laughed as the puppy skittered through the grass, coaxing the awkward youth to laugh with her, though his hands were shaking at his side. She turned toward the window where Ned stood with the marchioness.

Lizzie, Ned's own sister, acting her best beautiful self, living in the house of Tom's enemy.

18
A Barrister

PERRY JOINED TOM AFTER sending Ned on his way early Wednesday morning. They ate breakfast at six different taverns near the Inns of Court, asking about the barrister Mr. John Mordaunt, to learn more of his reputation, other than being on the list of Hawkins' Heirs. People in this neighborhood said that:

His clerks considered Mordaunt a fair man who worked hard day after day to make the world turn.

Mordaunt had a small army of loyal proctors, solicitors, and clerks allied in business with him.

You must begin with Mordaunt if your case will go to proctors in ecclesiastical and admiralty courts.

You'd best choose Mordaunt if you have sufficient coin to pursue a disputed inheritance.

"Do you mean to say, he bribes judges and proctors?" Perry asked the clerk they were bribing with cold beef and hot bread.

The clerk Elisha Newton came from a village in Cambridgeshire. Tom suspected that homesickness led the pale, eager young man to join in a warm conversation with Perry and Tom. Elisha dipped a slice of cold beef in mustard, chewed it, then pointed his knife at Tom while he talked.

"Great men do business as they've always done in England," Elisha said. "Your purse matters for the law as for all else."

"Don't we know that for truth?" Perry poured ale from his own mug into Elisha's. "Any shiver-the-wink like us'uns haven't the guineas it takes to move action in any court."

"That's Mr. Mordaunt's view. A barrister must foresee possible gains before investing his time together with the coin he'll have to deliver to the proper pockets." Elisha swished the last bite of bread through the mustard on his tin plate. "Even when Cromwell's Puritans put a stick in the wheels of the law, the law remained on the side of those who could afford it. However, it's only common gratuities that Mr. Mordaunt expends, merely enhancing the sinecures great lords have allotted the judges and such like."

After they bid farewell to Elisha and walked away, Tom said to Perry, "I cannot eat another bite of bacon and bread. And before we meet Mr. Mordaunt, we need better clothes."

"Why ever must I be a deft fellow?" Perry tugged at the bright scarlet waistcoat Lizzie had given him. "Am I not as finely dressed as any man in England?"

"Your scarlet waistcoat does not declare that you are Marborne's overseer. Because—"

"Because your inamorata declared Mordaunt to be one of the Marquess of Withersea's evil minions. Hence, I must dress snug and smug as a man of business."

Weary of so many attempts to lay to rest that misconception about Aurora, Tom followed Perry to a pawn shop in search of good suits, both in agreement about the ethics of taking advantage of other men's unfortunate sacrifices in pawn.

Later, when they reached the door to the barrister's chambers, Tom said, "Perry, please observe what I might miss."

"Mayhap you can teach others to milk a pigeon, but this kitten," Perry tapped his chest, "knows how to lap cream."

When they entered Mordaunt's chambers, Tom purposefully confused the clerks about who they were to announce to their master. Consequently, Mr. John Mordaunt rose from his desk, his hand out in greeting.

"I'm happy to meet you, sir. I hope to be of real service."

Mordaunt attempted to get a fix on which of the two men might be the earl, until Tom stepped forward to shake his hand, which was long and boney, with skin that felt like old paper. He had a long face, like an old but handsome horse, though he couldn't be more than fifty, and he wore a well-tended brown linen coat, with no flash other than gold buttons and the gemstone pin in his cravat. The man might be called tall by some but he stood in Perry's shadow. He repeatedly cast his eyes over Tom's shoulder to Perry's imposing figure.

"Thank you for seeing us, Mr. Mordaunt. Allow me to introduce Mr. Peregrine Frake, the overseer for the Marborne estates. You can imagine why I've brought him along today. He's been tasked to ensure no Foxe cousin flies into unsure investments or legalistic commitments."

"Welcome to my chambers, Mr. Frake." Mordaunt gestured to encompass his entire chambers. "Lord Bagsham gave me strong reason to believe that Marborne and the Foxe family have much need for my services."

"Yes, sir." Tom hadn't released the man's hand to allow him to greet Perry. Instead, Tom took a step closer. "There's the title, plus my uncle's will and estates to settle. And, of course, the long-forgotten affairs of our other uncles who have passed. But first, I require your help with what I seek to do in London."

"Please take a seat." The lawyer indicated the guest chair close to his desk. Tom sat, arranging the skirts of his coat. Perry remained standing, still as a statue, a giant blocking the light through Mr. Mordaunt's windows, leaving Tom in shadows. "Upon my honor, I shall help in any way that I can. Let us begin with your needs in London. I understand that Lord Bagsham offered Viscount Bravewood's former residence."

"*Vero, vero.*" Tom spouted lawyerly Latin. "But we first need your help with an immediate crisis. Our uncle departed this earth last week. And our solicitor left England for the New World days later, creating a crevasse in management of our affairs, while our uncle's last testament left us with certain specific obligations."

"I see." Mr. Mordaunt picked a quill from the inkstand on his desk. "We'll send a solicitor to Cambridge first."

"Obviously." Tom waved one finger to dismiss that offer as mundane. "More to the point, my great-uncle Absolom Foxe, who fostered us all after the loss of our parents, left me with a personal obligation to protect the Foxe family."

"These chambers," Mr. Mordaunt said, "are your strongest allies for protecting all that you value. I promise to do whatever you require of me." The man set down his quill and lifted his hand to his heart, as if the lawyer believed he had honor to protect.

"Quite happy to hear it," Tom said, while thinking only of Mordaunt's name as part of Hawkins' Heirs. Was this man a weapon being used in Withersea's attack on Jacob? "Our uncle raised us with a strict regard for personal honor, to always incarnate it and to respect it in other men."

Perry shifted, drawing attention away from any note of distrust that might have crept into Tom's voice.

"Your uncle sounds to have been a good man." Mordaunt took up the quill again, tapping its ink-free barrel with his boney forefinger, as if he might be growing impatient.

"Better than any man on earth," Tom said. "Sadly, he's gone. But we all intend to abide by our uncle's guidance, which we call 'Doctor Foxe's Rules for Enlightened People.'"

"Few people today live by a strict code." Mr. Mordaunt tapped the quill on his desk again, though not so hard as to ruin its point. He wanted the conversation to progress.

"Shall I tell him the rules?" Tom asked Perry, who then proclaimed that all of England should know Doctor Foxe's goodness. Tom turned back to Mordaunt, speaking confidentially. "When Mr. Frake joined the family business, he eagerly chose to abide by our uncle's rules in all endeavors."

While Tom recited the rules, Mordaunt's knee twitched under the desk, though he retained the mask of his good manners.

"It's charming to know," Mordaunt broke the long silence after Tom's recitation, "that such men have been allowed to guide others as a teacher and...uncle."

"Thank you for indulging me. Uncle Absolom always intended that I become a barrister, for the sake of our family and parish. And for the sake of justice." Tom dragged papers from his pocket. "Our first business, therefore, is to negotiate a fee so that I might clerk in your chambers, to launch my life's work as a barrister in the Inns of Court."

"But I had been made to understand that you came from the king's service, guarding diplomats." Mr. Mordaunt, twitching, snapped the barrel of his quill, and yet quickly dropped a curtain over his surprised expression. "Your lordship, such an apprenticeship would be long and arduous, while you have new duties to take up."

"Lordship? Bless me, Mr. Mordaunt, how did you come to confuse us? Rowland and I are quite different men."

~

Tom set his papers on Mordaunt's desk. "I am Thomas Foxe. Everyone always believed I'd become the next Earl of Marborne, because I'm the older cousin. However, to our great surprise, it's my cousin Rowland who will bear that burden."

Mordaunt had turned stern and grey, as if he wanted to throw Tom out, but he'd come too far to do so gracefully.

Tom forged ahead. "I have completed the long apprenticeship you describe. First, I read at Cambridge under Doctor Primerose. Do you know him?"

"Y–Yes." Mordaunt begrudged the concession. "I read under him when I was at Cambridge. He is—"

"A strict master. That's old Primerose, it's true." Tom pretended to be oblivious to Mordaunt's discomfort. "Then I served my clerkship under a barrister in Cambridge."

Tom named his old master, but Mordaunt didn't know the man, so Tom hurried on. "He recently departed us for heaven." Tom tapped his papers on the desk. Mordaunt did not take his eyes off Tom. "Here is certification that my apprenticeship has been completed, so I am now free of my original articles."

"I'm not sure…" Mr. Mordaunt, England's famous barrister, was at a loss for words.

Tom breezed along. "We struck a bargain at four hundred guineas for my clerkship in Cambridge. Because you promised this morning to do whatever is required to help me, will one hundred guineas be appropriate for a half year to clerk under you at the Inns of Court?"

The barrister flinched when Tom repeated the barrister's earlier promise to help in any way he could. Then he stammered, "That…that…seems reasonable."

It was twice the sum Mordaunt should have named.

"Excellent!" Tom shook the barrister's hand again, while privately celebrating how he'd nuzzled his way into Withersea's legal affairs. "Lord Bagsham recommended that all our family business come to you. Here I am, prepared to do whatever is best for the Foxe family and our new earl."

"It is to be hoped." Mordaunt blinked, as if trying to comprehend what had just happened to him.

"Hoped? More like fated," Tom said cheerily. "For they say there's no other profession in England by which a man might make significant money so quickly. I'm ready to begin. Who will serve as my supervisor?"

A quarter of an hour into the meeting, the lawyer and his new clerk shook hands to seal their agreement. Perry, who'd spent his time in silence, excused himself to seek air on the street while waiting for Rowland.

Mordaunt walked through his chambers to introduce Tom to his partner, Mr. Erasmus Lutwyche, who took Tom to find a desk. Tom winked at Elisha Newton when he passed that clerk's desk, a finger to his lips to beg complicit silence. At a desk tucked into the farthest corner, Mr. Lutwyche explained Tom's duties. Tom listened, hiding a smile that wanted to overpower him.

Only eighteen hours since Aurora begged his help, Tom had scaled the walls of the marquess's barrister and had inserted a guardian into her house. Now, for his next heroic act, he must comprehend the filing methods in the chambers of Mordaunt and Lutwyche, to uncover Withersea's business.

Here he was, prepared to achieve what Absolom predicted, that Tom would use the law to protect the innocent. With Jacob as his first innocent.

He coughed five minutes later, when the dust in his assigned perch got to his nose. Then Tom coughed again, harder, which made him yearn, over only a single heartbeat, for Winwood's elixir, despite its bitter and foul taste.

Then he had to stop coughing, because the location of his clerk's desk and its totally insufficient partitioning walls allowed him to hear Mordaunt's conversations with clients.

19
Pocket Pickers

-ꙮ.ꙮ-

— TAMSIN —

IN THE WEDNESDAY MORNING crush, people did move along Fleet Street in a fleet manner. The trio seeking the King's Head had to shoulder their way among clerks hurrying to work, messengers streaking to deliver letters, chairs carrying lawyers and merchants to their daily toil, and those in rags intent on gleaning what others might leave behind.

Inside the tavern, the trio procured bread and cheese, taking a long time over it, neglecting their hot ale while observing that morning's doings in the tavern. Tamsin checked that no one followed them, whether sent by Leighton Fairchild or Cornelius Rosewurme. No one in the tavern seemed to be watching, but strangely (to Tamsin's way of thinking) Felicity did not look about on the street or in the tavern, though she'd had true bullies stalking her only the night before.

However, Tamsin found she was wrong.

"This room is remarkable," Felicity said.

"Indeed." Camilla wrinkled her nose. "So many pipes have been smoked here since Raleigh returned from the New World. It's like sitting inside a whitewashed casket filled with snuff."

"I shall not laugh at you, precious lady." Felicity did laugh. "But I meant to speak of the men in the place. There's five in the north corner that my maestro might like for hustling our scenery and risers, but I estimate they have employment that pays better than the theatre. They're dressed for rugged work, but not in rags. I estimate they even have wives, for each has a clean neckcloth."

Felicity gestured to a corner where four men in bag wigs and shapeless coats counted pennies for their reckoning.

"And if ever I did see a nest of waspish clerks, buzzing their desire to sting their master, those four be such an unhappy band. Each with red eyes from smoke and ale, and with grievances tugging their jowls and double chins into their limp cravats."

"Do not be so cruel," Camilla said. "One never knows the true stories that shape men's faces."

"Ah, will you tell me that you never choose a play for the sake of the handsome personage in the lead role? At the far table to your right," Felicity said, "sits a philanderer, a true professional, from whom I might have a pie at luncheon and champagne at dinner, if I were to eat my own scruples first."

A gentleman in a purple linen coat pointedly studied the dandy in their trio. He winked and tipped his glass when he found the dandy returning his gaze. However, when Felicity took Camilla's hand and kissed the soft fingers, the trifling man looked away.

After two hours loitering, learning nothing, Felicity released Camilla's hand (having performed a palm reading that was a cartload of pettifoggery) and nudged Tamsin.

A young fellow in worn gabardine, his collar starched and doubtless scratching his scrawny neck, approached the publican. "Hoy! I'm to say the watchword, which is 'bubukles,' then receive from you any messages for Mr. Cornelius."

The threadbare fellow (who couldn't be more than fifteen) received a bundle of letters and handed the publican tuppence.

"Tell your Mr. Cornelius that it'll cost an extra tuppence for any that come in here looking for him, and a groat if it's a woman who's got an abusive tongue. I'm not his valet."

Tamsin and Camilla locked eyes. Camilla nodded, as if she saw Tamsin's imaginings. They rose together and approached the publican, but Camilla tripped over a man's feet and stumbled into the scrawny messenger, falling so hard that the lad tumbled onto Tamsin, who wrapped her arms around him.

"Steady, sirrah." She pushed him upright, as awkwardly as she possibly could, making a show of twitching her skirts away, which lashed at his legs.

Camilla patted his arms. "Are you all of a piece? I do apologize."

"It's nothing," he said.

When the young man was gone, Tamsin sat back at the table. "Ah, Miss Felicity. The publican feels put upon. Your enemy seems to have more names than the two we've heard."

"The tremendous sins of Mr. Cornelius Rosewurme." Felicity heaved a theatrical sigh. "That 'cream faced loon.' And exactly the liar I suspected him to be."

"How do we proceed?" Camilla said.

"We go to his door and demand answers," Felicity said. "Or pursue him through the streets with a cudgel."

"No," Tamsin said. "To proceed with the best plan, we shall ask our friend Perry to prowl through his business."

"Is your Perry the answer to everything?" Felicity asked.

"No, just the problems that beg his peculiar talents." Tamsin had been watching Camilla for symptoms of fatigue, and now found her friend flushed. "Camilla, you look done in for the day. Let's wait for Perry at our lodgings. I'll call a chair for you."

"I prefer to walk," Camilla said. "We'll get there faster. Then we can read these in private." She held out the bundle of letters the publican had handed to the scrawny young man.

"You angel!" Felicity exclaimed. She stopped in the street to bow to Camilla. "You are the Madonna of the Light Hands and Golden Hair. Angels will sing your praises."

Tamsin agreed, but wanted Camilla indoors, propped with pillows, sipping a healing tisane. Not tumbling in a common room with messengers sent by a bad man.

~

At their lodgings, the trio found only Winwood present. He had packages of herbs and powders spread on the table in their hired salon and was busy concocting the physick with which he'd been dosing Tom for several weeks.

"Happy you've returned," Winwood said, "since I've been here all alone. Ned left early to see the agent who sells his paintings. Perry received a message from Rowland, who has removed to a house across Covent Garden. He and Tom have joined him, to meet with a lawyer."

"We can't afford a house!" Tamsin said. "We all went over the costs and agreed to keep to lodgings."

Winwood said, "A duke who visited Rowland last night. gave him a house to use."

"Gave him a house?" Tamsin felt a flash of alarm but tucked it away with an intent to ask Rowland how he'd earned a London house, as soon as she saw him.

"I can only repeat what Perry told us." Winwood shrugged. "What have you three found in London?"

"The correspondence of Cornelius Rosewurme," Camilla said. "Felicity's enemy."

"How…" Winwood didn't complete his thought.

"We are about to read the letters, Winwood." Felicity took the chair beside him, which Tamsin had been about to claim. "You will not believe how notorious Cornelius proves to be. Your sisters are great finders."

"How did you…" Winwood began, yet perhaps recalled his former endeavors to avoid knowing how Tamsin and her cousins nabbed justice without the aid of magistrates and lawyers. "Let's hear what you found."

Camilla read, since she'd snatched them from the threadbare messenger. She managed to get a few words out.

Mr. Knatchgull: This is to inform you—

"Blight the scoundrel!" Felicity exclaimed. "It's Spittlehame at breakfast and Knatchgull at lunch."

Camilla shushed her and read on.

—that I have engaged a solicitor, to counter your claims on my uncle's property where my late aunt was residing in the dower house. We are prepared to prove this property is entailed to the male line and saved for my aunt's use only in her own lifetime. Your brief marriage, which the parish records show occurred only twenty days before her demise, represents no legal standing on your part.

We shall also contest the obviously forged will that leaves you any portion of my aunt's personal effects. We expect that the chancery court will judge that all such material goods in your possession will be seized and held until the courts rule on all these matters. —Mr. J. Wright, Oxford

"By Gemini!" Felicity exclaimed. "He's done evil to more women than my poor aunt."

"But didn't we guess such after meeting the woman outside Chalgrove House?" Camilla said. "Tamsin, read the next one."

Tamsin obeyed.

My own darling Cornelius: I brought this letter to London myself, in hopes that this message will find you. It has all come about as you promised. My poor departed husband's distant cousin, who I never heard of before in this life, has relented. I now hold the deed to my cottage and garden.

Alas, the chancery court has ruled that the mansion and lands are entailed to the male line. Hence, the claim you advanced for me is lost. However, I am content to have my cottage, where you and I can be so comfortable together.

Please come home, dear husband. The last time I wrote, I feared having nowhere to live but under a hedgerow. Now I have a house! All I lack is you, my dear husband. I remain yours with all my soul. —Bridget

"Is there more?" Felicity asked. "I shall carve out his heart."

"Only two that aren't bills from a tailor or bootmaker." Tamsin read the first of these:

My dear little man: Let us rendezvous before meeting your barrister, so we tell the same stories. Two o'clock. —Dux

"Rosewurme is plotting with a lawyer to cheat me," Felicity said. "Together with those other women."

Tamsin nodded but didn't agree; it was unlikely that a bigamist might ask a lawyer's help. She read the last letter.

Mr. Cornelius: Am in receipt of yours from July. People here are still muttering about the Rebels' heads on pikes and the King's Declarations against traitors. I cannot unload your anti-Catholic rags. My last lad offering pamphlets on Papal Tyranny was called a Huguenot and told to go back to Spitalfields. With a Host of Militiamen here, I cannot find lads who will carry such pamphlets.

I can take fifty bottles of your Elixir for the coming Fair, guaranteed. But for the other, I fear the King's Men. And I hope you have a sturdy Protector. —Your own Benjy Nokes, Norwich

"This man Cornelius is surely dangerous." When Tamsin finished reading the last line, her fingers tingled in warning. "If he's working against the king, perhaps we'd best stay away."

"A magic-elixir peddler and a dissenter with no pulpit?" Felicity scoffed, then paced, waving her arms dramatically. "If he's about to be in trouble with the Crown, then I need to remove my chattel goods immediately. I shall weep if the Crown claims my aunt's treasures when Rosewurme proves to be a traitor."

She continued muttering about his crimes. *Traitor. Seducer. Bigamist. Thief. Phanatic.*

"I promised to help you, Felicity," Winwood said.

Camilla said, "You must be assured that, whatever it takes, we will be at your side tomorrow."

Tamsin had nothing to add. Because, privately, she reserved *whatever it takes* for efforts to protect Camilla.

~

Winwood left the lodgings in search of the powders and potions he'd failed to find on his morning hunt.

"My friends, for all you've done in so few hours," Felicity said, "allow me to procure luncheon."

She was gone in an instant.

"God keep my giddy cat! This is exciting." Camilla wiggled in her chair, playing with the stolen letters. "Isn't Felicity intriguing? She changes her voice, shifts her shoulders, and then she's someone else entirely. And she likes to tease me."

"Yes, she is an entire intrigue."

"It is admirable, isn't it? The way Felicity is pursuing justice, not letting the world trample her dreams."

"Justice? She only wants her aunt's furniture and keepsakes. Me. I have doubts."

Camilla's bright smile twittered away. "You doubt this adventure? Just yesterday you were eager to return to Revelstone, because you can find nothing to do in London."

"Yes, but..."

"What a horrible word to pause on. But what?"

"I can't estimate how much she's playacting. We don't know if any of her story is true, Camilla."

"It must be true. It's exactly what we read in those letters. Such an evil man!"

"Yet she leaves many large silences while telling her story."

"She's Winwood's cousin. We trust him."

"But Winwood hasn't seen her since they were children. Trust doesn't transfer in such an abrupt way."

"I'm surprised at you," Camilla said, "being so suspicious of such a good-natured person."

"She's an extraordinarily lively person, yet she came to England to be the quiet companion of an aged woman." Tamsin drew Camilla's attention to what bothered her the most. "Besides, this aged aunt was the wife of a baron who did many heroic things in the war. I wager that Felicity's story about the baroness is missing certain parts."

"If part of the story is missing, let's ask Perry to find it." Camilla seemed only more excited now, not made cautious.

"We'll have to find Perry. He's been gone with Tom all day."

Felicity appeared at the door of the hired salon, followed by Adam the footman. "Here's our luncheon, my beauties. Then I must be off to the theatre for rehearsals. I'll ask my roustabout friends at the theatre to help us tomorrow."

When Felicity was gone, Tamsin sat close by Camilla on their chamber's wooden settle.

"You're jealous, Tamsin." She snuggled her arm around Tamsin's waist. "Admit it. Though I warn you, I can see perfectly well how she tries to talk sweet with me, while ignoring you."

Tamsin leaned her head on Camilla's shoulders, wishing for a teaspoon of comfort. "I'm not jealous. Only uncomfortable with this rapid plan that might drag you into danger."

"Drag me into danger, but not you?" Camilla tilted her head away to examine Tamsin. "Are you seeking to protect me from some imagined threat?"

"I…" Tamsin took a shaky breath. *Yes, but not from Felicity.*

"Because, Miss Thomasine Foxe," Camilla drew herself up, moving away from Tamsin on the settle, "I can protect myself from danger. I can see clearly that Miss Oakes is using us for more than she reveals. That she keeps secrets."

"I'm happy you perceive that about her," Tamsin said, regretting that Camilla had moved away.

"If you have your doubts," Camilla said, "I shall undertake the adventure without you. It's not dangerous. Not like your restorations and gambols. We aren't undertaking anything that might bring the king's militia down on our heads."

"No, no, don't go without me." Tamsin voiced more alarm than she wanted to reveal. Teasing was her only escape. "It'll be a lark. Tom advised me to have a lark in London."

"Then you will join us tomorrow? And not merely to protect me? Honestly, Tamsin, it speaks badly of me, that you think I'm a child who needs your protection."

Painful pricks of confusion and dismay picked at Tamsin's heart and mind. What Tamsin wanted most—that is, to protect

Camilla—was what her friend decidedly did not want. Yet Tamsin could not let go of her raging desire to protect, which she needed to act on to calm her fears.

"I don't think badly of you, Camilla. I will come. What should I do for an entire morning, alone in London without you?" Having revealed her secret fears, Tamsin reached to change the subject. "I propose, sweet nutting, that we practice how you will tell your story to the attorney this afternoon."

"I have thought long on this," Camilla said. "I shall play the helpless child that the attorney must rescue."

"You just insisted you can take care of yourself."

"No, I insisted that *you* do not need to take care of me." Camilla changed her voice, soaring into high, frail tones. "But my husband has sworn in writing that he cheated me. My father is gone to the New World. I have no one to protect me without the help of the laws of England."

Tamsin laughed at Camilla's false voice—and stopped from saying what she thought.

The law has not protected you thus far. I have.

"You laugh?" Camilla poked Tamsin's shoulder. "You cannot laugh when I present my case to the attorney. He must feel compelled to do whatever he can to protect me from the perfidious Leighton Fairchild."

Me. I will do whatever I can to protect you. Always.

20

Chancery Lane

ROWLAND HAD HEARD NO word from Perry. He found a sword-stick in the wardrobe and buckled it onto his belt, though the blade felt too light to be of serious use. He didn't carry the flint-lock Lazarus recommended, since he was only visiting a lawyer.

The boy Peter held the door, bowing in a practiced way, while Rowland felt like a village lad in another man's clothes.

"Good morning again, Peter. Did you find Mr. Frake at the lodging house?"

"I left the message for him, your lordship. But the porter said Mr. Frake and Mr. Foxe departed early for breakfast."

God blind me! I'll have to face that barrister alone.

"I'm sorry, your lordship."

"You did well, lad. Thank you for taking my message." Yet the boy remained distressed over the imperfect result of his task. "And thank you, Peter, for the excellent work on my wretched shoes. You are my savior, since my feet are too big for any shoes in the wardrobe."

He didn't make it through the door that Peter held for him before he was waylaid by Isaac, the duke's footman, who also carried a message, that the duke's sword master was free at noon to offer lessons for his lordship.

Lord Bagsham intends to ride me like a horse.

"Thank you, Isaac. Please carry my compliments to his grace's sword master, but I am not free until Saturday. Ten o'clock on that day will suit me."

After crossing two streets on his way to the Inns of Court, Rowland noticed that he still wore that black-lace finger-free glove. No one he passed on the way out of his house—Lazarus, Peter, Isaac—had commented, blinked, or fixed their gaze on his hand. He jerked down one cuff of his coat, dislodged the glove, and shoved it into a pocket. He continued walking, repeatedly looking over his shoulder for bully boys and far more fretful than the meditative state he'd enjoyed at the theatre.

He indulged a fanciful imagining: appearing at the barrister's chamber in one of the viscount's gowns, seizing an advantage. But then, he knew from his adventures the previous week, dressing as a woman in the heats of August was oppressive and constraining. Still, Rowland wished to find an advantage over the lawyer, because he was feeling far out of his depth.

A brick wall surrounded Lincoln's Inn, separating it from Chancery Lane. Coming through the gate, Rowland stepped into a major building site, with the bang and scrape of masons' work, and bricks and dust everywhere.

To Rowland's relief, Perry stood at one edge of the square.

"Here you are, Mr. Frake," Rowland said. "I thought my message had gone astray."

Perry said, "Your barrister awaits you. And I shan't say a spider patiently awaits a fly. You'll see soon enough."

"You've met the man?"

"Aye. Your secretary also awaits within. Where did you find that whip-thin creature?"

Odsme. More interference from the duke?

The so-called secretary waiting inside proved to be Michel Chêne, with a cream linen shirt and minimal neckcloth added to his mouse-colored suit and vest. It seemed that Michel didn't want to be noticed, like how Rowland dressed in his former life.

"Good day, my lord. I'm here, for your protection again."

"Shall we chat in the street?" Rowland motioned for Chêne to join him with Perry on the pavement, then dragged him by the coat sleeve when Chêne didn't follow rapidly enough.

"How did you know to find me here, Mr. Chêne?"

"I followed Mr. Frake and Mr. Foxe from their lodging house, since I didn't know the location of your new home."

"You never did." Perry folded his arms and widened his stance, challenging Chêne.

"I did though, through all the taverns where you questioned law clerks." Chêne recited the names of half a dozen taverns. "That's the proper order, isn't it?"

Seeing Perry's color rising, Rowland let loose his own outrage. "You introduced yourself as my secretary? You are not associated with me."

"As I said, Colonel Kilbuck sent me to protect you. When he heard of your doings last week, he estimated you might be in more danger than what pursued you from Holland."

Perry interrupted. Or perhaps "erupted" would better describe his response. "Lord Marborne and I are skilled in protecting ourselves from enemies."

"Except," Chêne said, "you weren't there last night when Lord Marborne was attacked. And he was insufficiently armed to protect himself."

At that Perry turned on Rowland. "You were attacked?"

"Yes, but no matter." Rowland glanced at Perry, who kept his sternest face in place. "Mr. Chêne, it is unsuitable for me, or Miss Foxe, to be seen with Kilbuck's agents."

"Did Kilbuck truly send you?" Perry asked, his arms still folded, his face stern, which most people found disconcerting. "Why should we trust you, Mr. Chêne?

Seemingly unintimidated by Perry, Chêne whistled one note and said in Dutch, "'Thou whoreson zed. Thou art like the unnecessary letter zed!'"

Perry whistled the two-tone response to Kilbuck's last watchword, a forbidding expression still on his face.

"That's from the week you left Amsterdam," Chêne said. "A poor choice of watchword for friends seeking to find each other. Can we proceed now? Your brilliance as intelligencers—"

Perry snorted his disbelief. "Don't flatter. Fate allows good luck among the bad."

"Fate? Luck?" Chêne shook his head, denying that. "My father says—"

Rowland interrupted, his thoughts turning back. "Wait. You followed Perry and Tom? Then where's Tom?"

Before either Perry or Chêne could answer, the barrister's clerk appeared in the doorway. "Mr. Mordaunt awaits you, Lord Marborne."

~

In the barrister's inner chamber, Mr. Mordaunt's eyes darted among his three visitors, blinking rapidly, as if more wary of than curious about his guests.

Michel Chêne introduced himself as the earl's personal secretary. Perry subtly elbowed Chêne aside. "As overseer of Marborne estates, allow me to introduce Rowland Matthew Foxe, the Right Honorable Earl of Marborne."

I wager Perry never expected to utter such words even once in the past ten years we spent on the Continent.

While shaking the barrister's hand, Rowland found the man smelled of dust and snuff, despite the tidiness of his chamber and his austere but well-tended business clothes. Two fingers' breadth taller than Rowland, Mordaunt acted like a man who used his height to command others, all while keeping his nose in the air. However, when Perry insisted on shaking his hand, Mordaunt responded as most do, with a twitch, as if the tall man cowered at Perry's greater size.

When Chêne retreated to a corner with a wad of paper and a plumbago pencil, Perry expanded his presence to fill half the room, with Mordaunt stepping away, a subtle retreat that Perry kept forcing. But Perry only did that when he didn't like a man.

Fantastic! Now, I suppose I must again play nitwit.

After exchanging niceties, Mr. Mordaunt folded his hands as if in prayer and bowed his head to Rowland. "Forgive my direct inquiry, your lordship. The Duke of Bagsham presented me with your family's history when he referred your case to me. I understand that your uncle, Doctor Absolom Foxe—"

"My great-uncle, who passed recently."

"My condolences, your lordship. I understand that I must handle matters of inheritance."

"Since my head is empty of such, I shall rely on you to guide me through the courts and laws of England." Rowland tucked his hand in his pocket, intending to find his lucky coin, but instead found that black lace glove again, a reminder that he had experience and knowledge this barrister did not.

Perry coughed, then gazed just past the barrister's head, which caused Mordaunt to look over his shoulder before he said, "Let us begin, your lordship."

While Rowland played a dunderheaded lord from the fenwater shires, Mordaunt offered the singularly most boring lesson under heaven on the obscure ways of English law. Rowland's thoughts drifted, as he regretted not having Tom there to interpret, only Michel Chêne to keep notes. Hence, he found it jarring when Mordaunt suddenly changed the subject.

"Lord Bagsham told me of your great good luck last week. The king is enjoying that luck, what with his militia defeating Monmouth, then with your lucky contribution."

Perry glowered. Rowland raised his brow, wondering what the fellow insinuated. And why.

"Come now," Rowland said. "You cannot think that the James Stuart who fought the Great Fire is now relying on luck to run the kingdom."

"Oh, ah…of course not, your lordship." Mordaunt again blinked rapidly, his eyes flashing in Perry's direction.

Irritated, Rowland let his tongue run away. "The Battle of Sedgemoor and the work that Mr. Frake and I performed last week had much in common. Both instances required investigation and preparation for a carefully executed strategy."

Alack, I've tossed away my nitwit disguise.

Given the theme of strategy versus luck, Rowland pitched himself into it, but changing direction lest he sound like his old captain, complaining that today's new subalterns know nothing of battle strategy.

"The only luck last week fell to Tom Foxe, because the order of our fathers' deaths left me to serve as earl."

Mordaunt's brows arched into dark Vs, like a painted actor showing dismay. "One hates to see such conflict within families. Shall I ask the courts to resolve the conflict between you?"

"Conflict?" What was this fellow digging for? "If you saw the reckoning for all the champagne Tom poured when toasting me, you'd never take such a notion. Tom and I are in accord."

"That gladdens my heart," Mordaunt said. "I shall proceed on your word that no counter claims will be advanced against you." He then named a person in the consistory court that he intended to ask to handle the Foxe inheritance. "He accepts half the gratuity of any other proctor in all of England."

The lawyer went on to list the fees and benefices to be paid on Rowland's behalf. While Chêne scratched notes, Rowland kept his own tally. The court's affirmation of the Marborne title and the Foxe inheritances would cost more than the cows and sheep Tamsin wanted. Bagsham warned that this needed to be done, despite Absolom's long-time resistance. Rowland felt it to be corruption, and the notion made his skin crawl. What was it that Absolom sent in a letter after Rowland described the rot among lords in Paris? It had guided him all this time.

> When all around seems pure corruption, you will endure by way of your wit and wiles, your loyalty, and (I very much hope) your profound kindness.

At a pause in the barrister's recitation, Rowland said, "Last Friday, the king declared the Foxe claims to the title to be just and true. Yet I must bribe clerks and proctors and bishops for them to declare the justice of my claims."

"A coarse way of putting it, your lordship," Mordaunt said, his voice top lofty. "English law is the best mankind has mani-

fested. Ancient ways prescribe the fees and sinecures that reward men who have the honor of serving the law."

Blind me! I just did what Bagsham warned me against.

"As you say. Fees, not bribes," Rowland conceded, pronouncing *fees* to indicate disbelief. He owed Absolom at least that much
indignation. "Forgive my ignorance. Lord Bagsham warned me
that I also must pay emoluments to the lords' Committee on Friday. I should grow accustomed to it."

"Of course, your lordship." Mordaunt's condescension reeked.
Rowland had insulted the man's world of laws. That might be
difficult to overcome in the work ahead. "To proceed, I shall have
my clerks draft our agreement to begin the work. What time can
you come tomorrow?"

They agreed to meet at five o'clock Thursday, with Rowland
resolved to brush the man off the next day.

"Please allow me one immediate service, your lordship."
Mordaunt was rubbing his hands, which must presage more fees.
"If anyone proposes investments or other commercial business,
please allow me to investigate before you commit."

Perry coughed again. This time, his eyes almost popped from
his head.

Rowland sat back, folding his arms. He utterly abandoned
his faux idiocy, to save Perry from apoplexy.

"Mr. Mordaunt, do you know anything about what I've done
for the Crown for these last ten years? Perhaps Lord Bagsham
omitted such tales when he communicated with you. Please be
assured, if I lack the time to attend to new business personally,
Mr. Frake will unearth all that can be known about people who
approach me."

And about you too, Mr. Mordaunt.

The meeting seemed to conclude, so Rowland stood to leave,
having come to dislike and distrust this spider waiting in his web.
The barrister, however, rushed assurances that he didn't intend
to intrude on the earl's business, then dropped a Spanish grenade on Rowland's head.

"Because we now have Mr. Thomas Foxe serving as clerk here, I promise we shall take the greatest possible care of your family's business."

God blind me! What did Tom and Perry get up to?

"I believe," Rowland said it as brightly as possible, "you will find my cousin Tom to be ambitious and quick witted."

"I'm gratified to hear it," Mr. Mordaunt said. "Now that we are upon the dinner hour, I'd be further gratified if you'd take your midday repast at my house, Lord Marborne."

Rowland didn't think he could stand more of the barrister's company that day, but behind Mr. Mordaunt, Perry nodded, wanting Rowland to accept. Which meant that Perry wanted to prowl Mordaunt's house, likely for some business of Tom's.

However, Michel Chêne answered first. "It is kind of you to ask, sir, but his lordship has an appointment with Lord Bagsham and only barely time to cross town for the meeting."

Chêne, that rampallian, knows business I'd forgotten.

Perry and Tom are playing three-card loo, and hiding their cards.

The duke's barrister takes me for a gudgeon.

And the duke is riding me like a horse that's crowbait.

This peer-of-the-realm gambol is not joyful. It's like work.

~

Once they were outside the wall surrounding Lincoln's Inn, Rowland asked Perry, "How was Tamsin persuaded to let Tom run free in London?"

"Tom wants to be a barrister," Perry said. "He's straining at the bit. Doesn't want to miss the next race."

"How did he come to pick my barrister?"

Perry glanced at Rowland, then looked past him at Michel Chêne. "We spent the early morning asking clerks in the neighborhood who was the best barrister."

His former sergeant was an experienced professional in all situations that demanded prevarication, but not good enough to put his lies past Rowland.

Hence, Rowland said, "I pretend to be a nitwit, but I'm not one. Tom overheard my interview with Lord Bagsham last night."

"No," Perry said. "But the servants heard most of it."

So many more questions to be asked, but none could be spoken with Chêne standing there. Besides, Rowland needed to attend to what he'd just learned.

"Will Mordaunt send us a reckoning for Tom's clerking? It's bad enough that I must disburse so very many gratuities to bishops, judges, and proctors."

Michel said, "Yet it is good luck that Mr. Tom Foxe can watch over your best interests."

"Not luck," Perry said.

Rowland sighed. "You sound like our protocol tutor in Paris, claiming that things always turn out for the best."

"It's what my father says," Chêne said, nodding.

"That does not enhance my estimation of your father." Perry shook his head.

Chêne jerked, either startled or insulted. "My father—"

Rowland interrupted. "Let's quarrel later. What do you make of Mr. Mordaunt?"

Perry said, "The grave gentleman kept glancing up, like a chandler counting beads on a wire, calculating another fee."

"However, Mr. Mordaunt seeks to be your particular friend," Michel said.

Rowland wasn't convinced. "It's merely his profession, which I seem to have insulted. However, he has a bad habit of casting his eyes past the man he's speaking to, making it impossible to fix his character."

"It's as if he's checking whether a more important man than you might appear," Perry said. "The intelligencer who abides deep in my carcass yearns to learn the man's business."

"I cannot accompany you," Rowland said. "I must meet with Lord Bagsham. I believe I'm to be fitted for an oubliette."

Perry's face showed interest.

"The duke has appointed himself to be my tutor. I'm to undertake lessons in lordliness, which I missed in my cradle," Rowland said.

"God's teeth!" Perry smacked his palms together. "How it distresses me, Rollo, that you must now live such a life."

I'm comforted that you share my distress, friend.

"The duke also," Rowland paused, then took the risk of saying it in front of Michel, "wants me to play king's watcher among the lords who will be my new friends. I am obliged to take my first assignment this afternoon."

"Howbeit that…" Perry frowned. "I wager you are about to quote me a quote from your Bard about his mysterious Dark Lady." He seized Rowland's arm. "There's Tom walking off with Mordaunt. I must follow. Shall I see you at supper?"

"Come to my new lodgings, Perry." Rowland described the way to Xanthus House, longing to show Perry his spy cupboard. "I need your wit and wiles."

"After I've finished my chores for Tom." Perry took five paces, then came back. "Mr. Chêne, stay with Lord Marborne. I cannot guess your skill, but he does indeed need a guard."

Then Perry was soon lost in the mix of men heading off to their midday meal, leaving Rowland with Chêne.

"What chores," Rowland mused, "do you suppose Mr. Tom Foxe wants Mr. Perry Frake to perform?"

"I suppose," Michel ventured, "it's about wit and wiles and Mr. Mordaunt's private business."

Wit and wiles. Rowland considered again Absolom's advice about avoiding corruption. He needed a different attorney to do what needed to be done. How to explain to Lord Bagsham that he couldn't trust the austere Mr. Mordaunt?

"My lord Marborne?" Chêne had been begging his attention, apparently.

"Yes?"

"Shall we stop at an inn for a morsel before we meet Lord Bagsham? He might feed you, but likely not your secretary."

"Fine. But call me Rollo, as my friends do."

"It feels a trespass. Does this mean we are friends?"

"Give me a day to decide. You must admit that you've thrust yourself on me quite suddenly."

Near the Strand, they turned into The Lyre for luncheon. Rowland ate bread and cheese like an ordinary man, and soon found that he rubbed along quite well with the opinionated Michel Chêne. After they agreed on the quality of the cider, Rowland said, "Tell me again why you intruded in my life."

"Rumors followed you out of Amsterdam, which led Colonel Kilbuck to believe that you and Miss Foxe require protection. Last night proved his foresight was correct." Michel appreciated another taste of his cider. "And William and Mary need your help in England."

"God blind me! An utter stranger begs me to be disloyal to the king now wearing the crown."

"All that William seeks is to make sure there's peace when Mary becomes queen. He believes that means tamping down the antipapal fervor King James is igniting. Many people are uneasy with how he favors his Catholic friends. And how he seeks to keep King Louis's friendship."

"Yet I owe my title to the current Stuart king."

"The Stuart kings owe your family more than that. Now, to do my duty, I must ask about Miss Foxe's safety. The servants at Benson's lodging house don't know where she has gone."

Rowland held up his hand for silence. If any association with Kilbuck became known, Bagsham would close the trap he'd set, leaving Rowland like a rat in a box with the lid hammered shut.

"Mr. Chêne…"

"Michel."

"I'm uncomfortable with your deep knowledge of my doings. I never heard of you in Amsterdam."

"It was my father who suggested I come. I have been serving another lord." Michel named the laziest and oldest English lord living abroad in Amsterdam.

"And your father is…?"

"A stern and accomplished man who wants to see me surpass him in skill and success."

"I hope you informed the king's intelligencers in London that you are here as a visitor."

"I prefer not." Michel shrugged. "What use could they be? The king's intelligencers can uncover secrets but cannot protect secrets. Such as your whereabouts in London."

They paid their reckoning and walked onto the busy street. Michel began a different topic. "Will James still be king in ten years? Or even five? Would you prefer to work for the future?"

Rowland drew Michel close when a quartet of militiamen passed. "Don't talk treason when out in the open air. Let's finish the meeting with Lord Bagsham. Then I need to purchase a new knife since I lost mine last night." His new closet held several throwing knives, but he preferred to choose his own.

"There's a smithy that keeps a shop off Portugal Street. I think you'll appreciate their craftwork, Lord—Rollo."

Rowland once more quelled his touchy sense that Michel vaunted a superior sense of wisdom and knowledge, while he was far less experienced than either Perry or Rowland. Other than that, and the too-frequent topic of treason, Rowland had begun to enjoy Michel's company. Not least because it meant he didn't have to meet the duke as a solitary figure.

21
Holborn

— T O M —

"IT'S KIND OF YOU to invite us to dinner, Mr. Mordaunt," Tom said. "I am at your disposal."

Tom had watched Mr. Mordaunt watch his new patron walk down the street with the straw-thin fellow Rowland introduced as his secretary, a servant acquired overnight, perhaps the same way he'd acquired a house. Seizing the moment, Tom grasped Mordaunt's dinner invitation for himself, like a hero who keeps his arms ready at hand.

"Oh, I…" Mordaunt's eyes danced from side to side, clearly trapped in an invitation he didn't want to offer.

But why not? Tom had proper manners and was better dressed than Rowland, who wore what appeared to be a suit belonging to a Puritanical sexton.

"Certainly," the trapped Mordaunt said. "Let me get my hat. I always walk between chambers and home."

While Mordaunt was briefly absent, Tom glanced down at the paper on the barrister's desk, assuming his best nonchalant posture. The paper was signed by Lord Bagsham's secretary, introducing the duke's new protégé, the Earl of Marborne:

Articulate, due to his scholarly ancestor.

Made himself useful to diplomatic delegations in Holland. Yet surprisingly naïve about our English government.

The Duncombe affair brought him to the king's notice. Rewarded for pure luck? Assess actual skills.

Same luck landed him in his cousin's place as earl. Is there a family conflict?

Grossly unfamiliar with London society and court life. Please fend off predators in case his luck does not hold.

Already tutored for proper deportment before the Committee. I shall attend to any gaps in his knowledge.

After an initial flush of embarrassment for his cousin's sake, Tom saw that Mordaunt had worked through the list in his interview, prying at its points. Having just eavesdropped on Rowland defending his own wit, Tom instead felt embarrassed for the duke's under-estimation.

And he pocketed the note.

On the street, Tom began a conversation in a familiar way, pitching his voice such that Mordaunt was obliged to walk close to Tom, as if they were intimates. Over Mordaunt's shoulder, Tom spied Perry. That infused comfort from his heart to his toes. This gambol would succeed.

"Do you think, Mr. Mordaunt, that Lord Bagsham can fix my cousin's military manners? Did you know that the duke was Rowland's mentor when he served as aide to diplomats in Paris?"

"The duke said kind things when he referred Lord Marborne to my care. Your cousin seems…earnest."

"We've been separated for a decade," Tom said, "and only reconnected this last week. We were all young and relatively innocent when Rowland left for the Continent. But he is quickly understanding how civilized people conduct themselves in England. I feel obliged to help him now that he is our earl."

"A kind thought. Caution, sir!" Mordaunt warned Tom of a carriage bearing down on them. On their way again, he said, "I understand that it was you who was thought to be heir to the title. It's gracious of you to give up your claim."

Cheerily, Tom said, "Didn't want it, did I, sir? The law is my desire. From the cradle." He'd said as much to Mordaunt earlier, and Rowland confirm it. Why keep testing the notion?

They strolled on. The day wasn't as hot as London had been last week, yet Tom's neckcloth grew damp.

"Do you not agree that a man who takes up the law can do as much for his family as a lord with a seat in parliament?"

"Yes." Mordaunt tilted his head, considering the idea. "However, the Crown's recognition means much."

"Would you say, sir, that a title is worth more than the riches men are making off trading sugar and Black Africans?" Tom wanted to draw Mordaunt out, to know what his ambitions might be. And he wanted to know why Mordaunt's name was among those on the list of investors in the syndicate that called itself Hawkins' Heirs.

Mordaunt changed the subject rather than answering. "Your enthusiasm for the law will be a benefit for our chambers, Mr. Foxe. Here's my house."

Mordaunt's home was just off Holborn Road, likely as near to Bloomsbury as the man could afford. It was newer built than those that rose after the Great Fire. After a footman let them in, Mordaunt's pretty and very young wife welcomed them. Tom's unplanned appearance did not fluster her.

"My dear, this is Mr. Thomas Foxe, new to my chambers and also brother of the new Earl of Marborne, whom we've heard so much about."

"Charmed to meet you, Mistress Mordaunt. But I'm only the earl's second cousin. I hope my appearance as a beggar at your door is no inconvenience."

"I'm delighted to meet you, sir. And Mr. Mordaunt will tell you that I always welcome guests. Meeting a new friend is such a pleasure. Better than most diversions."

She did, however, draw Mordaunt back at the archway that led to their first-story dining parlor.

"Sir, it's the day when the boys hope to join you at dinner. They will be disappointed."

"Boys?" Tom intruded. Since Mordaunt had not yet given him a set down for brash manners, Tom had no reason to reform.

"You have sons, sir? I'd be flattered if you'd allow them to join us. I like a boy's company and it's a rare opportunity."

In truth, Tom couldn't avoid the company of the dozen boys who sheltered in Revelstone House when the village cottages had burned. He'd been ill, though, and the clatter added to his sick headache. This, however, might be an opportunity to excavate details of the lawyer's life, to find ways to help Jacob.

~

Tom learned that the plain but substantial midday dinner was to accommodate Mr. Mordaunt's bilious nature. He also learned that the wedded pair differed over the design of the back garden. Neither news was of value for Tom's gambol.

"We are in accord with everything in life, my love," Mr. Mordaunt said. "Except for the garden. Before winter comes, we shall visit the New Spring Gardens to see its superior aesthetics."

"I shall never convince you," his wife spoke with some fondness, "how much I require the comfort of flowers." She turned to Tom. "You can see much of it from the window. Tell me if it is not beautiful, even after the last several days' heat. The alstroemeria is in bloom. And the lilies. Love in a mist. Pinks. Joe-pye weed from the Americas."

"It is grandly beautiful," Tom said, having spied the riot of color framed by the mullioned windows.

"It has no design," Mordaunt said, "beyond the jumble you'd find in a hedge-witch's country hovel."

"One easily sees your garden's celestial order." Tom added to his list of complaints: that Mordaunt censured and quarreled (though mildly) with his wife in front of a stranger.

Mordaunt's sons came in to share the cheese course and (their mother's admonishments drifted from the hallway) to show off their manners. Mordaunt declared that the oldest, also called John, would go to court as a page next season.

Mrs. Mordaunt added, "Lord Bagsham promised to put the boy's name forward."

Tom said, "I've heard that Lord Bagsham considers himself your mentor," though he'd heard no such thing, only surmised.

"I owe much of my success to favors Lord Bagsham granted when I first came to the bar." Mordaunt spoke while distracted by his efforts to monitor his sons' manners. "I also have other champions at court, such as the Marquess of Withersea."

Mrs. Mordaunt bit her lip, looked down at her tiny porcelain plate of cheeses. The deeply embroidered bodice of her gown rose like a knight's breastplate. Then fell. Her eyebrows dipped.

Eureka! (Aurora would cry the word in Greek. Oh wait, the word was Greek.)

"Wherever time and tides carry our nation's leaders," Tom masked his curiosity about the dark frown on Mrs. Mordaunt's face, "it is fervently to be hoped that your sons prosper."

Now Tom felt impatient to spend his afternoon exploring details of Mordaunt's business with Bagsham and Withersea. Given Bagsham's advanced age, Tom didn't blame Mordaunt for seeking younger mentors. Many men found themselves stranded when the second King Charles died. The future under James II was as yet unknown.

But why did Mordaunt choose to associate with Withersea?

Tom also guessed that Mordaunt's fondest wish was to be Sir John Mordaunt. Like a rich bridegroom tossing shillings to the crowd, James had handed out common titles and beneficent grants in his first months on the throne, but Mordaunt had not been knighted. Why not? Tom added that to all else he had to learn about Mordaunt's business.

"Have a care, young John." Mordaunt raised a boney finger to correct his eldest son. "A gentleman catches his crumbs in his table linen."

"Yes, sir. I am grateful for your notice."

"Father, sir," his second son spoke, "will you take us to the Bear Garden? Our tutor says it's ever so exciting."

The lawyer's eyes flitted to Tom for a moment, then back to his son. "It is not fit amusement for gentlemen. We shall go to the royal menagerie in the Tower. We'll make that visit before we go to your cousins at Michaelmas."

"I think I shall enjoy the Tower more than the country," young John said.

"But your cousins promised to teach you to ride in a hunt. The same way they taught you to climb trees two years ago."

From the manner in which young John compressed his lips, Tom guessed the lad was dying to say he knew how to ride. And that both lads didn't feel any need to be taught tree climbing.

"Country gentlemen," Mordaunt said, "have their ways and traditions, which we as city gentlemen do well to learn."

"Will our cousins ever learn city ways?" the youngest of Mordaunt's sons piped.

Young John bit his lip again, though a squeak leaked out.

"You ask the question of the ages," Tom said, not interested in his host's answer. "My own country cousins are new to the city. It is unknown whether they can learn city skills. Pony riding may be useful here, but how might climbing trees benefit my cousins in London? Especially the ladies among them. You might well guess how I despair of their manners."

The boys laughed, but Tom hadn't completely relieved them of Mordaunt's desire to upbraid his sons.

"The polished gentleman does not point to the fault of his peers, his betters, or even his country cousins," Mordaunt said, without any apparent consciousness that he'd just pointed to his sons' (extremely minor) faults, and done it in front of a stranger. Which meant that he upbraided his sons habitually.

"My cousins," Tom said, "will find comfort in that thought. But I must forever seek diversions to keep them out of the trees, since scolding won't do for their rebellious ways. Just think of the scandal if the Countess of Marborne were to appear high in the boughs of a famous plane tree in St James's Park."

Each boy covered his mouth with his napkin, to hide the laughter Tom provoked. Before any more scolding could occur, the tutor appeared to take away his charges, which signaled the conclusion of dinner. The boys did well by their training in how they bid Mr. Foxe farewell and thanked their father for the opportunity to enjoy his company.

Which caused Tom to erase Mr. Mordaunt from Aurora's list of enemies to be caught in his gambol for Withersea. For the sake of the man's gentle wife and bright sons, Mordaunt must be guided back to using the law for the sake of justice, rather than ambition. And it would not reap more justice in the world if that family's life was up-ended in Tom's endeavor to ensure justice for Jacob.

~

Tom made a lengthy farewell, with artful expressions of gratitude to Mrs. Mordaunt, extending time for Perry to finish whatever he might be up to elsewhere in the barrister's house.

Meanwhile, Mr. Mordaunt stood on the street, impatient. In the middle of Tom's extravagant appreciations, Mordaunt called out, "I say, Mr. Foxe. I am late for an appointment." He had just then been joined by a small man with a preposterous nose and a too-bright orange damask coat and matching waistcoat. "I must be off. I shall see you at my chambers. Or better, tomorrow. You may take the afternoon to see to your own affairs."

The footman closed the door on Tom while Mrs. Mordaunt still waved her kerchief. Tom looked about, then walked east, believing he saw a figure tall enough to be Perry. At the corner of a cross street, Perry stepped forward with such force that Tom was knocked to the pavement.

"God's teeth! Please forgive me, sir. I didn't see you there."

Perry bent to assist Tom, making a great deal of preserving Tom's hat. He whispered, "Three rascals are following you. The same I spied loitering outside our lodgings last night. I'd know that one fellow's ridiculous hat if I saw it burning in perdition."

Tom stabbed a finger at Perry, miming an argument. Yet he said, "Mordaunt's wife is nice. His two sons are snapping good lads. Did you learn any more about him?"

"He keeps nothing of interest in his house." Perry knocked aside Tom's stabbing finger, then shook his own, keeping up the pantomime. "In her box of ribbons, Mrs. Mordaunt preserved a letter. It is indecent of me, but I pilfered it, and it is now in your pocket. You'll see Withersea and Bagsham connections run wibble-wobble through the lawyer's business."

Tom stood with his hands sternly on his hips. "At Withersea's house, you must look for Jacob's guardian bond and details of property and trade, especially any with other lords' names. I have not yet found scandal to level over the man."

"I shall delve into his mysteries." Perry shook his fist at Tom. "After I follow these bully-boys to their lair, I'm off to catch a kip at our lodgings. Your gambol leaves time only for a foot-guard's swift nap."

"The three of us didn't sleep much before dawn, Perry."

"Beware, hoddy doddy!" Perry bellowed. He dropped his voice. "After I seize a kip, I'm for Knightsbridge. Snooping there might take much of the night. Can you quit your lawyer's chambers for today? I'd like to see you inside our lodgings and free of those bullies."

"I need to poke around Mordaunt's files more. So far, I've found Withersea's papers for country and city properties. And he's entwined with shipping syndicates in complex businesses. It's too intricate to…to…"

"To plan a gambol to run before Friday?"

"Perhaps. We need to enlist Rollo's help, don't we?"

"Aye," Perry said. "Also, I yearn to learn more about his new amanuensis, who claims to be an intelligencer from Amsterdam, but carries a sword-stick, which our colonel's men never did. He's a riddle, else I'm my granddam's pet rabbit. Poke me."

"Michel Chêne is no nick-ninny." Tom mashed his thumb on Perry's chest, had his hand slapped back at him. "I was eaves-dropping when you all met in Mordaunt's chambers. I hope you can coax Rollo into revealing what trap Lord Bagsham set to snare him."

"It distresses my heart to think on it. Now, Tom, you dodge up this street. I'll follow those picaros to learn their business."

Blocking others from seeing into the narrow side street, Perry left no further opportunity for chatting, just pointed where he wanted Tom to be gone and began shouting imprecations in a thick Yorkshire accent. At the next corner, Tom glanced back and saw no trace of Perry nor the three rascals. No one on the street attended to Tom, who did as commanded and hurried back to the chambers of Mordaunt and Lutwyche, nearly losing his way while choosing alternating streets to Lincoln's Inn.

Elated from the adventure, Tom felt the purloined letter in his pocket. Perry! What a commendable fellow. He felt so lucky to have such a friend—fetched home to England by Rowland, who was still the best possible cousin, the same as when they'd sworn allegiance years ago as a band of brothers.

Gasping from unaccustomed exertion, a pain in his side, Tom paused to catch his breath outside the gate to Lincoln's Inn. Then he wiggled through a passel of street hawkers, declining all the pamphleteers' offers. He gave a lad two pennies for peppermint candies twisted up in a paper crescent. It wasn't Winwood's elixir, but the peppermint might invigorate him while he searched for a way to save Jacob.

In the far corner of the chambers where he'd been consigned to work, Tom sat for a moment to consider his next actions. First, to read the letter Perry had filched. He began to unfold it.

My dearest cousin Arabella:

Tom unfolded the rest, seeking the sender's name.

—Your truest friend and most loving cousin, whom you called Aurora Rôche when we laughed as children

Seeing that, Tom felt...Betrayed? Merely confused? Aurora had placed Mordaunt's name on her list but hadn't told him about this personal relation. He felt a petty and dishonorable resentment for the insufficiencies of Aurora's details when she came to him for help. In that purloined letter, he began to read about morning social visits, the promised flower seeds enclosed, titles of poetry and pamphlets to recommend. Then:

> I have read closely your letter telling of your excitement over what W promised John for his help in W's quests to gain new estates.
>
> I know you adore John as the companion of your heart. Now, please tell me, is John guided by you? Because if so, you must coax him away from any business with W.
>
> You can only guess how it pains me to write this. But I long to see you cared for, as you were when Lord B was your guardian. I implore you to think about how Lord B has helped your husband and has promised to help and promote your sons.
>
> I cannot commend W to you as a man to be trusted for either help or protection. Or to keep his promises.

Perry picks just one pocket—rather, one woman's ribbon box—and they learn that Withersea and Bagsham run, as Perry said, wibble-wobble through the lawyer's business.

And what more did Tom know?

The letter was dated two months before Easter. Yet Aurora said that she hadn't seen Withersea's true character until Jacob came to live with her. From this letter, Aurora had seen enough of Withersea's true self to warn her cousin against letting Mordaunt do business with Withersea.

Mordaunt's wife was Lord Bagsham's ward. And Aurora's cousin. And Bagsham was the barrister's (former?) mentor. So very cozy. Yet Aurora hadn't told him.

And W's quests to gain new estates? At the time of this letter, could it be Marborne he sought?

Aurora claimed not to know details of Withersea's business. But she'd been the shining star in Madstone's Greek seminar. She had sufficient wit to learn about business in her own house. What more had she failed to tell him that might have given him a better idea of what to seek in Mordaunt's papers?

Tom put a peppermint on his tongue and closed his eyes while considering what Perry and Ned needed to find, given that he had only a day and a half to ensure Jacob's safety.

Find Jacob's guardian bond. That remained most important for Jacob's protection, to keep him away from Withersea.

Find proof that Withersea is using the law to take properties, as Aurora hinted to him and in the letter to her cousin.

Earlier, he'd found files that showed how Mordaunt's chambers brokered sales of sinecures for the Lord Chancellor; those men received gratuities to be shared with bishops in consistory courts. Not a crime. Tom was not naïve. These records merely showed how the business of justice was managed in England. And although corrupt in the way Absolom saw it, nothing he'd found mattered for the business Aurora set him to undertake.

After this Friday's gambol to save Jacob, he must look for bonds and writs. He could feel it, in what Aurora told him, in how she'd warned her cousin: Withersea was involved in broad corruption. That cried out for justice such as must be pursued by those who lived by Absolom Foxe's rules for Enlightened People. Tom had to find a quicker way to proceed in the morass of papers and writs in Mordaunt's chambers.

His exhilaration from the run back to chambers and from his discoveries dissolved quickly. Instead, the immensity of what he needed to do threatened to overwhelm. He didn't see a way to find what was needed for a successful gambol, not in a mere day and a half, and his scheme needed to preserve Jacob's safety by Friday. He'd have to save further action against Withersea for a later time.

However, once Tom had foiled Withersea for Jacob's sake, it would be hard to come at the man a second time. Therefore, it all had to happen somehow on Friday.

He needed to find Rowland, to warn him that Mordaunt was playing in both Bagsham's and Withersea's business. And to ask for his help. He also needed to recoup from last night's lost sleep, from his efforts with Mordaunt, from escaping those picaros.

And who sent those picaros? Certainly not that incompetent fool Leighton Fairchild.

He ate two more peppermints.

Then he examined the towering shelves above him, filled with bound journals, ledgers, books, papers tied with the traditional red ribbons. Standing on the chair, he pulled volumes from the shelves and stacked them on the table, building a wall that kept him from being seen if anyone peeked in the archway that led into his alcove.

Tom put his head on the tabletop for a moment's daydreaming, giving in to the memories he'd been avoiding since Tuesday afternoon, of that precious time with Jacob in Cambridge, the dear fellow's jests, his head on Tom's shoulder while reading. Aurora whispering Greek poems in the night. Friendship and excitement and secrets amalgamated.

No, no time for ancient memories. He needed a few minutes' kip to sharpen his wits for the work ahead. Tom closed his eyes, smelling peppermint with each breath. Then voices in the next room roused him.

22
Knightsbridge

"LIZZIE!" NED, THOUGH ASTONISHED to see her, found his sister as beautiful as he'd ever painted her. He must always paint Lizzie wearing shades of gold, her face like a delicate tawny rose turning toward the sun. "You aren't in mourning clothes."

"Ned?" Lizzie stopped in surprise. Her playmate bounced a ball off her collarbone. She rubbed where she'd been struck, her white gloves showing stains from the ball. She called, "Wait, Jacob. Let's meet a good friend." She waved for her playmate to come closer.

"Do you know each other?" Lady Withersea said.

"She is my sister." Ned saw the marchioness's eyes searching between the siblings, one pale as silver, the other bronze and dark haired. Ah, people are always curious.

Lizzie said, "We didn't share the same father."

He repeated their ancient jest. "My father was Dutch. That's why I look foreign."

When Jacob stood beside the marchioness, she held his hand in hers, stroking it the way one calms a kitten. "Jacob, this is Mr. Wijck. Remember what Tom promised yesterday? This is Tom's friend, come to help."

"Tom? My Tom?" Jacob was tongue tied, like Caleb, the freckled lad of Marborne parish who begged to watch whenever Ned painted in the garden or village.

"I'm Tom's cousin. I'm called Ned." The lad ignored Ned's offered hand, so instead, Ned let the curious dog sniff his fingers. "You have a bonny dog, Jacob."

"It's Pip. His name is Pip." Jacob scooped the dog into his arms. Not just tongue-tied; Jacob was a natural.

The marchioness said, "Ned came here to paint your picture."

"Did he now?" Lizzie said, even more curious than the little sniffing dog.

Jacob said, "Paint Pip, too?"

"I will," Ned said. "Most certainly."

"It's time for your dinner, Jacob," the marchioness said. "Go find Emma and Cook in the kitchen. Cook promised a chop for Pip and a hot pie for you."

Jacob started toward the house, then came back to Ned. "Pleased to meet you, Ned. So is Pip."

"Pip is a good dog," Ned said. "I hope we'll be friends."

"Tom is my first friend." Jacob then bounded toward the end of the house, stopping only to set Pip down so the dog could run behind him.

The three, left alone at the edge of the garden, regarded each other, two of them prepared to begin that day's business, the third particularly suspicious.

The suspicious one said, "Tom sent you? Not Rollo?"

The marchioness said, "Tom sent Mr. Wijck at my request. But I didn't know you had a brother, Miss Foxe."

"My lady, how do you know my cousin Tom?" Lizzie asked, rather than responding to the prompt.

Lady Withersea offered a smile, as if keeping a secret, like a Celestial Queen in the old paintings Touchstone kept in a locked part of his warehouse. "I met Tom many years ago, when Jacob and I were visiting the Master of Trinity College."

Similar to, but not identical with, Tom's story.

While the two women talked, Ned concentrated on the chore Perry asked as the day's first task. Next to tall, dark Lizzie, Tom's old friend was small, pale, and comfortably plump, with a freely given smile. Bright grey, intelligent eyes glinted in the sunlight of an English summer's day. Those eyes, with a blink of long lashes, lifted her from common to intriguing. Hence, Ned judged that Tom had succumbed to wise eyes, a soft voice, and a gentle yet direct manner.

Lizzie, also with wise eyes, blinked at the marchioness's tale about meeting Tom, putting her in the grips of a desire (Ned knew that look) to ask for the real story. Instead, Lizzie turned her scorching attention to Ned.

"How did Tom know I was here? Or did Rollo tell him?"

"Tom doesn't know. And who knows what Rollo knows?"

Lady Withersea help up her hands prayerfully.

"Let us sit by the roses at the end of the garden, where we can safely share our confidences." She directed them to three benches set in a triangle near an abundant climbing rose. "We have much to do, and quickly. First, let us disregard titles and niceties. Call me Aurora. May I call you Ned? And you, Miss Foxe? Is it Ysabel?"

"Lizzie," Ned said. "She's always Lizzie among us."

"Yes, please call me Lizzie. What quick business are we called upon to do, my lady...uh, Aurora?"

Aurora nodded. "May I assume Tom told you all, Ned?"

Feeling awkward between a stranger and a woman who knew him too well, Ned said, "I have only modest directions from Tom, chiefly about protecting Jacob."

She turned to Lizzie. "Lord Withersea invited you—"

"No, it was Sir Duxwold, whom I'd met in Amsterdam two years ago."

"Who?" Ned asked.

"An overdressed baronet with the eagle's beak and huge hands," Lizzie said.

Aurora said, "He's one of the marquess's coterie."

"That faux-cavalier," Lizzie said, "wanted me to meet the marquess and invited me to bring the new earl, though Rollo declined to join me."

Aurora said, "Yesterday when we met, you said you were a distant cousin to the new earl."

"No distance at all," Ned said. "That is, only a second cousin who intends to marry Rollo."

"For the sake of your family?" Aurora asked. "Or for love?"

When Lizzie hesitated, Ned said, "Neither of them could afford love until last week."

"We need the king's permission." Lizzie sounded modest, though Ned knew for a certain fact that his sister had never been an unassuming person. "My grandfather married a royal cousin, for which he had to have the king's permission. He asked King Charles—the first Charles—to make all Foxe scions the king's wards if anything happened to their parents, and pledged that all Foxe children would seek the king's permission to marry."

"At least," Ned said, "that's the family story." He never believed he was a king's ward, but as a child, he'd been awed at the myth that his cousins were. Though, of course, no king of England had done one thing for them.

"A family story?" Aurora repeated.

Lizzie said, "Yes, though most likely neither Charles nor James ever heard such a story. Still, Rowland intends to ask the king's permission as soon as he is granted an audience."

Aurora said, "And you came here to visit because you are a good friend of Sir Duxwold? I did not observe the two of you in conversation."

"I came only for the chance to meet the marquess."

"Ah." Aurora's lips twitched, almost smiled. "Did Princess Mary send you to spy on him?"

"Indirectly." Lizzie dipped her head, the sole gesture to reveal that she'd been discovered in an untruth. "Certain men want to know whether the marquess might be ally."

Aurora said, "Unless I misapprehend what you mean by ally, the marquess disabused you of that possibility last night."

"I was rather startled to hear," Lizzie said, "that the king of England should be coaxed to give up the throne. And Sir Duxwold spoke as if it were a fact, that when Mary and William come to rule in England, they'll bring Dutch shipping here."

"The marquess believes the sooner the new royals arrive, the better," Aurora said. "But only because moving Dutch shipping to London's harbors will mean a windfall for all his investments. He's spreading his tarps to catch the wealth that's coming to England."

"Late last evening," Lizzie said, "they invited us all to invest in a syndicate that promises enormous returns."

"That's why everyone was invited for supper," Aurora said. "The marquess is short on funds. He needs investors to proceed with his various businesses."

"Such as a syndicate that's sending merchants to China or the Dutch East Indies? Because…" Lizzie switched tones, imitating the marquess's sneer, the same sneer as when he'd castigated Jacob that morning. "'Because every rascal in Asia steals whatever he can, then passes it off as treasure, while—'"

"While," Aurora finished the quote, "'ignorant of what it's worth in the civilized world.' The marquess was overbold in his assertions last night, because he's short of funds and needs new investors."

Ned's thoughts drifted to the marquess's treasure trove and that stunning snuff bottle.

"Meanwhile," Lizzie said, "no sane man should be bold about persuading James to give up the throne. Not this soon after the Duke of Monmouth's invasion."

Ned said, "Perry insists…ah, and Rollo too…that James remains in pursuit of all who supported Monmouth's cause."

Lizzie swiveled on the stone bench, her eyes piercing Ned. "Is that why you came here? To spy on the marquess?"

He said, "I'm here only because Jacob needs protection."

"Yes, that's the real business," Aurora said. "The marquess intends to send Jacob to his holding on the Scottish border. Friday, he'll ask the king to put the Cloudesley title in abeyance. Then I believe he'll offer the king emoluments to buy the title for himself." She clasped her hands tightly in her lap. "Meanwhile, the man now claims to be short of funds. I believe he's selling anything of Jacob's that is of value."

"Buy Jacob's title?" Lizzie was shocked. Then her dark eyes again bore down on Ned. "Why didn't Tom send Perry if Jacob is in danger?"

"Perry is coming tonight," Ned said, bravely ignoring that Lizzie had just slighted him.

"Tell me, my lady…uh, Aurora, how shall we help?" Lizzie asked for instruction, which was like Lizzie: ready for action. "Claim me as your ally."

"We shall both do whatever it takes to help, because," Ned imitated Uncle Absolom, "'my family obligations—'"

"'Are sacred.'" Lizzie spoke earnestly to Aurora. "Our honor calls us to restore justice where we find such a need."

While Lizzie and Aurora talked, Ned considered how Absolom's moral guidelines made allowances for restorative forgery, swindles, and highway robbery (actually, just country-lane pilfering). He'd have to admit, if Perry pressed him, that he'd long relied on Tamsin's moral reasonings. This was the first venture in which he accepted a rationale from Tom about polite deceptions in pursuit of civil and personal justice.

"Jacob is in this dangerous position," Aurora was saying, "because my family never thought our entire heritage might come to Jacob. My two older brothers were to be adequate insurance for the Cloudesley title. And Lord Kettlebottom was to be Jacob's protector as a bonded guardian. But he too died at Easter time."

"Our family suffered once in a similar way," Lizzie said, "I'm sure my father and uncles thought they had each other and their sons to protect Marborne."

"Fate is fickle." Aurora smiled, warmly now, not hiding secrets. "We must laugh at the machinations of the gods, because after a while, one is drained of tears. I need your help to do more than weep." She took a breath, and became steely, rather than the soft, warm woman he'd first met. "Now, for our work. The marquess has departed for London. Ned, can you begin painting this afternoon? If he returns, I don't want him to suspect you to be more than a portraitist."

"Yes. Though my brushes aren't sturdy weapons."

"What shall I do?" Lizzie asked.

Aurora said, "After the marquess departs, you can join me in searching his private rooms."

Ned said, "I do not recommend that. Wait for Perry."

"Is Perry a friend of Tom's?" Aurora asked.

Just then, that yappy little dog was upon them, barking furiously at Aurora, nipping at Lizzie's hem.

"Jacob!" Aurora leaped to her feet. "Where's Jacob?"

She scooped up the dog. Lizzie ran after, with Ned close behind. They ran toward the back of the house, the dog howling, until it leapt from Aurora's arms and ran toward the Knightsbridge Road.

~

An ear-piercing shriek swept like a high wind through the sticky-hot air.

Running ahead of the women, trailing Pip, Ned rounded the last corner of the house and reached the road to find a small riot in progress. Daniel and Neriah beat at two large men with long willow switches, each whirring lash striking with a snap.

One man, dressed like a dockwalloper in dusty canvas, had his arms around Jacob, who shrieked as he struggled to stay out of the reach of the snapping willow switches.

The other man, in dirty and torn black leather, lunged for one of the young Frake brothers, missed, then shouted hideous oaths when the other boy's switch struck him across the face.

The yapping Pip bounded to Jacob's side just as Ned dove in to extract Jacob from his captors. Pip went for the dockwalloper's ankles first, then leaped to nip at the fork in the man's canvas breeches. The man kicked at Pip, who dodged the boot.

Jacob shrieked at a higher pitch, then bit the man's hand.

The man shouted in pain. Ned punched the man's right shoulder but hit his clavicle instead. At the same moment that Ned heard the fellow's clavicle crack, devastating pain shot through Ned's hand. The walloper fell to his knees. Ned got his arms around Jacob, keeping him from falling when the walloper did. Ignoring the pain in his hand, Ned struggled to hustle Jacob out of the mêlée. Regrettably, his back took two willow whips meant for one of the captors.

Jacob, unhappy at being held, ceased shrieking but writhed, while Pip jumped up to nip at Ned's arm, then scratched frantically at Ned's breeches, trying to get to Jacob.

The one captor was still standing. His black leather coat resisted the snapping whips better than did the walloper's canvas (or Ned's coat). And he now had a knife in his hand.

"Stop!" Lizzie's voice rose above Jacob's shouts and the ruckus of the mêlée.

A pistol shot rang out, close by.

Jacob wailed, trying to get his hands over his ears. Ned loosened his hold, yet wrestled Jacob upright and steered him out of the fracas.

A stone hit the man with the knife, knocking the blade away.

Pip leaped out of the crook in his master's elbow. Jacob wailed again, his fists over his ears. Ned had to turn Jacob and himself to find who was shooting whom.

Lizzie held a small, smoking muff pistol, black powder streaking her white gloves. Aurora had a stone in her fist.

The two attackers scuttled down the road, the knife-holder helping his comrade along. Ned shouted execrations at them.

"Run you pestilential, swiving mongrels!"

At the turn in the road, the two climbed into a waiting carriage, which jerked and sped away before its doors closed.

"Pip! Come!" Jacob called for his dog.

Pip jumped on Ned's aching hand as a mounting block to reach Jacob, who wrapped his arms around the dog.

"Blast and damnation!" Ned gritted his teeth against the pain, then lowered his voice when he saw Jacob cringe. Zooterkins, he knew to be peaceable with the fellow. "Have no fear, Jacob. I'm only grousing because that picaro broke my sarding hand. Hurts like the burning devil."

"Are you hurt, Jacob!" Aurora called. "Come, show me that you are well."

"Hurts like the burning devil." Jacob pulled up his torn shirt. Red welts promised to turn to bruises.

While Aurora and Lizzie exclaimed over Jacob, Ned greeted the Frake brothers, dismayed that he didn't know one lad from the other. "Daniel, Neriah. Are you hurt?"

"No, sir," one said.

"We gave better than we got," the other replied.

His hand throbbing, Ned slipped coins from his pocket, holding out two shillings. "You were both magnificent. And you deserve an extra reward when we are done here. Now, which one of you will fetch Dr. Oakes from Covent Garden? Ask the doctor to hire the fastest carriage, so he can come to make sure Jacob isn't hurt."

Ned made sure he sounded calm, reassuring. Yet his heart was beating faster and harder than the puppy's.

Aurora said, "My driver, John Coachman, will take your lad to fetch the doctor." She beckoned to a man who'd just arrived at the edge of the scene. "John, please depart immediately for that same lodging house in London. Also, please make sure neither of these two lads took harm."

"Yes, my lady." John motioned for Daniel and Neriah to follow him to the stables.

When they were gone, Ned shook his finger (on his good hand) at Lizzie, admonishing her. "A loaded flintlock in your pocket? Did you learn nothing when Camilla got herself shot?"

"I gave her a pistol from my pocket," Aurora said. "You didn't see us while you were helping Jacob."

"A pistol, my lady? In your pocket?" Ned worried about the two women, which kept him from worrying about his throbbing hand. "How have you both not injured yourself?"

Aurora said, "John Coachman, who is clever, added a bracket and pin to keep the powder from emptying into my pocket. I have carried it out of worry that the marquess might attempt just such a crude taking."

"The marquess? This was his doing?" Lizzie asked.

"He wants Jacob out of sight and away from me. Which would ruin Jacob's life." She answered Lizzie, but her attention remained on Jacob. "Did those men frighten Pip, dear heart?"

"Pip is good." Jacob didn't look up from where he stroked his dog, hugging it to him. "Too much, Rory!"

"Too much what?" his sister asked.

"Noise!" Jacob said. "Scared Pip."

Ned said, "Pip is a hero. He told us to come find you."

Aurora dropped her voice to the kindest tones. "Dear heart, why were you by the road? You know it's not safe."

"Cook sent me. To give a man a note. Didn't she?" He held Pip up, wanting his dog to agree. "But he grabbed me. The other bad man kicked Pip."

Aurora sighed at Jacob's story. "Ned, please come with me to the kitchens while I turn out the cook. Help me see who among the staff expects a similar dismissal. They must go too."

Ned followed, tucking away his feelings of failure. He was supposed to protect Jacob, but the two women did as much as the two Frake brothers. And by tonight, he'd have Perry scolding him for fighting with his fists. All the pride he'd felt earlier, when he'd gained entry into the household and made it past the marquess, drained away in the afternoon heat. He had to do better, since Tom had trusted him to protect his friends.

23
Tidying Up

As IF SHE NEEDED an escort (while smelling of gunpowder), Lizzie placed her hand on Ned's elbow. She grasped his arm to hide her shaking hands and guessed that was why Aurora took Ned's other arm, while Jacob held her other hand. It wasn't fear Lizzie felt. Rather, it was the bang of the pistol that had alarmed her bones. She held her breath a moment, to let her bones and heart catch up with her rational mind, which knew they were now safe.

"The black powder ruined your gloves," Aurora said. "Let me give you another pair."

"No need," Lizzie said. "I have another pair. I ruined these earlier, playing ball in the grass." She took a breath again, making her rational mind rule. "I suppose, my lady, that the other guests here will be sent packing."

"I'm sure you are right, Miss Foxe," Aurora said, as cool as ice saved in straw. "I can't entertain if I turn most of the staff out onto the streets."

Likely pretending a similar cool-minded nonchalance, Ned said, "I can fetch bread and cheese from the World's End inn."

"Bring back a bottle of wine," Lizzie said, "so we can pretend to be civilized, enlightened people."

"Perhaps an entire bottle for each of us," Aurora's voice sounded a bit shaky, "might be in order after—"

"Ned!" Lizzie exclaimed, now seeing the jutting broken finger. "Your hand!"

ANNIE PEARSON

"It's nothing." He hid his hand. Which was just like him.

"It's not nothing." Lizzie turned his arm to see his hand, then regretted it, since he winced in pain. "At least one finger is hurt badly. Broken, I think."

"Swiving mongrel broke his sarding hand." Jacob nuzzled his pet, whispering comfort in the ear of his over-excited dog.

"Jacob, dear heart, it's not good manners to echo a friend." Aurora spoke with tenderness. "Ned was your helper."

"Forgot." He hugged his dog. "Sorry you broke your sarding hand, Ned. My friend."

"And Miss Foxe, too. She is also our hero." Aurora paused by an open door at the back of the house. "I loathe turning people out. But it must be done."

"Let me do it," Ned said.

Aurora agreed, then told him what to say.

Lizzie listened, too aware that she'd longed to be a countess and yet had no idea how to run a large house, only how to attend a princess. She now wished to be friends with Aurora, to learn from her.

What a selfish thought! Why was she the only Foxe cousin who'd been born selfish? She turned her attention to Ned, intending to partner with him to help rescue Jacob.

With his good hand, Ned opened the kitchen door wider. Ten busy workers, except one small girl on a stool by the butter churn wept into her apron. All stopped amid their chores when Aurora came in.

"Who among you sent Jacob out to the road?" Aurora studied each person in the room, all of whom looked pale with guilt. "Into the hands of bad men?"

The weeping girl looked up, her face destroyed with tears, but didn't speak until Jacob came up beside Aurora. "Oh, Jacob! You're still here! I'm so glad. You are my only friend."

Pip jumped from Jacob's arms and ran to the girl, who dished buttermilk into a bowl.

"Pip likes you, Emma," Jacob said.

Lizzie felt sad dismay, seeing that everyone else in the room was astonished to see Jacob. They'd either known about it or participated in snatching Jacob.

And none of them had expected to be ousted on this hot August day.

"The marchioness wants all of you to pack your belongings and depart," Ned said. Beside him, Aurora nodded as he spoke. "You have until the bell strikes one o'clock at the Church of the Holy Trinity." While everyone murmured in shock, Ned added the detail Aurora wanted. "Gabriel the footman will meet you at the World's End at three o'clock to dispense your final wages. Go now, all of you."

A woman was kneading bread on a long wooden table. The weeping girl ran to her and buried her face in the woman's apron. The dog yelped and leaped out of the way.

"Emma, stop," Jacob said. "You scared Pip."

Alas, the weeping Emma was to be turned out along with her mother or guardian or whoever the granite-faced woman was that only now brushed flour from her hands to put an arm around Emma.

When Aurora and her coterie left the kitchen, Lizzie said, "Now for your other guests?"

"Yes," Aurora said. "Though most departed after breakfast, and Sir Duxwold left with the marquess. Only the ancient Sir Didlington and his cousin Mr. Cokayne are malingering in their borrowed bedchambers."

Lizzie said, "Perhaps you can say Jacob has a putrid sore throat. And that when the doctor comes, he'll surely quarantine the household."

"That should scare Sir Didlington and Mr. Cokayne out of the house immediately," Aurora said, pleased with the suggestion. "Though they'll run to the marquess in London with this story."

Lizzie whispered, "I too feel a fever coming on."

Aurora said, "I'd best say farewell in the foyer while Lizzie takes Jacob out of sight. Ned, will you stand by me?"

"Aye, yet I won't shake any hands for fear of infection."

Blessedly, it took only few more moments until the two guests beat hastily away, because Jacob was keening softly when Ned came in. Ned began to set up his paints and gear as if portrait painting were truly his task. He picked up a jar of brushes, set it down awkwardly.

"Blast and damn! My hand hurts like the devil. I hope Winwood gets here soon."

"Blast and damn." Jacob pulled at the length of linen rag that Pip gripped until the dog hung in the air, not letting go.

"Some people," Lizzie said, "need to hold their tongue, rather than give others new imprecations to echo."

"Zooterkins!" Ned, grasping the wrist of his injured hand, glared at her for scolding him. "When Perry arrives, will you scold him too?"

"When Perry arrives," Lizzie said, "he'll burn the ears of every grandmother in York while reproaching you about endangering your hand."

"You distress me." Ned imitated Perry. "Your foolishness takes the cheese."

Jacob looked up. "You are the man in the moon. Like Tom."

Ned laughed, though Lizzie didn't understand why. "Come help, Jacob. While we wait for Winwood and Perry, let's see if it's possible to hold a brush when one finger points the wrong way."

His kindness with Jacob shouldn't amaze her, since Lizzie had seen Ned with the village boys. What amazed her was to find that she had so quickly bonded with Ned over Tom's crisis. But why should that be amazing? It was only a different house from Revelstone. They'd been united since she'd come back from Holland, when they all needed to protect Tom because of his illness.

~

Wanting a few moments to herself, Lizzie went to tidy her gown, claiming that the romp with the rogues in the roadway had likely ruined her hem.

"Lizzie." She heard Ned whisper as she turned into her guest chamber. He followed her in and closed the door. "You have to help me, before Perry gets here."

"With your hand?"

"No. Perry wants to know whether she loves Tom back. Don't you want to know, too?"

She opened her mouth to speak, but Ned rushed on before she found words.

"You know how Tom's always cutting up, but even a blind cove can see he's hellish lonely. He came home from Trinity in a dead funk. He must have been pining for her all these years."

"I didn't know. I wasn't at home then." She wasn't sure she knew now, still struck by surprise.

"Now she's come to him, asking Tom to play hero for her. It's like to relight the candle he carried for her after Trinity."

"How do you know he was in love with her at Trinity?"

"That's a cat's whisker, Lizzie. What fellow is going to let a woman live in his room unless he's in love? If Tom was going to allow such, why didn't he let Tamsin hide out at Trinity in breeches? I'll tell you why not. Because the affection a fellow has for his sister isn't the same. Perry spied it the very moment as I did. Tom's heels over his head. He's in love."

"Why tell me this?"

"You have to ask her if she feels the same as Tom."

"I will do no such thing. I'll leave that sort of pickthank gossip to you and Perry."

"It's how women talk with each other. A fellow can't ask such a question of a woman."

She stepped back, feeling as if her brother had trapped her against the wall. "Let me practice on you." She had her hand to his breastbone, easing him back. "Are you in love? Do you return the affections lavished on you?"

He gaped at her. She opened the door and pushed him out.

Alone finally. But before she undertook repairing her gown, she sat to write another message. With John Coachman already gone to London, she'd have to give it to Perry that night to take away with him. She wrote with faith in her ability to make happen that which she needed.

> Midafternoon, the eighth of August
> My Lord Marborne: It speaks ill of my own breeding that I write to beg a favor of your lordship. Below is a pattern for a lace border of my own invention. I beseech that you might be so kind as to carry it to Mrs. Gamlingay, our rector's wife. I shall be forever grateful. Just as I have the honor to remain, —Your Lordship's obedient servant, Ysabel Flores Foxe

Again, she cast code, in less hurry than her last letter. Tom must have alerted Rowland, yet it felt imperative that she too warn Rowland about the marquess. Folding and sealing the page, she wrote across its face in bold letters:

> The Right Honorable the Earl of Marborne
> Benson's Lodgings, Covent Garden, London

That should be sufficient direction to reach Rollo. She had to believe (rather than merely hope) that the line of poetry at the end of the coded message would touch his heart. She'd ask Perry to carry the missive to London.

Just then, though, she concentrated on getting grass and gunpowder stains out of her new gold silk dress.

24
Lincoln's Inn

ALONG THE COBBLED STREETS that led to Lincoln's Inn, Cornelius's heeled shoes tapped a beat while he silently mouthed what he'd say at the accounting his patron had commanded:

My lord, your task proceeds as well as can be in the green and comely countryside. I have, however, ceased activity in Westminster for the present. May I beg that you—

Bah! Beggary. Best if he took another stance. Cornelius practiced it, so he didn't sound like a common villein or like mendicants on a street corner.

My lads cannot flog pope-hating pamphlets near Parliament or royal offices. It's too dangerous. Please allow me to recommend a new message.

Clattering up Chancery Lane with these meditations, Cornelius arrived at Lincoln's Inn in a heat. Near Mr. Mordaunt's chambers, he caught his reflection in a mullioned window. From habit, he tugged his cravat out of his coat collar to cover his neck. Perhaps he shouldn't have worn his dusky-pink velvet suit with yellow piping. He should have chosen the suit his wife liked best.

Alack, he'd let that condescending note from Duxwold—*Sir* Duxwold—get his back up like a heron on a branch. Cornelius had naught to gain from showing his ire to his patron. A mere *aide-mémoire,* as his dear wife would say, a reminder to get out from under that yoke before summer's end. He was now a man of wealth and property, yet still being treated as an errand boy, when by dint of his own hard work, he'd advanced to his current heights. However, he had no ability to cry "No!" until his so-called debt to his patron had been paid through new services.

"Rosewurme!"

Outside the barrister's chambers, Sir Duxwold lounged against the wall, as if waiting for him. Not seriously taller than Cornelius, the knight had a face like a white-tailed eagle. The alabaster curls of an immaculate periwig dripped over the shoulders of his shiny orange coat with its vastly wide skirts. Though Sir Duxwold lacked power in the king's court, he'd made himself useful to a small circle of lords. The always-cordial fellow greeted Cornelius with a jolly handshake, as if he hadn't laden his summons to this meeting with insults. Duxwold never lost his smile, never appeared to take offence, had even laughed when an earl called him a drummer for lords' purses. "Someone has to do it," Duxwold had replied jovially.

"My last note called for you and I to meet an hour gone past." Sir Duxwold pushed at the door to Mordaunt's chambers. His widest smile: "Don't muck it up for me."

"I had no such note, sir."

A bell tingled, set to ring when the clerks were out. Cornelius announced himself rather than being made to feel an intruder. "It's Mr. Rosewurme, sir. With Sir Duxwold. We've come at your particular invitation."

"Come to the back, gentlemen," Mordaunt called. "It's only us here. We're in my own work room."

There he found Mr. John Mordaunt, a tall, spectral man with a faint Puritan whiff about him. And, for the day's surprise, Lord Withersea in the flesh, looking jolly, over-fed, and sunburned from riding in the summer heat. Mordaunt was accepting snuff from a small crimson jar the marquess offered while his lordship finished a story about how he'd bargained for the snuff bottle and so got it cheap off a captain on a trader from Batavia.

"I'm pleased that you admire it, Mr. Mordaunt. I prize it highly among the many antiquaries my captains have brought from the Indies trade." The marquess then offered the crimson bottle to Sir Duxwold, who declined.

No snuff was on offer to Cornelius.

Mordaunt nodded to Cornelius in greeting, but Withersea didn't look up, busy pocketing the snuff bottle. The barrister poured what appeared to be port from a decanter into a Ravenscroft crystal glass, like those in Cornelius's wife's cabinet of treasures. Cornelius was not offered this hospitality either, yet governed his face and rising shoulders, quelling resentment. After all, he wasn't an admirer of port wine and found its scent in the room too heavy for a business meeting. Lord Withersea accepted the glass and sipped it with a sigh of pleasure.

"I shall not importune against your time, my lord," Sir Duxwold said. "Let me do what I can for you and be gone."

With that, Lord Withersea handed him a parcel, and Mr. Mordaunt waved a paper, setting it down on the desk for Sir Duxwold to sign.

Then Sir Duxwold was gone with sunny farewells. Cornelius retained the innocent face with which he'd been born, while the inner face of his soul sneered: Duxwold was merely this lord's footman, no loftier than Cornelius.

"Lo, it's Mr. Rosewurme," Mordaunt said. "It's a beneficent happenstance that you have appeared at just this moment. We were discussing the need for your services."

Amazing happenstance, given that the message Cornelius had stuffed into his pocket read: *Lord W requires an accounting…*

"How may I be of service?" Cornelius bowed, hiding how he preferred to dodge any such service, except now a debt was held over him for those four properties he received, which had been sent as gifts to women for whom he'd had a *tendre*.

"When we came to the gate of Lincoln's Inn this afternoon," Mordaunt said, "your hirelings were being shouted out of the street by mercenaries working for Gray's Inn barristers."

"Mordaunt thinks," the marquess stuck in his oar, "that you'd best find new hirelings for Friday's business."

"Have done so already, good sirs." Cornelius still had his hand in his pocket, keeping his resentful fist out of sight. "Yet such gangs are costly. If you wish to hire more men—"

"It's between you and Mr. Mordaunt," Withersea interrupted, "to agree on how your expenses are covered. In my absence. As we have always done."

"Yes, your lordship, but—" Cornelius began.

The marquess had more to say. "As we have long agreed, there is no bridge from you to me, and only a thread between Mr. Mordaunt and myself. You do understand, I am certain."

Cornelius did understand. It had been his work to find properties with unproved inheritances, and to bring Mr. Mordaunt the details he could uncover for such cases. Then Mordaunt froze each claimant's hopes in chancery, leaving the purported inheritor like a wigeon skidding on a frozen pond. Once a claim was abandoned, or when the chancery court ruled, Mordaunt guided the outcome to allow Withersea or one of his peers to stake a claim, without the land reverting to the Crown.

From the beginning of any such case, it was Cornelius's task to ensure no bridge could be found between the men who paid gratuities and emoluments to the procurators, bishops, and judges in the chancery courts. In dire cases, Cornelius employed Merryboy's hard men to scare off claimants.

"I am always discreet," Cornelius said, as haughtily as he dared. "More than any other man in England." For his personal discretion, however, he kept certain papers stored in his study at home. What had old Fowlmere taught him in Oxford? Look out for yourself first and always.

"That's exactly what the Duke of Bagsham claimed when we were first introduced," Mordaunt said.

Withersea heaved a sigh of impatience. Cornelius waited to hear what the marquess had to sigh about. At least the odor of port had lessened since the two men had emptied their glasses. Now Cornelius smelled peppermint, though he didn't know which man might be the source.

"The Duke of Bagsham?" Withersea frowned. "It's years gone since I've invited Lord Bagsham to join my projects."

"Indeed," Mordaunt said, seeming to ingratiate himself with the marquess, "the death of Lord Bagsham's heir took him hard. As if he has no wind to fill his sails. My wife claims—"

"Your wife?" Withersea wasn't frowning; he was squinting into his crystal glass, seeking more port. "Oh, yes. She was the duke's ward. No matter. Bravewood being 'lost in battle,'" his voice tilted as he smiled a crooked smile, "took Bagsham off the list of men to worry about. Let him think we are allies, but the man is a captured rook, left by the side of the game board."

Mordaunt blanched, if such a pallid man could be described thus. He didn't answer, just poured port into the lord's glass.

Withersea turned solicitous. "If either of you still performs services for that ancient relic, I advise that you cease. The duke's usefulness in England diminishes by the day."

Mordaunt nodded, his lips pursed like a judge in court. "As you say, my lord. I've been directing the duke's work to my partner this past half year. Which leaves me more time for your needs, my lord."

"I came at your calling," Cornelius said, the heat rising in his breast again, disliking to hear his former mentor denigrated. "What do you require of me, my lord, in the way of service?"

"On Friday this week," Withersea said, "two new cases will come before the Committee. You must help make sure that day's proceedings are agreeable to me."

"While leaving no sign that his lordship has a hand in the Committee's doings," Mordaunt said, unnecessarily.

"The Committee?" Cornelius detested being forced to ask for information, as if he were ignorant or unrefined.

"The Committee for Privileges and Conduct, which convenes in chambers kept by the House of Lords." Withersea's tone implied that a child should know this. His nostrils flaring, he glanced at Cornelius. "You will appear there at ten o'clock Friday morning. In your most solemn and respectable clothes."

"The House of Lords?" Cornelius spoke in his brightest voice, as if he hadn't just been insulted again. And he had no desire to be pulled even deeper into Withersea's corruption. Which had to be what this business intended. "Perhaps a man such as Sir Duxwold might best—"

"No." Withersea slapped his hand rather too firmly on the desk. "I don't want any others to know my business. You are the best man for such delicate affairs."

Before Cornelius could enjoy that compliment, Mordaunt condescended to explain what they expected of Cornelius, describing a task that a child could do.

"Read a pair of writs? I can do that," Cornelius said.

"As your most auspicious self," Mordaunt added.

Cornelius merely nodded, struck deep in his heart that he had no need of the barrister's admonishments.

"Naturally you can do it, Rosewurme." Withersea became his jolly self again. "Or did you not hear from your hirelings at Easter what happens to men who fail me?"

Cornelius covered his face with his handkerchief to cough politely. Withersea had levied a casual, perilous threat. Just as Merryboy had foretold. Now was the time to be bold, as Fowlmere had long ago taught him.

"Will this satisfy my remaining debt for those properties in Oxford and the south of England?" He forced a warm smile. "Or will there be additional reward?"

"Why, yes to that debt. I'd forgotten. And also..." The marquess's eyes darted as he considered an answer. "Gold to buy your lady fine silks and pearls to bead her gown."

"My lady wife has been dead these two months."

"Ach, sorry to hear, my dear little man." The marquess offered shallow condolences. "Then the gold will be your own to do with as you will."

A great sadness rushed into Cornelius's heart, like a rising tide, as great as the day he'd laid his dear, dear wife to rest in the cold church vault. He blinked to hide it.

This lord would never help him to a title. This lord considered him a servant. Or worse perhaps. One of the dogs chasing cattle on his estates.

"Now for the accounting you were called to offer," Mordaunt said. "About his lordship's pamphlets."

"Too busy with your personal affairs to do the work you committed to?" Withersea said it pleasantly enough (having made threats only moments before).

I just told you that my wife died. Did you not hear?

"It is true that my personal affairs have taken me away from other work."

The man remained unaware of how he'd overwhelmed Cornelius with slights to his wife's memory.

He hoped Mordaunt might speak up about the help Cornelius provided in preparing the marquess's cases for the chancery courts. He wanted to say to Mr. Mordaunt: *Lord Bagsham was patron and mentor to us both. What are we doing with this lesser man?*

He hoped Mordaunt might speak up, yet the man presented a heart of stone. Mayhap he learned it in barrister school.

"Yet you promised results," the marquess said. "Where are your lads? Howbeit, not a single lad approached me from the time I left my house in Knightsbridge until I came to Lincoln's Inn? I need more, and better, before autumn comes."

"I did as you asked. At Grub Street, I paid scribblers for better writing. 'The Hazards of Untrue Communicants' is quite popular with the gentry. I offered my agents in the countryside splendid terms for large orders." Cornelius loathed explaining his business to men who didn't understand. Or care about his lads.

"But that does not explain," the marquess said, "why I have not seen my pamphlets in Westminster or near White Hall."

"We'd do better with a new topic, my lord." Cornelius held onto his courage, as if he cupped it in his hands. "Since the Duke of Monmouth's invasion, my lads have had a hard time from the militia. Several were beaten and their pamphlets burned. They say the king wants to smash all anti-Catholic sentiment."

What he didn't say: Last week in Oxford, Cornelius had himself tossed in a gutter all the anti-Catholic pamphlets his lads had been hawking there. He didn't want to see his lads crosswise with the king's men.

"Yes, James persists." The marquess drummed his fingers on the desk, as if this bored him. "The fool seeks to put his Catholic friends into the House of Lords—and Commons, too."

Mordaunt's eyes twitched, as if he sought words to answer. "Lord Bagsham complains—confidentially, you understand— that James is bringing his friends into his court as advisors."

"There's Lord Bagsham busy failing again," Withersea said. "The old fool cannot persuade the king to turn away from promoting his Catholic friends."

Cornelius took a breath. "The militia in Oxford seized that last pamphlet. 'Jesuit Devils Are Returning to Your Pulpits!'" It wasn't wise to argue, but his poor lads had taken the lash for the marquess's sake.

Mordaunt said, "I had been unaware you nursed such a strong antipapal persuasion, my lord." He spoke as if it were a matter of idle curiosity, not the lashed hides of young lads.

"I don't." The marquess remained bored, examining his fingertips. "I don't care which priests stand in English pulpits. But people's animadversion for the pope is our best lever for prying James from his throne. We need a strong man, like William in the Low Countries. Not a man afraid of his nephew's shadow, like James."

S'welp me! The marquess seeks to draw me into sedition!

Cornelius watched Mordaunt, who crossed his legs and folded his arms tightly, his eyes cast down. Shame for the association? Afraid to speak up?

Was that Cornelius too?

While his lady-love lay dying in the late spring, he'd been pressed to take on the marquess's tasks. At the time, he'd only worried that the anti-Catholic pamphlets might displease his wife, but she'd died, never learning of it. He then worried for his lads' safety. He hadn't conceived that this work might be helping foment rebellion against the Crown. Cornelius didn't have the mettle for it and wasn't ashamed to admit it. His royalist wife would rise from her tomb if she knew he'd become involved in such endeavors.

His face stiff as stone, Mordaunt still hadn't spoken. And Cornelius had taken too long to answer the marquess.

"I am..." Cornelius needed to be more politic than he'd been in his life. "I am unwilling to partake in rebellion. The Duke of Monmouth brought catastrophe. The heads of half of Bristol are now on pikes above that city's gates."

"This isn't about rebellion." Withersea sucked a breath through his teeth. "We only seek to encourage James to remove himself." He had his snuff bottle in hand again. "Have we concluded our business?"

"One more item, my lord." Cornelius held up a finger. "About Friday? I've enlisted new men. The present lot bloodied their knuckles while pursuing the Earl of Marborne—"

"The Marborne Pretender," Withersea said, correcting him.

"He and his coterie attacked your hirelings. The earl travels with other men who are handy with sword and pistol."

"Find better quality picaroons," Withersea looked down his nose. "Men with enough wit and speed to avoid a brawl. But do not spend a fortune on it. I'm not made of silver coin."

Cornelius had his fist in his pocket again, though it destroyed the tailored lines of his coat. How much condescension was a decent and honest man to endure?

"As you say, my lord," Mordaunt said. "It will be an entire year before you can petition for release of the funds the king has frozen. The Crown took far too much without a trial."

"Curse the Fates!" Withersea still spoke in a passion, perhaps not wisely considering his words. "I may as well have played faro and hoped for a better outcome. Why did I let Duncombe talk me into investing in his farrago? Now my money's been carted off to the king's exchequer."

Cornelius was both startled and confused by the marquess's passionate declamation.

The marquess mashed his fist on the table. "That pestilential Duncombe will likely as not trade my name to the king's enquirers. He's just the sort of mercenary traitor to betray his friends. And what can I do to stop that?"

Mordaunt put up his hands, as if placating his patron. "Lord Bagsham puts Duncombe's arrest down to happenstance, especially since Mr. Foxe arrested Duncombe and came into the Marborne title on the same day."

"Marborne arrested Duncombe?" Lord Withersea's voice pitched close to a screech. Worse, his eyes shifted, glowing with more than surprise at Mordaunt's comment. "That upstart who now calls himself an earl? That man arrested Duncombe?"

Mordaunt became cautious.

"I have it from Lord Bagsham. The whole affair is not widely known beyond the Crown intelligencers. Mr. Foxe produced the evidence that a militia captain used to arrest Duncombe. Then the king froze all the funds on deposit in Duncombe's business. Others arrested were—"

Withersea shouted more expletives than Cornelius knew the king's English offered. "I lost a fortune to a Foxe bastard?"

"Your funds are only f–f–frozen," Mordaunt stuttered, "not lost. If you didn't join the syndicate supporting Monmouth."

Withersea wasn't listening. "The last earl, Samuel Foxe, cut me in front of Charles. And it was at the king's feast when I came to my own title."

The marquess's voice rose on his last words. He stopped, fiddled with his snuff bottle, poured out a pinch, and inhaled. He sneezed and wiped his eyes before continuing his rant. "Samuel Foxe spent the evening recounting with Charles how they'd escaped the Roundheads together. How did a noble English title fall on that black knave? And now a Foxe brat has his muddy shoes on the funds gathered to help Monmouth."

Withersea only vented his spleen, showing no interest in what Mordaunt or Cornelius thought. Cornelius, never low-witted, perceived a great deal more than Withersea's ire over his frozen funds.

First, Mordaunt was alarmed to hear that the marquess had staked money on Monmouth. From how rapidly Mordaunt blinked while his eyes searched the room, the barrister was aware that he'd been cast, however unwittingly, in the role of accessory to rebellion.

Second, Withersea—turning red and sputtering—wanted blood-vengeance. He couldn't utter the names Marborne or Foxe without spitting more poisonous words.

And third, Cornelius needed to quit Withersea's business as quickly as he could. Treason was too heady a brew for his tastes, however secretly this lord thought he'd managed the affair. If Mordaunt and Cornelius now knew of it, then others also did, or would soon. Sir Duxwold, for example, who transported the money for Withersea's business exchanges.

Cornelius rose, thinking the day's brutal business was done.

"Sit down, Rosewurme," Withersea demanded. "We need to discuss our business before the Committee on Friday. I want Lord Marborne broken and despised by the end of the meeting. In the best of worlds, the king sends him to the Tower."

Cornelius couldn't keep from glancing at the door, needing to run, but requiring a cautious path for his escape. He cast a look at Mordaunt, imploring the man to speak up, but barely caught his eye.

You are a barrister, a great man. You stand for the law. Stop this.

No, the wise and powerful barrister must have seen what Cornelius had discovered: they were in danger from this lord.

With no possible retreat, Cornelius cast his eyes down. Best to let this lord believe he had the upper hand. And best not to ask about any business that touched on the rebel Monmouth. Cornelius now felt as if he were among the fear-struck boys flogged for peddling seditious pamphlets.

"The most important business tomorrow is to attain the guardianship of my wife's useless brother." Withersea explained his plan for the Committee meeting.

Mr. Mordaunt had his head in his hands. "What shall we plan for the second part of the meeting? When the lords consider the Marborne title?"

"For that," Withersea said, "I shall deal with Marborne in the same way I dealt with Bravewood. Which is fitting, since they are both dangerous to the future of England."

Cornelius's throat had closed in fear and anger while listening to this evil lord. But he had to ask. "Have you any more instructions for the hirelings you requested for Friday?"

Withersea rose. "Sir Duxwold has directions and payment for your brigands' work. Good day, Mordaunt. Rosewurme."

The bell rang when Withersea closed the door behind him. Cornelius's angel looked down from heaven, shaking her head sadly, letting tears fall. He gathered himself together, nodding to Mordaunt, barely managing to say, "Good day, sir," while wishing he never saw the barrister again outside of heaven.

How to deal with the fury in his belly when there was nowhere to strike? Mordaunt betrayed their years-long collaboration. Withersea threatened him. Just as Merryboy had hinted might happen.

How to escape while keeping his skin and fortunes intact?

25

St James Place

— R O L L O —

By WEDNESDAY AFTERNOON, ROWLAND had a new house, a new
lawyer, and a secretary whose youth and know-it-all air made a
decent disguise for a personal guard.

The Duke of Bagsham's house was across town in St James
Place, so their transit was frequently interrupted by hordes of
chair-bearers carrying their human burdens, footmen delivering
packages, and street hawkers at every corner, together with shop-
keepers chasing away such lads with brooms.

Rowland said, "When we meet with Lord Bagsham, what
shall I say about how I found you?"

"We knew each other in Holland, where I served Lord T—,
recently deceased. A new diplomat has taken his place, bringing
his own men into service, which left me free to find new work."

"Do you have an answer for everything, Michel?"

"I must say yes, if only to advance your confidence in my
skills. And I am aware, from the examination Mr. Frake made of
me at the lawyer's chambers this morning, that I shall have to
labor long and hard to convince your friend of my worth."

"Did you meet Mr. Frake and Tom Foxe before this today?"

They dodged a mover's cart that threatened to tip chairs and
dusty straw mattresses into the street.

"I was determined to wait for you to introduce us. However,
Mr. Thomas Foxe set upon me after church on Sunday, asking if
I knew the best barber in the neighborhood capable of restoring
a periwig so it's suitable to wear in the king's court."

"Tom Foxe has been an invalid since February. He is now often quite eager to meet people as he was used to."

"I cannot speak to his health. But if I had such a cousin, I'd advise keeping limits on what the tongue boasts."

"You mean to say, when seeking a barber, it's best to leave off saying 'capable of care suitable for the king's court?"

"If it were my relative, I'd say so." Michel nodded, to punctuate his advice.

"Except my relative caught you watching me in church and provoked you into conversation. Tom, you will see, has depths. You might find that he uses his seemingly enthusiastic naïveté for his own purposes."

They stepped aside to allow a governess and a passel of children to come down the way to the park.

"Here is your mentor's house, my lord. Allow me to knock and announce you."

Rowland waited, dressed in another man's suit while yet another fellow knocked on doors for him. He'd been promoted in life such that, it seemed, he no longer lived his own. Perhaps soon Rowland would be required to employ urchins to eat his meals for him.

But who am I now, while the world rushes to the new earl?

The Duke of Bagsham lived just north of St James Palace in a stone-block and porticoed home also best described as a palace, though it was called Littlecote.

The footman Isaac took Rowland's hat with a warm greeting. "His grace has cautioned us to make you welcome for your frequent visits. Whatever we can do for your comfort, you must be free to ask."

"Thank you. This is my secretary, Mr. Michel Chêne. Please announce us to his grace. I am here at his particular invitation."

Isaac took Michel's hat with a coolness that indicated an expectation that the Earl of Marborne was to come alone.

Lord Bagsham invited Rowland to sit at his right hand at the head of a table that seated twenty and had been polished to mirror-like brilliance. The two secretaries shook hands, Michel showing great deference. They took seats opposite each other at the foot the table and never spoke again.

So, Rowland was offered coffee, Michel nothing.

"My kitchen prepares delightful coffee. Richard says that," the duke referred to his secretary, "coffee has set London a-buzz. Ha ha. Do you perceive his wit?"

Rowland received his coffee along with a grim plate of cold sliced meat, a bite of cheese, thinly sliced bread, and nothing to dress it with, apparently the portly duke's slimming meal. Sipping the thick, over-sugared coffee, Rowland was grateful Michel had led him to dine before attending lordship school. He waited for the duke start the conversation.

"How did you get on with Mr. Mordaunt?"

"The man seems quite capable, duke. Talented even, but…"

Rowland prepared to rush into it, to declare that he didn't like the man and would be seeking another lawyer; however, his softly voiced comment dropped like crumbs on a carpet.

Bagsham interrupted. Or hadn't listened.

"Good, good. John Mordaunt was already a fast-rising barrister when he married my ward. The success of the man and the match are both delightful to me. Arabella Mordaunt is the kindest, wisest woman in London. I feel fortunate to have helped her get on in the world."

Rowland tucked away what he intended to say. He'd find another lawyer without dragging all that into his complex affairs with the duke.

The duke brushed his hands and set aside his meager meal. "We now have work to do."

As the tutorial began, Rowland felt like a child being made to repeat his lessons over and again: *I must always behave as a peer of the realm.* To endure the perishing tedium, Rowland kept busy taking the duke's measure and observing the two secretaries. Michel wrote industriously; Lord Bagsham's secretary took up his pen only upon rare occasion when the duke said, "Make a note of that, Richard. We shall have to prepare." The duke seemed proud of his condescension to Rowland. And Rowland listened to what other lords absorbed in the cradle.

The proper way to approach, bow, and address the king. (A bit less onerous than the customs Rowland had observed around Louis in Paris.)

The correct sort of compliment to offer the king before saying anything else. ("So important," Lord Bagsham murmured twice.)

The promises to be made as a peer while standing before the Committee for Privileges and Conduct. (Not as strict as Absolom's Rules for Enlightened People.)

The amount to pay as bribes, called emoluments, to other peers of the realm. (Bagsham uttered "emoluments" as if speaking of spices and sugar.)

The protocol when paying such bribes. (Never directly to a lord, "Only from your trusted aide to his aide," which caused Rowland to see anew the nature of his work that first year in Paris, carrying "messages" to lords' aides.)

The proper raiment when he and members of his family were received at court.

"My family is in mourning," Rowland said. "We won't wear bright colors, after the style the Continental courts have chosen."

Because Tamsin suggested, then Lizzie commanded it.

"Good, good. Nothing to be gained by appearing as peacocks." Lord Bagsham intoned more details, ending with: "Oh, and remember, James shuns any demand to perform the king's touch, but only because he fears infection. Just as well, to my mind. Few in England want to see a confirmed Catholic heal even one soul by the laying on of hands."

"I suppose not, your grace."

"Now, as for prayers," Lord Bagsham said. "Is there any chance you are a secret Catholic?"

"No. We follow the teachings of our parish rector." *Who debated ideas with Absolom that might have put them on a pyre a century ago.*

"Ah, yes. Didn't Doctor Foxe testify for several dissident rectors after Charles's restoration, including the man in the Marborne parish?"

"Indeed. My uncle was a well-known moral philosopher."

It irked that the duke knew such a detail about Absolom yet hadn't lifted a hand over the Marborne title lingering for years. Rowland steered the discourse toward his own desires.

"Your grace, my cousin Ysabel Foxe and I intend to seek the king's permission to be yoked in common cause. But how do we ask?" He kept talking because the duke didn't answer or even blink in response to Rowland's question. "Asking the king is, Doctor Foxe told us, a family tradition. The connection goes back to a forebearer who married a royal cousin." Rowland stared at the duke while waiting for an answer, as stern as he dared to be with a man who had threatened him. "Miss Foxe and I each served the Crown of England for a decade."

The duke sat for a moment, which increased Rowland's uneasiness. "Let me think on it, Lord Marborne. Richard, please take a note." Then he pushed his spectacles up his nose with those tiny hands. Rowland now knew to expect ill fortune whenever the duke smeared his fingers across his spectacles. "Mr. Chêne, Richard. Please excuse us for a moment. I have private business with Lord Marborne."

Michel rose without a change of expression and was out the door ahead of Richard, who moved like a much older man than he appeared to be and who cast a resentful look over his shoulder before walking under the ornate archway and closing the door behind him.

Then came the moment Rowland had dreaded.

~

"Now, Lord Marborne. Let us pray your famous luck abides," the duke said. "I have your first task as the king's watcher."

"It's not luck." Rowland said, hiding the same ire as rose when Mordaunt asserted that claim. "I am skilled. An expert."

The duke wasn't listening, and Rowland didn't want to be arguing the degree of his capabilities for work he didn't want to do. Bagsham handed Rowland a pamphlet like the hawkers had pressed on him outside the theatre. Printed on the cheapest paper, replete with creative spellings, the pamphlet decried King James and Louis of France as the pope's puppets.

"Lord Marborne, please find this particular provocateur so that we may stop him. I should like to speak to the king about your success when we next share a late supper."

"Where do I begin to look for the man who," Rowland rubbed his fingers on the rag and came away with blacked thumb and forefinger, "poorly performs provocations."

"You frown. You are offended by such a trivial request?" The duke lifted his eyebrows so they wiggled above his spectacles, which sent the spectacles slipping down his nose. He shoved them back in place.

"I'm honored to be trusted with this request." Rowland did his best imitation of an honest man while speaking a falsehood. His heart and soul wanted to flee, but not from the chore, rather from being coerced into it. "What I first need to know—"

"Shall I explain why it matters to the king?"

"Be assured, your grace—"

As was his way, the duke interrupted. "It matters that Parliament remains free and of service to the king. I do not care about issues of faith, only that it affects how Parliament deals with a monarch who is seen by many as indebted to France. I don't worry about the pope, only about Louis wanting to rule all of Europe."

"That tells me why it matters to you, duke, but—"

The duke lifted another pamphlet, looked over the top of it, but dropped his eyes when he caught Rowland's gaze. Which left Rowland more curious about what the duke intended and about what he wasn't saying.

"You found your house to be satisfactory, Lord Marborne."

A statement, not a question.

"You have overwhelmed me, your grace. It is too kind of you to lend it to me."

"It's yours to have, Marborne. Given our agreement."

"I understand it was your nephew's house. Please accept my condolences."

I feel as if I awoke in another man's life. The man who must have been your spy, and now I am to wear his clothes and be your puppet.

"Aye, he was my grand-nephew. I named him as my heir, but he died at Sedgemoor. Left no wife or child." Lord Bagsham didn't falter, his eyes didn't drop. "There's no reason to leave the house empty."

Rowland's questions about where to start were ignored. He didn't indulge his desire to ask if he should search for the malefactor while wearing the pink gown or the missionary's wife's grey dress. Instead of speaking to what mattered at the moment, the duke gave him a list of the Committee members, who must be bribed. Rowland was then dismissed with one final caution:

"Court shoes, Mr. Foxe. Yet I advise against red heels. Your austere ways will do well with King James."

Rowland bowed as he'd been taught, then joined Michel in the foyer. When they'd traveled two streets over from Lord Bagsham's palace, Rowland explained that the duke wanted him to search for a political provocateur.

Michel said, "But you quit the intelligencers."

Though annoyed about Michel knowing that, Rowland stayed on mission. "Lord Bagsham says the king requires my service, without asking Richard to make a note of it."

Michel said, "He's afraid of you."

"Richard the secretary? But I paid him no mind."

"I mean the duke. Each time you spoke of your past service or your family's service, or mentioned the Duncombe Affair, the duke blinked wildly, ducked his head, averted his eyes from your fearsome gaze."

"The Duncombe Affair?"

I wish I'd been fearsome instead of fearing. For Lizzie's sake.

"Whatever you choose to call it," Michel said. "You made it possible for the king's men to arrest Danvers Duncombe and seize his assets. You uncovered other traitors, didn't you? That left the duke uneasy about whether you uncovered other men who played traitors by way of the purse. Men he might know."

"Friends who gave money to support the rebel Monmouth?" A good guess. The duke had prodded in their first meeting about missing pages in the ledger where Duncombe had recorded the names of men who participated in his traitorous syndicate.

"Or," Michel said, "perhaps the duke worries about his nephew's loyalty and what you might know."

"The duke's nephew was killed at Sedgemoor, fighting for James. The nephew seems to have been a royalist and to have been puritanical in his personal life."

"But are you sure? Did the duke have his nephew's house thoroughly cleaned? Did he leave anything for you to see?"

"Michel, you have a suspicious mind."

"It's how we were both trained. Here's a bootmaker's shop. Do you want my advice for court shoes?"

"I can manage," Rowland said. *I have only to avoid choices that repel Lizzie.*

After the bootmaker's, Michel pointed out the smithy's shop where Rowland purchased a well-honed and nicely balanced blade with a comfortable horn handle. Back on the street, they turned a corner near Charing Cross. The well-nourished portion of the crowd wore more colors than Joseph's coat and appeared puffed up with greater importance about their corporeal beings than God intended. The other part of the teeming crowd suffered in layers of filth and poverty, some sinking by degrees, some nearly indistinguishable from filth and tatters left for the bone-and-rag men.

A riot of young hawkers and pamphleteers accosted them. One youth, no more than twelve, in tatters and barefoot, shoved a pamphlet in Michel's hand.

"Hoy, sir. For your edification." The lad's face was ravaged with pimples and infected scratches.

"Here's a penny to leave us alone." Rowland tossed him a coin but refused a pamphlet.

On their way again, Rowland showed Michel the duke's pamphlet. "This is from the provocateur I am to find." He read the title aloud. "'Calling All True Christians to Action.'"

Michel stopped in the street. He took the duke's pamphlet, studied it, then passed it back to Rowland. "The one the lad hawked at Charing Cross is from the same press. You can tell from the broken letter E."

They returned to Charing Cross, seeking the tattered boy.

"Here, lad. I'll take all your sheets." Michel offered a shilling. "Is this fair coin for your troubles?"

"Oh aye, sir. G'bless you."

"Who pays you to stand here and pass pamphlets?"

"To stand here? This is always my corner. Every lad here knows it be mine. It came to me, fair and true blue, when my gran'fa went to heaven."

"But who pays your effort?"

"It's whoever catches me early in the day. It's usually Mr. Knatchgull, at the King's Head. He's got the goods for people who like cursing papists. But we got to be careful. Last week, the king's men gave us a good thumping and stole our goods."

Rowland nudged Michel. "We'd best get an early supper at the King's Head. Let me treat you."

For the first time since they'd met, Michel burned crimson, as if in a passion, excited during the entire walk to the King's Head, muttering, "Providence!" and "Fortuity!" and once, "The gods shine their faces upon us!"

Rowland patiently waited, intending to use the noise of the tavern to cover his inquiry into Michel's exhilaration.

The King's Head, on the west corner of Chancery Lane, must have been built in the time of the Plantagenets, its ground floor now devoted to a greengrocer and a bookshop. They walked up to the first floor. Inside, they had no luck finding any fellow called Mr. Knatchgull or even getting a response to their inquiries.

While waiting for food (and finding they'd attracted everyone's attention by asking about Knatchgull), Rowland noticed details while spinning his angel coin over his knuckles, disliking what they'd walked into. A half-dozen men wore shabby knots of green ribbon on their hats. They stared at Michel and Rowland more than others in the tavern.

The Green Ribbon Club! Rowland felt slow-witted for how long it took him to notice that he'd entered a room with left-overs from the last anti-Jesuit plot. Hard-looking men brave enough to still wear their ribbon-badges. Which likely meant the room was filled with shades of Monmouth supporters. Rowland kept his eyes on his trencher, given that the men here clearly didn't like curious strangers. Michel, however, seemed oblivious to the nature of this crowd. He gulped his ale in a less refined way than he had at luncheon. Perhaps details of the turmoil stirred by the Green Ribbon Club never reached Michel on the Continent. Rowland pitched his voice in conspiratorial tones.

"Why did you lead me into a den of dissenters, Michel? Is this a trap laid for me? I thought you were sent to protect me."

"What? Why, no, my lord, no plot. We are looking for the purveyor of that pamphlet."

"You've been excited about my new assignment. Why?"

"Colonel Kilbuck sent me to do more than assist you and Miss Foxe. Fate has wedded the two."

"I cannot wait one heartbeat more to hear about our Fate."

Michel missed Rowland's sarcasm and so answered solemnly. "There's been a disruption among supporters of William and Mary. Most support rightful succession, but suddenly some are now virulently antipapal. That's not good for Mary's cause."

"That's what Lord Bagsham's task is about."

"These pamphlets," Michel pointed to the stack from the boy at Charing Cross, "were printed by the same press that Mary's supporters have used for years. If we don't find this printing press before the king's militia finds it, William and Mary will be associated with traitorous provocateurs."

"Whatever we do, it must be for the Crown," Rowland said. "I'm not in the business of helping Mary's supporters."

"Colonel Kilbuck says that when Mary becomes queen, William wants her to come to a peaceful England. Finding the press would contribute to that peace."

"And am I to understand that you, who have been in London for what? Five days? You can help me find that printing press? As Bagsham commanded me to do."

"I can." Yet Michel continued to fidget. "After a hiatus, the press can be put back to other useful work."

"No, Michel. I'm not bargaining." After years of being paid (poorly) to spy on and trick other men, Rowland felt the same methods being used on him, while it also nagged at him that both Bagsham and Kilbuck cared about the same business. "We merely find the press, so I can satisfy Bagsham."

"I feel compelled to bargain, sir. Especially since I'm confident that I know where it is."

"Perhaps I'd bargain if you'd share all you know. I feel I'm being led blindfolded into an unknown future."

"I can explain more after we find and remove the press," Michel said. "We'll leave these pamphlets behind and then call the king's men down on the house where we will have found it."

"Lord Bagsham also wants the provocateur." That was all with which Rowland could bargain.

"We can do that, and then claim to have lost the press. Surely we are nimble-witted enough to invent a believable story about how a printing press came to be lost."

"However," Rowland held back complete agreement, "we will revisit what I've agreed to after we find the press and you explain why Colonel Kilbuck seeks the same thing as Lord Bagsham. Right now, there's too much I don't know."

Rowland felt partially persuaded yet reserved his many suspicions about Michel and what he (and Colonel Kilbuck) wanted.

Yet it gnawed at Rowland that he was voicing hesitancy like Perry did whenever Rowland instigated a risky gambol: *Insufficient information. Suspicious actors. Too many unknowns.*

Michel seemed oblivious to Rowland's hesitancies. Rowland changed the direction of his worries. "No use quarrelling now when we haven't yet begun to find the provocateur."

"We needn't wait," Michel said. "We can act now."

The fidgety Michel barely allowed Rowland to swallow his supper. He hurried them to Covent Garden, but wouldn't say more than, "I know what to do next," while smiling like a cat who'd licked up the last of the cream in the buttery.

"Where are we going?" All of Rowland's distrust and suspicion increased when Michel prodded him into action.

"Trust me," Michel said. "You'll like this."

"Trust you? Why? Because you know last week's watch word and Kilbuck's name? And—"

"And I saved your life. Also, I know how to find what you are assigned to seek." Michel walked ahead of him. "Besides, you're a gambling man. So, come on, man. Let's go."

~

The late-afternoon sky had clouded over, the London air now sticky and thick. Repeated gusts swept the overheated streets.

"I haven't ever longed for rain more in this life." Rowland rubbed the back of his neck with his kerchief, fortunate to have not fallen into vanity while dressing that morning. He'd tied his hair back with a ribbon instead of choosing one of the deceased viscount's periwigs, else he'd have perished in the August heat.

Michel led the way to Covent Garden, then down an alleyway. Midway along the huddle of townhouses, Michel pointed to a barrel beside the garden wall. "You are taller than me, your lordship. Stand here."

When Rowland mounted the barrel, it allowed a view into one house's garden, mostly filled with late-summer flowers, plus a mound of kitchen greens.

"I am certain the printing press is here." Michel barely suppressed his excitement. "Whenever I've had a moment since Saturday, I've stalked here, hoping to spy a way to enter. I knocked at the door, but a rather shoddy servant insisted the tenant is never home."

"Why do you believe—"

"I'll reveal all when we find that printing press here."

"You're sure it's here?"

"If it's not, it will have left a trail."

The kitchen door opened, and two women and a young man emerged. They sat on a bench that backed up against the house wall. They drank from mugs, but one could only guess whether they drank ale or buttermilk.

"Michel," Rowland said quietly, "how much grief will we find if you're wrong?"

"I'm not wrong. Therefore, no grief."

"Fine," Rowland said. "Here we go then."

He jumped down from the barrel. The garden gate had only a simple latch, which Rowland sprung.

"Heigh ho!" he called. "A word?"

The young man looked to the older woman, likely the cook, who nudged him toward the gate.

"Good evening." Rowland held out his hand in greeting. "I'm David Caius." He hastily adopted his great-grandfather's name, and then stole Winwood's name to use for Michel. "And this is Michael Oakes."

Michel looked startled, which again raised Rowland's cautions about the fellow. Didn't Colonel Kilbuck teach quick-witted prevarication?

"Sir? How can we help you?" the older woman asked.

"We seek to help you," Rowland said. "You see, the king's men will be here within the hour to raid this house for traitorous activities. As the king's pursuivants, we've watched this house for days. It's been a quarrel among us, but," he pointed to Michel, "Mr. Oakes avers that you are not rebels who should be taken up."

"Odds bodkins!" The lad turned whiter than his linen shirt.

Rowland tapped the lad's chest. "But we can only prevent you being taken up if you depart now."

The lad ran for the house, the two women following. Rowland and Michel stood around the corner, so the servants might flee without the king's pursuivants hounding them.

"Well done, my lord." Michel peeked around the corner. The three servants trotted down the alley, clutching goods they'd tied up in cloths.

"Now, we enter the house," Rowland said.

However, the frightened servants had taken the time to lock the doors. Rowland tried an iron-strapped door that led into the cellar, but it seemed to be locked from the inside.

Next, he inspected the kitchen door.

"Can you open this lock?" Rowland asked, because Michel claimed to know what was inside the house.

"Not my skill, my lord."

Having learned years before not to rely solely on Perry, Rowland kept his own slim tools in an inner pocket, wrapped in a calf-leather pouch. However, he couldn't achieve the click of an unlatching lock that he sought.

"The only open window," Michel said, "is in the garret."

"We can't try the front door until dark."

"That's hours from now," Michel said. "I propose we enter the empty house next door. It has an open window on the second floor." Before Rowland answered, Michel had vaulted the fence next door and was climbing a drain spout. "Then we make our way across the roof."

Rowland followed, though he wasn't dressed for scaling spouts or traversing a slate roof. Neither was Michel. However, from past years' practice, Rowland was capable of undertaking such a venture. Other watchers serving the king, under whatever principles they followed, might perhaps take longer to decide or have been less agile.

Inside the deserted house next door, they climbed the stairs to the garret. From there, they climbed out onto the roof. The fortunate thing about not yet having new shoes? Rowland could climb through windows and scamper across roof tiles.

But then, fat drops of that sweet elixir, summer rain, began to fall, making every handhold and foothold slippery. The suit from the Xanthus House closet, unfortunately, wasn't made to be dragged at the knees across tiles, or to pass unscathed through a narrow garret window.

The rain increased and a wind rose.

After moments of intense caution, they made their way past the racks of laundry drying in the garret, while their own clothes dripped from the sudden rain. As they tiptoed down the stairs, no sound of inhabitants echoed up to them.

"If anyone comes," Rowland began one possible prevarication, "I indignantly claim to have purchased the property. Then I shall show great remorse at being in the wrong house."

"A reasonable tale, my lord."

They moved stealthily through each floor, until they reached the ground floor, where they examined the kitchen. Rowland unlocked that outer door from the inside and left it ajar for quick exit. They searched the remaining rooms at street level. None contained a printing press.

"Look here. This must be the passage to the cellar," Michel called from the grand foyer. "But it's locked."

For this door, Rowland's pick-tools worked quickly. They stared down a set of steps to what had once been a buttery.

Michel hesitated. "One of us should go down while the other remains here."

"We saw the cellar door in the garden." Rowland had spent too many childhood hours hiding in Revelstone House's dark spaces to worry about cellars. "No one carries goods into a cellar from this handsome hallway."

Michel rummaged in the foyer and found a candle and a punk box on a table. The candle revealed a printing press in the cellar shadows. Michel hesitated, offering no resistance when Rowland held him back by the collar.

"First, Mr. Chêne, a complete explanation, please."

"It's a simple story." Michel hovered close by. "My extended family, since before the time of the regicide, has served the royalist cause. When Charles and the Duke of York fled to France, my family operated a courier service that connected royalists in England with those on the Continent. We helped prepare for the restoration of the rightful king."

Rowland said, "Does your family work to benefit our new King James?"

In the candlelight, Michel's eyes could be seen to dart left, then right. "We are joined with those who believe a strong Parliament is best for the king's success. Some people worry that James might plunge the country back into chaos."

"How did you know this press was here?"

"Our leader in England died recently, after using that press for thirty years to print broadsides in support of a loyal Parliament. It's why my father wanted me to take this mission. Because whoever has possession now, they want to foment unrest among people unhappy to have a Catholic king again."

"Hence, for the king's sake, we'll call the militia," Rowland said. "Bagsham wants the person who is using the press. Doesn't Colonel Kilbuck want the same?"

"Not necessarily." Michel's eyes darted, confirming to Rowland that he did not yet know all the truth.

"We'll come back with some roustabouts to help move it. And we'll resolve our disagreement tomorrow," Rowland said. "Let's leave through the kitchen instead of back over the roof."

Michel's eyes darted again. "I must insist on restoring this press to the consortium of couriers which my family leads." He started down the steps.

Rowland followed. "Michel, I insist that we—"

The wind from that storm rushed through the hall. A door far away in the house banged. The candle in Michel's hand guttered and died. The door above their heads slammed shut.

26
Pillar to Post

AT BENSON'S LODGINGS THAT afternoon, Winwood was still out searching for herbs from London apothecaries. After Felicity left for her afternoon's work at the theatre, Tamsin and Camilla set out for the Inns of Court for Camilla's legal appointment.

First, though, they visited the stable that belonged to a cousin of the for-hire carriage driver who shuttled between Cambridge and London twice a week. For the next good luck of the day, they learned the stable had a cart that could be hired.

"We'll need the cart early tomorrow morning," Tamsin said while counting out coins.

On their walk to the Inns of Court, they rehearsed Camilla's plans for meeting the lawyer who was to advance her annulment from Leighton Fairchild. Camilla intended to play a helpless innocent, because, she said, "I need to see what kind of man he is. With Leighton, if I sought to discuss things in a rational way—like you and I do—he'd strive to prove me wrong and ignorant. I want to hear how this man explains the law to me."

"I'm sure you'll play your part as well as Felicity Oakes does on the stage. But I do wish Tom were coming with us."

"Yet I'm prepared to prosecute this business myself." She paused. "But promise me, Tamsin. Do not rescue me like you have been rescuing Tom. I shall sink or rise on my own."

That felt like a blow to Tamsin's heart.

"It's true about Tom. I'm trying to do better. But I know how Leighton trampled your soul." Tamsin touched her gold angel.

"I promise no rescue. I'd grasp thorns before I'd restrain whatever you want to do in the world."

Tamsin and Camilla arrived at the chambers of the lawyer that their neighbor Viscount Heydon had recommended. Outside the door, Camilla clenched Tamsin's wrist. Then she took a breath and they entered.

A clerk greeted them. "I'm Elisha Newton." He bid them wait while he spoke with the barrister. "Please be comfortable on the guests' bench." Just after the local bells rang the five o'clock hour, Mr. Newton led them into the lawyer's cluttered, suffocating chambers, which had only one window, high on the wall, seeming to open only onto another room.

The barrister rose to greet them. Although Mr. Mordaunt might be any age between forty and sixty, his dark brown wig aged him, its color wrong for his chalky skin. He'd dried down to mere sinew, as if forced to fit the confines of his chambers, like forcing a large foot into a small boot.

"Good afternoon, Mr. Mordaunt. I am Camilla Candecote."

"How do you do." The attorney pressed his hands in a prayerful gesture and offered a bow.

"This is Miss Foxe, who is my companion. I live at her house in Cambridgeshire."

"Miss Foxe?" Mordaunt bowed again. "I believe that I met your relations this morning."

"Cousin," Tamsin said. "One of many Foxe cousins."

They traded polite greetings. She glanced down to see if a cloud of powder rose where he continually rubbed his hands.

He's dry as dust.

"Welcome, ladies. Mr. Newton, sherry for my guests, please. You must surely be exhausted, being abroad in London this late in the day. Please be seated, Mrs. Fairchild."

Tamsin tensed at the lawyer's condescending assumption. Yet Camilla's face showed only a curious smile.

"Thank you," Camilla said. "I am not in need of refreshment. And please address me as Miss Candecote, my own name."

Niceties over, Mr. Mordaunt settled into his chair, advising Mr. Newton to take notes. "What can I do to bring the laws of England to your assistance, madam…uh, Miss Candecote?"

She reached her hand to Tamsin, who produced from her satchel the writs Viscount Heydon had coerced from Camilla's father and husband a week earlier. "I have a writ from the man I married in February, declaring our marriage null, vowing that he entered into the connection under false pretenses. And that the marriage was never con…con…"

"Consummated," Tamsin said. Good stars! She'd already performed a rescue. She bit at her lip, forcing herself to silence.

"Yes. That. Mr. Mordaunt, I'm asking your help to present this writ to the court. It is signed by Mr. Fairchild and two witnesses, including our parish rector." Camilla then proceeded as Tom had advised, asking questions for which she knew the answers. "Can you advise which court is appropriate?"

"That is the bishop's consistory court, Miss…Candecote." Mr. Mordaunt continued with an unnecessarily lofty manner, as if Camilla were a child. "You should have no worries as I am most familiar with the customs and methods in that court. Is your husband available to speak in court?"

"No. The issue of his 'false pretenses' is a special case." Camilla spoke in a frail-flower voice. "He subscribed to a syndicate in support of Duke of Monmouth's rebellion."

"Oh dear." Mr. Mordaunt grasped the arms of his chair, licked his lips as if anxious. A decidedly dramatic response.

"Mr. Fairchild has begged the king's forgiveness and departed England." Camilla waved her hand, signifying her disgust with and dismissal of Leighton. "You must see why I wish this annulment to conclude as quickly as possible."

"Yes, I do see." Mr. Mordaunt examined the writ she had handed to him. "It is a delicate matter."

Treason always is, Tamsin thought.

Camilla said, "I hope you can help, sir, given that I have been betrayed as badly as has our king."

Mordaunt took a breath that quavered midway. Then he nodded as if resolute, though Tamsin marked the initial hesitancy against him, as well as his reaction when Camilla first mentioned Monmouth's rebellion. Perhaps Heydon didn't know everything he might when he'd recommended this man.

"We can help you, Miss Candecote. Now I see why you prefer to be addressed by your…uh…own name. And that you want to proceed immediately."

"Yes," Camilla said. "Viscount Heydon vowed that I could trust you with this business. Shall we shake upon the agreement, so that you can begin in a speedy manner?"

"Yes, Miss Candecote." He shook her hand.

Tamsin wished Camilla had hesitated, that they'd taken time to discuss the man and whether Heydon's vow was sufficient for Camilla to trust the barrister.

"There's more," Camilla said, holding onto her second paper. "My father is Isaiah Candecote, a baronet. His wife was lured into the same scheme. Hence, my father has also begged the king's forgiveness, vowed to no longer use his title, and departed England for Barbados."

"Good lord!" Mordaunt said. "You are alone in the world?"

"My friends are quite helpful," Camilla said. "I have this from my father." She handed the second paper to Mordaunt. "He assigned all his land and wealth to me, as the sole heir of his body. I have no cousins, uncles, or such that might plead for their share. Can you free all property and funds for my use?"

He studied the writ. "We shall begin by establishing a trust to manage disbursements while the courts proceed."

"A trust? I'm of age, and nothing is entailed. My father's wealth became mine as soon as the witnesses signed this writ."

Camilla held out her hand for the paper to be returned to her possession, but Mordaunt didn't notice. Instead, he proceeded to explain the law, often turning to Newton the clerk as if lecturing a point. The clerk kept his head down, busy writing notes. Camilla listened patiently, seldom blinking.

Mordaunt said, "Now, do you understand the way ahead, Miss Candecote?"

"I believe I do." She reached over the desk to take back the paper that promised her father's wealth to her. "I was made to understand from Viscount Heydon that you have the most efficient methods and alliances for moving the annulment of my fraudulent marriage through the bishop's court."

"Which requires certain emoluments and other payments," Mr. Mordaunt said.

"Yes. I came prepared to lodge a sum with you." Camilla named the sum Tom had said to expect. "Then you can proceed with the gratuities and bribes required to hasten the courts."

Mordaunt didn't blink at Camilla's choice of words. "My clerk will prepare an agreement that authorizes me to proceed with your annulment. As to your father's estates, our fees together with emoluments are twice the amount you named."

"Never mind." Camilla handed the retrieved paper to Tamsin, who tucked it away in her satchel while feeling a thrill that Camilla had kept her trust in reserve. "I shall find a solicitor who won't ask me to pay a significant fee merely so I might access my own wealth."

"Miss Candecote, truly, I assure you. I recommend only the common course for women who inherit—"

Tamsin coughed. Did Camilla distrust the barrister too?

"Common?" Camilla expressed disdain in that one word. "Mr. Mordaunt, how many such cases do you manage each year, where living fathers give their wealth to their daughters? A dozen? I shall assume from your silence that it's fewer."

"Madam, it is because your case is so uncommon that I recommend proceeding with great caution, employing all possible legal protections." Mordaunt had not yet perceived that his condescending tone would not win Camilla's trust.

"I prefer to seek a resolutely brave solicitor to help free my wealth." Camilla stood. "May I wait while your clerks prepare papers that authorize you to prosecute my annulment? You have heard why I am eager to begin."

Mordaunt sat back in his chair, astonished, rather like he'd had the wind knocked out of him. Tamsin burned with pride for Camilla's resolve.

They returned to the outer room and sat on the bench where they'd first waited for Mr. Mordaunt. Camilla whispered, "I don't like him. But the viscount said this fellow would advance my annulment with the greatest speed."

"You were wonderful. I only wish I had come with Tom—"

"But we didn't need Tom."

"Dear heart, I wished I'd come wearing Tom's suit, carrying that sword stick, and standing behind you with a threatening frown. We weren't five minutes into the interview before I felt that the man needs a thrashing."

"Oh, trust me to say, you appeared quite foreboding in your own clothes." Camilla laughed, holding Tamsin's hand under where their skirts spread on the bench. "It makes me giddy, to think of the look on the man's face when I said Leighton had supported Monmouth's rebellion."

In a quarter of an hour, marked by the ticking pendulum clock in the clerks' workroom, Mr. Mordaunt appeared again. He had his hat in hand, as if prepared to depart.

"My clerk will present papers for your signature in a moment. I am pleased to meet you, Miss Candecote." He wasn't pleased. Tamsin didn't merit even a farewell nod.

"Likewise, Mr. Mordaunt. Thank you for your time."

"My clerk will give you a date for when we shall meet again to advance your business in the consistory court." He bowed and was out of the door before the clerk appeared.

The clerk who offered the paper for Camilla's signature was not Elisha Newton, but rather, Tom Foxe.

27
Two Pounds Sterling

"I PREPARED A RECEIPT for the funds you will deposit," Tom said, as if he always appeared by magic.

"What are you doing here?" Tamsin had seldom been as astonished by one of Tom's hoaxes. Camilla was already handing Tom the deposit the Mr. Mordaunt had named.

"Rollo's lawyer agreed to take me on as an apprentice. I need six months at the Inns of Court if I am to become a barrister, the fate Uncle Absolom intended for me."

Tom held out his open palms to indicate honesty.

"Must you apprentice again, just because your master in Cambridge died?" Camilla asked in her truly innocent way. She'd never guess that Tom was up to something. But Tamsin could smell secrets emanating from her brother.

"It's because I spent all year in bed." Tom grinned when he answered Camilla, not letting Tamsin catch his eye. "Now, why are you two walking around London alone? Was Winwood not available to accompany you?"

"We know how to be safe on the street," Tamsin said.

"Yet I wonder whether it is wise," Tom said.

She frowned, since the day before he'd discounted her fears about Leighton's threat. However, she said, "The wisdom to be questioned is whether you, dear brother, are well enough for your new enterprise."

"Ah, but you forget the efficacy of Dr. Oakes's Astonishing Elixir," Tom said. "That potion will make Winwood as rich as a

Dutch trader. He will offer my history as a testament on his labels and leaflets." He gave Camilla a quill and nudged an inkpot near to her. "This is where you are to sign, Camilla."

Though Tom was resolute about his new work, Tamsin said in a low voice, "Tom, how can you work under that man? Mr. Mordaunt will suck on your life's essence and spit out your soul to seal the bribes he sends to judges."

Tom said, "Rollo was sent by his mentor, the Duke of Bagsham. I can be useful, watching his business. Camilla's, too."

Tamsin was, to say the least, not assured. "You and Rollo are both working with this cadger?"

"I took a clerkship, in order to quickly become a barrister and also to protect Rollo's business." He sprinkled pounce on the paper Camilla had signed. "Mordaunt can nudge Camilla's annulment forward quickly. And, Camilla, you are wise to seek elsewhere to free your estate, since Mr. Mordaunt's way of doing business will cost you…uh, more than need be."

Before Camilla could speak, Tamsin asked, "Did you warn Rollo about your new master?"

"I think he made the same observations that you just did. I'll confer with Rollo when next I see him."

"At his new house? That the Duke of Bagsham gave him?"

"We'll both ask him," Tom said, "when we see him next."

"How shall I find another lawyer?" Camilla asked, guiding the twins back to her own business.

Tom said, "I shall write an introduction to Mr. Luke Holywell, who shares chambers with his father just across the courtyard. He and I read together at Cambridge. Perhaps he will remember meeting you from those years."

"Will your Mr. Holywell also seek to hold my funds hostage?" Camilla asked.

Tom said, "Luke is the most honest man in England." He wrote that introduction, while Tamsin hung close by. "Can you step back, Tamsin, and leave me room to write?"

"You smell of peppermint," she said.

"It covers the taste of Winwood's physick," Tom said. "I've drunk so much it's coming out through my skin. Can't eat for always tasting his elixir inside my mouth."

"I shall order supper at our lodgings for half past eight." Tamsin wanted it to sound like an invitation, not a command. "We'll share a repast while hearing about your new venture."

"I might be late," he said.

"Pray, don't be!" Tamsin said. "Else, I worry for you."

Tom rose quickly from where he'd been writing. He swayed, blinking wildly. Tamsin caught him just as he was about to fall.

She didn't remark on it. He'd hate it if she did. Instead, she said, "If you can't join us for dinner, then you must send for food to be brought here. Oh, don't look at me like that. I'm not trying to bully you, since it never works. But if Winwood isn't around, you often forget to eat."

Rather than answering Tamsin, Tom said, "I've rethought the case. Rather than giving you a letter, let me walk you across the way and personally introduce you to my friend Luke."

Despite appearing at Mr. Holywell's chambers without an appointment, Camilla and Tamsin were welcomed because of Tom's introduction. Mr. Holywell seemed youthful, free of stress. His sole mannerism was to repeatedly push his periwig back into place. He offered a buoyant smile and a warm greeting, remembering both Tamsin and Camilla from his days at Trinity.

"Tom's invitations to Sunday dinner at Revelstone House," he said, "saved my spirits and my belly on a dozen occasions." Then he turned sober. "I am sorry to hear you have lost Doctor Foxe. He was a tremendous spirit and a good man."

They advanced Camilla's business in a friendly and agreeable manner, just as Tom had promised. Camilla was allowed time to explain her business in a leisurely way.

"Come again tomorrow at three o'clock," Mr. Holywell said, when they'd finished that day's business. "We'll have the first tasks ready for your review, and we'll discuss how to best proceed from there."

~

After leaving the Inns of Court behind, Camilla said. "Oh, God keep my giddy cat! I nearly burst into a violent ebullition of laughter when Tom appeared!"

"One wonders what my brother is up to."

"I'm eager to hear his tale. Especially the part he didn't choose to tell us just now."

Tamsin said, "You did well with Mr. Mordaunt, especially in addressing how much coin he seeks to gouge from a frail and helpless woman."

"Except," Camilla smashed Tamsin's shoulder with her fist, "you promised not to rescue me. Then you couldn't help it, saying the word I was loath to speak."

A broken promise. A battle raged deep in Tamsin's core. *I must protect you. I must regard your wish to protect yourself.*

"I'm sorry, Camilla. I beg you to forgive me."

"You are as bad with me as you are with Tom, acting like we're children in need of your care."

"I'm not, Camilla. That's not true." *I must do better.*

"Well, please try not to treat us as infants. And yet, I suppose that I should have rehearsed saying that word. Consummate." Walking close beside Tamsin, Camilla began chanting the word until Tamsin put her hands over her ears.

Laughing, Camilla said, "It's this thick, oppressive air. Let's scurry home. There's a summer storm in those dark clouds."

Tamsin heard her heels beating against the pavement. *I must protect you. I must protect you.*

And heard Camilla's heels tapping a counter rhythm. *Stop protecting people.*

At the lodging house, Camilla ran upstairs. Tamsin, still in the foyer, heard voices and greetings, then encountered Perry, carrying a bag down the stairs.

"Oh, hello," Tamsin said. "I understand that Lord Bagsham lent Rollo a house. Are you removing to join him?"

"No," Perry said, offering nothing more.

"Where's Ned?" Tamsin asked, hoping to extract more information. Perry and Ned had been living in each other's pockets since coming to London.

"Ned has a commission to paint the portrait of a great lord. He's living at the lord's house while painting."

"How unexpected," Tamsin mused. "Rollo's moved out. And Tom's off clerking for the strange Mr. Mordaunt. And Ned's gone away to paint."

"Paint portraits. Exactly what he has wanted." Perry folded his arms. "You too found Mr. Mordaunt to be less than canny? I wonder why Tom let Miss Candecote consult with that man."

"She sought him under Viscount Heydon's advice," Tamsin said. "Mordaunt is only managing her annulment. Camilla took her other business to Tom's friend at Lincoln's Inn."

Without advancing the conversation, Perry said. "I have to go now. They need a doctor at the house where Ned is staying, and I'm escorting Winwood there."

"Will you be here tomorrow, Perry? We need a favor. Winwood's cousin has been cheated out of a legacy. We've learned today that the villain pretends to be more than one personage in England." Tamsin described their morning's discoveries at the King's Head about Felicity's enemy. "Therefore, if I might ask—"

"You want me to prowl the villain's business?"

"Yes," Tamsin said, "that would be excellent."

"I shall attempt your tasks and hope to be in time for a second breakfast. Tell me again about the business at the King's Head. I shall remember the watchword when I go there."

Winwood came down the stairs, also carrying a bag. He said, "Tamsin, please make sure Tom takes his physick tonight and in the morning. And stop him from—"

"Indulging in too much wine? Eating salty meats? I shall endeavor to persuade him."

Per her own resolve, she wasn't to interfere, to let Tom take care of himself. Now, how to watch out for someone's well-being when they don't want it, but they need it?

After Perry and Winwood left, Tamsin went in search of the landlord to ask for a change in their rooms. One of their rented rooms could be given up (to save the fee), and another be made for Felicity's use, while Tamsin would be able to listen to her heart's content to Camilla breathing in her sleep.

Waiting, the two women sat companionably, reading by candlelight, listening to the wished-for rain, which lifted spirits as it cleared the air. They were tucked safely in their lodgings, and no one needed Tamsin to worry about them.

Or so she told herself.

Yet deep inside, all the unknowns churned within, stoking Tamsin's habitual cares, frustrating her inclination to undertake action that might offset worry. She was built to worry; it was born in her nature. What she didn't know plagued more than her curiosity. Tom could be in danger from Leighton's assassins, or from Mordaunt's unknown machinations, or from his health and his own obstinate nature. Ned had gone off alone to a rich man's house, not a situation where his shy reticence would find comfort while waiting for Perry to join him. Rowland had—what? Her unease came from more than not knowing. A sensation tickled at the back of her head, as it had over the past year, that something bad might happen and she wouldn't be prepared to fix things.

"It's nice, isn't it?" Camilla murmured. She rested her head on Tamsin's shoulder, in the way that often felt comforting. "Sitting peacefully together. The day's work done. No cares to plague us."

"I wish Tom would appear for supper."

"I agree," Camilla said. "I'm ravenous with hunger."

That wasn't what Tamsin meant. She wanted to shake Tom's secrets free. But she rose to find the footman and ask for their evening meal, though her stomach carried her worry, leaving her uninterested in food.

None of her stern resolve was working. She wasn't becoming a better friend or sister. She'd never learn.

Yet when rain threatened and Tom did not appear at supper, Tamsin worried about whether Tom might wend his way through London's filthy streets, drenched as a wharf rat. But why should she doubt whether her brother had enough wit to stay out of the rain when the skies clattered and moaned?

— TOM —

WITHIN THE WALLS OF Lincoln's Inn, Tom surveyed the stacks of papers from the archives of Mordaunt and Lutwyche, Barristers. The papers had been organized solely by date.

Which meant no one could find anything without knowing the month when a case had concluded. Each month's pile of papers had no discernible organization, such as the name of the person Mordaunt and Lutwyche had represented.

Yet Tom persevered, happy to undertake the work for Jacob's sake. Every time a barrier appeared, that new organ Tom had discovered, the one that wanted to go to battle, found ways to leap over the barrier, or stand on it and dance.

Late into the evening, Tom had to admit he couldn't succeed by Friday under his current method. He needed days to sort out cases that proved Withersea's corruption. What he had so far:

Writs and records of transfer where chancery courts had rewarded the marquess with ten properties.

Ownership records for three houses in London that came to be owned by the marquess.

He hadn't found what he most wanted: the bonds for Aurora's marriage portion and the guardian bond for Jacob.

And yet: what he'd heard in these chambers proved to be monstrous: Withersea dabbled in treason, sponsoring anti-Catholic pamphlets and lodging funds with Danvers Duncombe.

The marquess intended to attack Rowland at the Committee meeting on Friday but hadn't told Mr. Mordaunt what he intended to do. Tom had to warn Rowland—and ask his help about what to do with these eavesdropped insights.

Mr. Mordaunt had hesitated or fell silent in that meeting. Lord, how Tom wished he'd seen the man's face to know, but he felt he could pull Mr. Mordaunt back to the side of justice. Especially if the barrister's wife had been working on him.

Yet Tom's gambol was doomed if Perry didn't have better luck in Knightsbridge than Tom was having in London. And it was too dark to continue work even with a lamp. He'd read enough and overheard enough to know who to see and what to do the following morning. He tidied up his personal pigeonhole and moved all the quills back into the business's common stores.

When he opened the chamber's front door, a strong wind blew dust over him from the masons' yard and ruffled his modest wig. Thunder rumbled. Lightning lit up the horizon. The air held a miserable stillness that promised a storm. Rain had to come, to relieve the tension and this stifling humidity.

A man stood at the chamber's front door, about to knock. He wore an orange suit, the color that Ned called Lusty-gallant. The wind lifted the white locks of the man's periwig, so that for a heartbeat he resembled a mummer out to haunt on All-hallows' Evening. Tom jerked in surprise, on edge from the pending storm.

"Avast, *mon frère*. Didn't mean to startle you."

It was the voice from earlier that day. Sir Duxwold, who'd come in with that Rosewurme fellow to do business with the marquess. Tom hadn't seen him, only heard his voice, and was surprised to be saying good-evening to a gentleman with a face from a bestiary, dressed in bittersweet colors that overpowered his complexion. Lizzie would have her head in her hands, dismayed to see chaos worn as a costume.

"Mr. Mordaunt is gone for the day." Tom croaked, his voice dust coated and wind bothered.

"You're one of the great man's clerks?" The man leaned forward to examine him. Young Elisha would never stay so late."

"I'm new." Tom wasn't about to introduce himself as a Foxe kit. "I'm Thomas Caius, previously under a barrister in," not Cambridge, "Bristol."

"Ah. Pleased to meet you. I came to leave a package for Mr. Mordaunt."

"Of course. Do you need a receipt?"

"If you can oblige me."

"Of course, sir."

Tom stepped aside to let the man in, then pushed the door closed, which took effort against the wind. While Tom lit a lamp and prepared everything, Duxwold perpetually stood too close, leaving Tom to quell his inclination to step back. Or to thrust out his arm for more room.

"What shall I write on the receipt?" Tom asked, once he had quill, ink, and paper in order.

"Received, two pounds sterling from friends of Leighton Fairchild, for disbursement as arranged. Our friend's name is spelled L-a-y-t-o-n."

Tom wrote it, misspelling the name as directed while clutching the quill so his hand didn't shake, and designating it as received by John Mordaunt, barrister. "Please sign here, sir."

The visitor signed his name: Duxwold Cuthbert, baronet.

It took an eon for the ink to dry. Tom shook off the pounce, letting it fall onto another piece of paper, then folded the receipt in a tidy way for Sir Duxwold. He escorted the baronet out, the wind causing the flame of the lamp to flicker.

Tom returned to extinguish the lamp and put away the quill and ink, disappointed to learn that his life was worth only two pounds sterling. Wait, it was two pounds for Camilla and Tom together. Laughing at his quick decision, he pocketed the packet with its two pounds sterling. After all, it was meant for his sake. He'd carry away the coins to share with Camilla.

He wasn't about to disperse the funds to assassins.

Out on the street, Tom trudged a dozen steps on the cobbles before two notions knocked him awake from the thousand ideas racing about his brain case. First, Perry's warnings about danger caused him to look around for the picaros who'd tried to follow him from Mordaunt's house.

Second, his shoulders and knees warned that he'd exhausted his wretched carcass.

A massive clash of thunder struck, and the rain began. At the corner, he hailed a sedan chair, hoping that resolved both problems. He gave the chair-bearers direction to Benson's lodging house, then sat back, hoping Tamsin had saved dinner for him, and that he might catch a nap while he waited for Perry to return from prowling in Knightsbridge.

Besides wishing for supper, Tom also hoped Winwood and Tamsin never learned about the mammoth tax Tom had levied against the body they'd worked so hard to save and repair.

28
Arcadia House

NED COULDN'T REMEMBER SUCH pleasure flooding his senses as that evening when Perry arrived at Arcadia House, nor having felt as much pain as when Winwood set his broken little finger.

Both visitors arrived wet, John Coachman having brought them through a summer's thunderstorm. However, Gabriel the footman had already kindled a fire because Jacob wouldn't come in out of the rain until a peal of thunder startled him. Ned had been sketching Jacob and Pip as they huddled under a blanket on a wooden settle. Jacob drank a tisane Lizzie had made over the fire, and Pip gobbled the bits of cheese tossed to him.

Winwood came into the room first.

Pip leaped up. Jacob splashed tea everywhere while calling "Pip! Pip!" to stop his dog from worrying at Winwood's ankles.

Then Perry entered.

Ned had become used to his new friend's massive frame, but in this room, with the diminutive marchioness, Jacob on his knees calling his dog, and Lizzie folded up in a chair with her embroidery, Perry appeared as one of the giants who'd walked the earth in ancient times.

Yet Perry moved in a graceful, determined way now familiar to Ned: he scooped the yipping Pip into his arms, holding it loosely while scratching between the dog's ears.

"Settle, my good boy, settle."

Perry hummed while letting the dog sniff and lick his fingers, then sniff and lick his face.

"What a good boy! Whose good boy are you?"

"Mine, sir."

Jacob retreated to the tea-drenched blanket, hesitant to come closer to Perry, yet his hands rose; he wanted his dog back. However, Pip hadn't yet had enough strokes and kind words from Perry. Ned swallowed a whisker of jealousy, also wanting to be greeted by Perry.

"He's Pip, sir." Jacob held out his arms for his dog.

"Pip, is it? You have a wonderful dog." Perry handed the dog over with care. "I should be so lucky as you, my lord."

Of course, Perry also knew how to settle the tousled young man in a damp shirt, the lordling Tom wanted them to protect.

"You've got a good way with your hound, my lord. He likes your gentle, kind hands."

Then Perry looked at Ned and nodded. Smiled. Which settled Ned too, so he laid his sketchbook down, being like Jacob, unable to attend to anything but Perry.

Meanwhile, Winwood listened to Aurora explain what had happened with Jacob, then asked quiet questions. "How well does he like it when his own physician examines him?"

"He can tell you, if you listen closely." Aurora called Jacob over. "This is Dr. Oakes, who is Tom's friend."

"Tom is my friend," Jacob said, ignoring Winwood's offered hand.

"Mine too." Winwood's melodious voice did its soothing best. "Tom was ill this year. He was in bed from February until July."

Jacob looked afraid, holding his dog close. "My Pip, my other Pip, was ill. He died."

"Tom is fine now," Winwood said.

Jacob nodded. "Saw him yesterday."

Lizzie said, "Dr. Oakes made Tom better, so Tom sent him to make sure you are well."

"Are you hurt?" Winwood asked tenderly.

"Yes, sir."

"May I see where you are hurt?"

Jacob had Pip cradled in his arms. "Here." He pointed to the dog's ribs. "And here." Shoulders. "And here." The dog's equivalent of upper thighs.

While the doctor's slow, gentle questioning continued, Perry sat near Ned, which was a greater balm than Lizzie's willow-bark tisane. He took Ned's hand with great gentleness, turned it until he saw Ned wince. Instead of the invectives Ned had expected, along with a scolding for risking his hands in a fight, Perry only whispered, "What fine mettle you have. My true gallant."

It was more praise than Ned deserved for his afternoon's exertions, yet so consoling that his inner being grew warm and comfortable. Except for the throbbing pain in his finger.

Across the room, Winwood coaxed Jacob into opening the ties on his shirt. Jacob pointed to where he hurt.

Collarbone. Sharp shoulder tops. Ribs above his lank belly.

But he didn't let Winwood touch the large dark bruises. However, Winwood's soft words and kind encouragement gradually unbent Jacob's stiff resistance. Winwood arose from where he sat by Jacob.

"Could you all excuse us, to allow Jacob privacy with his doctor? That's what Tom wants when he sees the doctor." Winwood shook his head when Aurora asked to come along. "All Jacob needs is Pip. And Tom's doctor."

~

"Neriah expounded upon your adventures when he fetched the doctor," Perry said as Aurora led them across to the study. "I'd have joined an exaltation of larks to have come earlier."

Aurora said, "I am grateful you've come now, Mr. Frake. Do you live by the same rules as Ned and Lizzie?"

She asked it as if inquiring about the kind of biscuit Perry might prefer. In the study where the marquess had first greeted Ned, Gabriel lit three branches of candles, yet the dark walnut panels and shelves seemed to swallow the light, so that nooks and cabinets and doors cast a maze of shadows.

"Aye, my lady, that I do," Perry said. "Doctor Foxe's rules for enlightened people fortify the mind and soul."

Aurora said, "I've begged my new friends to use personal names. Will you please call me Aurora? May I call you Perry?"

Perry flinched before he nodded. "I shall do whatever any lady asks of me. As Miss Foxe will attest."

"Lizzie. Call me Lizzie."

Perhaps Ned alone saw Perry twitch as he surrendered to the idea of addressing two women by their christened names.

"Do you bring news from Tom?" Aurora asked.

"Afore I came hither," Perry said, "Tom wiggled his way into becoming a clerk in Mr. John Mordaunt's chambers."

Lizzie exclaimed, in whispers, "Upon my soul! He didn't!"

"Yet he did," Perry said. "He's scavenging the lawyer's chambers for inklings of Withersea's business. I expect he'll have matters in hand by…oh, by this very moment. Likely, he's home now and toasting his own success."

"That comforts me," Aurora said. "But perhaps we can still help. This is the room we need to explore. Ned bade us wait for you to lead the effort."

"We must prowl among these baubles and anticks?" Perry said. "It's like to make us all busy as a hen with one chick."

"What are we looking for?" Lizzie asked.

"The details of my brother's inheritance. Any records of the marquess's business dealings." Aurora paused when Winwood's voice drifted from the room across the hall.

"I have an idea of what Tom wants us to find," Perry said, "since he set me to searching Mr. Mordaunt's house."

"My cousin Arabella?" Aurora looked startled.

"Be not distressed!" Perry wagged a finger. "Tom says she's a very good woman. He wants to make sure that her husband's business does not lead her into harm."

"Has Tom set out to protect all of London?" Lizzie asked, then answered her own question. "Yes, of course he has."

"Beware," Perry cautioned, stopping Aurora from opening the marquess's desk. "This drawer has a wee trap to reveal trespassers." He held up a black thread. "Let me find and remove these. I'll replace them when we are done."

Then Perry taught them how to search in an orderly and thorough manner. "Open every book. Lift every box and antiquary's treasure."

"So many books, so many boxes," Lizzie said.

"So many cabinets with filled with treasures," Ned said.

Perry's first discovery: a walnut panel gave way to reveal stacks of pamphlets with blaring titles:

> The Implausible Arguments of the Pope's Priests
> The Tyranny and Impiety of Popery
> Popish Idolatry: A Warning to Good Men
> The Pope's Plot: Fire, Plague, Poverty, Riot

Lizzie said, "The marquess pounded the table at dinner last night, asking us to help spread anti-Catholic rumors across England. Because he wants James to resign the throne."

Aurora said, "It's only a facet of his many doings. I don't know how it might help Tom with his endeavors."

"I'm getting an idea," Perry said, but shook his head when begged to say more.

Ned's next task was to study the journals Perry found, which required only one hand to turn the pages and a candle set closely enough that he could read. The journals were redolent of snuff and of ink more expensive than Ned could ever afford. He intended to fully attend to the task, like he did while painting.

Yet when he painted, Ned was alone or had only the lad Caleb as a silent companion, not working in a clutch of people chatting. Lizzie imitated a guest from last night's dinner, which sent Aurora laughing. Ned composed in his mind the image of two women becoming friends by candlelight. Was that beyond his skills? At Revelstone, he'd spent many hours thinking about composition and color and texture. If he was now to begin true portraits, he'd have to reveal more about what happens between people when they sit together.

Whenever Perry spoke, his deep voice sent Ned's thoughts up into the stars. *For thy delight each May morning...* But instead of singing, Perry was teaching the women how to search properly, or exclaiming over treasures he uncovered, or asking Gabriel if another biscuit might be on offer.

And each time Perry set down a new journal for Ned to examine, he laid his hand on Ned's shoulder, transforming their simple tasks into the profound work of comrades. Ned reached up once to touch Perry's hand when he gripped Ned's shoulder, but he used his bad hand, which sent such twinges of pain to his elbow that he regretted the motion. Almost.

Aurora pulled down books from a shelf over her head, stretching to reach each one. Dust cascaded. She sneezed, then exclaimed, "This is the revised marriage settlement that my father made, which I've never seen." She read silently. "He made provision for a dot. That means..."

"A dot?" Lizzie paused from searching a box of icons. "That means your...husband...can take only the annual interest. There's money that's solely yours."

"I need only to find who holds those funds." Aurora set the paper aside. "John Mordaunt can help with that."

Perry said, "I believe Tom would warn you to be cautious about trusting Mr. Mordaunt."

"I'm not surprised," Aurora said, "that Tom learned about Mr. Mordaunt so quickly."

Ned pointed to the marriage settlement. "We must give that to Tom to study for the sake of his gambol."

Lizzie went very still, then came to stand over Ned. "My dear brother. What gambol?"

"Tom wants papers he can use to advantage for Jacob. Which is why we especially need to find Jacob's guardian bond." While explaining, Ned worried for the first time that his throbbing finger might endanger Tom's gambol.

"What gambol?" Lizzie lifted one brow, which was Rowland's habit. "Oh, of course. Tom asked you to create forgeries."

"Do not chafe yourself, Lizzie. No one ever challenges my work." Ned covered his hurt hand when he saw Aurora had paused to listen. "Tom's plan seeks the most impact with the least danger to any of us."

"Tom has a plan?" Lizzie asked. "What does Rowland say? And we cannot hope to take on a gambol without Tamsin."

"Cease blethering, Miss…Lizzie," Perry interrupted. "Rollo and Tamsin are worn to a nub after last week. We can manage this with only Tom's brain and Ned's wonderful hands."

They were interrupted when Winwood came in. Jacob stood at the threshold as if iron bars kept him out of the study.

"Come in, Jacob," Aurora said. "This is a special night." She glanced at Winwood, a question in her eyes.

"Jacob is well," Winwood said.

"No medicine!" Jacob announced, laughing. "No doses. Dish took the spoon!"

Because Tom has warned both Ned and Perry how to respond, Perry said, "And you are the man in the moon."

"You know Tom!" Jacob said.

"I promise you," Ned said, because it needed repeating, "we are all Tom's friends."

Winwood spoke to Aurora. "Bruises. No broken bones. I should like to see his jerry pot come morning. To know he took no hurt inside."

Aurora exhaled, relieved. "Now, if you'd be so kind, sir, Ned needs your attention."

Jacob sat beside Ned, watching intently as Winwood began the torture of first prodding, then splinting that little finger. Winwood said, "This time next year, you won't even remember this. Over the winter, though, you might feel twinges to remind you."

"To remind you, chucking, not to use your fists," Perry said, the only upbraiding Ned received. A shiver ran up Ned's spine at the odd pleasure of a scolding cloaked in a kind notion.

~

It took forever for Winwood to finish with Ned's finger. When he was packing up his medical kit, Winwood dropped a strip of linen. Pip pounced on it, dragging it under the marquess's desk. Jacob was under the desk after the dog, coaxing with a few bad words that he must have heard from the marquess.

When he emerged, Jacob had the linen strip and a letter in his hand, which he gave to Perry, who unfolded the intricate paperlock.

Ned guessed that he'd seen similar before. "Withersea was stuffing a bag with several letters like that one when I arrived this morning."

A coin dropped out of the letter when Perry undid the last fold. Again, Pip chased the rolling coin under the desk, with Jacob in pursuit. He emerged, holding up the coin. "A prize!"

Ned coaxed Jacob into showing him what proved to be a five-guinea coin, inscribed with King Charles's name.

Perry was reading the letter aloud. "'God grant us good lords, good kings, and peace.'"

Aurora was at his elbow to see it. Perry passed it to her. She said, "It's one of the customary emoluments for members of the Committee for Privileges and Conduct. Where the marquess will ask that the Cloudesley title be put in abeyance."

Perry sat on a corner of the desk, his leg brushing Ned's. "Let's think on it. The Duke of Bagsham let Rollo know that he's to pay emoluments to the Committee."

His eyes lighted on Ned, who nodded.

"It is a delight to my heart," Perry said, "that our thoughts coalesce so quickly."

Ned rummaged for paper, finding a shelf with the same sort as what Jacob had pulled from under the desk. Meanwhile, Perry had been opening boxes, coming to Ned with a wooden box of mostly silver half crowns and shillings, shoved far into a back corner and abandoned years ago. He fished out several silver pound coins, most shaved and nicked.

"What shall I write and how many?" Ned so enjoyed having the same ideas with Perry that he forgot his finger and hummed while he prepared to work.

"Write, 'For men among Hawkins' Heirs and Duncombe's syndic.' Can you do it like the writing in the journals?"

Lizzie said, "What will you do with these?"

"Cannot yet know, can I?" Perry shrugged. "Tom needs to uncover secrets for his gambol. These might be useful."

While writing, Ned kept glancing up at that picture, which faithfully imitated one his father had painted. Dutch money-men weighing coins and writing in ledgers, all serious about their business, and all dressed in old-fashioned starched lace collars. The painting wasn't a forgery precisely, since his father had supervised Ned's attempts at imitation. And his father had indeed studied in Rembrandt's workshop, as he'd signed it. But the actual workshop where this copy had been painted was a mullion-windowed gallery at Revelstone. The truly forged piece was the letter of provenance Ned presented when he sold that copy, the proceeds of which had kept Revelstone and half of Marborne fed through a hard winter.

When the ink had dried on twenty letters, Ned began folding each into a letterlock with a shaved pound coin inside. It took a couple of attempts to copy the pattern of the one Jacob had found, but after four attempts, he'd mastered it.

Jacob, on the floor near Ned, made two attempts to imitate the letterlock pattern. Then he folded several letters faster than Ned managed. Perry had been searching boxes and shelves, but paused, seeing Jacob busy. He caught Ned's eye again.

"Jacob, my friend," Perry said. "Have you a tutor?"

"No, sir."

Aurora had been watching too. "My father set my brothers to teach him." She seemed to read what Perry and Ned meant, watching Jacob. "You think he knows more than he was taught."

"Mayhap," Perry said. To Ned it didn't sound like a guess. "Jacob, here's a velvet sack. Please put the letters in it."

"Wait," Ned said. "I need to write a W across the fold like the one Jacob found."

Jacob waited patiently, then dropped letters into the sack, counting to ten twice until he had finished all of them.

After that, Ned returned to his work studying Withersea's journals, wishing Tamsin was there, since she was brilliant at accounts. And he could ask her about what their Rules allowed.

Throughout their work, Ned kept an eye on that painting hanging among the marquess's treasures. He considered whether it could be restored to him as part of Tom's gambol. Alas, the glorious snuff bottle must be in the marquess's pocket, but another carved ivory piece sat on a shelf. Except for Lizzie, neither Ned nor his Foxe relations indulged in pilfering others' personal possessions. However, Ned began to silently interrogate the Restoration Rules, to determine whether an exception might be allowed for that painting and the carved ivory to fall into hands that respected the true value of precious art.

When Jacob caught Ned staring at the carved ivory piece, he reached up and took it from the shelf, placing it on the desk where Ned could see it.

~

Aurora sighed while reading a letter Perry had found. "This is a collection of witnesses who claim my father asked the marquess to serve as Jacob's guardian."

"Am I to forge an alternate?" Ned asked, dismayed at the letter's many pages.

"No." Perry took the letter from Aurora. He used a candle to set each page afire, laying them to burn on the hearth. "Tom wants you to write a bond for the Earl of Cloudesley's guardianship. If you are done with the journals, you might start this task. Here's the model he sent."

Ned examined the document Perry extracted from his waistcoat pocket. "I can do this."

Perry said, "The complication—"

"There's always a complication," Ned said, "if it's a Foxe kit asking or if it's about the laws of England."

"It distresses me to hear such dispiriting words," Perry said. "The complication is that the bond must be written by the person who needs a guardian."

Aurora shook her head. "Jacob can only write his name."

"And Pip," Jacob said. Though distracted by his own amusements, he'd often proved to be listening, at least to Aurora. And Perry. "I can write Pip's name."

"Do not fuss yourself, my lady," Perry said. "Tom tells me that Jacob wrote a book called *Ajax*. He's sure that the book's publisher will swear it's Jacob who wrote it."

"I shall send a message to the publisher come morning," Aurora said, "to remind him of promises made."

Ned had another notion. "Jacob, you helped with my paints and brushes. Can you sit by me and help write this letter for Tom? It's brutally long, but Tom says—"

"Tom is my friend." Jacob slipped onto the bench beside Ned again. He was, it seemed, righthanded. Being lefthanded, Ned could guide him without making the lad uncomfortable.

"Then you'll do this for Tom?"

"If Tom says so."

The work took a long time, but only because Ned's hand ached so while guiding the pen through each word and letter.

> Know all men by these present that I Arthur Jacob Rôche the lawful child of Charles Arthur Rôche of Cloudesley in the county of Kent…

Jacob lost interest after Ned explained where Kent was, but by that point, Ned could imitate what the script looked like when Jacob had his hand wrapped around Ned's. He read every few words to Jacob, who became absorbed in tossing a wad of foolscap for Pip to retrieve, then tossing it again.

> …my father deceased, and I being under the age of thirty years as specified in my father's testament and therefore incapable of recovering or receiving the rents, issues, and

profits of all those lands and tenements and hereditaments lying and being in Cloudesley aforesaid given and devised unto me in and by the will of my said late father, and of giving a discharge for the same in my name, do hereby elect and make choice of Thomas Caius Foxe of Revelstone House, Cambridgeshire…

"That's Tom's name," Ned said. He pointed to where he'd written the name. "Thomas Caius Foxe."

"That's Tom?"

"It's how his name is written. No, please don't touch it. The ink dries slowly, remember?"

"Can I have Tom's name?"

"*Ja.*"

"*Ja?*" Jacob imitated the word, perplexed.

"That's how my father said yes." Ned took up a scrap he'd used to test his pen. "Do you want to learn to write Tom's name?" He wrapped his aching hand around Jacob's again, to ink the letters. "T. That's easy. Do you agree, Jacob? Next, draw this letter, called O. You drew the circle very well, my lord. Now comes the only hard letter, called M. Like two mountains pushed together."

"Tom." Jacob studied his work. "Why is Tom's name on your big paper?"

"Because you and I are writing the bond that makes Tom your guardian."

"Like a soldier to guard me?"

"A bit. It means Tom is to be the only person who can tell you what to do."

"Not Rory?"

"Oh, Rory too."

After that, Jacob took Pip into his lap and closely watched Ned at work.

…to be my curator or guardian to all intents and purposes in law whatsoever. And that this my election and choice may have its due effect in law, I do hereby nominate and appoint a procurator of the Consistory Court of Canterbury to act for me and in my name to appear before any competent judge and to procure and desire this my proxy and election to be admitted and enacted, and the said Thomas Caius Foxe…

"That's Tom." Jacob held Pip up to see. "Careful! It's wet!"

… to be assigned my curator and guardian to the purposes aforesaid and to all other effects and purposes in law whatsoever, and to do and perform all other acts and things requisite and necessary to be done in the premises.

In witness whereof I have hereunto set my hand and seal the eighth day of August in the year of our Lord one thousand six hundred and eighty-five.

"Jacob, you have to help me again with the last part. Just put your hand on mine."

Sealed and delivered being first Arthur Jacob Rôche,
The Right Honourable the Earl of Cloudesley
Duly stamped in the presence of
Eduard Wijck
Peregrine Frake

Ned said, "That's my name, where I shall sign it. This is where Perry will sign it. And after Perry signs it, he will take it to Tom."

"Now Tom is my soldier?" Jacob asked.

"From this moment on." Aurora swiped at her eyes with the sleeve of her gown pulled over her hand.

"Crying, Rory?" Jacob looked alarmed. "But Tom is my soldier now."

"Never mind. It's just…" She touched Jacob's shoulder, as if to console him, though it looked to be the other way around. "I'm not used to being in a room filled with friends."

"Never be in this room," Jacob said. "Never. We are bad."

"We," Perry said as he signed Jacob's bond, "are more than usually wicked good."

Ned sprinkled pounce to dry the ink, then jiggled the paper to make sure no sand stuck to the ink, and finally spilled the sand onto another piece of paper, all the while thinking that this was true, not a forgery. Jacob did write portions, and he did want Tom to be his guardian. Ned closely examined his first genuine legal document, pretending to look for flaws, hoping no one caught him admiring his own work.

"You've performed a miracle, like a true saint," Perry said, startling Ned from his reverie. "Even the lowliest dissenter must know your hands were touched by angels."

A fire ignited behind Ned's ribs at the compliment. Then Perry took back the model Tom had sent, running his hand down Ned's arm, gently enough that he didn't awaken the broken little finger. But it did send shivers down Ned's spine.

"A true angel," Perry said as he set the model document to burn on the grate. "A guardian angel."

"Tom is my angel," Jacob said. He looked puzzled again. "But angels are in–in–invisible. Can't see them."

"Our new friends have done the work of angels," Aurora said. "They are true friends and helpers who keep—"

"Promises," Jacob said. "Tom promised."

He tossed what appeared to be a small stick for Pip to fetch, but it proved to be a finely carved piece of wood with ivory and gold inlays.

And now, with a puppy's teeth marks.

29
Epiphany

WITHERSEA'S DEGRADATIONS AND THREATS put Cornelius into a brown study.

A pox on the man. May his nose fall off!

After he departed Mr. Mordaunt's chambers Wednesday afternoon, Cornelius began a perambulation across London. First, he'd walked along the Strand, passing the stone lions atop the Water-Gate entry to what was once a Norwich mansion house. He popped in to familiar inns as was his wont, to offer his usual greetings, seeking friends who might lift his spirits. He wandered up Fleet Street toward Ludgate Hill. He still missed the cathedral spire lost in the Great Fire; that sentiment left him wishing the workmen might hurry its replacement.

Then he trudged along Cannon Street to Fenchurch Street, where the bell tower of the new St Dionis Backchurch rose. It was mawkish of him to prefer the old one, from before the Fire. When had he lost his admiration for the new and modern? Perhaps it came from living in his lady-wife's beautiful house.

The sun caught the sign above The Cock tavern, making the rooster's feathers glow crimson. Inside, he didn't find any of his usual fellows but did encounter a pair that Merryboy had hired as knights of the post in the past season. He didn't want to open that connection again, so departed quickly, offering no more greeting than, "A fine summer evening, isn't it?"

Except it wasn't. The sun had disappeared. A London summer's thunderstorm threatened.

Hence, he went to The Bell. He liked the place because of a lass who worked there, the one christened with an old-fashioned Saxon saint's name, Frideswith, but who bade her friends to call her Princess. She joined Cornelius while he dined on a potato-and-leek pie and waited out the thunderstorm. When the tavern owner emerged from the kitchen and called her name, Princess left Cornelius with heart-felt apologies. Distressingly, though, he heard her describe Cornelius to her master as "an old uncle come to say her aunt had died."

Then he passed along the wet lane, inhaling the divine scent of rain-washed cobbles, until he came to The Half Moon off Bishopsgate Street, the tavern holding onto the bottom of what was said to have been Sir Paul Pindar's mansion. But that was before Cornelius's time and so roused no sentimentalities. Inside, he asked for Audrey, always a good friend to laugh with in the wee hours. Alas, he learned that she'd gone away at Lammas, married to that aging tailor she'd long had her eye out to capture.

He'd begun his perambulations while contemplating the humiliations Lord Withersea had dispensed so freely. Instead of being released from those mortifications, Cornelius became too aware that his London world was changing around him. Old friends lost to time or to others' arms. When he'd worked under the Duke of Bagsham, he was used to hearing kind words and being paid fair recompense. In those days, Cornelius could serve a lord and make good money on the side by selling his elixirs. The good seasons of time past, before Lord Withersea became his patron. Now he had to hire hawkers, who shared his income.

He'd often listened to Merryboy's rough warnings, that Cornelius let soft lords and soft beds corrupt his soul. Of all things! Merryboy who chased and beat men to earn his coin. Yet with the Marquess of Withersea, Cornelius came to know he was a cog in the wheels of that lord's corruption.

His ladybird wife used to say, "You are a good soul." But she didn't know all he'd done that sucked at his soul, like pulling one's boots out of muck. He needed a way to cleanse his spirit.

And to avoid the threats that Merryboy had foreseen, and to keep Withersea from dragging him to Hades.

Late into his long tour, he'd wandered far from home. He sluiced his gob like in the old days, drinking Canary sack at a tavern in one of the Tower Hill hamlets. Too tired to wend his way home, he'd asked (under the usual terms) for a night's lodgings. That sweet bird, Magdalina, had inherited the tavern when her husband died in one of the Dutch wars. The years since he'd first known her were beginning to tell, but he felt that only made her a comfortable companion.

Sighing to ease his soul, he fell asleep on a soft breast, escaping all fears about keeping alive on God's green earth.

Day 3, Thursday:
Discoveries

He, laid, and covered well with curled wool
Woven in silk quilts, all night employed his mind
About the task that Pallas had designed.
— The Poet Known as Homer, *The Odyssey*
(George Chapman, translator)

—

No, no, the bell: 'tis time that I were gone:
It was two ere I left him, and now the clock...
— William Shakespeare, *A Comedy of Errors*

30
Polity

❦

− R O L L O −

"AIIEEE!" MICHEL CALLED IN the sudden darkness of the cellar. He clutched Rowland's arm. "We're trapped."

Rowland's first housebreaking without Perry leading the way was not yet a great heroic adventure. He'd located the printing press that Bagsham commanded of him but was now further from freeing Lizzie from the duke's threats.

"Mr. Chêne, didn't your captain teach you to be prepared?"

Rowland relaxed to loosen Michel's grip, though his own hands shook from being startled into the pitch dark. He felt in his waistcoat pocket for what he'd long ago learned to carry: phosphorus paper and a sulfur-coated wood splinter. Making his kit work to light the candle Michel held proved to be an inelegant struggle in the dark. The splinter flared up in Michel's face, a spark stinging his hand. With a yelp, he jerked away and the candle flashed out.

A thud.

After shuffling in the dark, Michel said, "It's lost."

"Fear not, Michel. We'll feel our way to the door that opens out to the garden."

Moving cautiously, Rowland held his hands out in the darkness to feel barriers. Michel kept too close.

"This is like games we played as children." Rowland forced a bright voice. "We used to hide in seriously dangerous places. The cellar below the old mill. The priest hole in my uncle's house. We never think of it now, but those fleeing Jesuits did not have a sweet time of it. It's a blessing there aren't caves on the edge of the fens. My cousins would never have resisted such a lure."

Rowland persisted with this chatter, querying irregularities in the wall and offering creative curses when he stepped too close to that hulking press and bashed his elbow, sending shards of surprised pain up and down his arm. Twice he tripped over bundles of paper pushed close to the cellar wall.

They reached the door to the outside but found no way to open it. The latch couldn't be moved by any method they tried.

"Here. We're back at the stairs. We'll sit until we hear voices. Then we'll shout until heaven hears us."

"And draw steel to defend—"

"No, I'll tell my story. My solicitor sent me round to look at a house he purchased for me." Rowland was good at making up plausible tales. "We found the garden entry unlocked, as my agent said it would be. We shall be confused and humble."

"Your agent?"

"Be assured, Michel, I am very good at being stupid and innocent, and grateful for rescue."

"What if they don't open the door for days and find our deceased selves?"

Rowland laughed, punching Michel's shoulder like fellows do. "Whoever is using this press will appear before we expire. While we wait, tell me your story. You've revealed only that you know one of my former masters."

Michel, who'd mashed up against Rowland's side when they sat on the steps, needed to be distracted. The audacious swordsman had lost his bold confidence. And they were both sitting on a cold stone step in rain-drenched clothes.

"When I left my tutors," Michel said, "I went to work under my father, learning the profession he'd inherited from his father."

"Like the Foxe family?"

"Except we rely on steel, not land. Your Foxe heritage, my lord, is about land stewardship and feeding your villages. We're more like landless knights serving dukes and earls."

"And now you hold a commission in a militia?" Rowland still chafed over Michel criticizing his poor form at arms. "Where did you learn sword play?"

"My father served among the protectors when William of Orange was a child. I trained under my father, who is a much stricter instructor than any you may have known."

"What's that like, having a strict father?" Rowland wanted to keep Michel talking. The young man shivered enough to rattle Rowland's hand, where Rowland had taken to rolling his gold angel coin over his knuckles. "I never knew my father. The uncle who oversaw my education…ah, well, he was more like a negligent shepherd than a strict master."

"My father is a stern guide, whom we honor and obey."

"We say the same about my uncle Absolom. Except for the stern part. He taught us proper conduct, but without the promise of heaven or threat of hell."

"My father doesn't use childish threats either. Just the promise, or withholding, of his blessings." Michel shivered violently. "You might say I'm in thrall to him."

"Um, Michel? Did your father not teach you how to stop shivering in the cold?" He didn't receive an answer and so preached a lesson about loosening muscles instead of tensing to resist the cold. "I learned it from my cousin Ned's father, who dug drains in the fens, when England wasn't generous with coats and blankets for prisoners of war."

After Michel managed to stop shivering, Rowland returned to his distracting questions. "Why didn't your family come home to England at the Restoration?"

"We had…ah…no significant property to return to in England. My great-grandfather's property in England was seized by Parliament. My father and grandfather married women from Amsterdam who owned property. You must understand how possession of property protects one's family."

Michel then fell silent, either exhausted or unenthused by whatever Rowland attempted for conversation. With no way to tell time, Rowland didn't know how long they sat in the dark, waiting with each heartbeat to hear whether anyone entered the house. It wasn't cold enough to be a hazard, but it wasn't warm enough to dry their clothes, like a pair of horses put up wet. No comb. No brush. No blanket. Only darkness.

"You're shivering again, Michel. Try once more, the way I showed you, to find repose."

~

It had to be after midnight. Michel fidgeted. Rowland quelled his annoyance that Michel's fear of the dark was greater than his own. They were, after all, in dire straits.

Rowland focused on the coming possibility of release. He was supposed to have met Perry for a late supper some hours earlier, so Perry would come looking for him, beginning with...alack, no one knew where Rowland had gone.

Into the extremely black darkness.

The cold darkness.

The silent darkness—except for scrabbling below where they sat on the steps, which Rowland didn't like to think about.

As the night wore on, Michel resolved his fidgets by talking, but of nothing more interesting than the politics of kings. "People worry more about Louis in France than they worry about James in England. Because Louis might soon revoke the Edict of Nantes. Every Protestant on the Continent is concerned that Louis will once more persecute Huguenots."

Rowland did his best to engage, since Michel didn't fidget while talking. "Men in England worry that King James yearns to be friends with Louis of France."

"Those of us who serve William of Orange are certain that Louis seeks to destroy the United Provinces and return Europe to living under papal edicts. They'll do whatever it takes to keep their Protestant ways."

"What do you see in England?" He prompted Michel to keep talking. "What do your masters worry about?"

"Most are concerned that King James has retained his militias, even though the Monmouth rebellion is destroyed."

Rowland said, "We have our Loyal Parliament, who will keep James in check." He didn't know that was true; it was what Lord Bagsham had repeated as common knowledge.

"Yet James is placing Catholic officers over his cavalry."

"England's lords," Rowland said, "do not like a king to keep a standing army. Parliament will end his notions."

Rowland had no proof of that. He pondered the future of officers he knew who hoped to advance but were now competing with James's favorites. For a heartbeat, he missed court life, where one learned a great deal while stewing in intrigue.

"James might prorogate Parliament," Michel said. "You must ask Lord Bagsham about this at your next meeting."

"I shall ask the duke," Rowland said, "when we report that we found the press which has worried him. To show how we've served the Crown of England."

Michel settled into silence for a long while. Then he said, "Why do that? Why serve the Crown of England? What have English kings done for us, you and me?"

"You ask all the hard questions, Michel. Why can't I fight with a sword? Why didn't I notice when I was being followed? Why serve the king of England?"

"But why?"

"An inherited predilection, I believe. About serving the king, I mean. My forefathers have no responsibility for the lapses in my awareness on the night you and I first met."

Rowland finally talked Michel to sleep by telling the world's most boring story about gambling with diplomats' attachés in Paris during the long, cold winters he spent there. Michel breathed evenly by the time Rowland finished the story by saying, "They all cheat! Worse than my cousin Ned."

Listening to Michel's shallow breathing, Rowland pondered the change in the young man, from the bold protector after the theatre to the fidgety fellow preaching politics to calm himself in the dark. When Michel's head lolled, Rowland put his arm around the lad so he rested on Rowland's shoulder. Like how Rowland had long imagined that his true love, his Dark Lady, might one day accept his comfort.

As much as Michel's history resembled his own, Rowland hadn't ever had faith in the political machinations of diplomats and spymasters, or the kings they served. Rowland mined for nuggets of golden insights while playing intelligencer for the Crown. The only golden nuggets he possessed came from Absolom's tutelage and too much Shakespeare, which had left him perpetually dubious.

Rowland had ranted years before, when Absolom named the Foxe kits' destinies: *"Why serve a king we cannot trust or hold in awe?"* Until last Friday, the restored Stuart kings had done nothing to help the Foxe family, who'd lost everything in helping Charles escape Roundhead enemies. Yet Absolom had assigned both Lizzie and Rowland to serve the Crown.

"Because," Absolom had said, "in the way our world is constituted under the monarchy, the people of Marborne parish are powerless unless someone holds power for them, someone who also holds goodness."

Rowland now held the title again but had yet to understand how best to use it. He was fated to serve a king. He had to trust that all the values he'd learned from Absolom would make him good enough to serve. At the same time, he judged poorly the moral worth of the English kings while corruption ran rampant in England, since it took two decades for a Stuart king to be moved to restore the Marborne title.

None of those who held power in England—Parliament, the king, his advisors, the Church—had been moved to help people in Marborne parish, who'd lost so much in the wars, through no fault on their part.

Waiting for rescue, Rowland washed through a whirlpool of more philosophy than he usually swam in between Twelfth Night and Michaelmas. Next, he pondered Lizzie's predicament, given that her allegiance to Mary placed her in political danger. Rowland squirmed, wanting desperately to act, to prove that Lizzie was no danger to King James.

The night before, he'd lain in comfort on his new bed, seeking his next action to protect Lizzie and his cousins. This night, he needed to accept his instant failures, especially that he'd surrendered to Lord Bagsham's threats. He'd yielded once and therefore should assume that the duke's black persuasion would continue into the future. He must take back his own future from the duke. To do that, he needed to learn details of the duke's business, plus how the duke knew about Lizzie's commitments.

No. Better that he first join Lizzie and help with her task. He must take up Absolom's duties as a protector. He had to do as Tamsin had done, serve England by protecting his patch of this sceptered isle, using all the tricks he'd learned as an intelligencer.

Then the cellar door opened, casting morning light on the two men huddled on the stairs like furtive lovers.

"God blind me!" His voice cracked in surprise, though he'd waited all night for the door to open.

"*Nom de Dieu!*" A voice shrieked in answer.

"I'm glad someone's come at last!" Rowland prepared to perform the falsehoods he'd rehearsed hours before. "We found ourselves in the wrong house, then we couldn't get out."

31
Treasures

— N E D —

AT ARCADIA HOUSE, THEY worked diligently past the midnight chime of the pendulum clock, when Winwood begged off to nap in the bedchamber set for Ned's use. The others carried on until after one o'clock. Two o'clock. Three.

"I must return to London," Perry said. "Tom needs what we've found. Miss Foxe, do you want to return to London too?"

Lizzie glanced at Aurora. "Not if I can be useful here. Aurora, if you wish it, I will stay."

"Please," Aurora said. "And thank you."

Perry said, "As you will. My brothers are sleeping at the World's End. I'll send them over to resume their watchman work. And to run messages if you need them."

Aurora called for Gabriel to take a message to John Coachman, that Perry required a ride into London. Meanwhile, Lizzie packed a satchel with what Perry was to carry away:

Jacob's new bond, declaring Tom Foxe to be his guardian.

A selection of traitorous pamphlets.

A "revised" version of Aurora's marriage settlement, dated from before her father died, allowing her to withdraw funds at her own discretion now that she'd come of age.

Perry said, "You aren't out of jeopardy yet. Howsomever, Tom hopes he can make Jacob safe with this new bond."

"Take these journals and deeds to Tom," Ned said. "They show a series of schemes to seize people's properties."

"I asked Tom to undertake too much." Aurora blinked twice as an entire history of emotion crossed her face.

"Nay," Perry said. "We just haven't yet found the means to destroy Lord Withersea as you asked. Tom might have found what he needs while we stayed busy digging like badgers."

"We'll keep looking," Lizzie said. "Now that Perry has taught us how to do it."

Jacob said goodbye to Perry briefly, then turned to where he was writing TOM on a scrap of paper with a plumbago pencil.

Outside the door, Aurora's coachman waited to carry Perry away. In the foyer, Ned offered a restrained farewell.

"Perry, please tell Tom that I saw the sketch of Jacob's mother in Touchstone's warehouse. It's by an artist called Lely. Give Touchstone my name, and likely we can buy it back. Or learn who Touchstone might have sold it to."

"I shall do. Tom will declare you a hero."

Ned rubbed his hands on his breeches, wishing he didn't have to part with Perry.

"We say farewell only until Friday," Perry said, as if reading Ned's heart.

"An eternity."

"Thirty-three hours, as I estimate." Perry looked over his shoulder, then bent his head to offer a restrained but now familiar kiss. He sang just a snatch of that song again.

> If these delights thy mind may move,
> Then live with me and be my love.

"Anon," Perry said, then closed the door.

Perry wasn't gone but five moments before Lizzie said, "Upon my soul! My letter was to go in Perry's satchel. But it's here under this map of…what is this a map of?"

Aurora looked over Lizzie's shoulder. "Batavia. The Dutch East India Company has a trading post there. The marquess has been negotiating to put his own permanent agent there."

"Alas alack. My letter to Rollo got lost under the other side of the world. He'll laugh when he hears."

Ned had returned to his tasks in the study, imagining for the first half hour that his lips burned, but he had too much work to take any time to examine the unfamiliar sense of emptiness at Perry's departure.

Lizzie yawned.

Therefore, Ned yawned.

Jacob yawned. Aurora said, "Surrender to sleep at last, my dear heart."

"Not tonight." Jacob shook his head. "Doing Tom's work."

He'd gathered several whatnots from the shelves and was carefully rattling boxes, then opening them to examine the contents. He arranged what he found into a collection on the broad seat by the window.

A peacock feather.

A stuffed red-breasted songbird in a gilded cage.

A fan, with an inky picture of a mountain, a tree, a red deer, a thatched cottage.

Several carved boxes, all painted scarlet red. The first box Jacob opened held three rocks that sparkled with crystals. The second, five coins with holes in their centers.

While Ned continued to review journals, Lizzie studied a papers Perry had found just before he left. Aurora read every letter from a bundle Perry found in a hidden cupboard.

"We've made a shambles of his study. Will this create havoc for you, Aurora?" Lizzie asked in the wee hours. "When the marquess comes home, I mean?"

"He won't return until Friday. I won't be here."

"Where will you go?" Lizzie asked.

"Going?" Jacob looked up, though he'd been absorbed in opening and closing boxes. "Stay here, Rory."

"You and I, dear heart, are going together," Aurora said.

"Where?" Lizzie mouthed, out of Jacob's sight.

"I don't know," Aurora said. "Somewhere warm. Rome?"

Lizzie and Aurora quietly named every person they knew in Amsterdam who might offer refuge along the journey to Rome.

Lizzie made the notion of a removal by way of Amsterdam sound easy. However, Ned remembered the extreme labor required last winter to remove Lizzie from the Low Countries.

When Tom had presented his scheme the previous morning, he didn't have a final act for his gambol and hadn't mentioned "Jacob leaves England" as part of his scheme. Did Tom have a plan for whisking the young earl and his sister out of England?

If so, such a plan must be put into action before Friday. Before the Committee meeting.

Before Ned saw Perry again.

Ned shifted to examine a new journal. The entire night's work left him seeing the marquess as too formidable, too great of an enemy to defeat with a few scraps of forged papers. Though Ned's work was always perfect.

And Perry had admired that skill the first day they met.

~

The search of Arcadia House had slowed. For a bit of time, Ned gave up on the infernal stinking journals and prowled the pirate's treasure that filled the marquess's shelves.

A dozen pieces of intricately carved ivory, nearly as beautiful as the snuff bottle Ned coveted. One, a fisherman in a cone-shaped hat. Another etched with intricate graphical braids. A third was a fantastical bird carved in jade.

Painted fans, most with garden scenes. Flowers and trees. Some with women (he guessed they were women) in flowing robes unlike anything a queen of England ever wore.

A telescope, the lenses wrapped in polished wood of a kind Ned had never seen. He reached for the telescope, but Jacob said, "Don't touch. Flaming twit."

Ned, two nights without sleep, nearly argued that he wasn't a twit. He'd spared enough wit, though, to hear that Jacob merely repeated an insult the marquess had chucked at him. So, Ned returned to his sad journals. Yet it wasn't just Ned who'd slowed his efforts. The others all suffered from no sleep, though Gabriel had brought them a modest supper of cheese, bread, and watered wine.

Jacob sat on the carpet playing with a smooth lacquered box from one of the highest shelves. He tapped Pip on the nose with the box. Pip, who'd been sleeping, woke with a yip. Jacob tapped the terrier softly again, while saying, "Never touch. You damn freak. You sick wretch. Never touch."

Aurora, alarmed, sat beside him, her voice low and sweet. "Jacob? Are you well?"

"Doctor says yes."

Jacob pushed and pulled at lozenges along the edge of the polished box. When he pressed one projection, another slip of wood protruded on the other side. Then the box sprung open. A roll of paper escaped the opened box and unfolded itself on the carpet where Jacob sat. Pip scrambled for it.

"Oh-oh. Pip, you are bad."

"Don't put it back, Jacob," Aurora said. "Please let me have it." She read it, then handed it to an impatient Lizzie, whose hands shook so badly it was a wonder she could read it aloud.

I first learned of that empty seat from Viscount Heydon. Now I've heard that bastard Heydon wants it for himself. He's talked with the king about it. With two of us begging him, the king will demand an even larger garnishment. Not to be caught backfooted, I have a scheme to free funds by way of my agent's hirelings (the same rogues we used for Lord K—). But I confess, I'd be happy to send that blasted viscount on a crimping voyage to Batavia. Too fantastical, you'd say.

"Crimping voyage?" Lizzie puzzled. "What's that?"

"It's when a man is kidnapped and sold as a sailor on a ship." Ned had heard fantastical stories of such doings when he and Perry toured London taverns on Tuesday. "It's a bad thing to wish on Viscount Heydon. He's been good to us. Read more."

I'd send Bagsham too, but he's too old and too slow to bother speeding his way to the devil. However, I want that earldom in Cambridgeshire. Desire beats hard in my heart because of the way in which Samuel Foxe cut me at the king's feast. It burns like gall in my belly. Possession of Marborne will be my revenge, even if the blackguard is dead in his grave these twenty-five years.

"Upon my soul!" Lizzie said. "What an absolute rapscallion."

"It's blotted at the end," Ned said. "He must have cast a second version. It's a wonder he saved this."

"I'm proud of Tom, that he is acting for Jacob," Lizzie said.

Ned said, "And that he already thought Marborne might be in danger."

"Good work finding this, Jacob." Aurora combed her hand through Jacob's hair. Tears streamed down her face, but Jacob didn't see, being busy pushing pieces of the puzzle box.

"Jacob," Lizzie said. "Would you please see if there is more cheese in the kitchen? I'm famished."

He went, Pip trailing behind.

"Aurora." Lizzie rushed over, knelt, and stroked her hand, the way Aurora stroked Jacob's hand. "He must have had Jacob's guardian killed."

Ned wasn't stupid, so he put it to exhaustion, that he'd paid too much attention to the scheming around Marborne. But clearly, the letter confessed to the murder of Jacob's guardian.

Aurora had just wiped at her tears when Jacob returned, saying, "Cheese is gone."

"Jacob," Ned called, hoping the young man wouldn't notice Aurora's tears. "Come sit here and tell me what you think of these sketches."

Jacob sat on the floor by Ned, petting Pip and leafing through Ned's sketchbook, crying out when he recognized people. "Tom's doctor! Tom is in bed! Miss Foxe!" He turned a page. "Pip! Look, it's you, Pip. In a picture."

Lizzie spoke softly. "I'm trying to stop myself from running to Rowland with this, so he can help solve all this for us."

"I want to take it to Tom," Aurora said.

Ned wasn't sure of the urgency for bringing it to Tom, since he didn't see how Tom could do more than he'd planned. And the king had already recognized Rowland as the earl. Still, he said, "Lizzie and I should go to London together."

Aurora stood. "I feel that I must carry this to Tom."

"How will it help Tom?" Lizzie asked.

"Can't you see?" Aurora smiled, but it was cold, given the warm friendship the two were building together. "I must make Tom aware of the marquess's evils. And I can visit my...Jacob's publisher with a reminder that Jacob wrote my...the *Ajax* book. I'll also visit Mr. Mordaunt, to inquire about how I can take funds from my marriage settlement. I'll need funds to travel. And..." She stood and was gripping the back of her chair so tightly that her knuckles gleamed white. "And I must urge Tom to do more. I need him to utterly destroy the marquess."

"Understandable," Lizzie said, as if they might be discussing a book. "My heart goes with you, but you cannot go alone."

Ned said, "And you cannot take Jacob with you, my lady. He's safe with us, and he likes me. He likes Lizzie."

Aurora said, "John Coachman can take me when he returns. Though he's been up all night."

"Then," Lizzie said, "you can also carry my letter for Rollo, the one that didn't make it into Perry's satchel. In fact, I want to write another letter."

"I am at your service." Aurora spoke as if numb. She turned to Jacob. "Now, dear heart, 'surrender to sleep at last.'"

This time, Ned heard that she was quoting a poem.

"No," Jacob said. "Must help Ned. And don't scold."

Aurora didn't scold. She muttered, what must have been a line of poetry. "'So, surrender to sleep at last. What a misery, keeping watch through the night, wide awake.'"

When Aurora went to dress to go to London, Ned waved Lizzie to his side. "Marborne isn't out of jeopardy. There may be other papers. Perhaps the marquess collected names to help him, like he did in hopes of seizing Jacob's guardianship."

"Yes, it nags at me," Lizzie said. "I hope Tom discovers what the man intends for Marborne." She left then, to write her letter.

Ned let the idea nag him. Ignoring the pain in his hand, Ned wrote another letter on aged paper, dusted it, and let the ink dry, then rolled up his artful replacement to place it in the puzzle box. However, he needed Jacob's help to open and close the box again.

"Oh-oh," Jacob said. "Your fingers are black."

Ned wiped at the ink stains with a wet paint rag, finding that good quality ink doesn't wash away easily. Then he saw dots of ink on the sleeve of his new linen shirt. Naturally. When he wore his coat, no one would know. Not even Lizzie, who'd chosen Ned's shirt and suit.

— LIZZIE —

SHE KNOCKED ON AURORA'S door, which was open, knowing she wouldn't undertake to intrude if she'd had sufficient sleep.

"We've only begun to be friends, but I'm about to be brazenly impertinent." Lizzie rubbed her hands, more nervous than when she'd let a viscount announce that they were to be married, which was a mistake she still regretted.

"Go ahead," Aurora said. "Though I am beyond fatigue."

"Yes." Lizzie seized the chance to change the subject. "Isn't it best if you nap while waiting for John Coachman to return? We are all exhausted."

"Perhaps. But what did you want to say?"

Embarrassment rose as a heat on her neck before Lizzie found the first words. "Ned believes Tom loves you. He's worried that Tom might be pining for you."

"Tom pining for love?" Aurora looked thoughtful. And exhausted. "He never said a word of such feelings."

"He wouldn't, would he?" Lizzie sensed that she needed to do better by Tom, having let Ned guide her into this foolishness. "Ned wants me to ask whether you return Tom's affection. I sense that Ned believes he is working here for the benefit of Tom's heart, as much as to help Jacob."

Aurora shook her head, denying the notion. "I've seen Ned's sketchbook. He has romantical notions."

Though Lizzie knew that to be true, she felt a duty to ask one last time. "Then Tom wasn't in love with you at Trinity?"

"Gracious, he was a good friend to Jacob and me. Not a..." Aurora rubbed her hands, a mirror of Lizzie's earlier unease. "We were children then. For a time, I misunderstood my gratitude for his friendship as an affair of the heart. That is, my heart, not his. Surely you too got caught up in imaginings at fourteen? Fifteen?"

Only for one forbidden young man. Rowland. Lizzie nodded as a confession.

"I knew it was never possible," Aurora said. "Tom never showed interest then. Now the world is too chaotic, and I'm too careworn to indulge in poetic devices such as love or affairs of the heart. My heart is bound up in anger with the marquess."

Lizzie said, "I shall redirect Ned's romantic notions." She was out the door, but leaned her head in to say, "After you pass through the chaos, I shall recommend Tom Foxe to be as good a man as any on this earth."

As Lizzie set up paper, quills, and ink on the table in her bedchamber, she considered the confusion of mistaken affairs of the heart in a world that make such impossible. Rowland had persisted, gently, past her beliefs that it was impossible for them to indulge notions of love. Perhaps there was a chance that Aurora and Tom might know each other's true hearts on a future day.

Lizzie had written the night before that Rowland knew her true self. But did he? In her secret and less confident heart, she feared that no one in the world truly knew her. Not Mary. Not her brother Ned. Yet at least Rollo *wanted* to know her, to understand her, which was a blessing, since she'd come home from Amsterdam with too much advice from too many people.

"Marry a man who won't create problems," Mary had said. "The better the title, the less likely he is to interfere with you." Perhaps that was Mary's experience, marrying William. Aurora wouldn't agree.

Colonel Kilbuck had advised her: "Find an old man, so you won't linger long in the married state. We can use you again when Mary lets you return to court."

Lizzie scribbled a note for Aurora to carry away. During the search, she'd meditated on lines she wanted Rollo to read.

...I cannot live with visions of harm done to you...

...I wish that Tuesday last we'd never parted...

...Pains of love be sweeter far...

But she didn't have sufficient time to send him her heart. Instead, she wrote only:

Your lordship, you may chide me for again making you my message boy. But please forward this lace pattern to our mutual friend.

Then she scratched "lace" code quickly enough to avoid the possibility of any emotions overtaking her.

Aurora called Lizzie's name. Hence, Lizzie folded and sealed the letter before it had thoroughly dried.

32

Commerce

― C O R N E L I U S ―

IN THE HEART OF the Tower Hamlets, Cornelius woke early Thursday morning with a sore head and the profound knowledge that today was the best time to leave off all affairs with Withersea. With that in mind, he crossed town to meet Merryboy at the King's Head, as they'd arranged.

He needed to proceed with care, not revealing that he considered Merryboy his understrapper. Rather, he was about to offer his old friend a step up in the world.

A world Cornelius wanted nothing more to do with.

Spying Merryboy at their usual place in the tavern, Cornelius retrieved a purse from inside his waistcoat and heaved it onto the table, as if it weighed more than it did.

"Here's the rest of the coin for your hirelings' last work."

Merryboy lifted it, feeling its weight. "My thanks to you, Neely. A bit heavier than I'd expected."

That was because Cornelius had included his share of the filthy pay.

"I'm leaving my business, Merry. You'll have to meet with my patron's paymaster to learn what's to be done this Friday."

"Turning me adrift, Neely?" Merry spoke that name with a hitch, an unhappy note in his voice.

"S'welp me, it's not about you and me, Merry. We've rubbed along these many years without that." Cornelius cleared his throat. "By my troth, I am leaving England, which is why I'm giving you my business. Think of it as a legacy."

"Your lady left you too thick in the pocket to waste it with us," Merry said flatly.

"Not so thick as that," Cornelius said. "I have a chance to see the world. Like as not, I'll crawl back skint in a few years, begging you for a bit of work as a peterman."

"Do you know aught about the business on Friday? Is it to be more for the same gudgeons we been pursuing?"

"Aye. The meeting place is in Westminster." Cornelius detailed what he knew of the plan, grateful to be free of it.

"You're giving me all your fancy business, Neely? From here to the end?"

"Just so. I trust no other soul in England as I do you." In truth, with his wife gone, Cornelius trusted no one.

"But you've kept your gob shut these many years about who your patron might be. How am I to find him, to tell him I'm now his man of arms?"

Cornelius said, "Ask for Sir Duxwold in Covent Garden. Tell him I'm pursuing new business interests on the Continent. He'll be your paymaster."

He was keeping his gob shut now, since he'd learned that Merryboy did quite nasty work for Withersea.

"You taking up with frenchies?"

"King Louis be damned. I'm sailing for the Low Countries. No Catholics there."

At the front door of the King's Head, a lad stood, craning his scrawny neck. Foolish boy. Drew the attention of half those in the room, who'd likely grouse to a constable for a penny. Cornelius motioned for the boy to come to him.

"Are you Mr. Knatchgull? Billy Sly said I was to find him."

"Need your breakfast, lad?"

"Not here, sir. Billy sent me to say two of the lads were taken up yesterday on account of the popish papers. They was the king's militiamen, calling the papers sedition. We'uns are scarpering off for a bit. Mayhap for Southwark."

With that, the boy was gone.

Merryboy aped a show of sympathy. "Were your politicking papers ever a good and profitable business, Neely? I wager you aren't giving me that pitch. It's not the sort of thing I do well."

"Let's take it as a sign." Cornelius lifted a finger to signal the lad who drew ale in the morning, to settle his chit.

This must be the last time in the King's Head for him. Odspitikins! What about his elixir business in London? Merryboy was not capable of that. He'd have to find a competitor and offer to sell out, beg that his young hawkers be taken care of. It felt like a devilish plan to sell his dear lads to English slave-masters.

Before shaking hands, they spit on their palms. Merryboy didn't let go, crushing Cornelius's hand in his big paw. "Now, Neely, don't you be selling all this job to another body too. I know you like to double up your sales. If you do that to me, I'll find you. I always do."

"Merry! Of course, it's only you. It was always you had my back when the watchmen got after us as lads in Oxford."

"Good man!" Merryboy grinned, an evil smirk Cornelius didn't like to see. "Course, you know it'd be as easy to do away with any man that crossed me. Even easier than doing old man Rôche and his son. Or that doddering lord we took at Easter."

At that, with Merryboy's invisible blade shivved in his heart, Cornelius said adieu. Walking away, he determined that it wasn't safe to wait until the courts granted his right to his wife's estate. He'd find an agent to see that business through. That would not be Mr. Mordaunt, who had not stood up for Cornelius in the meeting with Withersea. Hadn't stood up for his own self either, had Mordaunt.

No. He'd heard Withersea's threat, to do away with any man who betrayed his trust. Cornelius must leave now. He could use messengers to find an agent. He assayed forth to gather from his house that which was most precious to him. Then he'd return to the haven he'd enjoy with Magdalina at her tavern near Tower Hill. He'd best shelter there, far from his usual haunts, until he got passage on a ship departing London for the Continent.

33
Chalgrove House

– T A M S I N –

THE BED BEING MUCH too warm, Tamsin rose Thursday morning when the Dutch clock below stairs struck six o'clock.

As she was part way through dressing, a stray sunbeam fell on the bed, lighting Camilla's flushed face. Dull eyes watched Tamsin dress. Biting back the impulse to insist that Camilla stay in bed, Tamsin said, "Good morning, dear heart."

"Winwood warned me, didn't he?" Camilla said. "My wound from last week aches again, like the devil kicked me."

"Will you stay in bed now?"

"Yes. I possess at least a bit of the wit my mother left me."

Having given up on the adventure, Camilla watched listlessly while Tamsin pulled on breeches under her skirts.

"It's just in case," Tamsin said before Camilla could object.

"In case of what?"

"In case I need to move freely."

Felicity came in then, bright with excitement. "Bonjour! Today is the day we seize justice!"

Camilla winced. Felicity flew to her side and coaxed out the story of illness and fever while stroking Camilla's hand and expostulating her dismay. "How dark our day of victory will be without your company, my dearest Mademoiselle Camilla."

Tamsin stepped out to take care of business: order breakfast; request willow-bark tea for Camilla; ask the footman to take a message to Luke Holywell in Lincoln's Inn to put off that day's meeting. Amid that flurry of tasks, she learned Tom and Perry

279

had departed early, leaving no message. Winwood had not returned to the lodging house. Rowland had sent no word about what he was up to.

Which meant Camilla would be left alone, without either Tom or Winwood as company. An uncommon resentment bubbled up within, that everyone had abandoned them. She shook it off and asked the upstairs maid to help with Camilla's care: a tisane every two hours, hot water for washing, a light luncheon. A gratuity passed in advance of service.

"Will we ever start out?" Felicity hadn't finished breakfast.

"We should wait for Winwood." Tamsin felt uneasy, though this undertaking didn't pose as much danger as her own highway restorations. But the affair lost its luster without Camilla. Whom Felicity fawned over, posing like an actor on stage.

"If Winwood has been out all night performing his physician's duties," Camilla said, "he won't be ready to join you."

When the Dutch clock struck nine times, Tamsin finally said farewell to Camilla and went off with Felicity to meet the helpers Felicity had recruited from among her theatre friends. Those four men were brothers, all huge, who laughingly asked that each be addressed as Mr. Buckworth, which promised confusion. Felicity and Tamsin rode to the house in the hired donkey cart, with one Buckworth brother driving. As they rode, Tamsin asked more about Felicity's aunt.

"She held a title in her own right?"

"Eventually. She and her husband, Sir Stephen, helped the Prince of Wales escape to France. Uncle Stephen was killed in battle not long after. As a widow, Aunt Letitia was ignored by those seizing power."

"A lucky stroke," Tamsin said.

Felicity tapped the cart driver's shoulder. "Mr. Buckworth, please turn right at this corner."

"How did your aunt manage in the interregnum with no husband?" Tamsin prompted for more story.

"She hid Charles's agents in London."

"Good lord! Such a risk. Did her family approve?"

"Most had fled for the Low Countries or France like my family, or to Switzerland like Winwood's."

"But Charles returned to England more than twenty-five years ago."

Felicity said, "At the Restoration, the king granted my aunt a generous pension and made her a baroness in her own right, though she never made me say 'my lady' or bow to her."

"Heroic!" Tamsin said. "I understand why you feel you cannot wait for English law to serve justice."

"*Oui*," Felicity said. "It'll take years and a small fortune in gratuities and emoluments for the courts to proceed."

"Your aunt's house seems large. How much can we recover today? Must we return a second time?"

"We'll carry away all that matters to me this morning."

The bells in the neighborhood churches rang ten o'clock just before they drove the cart into the alley behind the house.

"This is where I go to work?" one of the brawny roustabout brothers asked.

Tamsin whispered, "Felicity, you said you were inviting an actor friend to help." She didn't lower her voice enough.

"Ah, yes. It is I who shall help." The brother bowed, whichever one it was. "I've shared the stage with Thomas Betterton and John Verbruggen in my time. I played Celia beside Nell Gwynn as Rosalind."

"You must have been a tall Celia," Tamsin said.

"It was in my younger days," he said.

"Go to work, Mr. Buckworth," Felicity said. "We need to be at rehearsal when the bells strike one."

"I've got my copper crucifixes." Buckworth held up a basket. "Always happy to scare Puritans."

He stomped off to the gate Felicity indicated and disappeared inside the garden. They waited, expecting to see the servants flee once they learned Catholics were coming to burn Protestants in Covent Garden.

But the fellow popped out the gate in only a moment.

"Your aunt's house is empty. No answer at the door. No sign of servants. No smoke from the chimneys. I flipped the latch and the door swung open. Your stage is ready for your play."

Felicity's restoration commenced, her excitement soaring each moment, while Tamsin's enthusiasm sank to the horizon. Tamsin had come because Camilla wanted an adventure and because Tamsin wanted something worthwhile to do while waiting to go home to Revelstone. But Camilla was alone at the boarding house, while Tamsin felt a growing sense that she hadn't confirmed how truly worthwhile this effort might be.

The crew entered a kitchen much like the one at their lodging house, though with nicer tiles.

Felicity thrummed like a hummingbird.

Tamsin tucked her skirts under her coat and into the back of her breeches, preparing to go to work. "How do we begin?" They hadn't planned this step. Perry would cry for shame at the lapse. "Where did your aunt keep her most precious possessions?"

"Come in here," Felicity said. "Gentlemen, please follow."

They entered a long oak-paneled hallway. Tamsin halted by a magnificent painting. "Is this your aunt?"

"Yes, one of the few times she dressed as a baroness. She claimed no one is situated so well in this world as a woman with a title and no husband." Felicity continued to talk as she fiddled with a door in the hallway. "She lived a charmed and exciting life. I regret that I failed her, letting that hideous bigamist inveigle his way into her house."

"You cannot blame yourself," Tamsin said, as one does, when someone beats a drum of regret.

Just then the English clock on the wall chimed, its tones as silvery as its domed-shaped bell.

"Someone was here today." Tamsin's trepidation increased. "The clock's been wound. See, its weight is raised."

Felicity didn't answer, busy tugging at a door latch. "Locked," she muttered. She felt under one of the marquetry tables in the hall, its polished top an ornate pattern of veneer flowers. She produced a key, then found a candle and lit it from a punk box. When Felicity turned the key, the door opened, revealing an unlit cellar.

"God blind me!" a voice called from below.

"*Nom de Dieu!*" Felicity cried, more in anger than alarm. "*Qu'est-ce que tu fais à Hadès ici?*"

"God's bodkins!" Tamsin breathed the words.

"Someone's come at last!" An unfamiliar voice called from the darkness. "We've found ourselves in the wrong house and couldn't get out."

The first voice called again from the cellar. "Here are angels sent to deliver us."

"Rollo!" Tamsin drew Felicity back from the door. "What are you doing here?"

Rowland cuddled his arm around a slender man whose features remained hidden in the shadows. "We're waiting for you to open the door, Tamsin. Who are your friends?"

"What are you doing here?" Tamsin repeated, though she had many more questions. Relief and confusion flooded her senses for a moment. She motioned Felicity to keep quiet, which wasn't likely to succeed.

— ROLLO —

"BY A SERIES OF unfortunate actions, the cellar door closed and trapped us here." Rowland said, breathing fast to catch up with both astonishment and relief. He instantly discarded the fiction that he and Michel had agreed upon to explain their presence. "We came here as a duty to the English Crown."

"But you no longer work for the Crown." Tamsin tilted her head as if curious, seeming to have conquered the sense of surprise that Rowland still couldn't sort logically.

"Lord Bagsham sent me to find this printing press." Rowland pointed into the dark cellar. "To stop anti-Catholic pamphlets spreading in London. Why are you here?"

"This is my house. My property," Tamsin's companion said, a young woman who stood with her hands on her hips. "It was stolen from me. If the Crown has a problem, it is with that thief."

"Who are you?" Rowland demanded.

"Me? I am the person who owns this house. Who are you?"

Tamsin said, "Rollo, this is Felicity Oakes, Winwood's cousin. We came to retrieve her stolen goods. This is my cousin, Rowland Foxe." Then she added, "The Earl of Marborne."

"*La foudre de Dieu!*" Michel emerged from the cellar. "Miss Felicity Chêne, our father ordered you to come home. He asked *me* to solve this problem."

"It's mine to rescue from our enemies, Michel." Felicity pronounced his name in an exaggerated French accent. *Mee-shell.* "Father no longer commands me. I have managed this far without your help. In fact, it looks like you need to be rescued."

"You two are related?" Rowland asked in surprise, though it was obvious when they stood beside each other. Not twins, like Tamsin and Tom, but obviously brother and sister.

"Yes," Michel said.

"No," the Felicity creature said. "Not if Michel is about to steal my property."

"No matter who you are, Miss Felicity." Rowland kept the professional calm he'd learned a decade earlier, but he intended a less than professional interrogation when he had Michel alone again. "That printing press in the cellar produces pamphlets the King of England considers treasonous."

"*Ça me fait chier!*" She stamped. "*Ce branleur!* Rosewurme!"

"I too am annoyed." Rowland felt the same expression of his face that Tamsin had on hers. "As an agent of the Crown, I am seizing this press and shall deliver it to the king's militia."

"No," Felicity said. "This press belongs to me. My aunt never used it for treason."

"True," Michel said. "But we need to move the press to some other shelter."

"*Mes amis!* Buckworths! Take it away now." At Felicity's command, four roustabouts brushed past Rowland, descended into the cellar, and began banging at the printing press.

"Good stars!" Tamsin grabbed Felicity's arm. "You dragged me into a dangerous scheme, saying you needed justice."

"I do deserve justice. And I'm no traitor. That's Rosewurme!" Felicity wrenched her arm away. She whirled on her brother. "And you, Michel, if you help that man, you are a traitor to everything our aunt fought for." She pointed her finger at Rowland like a weapon.

"You flaming dulpickles!" Rowland dropped his voice. "Just stop for a moment. I need a drink of water and the jakes."

Michel said, "Aye, the first thing."

After they found what they needed in the garden, Rowland discovered a stone water cistern in a corner of the kitchen. He slaked his thirst and rubbed his eyes to conquer the remaining sense that this muddled scene rose from a sleepless night's scrambled imaginings.

Michel, returning from the jakes at the back of the garden, joined him at the kitchen cistern.

"Michel, you know what I risk. You said Colonel Kilbuck was involved in this."

"Upon my honor," Michel said, his face empty of guile, "I intended to tell you about my family's concerns."

"Indeed? What matters to me is my family. And the villages we are responsible for." Rowland tried not to sound like he was begging to be understood. "It is only for my family's sake that I am doing the duke's bidding. I must seize that printing press."

"I also work only for my family's honor."

"It's not honor," Rowland said. "It's…" Absolom's principles, his cousins' personal fates, Lizzie's safety. "What you tricked me into…when did you plan to tell me?"

"Today."

"Tell me now. All. Especially how Kilbuck is involved."

"He only sent me to warn you that enemies might have pursued you from Holland. My father insisted it was my chance to fix how things had gone awry with Felicity."

Then Kilbuck and Bagsham aren't pursuing the same end?"

"Colonel Kilbuck knows nothing about our printing press."

Rowland muttered words he'd first learned from Perry as they walked back to join the others in the foyer.

"By removing the press from this house," Michel said, as he had just confessed to significant falsehoods, "we stop the anti-Catholic screed. Then we can tell the duke—"

"What?" Rowland said. "It has to answer to the duke's command to seize the press."

"The Duke of Bagsham?" Tamsin asked, but Rowland didn't have the wit to answer her.

"We'll say that the wherry we used to move it upended," Michel said. "Now it's at the bottom of the Thames."

Michel seemed sure of that idea. Rowland had to decide quickly, and yet paused. "Perhaps—"

"No." Felicity crossed her arms. "Aunt Letitia consigned its care to me, Michel. Don't you dare to take it from me."

"Our father wants this press out of radicals' hands, Felicity." Michel spoke her name with a hiss. "The fanatics cannot be allowed to divide England again. You know his command. No more wars over religion."

"Cease!" Rowland exclaimed. "We all agreed that the crucial work at this moment is to remove that press."

Felicity, cursing in French, pushed past Michel and called into the cellar: "You know where to take it, *mes amis*. Please leave the donkey cart at the theatre. I'll fetch it anon."

A chorus of voices answered, in whimsical fractured French. "Wee, ma-DAM ACK-truss. Mercy buttercups."

Another voice echoed up from below. "It's ma-DAM-more-SELL, you clodpates."

Rowland said, "It appears that your dockwallopers are—"

Felicity said, "They are professionals. Men of the theatre. We are a company of great renown, that most call the king's own company." The whisker-thin girl folded her arms.

Rowland had no time to join new conflicts, and this woman appeared to relish tiffs. He needed to waylay her over-abundant anger. "I saw Tuesday's performance. Did you play Dromio? Most excellent!"

Felicity preened.

"If you, Mademoiselle Felicity," Rowland said, "can guarantee no dissidents' pamphlets will ever again come from that press, then I'll release the press to you."

"More than that," Michel said. "We'll exchange its letter cases with another printer outside England. Perhaps Scotland."

"What's a letter case?" Tamsin asked. Rowland sensed she simmered under her usual calm and sensible demeanor.

"The trays that hold the letters for the printing press," Michel said. "From the broken letters in the dissidents' pamphlets, we knew they were printed on this press."

"No, *you* knew it, because you already knew this press was here." Rowland prompted, not able to quell his irritation with the upstart he'd spent the night protecting in the cellar. "You cannot insist that finding this press will serve only your needs."

"Not Michel's needs," Felicity said. "Our father's needs. Which are not the same as Aunt Letitia's intensions."

"Did you mean to deceive me?" Tamsin demanded of Felicity. "And you, Michel Chêne? How are we to trust you?"

She stood beside Rowland as if they were allied with each other, which felt…

Rowland checked his senses. Good. Very good.

Another voice carried down to them from the upper hall. "I'm so glad to find you all here. It saves me chasing across London to ask for help with my gambol."

At that sound, Rowland felt his intelligencer's need to control this situation fall away, as if a gaping hole opened in the floor. Too many voices made demands over the printing press—which he *must* control. Now, too many forces swirled, with too many unknown demands.

But it was Tom who appeared.

That new voice meant Rowland must turn his attention to his cousins' needs, rather than running about as a watcher serving Lord Bagsham's demands for black tribute.

— TOM —

TOM INTENDED TO HOLD his tongue for the rest of his life before uttering one word of the thrill and wonder that struck when he found his cousins in this house.

He'd been up since Perry returned from Knightsbridge. Once he'd heard the news and collected the messages from Ned and Aurora, he'd let Perry sleep while he ran his own errands.

Knocking on the Touchstones' door to deliver Ned's message about the Lely sketch of Jacob's mother.

Sending a boy to carry Aurora's message to Mrs. Mordaunt, plus his own message to her husband to announce he'd be tardy that day.

Studying Ned's work on the guardian bond to be sure not even one dot fell by mistake.

He didn't have to alter plans based on Aurora's message, because he'd already decided that he must destroy Withersea. He'd come with Perry to begin their day's prowling here, where they'd uncovered great gifts to Jacob's cause. Then he'd lurked in the upper hallway listening to the commotion below. His hands trembled, but not from fatigue. Rather, he was delighted to find Tamsin and Rowland here, yet anxious about their judgment, since both knew a great deal more about planning a restoration than he did.

He announced his presence only after he'd heard enough to guess at what they were about, and after hearing the surprise: Lord Bagsham wanted a printing press kept in this house.

"I'm so glad to find you all in one place. It saves me chasing across London to ask for help with my gambol."

Tamsin said, "What gambol, Tom?"

Not a hello, not an exclamation of surprise. At least she didn't first chide him for gadding about London. And no response from Rowland, who remained in a passion over that printing press.

Tom raised his voice, to impress the importance of the work ahead. "Your pressing business…ah, ha ha…must be set aside for now." He coughed, to clear his voice and lower it to conceal his excitement. "Mr. Chêne, I have just overheard your name and that you care deeply about the printing press. Will you and your sister please depart with it now? It is most important that I speak with my sister and my cousin at this very moment."

This prompted a tussle again between Michel and his sister. Felicity raised her voice. "Most important right now—"

"Most important right now," a new voice carried from the end of the hallway, "is to explain what you are doing in my house, Miss Oakes, with this clutch of bandits."

"You! Cornelius Rosewurme!" Felicity shouted. "Bigamist! Thief! Traitor!"

"S'welp me, this is my house."

Heigh-ho! This gangly little fellow was the man Withersea bullied in Mordaunt's chambers the previous day. After Mordaunt left for home, Tom had shuffled papers to discover the man's name and where he lived, curious about what he'd find here. Now the fellow appeared in the flesh, declaring, "You are the thieves."

"Pistols!" Tamsin hissed.

The diminutive man stood by the staircase, wobbling on high-heeled shoes, holding a pair of wheel-lock pistols, weaving his aim to cover the five people in the hallway.

Felicity, Michel, and Rowland each drew sword-sticks. Tamsin also drew one, surprising Tom. However, even four sword-sticks had no advantage over pistols.

"God blind me!" Rowland's voice again rose just shy of a shout. Tom twitched at the command ringing in his cousin's voice. "Stand down, in the name of the king, sir." Rowland turned on his companions. "You too, you pestilential lunatics!"

"God's teeth!" Perry came up behind Rosewurme, instantly disarming the fellow and sending him to the floor. Perry pressed his knee into the man's back. "You all distress me grievously. How am I to protect even one of you when you all jump in the fetid swamp like untrained puppies?"

"Where did you come from, Mr. Frake?" Michel asked.

"He's been prowling this house at my behest," Tom said.

"Whoever you are, sir—" Felicity brandished her sword.

"I am Peregrine Frake." Perry raised Rosewurme to his feet, holding him with one hand in what must be a painful grip, then batting the slender sword from Felicity's fist. "You are Dr. Oakes's little cousin who's in the playacting business?"

"I am Felicity Oakes, the owner of this house."

"I am the owner." Rosewurme managed to sound indignant, though held in place by Perry.

While Tom had eavesdropped in Mordaunt's chambers, Lord Withersea heaped scorned on Rosewurme. However, that spindly creature Perry held was not what Tom expected. As ruddy as a Scotsman, Rosewurme's head was out of proportion to the rest of him, and he was surely too old to be dressed as a popinjay who'd spent a rough night away from home.

Yet Rosewurme's appearance in this mêlée was providential, if one believed in that sort of thing. Tom formed an idea quickly, with a stronger impulse than he'd ever felt driving him forward: He must enlist the fellow in his cause.

Tom said, "Mr. Rosewurme is to be the hero who will save us all. He just doesn't yet know how much he wants us to be his new friends."

"Cornelius Rosewurme a hero?" Felicity Oakes spat on the fellow's high-heeled shoe.

"Alack, you whipperginnie!" Rosewurme drew up, raising his shoulders, indignant. Perry pressed him back down. "You believe the Almighty God owes you a cake but delivered only half a stale loaf. After all my dear wife did for you, you still declaim your lot to be unjust."

"Mr. Rosewurme is a nostrum quack." Felicity spoke to Tom while shaking her finger at the little man. "He's a bigamist who exploits widows. He stole the legacy my aunt left me." She jabbed a finger at Cornelius. "*Vous êtes un voleur grossier et traître.*"

"Must you curse in French?" Rosewurme, despite being under Perry's control, seemed unperturbed. "It's a deplorable language. And such profanity is filthy on your tongue."

"I shall call the force of English law down upon your head," Felicity said. "You swindler!"

"We have larger problems to discuss," Tom said, drawing on every ounce of patience he possessed. While he was pleased to find Tamsin and Rowland here, the chaos was exasperating.

"But my legacy—" Felicity began.

Perry, having been prowling, drew a paper from his waistcoat. "Miss Oakes, I found the baroness's will upstairs. Take it, so Tom can conduct our business without your screeching."

Felicity took the paper from him, reading quickly. "'To my niece, Miss Felicity Oakes, I leave my house and all its contents to her free use and care.'"

"One does wonder," Perry said, "why this miscreant didn't destroy it after he'd forged another testament."

Rosewurme didn't respond to Perry's goading, his face as innocent as a young child's, proving what Tom had guessed when eavesdropping: here stood a truly unique person.

Yet Felicity said, "Tell me, Mr. Rosewurme, how you finagled your way into Baroness Rôche's graces." She continued to disregard Tom's request for attention to his business, piquing his impatience. "First, you're a Nonconformist seeking funds to bring Huguenots to Spitalfields. Next, my dear aunt is dead and you're inhabiting her house, calling her your wife. She'd never marry a goat's pizzle such as you."

"You are rude to ask," Rosewurme said. "It's an abomination to pry into the ways a man and his wife love each other."

"*Voleur. Tricheur.*" Felicity, hands on her hips, shook a finger. "Thief. Cheat. Lord Marborne, give him to the king to judge."

"You are overwrought, my dear," Rosewurme said, which further raised Felicity's ire.

"*O merde de vache! Ça me fait chier. Bon sang.*"

"You distress me, Mr. Rosewurme." Perry took a tighter grasp of the fellow. "Let me hear it in my mother tongue, not in French, mademoiselle. And no more blether from you, tosspot."

"Aye, sir, I—"

"Shut it." Perry turned to Michel. "You, Michel? The so-called secretary? Resolve your family business. This moment."

Michel said quietly, "Felicity, if you cannot conduct yourself with honor, which you owe our father, then at least honor our aunt, the baroness."

"I will," Felicity said. "If you acknowledge that I am guided by our aunt's wishes, not our father's."

"Michel." Rowland spoke in a low voice, which Tom saw made people attend to him. Tom wanted to learn that trick. "Please go with Felicity to remove the press."

Michel nodded and followed Felicity into the cellar.

"*Ceteris paribus,*" Tom said, wondering why neither Rowland nor Tamsin ever had such problems directing people into the actions they must take. "We have work to do."

"All things being the same?" Tamsin said, translating his words with a puzzled frown. "What things are the same in all this chaos?"

"I shall explain," Tom said.

"At last!" Rowland said.

"I hope it's not in Latin," Perry said. He held up Rosewurme so his red-heeled shoes left the floor. "Where do you want me to put this fellow?"

"Let us all sit in the dining salon," Tom said, "and discuss our business in the manner of enlightened people."

He smiled, hoping to encourage them, though the organ behind his rib cage that held his wishes was knotted like a wire-and-ring puzzle. From Tamsin's expression, she didn't yet believe in the business. Or perhaps she feared that he was about to perish.

"Trust me," Tom said to Rowland and Tamsin, the pair he needed the most. Then, to advance his new wild idea: "And you, Mr. Rosewurme, must also trust me."

34

Revelation

— C O R N E L I U S —

ODSPITIKINS! HE'D ONLY COME to Chalgrove House to retrieve what mattered most before sailing to the Continent. This must be what a sailor feels when his ship has been pirated. Nothing to do but surrender and salute the new flag.

It seemed that Cornelius had no choice but to put his faith in the words: *Mr. Rosewurme is to be the hero who will save us all...his new friends.*

A crash rose from the cellar, turning everyone's attention. Four Kentish-looking giants hauled pieces of his dear wife's printing press up the stairs, through the kitchen, and into the alley.

Alack, he couldn't sell the press to add to his portable fortune. No matter. With the king's agents searching for it, that press presented more risk than any future remuneration might be worth. Let Miss Felicity Oakes worry about what the king's militia might say about a printing press being carted through Covent Garden. Cornelius only hoped these pirates might not seize the physicks in the still room. He needed his savings and that income, since Felicity Oakes had snatched away his wife's house, the greatest of his new fortune.

Now shed of the disruptive Miss Oakes, Cornelius sought to learn what his captors intended. The giant holding him was a greater force than he could overcome. His servants had deserted their posts, so Cornelius held no hope of rescue.

The smaller man, their leader, directed them to the dining salon and sat at the head of the table, which in happy times had been his beloved's seat. As the others found chairs, Cornelius took stock of his captors. They all dressed—rather uncomfortably—in new clothes, or perhaps seldom-used Sunday best.

"I'm Tom Foxe, Mr. Rosewurme." Their leader wore the suit of a London man of business. Despite his affable air, the man appeared to be neither a coxcomb nor a fool.

"You are to be the Earl of Marborne?" Cornelius asked.

"No, that is my cousin, Rowland Foxe, whom you should address as Lord Marborne." Tom Foxe pointed to the tall fellow at the end of the table, who had a reasonable visage, although overly quizzical about the eyes.

"How do you do, Lord Marborne." Cornelius nodded to the man he must appease. The earl might have emerged from his closet dressed as a wealthy Puritan, but now resembled a sexton several hours after the day's last funeral.

The earl raised his hand in a modest greeting. Cornelius continued to look to the earl, but he did not seem to pose a threat, like the Goliath did. Hence, Cornelius looked to Tom Foxe, but that man also had his gaze directed elsewhere. They all fixed their attention on the fellow at Tom Foxe's right, whose nods of agreement satisfied them. That fellow resembled Tom Foxe enough to be his twin, but likely a Ganymede.

These first exchanges proceeded well and good. Civilized. Enlightened. These hellions treated him with more decency than he'd endured with Withersea and Mordaunt.

"Seated beside you," Tom pointed to the Goliath, "is Mr. Peregrine Frake. Although he is wearing his leather cuirass and not his crimson coat, Sergeant Frake has long been in service to the king, where he has always been obliged to report to his captain any crimes he uncovers."

"I am honored to make your acquaintance, sir." Cornelius blinked in the way he'd learned from old Fowlmere, to appear as innocent as a June day is long.

Tom Foxe said, "Perry is a kindly man, but he's compelled to keep you here. Do not attempt to leave our company."

"S'welp! I would never," Cornelius said, having taken to his heart that these men controlled his future. "You have my word before God."

"Whatever that's worth." Mr. Frake released his grip. Cornelius's fingers had grown red and painful. "I shan't harm you. Howsomever, you did direct your pistols at my friends."

"Yet you," Cornelius said, "must acknowledge that my home has been invaded."

"If you will acknowledge, sirrah," Frake said, "that Miss Oakes has a testament that shows it to be her house, not yours."

"You scoundrel, Perry!" The Ganymede beside Tom Fox glared at Mr. Frake. "I asked you last night what Rollo and Tom were doing. You didn't answer with what you knew."

Mr. Frake said, "I had no knowledge that Rollo planned to decamp to a cellar with Michel Chêne. Or that either of them had aught to do with that press."

The fellow persisted. "Yet you are bound up with Tom in this business. You omitted truths in your answers last night."

When that glaring fellow crossed arms to appear stern, Cornelius finally recognized a lass. He drew a breath out of disappointment at being taken in by such a cobweb cheat.

"This," Tom Foxe pointed to the glaring creature, "is my sister, Miss Thomasine Foxe, who is both careful and bold. I recommend that you attend to our Tamsin with care. She is always right and always ready."

That compliment appeared to appease his sister, who rested one hand on the table, the other in her lap. Cornelius had observed that this gang looked to her for approval; hence, she must be the queen of these pirates. He'd met such queens before, but only among the most ruthless of gangs in the Pool of London. He must take care of how he dealt with such a dangerous and powerful being.

They were calm and, unlike the impudent Felicity Oakes, well-mannered. He therefore set aside most of his fears, hoping that Perry Frake did not again threaten to break his hand.

"Ah," Tom Foxe said, "now we come to the business that must command your attention today and your help tomorrow."

"Especially your attention, Mr. Rosewurme." The Frake fellow sounded warm and friendly, frightening Cornelius more than Merryboy had.

Tom Foxe addressed his cousins. "Given what Uncle Absolom taught us, we are required to perform a restoration, for the sake of innocents you have never met."

Cornelius's thoughts tossed about in a jumble. He wasn't sure what Mr. Foxe proposed. Miss Foxe nodded as if to agree with Tom Foxe, her expression grave. Lord Marlowe looked at Mr. Frake, who grinned like a gargoyle. His lordship broke the silence. "Tell us all, Tom."

"Tomorrow, the Marquess of Withersea will appear before the Committee for Privileges and Conduct to submit a dastardly claim against my friend, Jacob Rôche, the Earl of Cloudesley. We must stop that travesty."

Given what was discussed in Mr. Mordaunt's office the day before, the name Rôche surprised him.

Lord Marborne frowned, then voiced what Cornelius felt. "I'm just a mite confused. What are we doing here?"

— ROLLO —

"IS THERE ANY WAY, Tom, that you can tell your story before tomorrow?" Rowland said, minding that he was not only beyond famished but also expected at the Duke of Bagsham's house. He'd listened to Tom while also composing the tale he must spin for the duke. But Tom's tale grew longer by the moment. "Please explain who under the celestial heavens your friend might be. And why he is our concern."

"In a moment," Tom said. "But this part is my personal business. Perry, for just a few moments, will you please help Mr. Rosewurme excuse himself?"

From the hallway, Perry called into the cellar. "I say, gentlemen, can I beg you to entertain Mr. Rosewurme for a moment?"

Once the press-removers took Rosewurme with them, Perry came back, saying, "Now it's just us. Speak, Tom."

Tom said, "Jacob Rôche is the Earl of Cloudesley, a sweet, joyful young man who claims me as his friend. He is also a natural, with few words and his own peculiar focus on the world." He held out his hands to Tamsin, as if pleading with her to understand. "The Marquess of Withersea seeks to cheat Jacob of his birthright and fortune, and then to send him into exile on the northern border."

"Despicable," Tamsin said. Rowland agreed.

"On Tuesday," Tom said, "when he came with his sister to ask my help, Jacob had my picture, one Ned drew. He has carried it in his coat cuff for a decade." Tom coughed. "You, see, he calls on me to be the friend I once promised him I would be. I must do everything I can to save him."

"Of course, you must." All of Tamsin's irritation seemed to fall away with just this short story. However, Rowland felt...well, he felt a lump in his throat. Had anyone ever offered him such a wholly awesome friendship?

"I promised only my own help," Tom said. "Then Ned and Perry agreed to assist. I didn't commit you, Rollo. Or you, Tamsin. But I hope you'll want to join us, because the problem continues to grow, by the hour."

"It distresses me to know this, but I shall tell you fair," Perry spoke emphatically, "that the Marquess of Withersea abuses young Jacob in monstrous ways. I've seen the bruises and whip marks. I understand wholly why Tom has promised to help."

"It's exactly what one might guess that Tom would do," Tamsin said. Rowland, still trying to swallow the feelings left from Tom's story, felt the lump swell.

"It touches the heart," Perry said, "how Jacob has placed his faith wholly in Tom."

"It's a bit overwhelming, being responsible for a man's life."

This story had now shaken Rowland out of his private worries about Michel and the press. That business could be made to wait. "We should all want to help you. But how do you know Withersea's business?"

Tom opened his mouth to answer, but Perry intruded again. "Last night Tom asked me to prowl the marquess's house to find papers to help Jacob. While we searched, the marchioness told us how Tom rescued her from drowning in the River Cam, then made friends with her brother. You see, the marquess's wife is Tom's old school fellow from Trinity."

"Old school fellow?" Tamsin echoed Rowland's surprise.

"Just so." Perry's smile crinkled around his eyes, quite pleased to share this news. "She is quite nice. And pretty, in her own way."

"Old school fellow?" Tamsin repeated.

"That's much too facile an explanation." Tom spread his hands, which Rowland took to mean that deep secrets were being opened. "I knew Aurora Rôche at Trinity, long before she became Lady Withersea. At that time, she pretended to be her older brother, because of a burning desire to learn Greek from the Master at Trinity. I invited Jacob and Aurora to live in my chambers."

"You never asked me do that," Tamsin said, "all while you knew I was so very jealous of your days at Trinity."

"Aurora possesses more Greek than a bishop," Tom said. "She was driven to pursue her dream. And the pair of them needed protection."

"Did Uncle Absolom talk you into protecting this woman at Trinity?" Rowland asked, noticing that Tom offered a poor response to Tamsin's complaint.

"Our uncle didn't know a woman in breeches lived in my chambers. At the time, I didn't even tell Aurora that I saw through her disguise. And it was Jacob whom I served then and seek to serve now."

"The younger brother?" Tamsin seemed to be sorting out the story better than Rowland felt he did.

"Then Tom sent you to protect Jacob?" Rowland asked Perry, who was far too delighted with this story.

"No, my task was to prowl," Perry said. "Ned is the real savior. He created a new guardian bond for Jacob, to help keep the marquess's hands off young Jacob."

"Ned created..." Tamsin began, then shook her head.

Rowland, meanwhile, was losing patience. "Perry, you're taking as long as Tom with this story. Tom is a bad influence."

"It's a simple plan," Tom said. "Ned went to Aurora's house to paint a portrait as a disguise for protecting Jacob."

"Ned? A protector?" Rowland immediately perceived the stern look on Perry's face. "I didn't know he had such skills."

"Ned has proved to be a worthy cavalier," Perry said. "He wrote those...the new bond beautifully. You might even say hero-ically, given the splint on his broken finger. I saw in his eyes that it pained him. But Winwood insists we not worry. The break will heal soon enough."

"Winwood? Ned broke his finger?" Tamsin said. "What circus is this, Tom?"

"Jacob," Perry said, "needed a physician to assess damage done when picaros attempted to abduct him. In that calamity, Lizzie proved as valuable as Ned amid all the danger."

"Lizzie?" Rowland's heart stopped, as if the sun stood still in the sky. "But Lizzie is visiting friends in the country."

"In Knightsbridge. At Aurora's house. Lizzie has..." Perry stopped, as if he recognized the effect of saying that Lizzie was involved in this chaos.

Rowland felt a cringing sensation in his scalp, his shock doubled by hearing Perry say *Lizzie*. Until that day, Perry had always called her Miss Foxe. But now, it seemed, they were friends. A good deal must have happened the previous night.

"Yes, by our great good luck, Lizzie is there too." Tom did not seem to see that Perry's words had struck Rowland like a fist to his ribs. "She's helping to protect Jacob. Lizzie and Aurora rescued Jacob from the abduction, using pistols."

"Gah...God's heart!" Rowland choked on the words, his throat tight with distress. He watched Perry, as if to bore into his skull what he needed to hear. Could be mere coincidence? And did Bagsham know where Lizzie was, what she was doing?

"Ned and the ladies were reluctant to tell all about the attack." Perry glanced at Rowland, as if he saw his heart thump. "They have remarkably kind ways with Jacob. And I think Jacob has more wit than his tongue can form words."

Fear for Lizzie sizzled in Rowland's veins. She'd gone to visit Princess Mary's friend, while he'd spent a night in a frigid cellar because he hoped to protect her from Bagsham's threats.

May the King of the Dead fry me in Hades! Lizzie is in jeopardy!

He wanted to run to Knightsbridge. Now. It took every bit of what he'd learned from Absolom, from Perry, and from hard-won experience to master impulse.

"Can you assure us that Lizzie and Ned are safe? And Winwood?" Tamsin could speak. Rowland only stared at Perry.

"Lizzie is safe," Perry said, too coolly for Rowland's needs. "They all are. Withersea is in London and will not return to Knightsbridge until Friday night."

Rowland took a breath while seeking words from the Bard, *"that might cure the fever in my blood."* He scrummaged enough resolve from his empty belly to speak. "How are we to help?"

Tamsin said, "Will this gambol keep me from going home as I've planned? How many days will this take?"

"We have only until tomorrow," Tom said. "When the lords' Committee meets in Westminster, the marquess will attempt to seize Jacob's title. But Perry has brought the guardian bond Ned created to protect Jacob."

"By devil drawing?" Tamsin asked. Rowland couldn't read her expression. Pride perhaps?

"No," Tom said. "It's a true bond, witnessed, with everything the law requires."

Perry said, "I saw the Earl of Cloudesley write it, and signed my name as a solemn witness."

"For tomorrow at the Committee," Tom said, "that's all we need to save Jacob's title. Afterward, we will have to do more to protect him from Withersea's wrath. Likely as not, I shall have to remove brother and sister from England. But that's another day's worry."

"After tomorrow's meeting," Perry said, "I shall do my best to help protect Jacob from further travails."

Rowland relaxed, breathing out the fear for Lizzie's safety that had bound his heart. He accepted Perry's reassurances about Lizzie's safety. He needed at this moment to be as noble and willing as Tamsin was to help. It was only hunger that left his belly still in knots.

"Perry, would you fetch Mr. Rosewurme?" Tom said. "We need him to help address our other worries for tomorrow."

"What other worries?" Tamsin asked. "Rollo is right to complain about how long you take to tell your story."

"It's the unexpected news I learned yesterday while eavesdropping in Mordaunt's office," Tom said. "Lord Withersea is sore wroth and swears to destroy Rollo and Marborne."

Not just a knot of hunger then. Rowland wanted to sound rational, though a squeaking animal panic rose deep within his core being. He stilled that panic, seeing how Tom enjoyed himself. Rowland folded his arms. "And we roll along on 'Giddy Fortune's furious fickle wheel.'"

35

Confederation

— C O R N E L I U S —

"WELCOME BACK, MR. ROSEWURME," Tom Foxe said when Cornelius returned, that fellow Frake right on his heels. Sounds echoed up from the cellar where those roustabouts were destroying Cornelius's livelihood. Blessedly, someone closed the cellar door, so the noise of destruction didn't assault Cornelius's ears. "I am about to explain to my cousins that Lord Withersea is our archenemy who aims to harm Lord Marborne. To defend against that, we shall need your help."

"I have never met this marquess!" The earl's brow shot halfway up his forehead. "Whyever does this Lord Withersea want to attack me?"

Tom Foxe said, "Can you, Mr. Rosewurme, tell the story? I was only an eavesdropper rather than the true witness."

"Aye, Mr. Foxe," Cornelius said. "Your lordship, the marquess recited an angry complaint in Mr. Mordaunt's chamber. At the feast when the Marquess of Withersea's title devolved to him, King Charles accepted the marquess's homage, then never spoke to him again that night. Instead, the king spent a long hour with Samuel Foxe, recounting their adventures when Charles escaped to France."

"When I listened through the wall," Tom said, "the marquess spit the words, beyond angry with bitterness and spite."

"So it was." Cornelius nodded. "Under the influence of French brandy, King Charles made extravagant promises to Samuel Foxe, whom the king called his rescuer."

"However," Tom Foxe said, "Withersea never acted on his spite, because days later we lost all our family to the plague."

"This—this—'Poisonous bunch-backed toad!'" Lord Marborne seethed. "If that is Withersea's reason, it's the most trifling excuse for malicious revenge I've ever heard."

"This maungy marquess intends to attack Marborne." Perry Frake uttered it flatly, not questioning the intent.

"We are to be punished because the king spoke more with Lizzie's grandfather than with this corrupt, festering lord?" The earl was outraged.

"There's more." Tom Foxe gestured for Cornelius to speak.

"Lord Withersea was unhappy because the king froze funds held by his agent, Mr. Danvers Duncombe. About then, Mr. Mordaunt took a fright." Cornelius paused.

Tom waved Cornelius on to say more. "Come, Cornelius. May I call you Cornelius? And you shall call me Tom. Describe the part that frightened Mr. Mordaunt."

"Tom." Cornelius felt uneasy speaking his christened name.

"You can call me Mr. Frake," the Goliath said. He jerked a thumb at the earl. "And you'll call him 'your lordship.'"

"Go on, Cornelius," Tom said.

"To my eye, Mr. Mordaunt took a sincere fright when the marquess complained about having invested in what he called 'Duncombe's farrago.' Then Withersea erupted in anger when he heard from Mr. Mordaunt that it was Rowland Foxe, the new Lord Marborne, who arrested Duncombe for treason."

"Nobody knows it was Rollo!" Perry Frake set his fist rather too firmly on the table. "Except a few militiamen."

"The king's confidantes know," Lord Marborne said. "Is the marquess a confidante of the king?"

Cornelius said. "Mr. Mordaunt learned it from Lord Bagsham. When he repeated it, that's when the marquess remembered Samuel Foxe, and his wrath turned into a bonfire."

The earl raised one eyebrow. "I have never met this marquess, yet he intends to do us harm."

The earl seemed cool as a winter's day, despite what he'd just heard.

"What exactly does he intend, Mr. Rosewurme?" Perry Frake glared at Cornelius, sending shivers up the back of his neck.

"I don't know," Cornelius said, speaking pure truth. "The marquess told us he has something planned for the Committee meeting tomorrow." Cornelius had heard Withersea say he'd deal with Marborne as he had dealt with Bravewood. But Cornelius didn't know the true facts about what had happened to Viscount Bravewood. Therefore, he had nothing of value to say.

Tom said, "Withersea does not trust Cornelius or Mr. Mordaunt at this point. Which is to the credit of both men."

Miss Foxe had grown impatient. "How do we defend against our enemy if we don't know what he intends to do?"

"We must commence our own battle," Tom said. "I do know that the marquess has, in the past, offered the king emoluments in return for titles held in abeyance."

"The king returned the title to the Foxe family last Friday," Miss Foxe said, a tone of disgust in her voice. "The marquess cannot take the title. Is that what you think he's about to try?"

"Not possible to know," Tom said. "What we must do is advance a gambol that reveals a wide scope of the marquess's corruption. That's why I need Mr. Rosewurme's help to prove that Withersea bribed officers and clerks of the court to grasp the wealth he feels he is owed."

"Bagsham and Mordaunt consider such to be customary fees," the earl said. "I have to pay a small fortune in such fees to move Marborne and Foxe business through the courts."

"It's a matter of scale," Tom Foxe said. "Paying customary fees as compared to buying entire seats and the full devotion of the men holding those seats, then paying more to sway the inheritance of properties."

"Hold thy horses with a much firmer rein, Tom," Frake said. "I didn't understand all such this morning. How shall we ever find which magistrates haven't been bribed?"

"I am confident we can find a magistrate and make a case with Mr. Rosewurme's help," Tom Foxe said.

"How?" Miss Foxe folded her arms. "He's a swindling Captain Sharp, exactly like the marquess."

Cornelius felt this as an unkindness but offered no defense.

Tom said, "Am I correct, Mr. Rosewurme, that you'd very much like us to help you be free of your former master?"

"Not master. Rather, only a client," Cornelius said. But after yesterday's threats from the marquess, he must hope that these Foxes might offer some safety until he fled to the Continent.

"And so, you will help us, Mr. Rosewurme?" the Frake giant asked, infuriatingly pleasant.

"Stop, Perry. You can't coax a man's help by frightening him," Lord Marborne said. "Yes, people try to do so, but then you have to watch your back forever more."

"He's afraid, but not of us," Tom Foxe said. "The marquess uttered dire threats against our friend yesterday. Mr. Rosewurme is far better off if he chooses to help us."

Miss Foxe cast her dark brown eyes on Cornelius. "Tom trusts you, though I do not yet see why. However, if he believes you can help, then you must do so."

Cornelius had never seen anyone as adamant as Miss Foxe. Perhaps Mordaunt and Withersea could learn from her, how to be resolved without flinging threats about. Her fierce glare convinced him to act, though he had one nagging worry, with that giant pressed too close to him.

"Your lordship, I hope to be of help, if only I might have your assurances of my safety afterward. That you will trust me to remain silent."

"Your safety?" The earl tipped his head, looking surprised. "What a bewildering request. Why would...God blind me! You fear that we'd gain your cooperation, then dispatch you?"

"Dispatch?" Miss Foxe frowned. "You think we'd..."

Perry Frake laughed, rudely. Tom Foxe put his head in his hands, his shoulders shaking, because he too was laughing.

Miss Foxe said, "Please tell him there's a rule against that, Rollo...um, your lordship. It might ease his mind to hear our Number One rule." She tapped the table to stress each of her next words. "*No one dies.*"

"You have our word," Lord Marborne said. "We will protect you from harm, from all quarters. Is that what you need?"

"It is." Tom answered before Cornelius could speak. "Mr. Rosewurme suffered distress, I believe, when he learned that the Marquess of Withersea hired mercenaries to dispatch Jacob's father and other significant persons. That's what else the marquess spoke of, isn't it?"

"I wasn't that surprised to learn it," Cornelius said. "But I believe Mr. Mordaunt was swept away."

"Can we prove that against Withersea?" the earl asked, sitting up as though excited. "Or can we convince your mercenary friends to give evidence to a magistrate?"

"No!" Cornelius sat back, aghast. "If you even whisper such stories to a magistrate, any alleged...um...mercenaries would be found to have disappeared from London. The marquess has a long reach."

"Such knowledge tells us," Tom said, "that we pursue an evil soul and that we must be cautious."

Cornelius remained unsure whether he should say more or simply seek a handshake to seal an agreement to work together. Perry Frake, however, wagged one of his immense fingers at him. A warning.

Watching the preternaturally calm Tom Foxe, Cornelius began to see a better future than he'd planned for himself the night before. Their pirate queen no longer glared at him. The earl still masked any expression other than curiosity. Whatever Tom Foxe might have planned, Cornelius felt Withersea's threat wafting away, as if a burden were lifted from his shoulders. He sighed. Alas, that sigh caught Perry Frake's attention. That Goliath's eyes again fixed on him. Cornelius bravely gazed into those blue orbs.

"I shall do," Cornelius said, "whatever you require."

Cornelius smiled in the way that always made him a friend, while he calculated how many days he'd collaborate with these pirates until he could escape, retrieve the hoard cached under the still-room floor, and sail for the Low Countries. Forsooth, Amsterdam was the best place for a man with a head for business and seeking to carve a new future for himself.

"*Aspirat primo fortuna labori*." Tom Foxe turned to Mr. Frake. "It means fortune smiles on our first effort. Now let's study the real business needed to protect Rollo and Marborne."

— TAMSIN —

HER BROTHER TOM SAID, "We still have mysteries to unroll."

For her private consolation amid all that turmoil, Tamsin touched the gold coin dangling from the chain around her neck. She rubbed at the Archangel and dragon to release her agitation, all while staring at the side table, its top of exotic wood and ivory inset in delicate circles. She'd been working for Felicity and worrying about Tom's fragile state, while he'd been running all over London with Perry, seeking a true restoration. Whatever mysteries Tom had discovered, his lips twitched and his eyes gleamed, which meant he was enjoying this and he'd take an eternity to reveal his mysteries.

Tamsin swallowed the complaints she longed to utter, not just to Tom, but to Rowland and Perry as well. *You didn't ask me to help with your many secrets. And now, I wager this gambol means I can't go home on Saturday, like you know I want to.*

Tom said, "Please tell us, Cornelius, about the bullies Withersea asked you to hire to harm Lord Marborne. I assume the same bullies chased me on Holborn Road yesterday."

"I hired bullies? To harm his lordship?" Mr. Rosewurme drew up indignant once more, displaying the excessive astonishment of a painted stage actor. Tamsin found him repulsive, like the villainous corn-merchant who'd cheated Marborne village last winter.

"Again," Tom said, "I heard what transpired with Withersea yesterday in Mordaunt's chambers."

"That was merely business." Mr. Rosewurme waved his hand, as if to signify his innocence, while Tamsin saw the pleas of an inveterate liar. "My lord, I beg that you'll see my former employment as mere business, nothing personal."

"I do not take any afront, sir." Rowland folded his hands and closed his countenance, so no one could read his thoughts.

"You also sent hired bullies after Felicity Oakes." Tamsin meant to sound factual, to hide her disgust that Tom wanted an alliance with the hideous, vain fellow.

"Only one time, to keep her away from my door," Rosewurme said. "They never laid hands on that woman."

"But I was there when your picaros came for her after the theatre Tuesday." Tamsin fumed. "We sent them on their way with bruises and spilled blood."

"I did not send men after Felicity Oakes on Tuesday night." Mr. Rosewurme seemed confused, rather than prevaricating.

"Then who attacked us?" Tamsin touched her gold angel. Tom stared at her. She blinked under his gaze.

No, Tom, I didn't tell you about that attack on Tuesday.

Felicity claimed those picaros were after her.

Mr. Rosewurme said, "It's likely that certain knights of the blade were hired—"

"Mercenaries," Perry said. "Or shall I say, assassins? As we discussed just moments ago, I believe, about the last Earl of Cloudesley that was."

"As may be, sir." Mr. Rosewurme nodded affably. "I have refused to be involved with any such business."

"Yet, one of Withersea's confederates came to Mordaunt's chambers late yesterday," Tom said. "He left two pounds sterling to pay rogues to pursue me, not Lord Marborne. Two pounds from Leighton Fairchild."

"God's bodkins!" Tamsin cried. A landslide of emotions tumbled from her heart. Indignation knotted her fists. Fear pounded inside her ribs, banging like the roustabouts working in the cellar.

I was right to worry. Leighton made good on his threat.

And now, Tom: Who's protecting which secrets?

Tom didn't blink when he caught her frowning at him. He continued questioning the little man. "Did you help to take revenge on behalf of Mr. Fairchild?"

"No, not I," Rosewurme said. "I am no longer an agent for any such business. I believe you met Sir Duxwold."

"Duxwold? That's the fellow who gave me a pass to the theatre," Rowland said. "That's how the marquess's rogues knew where to find me after the play."

"While Leighton's rogues found Camilla at the same theatre." Tamsin resisted fear, allowing only calculated caution and resentment for Leighton to flow in her blood. She resolved again not to tell Camilla, who still suffered from the injuries incurred when Leighton shot her. Last week, Leighton had sought only to frighten her, yet never apologized for hurting her. No matter. She would ensure that Leighton never again came near enough to make Camilla afraid.

Her other feeling: dismay that Tom had been carrying all these worries, while she'd wasted time on a mistaken lark with Felicity. Whatever mysteries Tom had to reveal, Tamsin held tight to her core resolutions, the way she still knotted her fists, determined.

Never waste time on idle diversions.

Never allow Leighton to harm or frighten Camilla.

Never spend a day longer than needed on whatever Tom is about to propose, so she could go home.

And forget her ill-managed resolve not to interfere or worry about her cousins. The sense that had been creeping at the back of her head? The tension in her stomach? Both proved valid. She *should* worry about her relations and friends.

Especially Tom, who looked fatigued near to death. And did she have to interfere with Rowland, too? Would Perry step up for his friend? Or did she have to nudge him into helping?

Meanwhile, Mr. Rosewurme justified his nefarious dealings. Tamsin felt a flutter rise within her, like a bird winging from its nest into sunshine after a wretched storm. She deeply wanted whatever adventure Tom was about to propose.

"Tom seeks our help, so I promise to join you," Tamsin said. "I'll do what you need, Tom. Just tell us, so we can start now. Will it all be done tomorrow?"

She wanted to keep that promise, but she also wanted to go home as soon as possible.

— ROLLO —

ROWLAND IGNORED HIS BELLY'S continual complaint about no breakfast. To keep from staring at the Rosewurme creature, he'd been studying the overly ornate fire screen, its needlepoint cover showing two men in a forest. With swords. Why place such a scene in a lady's dining salon?

This day had twisted out of Rowland's control when he lost the printing press, just like the day before, when he'd been commanded to find that infernal machine. His resolve when he came to Xanthus House—to just make it through the next few days— was in tatters. He must first make it through Tom's gambol. He fished the gold angel from his pocket again and rolled it over his knuckles. *"My soul's in arms, and eager for the fray."*

That feeling came back, from the previous week's gambol. That his cousins were the best of enlightened people. And Tom clearly felt a need to serve as his friend's hero.

Rowland might feel better if Perry weren't just then listing comprehensive categories of catastrophes that Withersea might perpetrate, with Tamsin responding like a chorus in a Shakespearean spectacle.

"Please cease your dramatical debate," Rowland said. "First, I will call the man out for a duel if he attempts to accuse me of treason. And if the man tries any other tactics, I vow to keep him stuck in chancery for another quarter century. And I'll pay a gang of paupers to shout 'Samuel Foxe saved the king!' outside his window every night but Sunday."

Perry slapped his shoulder. "Lord Merry Andrew. It eases my heart that you can laugh at adversity."

"I'm laughing because weeping would be unmanly."

"Cease fretting about the unknown," Tom said. "As I said, we must attack rather than wait to see what battle the marquess intends to mount." He drew from his waistcoat a packet of papers tied with a barrister's red ribbon. "Let us now draw Cornelius close into our capers."

"I am ready, my lord." Rosewurme nodded to Rowland.

Shall I ever become accustomed to that appellation?

Tom said, "I've uncovered two dozen estate settlements recorded in Mordaunt's chambers, each altered to hide disbursements to you, Mr. Rosewurme, and to Mr. Mordaunt, and larger than customary gratuities to men in the consistory and chancery courts. All prepare the way for certain lords to take possession of disputed lands." Tom's eyes grew harsh in a way Rowland had never seen. "In short, you have helped Withersea and other lords swindle poor innocents from their property."

The Rosewurme fellow waved away the accusation.

"My work was within the bounds of the law. Mr. Mordaunt is too good at his work for any to find fault with it."

"Explain your part in this work, please." Tom had quickly learned the posture and tones of a stern barrister. Which Rowland found comforting in this chaos.

"I help find properties where the inheritance is in dispute."

"Then Mr. Mordaunt helps in what ways?"

Rosewurme said, "He works with the courts to resolve disputations over lands that would otherwise fall to the king."

"Then," Tom said, "you can help me identify lords who cheated the Crown as well as swindling from poor innocents."

Rosewurme paled and didn't speak. That was when Rowland perceived all the face-paint the man wore.

Rolling his coin across his knuckles under cover of the table, Rowland felt excitement defeat the panicky creature Tom had roused in him. And Fate, dressed in Tom's clothes, might now identify nefarious rich men who deserved righteous reaving. "Which lords, Tom?"

Tom named two earls and a baronet, then finished: "But principally, it's the Marquess of Withersea with his minion, Sir Duxwold. However, in one case, that same trickery was used to gain property for the Duke of Bagsham."

"No one was harmed by that." Mr. Rosewurme interrupted, then shrank when everyone turned to look his way. "The man who originally claimed the property died without heirs."

"Is that your same duke who wants the printing press, Rollo?" Tamsin asked.

Rowland agreed, aware that he hadn't answered her earlier question, but he didn't want to discuss the duke with Tamsin and Tom at this moment, to reveal how he'd been compromised, forced to become the king's watcher. However, he felt Perry's eyes on him, which likely meant his friend had guessed as much. He slipped his hands into his pockets to cover any display of trepidation.

And touched that black lace glove. From a spy's closet.

The king's new watcher needed to learn quickly how Lord Bagsham was involved in property swindles and other corruption spreading from Withersea. He had power and skills to act, to help Lizzie and Marborne villages and Tom's friends.

And knowing that about the duke, Rowland felt his worries over that press began to ease. The compromise Michel Chêne had maneuvered him into didn't seem such a moral quandary in comparison to how the duke had acquired property. Or had blackmailed Rowland into becoming a watcher.

"Several disputations," Tom said, "involve widows who were denied their inherited portion by distant cousins. In at least three cases, claims were denied because the widow had remarried. I am right, sir, that you are the various Corneliuses who breached those widows' defenses?"

"He's a bigamist," Tamsin said, her lips tight with disgust. "Felicity has letters from a host of women. She wants to hand this fellow over to a magistrate."

Rosewurme didn't even blink at the accusation or voice a defense. Watching the man, Rowland could not yet perceive why Tom had picked such a uniquely strange new friend.

Placid in his inquiries, Tom asked, "Who were the long-lost cousins who made property claims, Mr. Rosewurme? Mercenaries you put in place at the behest of your masters?"

"Is this a tribunal?" Rosewurme asked, indignant. "Do you, the land pirates who invaded my home, seek to judge me?"

"Aye, we are a tribunal," Perry said, in that amicable voice which signaled jeopardy. "Mayhap, I'm minded that's three judges, and we are four."

Tom might need this new friend, but Rowland knew Perry. His old friend disdained this fellow.

"And you stole this house from Felicity Oakes. We are a rescuing militia, not pirates." Tamsin did not like the fellow. Most definitely. Her expression reminded Rowland of the week before, when she mistakenly believed Rowland to be a traitor.

"Also," Rowland said, hoping to contribute to Tom's work, "as an officer of the Crown, I can arrest you for slander and treason against the king, given the pamphlets in your cellar."

"Stuff it for three minutes, your lordship," Tom said. Which surprised Rowland into silence. "Mr. Rosewurme is still in the midst of learning how very much he wants to help us."

Rosewurme said, "S'welp me, Mr. Mordaunt is a great man of the law. Those papers you purloined from his chambers won't stand before the law as judgment, either against my own self or any lords or common men cited within them"

"Yet we found this in your study." Perry removed a ribboned packet of papers from inside his cuirass. "It distressed my heart to see, friend Rosewurme, that you've gathered documents that trace your mentors' cheating ways. Bless me, are you planning black tribute?"

"I–I need those papers to protect myself." Rosewurme's ruddy complexion paled again when Perry flashed the smile of a wolf who'd found a solitary sheep. The fellow reached for the papers, but Perry held them away at arm's length. Rosewurme, obviously intimidated, mouthed silent words while frowning so hard he'd closed his eyes.

"We need these personal papers of yours to prosecute Withersea," Tom said. "I appreciate how you've helped us thus far. And beg that you'll continue to help with our quest."

"You've said it, but," Perry leaned forward, "tell me again why he'd help rather than deserting at his first free moment."

"Mr. Rosewurme does not trust his partners," Tom said. "Yesterday, Withersea drove spikes of fear deep into his heart. That's why he wants to help us."

Rowland set his hand on the table and rolled his gold angel. All he needed was patience, waiting for Tom to tell how his gambol would work—giving Rowland a chance to show Bagsham exactly how Absolom's enlightened Foxe kits served England.

36
Visitant

THEY ENJOYED A PLEASANT and quiet day at Arcadia House.

At dawn they'd congratulated each other after restoring the marquess's study and bedchamber. Before he'd left, Perry had replaced the threads on the marquess's desk drawers. Aurora said, "I'll blame one of the discharged maids for clumsy dusting if anything is wrong."

"However, we will be gone before he discovers aught," Ned said while surveilling the study they'd plundered, sure that Perry would praise the quality of their restorative housekeeping. "The marquess isn't due home until Friday night."

Before Aurora left for London, she'd talked Jacob into a nap. While he slept, Ned sketched, starting with his idea of showing two women becoming friends, which he thought should best be expressed in how he arranged their hands. He was about to begin a sketch of Jacob, but then had another idea, which was ready when Jacob came in, rubbing his eyes, his hair tousled.

"Rory home?"

"Not yet, Jacob. Come see what I made for you."

Jacob sat on the floor by the chair where Ned was working. He took the sketchbook, laying his head on Ned's knee while he studied it.

"It's Mother. You made Mother."

Ned had drawn from memory, guided by that Lely sketch at Touchstone's and by Aurora's face.

Jacob sat up, bent his head over the sketch. his head in his hand. A tear dropped on the sketched page. Jacob moved the paper away, scrubbing his face.

"Tom promised to bring Mother back."

"I'm sure he's still working on it," Ned said. "I thought you'd like to have this until Tom finds your own sketch."

The sketch served a second, unplanned purpose. By propping it where Jacob could see, he sat still long enough that Ned could draw his likeness on the canvas. When Jacob grew tired of that, Ned painted Pip in the portrait while Jacob sat nearby, sorting Ned's brushes by length, then by color, and explaining to Pip that they must help Ned because Ned was Tom's helper.

While Ned painted, he learned that Jacob had a unique and deeply colored view of the world, and that he rarely forgot anything, only sequestered things he didn't want to remember. Though tongue-tied, Jacob told Pip about the cold winter when Tom was his friend. How they ate cheese and mutton stew and drank hot cider. How pens often ran away and hid from Tom. How Rory was always reading, so Jacob and Tom played tag. The loser was the man in the moon, and Tom always lost.

That story gave Ned an idea. He wrote "Man in the Moon" on a page in his sketchbook and gave Jacob a plumbago a pencil to try to copy it. That snagged Jacob's attention long enough that Ned could paint his face and hands.

Lizzie plied her needle to embroider over grass stains on the hem of her dress. As the morning advanced, Winwood read aloud Aurora's translation of a Greek comedy.

"When will Rory come home?" Jacob interrupted Winwood's reading three times, as if he didn't hear the tenor tones of the doctor's voice. "When is Tom coming?"

Lizzie answered each time, saying "Soon." But that begged the question: was "soon" in moments or before nightfall?

"Tomorrow?"

"Today, dear heart," Lizzie said. "Or tonight at the latest."

"Jacob." Ned called to him. "Is my picture of Pip good?"

The young man studied it, hovering close over Ned's shoulder. "Who is that man with Pip?"

"It's you, Jacob."

Jacob studied it for several more heartbeats. "Needs a ball." With that, he ran to the garden to fetch Pip's ball. He arrived at the threshold at the same moment as Gabriel the footman, who hissed, "His lordship the marquess just this moment rode into his stables, coming in at a heat. He demanded a fresh horse."

"Zooterkins!" Ned muttered, more like a curse than out of surprise. But he knew immediately he should not have said it.

"Zooterkins!" Jacob echoed. He glanced toward the stables, though they were not visible behind the garden hedge. "Hiding," he said, and disappeared, Pip scampering after him.

Winwood sighed. "*Bon sang.* We can't lay hands on a peer of the realm to stop him in his own house."

"Do you mean the marquess or the earl?" Ned said.

"Ha!" Winwood said. "Perry is a bad influence on you. And you sit as cool as he would, while my heart's thundering."

"Upon my soul!" Lizzie set aside her needlework and rose from the settle. "We made a plan before Aurora left. You all know what to do."

Gabriel nodded and left them, then reappeared. "I forgot what it's supposed to be."

"Scarlatina," Winwood said.

He followed Lizzie, who hurried up to Aurora's bedchamber. Ned kept painting, grateful that Winwood saw him as fearless, all the while he'd had to quell his own fears as they'd moved into action, executing the plan Aurora had insisted they make.

The marquess announced his presence by the clatter of hard leather heels on the parquet floor.

"Where's John Coachman? Why in flaming Hades are you here, Mister...what is it? Wicket? Whelks?"

"The driver is delivering departing guests to their London homes." Resuming the Dutch accent he borrowed from his father,

Ned answered the first, then the next inquiry. "Lady Withersea begged me to stay, so there's someone with Lord Cloudesley. Our work soothes his worries about his sister." Ned didn't answer the last part of the question, considering it more of a sneer than a query.

"Where is Jacob? That ninnyhammer!"

"Lord Cloudesley?" Ned persisted in citing Jacob's title, hoping to irritate his inquisitor, while also hoping Jacob wouldn't reveal his hiding place. "I believe he took Pip into the garden, with a promise to go no further than the roses. Did you hear about yesterday's scuffle?"

"Unbelievable," the marquess muttered, with no indication of what he didn't believe.

"Yet quite understandable, your lordship," Ned said. "Pip chased a ball into the road, and his lordship the earl followed. Afterward, Lady Withersea chided him sternly. Then the dog found itself caught between passing strangers and his master. Most dogs will attack in such cases, don't you agree?"

The marquess stood at the threshold, looking out at the garden, showing no response to Ned's tale.

Ned continued. "The encounter only grew as it did because the passersby were afraid of the dog and beat about with sticks. And Pip is a young terrier that barks when frightened."

"I don't see him in the garden," the marquess said.

"Perhaps he went up to rest." Ned glanced up, as if thinking. "Dr. Oakes did insist he rest."

"Doctor?" The marquess looked startled.

"Lady Withersea sent for a doctor when she woke with the same fever as the cook's child. He advised that your servants and guests depart, lest they find themselves in quarantine."

"Quarantine? Only children get scarlatina. And I rule this house, not an unknown doctor."

"Yes, your lordship." Ned observed the marquess's increasing redness...ha, without scarlatina! He fearlessly determined to raise the man's irritation. That's what Perry would do. "Yet the doctor says scarlatina is highly infectious. He's been at Lady Withersea's bedside since the guests and servants departed, except to check every hour that Lord Cloudesley is well. If you want, I shall—"

Lord Withersea stalked from the room.

~

Ned, wanting to protect his friends, resisted leaping up to follow. Or to pace. They had a plan. And they knew what to do.

Brush in hand, still favoring his broken finger, Ned teased at the shadow details for the scarlet piping on the jacket in which he'd painted Jacob. That jacket hung on a chair, Jacob having refused to wear it. ("Scratches. Too hot.")

Everything would be fine: upstairs in Aurora's bedchamber, Lizzie in a nightcap, immured under a heavy quilt, face down, was pretending to be the feverish Lady Withersea, asleep. Winwood was sitting solemnly at her side, perhaps feeling her pulse. Or bathing her feverish temples with vinegar. Nothing ever perturbed Winwood, and no one ever came between Winwood and his patient. The marquess would need to raise a pistol if he wanted to see more of his wife than the moaning figure in her bedchamber.

"Gone?" Jacob whispered behind Ned's head, like a ghost.

"Still in the house," Ned murmured. "Where are you?"

"Hiding." More shuffling, like mice. Then the room was silent except for the *whish* of Ned's brush on canvas.

He paused for a drop of mineral spirits. The miniscule dot of scarlet for the coat's piping had grown thick on his palette. The stirring of paint was the only sound breaking the portentous silence, while he strove to hear other sounds in the house. Then banging doors echoed.

"Gabriel!" The marquess shouted. "Pack my trappings for two nights in London. And for a state dinner tomorrow."

"Yes, your lordship," the footman answered. "What do you require for tonight?"

"I'm intending the theatre," the marquess called. "Make it linen. And light. This cursed heat." Then Withersea was in his business room. From the banging and clatter, he was opening drawers and boxes.

Ned held his breath, considering what Withersea might find altered or missing. Then he took a deep breath. What had Perry taught? *Do not fuss, chucking. Just be ready for whatever might come next.*

Ned clenched his fists, to be ready for what might be needed to protect Jacob. The pang from his little finger begged to be felt as a message: *Sweet chucking, your bare hands are never to be offered in a brawl.*

"Gabriel!" The marquess's voice echoed from his study. "Where have you gone, you absolute arsworm?"

"I'm here, my lord." The lad's voice came from upstairs. "Packing, as you commanded."

"Find a carriage to take Mr. Wicket—"

"It's Mr. Wijck, I believe, sir."

"Send that Dutch sharper back to London with his brushes. I shall not be responsible for his comfort or any diseases he might try to catch. And send that damnable London leech to my study. I want to hear what the doctor says about this prurient fever."

Ned had come to know the soft sounds of Winwood's steps, after the long winter and spring the physician spent tending Tom. He imagined Winwood's unyielding expression while Withersea quizzed him one room away from where Ned now only pretended to paint.

"You are the doctor?" Withersea pronounced "doctor" as if it were a challenge.

"Yes, your lordship. Dr. Winwood Oakes. I am wholly at your family's service."

"Oakes? Never heard of you. Why didn't my wife send for our usual physician?"

"I was at the World's End when the servants came in and spoke of a fever in the household. The landlord drove them off for fear of contagious, and I came here directly in hopes of being of service."

"You aren't from London. I cannot place your accent."

"Switzerland, my lord. I studied there under the famous Doctor Gessner, the physician who has revived and extended his ancestor's work with infectious diseases."

"But scarlatina is a child's sickness."

"Your wife has contracted a severe case." Winwood spoke as mildly as ever, then proceeded to quietly share more information, which must only heighten the marquess's rage. "The cook's child, who likely carried it into the house, had only a flush face and hot hands. But when a mature person takes up a child's disease, the effects can be dire. I attended a man last winter who was brought near death's door by chicken pox."

"Can she be moved?" Withersea asked. "I want my doctor in London to attend her."

"Not today. Her fever must abate before any removal. Perhaps tomorrow, or the next. I'm using vinegar sponge baths, plus an elderflower-and-mint tincture that the apothecary in Knightsbridge was quick to send at my urgent request. I believe—"

"Go tend your patient. Wait! How do you manage your doctoring chores with no female servants in the house?"

"Your footman has been gracious about bringing food and water, though I have to lay out my own funds for it, since her ladyship could not put her hands on any coins."

"But the vinegar baths?" Withersea, in asking the question, sounded ready to pound Winwood into the floorboards.

"Your lordship! Do you fear that I have impinged on Lady Withersea's privacy? Please be assured, I follow the best methods, as taught by my mentor, the famous Dr. Theodor Gessner, for preserving modesty in the course of treatments."

The sound of coins hitting a wood surface echoed. "Here's for your troubles, doctor." The marquess sneered at the title. "Your services are not required after tomorrow morning. Here's sufficient coin to take you to your next destination."

Ned listened, while his heart thumped loudly enough to echo into the next room where Winwood endeavored to reduce Lord Withersea to boredom. Ned silently praised Winwood's ability to weave a ring of falsehoods. Until that moment, Ned had not believed Winwood capable of telling lies.

"Gabriel!" The marquess shouted again, after Winwood had gone back upstairs. The footman must have appeared quickly, because Withersea next said, "Inform John Coachman that I want my wife and her brother at my house in London tomorrow morning. And you! Pack all of Jacob's clothes and gewgaws. All of it. He won't be returning here. John Coachman can send that baggage to my most northern country house by separate carriage. He knows the direction."

"Yes, my lord."

"Since she's so very ill, you need not inform my wife. Do you hear me?"

"Yes, my lord."

Exactly what Aurora had forewarned: that the marquess intended to exile Jacob to the Scottish border. Ned clenched his fists again. This time the pain streaking up to his elbow reminded him of how once Perry had calmed a belligerent drunkard with a single thwack on the temple.

But Jacob's friends had another plan.

~

"Gone?" Jacob whispered again.

"Yes, Jacob. It's safe," Ned said. Withersea had stomped through the house, shouting curses and commands at Gabriel. Then peace descended after they heard his horse clatter in the lane, the sound soon lost in the distance.

Jacob emerged with Pip from behind the second canvas Ned had propped on a wall. Lizzie appeared a few moments later, her gown still rumpled from hiding under heavy blankets, but her hair tightly braided and pinned down. Winwood came down the stairs behind her, Gabriel trailing the doctor.

"Lad!" Ned exclaimed, seeing how pale and shaken the footman was. "We're all safe now."

Lizzie dragged Gabriel into the study, where she poured brandy from the marquess's gilded decanter and ordered him to drink it. She had a glass in her hand when she emerged from the study, and Ned had to point two fingers at her before she remembered to console Winwood and Ned, too.

"Do we send one of Perry's brothers back to Covent Garden?" she said, as if reading Ned's mind. "Perhaps we need Perry to come here with...uh...guardians?"

"No," Ned said. "You should help Gabriel pack, so we're ready for the next action when Aurora returns."

"Pack all of Lord Cloudesley things?" Gabriel asked, not thoroughly fortified by a dram of brandy.

"I don't think so." Ned consulted Lizzie. "What does he need? Where will they go?"

"Rome," Lizzie said.

Jacob said, "Rory says it's warm."

Rubbing her wrists like she did when thinking, Lizzie said, "They'll have to purchase what they need later. Gabriel, pack whatever Jacob might need for only two days. I'll come up in a minute and pack for the marchioness."

Gabriel seemed relieved to have a task to undertake that was of a size much less than "pack everything."

"Take Jacob to help you, Gabriel," Lizzie said. "He can tell you what is most important to him."

After Gabriel and Jacob went upstairs, Winwood said, "Do we take Jacob to London with us? He's clearly not safe if he's within the marquess's reach. One of us can stay behind to meet Aurora when she returns."

"Let's wait for her," Lizzie said. "I'm sure Aurora will prefer to decide the next step."

"Since it will be a rather large step," Ned said. "We need to explore the marquess's study again. What do you think he was doing in there with all that banging about?"

When Ned came into the study, with Lizzie and Winwood trailing, he banged open the desk drawers. Until a thread flew up and caught on his finger splint, Ned hadn't noticed that he'd abandoned any desire to preserve the secrecy of their incursion into the marquess's business.

Was it the manifest threats against Jacob?

The man's utter disregard for his wife's health?

Certainly, it was nothing so petty as the scornful way the marquess treated Ned and Winwood.

Ned shuffled the bottom drawer's contents, not seeing any change. He opened the top drawer. That exquisite snuff bottle had been tossed on the pen wipes and pounce.

He pocketed it. He didn't check for Lizzie's approval, remembering Absolom's funeral feast, where he'd seen her steal gold buttons off a man who was too impertinent.

Lizzie toyed with one of the painted fans while she watched Jacob with the three puzzle boxes, which were now scattered on the window ledge, rather than tucked into their places on the highest shelf.

He pressed the lozenges on the box that had held the letter condemning the Foxe family. It was empty.

For Ned, that meant the marquess had carried away the altered version. For Jacob, it meant the box was no longer interesting, it having been left open. He selected another box and played with all the depressions and carving that might unlock the puzzle. When it opened, Jacob retrieved a coin.

"Gold!" He rubbed it on his sleeve. "Are we rich?"

He showed it to Ned. It was a gold louis with shaved edges.

"Almost," Ned said. "Keep it in your pocket."

Ned was pondering how to steal back his own forged painting. Take it off the frame, then put it with his paint kit?

Jacob popped the third puzzle box open.

"No gold. Just paper."

He had it out, studying it. He frowned. "Tom's name?"

"N–No." Ned read it slowly. "It says 'ten,' not Tom."

He handed it to Lizzie, who read it aloud. "'Pay to the bearer five hundred and ten pounds sterling.' This illegible part must be the marquess's signature. The stamped image is surely his sign."

When Winwood whistled, Ned found he'd been holding his breath. He asked, "Why the ten additional guineas?"

"We don't know what the five hundred guineas are for," Lizzie said. "But even if Tom's gambol fails, Jacob has found the means by which he and Aurora can leave England."

"I am good?" Jacob asked.

Ned said, "You, my friend, are very good." He petted Pip, since Jacob wouldn't let anyone other than Aurora and Winwood touch him. "Did you finish packing with Gabriel?"

"No," Jacob said. "Pip wants two balls."

Lizzie said, "You have to decide, dear heart. The red ball or the blue one?"

That took Jacob's attention for half an hour, while he tossed both balls in the garden, prompting Pip to choose.

Meanwhile Lizzie, Winwood, and Ned decided about the marquess's treasures. Lizzie said, "A true restoration requires seizing it all. I'm sure Tamsin would agree."

"There must be a handcart in the gardener's shed," Winwood said. "And Perry's brothers strike me as quite a sturdy pair."

"The two boys can't drag all this to London in a handcart," Ned said.

"It must take our blessed Savior," Lizzie said, "to make the blind man see." Her voice rang in her own special way, to indicate how foolishly shortsighted he was.

"Ach, of course." Ned wasn't that thick headed. "I'll go to the World's End to buy supper for us. And pay the landlord to hold the Frake brothers' room for extra days."

"I'll ask Gabriel," Lizzie said, "for linen and lint batting to wrap anything that might break."

Later, returning hot from the walk of an August summer's evening, Ned carried their dinner wrapped up in a tablecloth, along with a stone bottle of wine. It was awkward work, since he kept forgetting to favor that bad finger, and so had to repeatedly shift the load. He found Lizzie in a chair near Jacob's portrait, likely because that was the room's best light, because she was again busy with her needle and damaged hem. She looked up when his shadow fell on her work.

"Thank you, Ned." She smiled, like she had when she made Aurora laugh at her imitation of stuffy lords. "If it weren't for this adventure, I'd have taken too long to see what's obvious."

"That we must seize everything as part of Aurora's restoration? But you saw that first."

"No. That you, dear brother, are more than a nice man with good hands." She pointed to the painting with her little gold embroidery clippers. "Beyond your magnificent talent, you have a good, kind soul and you aren't afraid to show it."

Perhaps it'd have been better if he'd been struck speechless, but Ned blurted, "That's what Uncle Absolom said to me."

She blinked, nodded, brushed at her eyes. "If only we'd had more time with him. If only I'd been with Uncle Absolom instead of the ten years I spent at court. Perhaps I'd have grown a better, kinder soul."

"You are adequately kind," Ned said.

But she'd led him into pondering Absolom and his own fate. Yes, he was about to enter the future he'd longed for, with his paint and brushes, with the unexpected addition of Perry coming to live at Revelstone. But that thought dislodged an unlooked for worry about what Perry meant when he promised his mother to take up the reins for his family. Instead of worrying, Ned closed his eyes, seeking to be united with Lizzie for a moment in grief and regret over losing Absolom.

Jacob dashed in through the garden door just then.

"Blue! Pip wants the blue ball."

37

Three Weaknesses

THE PENDULUM CLOCK IN the hallway struck at the same moment as the bells rang in nearby churches.

"Then we will perform your gambol within a day?" Tamsin asked, interrupting whatever intimidation Perry intended for Mr. Rosewurme.

"Unlike last week's restoration, we know which rotten and rich rover we must reave and ravage," Rowland said.

"And you will keep me safe from Withersea's revenge?" Rosewurme asked.

"That's what I've promised," Tom said, "if, for the sake of your many trespasses, you will act as I ask."

"Aye, s'welp me," Rosewurme said. "There is one more—"

Felicity and Michel emerged just then, trailing behind the men carrying the last loads from the cellar.

Michel said, "I left the font case, your lordship. You can use it to prove to the duke that you found the press he wanted."

In the middle of Rowland offering his appreciation, Felicity waved it off, seeking to interrupt, as she so often did. "*Pardonnez-moi, s'il vous plaît.* My brother Michel assured me that you will assist my business, to move the press to a new private space. And you will replace the letter case he insisted that we must leave."

"I didn't say that," Rowland began.

Felicity didn't answer to Rowland's denial. Instead, she turned her sweetness on Tamsin, which felt cloying. "I appreciate your help, Miss Foxe. I beg you to kiss the beautiful Miss Candecote for me, to share my thanks. You both have my lifelong gratitude."

"Think nothing of it." Tamsin felt mostly resentment and impatience just then.

Felicity then went to the kitchen and, in a heartbeat, the house was filled with the sound of glass shattering, followed by the ragged thunder of something larger smashing on a stone floor. Her voice rose. *"Je maudis le sol sous tes pieds."*

"My elixirs!" Rosewurme seized at his heart, wrenching at the rich fabric of his waistcoat. Perry had a hand on his shoulder, keeping Rosewurme in his chair.

"Une malédiction," Perry murmured. Of course Perry knew French; he'd lived in Paris for half a decade. "The glimflashy girl said, 'I curse the ground under your feet.'"

A moment after the house became quiet again, Felicity called, "Promise to remove that picaroon from my house."

"We shall," Perry called after her.

The kitchen door slammed shut.

Rosewurme rubbed his hands, then his face, glancing rather wildly about the room, not attending to anyone there. Tamsin bit at her lip, resisting the impulse to feel sorry for his distress.

"Now, Cornelius," Tom called him back to attention, "as part of our promise to protect you, can you make sure that the attacks on all of us cease?"

"I can do my best," the man said.

"What do we do, Tom?" Tamsin asked, "I mean, each task, at each turn of the clock tomorrow."

Tom said, "We'll meet in Westminster when the bells ring at nine o'clock. Perry will take a crew with him to guard the way to the Committee meeting, which begins at ten o'clock."

"I shall take Miss Thomasine with me," Perry said, "plus several lads I know from the London militia. After the Committee meeting, I shall lead my misfit army to defend Rowland against any threats."

"Will it be safe enough for Camilla to come too?" Tamsin said. "If she's well enough. I don't mean that this is just a lark. It's as serious as any of our roadside restorations."

"Not the best idea," Rowland said. "I mean to say, Perry, you should not include Tamsin and Camilla. But as for lads from the barracks, I heartily approve."

Tom said, "I don't want to see either Tamsin or Camilla in jeopardy for the sake of this gambol."

Tamsin crossed her arms, not bothering to hide her annoyance. "How can we be in danger, just observing from the public square in Westminster?"

"Tamsin and Camilla can serve as lookouts and will be quite safe," Perry said. "This will not be a sanguinary event."

"No blood?" Tamsin said. "That is good news."

"But you must swear to do exactly as I command."

"I thank you for allowing me to come. I do so swear." She solemnly touched the gold coin dangling from her neck.

Tom smiled brightly. "You can call your army the Knights of the Marborne Fens."

Perry said, "It distresses me that any of you might be called knights of any kind, however much you beg me."

Not appearing to attend to the exchange between Perry and Tamsin, Rowland asked, "Is the Earl of Marborne to walk into the Committee as a naïf, like a lamb to slaughter?"

"Crudely stated, but yes," Tom said. "You must perform as Lord Bagsham teaches you today."

Rowland twitched as if startled. "How do you know what the duke intends?"

Tom said, "I saw a note the duke sent Mr. Mordaunt. Also, Rollo, you must dress your very best tomorrow."

"Mayhap," Perry said, "Rollo will play a pudding-headed fellow. You perform that role so well, your lordship."

"Thank you," Rowland said. "I appreciate the notice of my manifest skills, Mr. Frake. Tom, what part do you play?"

"I shall travel with Mr. Mordaunt as his clerk. Correct me as needed, Cornelius." Tom turned to the Rosewurme fellow. "In the first business before the Committee, Mr. Mordaunt will ask you to read a document for Jacob Rôche. But you will read a new bond. The marquess is not his guardian."

"Is the new bond Ned's work?" Tamsin asked.

"Aye. He's fantastically talented," Perry murmured.

"Mr. Foxe...uh...Tom, are you not," Rosewurme asked, "merely maneuvering the apostles?"

"Robbing Peter to pay Paul?" Tom said. "Substituting one lie for another? The bond you'll read contains pure truths as opposed to Withersea's lies."

A slow, quiet smile crossed Rowland's face. "When Withersea complains, the Earl of Marborne will be indignant about his interruption of the day's business."

"What follows next?" Tamsin asked.

To Tamsin's mind, in relation to any of their earlier restorations, Tom's seemed as good as any. No truly unnatural acts. No costumes or playacting. She felt inordinately proud of him.

– TOM –

DURING ALL THE REVELATIONS with his cousins, Tom was still recovering from his sensation that he stood naked before them. Rowland, Tamsin, Perry, and Rosewurme all looked at him, each with eyes filled with expectation.

"The next order of the Committee's business," Tom said, "will be to approve the king's acknowledgment of the Marborne title. That is when...ah...assaults might occur."

"I shall not enjoy that," Rowland said.

"Except Perry will have seeded distractions." Tom had not finished his errands, but he had retained faith that some portions would function. "I too will have more disruptions."

"For example?" Rowland said. "Or wait, I can guess from what I've heard so far. Some lords on the Committee, those whose names appear in Mordaunt's papers, will have messages that warn them about the risk of business with Withersea."

"I am working through a set of lists," Tom said. "Aurora gave me a list of men who joined in Withersea's investment schemes. And I've made a list of names from Mordaunt's papers." He passed to Rowland the list of men who invested with Withersea as Hawkins' Heirs. He also passed a copy of a writ from Mordaunt's documents that transferred property to Lord Bagsham.

Rowland studied it. "This might be useful in convincing the Duke of Bagsham to work with us. Tom, here's a list of Committee members." He produced it from a pocket.

"Excellent," Tom said. "I shall explain my other diversions after I've searched for more information."

"We are taking so many risks," Tamsin said. "What if—"

Tom flinched, not liking the sensation when his sister repeated his private trepidations. But he still intended to win the coming battle by force of wit and will.

"You simply must trust me," Tom said, "to prepare sufficiently to distract the Committee from Withersea. I will tell you before the meeting begins exactly what I have prepared." He spread his arms, like the rector at the benediction. "At the end of the Committee meeting, considerable commotion will arise. It will be important for Rowland to take great care in departing the meeting hall, since we do not know what Withersea has planned."

"It will be my duty," Perry said, "to ensure that Rollo is never vulnerable to Mr. Rosewurme's knights of the blade."

"As I avowed," Rosewurme said, "those knights of the blade are not mine."

Rowland said, "My secretary Michel can be allowed into the Committee room. He can contribute to our safety."

"Do you know," Perry asked, "where Mr. Chêne went when he departed with his sister? Can you find him again?"

"I don't have to look," Rowland said, "because he turns up all the time, unasked."

"Fine. In advance of our gambol," Tom said, "I shall mollify Mr. Mordaunt, who will quickly see the virtue of working with me to restore those fraudulent estate transfers. I shall prey on all the unease he felt yesterday."

Tamsin said, "What will become of Lord Withersea?"

"My preference," Rowland said, "is that he's in the Tower with Danvers Duncombe by dinner time on Friday. I know I've decried James's over-eager desire to punish his enemies, but this enemy needs punishment."

"What the marquess will have at least," Tom said, "will be magistrates and militia captains pestering him to open doors for the king's men to search out whatever he has hidden."

"And Mr. Rosewurme?" Tamsin said.

"He will," Tom clapped his hand on the fellow's arm, "in all his wisdom, disappear from London."

"I do have plans to depart England," Rosewurme said. "Perhaps you can expedite my plans."

Tom nodded, though he was not prepared just then to explore such details. Tamsin's probing glare meant Tom had to resolve her feelings as well as his own about rewarding Rosewurme. He'd worry about it later.

"Three weak points in this plan distress me." Perry held up three fingers. "Through no fault of his own, Tom might fail to substitute Jacob's bond." He folded down his right forefinger.

Tom flushed. "But—"

Perry held up his other forefinger to hush Tom's objections. "If...that is, *when* a new guardian bond is presented for Jacob, the Committee might not accept it." He folded a second finger.

"I'm profoundly certain," Tom said, "that the new bond cannot be disputed."

Perry waggled that hushing finger again. "Some lords on the Committee might have joined in Withersea's syndicates and schemes, leaving them prejudiced against Rollo, instead of prone to encouragements that Tom creates." The third finger folded.

"If the Committee rejects the king's approval or accepts the marquess's claims, then Rollo won't be the earl."

"That's four weak points." Rowland raised a rude finger. "I have another. This gambol seeks justice. But it cannot earn Marborne even one farthing for undertaking this caper."

"We will have kept Marborne safe," Tamsin said.

"And Jacob will be free of Withersea," Perry said.

Tom, gratified to hear their instant answers, voiced his second goal. "I also hope to restore the swindled property to rightful heirs, wherever possible. After all, Absolom said it was my fate to serve justice."

"I think it's fair," Rowland said, "to want to earn more."

Tom stopped him. He asked Perry to go upstairs with Mr. Rosewurme to retrieve any personal articles that their new partner might want to carry away. "Perry, please ask him to write the history that you and I discussed."

"It will be my pleasure."

~

After Perry marched Rosewurme upstairs to pack his goods, Tom said, "Are you about to propose, Rollo, that we need a fee for reaping justice?"

"Consider what your Restoration Rules say. 'Reave when sins are ripe.' Let us relieve Withersea of his wealth."

"You mean, take more than what belongs to Jacob and the marchioness, and those who lost property?" Tamsin said.

"Yes." Rowland folded his hands while arguing. "All the courts and lords and lawyers have reaped wealth, taking emoluments and gratuities on every hand. If Tom returns property to those swindled, why can we not glean what remains? Especially if we end with Withersea in the Tower where he belongs."

"I haven't considered it," Tom said. "I confess, I don't know how to think about it now."

"Let me think about it," Rowland said. "You are a bit busy at the moment, juggling so many balls for the gambol."

Tom felt knots untying, in his neck, hands, around his ribs. "When we next rescue any unfortunates, you can lead, Rollo. It's really a bit of bother."

"What I was about to ask earlier, Tom," Tamsin said, "is why are you so resolved to repair the property frauds? You said at breakfast the other day that gratuities and emoluments are the grease that keeps business running in England. Have you changed your mind?"

"No. Except when it's personal." Tom hedged, unsure how Rowland would see it, since he'd been so adamant about refusing gratuities. "In the papers from Mordaunt's chambers, I found two cases from when I was a clerk in Cambridge. We failed to protect two widows who suffered great losses. After that failure, I invited them to take shelter in Marborne—"

"Barbara Hinxton and Hannah Barton?" Tamsin asked.

"Aye. Then our village burned, so I still haven't made those women safe. That spurred me to resolve all the cheats in which Mr. Mordaunt assisted, to pursue justice for innocents."

"Are we to punish Mr. Mordaunt along with Withersea?"

"No," Tom said. "It'd also punish Mordaunt's wife and children. How can I seize justice for certain innocents by condemning other innocents? After yesterday, he surely sees the value of backing away from Withersea. I shall coax Mr. Mordaunt into helping repair the damage from his misguided application of the law."

"Can I help?" Rowland asked.

"Perhaps. I'll need to find a judge who can issue warrants. For example, there's a portrait of Jacob's mother that Withersea sold without permission."

Rowland cited one judge's name, denying knowledge of any others in London.

"No, that man won't do," Tom said. "He's on the list of men who invested with Withersea."

"Hmm, I'd wager than I can put that list of Hawkins' Heirs to use," Rowland said.

Tamsin said, "Can you ask your duke to recommend judges that can be trusted?"

"I don't trust my duke," Rowland said. "And his deceased nephew, Viscount Bravewood, is one of Withersea's investors."

Perry released a few typical expletives. "Why does everything have to be so difficult?"

"Tom, it is difficult, and I admire your resolve," Tamsin said. "Absolom said you'd bring justice by serving the law."

He closed his eyes, letting joy flood over him: She agreed with his choice for the future.

"Tom," Rowland roused him, "did you seize this entire plan out of London's mucky blue skies?"

"The details," Tom said, "came to me with Rosewurme's papers, which Perry and I found this morning."

"You made your plan while standing right here?" Tamsin didn't show any surprise, which he should expect from her.

Rowland scratched at an eyebrow. "Perry is satisfied with that? He always complains when I make hasty plans."

"Did you take longer to tell the plan than to make it?" Tamsin asked but didn't wait for an answer. "But now, we shall work as a crew at oars together. No more secrets, like we promised each other last week."

"Tamsin," Tom prompted. "Tell Rowland your secret."

"Very well," Tamsin said. "Leighton sent a letter, threatening Camilla and Tom with assassination."

She carried the letter in her coat pocket (which, Tom noted, was in fact his coat). She handed it to Rowland, who read with his whole face screwed into deep concern.

Rowland shrugged it off, handed the letter back. "I struggle to believe that weaselly sot Leighton Fairchild has friends."

"Not competent ones," Tom said. "I pocketed the fee that Duxwold intended to pay those rogues. Two pounds sterling is enough to raise a feast when we finish our work tomorrow. We can invite Captain Starbuck and his militia men."

Tamsin changed the subject, which Tom guessed was because she didn't want to talk about Fairchild. "Now, Rowland, your secrets? You resigned as an intelligencer on Tuesday. But you came here in pursuit of dissidents."

Rowland succumbed to her piercing glance, the same way that Tom did whenever Tamsin put a sharp eye on him. "Lord Bagsham persuaded me to act as a king's watcher."

"How did he manage that?" Tamsin said.

Rowland took a breath. "He begged black tribute, to stop him from repeating words that might endanger Lizzie. I cannot say more."

"What? That Lizzie is a spy for Princess Mary?" Tamsin said. "We all know that."

"Yes, but…" Rowland, pale, tugged at his ear as if distressed. "That's why she went to visit friends in the country, to meet others who support Princess Mary."

"We can help with Lizzie's case," Tom said, "when we finish this gambol."

"Lizzie can help herself," Tamsin said, frowning.

"However," Rowland said, "can we agree that we've all kept secrets, but only to protect our friends and cousins? Which is a good thing for all of us. But I especially appreciate your efforts. Now, Tom, what about your secret?"

"I've been in bed since winter, Rollo. I don't have secrets."

"I saw Perry's eyes sparkle." Rowland shook his head. "Tell us about your inamorata from Trinity College."

He felt heat rise up his neck, because Tamsin stared so. "Oh, that. Perry is wrong. The marchioness and I are only friends."

"Truly?" Tamsin could read him like the New Testament, but Tom couldn't read what she felt in asking that question.

"I swear upon our best oath, as brothers in arms. This entire gambol comes from the need to protect Jacob and Rollo."

"That's too bad," Rowland said. "I mean, it's a blessing that you are Jacob's friend. It's too bad you don't have a lover."

"I…" Tom was confounded, seeking a way to reply to that well-intentioned sentiment. "Jacob's friendship is important to me. And I have all of you as friends. Which I am learning is most important in this world."

"In Perry's words, you console me," Rowland said. "I can only succeed as the confounded Earl of Marborne if we are all true partners. And I like the image of Ned and Perry nodding at the idea of privately helping you. But next time—"

"Next time?" Tamsin said. "Shall we continue a career of gambols and subterfuges like a band of pirates?"

Perry came in with Mr. Rosewurme, preserving Tom from speaking more feelings he was only beginning to understand.

"Perry, tell me again. That…everyone in Knightsbridge is safe?" Rowland sounded casual in asking, but Tom saw his chest rise and fall from a large breath.

"Aye, Lizzie is well and fine," Perry said. "Ned and Jacob and Aurora are safe, too. Withersea came to London and has no plans to return to his house in Knightsbridge until Friday night. We'll go fetch them back to London after Friday noon, as soon as that Committee names Rollo as the earl."

And, Tom intended, Jacob would be free from that monster when the Committee finished. His resolve hardened, determined to ensure that future.

"Are we done here?" Tamsin asked.

"If so, let's keep Mr. Rosewurme at my new house until tomorrow," Rowland said.

Perry said, "Tom, you should stop there tonight, also."

Tamsin said, "Yes, Tom. Go rest at Rollo's house before you find yourself back under Winwood's care. I shall return to our lodgings to see how Camilla is fairing."

Perry said, "Let's all be safe tonight, Miss Thomasine. You and I can gather Miss Candecote and go to Rollo's house."

Rowland said, "Take a chair to my house, Tom. Tell Lazarus at the door to expect me in a few moments. He'll give you a room for your rest."

"Aye," Tom said, not interested in sleep, since the morning's work left him in a particularly fine state. All Tom felt inside his ribs now was his gently beating heart. He wasn't alone in this restoration. He had his cousins and his friend Perry to help, though he still had tasks worthy of Hercules to complete that night. When he returned to Mordaunt's chambers, it would only be to wrestle with dust and bad quills.

"Rory hid your pens." "Cat ate your shoe."

Each time Tom had told the tale of Withersea's cruelties, people responded with shock, proclaiming the man to be a monster. Even Perry cringed. In fact, Perry showed the greatest animosity of all of them, because it was a man hurting another who had no defenses.

Tom had never met the marquess, but after the shock when he'd first heard about the cruelties, his meditations on the monster produced laughter in response to outrage. Just as well that Tom had never met the man because he'd certainly burst into laughter. Why choose to be a monster when one can rub along quite pleasantly without harming others? Take Jacob as the best example. Why plague the sweet fellow and cause him pain? Dear Jacob was affectionate and utterly devoid of mercurial humors. And incapable of doing evil to others.

He set out to finish the day's work for the sake of the Man in the Moon.

38
Black Tribute

ROWLAND HAD LONG KNOWN to put forth his best self when conversing with men he did not trust. He towed Mr. Rosewurme on that humid walk across Covent Garden to Xanthus House, clutching the foppish lace of the man's cuffs and practicing patience.

"I have no reason to flee, your lordship," Rosewurme said. "You offer more safety than I can find elsewhere."

"Odsme!" Was this the beginning of his new life? Would others, besides the Foxe kits and Perry, need him to take action? He'd made resolutions to right wrongs, to do what must be done for others, but he hadn't ventured to take on any act as immense as what Tom had committed himself to do. His own resolution presented a test of skills he wasn't yet sure of, to know what must be done for other people. Rowland took a breath to begin his first attempt. "Indeed, Mr. Rosewurme, pray tell me what you fear. Then I'll know how to protect you."

"It's only a crawling suspicion, creeping up my spine, my lord." Rosewurme, in his high-heeled shoes, was not a fast walker. "There's them I know what had a business connection with the marquess who are now gone from London with no word left behind. Just gone. From England, for all I can tell."

"Yet you took on the risk of working for the marquess."

"It came on gradual," Rosewurme said. "For years I did certain business for several lords." He named them, including the Duke of Bagsham. "Nothing that even a Puritan might call a sin, just helping to distribute news in the countryside, to encourage elections of, uh, compatible Members to the House. Such work fit right nice and tight with selling my elixirs at fairs, and so on. I did it well enough that one lord nodded at the idea of suggesting to King Charles that my service should be recognized. That I should be a Knight Bachelor."

"But that never came to be?" Rowland prompted him, while striving to ignore the scent of hawkers' pasty pies and fig tartlets at street crossings. No breakfast. Now, no luncheon.

"S'welp me, no." Rosewurme shook his big head. "About the time I felt I must give up hope, Mr. Mordaunt introduced me to Lord Withersea. Mordaunt's stable of lordly mentors and patrons had grown long in the tooth, leftovers from the heady days of Charles's restoration. The marquess had ambition. And Mr. Mordaunt, I believe, also longs to be called Sir John. And so together we entered into the marquess's mire."

"The politics of the peerage are complex."

"You and I know that to be true, your lordship. I understand that you and your family have also suffered the pangs of interminable denial, your ancestors' title unfairly withheld."

"It has been said."

Rowland's anodyne comment obscured his true response: No lord would ever help Rosewurme achieve his goal; but some might dangle that impossibility to draw him in. Rosewurme was a scrawny thing, but his counterpart in Shakespeare was John Falstaff, believing his fortunes would rise with Prince Harry's.

'Twas never to happen.

"Mr. Rosewurme, do you continue to hope for beneficences from the marquess?" Rowland asked.

"No, not at all." Rosewurme banged his hand on his thigh as he said it. "Not one dot. My hope is that I am not disappeared out of London for failing to do the man's bidding."

"We shall prevent that, sir." Rowland retained his hold on the man's lace cuff, as if a part of the promised safety. "We just have to make it through tomorrow's work, denouncing the marquess's many crimes."

"My fate is in your hands, your lordship."

"Ah, indeed." Rowland's worries increased, that Tom's plan lacked details, such as how to protect them all if any element failed. He'd to put his wits to work to deepen Tom's plan as soon as he had a meal.

They crossed an alley where the summer smells of carbonadoed meats floated on the heavy summer air. Beef. Rowland's hunger identified it precisely. Yet he squelched the pleas of his ravenous belly in hopes of finding food at Xanthus House. Except just then, the bells of a church rang, reminding Rowland that he was due in St James Place to meet Lord Bagsham in an hour.

Rosewurme began a recitation on the quality of the ale at The Lion's Head. Rowland interrupted.

"Tell me more of what you know about the marquess's enmity for me."

"I've met the marquess in person only a handful of times. I mostly ran packages for his henchmen and published pamphlets at his behest. He did send me to learn details about Marborne and a pair of other titles in abeyance." Rosewurme then broke off to praise the soup on offer at The Mitre.

For Rowland, the connection struck like lightning meeting between heaven and earth. "One moment, sir. I must ask you. Did the marquess know that Danvers Duncombe held the mortgage on Marborne lands, and that he wanted to offer the king a garnishment for the title?"

"Aye, my lord. When I brought the marquess that news, he spewed the devil's own wrath. He intended to take his offer to the king. But then you appeared. Hence, through your doings last week, he lost funds and the possibility of a title he wanted."

"He had you peddling anti-Catholic rags? Did you know that the king considers that to be treason? You are brave to undertake such work for him."

"It paid well. And until my lads began to take beatings from the militia, I believed it was only the marquess's hope that the French might not take advantage of the Catholic James."

"Here's my house." Rowland was grateful to have arrived, because the heat had left his coat and shirt damp again, and because he hoped to find food behind the door.

"Ah," Mr. Rosewurme said, "this is one of the houses I found for his grace, the Duke of Bagsham. This, and the house where Mr. Mordaunt resides."

The idea burst in Rowland's mind like a Spanish grenade.

A few years ago, he was assigned to train with English grenadiers for thirty days. His role was to stand in close quarters, trying to block the grenadier. If he'd been born with a better throwing arm, he'd have had a better role.

But Rowland was good at dodging, so surely he could figure what to do with Rosewurme's newest grenade. Best solution: toss that damnable grenade back in the duke's direction.

~

"Good afternoon, your lordship." Lazarus opened the door to Xanthus House before Rowland could knock. "The Duke of Bagsham awaits you. If you will forgive me, I took the liberty of placing him in the rose salon and provided refreshments."

That was the day's best luck, not having to cross the city to the duke's palace. The dim side of that luck, however, was that Rowland had no time to find whether the cook might feed him. And he could not face the duke as a tatterdemallion once again.

"Thank you, Lazarus. Please tell his grace that I will join him in a moment." Rowland then gestured to his companion. "This is Mr. Rosewurme, who is my guest for tonight. Can you please show him to the yellow chamber at the top of the house? And please give him luncheon. And coffee."

"I prefer a tisane," Rosewurme said. "Chamomile is best."

Leaving that business to Lazarus, Rowland took the stairs three at a time up to his bedchamber. He'd spent a decade living in a barracks and, hence, knew how to change clothes in a flash. He kicked off his shoes, threw aside his foul linen for the sake of fresh, snatched yet another of the former owner's austere suits, and tugged on his shoes again, all while entertaining the thought of donning clothes from the secret closet. That reminded him to fetch that crumpled black lace glove from the pocket where he'd carried it for the past day.

He emerged from his bedchamber, tucking Tom's papers into his coat cuffs, just as Lazarus led Rosewurme to the stairs.

"Lord Marborne, his grace the duke was kind enough to greet me." Rosewurme paused at the first tread. "As I said, he's an early mentor of mine. He heard my voice and called a halloo to me, surprised to see me here. It is gratifying to know that he has not forgotten me."

"He is often kind." Rowland rushed past, then stopped. "Lazarus, can you please entertain the duke's coterie in the dining hall while I meet with his grace?"

"I have set them in the blue salon," Lazarus said. "Please ring the bell if you need me."

"Thank you, Lazarus. I am grateful for all you do."

Was that correct? Do you tell servants you're grateful? Would Lazarus resent the familiarity? Was there a book of rules a lord must follow, perhaps in the library downstairs?

No matter now. He had to face the duke, who insisted on being his mentor while threatening Lizzie. A great lord whom Rowland could not classify as a true friend.

At the rose salon, Rowland stopped his run and pushed the door open, but with too strong a hand. The door banged into a chair, tipping it over, with only the carpet preventing a momentous crash.

"Your grace! Welcome!" Rowland bowed the way he'd been taught in Paris. He set the fallen chair to rights. Believing it proper to shake hands, Rowland extended his. The duke took it up into his small, damp hand.

"Good afternoon, Lord Marborne." Lord Bagsham pressed at his spectacles to examine Rowland. "I was passing through the neighborhood and thought to save you the trouble of traveling to St James Place."

"I am heartily glad that you did, your grace." He sat on a stiff chair opposite the duke. "I have good news for you. That roguish printing press has been captured."

Of all the possible words Rowland thought to hear from the duke, he did not expect to hear: "Ah. That must be why Cornelius Rosewurme came home with you."

Rowland retained control of what his face might reveal, as his first captain taught him. Then he lied as he'd learned under the same captain's tutelage. "We found Mr. Rosewurme by inquiry, when searching those who know the more prolific pamphleteers in London."

"He is that," the duke said.

Rowland could not interpret the color in the man's voice, so he pushed into the business directly. "Your grace, did you believe yesterday that Mr. Rosewurme was associated with that particular printing press?"

"He performed services for us while we were securing the restoration of the Crown, then again when we were advancing peace in the countryside. I should have surmised he might still have his finger in that pie."

"Had I but known, I might have begun my hunt on a more solid footing." Rowland kept all bitterness out of his voice. The duke wasn't likely to reveal why he had not shared information about London's pamphlet publishers. "No matter. I found the printing press, seized it in the name of the king, and commanded its safe removal."

"Your quick work astonishes me."

"Did not my former captains advise about my efficiency in most matters?"

"Indeed." The duke shifted in his seat, a hard expression on his face that Rowland couldn't read. "Did you find the dissidents who were using it? Are they in the hands of the king's men? Was Mr. Rosewurme among them? That would surprise me. He has always worked on the side of Stuart kings and Parliament."

"Mr. Rosewurme advised us. But we found it in the cellar of an empty house. It took four men to remove it."

"Then you brought it to your…ah…former colonel?"

"We tried. We loaded it onto a wherry to transport. Alas, the wherry upended." He and Michel had argued over this fiction enough that Rowland spoke with a solemn face. "That press is now rusting at the bottom of the Thames."

"What a wild tale for me to bring to the king." The duke spoke slowly. Rowland detected doubt—nay, suspicion.

"The king believed my tale last week," Rowland said. He pulled his hand fully into his wide coat sleeve and rolled his lucky gold angel over his knuckles. "Please tell the king that I am able to achieve magical results from thin air, even though you offered no insights to help my work."

Lord Bagsham shifted in his seat again. "I suppose, Marborne, you expect a gratuity for this service."

"Never, your grace. I am no friend of the English custom of emoluments for service rendered. I merely did my duty. I am happy to be rewarded with your friendship. Especially since you gave me a house as your sinecure."

Was he laying it too thick? How not to appear subservient when an earl stood two steps below a duke? As Rowland groped his way forward in this new world, he had to be sure the duke wouldn't rip the ground from under his feet.

The duke offered no answer to Rowland's mention of friendship. At that awkward point, Rowland spied the silver bell on a side table and did what Lazarus had instructed. The bell had only just rung when the man appeared.

"Lazarus, may we have a flagon of wine?"

"Will a light wine from Montilla be appropriate, my lord?"

"Yes, thank you." Rowland had no idea.

Lazarus bowed his way out of the room.

While waiting for the wine, Rowland said, "Your grace, I've given considerable thought about my loyalty to our king."

"Yes?" The duke tipped his head as if curious.

"My meditations rose from the peculiar circumstances in which I find myself." Rowland stood and paced. "We who possess villages and forests and farmlands, we owe care for people's safety and peace. If we are attacked from without, like the armada in Queen Bess's time, we owe them defense. If we are attacked from within—as happened with Guy Fawkes and Cromwell—then we must rise to defend the peace inside England."

"A fair encapsulation."

Lord Bagsham pushed at the bridge of his nose, again shoving up his spectacles and smearing the lenses. Rowland consigned the duke's odd habit to a diplomatic endeavor to pretend blindness. Hence, he stepped into a bold challenge.

"Then, your grace, please tell me what I must do for you to acknowledge that I carry in my bones a hardened loyalty to the Crown. As do all my family."

Lord Bagsham folded his small hands over his belly. "I shall take your sworn word."

"Ah, then you are the man I believe you to be," Rowland said. "Can we agree that henceforth, you will request my support in good faith, rather than using what the Scots call black tribute?"

At that moment, Lazarus returned with a tray bearing a crystal flagon and six shortbread biscuits, the sugar crystals on their tops glistening in the afternoon sunlight streaming through upper mullions of the tall windows.

The duke gratefully accepted a glass of pale wine from Lazarus, who then divided the biscuits onto tiny China porcelain plates. He set one on the table beside the duke. Rowland refused the wine and reached for his plate of biscuits, rejecting the childish notion that he might seize all of them to gnaw in the corner.

Lazarus said, "Anything else, your grace? My lord?"

Both Rowland and the duke demurred, and Lazarus departed. The duke said, "The king will be grateful to have a man of your talents among his watchers."

"My talents? I'm a friendly borachio, playing the tipsy pigeon while losing all the silver my captain invests in me. Or while listening to conversations in a tavern. Or in a barracks. Or at a fête for diplomats."

"You are modest. Which is itself a fine trait."

Rowland let a beat of silence remain before he pushed again. "Your grace, you know my lifelong loyalty. And of my family's loyalty. Please, no more blackmail."

The duke nibbled a biscuit delicately, speaking between bites. "A man with my responsibilities must retain every arrow in his quiver, to ensure he can do what he must."

"But will you acknowledge, sir, that I have never given you, or any of my captains, even one reason to doubt my loyalty?"

"You have seen the world, Marborne," the duke said. "Surely you understand I am constrained in how I must act."

"Yes, your grace. But from my life on the Continent, I learned that the fair-weather winds of loyalty blow both north and south. Yet I remain steady."

"That is what your captains have given me to understand."

"Duke, you chose to serve as my mentor. And I've sworn my loyalty. What will happen if, for example, my loyalty is impugned at the Committee's gathering tomorrow?"

The duke had finished one biscuit, his tiny wine glass in hand. "Ah...ah..." He coughed, then coughed again, harder. He set his glass on the table, but too hard, so that it tipped and splashed Rowland's coat before falling to the carpet. The duke still coughed, now clutching his throat, his face turning red, then as purple as the cuffs of his long coat.

"My grace. Forgive me."

Rowland grasped the duke's upper arms and hauled him to his feet, then circled him, holding the little round man with one arm while his other hand repeatedly struck hard between the man's shoulder blades.

Finally, the duke coughed successfully. Rowland quickly offered a linen napkin that Lazarus had left on the table. The duke coughed into it, then folded the napkin and set it aside.

"More wine, I think." Rowland poured two sips into the unused glass that Lazarus had left. "Please forgive my heavy hand. Should I withdraw while you collect yourself?"

"No, please sit, Marborne. I appreciate your effort."

The duke sipped in silence for several moments. "I believe you are a worthy and useful subject of the king, Marborne. It would take strong evidence to prove otherwise."

"What if I were accused by a man with a loftier title than mine, however thin the evidence? Would you grant credence to a man with greater status than mine?"

"Marborne, I have faith in my ability to act as my position requires." The duke sipped at his wine, eyeing the plate of biscuits but abstaining. "I shall always weigh facts and evidence, and I favor only true justice."

"Forgive my insolence, your grace, but I do not know that you can be trusted to take the side of justice. I possess enough evidence of your own corruption, that I cannot be sure your conscience will protect me."

The duke choked in the middle of sipping his wine, spewing it on Rowland's sleeve. Rowland again rose to assist him, but the duke waved him back.

"Are you threatening me, Marborne?"

"I am only offering information, your grace."

At last, they were coming to the heart of matters. Instead of the agitation of nerves he endured at their previous meetings, Rowland felt only a steely resolve in his belly, to do what must be done for Marborne and his cousins. He hoped he wasn't mistaking hunger for his sense of strength and determination.

"I have been made aware that the Marquess of Withersea, whom I have never met, holds special enmity for me that I hope you can help me address. It rises, I believe, from his belief that Samuel Foxe the Elder slighted him before King Charles."

The duke nodded, but didn't show other emotion, or even push up his spectacles.

"I know little of that," the duke said, "except decades past, Withersea asked me to join in a charge against Samuel Foxe, based on quite thin pretext. I was adamant that it was bad form to go against a man favored by the king without strong proof. Just weeks later, poor Samuel and all of them were dead of plague. I assumed the marquess forgot the slight."

"Not for a heartbeat. He sought this year to bribe the king for the Marborne title and now—"

"It's a garnishment, not a bribe. A king's prerogative."

"But now the marquess is stymied. The king has recognized an heir—the man who led the king to freeze all funds held in the investment bank managed by the traitor Danvers Duncombe. You can therefore see that I incarnate a barrier to the marquess's desire for both vengeance and the Marborne estates."

"You began your tale with concerns about what might occur tomorrow. What can Withersea do then?"

"I don't know." Rowland tucked away his angel coin lest he appear agitated. "But he told Mr. Mordaunt and Mr. Rosewurme that he intends something dire. I must be prepared."

"How will you prepare for the unknown?" The duke held his wine glass to the light. "More of your magic from thin air?"

"No, your grace. Rather, I have done as I did when searching for your printing press. Having no information at the beginning, I have looked for how to defend against an enemy who seems to be planning an unknown attack."

"Ah, the king's watcher goes forth."

"As you say. What I have to begin is the sworn testimonies of Mr. John Mordaunt and Mr. Cornelius Rosewurme that Withersea stated in front of them that he'd invested in Duncombe's syndic in support of the Duke of Monmouth."

Bagsham may believe he offered no reaction upon hearing the marquess had committed treason, but Rowland saw all: the triple blink of his eyes, a subtle tremble of the pale wine in his glass, one foot shuffling, as if the man needed better balance.

"Only two witnesses, Marborne? And one is Rosewurme?"

"I have a third in my pocket, as good as the barrister." But he didn't yet. "I am also seeking that lost page from Duncombe's ledger, the one you asked me about. I haven't found it yet. However, in my mind's eye, I see Withersea's name there."

The duke yawned, covering his mouth with the back of his tiny hand, which Rowland took as a counterfeit of nonchalance. "Didn't you begin by saying you needed me as an ally? If you find that last page, then you have no problem defending against any attack the marquess might make on you."

"But you see, duke, there's a complication." Rowland had Tom's list from his coat sleeve. "Viscount Bravewood's name is also on the lost ledger page. And his name and yours are on the list of investors in Withersea's African shipping business." He unfolded the list. "I mean the syndicate called Hawkins' Heirs."

Bagsham showed no emotion that Rowland could discern as he studied the list. He pushed his spectacles up his nose, then dangled the note, forcing Rowland to rise from his chair to receive it.

"Of course, Bravewood's name is on Withersea's list," the duke said. "He joined in Hawkins' Heirs simply to learn more about the men involved. I lent him my name as an introduction to the marquess. I shan't be surprised if Bravewood's name is also on Duncombe's list. You must know—"

"That your nephew was the king's watcher? I am not as naïve as you first judged me. But even if I were, it's plain from living in the man's house what he had been up to."

"You should, Lord Marborne, hope to do as well for the king as my nephew did."

"I am, duke, truly sorry for your loss. I also regret that what I said sounds like a threat." Having stepped into forbidden territory, Rowland couldn't find a trace of fear within. Because he knew what he held, and knew he'd found a right, true path. "However, if it should arise that I cannot count on you to deliver justice, then I also need every arrow in my own quiver."

"What do you mean to say, Marborne?"

From inside his other coat sleeve, Rowland removed the writ Tom gave him earlier at Chalgrove House. "You sent me to Mr. John Mordaunt, the barrister who is married to your ward, the Marchioness of Withersea's cousin. Despite his wife's efforts to convince Mordaunt otherwise, he has been working closely with Withersea." Again, the duke blinked three times, and Rowland counted that as a score. "You know that Cornelius Rosewurme often works as Mr. Mordaunt's agent."

"One must always remark on how Mr. Rosewurme's unusual name suits such a very peculiar man."

"My cousin Tom Foxe now clerks for Mr. Mordaunt. He encountered this deed." He handed over the writ, which transferred property outside Oxford to Lord Bagsham himself. He waited, finally munching his own biscuits, while the duke read. When the duke looked up from his reading, Rowland handed him a second paper, which Rosewurme had written under Perry's supervision.

"Mr. Rosewurme has sworn to this bond, as to how supposed heirs came to lose properties under rulings by clerks in chancery courts who owe their sinecures to—"

"To the Lord Chancellor," the duke said. "Who possessed scarcely a farthing when he married my sister. I perceive the nature of the arrow in your quiver."

"Mr. Rosewurme, who is helping the Foxe heirs with other matters, is willing to write out his bond again, omitting any names to which you might point."

Lord Bagsham sipped the last drop of his wine. "You will ask me to return this version, so that you might retain this writ in your quiver."

"We are enlightened gentlemen," Rowland said. "We are not like old-time Scottish chiefs demanding protection money from their neighbors. All I shall ask of you tomorrow is this, that you retain faith in my loyalty to the Crown. And will assert if need be that I am worthy of justice under English law."

The duke set down his wine glass. The two papers shook in his hand. He pushed up his spectacles.

"I see," Rowland spoke the word with exaggerated emphasis, "that you are not fond of my request. However, in good faith, I leave Mr. Rosewurme's bond in your possession. It is the sole fair-hand copy that includes your name."

"You prove to be more remarkable than I was given to understand, Marborne."

"Can you and I continue our business, without either of us resorting to black tribute?"

"Ah…" The duke faltered, but he wasn't choking this time.

"Your grace, I can swear a great oath, if you prefer. Perhaps the oath that I share with my cousins." Rowland rose from his chair, hand on his breast. "We have sworn on our ancestors' bones to be true to each other until either angels or demons take us from this green land. Would such an oath suit you?"

"I don't understand the currency of such oaths," the duke said, looking down at his empty glass, not meeting Rowland's gaze. "Does your service require emoluments? New titles? Deeds of land?"

"No." The question chilled Rowland, who'd mistakenly believed he was making progress with the duke. "It requires only that two men respect each other's honor."

"I don't know how to enter into such a dramatic oath," the duke said. "But I will promise to respect your honor."

"Thank you, sir. I ask no more than that."

"May I ask a different question?" Lord Bagsham said. "Did you truly find the dissidents' printing press?"

"Yes, your grace. Within three hours of your request."

"But I cannot see the press?"

"You can see the pamphlets we seized. And we have the printer's letter case, which shows we found the right press. But the press is at the bottom of the Thames. Upon my honor, you'll never see treasonous slander from that press again."

Rowland felt perfectly comfortable with prevaricating while swearing on his own honor.

The duke rose. "I must be on my way."

"I'm thankful, your grace, that you lingered here with me." Rowland reached out to shake the duke's hand. "And that you will forego any future threats to Miss Ysabel Foxe. And I hope you will help my cousin Tom's efforts to lead Mr. Mordaunt away from Withersea's influence and back to the path of righteousness." He dropped his voice and leaned closer. "Your ward Arabella can use your assistance in convincing her husband."

The duke blinked three times while pushing up his spectacles. He finally took Rowland's offered hand. "Marborne, you must come to dinner at my house on Friday evening." The duke's voice took on a lighter tone. "We'll celebrate the Committee's work. Bring Miss Foxe. Bring all your cousins."

"We are rather a crowd, duke."

"I have a large house and can provide a feast to celebrate the Committee's confirmation of your title."

Rowland walked the duke to the door. Lazarus must have signaled to the duke's retinue, because as soon as the duke stepped out of the salon, his men appeared to guide him into a waiting sedan chair.

The new Earl of Marborne waved from his doorstep, wishing he could boast to his cousins about his ability to prevaricate while pledging his honor. He'd convinced the duke that he had magical abilities to uncover information (using Tom's work to do it). He'd blackmailed the duke to ensure fair play and to protect Lizzie from unjust politics.

He still didn't know whether the duke was a trustworthy ally or yet another corrupt English lord seeking to take advantage of him. Likely, he couldn't resolve that question before the next day. Absolom had written to him about confronting corruption, and Rowland aimed to do what he remembered from that letter:

> When all around you seems pure corruption and beyond any use in the universe, you will withstand it by way of your wit and wiles, loyalty, and (I hope) kindness.

39

St James Square

— T O M —

WHEN HE WAS OUT of sight of the others, Tom gave the chair-bearers new directions, asking them to stop on Portugal Street.

The clerk from Tuesday morning remembered him (a return on Tom's overly generous gratuity) and helped Tom into the red linen suit he'd spied on his previous visit. He added a lace cravat atop his own shirt and had barely finished tying it when the boy he'd sent to the nearest barber appeared with a wig that answered to Tom's request for "French style at two guineas."

"Do I look like I belong in St James Square?" Tom asked the clerk when he laid out coin for his outfit, which included ridiculously heeled shoes that wouldn't last one day at Revelstone House, plus a soft leather satchel such as the finest London business men might carry.

"You've chosen as well as Lord S— did for himself, sir. Though the grand old gentleman perished before he got even a day's wear out of that suit."

"That lord's suit came to your shop because…why?"

"Lord S— didn't leave his nephew a feather with which to fly, as often happens."

Tom left another gratuity after the clerk lent a quill and ink, with fine paper to write the note Tom needed, and another coin for a lad to carry his old suit and shoes to Rowland's house.

In the sedan chair on the way to his next visit, Tom wrestled with the mechanics and morality of what he intended to do. Withersea had committed crimes against individuals and English society—against the throne of England, for that matter. Yet to achieve what justice demanded was complicated. He lacked proof that Withersea had paid to dispose of Jacob's father, brothers, and guardian. It would take months to prove in the chancery that Withersea had cheated heirs out of their lands.

Tom had few provable facts in hand and an immense challenge in placing evidence where justice could find it. His slim collection of proofs?

The Lely sketch, which the marquess had sold without its owner's permission. That proved thievery of a valuable object and then fraud against the art agent. (But could Tom obtain a warrant in a timely way? Was it a dire enough crime to impinge on the freedom of a lofty peer of the realm?)

The pamphlets in the Chalgrove House cellar, for which Withersea paid to publish and distribute. (But could Tom prove they belonged to the marquess—and therefore obtain a warrant?)

The names from the marquess's journals of favors owed and favors due. (Ned had scratched the list in haste, without enough details to determine who in England could be persuaded to testify against a corrupt lord.)

The details in Rosewurme's black tribute papers. (Could Tom find any that'd lead a judge to issue a warrant?)

Besides needing time to find and recruit a judge, Tom needed to act on other kinds of truth that could be put to use. He had to provoke Withersea to show his character.

A love of costly artifacts. (Ned supplied that insight and a tangible enticement.)

An outrage that his funds had been frozen upon Danvers Duncombe's arrest.

An irrational hatred of Rowland Foxe as the intelligencer who'd arrested Duncombe and as a stand-in for Samuel Foxe, the source of an imaginary snub years ago.

A strong desire for King James to be gone from England.

Any exchanges with the Duke of Bagsham, who'd intruded into Rowland's business (and whose name appeared on Ned's list of men owing Withersea favors).

Emerging resolute from the sedan chair, Tom paid the chair-bearers, then adjusted his cravat and over-stated wig. He knocked on an oak door thickly coated with a dauntingly deep black color that Ned called Mortal Sin when he used it in his art.

"Good afternoon. I am Leighton Fairchild." He stole a name from his sister's enemy. "I was sent to discuss sensitive business matters with his lordship."

Tom offered the footman the letter of introduction he'd just written on the shop table in Portugal Street, stamping the wax wafer with the pawned signet ring of Lord S——, whoever that deceased worthy might be. Such a trifling forgery did not morally complicate Tom's sincere mission.

"If his lordship is not immediately available, please help me understand when I might call again."

"His lordship has been out, but I shall see if he has returned."

Tom was invited into the cool foyer and left there while the footman tapped up the wide wooden staircase at a measured pace, seeking whether his master was available.

~

"'If only the gods are willing.'"

Tom repeated a single line in Greek, one of the few he still remembered. But his wait was quickly over. His lordship had just come in from riding and was at home to hear sensitive business. A voice thundered from the top of the first flight of stairs.

"Lord S—— was an utter wastrel. World is better without him. Whyever did that beetle-head send anyone to me?"

While a giddy bubble formed behind his breastbone, Tom presented his warmest affability as he entered the salon. The lord sipped wine with a woman dressed in a gown of sea-water blue.

"My lord, thank you for seeing me."

While Tom bowed, the woman was shooed away with a flick of the man's wrist. Tom faced the monster he'd sworn to destroy.

Who was merely a man. A man who was too large to be battering Jacob and too old to be in a marriage with Aurora.

Perhaps five years ago the marquess had been handsome, but now, bitter lines etched across his forehead, and sun and wine had roughened his face. Though Tom stood a distance away, he could smell horse and leather and sweat on the man, with rose water splashed over.

"Lord S— is dead as a dog," Withersea said, without offering a greeting. "How did you persuade a dead man to write an introduction for you?"

"He wrote it some weeks ago, your lordship, saying you might find me useful. But I've only just returned to London on a task for him and, alas, too late." Tom shrugged and shook his head; wiping away a tear would be too much, since Withersea didn't care a fig for Lord S—.

"What did you do for the old reprobate?"

"He sent me to fetch treasures he'd left behind when he was…ah…called home from Paris. Mostly paintings." Tom applied his recently won knowledge about that lord's poverty. "His nephew was happy to take the cache of art from me, since Lord S— died in straitened circumstances. However, he didn't pay half of what that lord promised me."

"Bad luck for you. Why come to me?" Withersea tipped his wine cup, checked it, then poured more from a crystal decanter.

"I believe Lord S— intended to approach you with a proposition to convert some of his Paris art to guineas." Tom smiled, making his face incarnate innocent joy. "I can introduce you to the nephew, along with other business I'd like to propose to you."

"Bit of a buzzard, aren't you, lad?" Withersea bared his teeth, as if he were a predator about to nick a sheep.

"Sir? No one I've served would ever say I'm easily called way from my promised service."

"But I can go find that man's nephew myself, without your aid. There is no service you can do for me."

"Ah." Tom bit at his lip, pretending to ponder this point. Then smiled again. "But you see, my lord, I still hold the provenance for that lord's paintings. And will keep it until the nephew pays what his uncle promised. For the services I offer gentlemen, it's wise to have assurances to fall back on. That's the nature of my business today."

Withersea barked a single rueful laugh. "So, you want to talk business. Yet I don't know any Fairchild. Who are your people?"

"My mother died at my birth. I lost my father when I was ten. He'd remarried, and that woman's family took me in. Her brother, my adopted uncle, has been kind enough to employ me, to teach me skills that men need to support their business."

"So, a mongrel, then?" Withersea wasn't interested in his guest and was only toying with him for whatever humor he might find. "Why would S— send me a mongrel and then die?"

"My lord, I help men find things they desire, especially art and things of beauty. That's why Lord S— sought to introduce me to your lordship."

The marquess lifted his brows; Tom had gained his attention. "Interesting work for an orphan. How did you come to it?"

"That uncle is Danvers Duncombe. He lent my services to Lord S—. And now, of course, I will need new employment."

Withersea's face grew as dark as his oak front door. "The king's men took custody of everyone and everything in Duncombe's chambers last week. All of Duncombe's clerks and agents are guests of the king's militia." He leaned forward, menacing. "Why did that wastrel S— send me a liar?"

At the man's modest threat, Tom didn't step back. "No one knows he's my uncle, except my stepmother, who has fled to Barbados, or one of those New World places. I serve him in the shadows, which is the kind of service I can offer you."

"How can *you*," the marquess studied Tom's forged letter of introduction, "Mr. Leighton Fairchild, serve *me*?"

"My uncle will be eager to...how shall I express it?" Tom drew it out, seeing how easy it was to make the man impatient. "He seeks to maintain the strong ties he has enjoyed with you, while his attorneys work through the misunderstandings with the king's militia."

"To my knowledge, sir," Withersea was darker than Mortal Sin now, "our business constituted a few investments in syndics. And it will take me a year to persuade the king to release my money, which Duncombe held only as a banker."

"Aye, sir. The syndics of Hawkins' Heirs." He watched Withersea straighten at that mention, his black tide subsiding. "I have come here to offer you specific assurances."

"How will you assure me?" Withersea flicked his wrist in dismissal again. "No, wait, Mr. Fairchild. Tell me first *why* I need such assurance."

Tom prevaricated with gusto. "I can promise that your name will never be spoken in association with Mr. Duncombe, however much the king's men might pressure him or any who served him, such as myself."

"What are you saying?" Withersea's color was rising again, the spidery veins across his nose and cheeks flushing his face purple-red beneath his sunburn.

"My lord," Tom threw up his palms, still pretending innocence, "you know Mr. Duncombe and the way he does business. His first question, and mine, would be: how much is his silence about your business worth? Three hundred guineas? Five hundred guineas? My uncle needs money."

Hot as fire, Withersea was on his feet, towering over Tom, breathing wine fumes in Tom's face, reeking of horse and sun-heated sweat. "Black tribute? You dare it, you clodpated dandy-prat? You are as rotten and worthless as your uncle."

Tom stepped back, crossed his arms as if to protect himself. The man's looming size and sudden heat, fists clenched at his side, promised more danger than Tom had prepared for.

"My lord! I see I've done a bad job of it. Please, forgive me."

Tom's simpering words and cowering posture mollified the marquess. The man again sunk into his chair. For Jacob's sake, Tom hated the man and again resolved to destroy him.

"Why should I care if any London merchant in the Tower or his sneaking clerk speaks my name?" The marquess sneered, then ranted. "Shouldn't you be begging that I won't speak your name? It'd do me well with the king if I reported what I know about Danvers Duncombe. And if the militia don't know that you work for the man, I'd best tell them."

"Please, sir, no. I only present for my uncle." Tom folded his hands and dropped his voice, imitating how his sister presented earnest innocence. "I am no fool, sir. Nothing my uncle or I can say would hold sway with the king in the face of a marquess."

Withersea sat back, folding his arms, ready to be appeased. "I will not pay any man black tribute for silence."

"Of course not, your lordship. I am deeply unhappy that you perceived my offer as such."

"I think rather," the marquess said, "that you should consider what I am owed, to stop me from speaking a word of the Duncombe business to the king."

"My lord? Oh dear." Tom let his mouth fall open in dismay and surprise. "Owed?"

"Come, come." Withersea wagged a scolding finger. "Duncombe didn't have all his worth within his business chambers. He had a couple of houses in the countryside. Has the king found those yet? Did the man bury any of his gold?"

"No." Tom summoned his best feigned empty-headedness. "What are you suggesting?"

Puffed-up smugness replaced anger on the marquess's face. "Let us do as did kings of old who wanted peace. Offer me a hostage to hold, as assurance of your enduring silence."

"Hostage?" Tom played thick headed, while still smothering the anger and fear that surged through his entire body when the marquess lunged at him. "Weren't such hostages usually princes? We have no young sons in any part of the family to send you."

"I truly have no desire to take possession of your brats. It is," it took the marquess a heartbeat to find the word, "a metaphor."

"Ah, ha ha. I appreciate your brilliant wit, my lord. With most of my uncle's assets seized by the king, I can offer little as a surety." Tom did his best to appear to wrack his brain, while seeing that he'd irritated the marquess enough that it was time to pacify him. He reached into his satchel. "I could place these 'hostages' in your care."

Tom passed what he'd retrieved from Ned's baggage early that morning, the list of paintings consigned for sale by Duncombe in last week's gambol. Withersea read the list in silence, his eyes showing hunger. But Tom couldn't afford silence. He'd baited the bear long enough and began to prevaricate freely.

"This portion of my uncle's wealth is under my protection. I intended to sell it, but perhaps it's better to let you hold his...ah, hostages until his difficulty with the king is resolved. He said you admired the one from Rembrandt's workshop, which he hung high on the wall in his business chambers."

Withersea licked his lips, rather like a lizard pondering a fly. His eyes bored into Tom's. "When shall I take these hostages into my protection? And will you provide provenance?"

"Yes, I, uh, see that it would be safer if you also held the works' provenances." Tom resolved to hold his tongue lest he grow giddy. "The 'hostages' can be delivered tomorrow morning. Simon Touchstone is preserving them for my uncle. Do you know Mr. Touchstone, who has a warehouse on Threadneedle Street?"

"Yes, yes." Withersea seemed thoughtful, his eyes fixed over Tom's shoulder. "I'm engaged tomorrow morning. I shall arrange for my staff to receive your...ah, hostages. Can your...What relation did you say Duncombe is to you?"

"My uncle by marriage."

"Can he provide a sworn testament of what this arrangement signifies? In a discreet way."

"I believe I can deliver it with the collection."

"Fine." Withersea rose. "A servant will show you out."

"Thank you, my lord."

Withersea was gone when the escorting servant appeared. Tom begged for a drink of water, it being another beastly August day. The footman paused, then agreed to take Tom to the kitchen, while Tom repeated "thank you" an obsequious number of times.

When the blackened oak door closed behind Tom, only thirty minutes had passed since the door first opened. He'd never in his life accomplished so much—or risked so much—in a mere half an hour. Now he had to find allies to purvey the "hostages" to Withersea's London house come morning.

Around a corner and down two more streets, Tom ripped off the two-guinea French wig and stuffed it in his satchel. He turned his new coat inside out, wearing the buff taffeta outward.

Quod infortunii! He'd failed to find out what Withersea intended to do with Rowland. Ah well, he couldn't go back now to ask. Just like the original, this false Leighton Fairchild would never again be seen in England or on the Continent. Or heard to utter his irritatingly cheery lies and assurances.

~

Tom sauntered down the street, though after he'd turned two corners, he had to stop and lean against a railing while he laughed, covering his mouth so he'd look like any ordinary man in London, choking on the hot fetid air. He had to laugh, though nothing was funny, because he needed to choke out the ball of fear in his gut. He'd stood inches from pure evil, telling lies to a man whose inclination was to bat Tom aside like an annoying animal.

And yet. Tom had achieved great things, using only the pretext of the note Perry had carried from Ned, which had launched his early-morning raid on Ned's baggage at Benson's lodging house, then a jaunt to Threadneedle Street to deliver two messages from Ned to Mr. Touchstone. The most important of these messages was that the Lely sketch in Touchstone's warehouse had been stolen from the Earl of Cloudesley, who was seeking a judge to issue a warrant for its recovery.

The second message did not alarm Touchstone the way the first message did, only asking that certain paintings Ned had lodged with Touchstone not be offered for sale, but instead returned to Tom's care if he asked for them.

While Tom had been searching Cornelius's house with Perry (yes, without a warrant, and therefore, yes, risking his future as a barrister), he'd plotted what to do with Ned's information, trading one idea for another a half-dozen times. Every possible use of the information ("W is wild about collecting artifacts and has one of my Rembrandt's Workshop devil-drawn canvases") seemed like it'd take days or weeks or months to act on. Tom had one day. And not enough time to enlist those Foxes who could best assist him. At least he'd had time during that meeting at Chalgrove House to rest his body, since he'd done a week's work since dawn.

When Tom leaned, laughing, on the railing around the corner from Withersea's house, it gave him another moment to gather his strength and his wit. He needed a meal and a sedan chair to go to Mordaunt's chambers, where he could rest his bones while his fingers managed the next tasks. He laid out pennies for bread and cheese at a tavern, then consumed it while a sedan chair carried him to Lincoln's Inn. To think, a month ago, either Tamsin or Mrs. Bell supervised every meal, catching his crumbs.

He had a wagonload of tasks for the late afternoon. People to find. Papers to create. Messages to send. He popped a peppermint from his pocket into his mouth, wiped his hands on the chair's upholstery, and emerged from the stifling air of the enclosed chair a few steps away from the Inn's gated entry.

"Hoy!" A cry rang from two streets up.

Three rogues pounded down the street in Tom's direction. Their shouting seemed silly for picaroons intending to attack a man on an open street. One, a scarecrow, had a face plagued with pestilence. Another, a bandy-legged fellow, had a shock of red hair. A third bigger man, with a jutting iron jaw below a broken nose and a narrow forehead, did the yelling.

Then Tom heard what they shouted.

"Stop! Thief!"

Tom took off running, still in treacherously high heels. The street around the walls of Lincoln's Inn were nearly deserted since it was the dinner hour. Not seeing anyone to beseech for protection, he ran up a narrow alley, circled around, and came down behind where the men had been. A carriage stood there. When Tom ducked around into the shade of the carriage, hoping to hide in its shadows, a tall man standing beside its open door lifted Tom as if he were a child and thrust him inside, slamming the carriage door behind him.

"Stay down!" A soft feminine voice spoke.

He was face-down on the floor, buried in wide brocade skirts, and heaving to catch his breath from the exertion. Tom's too-sensitive nose detected a bouquet of scents that he'd learned while ill. Chamomile and mint in tonics. Angelica and hyssop to purify his blood.

"Don't look up yet. Oh dear. They are peeking in carriages. John! A diversion, please!" She had Tom up, but covered in her skirts and thick brown locks and a feathered hat.

"Aurora!"

"Shh!" She murmured. "They've been loitering here as long as I have. Who'd guess they waited for the same man I did?"

She had her arms around him, her body covering his, so he couldn't see out the carriage window. They lay together like that for several sweltering minutes, listening while her driver argued that the rogues best be gone about their business. She turned her head, smiled at him, so close their noses touched.

Was she going to kiss him again?

She'd think it childish that peppermint coated his tongue.

She'd find him a poor, thin creature who trembled.

Just like at Trinity, she murmured in Greek.

But it had been ten years since the master's tutorials, so he couldn't interpret a word. It didn't tell him what she wanted. She embraced him, and he didn't know how to respond.

"It's safe, my lady," her driver called. "Let me escort you."

They untangled and awkwardly exited the carriage. Or he was awkward. Her driver helped Aurora down gracefully, then walked behind them into Mr. Mordaunt's chambers.

Elisha was leaving as they entered, pausing to say farewell. The coachman remained outside the door when Tom closed it.

"Zeus Apemios!" Aurora exclaimed. She grasped his forearms, more in the way fellows embraced than like lovers.

"What?" Tom stepped back. She dropped her hands.

"I called on Zeus as the divine healer. Your bones are barely covered by flesh. Are you ill?"

"Not anymore."

"Why didn't I see it on Tuesday? Too full of my own woes?"

"I'd prefer that you not notice," he said. "May I offer you refreshment? Sherry, perhaps?" He'd spied Mordaunt's sherry and port bottles the first time he'd scouted the chambers.

"Water, please. I'm so relieved to have found you, Tom. I've been searching since breakfast."

"Why are you here? Where's Jacob?" His voice echoed as he went to the back room to fetch water from the stone cistern. He found two cups nearby.

She said, "Jacob is with Ned and Lizzie. Did you know your cousin is staying with us? Of course, you did. Perry told you."

"He brought all you found. Plus, Jacob's guardian bond."

"We found more for you. And Lizzie sent letters for your cousin Rowland." She sipped delicately at her cup of water.

Tom found that he'd guzzled his water. He poured another cupful, certain that Winwood and Tamsin would soon ambush him over the wreck he had made that day of all their hard work healing him. Yet, he didn't feel wrecked. Only breathless.

"I shall give it all to you. I'm so happy to have found you. I didn't want to leave them at your lodgings because things might have gone astray." She set down her cup. "But first I am compelled to speak to you. Of love. And heroic rescues."

40

Yearning for Home

⧽⧼⧽⧼⧽

TAMSIN AND PERRY WALKED to the lodging house to bring Camilla to the safety of Xanthus House. At one turning, Tamsin stepped out of the burning sun into the shade near a well-tended stable. Her heart thumped as she inhaled the smell of horse and donkey and clean straw. An orange cat leapt down from the loft and curled around her ankles. Perry scooped it up, burying his face in the purring cat's fur.

"Good stars, I wish we were home." Homesickness gripped Tamsin like an ague.

"Aye, Miss Thomasine. I do recollect that you have mighty fine cats in your great barn."

She flicked her eyes at him, to be sure he wasn't teasing. He noticed. "I shall never choose to distress you, Miss Thomasine. I too am eager to embark on new adventures at Marborne. As soon as we finish Tom's gambol and fetch Ned home."

"Tom's gambol," she repeated.

"The notion rumbles my belly," Perry said, "but then, I had six breakfasts yesterday and none today. Rollo had best make good on his promise to feed us."

"Do you remember when I said on Tuesday, that I only want to go home?" Feelings spawned at the morning conference roiled inside her. "I thought all we had to do before going home was to finish Camilla's business and wait for Rowland's meeting with the lords who'll confirm his title." She rubbed at her hands, seeing they were still bruised from that mêlée outside the theatre.

"We must sit on cold needles, awaiting others."

Tamsin said, "For your virtues, you were recruited to help Tom. For my sins, I talked myself into helping Felicity Oakes, simply because it plagues me to be idle, with nothing to do."

Perry said, "Mayhap the Divine Creator will next assign you a better mission than taking care of all the Foxe kits and their mates, who can't always see their own way."

"We have a mission now, don't we? Thanks to Tom, we'll have a few busy days doing worthwhile work."

When they reached the boarding house, they found that Camilla was asleep. Tamsin insisted on not waking her, so it was after three o'clock when Camilla roused, avowing that her fever was gone. While Perry left instructions to send their baggage to Rowland's house, Tamsin helped Camilla dress, but they weren't on their way until after the local churches struck four o'clock. Camilla begged to walk rather than take a sedan chair.

When they set out to cross Covent Garden once more, Camilla tucked one hand in the crook of Perry's elbow and the other in Tamsin's. Whenever they had to part to allow others to pass, Camilla clung to Tamsin, who found it gratifying to be her friend's choice. Perry's presence gave Tamsin a sense of safety, yet Tamsin still looked over her shoulder, it having become a habit.

Along the way, Tamsin related the morning's events, how it had proved that Felicity most wanted to retrieve a printing press, wanting to continue intrigues that her baroness aunt had fostered for decades.

Camilla listened, her head tilted with interest. "Do I understand? Mr. Rosewurme tried to steal Felicity's house from her. Thanks to Perry, she gets the house, but what she most wanted is a printing press in the cellar, which Rollo claims was used to print traitorous papers. Tom has a new gambol, and he's put Mr. Rosewurme to work rather than punishing that malefactor."

"That sums our entire morning," Tamsin said. "Though it seemed more dramatic when we lived through it. I still wish Mr. Rosewurme to perdition. And I wish—"

A ragged youth shouted after them. "Hoy, here now! Doctor Roseworld's Elixir for the Heart shall heal you. Half a shilling!"

This was one of the lads who labored under Cornelius Rosewurme's many swindles. Yet Perry fished in his pockets for coins while the lad proclaimed, "Every penny of your purchase, sir, goes to Dr. Roseworld's work to bring the Good News to the New World. He has blessed this miraculous potion in the name of Our Father, just as the archbishop commands him."

Tamsin wanted to caution Perry. Had he not heard from Mr. Rosewurme about the many rigs he ran with his elixirs? Yet Perry counted the coins the young peddler wanted and engaged him in banter. Tamsin stepped away, dragging Camilla with her, not wanting to associate with any of Rosewurme's minions.

But then, a big-faced man appeared at Tamsin's elbow. Felicity's Monsieur Pear Head. Behind him was that carbuncled scarecrow and the carrot-pated manchild, looking more scared than menacing, with two more rogues behind them, each with neckcloths pulled half over their faces, their eyes hidden by slouch hats.

The rogues of Tuesday night weren't just Felicity's stalkers. They must also be Leighton's assassins! Tamsin thrust Camilla behind her.

Monsieur Pear Head reached around to tap Camilla's arm with a cudgel. Tamsin grabbed the swordstick from under her coat and swung it, still in its case, down on Pear Head's arm with a resounding thwack. The cudgel fell from his hands, and he cursed Tamsin with worse words than she'd ever heard. She swung to strike again as Camilla shrieked, "Help! Murder!"

When Perry elbowed carrot-head to get past him, the hawker lad snatched Perry's coins from his hand.

"Militiamen!" One of the hawker lads shouted.

The cry echoed down the street. "Militiamen!"

Another hawker shoved a sheaf of papers into Perry's hands, and the two disappeared in a grand dodge-and-dash through the crowd. The rogues also ran, abandoning their prey. Tamsin tucked her swordstick back under her coat and rubbed her palms on her sleeves, since they'd dampened from heat and fear. She hugged Camilla close to her.

Six militiamen in red coats rounded the corner, talking with each other. But at the sight of the fleeing and ragged hawkers, half their number shoved through the crowd in pursuit. The other three closed in on Tamsin and her two friends.

Tamsin's first, ridiculous thought: They've come to hang us as highwaymen. And this time, she couldn't blame Rowland for calling the king's men down on her. What she didn't expect was the sergeant's question.

"Hoy there! Be you them what was just at The Rose over on Russell Street?"

Perry said, "Not since Tuesday. Is there a problem, sergeant? I assure you we paid for our ale that night."

"Lads, the king has listeners everywhere. And those who watch The Rose say that tavern harbors anti-Catholic rebels. Were you meeting friends there?"

"We were stopping for a half-measure of ale," Perry said. "Would that I had a full measure now."

Another militiaman stepped close to Perry, holding his hand out for the pamphlets the hawker had thrust upon him.

"See, now," the sergeant said, "this is just the problem the king worries about. Them that cannot just live peacefully."

"Not mine," Perry said. "A lad pushed them on me."

The militiaman dropped the pamphlets in the street, pointed to his comrade, and together they grabbed Perry's arms. One prepared to tug off his coat, apparently thinking to search him.

Perry, that damnable man, seemed amused. He folded his arms, dragging the two militiamen half off their feet.

"We are loyal to the king. I'd like to step out of the hot sun and drink to his health," Perry said.

Behind Tamsin, the pursuing militiamen had returned. But she dared not look away from their sergeant, thoroughly distracted by the vision of the gallows' shadow the king's militiamen conjured whenever they appeared.

"Leave them!" A voice commanded. "You can see they are lost country folk with no more idea of rebellion than puppies."

For the second time that day, a man identified her with puppies. However, it was Captain Starbuck, whom she'd met the previous week. He'd helped Rowland arrest Danvers Duncombe. Perry reached out a hand in greeting, sweeping past the red-coated fellows who'd grabbed him.

"Captain Starbuck! It's a pleasure to see you, sir."

"Ah, Mr. Frake, a pleasure! And you too...uh, Miss Foxe." Starbuck had met her at Revelstone House when she'd been dressed as her brother Tom. He hadn't blinked an eye then, and he greeted her warmly now.

"Good afternoon, captain." How rapidly could every moment change on this day? "This is our companion and neighbor, Miss Candecote. What a coincidence to see you here in London."

"Yet it isn't at all," Starbuck said. "I am in search of Rowland Foxe, since this is the last night we can address him as Lieutenant Foxe, and he owes us a night of brandy and feasting. You are all at Mr. Benson's lodging house, I think?"

"We have been," Tamsin said. "But Rollo is staying at a house a few streets over."

"You should meet us there," Perry said.

"So that you and Rollo can rob me of a pocketful of gold louis at cards?" Starbuck twitched a smile.

"If that's what you'd choose for the evening," Perry said. "Mayhap, Rollo will want to discuss some business with you. Of a military nature."

"You've made me curious," Starbuck said. "My men are just ending their day's duty. We can come directly."

Starbuck received directions from Perry and promised to see them at Rowland's house.

Then Camilla begged to stop at a milliner's, describing her need for ribbons and pocket kerchiefs as urgent.

"Come along," Perry called when Camilla finished her purchases. "I'm gutfoundered, and Rollo promised us a supper."

Because Camilla couldn't walk rapidly, it was several minutes later when Perry pointed ahead of them. "His house is just here."

"Crivens!" Camilla exclaimed, a cruder oath than she usually uttered. "Wish I had a nice house in London like this."

That notion startled Tamsin. Before she could ask what Camilla meant, the door to Rowland's new house opened. The sound of carousing noises drifted down the hall.

Perry said "Ah, Starbuck's militia arrived, as he promised."

~

A slim, somber man had answered the door before Perry could lift the brass knocker. Perry nodded to the fellow, who took his hat and motioned them inside.

"I'm called Lazarus," the butler said after Perry had introduced all of them. "Lord Marborne asked that we do whatever we can for your comfort. Or perhaps you'd prefer to join the gentlemen's party?"

Perry accepted the latter suggestion and mounted the stairs, pursuing the cries of men's voices.

"Thank you for the invitation," Tamsin said, "but what we need most is a peaceful restorative."

Lazarus led Tamsin and Camilla to a bedchamber painted the delicate blue of a starling's egg, its chairs and benches covered in matching silk, the big bed draped in embroidered linen.

"If you wish," Lazarus said, "I shall bring you a supper."

"Yes, please!" Camilla said with enthusiasm.

After Lazarus closed the door, Tamsin sat on the bed. "I'm as wrung out as boiled laundry. It's been such a day."

"While I had all day to rest," Camilla said. "Then I dragged us into that trouble on the street by insisting we walk here instead of taking a sedan chair. You are kind not to chide me."

"I have nothing but kind thoughts for you, dear heart."

"But I let myself be seduced into Felicity's restoration," Camilla said. "Then I left you with all the trouble and stayed in bed. I know you are choking back a scolding."

"We both wanted an adventure," Tamsin said. "Though I suspect that Winwood will be upset to learn his young cousin harbors couriers for Mary Stuart's people in Holland."

"Do not forgive me so easily." Camilla shook her head. "It's as if I wanted to be beguiled, like at the theatre on Tuesday."

"Perhaps." At the theatre, Tamsin had been sunk in worry and fear caused by Leighton's letter. This was a good time to be honest. "There's something I must tell you, Camilla."

At that moment, Lazarus appeared, laying a tray on the table with a supper that might have come straight from the gods of Olympus. He bowed gravely when they thanked him, and left them alone again.

"How," Camilla asked when the door closed, "did Rollo come by this magnificent house?"

"The Duke of Bagsham lent it to him for the favor of finding the printing press in Felicity's cellar." She repeated what she'd learned about Rowland's business that morning.

"A house and a cook sent from heaven," Camilla said dreamily. "You and I shall do equally well once my funds are freed."

There was no reason for Tamsin to declare just then that she would never live anywhere but Revelstone House. Instead, it was time for confession.

"Camilla, I kept a secret from you. I received this letter on Tuesday." She had to fetch it from where she'd kept it inside her coat, then unfolded it before handing it to Camilla.

Camilla bent over the letter to read it, a hand over her eyes. She began shaking, a little at first, then violently. Tamsin came to put an arm around her weeping friend.

Except Camilla was laughing, so hard that tears spilled from the corners of her eyes.

"Oh, save my giddy aunt!" Camilla choked with laughter. "If only you could see your face. As if you'd confessed a grievous sin."

"I am confessing such," Tamsin said. "Not telling you about it was a severe transgression."

"Leighton harm us?" Camilla again choked on laughter.

"He shot you! He's been petty and abusive since the day he married you. Leighton is just the sort of fellow to seek revenge by hiring murderers."

"Leighton arrange a murder?" Camilla laughed again. "His horse won't leap a fence upon his command. His dogs won't hunt. His mother arranged his laundry, since I refused to do it for him. I have promised myself to never fear him again."

Tamsin struggled to name her tumbled feelings. She had *not* been a fool for fearing Leighton's plot.

"Camilla, Tom met a friend of Leighton's who paid for just such a plot. His mercenaries attacked us outside the theatre. The same men tried to stop us today."

Her friend sobered. She looked up at Tamsin. "Zounds! Such a secret burden you've carried."

"It shouldn't have been a secret. I wanted to protect you, but I should have told you, so you'd know to protect yourself. I shall promise no more secrets."

"What a clodpated fuddle-cap he is." Camilla stared into the distance over Tamsin's shoulder.

They lingered over the excellent food, then found a book they knew, a slim volume of Andrew Marvell's poems. Camilla read aloud, and Tamsin let that voice lull her, offering more consolation than she'd known since—oh, too long to ponder.

"'Let us roll all our strength,'" Camilla read, "'and all our sweetness, up into one ball.' How delightful a thought." The book fell into her lap. Her hand rested on Tamsin's shoulder.

"Camilla?" Tamsin stretched, feeling consoled by these close moments with her friend. Yet she couldn't fully rest. "There's more I must tell you, because many parts of Tom's gambol will unfold tomorrow."

She repeated the details of Tom's planned restoration, beginning with his friendships, through his investigations and interrogations, and into the plans for Tom's gambol. While she related those plans, Camilla's excitement rose, expanding to fill the room.

"Oh, shall we be Knights of the Marborne Fens?"

Tamsin sought to dampen the fire of her friend's excitement. "Camilla, this is not a lark, like when you joined our little highway restorations. Rowland's peril is serious. And Tom's friends are in dire jeopardy. You and I will help—"

"Of course. We must."

"But we will follow Tom's and Perry's commands and protect each other tomorrow. Then we are going home to Revelstone."

"Where you will no longer treat Tom or me as if we are helpless children."

"I didn't think I was that bad." And yet, Camilla raised an event Tamsin hadn't fully considered. "Anyway, I don't think Tom is coming home to Revelstone with us."

"Of course, he isn't," Camilla said. "Anyone can see that he's been dying to get away from...from his months of dying. He's wanted to be in London, pursuing the law, since he came home from Trinity. He's well now and finally has his own money. It's only right that he seizes his dreams at last."

"Anyone can see..." Tamsin repeated the words.

"That you can seize your dreams now, too."

"My dreams? I want to be home, doing the work that needs to be done."

"Where you won't have to expend yourself taking care of Tom and sheltering me from Leighton and searching out every penny for Marborne."

"But that was exactly what I was supposed to be doing."

"Yes? Tricking thieves into returning money that'd been cheated from the villages? Fighting in the street, hitting bad men with a sword? Are you including that in your dream?"

"Of course not." Tamsin still heard Camilla's earlier words about Tom. "I've been too much in Tom's business, haven't I?"

"You did help keep him alive, which was good."

"But you're saying I've interfered too much in his life."

"I'm only agreeing that while he is working in London, you need to be home, living in Revelstone House, helping to repair the village. Which is what you claim to be your dream. Except for when you become solemn and say that Absolom proclaimed that to be your fate."

"Yes, it's my desire. But I never considered that dream without Tom being there. I must have a thick, thick skull, because he always had large dreams."

"Yet just a moment ago you said that Tom's likely to stay in London. And of course, Rollo and Lizzie will stay."

"There'll still be Ned. And Perry." She knew that to be true, about Rollo and Lizzie, but hadn't let it rise in her mind.

"And me," Camilla said. "I'll stay as long as I'm invited."

"That's always, my dear, dear friend," Tamsin said. "I must promise myself no more fighting in the street. And no more rescuing my brother. The past is behind us, and he's well enough to manage his own adventures."

41

A Proud Heart Knows

-ɔɔ◍.◍ɔɔ-

– T O M –

"THAT LAST NIGHT AT Trinity…" Aurora began to speak, but then she sipped water, taking too much time to finish her thought.

Must we speak of love and heroic rescues?

This was to be Tom's most uncomfortable moments yet in Mr. Mordaunt's chambers. He wanted to protest when Aurora asked but sipped his water instead.

Perhaps she wanted Tom to be the hero in her story, but his own story was wholly about freeing Jacob. He did not want to revisit the last night at Trinity. However, …

"I worry," she said, "that I made a colossal mistake."

"I don't think so," Tom said, afraid to hear more. "We're friends, and if one of us made a mistake, the other would call attention to it and we'd resolve it."

"Truly?" She set her cup aside and sighed. "Your cousins believe you've harbored a secret passion since Trinity."

"No," Tom said. "I dissuaded Perry and Ned from thinking that, but they share a romantical bent and won't hear it."

"Oh? Yet I did spend time after leaving Trinity believing that I was in love with you." She smiled in a shy way, then removed her spectacles and polished them with a kerchief from her sleeve. While still blind, and not glancing his way, she said, "But then I saw that what I called 'my passion' was never real. I was confused the last night we were together. Likely I confused you, too."

"To tell the truth," Tom said, wanting to do nothing of the sort, "I did sigh often as days and weeks and months passed. Then

I understood that, rather than a passion, I was sighing over the lost paradise that the three of us shared."

"What an excellent way to describe it." She put her spectacles in place and looked at him, smiling warmly.

"*Vero, vero,*" Tom said. "I liked being Jacob's special friend and having a secret adventure, making sure no one discovered who you were."

"How do we explain it to them?"

"From my experience, it's a waste of time to try. But this is what I will say. You could have gone to people far above me, the Duke of Bagsham perhaps, and told the story of the marquess's bad actions. Or asked for the Crown's protection. But you came to me solely because I'd made a promise. Because you knew that I am forever Jacob's friend."

"Yes! That's it. Then we are truly friends? You aren't doing all this merely to keep your promise?"

"Being Jacob's friend, and yours, is a cornerstone of the promise I made then. Now, why did you come to London? Did you foresee in a dream that you'd have to rescue me?"

"Our little band of searchers decided it would be impossible to restore the marquess's rooms so he cannot see what's been taken. Hence, Ned sent this."

It was a journal, no larger than Tom's hand, bound in grey canvas, its pages filled with a spidery script that took more than a moment to read. Names and notes. "It's one of the marquess's journals that list favors owed and favors done. Ned sent some hasty notes with Perry, telling of this."

"Ned thinks," she said, "it will help you with the papers you are examining, to find who abetted the marquess in his swindles and cheats. Did you receive the note I sent with Perry?"

"Where you asked me to destroy the marquess, not only protect Jacob? Yes, but I'd already decided that on my own. My plan extends beyond Jacob."

"It must." She handed him another note from her reticule. "After Perry left last night...no, it was already morning...we found this letter. It expresses an enmity the marquess harbors toward Marborne and your family. I think the new Earl of Marborne is in danger."

While Tom judged the paper and the style of writing, she continued. "You'd laugh if you'd been there. We searched every cranny in the marquess's rooms. But Jacob solved the problem, finding it locked in a puzzle box."

"Jacob is cleverer than he's been allowed to show us." Tom spoke idly as he read, then read one line aloud. "'I want that earldom in Cambridgeshire. Desire beats hard in my heart.' Yes, I overheard Withersea express as much in Mr. Mordaunt's chambers yesterday."

"This letter proves as much." She tapped the letter he held. "The marquess planned to offer the king garnishments for the Marborne title."

Tom's heart thumped at one line in the letter. "I see how this brought you to London. But it doesn't prove a crime."

"But it shows he has had Marborne in sight, with greedy intent. And that he does not mean well for your family."

"From the date of this unsent letter, it begins an awful tale I have to tell you." Tom pointed at the terrible line.

I have a scheme to free funds by way of my agent's hirelings (the same rogues we used with R— and his two rotters).

He had to tell her now, though he'd hoped to avoid telling her until a time in the distant future. "I was surprised to learn this yesterday, as was Mr. Mordaunt, who I believe is married to a cousin of yours."

"Yes?" Her voice quavered with trepidation.

"The marquess paid mercenaries to murder your father and brothers, and also the lord who was to be Jacob's guardian."

He watched as an epic tragedy played over her face. When she began to wipe at her eyes, he couldn't stand there as merely a witness. He folded her in his arms, feeling soft tremors pass through her in waves. He'd been fighting his own feelings about this tragedy, allowing only anger, but now he began to tremble too, having just faced that man-monster moments earlier. He murmured the consolations Absolom had chanted while Tom lay ill, the words running together as they had in his fever dreams.

> *Be still my heart; thou hast known worse than this. The proud heart feels not terror nor turns to run. It is ill if I turn and fly before these odds. A hero must stand firm and hold his own.*

Saying it all over again, like a chapel choir repeating the chorus, he let Absolom voice the words for him until they were both still. Then she eased out of his arms.

"It took far too long for me to see what a monster he is," she said, wiping her eyes with that kerchief. "I lived in my private world with my books and poems, making lists of words and their meanings, conjugating verbs. I wanted to bring Jacob into my private world, but instead…"

"Jacob's danger is not your fault," Tom said. "No one could be expected to see what the marquess is, because we cannot fathom how a man could be so evil."

"Are you excusing me?" She shook her head, then wiped at her eyes once more and tucked away her kerchief.

"No, I'm describing my own thoughts," he said. "I met him just before you found me on the street."

"You met the marquess?" This stunned Aurora out of grief and back to her more familiar rational self. "How?"

"I went to his house, pretending to be someone else, to present him with a business proposal." As Tom told it, he heard that it sounded like the notions of a lunatic. "To understand him."

"What did you learn?" She seemed to be withholding judgment, or any other response.

"He's mercurial and dangerous. I must beg you to leave his house as soon as you can."

She nodded as if agreeing, but her eyes drifted. She was thinking of something else.

"Can you take that message to a magistrate?" She meant the undelivered letter she'd brought with her. "Can you beg a warrant, to arrest him for m–m–murder?"

"No. The letter doesn't prove it. And what I overheard is mere hearsay, even if I could convince Mr. Mordaunt to swear to it with me. We have no one who will confess to carrying out his terrible scheme." He caught her hands, since she was shaking them with impatience, denying what he claimed. "You must not give him any indication that you know. It would put you and Jacob in even greater danger."

She said, "If you cross him in battle but do not defeat him, he will rise to fight again, harder than before. You must be prepared to cut him down."

"I'd understand if you wanted him dead, Aurora. But I cannot do that."

She held up her hand, in that mild way with which scholars concede defeat. "As you said on Tuesday. I'm not seeking his death. But you can already see that if you confront him, he'll slither out of the first door he sees. And so."

Apparently, she'd finished what she intended to say about whether she wanted the marquess dead. *And so.*

"And so," he said, "I must deal punishment that ensures the Marquess of Withersea cannot rise again like a phoenix."

"I cannot conceive what that will be."

"I shall destroy his hold on Jacob at the Committee meeting. Seizing all his wealth and destroying his standing with the king will take a few more days."

"You intend to turn the marquess's tricks upon him."

"*Ita quidem.*" He could indulge Latin with Aurora. "Do you see what you have to do?"

"Yes. I must leave England."

"We will find a way, no later than Monday. For safety's sake, bring Jacob to London tomorrow. I shall hide you both until we've arranged your departure."

"Will you travel with us, as Jacob's guardian?"

"Perhaps later," he said. "I have uncovered much business that requires legal resolutions. Many of the marquess's victims will need help to find justice. And," he hadn't allowed this notion to fully surface, "you do not want it to appear that another man spirited the marquess's wife out of England."

"Yes. He'd pursue us. He only cares about my inheritance, and he'll never let go of any of his possessions. I need to protect Jacob. Yet at the same time, I fear for you, not just for myself."

"Come to London tomorrow. It's a big town. I'll make sure you are both safe. If London doesn't suit, Ned and Lizzie can take you to our house in Cambridgeshire."

She nodded, agreeing more sincerely this time. Then she seemed to shake off the morass of grief and fear, at least for the moment. "Did you read the new guardian bond for Jacob that Perry brought? You are lucky to have a great devil-writer as a cousin." No, she was still caught in dire emotions because she chattered, which Aurora never did. "However, as good as that work is, I believe Ned would much prefer to paint." Her voice caught. "I'm grateful to all of you for your kindness. Else, Jacob and I would be lost."

"Aurora, please do not underestimate how highly I regard your bravery and your efforts to help us."

"We are indeed friends, aren't we?" She poked a brave tone back into her voice.

"Always." He braced her shoulders, but not enfolding her again. He dropped his hands to grasp her fingertips with his. "What we are learning and doing together now forges a stronger bond between us than whatever happened that one confusing night at Trinity."

He'd said many things that weren't true in the last couple of days, but this felt truer than anything he'd said in a decade.

She said, "Aye. I feel it. Together, we will protect what's most precious to both of us. Then we shall—"

A forceful rap at the door stopped her declamation.

Tom and Aurora remained in the grips of powerful emotions, so he preferred not to respond to that interruption, but the rap sounded again, more insistent.

"Mr. Foxe?" It was Rowland's new friend, Michel Chêne.

"Oh, hello," Tom said.

"Lord Marborne sent me, to guard you on the way to his house, since—" Michel stopped, seeing Aurora.

"This is the Marchioness of Withersea," Tom said. "This is Michel Chêne. Did I remember your name correctly?"

Michel stared at Aurora, who stared back.

"Hello, Michel," she said. "We visited with your family in Amsterdam. Was it two years ago?"

He nodded, then his voice made it past his astonishment. "You are Baroness Rôche's niece. On her grandfather's side."

"Yes, we discovered we are cousins. And you showed us how to walk about in Amsterdam without getting lost," Aurora said. "It's good to see you in London."

"I was sent to guard Miss Ysabel Foxe," Michel said. "But she's visiting friends, so I've been with the Earl of Marborne."

"Lizzie is at my house in Knightsbridge," Aurora said. "The gods made such a small world."

Then, it was her carriage driver who appeared in chambers, having been waiting in the street for her.

"Thank you, John. We'll return to Knightsbridge now, before it grows dark.

When Tom said goodbye, he expected her to embrace him again, but Aurora had only a peck on the cheek for him. At the door she said, "Please eat more. And rest."

When she'd gone, Michel became excited. "Can you believe it, sir? Your cousin Miss Foxe is with my own cousin, safe and snug. Our two stories prove to be the same."

"Mr. Chêne, I believe you can be of much more use to me than merely providing a guard for my journey home."

Brimming with enthusiasm, Chêne promised anything in the world, if it helped Lizzie or Aurora or Rowland, none of whom did he refer to in any but the most formal way.

Tom agreed to the amazing coincidence, but other amazing things had happened that week. He explained to Michel, as much as he could trust a near stranger, tasks he needed performed.

"Which will contribute to keeping Ysabel Foxe safe and advancing Marborne's well-being. And preserving the well-being of the marchioness's younger brother."

"Who is my cousin Jacob."

Michel eagerly agreed to what Tom asked for that evening and promised to meet Tom again in the morning. After Michel departed, Tom found one of the messenger boys who loitered around Lincoln's Inn, seeking to bear messages for pennies, and sent the lad off to Rowland's house with the letters Aurora had brought from Lizzie.

Then Tom sat with quill, ink, and paper, to match names:

Ten names on a list titled Hawkins Heirs, of men forming a syndic to invest in the blasted African trade.

Twenty names, taken from Mordaunt's desk, of the men on the Committee for Privileges and Conduct, some of whom matched names in Withersea's journal of men owing him favors.

Two dozen names from Mordaunt's files matching dubious land settlements described in Rosewurme's papers.

He sketched his own short list of actions to draw Withersea into a weir net of the marquess's own making. He paused once more to convulse with joy. He could do this! He'd free both Jacob and Aurora. All he'd been able to do since February was to offer his family reassurances, usually by prevaricating: *I'm feeling much better today.* He now knew how a butterfly felt, leaving behind an old carcass, emerging to fly.

No, it was too grand, imagining his emergence to be that of a butterfly. Say rather, a moth. The kind that flies up in your face when you don't expect it.

42
Duties Not Dreamt Of

ROWLAND HADN'T CLOSED THE door on his ducal guest before his peace was interrupted by Valentine Starbuck, who implored him to open his purse and kitchen and cellar to celebrate with the half dozen militiamen crowded behind him.

"Come, Rollo, you are compelled to entertain the men who helped you last week."

While the militiamen were still in the foyer, Lazarus reported that Cook promised meat pies, fruit, and cold ale from the cellar.

Then Lazarus answered the door again, greeting a messenger boy. He handed over a penny to the boy, who bore two letters for the Earl of Marborne.

"These come by way of Mr. Thomas Foxe. I am to instruct that you are to read this letter first, your lordship."

Rowland received both, and held the first with two fingers. The sight of Lizzie's elegant script sent tingles up his arm. The small hairs on his neck stood on end when he saw how she'd addressed it: *The Right Honorable Earl of Marborne.* She must have written thusly to tease him. The second missive was addressed to *R. Foxe, Benson's Lodging.*

Rowland stepped away from his military friends, hunching his back to block others' sight as he broke the wax seal.

A single sheet, words not even stretching to the edges.

He allowed only one blink of disappointment at its brevity.

After all, he'd see Lizzie again come Friday. No use in allowing disappointment overcome good sense. He'd be with her in one more full turning of the sun. Yet it took a moment to see what was written on the page; instead, he saw her smiling under candle-light, touching a rose to her face, the yellow one he'd bought for two pennies at a hawker's cart on the Strand.

Then he read the letter which asked him to send a lace pattern to the Marborne rector's wife. His heart was frail and his emotions childlike, so it took him a moment to remember that Reverend Gamlingay of Marborne parish had never had a wife.

It was a tortuous quarter hour before he could slip away from his friends by claiming he needed to change his wine-stained coat. In his bedchamber, he sat on a bench and unstitched a pocket in his best and only embroidered waistcoat. He retrieved a sheet from a crudely printed pamphlet that contained seven of Shake-speare's sonnets.

Because he'd discarded any notion of continuing life as an in-telligencer, he'd wiped portions of his memory in order to grapple with new duties not dreamt of in his previous life, as the Bard might say. Therefore, he translated clumsily. The first message cautioned him about Withersea, which he'd earlier learned from Tom. But her words warmed him.

> Lambkin: Lord W incarnates a monstrous spirit of corrup-tion. And he schemes to destroy you.

> Heed me: Do not go unarmed or unguarded, even within the chamber where you sleep. Also know: W and Sir Dux-wold likely invested with your traitor, Mr. Duncombe. I shall seek further proof here. Mayhap you can look about in London. W wants James gone from the throne so that William of Orange can bring Dutch shipping to London. He'll grow rich from property he owns along the river. That plus W's antipapal screeds should be a warning flag.

> Please let your former master know of this. Better still, can you join me here? I long for the day when you and I fight for justice together, since I am now among, as my poet says, 'the scum that still rise up most when the nation boils.'

My poet also says: Pains of love be sweeter far than all other pleasures are. And I am in such pain. I am she who would be yours, if Fate allows. —Y

Was that the trace of a tear that marked the bottom of the letter? It contained an encouraging line: "I long for the day…" Yet, however much his heart raced, it was impractical to run to her side that very evening. The other matters she raised, he felt to be in hand, due to Tom's work and Rosewurme's help. He broke the seal on the second letter, written that day in an obvious hurry.

Rollo, if all our messages fail to reach Tom, you must act in his stead. W intends to discredit and disinherit you, though we don't know how. Perhaps he'll attempt something at the Committee meeting on Friday. Take care that W's corruption does not touch you. Ned and I will return to London tomorrow. —Yours, Y

He held it under candlelight to better decipher the end.

You may chide me for my reckless obedience to our former master and disloyalty to you.

No, he would not. Perry had assured him that Lizzie was safe. All else that mattered: Lizzie loved him.

"Lazarus!" he called, not really raising his voice.

The man appeared like a hovering ghost. "Yes, my lord?"

"Can you please help me find paper and ink?"

"There's fine linen paper in the library, my lord."

"I'm wanting ledger paper, not linen rag."

"Just a moment."

Lazarus returned with paper, ink, fresh quills, and a penknife. "Shall I bring you—"

"No, Lazarus. This is perfection. I'll be only a moment."

Famished as he was, he had to spare necessary moments on this task, remembering as clearly as he could the names on the coded ledger page he'd given Viscount Heydon the week before.

His life presented yet another occasion when omitting someone's name in a surveillance report might give him power. After he'd finished that ledger sheet, he went to the upper floor to visit Rosewurme, to ask that the man rewrite his bond in a way that omitted any mention of the Duke of Bagsham. Then he joined Valentine and his noisy militia friends in the dining salon.

~

Rowland stopped at the door to the salon, dismayed at the sight of empty platters scattered on the table.

"If I may, my lord." Lazarus was at his elbow. "Cook bade me say, she's saved a new batch of meat pies for you, sir."

"It's Mrs. Flurry, isn't it?" Rowland turned as Lazarus set off down a hallway. "I must offer my gratitude."

This was his first visit to the kitchen, other than the brief peek when he'd toured the house. A half-dozen faces looked up from their tasks when he entered, several wiping their hands and dipping their heads in his direction.

"I didn't mean to interrupt," Rowland said. "I just wanted to thank you all for your efforts. Where is Mrs. Flurry?"

The smallest woman in the room stepped forward, rubbing her hands on a towel. "Yes, your lordship?"

"I wanted to express my gratitude for the sudden imposition of my friends."

"It's a pleasure to serve, my lord." She waved her hand over the other workers, among whom Rowland recognized only Eve, who'd been introduced as the scullery maid. Mrs. Flurry said, "We sent out for help from our best neighbors, sir. And I'm sorry that we did have to fetch victuals from a tavern for the first serving. Howsomever, we shall soon be ready to serve such as will make you proud."

"I cannot sufficiently thank you." He hadn't given thought to how much work it took to entertain ten unexpected guests.

"Will you, my lord, try one of my own meat pies?" She didn't wait for his answer, just served up food from the hearth.

"May I intrude to eat here?" he asked. "You see, I haven't eaten since about this time yesterday."

Eve quickly cleared a place at the end of the work table and set a chair for him. Mrs. Flurry placed before him a tin platter of fried meat pies, still steaming from her kettle. Eve offered a plate of cheese, warm rolls, and vegetables. She laid down a spoon and dining knife. As the pies were still too hot to eat, he speared a piece of cheese and wrapped it in one of the rolls. The cheese and soft bread dissolved as he bit in, filling his senses with a pungent scent while the inside of his mouth felt as if it had been coated with sweet cream.

"Exquisite," he exclaimed. "What district sends cheese like this to London?"

"I…that is, we make it here, my lord. The milk comes from the Bravewood country estate."

Before Rowland said more, the meat pies called to him, being now cool enough to be taken in hand. He finished one in three bites, unable to voice what he tasted.

"Marvelous, Mrs. Flurry. How do you do it?"

She flushed bright red, having milky skin that easily betrays blushes. "We fry them in butter, sir."

"From the same cows as the cheese?"

"Aye, my lord, and filled with milk-fed veal. We are happy you are pleased."

Since he didn't want to embarrass them by gobbling the plate of pies and cheese, Rowland instead prompted each of the workers to tell him their names and where they came from. Three were from London; the rest were all working in town to send silver back to their families in nearby counties.

Just as his plate proved to be empty, when he was resisting sweeping up crumbs with his fingers, Mrs. Flurry said, "We're ready now to serve your guests, my lord."

The women carried their platters to the dining salon. Lazarus followed with more pitchers of ale.

The militiamen, who'd taken up card games in trios, looked up when Rowland entered. They stood. Valentine, also standing, raised his cup. "I give you the Right Honorable Earl of Marborne.

And Lieutenant Rowland Foxe, our own servant to the king of England, and author of the feast."

They cheered. He laughed.

Author of the feast? He'd never treated his own barracks mates to more than a round of ale. Now he owed a feast to these men. By some quirk of fate, he could afford what he owed them and was also master of a staff who could arrange it.

"Wait until you taste these pies," Rowland said, in an imitation of modesty. He wanted to call Mrs. Flurry in to receive their applause, but first he had to verify with Lazarus what was appropriate. Meanwhile, he sat, accepting a cup of ale from Lazarus, then rolled his gold angel coin along the backs of his fingers, able to relax for the first time since Lizzie ran off to meet friends in the country.

43
Regard the Gods

꧁ · ꧂

— TAMSIN —

CAMILLA HAD FALLEN ASLEEP a half hour before Tamsin heard Rowland and Tom in the hallway. She wrapped her coat over her nightshift and opened the door wide enough that those two knew she overhead. Perry appeared at the same moment.

Tamsin said, "Should you be conversing in the hallway, where the servants might hear?"

"Not to worry," Rowland said. "This house has what might be the most loyal staff in England."

"How did you manage that?" Tom asked.

"Pure luck on my part." Rowland said. "Without their help, I'd have no insight into how to manage this house."

"Michel Chêne was to stay with you, Tom," Perry said, hands on his hips. "How are we to keep you safe?"

"I took a sedan chair." Tom yawned. "That's safe, though a bit more silver than one likes to see leave one's pocket."

"Where's Michel?" Rowland folded his arms, as stern as Perry, who hadn't learned yet that it's useless to scold Tom.

"He's with his sister at Chalgrove House, seeking what else is to be found in Rosewurme's lair." Tom shifted in a familiar way, which Tamsin recognized as an intention to change the subject. "The marchioness came to London and brought Lizzie's letters. Did you receive them, Rollo? I sent them here with a messenger."

"Yes." Rowland unfolded his arms. "Thank you for that."

"Our friends' search at Arcadia House," Tom said, "unearthed an unsent letter about the marquess's lust to have the Marborne title for himself. Aurora came to London to warn me about how dangerous the marquess is."

"She's nice that way," Perry said.

"However," Tom said, "I'd overheard such in Mordaunt's chambers. And I experienced the fire of the marquess's evil scorching my own self at his London house this afternoon."

Rowland gaped, seeming to forget to scold.

Tamsin had foresworn her inclination to manage Tom just an hour before. She could only wait for him to explain.

Perry apparently felt no constraint. "Thou art known to be God's own berk! Playing Daniel in the lions' den? Alone?"

Tamsin saw that Tom wouldn't answer. She asked, "You say the marquess was angry with you?"

"*Vero, vero.* 'Achilles' baneful wrath resounded, O Goddess, that imposed Infinite sorrows on the Greeks.'"

"Is Withersea a tragic Greek figure?" Tamsin frowned, not liking the idea of Tom in the man's house.

"I meant it as hyperbole, which is a rhetorical device—"

"No Latin. No Greek. No Hyperboreans." Perry put the evil eye on Tom.

"No," Tom began a correction. "The Hyperboreans are—"

Perry crossed his massive arms. Set his jaw.

"Fine," Tom said. "No Greek tragedy. A simple story."

"Which you will take forever to tell us, as you like to do," Perry groused.

"No, quite simple. I went to the marquess's house to provoke him into joining in my gambol at his own choice." Tom grinned, the Puckish smile that meant he was pleased with himself. "Tomorrow, Michel Chêne will deliver some paintings to the marquess's house which Danvers Duncombe consigned to Ned last week. That is, Ned disguised as an art dealer."

"That's a portion of the bounty we reaped in trapping Duncombe," Rowland said. It sounded like a complaint.

Tom said, "It will be only those paintings that are Ned's devil drawings. You may think it foolish that I went there alone, but I led the marquess to demand that I deliver evidence of transgression. *Gutta fortunæ præ dolio sapientiæ.*"

Perry sighed, theatrically. "You can debate your morals and metaphysics without the Greek. I find it rude."

"It means that it's better to be happy than wise," Rowland said. "It's Latin, from the third page of the text Absolom used to torture us, starting at about age...What? Age eight?"

"More like, it's better to have a drop of good fortune rather than a cask of wisdom." Tom shifted away from Perry, which foretold another shift in what he intended to discuss. "I say, Rollo, that fellow Michel is no secretary at all. What a rum story to spin. He came to England to guard Lizzie. Why does our cousin require a guard for protection?"

"She doesn't," Rowland said. "I extracted promises from Lord Bagsham today to protect us. He will ensure justice for Marborne, whatever the marquess might try to do tomorrow."

"You now trust your duke?" Tom pulled a note from inside his pocket. "This is what the duke thinks of you."

Rowland studied it. "I'd ask these questions too. I am offended by the word 'naïve.' Plus, I've been in England a fortnight. It takes time to learn current politics." He folded the note and passed it back to Tom. "And I can damn well fend off predators on my own."

Perry said, "We agree about that, since you seem to have wrung cooperation from your duke. How?"

"I told him what I've learned about his nephew, and about how Rosewurme helped him buy this house."

"You threatened him with that?"

"No, we agreed we wouldn't blackmail each other. I hinted that I have proof Withersea supported Monmouth's rebellion."

"But we don't have proof," Tom said. "It's only hearsay from a conversation in Mordaunt's office."

"No," Rowland said. "I found a missing page from Duncombe's ledger. It identifies others who contributed to the syndic that supported Monmouth's rebellion."

Perry stared, started to speak, stopped.

Which Tamsin guessed meant that Rowland's missing page was problematic.

"Then," Tom rubbed his hands, "given what Aurora and Ned have managed, and what Perry and Rollo have done, our plan should proceed as if favored by the gods."

Tamsin wished she could force Tom to rest, knowing better than to try. Therefore, she said, "We should all sleep now. We can tend to the remaining details at dawn. Neither of you slept much last night. You all need your wits tomorrow."

"Later. I must return to my guests," Rowland said. "If you stay up reading tonight, Tom, don't let your candle set the bed curtains on fire. It's only a borrowed house." With that, he left them, and Perry followed.

"I do need to read more tonight." Tom yawned again. "It will take more than tomorrow to uncover all the cases that can be recalled to the courts."

"Wait a moment, Tom." With her hand on his shoulder, Tamsin asked to relieve more of his workload, since he couldn't be at the Committee meeting while also reading writs in Mr. Mordaunt's office.

Tom took only a heartbeat to acknowledge it might work if she took half those chores. "You can help, especially since you read every text with me throughout my clerkship. Wear my best suit tomorrow and come with me to Mr. Mordaunt's chambers." He dropped his voice, as if concerned for the first time about being overheard. "Camilla cannot come with you. She must stay with Perry's Knights of the Marborne Fens. Will she mind? It's hard to pry the two of you apart."

"I'll convince her."

While he thanked her, she felt waves of worry emanating from Tom like a fever. Yet she refrained from calling attention to the ash-dark circles under his eyes. Her hopes rose when he began to mount the stairs to his bedchamber, but he paused with one foot on the first stair tread and looked back.

"Aurora plans to go to Rome, to be safe from her husband's wrath. But it will take time to make the arrangements. Can we shelter Aurora and her brother at Revelstone House until they are ready to sail?"

"Of course, but it's your house too. You don't have to ask permission from anyone."

He nodded, but still hesitated. "How can I be certain that it's morally right to spirit another man's wife out of England?"

"If you have doubts," Tamsin said, "then I'll help her in your stead. Or Lizzie or Ned can. You don't have to carry it all."

He looked befuddled with fatigue. "We are all so fortunate to have your vigilance."

Was this more of his teasing? Before she could ask him, the butler appeared, a candle branch in hand, and led Tom upstairs. Tamsin crossed her fingers with the hope that once Tom got into his new bed, he wouldn't be able to stay awake long enough to read a single paper.

When Tamsin returned to their bedchamber, Camilla said, "I heard it all. I'm to dress as one of Perry's knights come morning, while you go off with Tom."

"Are you annoyed with me for deserting you while I help to lift the burden from Tom?"

"Of course not," Camilla said. "I'll be safe without you, since I'll have my pistol in my pocket."

Tamsin snuffed out the candle. Camilla cuddled against her despite the lingering warmth of an August night. After several long sighs, Camilla turned on her side, then was deeply asleep.

Leaving Tamsin awake, staring into the dark.

How to persuade Camilla to leave her tiny pistol behind? Would it be ethical to hide the cursed thing?

Why did all aspects of every gambol feel so morally fraught? They endeavored to protect the innocent, the helpless. *Reap justice, shun revenge.* They followed their Restoration Rules. Yet each rule required endless equivocation, corollaries, and axioms.

Tamsin rested her arm in the deep curve between Camilla's hip and ribs. She tucked her knees up behind Camilla's, inhaled the lavender scent in her hair. She didn't have to make an ethical decision on Camilla's behalf. It was up to Perry to make and enforce the rules for his Knights of the Marborne Fens.

— ROLLO —

AT MIDNIGHT, ROWLAND TAPPED his comrade's shoulder. "Let's talk, Perry, now that we are alone."

The rioting militiamen had departed Xanthus House. Starbuck and all the others remaining in the house for the night had gone to bed.

"Are you about to castigate me," Perry said, "for keeping Tom's plan private until today?"

"No. I approve of Tom's impulse to keep Tamsin out of this. But I wish I'd known about Leighton Fairchild's threat."

"I rather wish I'd known, too. But we are right and tidy now. What do you want to talk about?"

Rowland said, "Tom's frolic needs more chaos than his plan calls for. Let us think more on this."

Perry said, "I suggest we ask Captain Starbuck to bring his men as escort to and from the meeting. Better his men than others from among the intelligencers we've met in London."

"He lost four guineas at pharo tonight," Rowland said. "I wager he will happily help if I return the voucher he wrote on his dining linen."

Lazarus appeared, again as if from nowhere. "I put Captain Starbuck in the green room. Will you allow me to assist your guests with their morning toilet? It would be my pleasure, my lord."

Perry cast a glance Rowland's way, likely worrying about how much of their conversation had been heard.

"Thank you, Lazarus," Rowland said, having complete trust in the man. "I appreciate your service. Will you please let Mrs. Flurry know how much we enjoyed the repast? And I apologize for the extra work I've caused all of you."

"You have no need to apologize, my lord. We are happy to have you in residence."

After declining Lazarus's assistance, Rowland pulled Perry into his chamber, to further plan for a chaotic Friday. Perry's first words in the privacy of Rowland's bedchamber: "You certainly trust the servants here more than I've ever seen done in this world."

"Lazarus assured me. He's not a man who'd be trifling about promising his trust." Rowland prepared to reveal more. "I believe Lazarus and the others are both trained and habitually loyal in their trustworthy ways."

"Few lords we knew in either Amsterdam or Paris expressed trust in their servants."

"The previous resident here required greater discretion than typically expected from people in service. And I'm nearly certain that Bagsham, who pays them, asked that their trust come to me."

"Tom would use Latin for how hard this is to believe. You saw the impudent note from your Bagsham to Mr. Mordaunt."

Rowland waved Perry over and showed him the wall that turned into a door. He opened the box that contained several knives. This time he opened the box beneath it, which contained five different pistols.

"Also, if I need to leave England in a hurry while dressed as a Catalan viscountess, it all fits me."

Perry inspected all of it, of course showing no surprise. Taking his time to comment, he finally said, "The pink gown doesn't favor your coloring, Rollo. Perhaps a white shawl will keep your chestnut curls from clashing with the silk."

When they returned to the bedchamber proper, Perry reclined on the bed, dangling his shoes over the side.

"Rollo, I've been thinking. We must excuse Tom from participating in the final scenes of tomorrow's gambol."

"Yet Tom longs for this adventure."

"Howbeit, I surmise that his old Trinity friend—a sweet and gracious woman—needs the marquess dead to truly escape from how he terrorizes her. Though she'd never think that, much less voice it. You know Tom cannot do that for her."

"We can? No, Perry, we can't. *No one dies.*"

"I only argue that we must ensure greater justice is called to bear than merely stopping the man's machinations," Perry said.

"I intend," Rowland said, "that the marquess will be in the Tower before the sun sets tomorrow."

He explained what he'd learned about Withersea's investments with Danvers Duncombe, the man he and Perry had sent to the Tower the previous week.

"Lord Bagsham threatened to call into question the missing pages from Duncombe's secret ledger. But my 'discovery' of the rebels' press freed me from that. Now the duke has pledged to confirm that I speak truth no matter what happens at the Committee meeting."

"What truth do you intend to speak?"

"We know Withersea invested in Duncombe's treasonous syndic. Tom heard him say as much. The missing ledger pages will be discovered and submitted to a judge for a warrant."

"What? You have the pages back from Viscount Heydon?"

"Never mind how I…uh…found the pages. I am certain it will work, and only you know how I shall contrive to do it."

Perry said, "But consider, do we trust the Tower to hold such a lofty lord?"

"Perhaps not. Yet given what Tom has learned and what I know about the investment in Monmouth's rebellion, we can severely damage the marquess in the king's sight."

"If only Viscount Heydon could send this enemy off to Barbados like he did Absolom Foxe's enemies. You'll have to do it this time."

"No, Perry. I don't want to be associated with the marquess's arrest. I want people to think Valentine found the papers and brought them to a judge."

Rowland, without thinking, had his gold coin in hand, riffling it over his knuckles.

Perry watched the coin roll. "It will distress you, Rollo, but I must remind you that you will be required to lay out large gratuities and emoluments to accomplish our goals."

"You are right." Rowland rolled the coin across his knuckles a fifth time. "I should learn to be inured of it."

"I have a plan for that. Will you allow me to surprise you when it unrolls?"

"Yes, the gratuities English lords and bishops believe are due to them are not significant worries. Rather, I am seeking a way to reduce Marborne's poverty as part of this affair."

"Tom is busy reaping justice." Perry voiced what Rowland had been thinking. "I believe you have fixed on a different rule: *Reave when sins are ripe.*"

"Yes, exactly so."

"Then, behold, we have a guilty man to reave," Perry said. "If I know you, Rowland Foxe—and I do—you've been thinking on the problem all this day. I shall delve into my brain-pan, too. Mayhap, together we'll find a way."

"We always have done so before," Rowland said.

Day 4, Friday:
To Undreamed Shores

O how falsely men
Accuse us Gods as authors of their ill,
When by the bane their own bad lives instill
They suffer all the miseries of their states,
Past our inflictions, and beyond their fates.
— The Poet Known as Homer, *The Odyssey*
(George Chapman, translator)

—

By my troth,
your town is troubled with unruly boys.
— William Shakespeare, *A Comedy of Errors*

44
How to Flee

⊸⊶⊙.⊙⊷⊸

— NED —

NED HAD SKIPPED THE quick breakfast Gabriel procured from the World's End, and therefore he could not identify exactly what his belly scraped against. He hoped it wasn't fear.

That Friday morning, before dawn, everyone in the house prepared for the journey to London. After hearing Aurora's report of Tom's doings, Winwood begged a horse so that he could be in London faster than the carriage would take him.

Ned, however, argued for Tom's safety. "Tom might have escaped from Tamsin's care, but you can trust Perry to have Tom firmly in hand."

"Tom Foxe can be wily." Winwood mounted the horse, intending to be in London long ahead of them. "I'm certain that he's dipped too far into his reserves."

John sat on top of the coach with Gabriel, Daniel, Neriah, and Ned, all armed by John so they could serve as protectors. Aurora, Jacob, and Lizzie rode inside. The road to London was smoother than a country lane. From his seat atop the heavy carriage, Ned kept checking the flintlock pistol John Coachman had given him, making sure it was ready, tracing the carving and silver-work on the handle, imagining a situation where he must point it, fire, resist the recoil, and reload while it was still hot.

This adventure had grown far beyond what Tom had initially asked Ned to do, which was merely to protect a young man from an ill-natured batterer. Now Ned (and his new comrades) must defend against the onslaught of a ruthless lord who had destruction in mind. Whenever Ned's thoughts wandered, he felt nagged that it might be beyond his capabilities. And yet: Tom had trusted Ned with this work. And, more, Perry believed in him.

In the end, they weren't waylaid. The coach proceeded slowly because of its weight, although Lizzie had instructed everyone to pack lightly. Aurora brought only one satchel, which could contain no more than a change of clothes. However, John Coachman had loaded a box of books without which, Aurora insisted, she could not live.

Ned, Daniel, and Neriah were let off the carriage first, while the others pursued separate tasks. Ned sent the two brothers to find Perry, to tell him that Aurora was seeking passage in the Pool of London, intending to flee England today rather than next week, as she's previously discussed with Tom.

Rowland was to meet the lords' Committee that morning, and so Ned guessed the best place to find Perry must be in Westminster. The two lads swore they'd find their brother wherever in London he might be. Although Ned would prefer to be the one seeking Perry, at least this arrangement meant that Ned wouldn't be the one to tell Rowland that Lizzie was on her way to Amsterdam.

Ned's task was to retrieve a portion of Withersea's wealth from one of the man's bankers, to amass sufficient funds to assist Aurora's and Jacob's escape. He had experience with bankers. A week earlier, when he'd come to London with Rowland, they'd visited bankers to redeem what they'd won in the gambol that defeated Uncle Absolom's enemies. Ned hadn't intended to make bank raids a habit, but here he was, presenting a writ that identified him as an agent for Lord Withersea and submitting a cheque for five hundred and ten pounds.

"His lordship has a transaction this morning that requires these funds." Ned aped the man's diction and manners as he expressed the need. "He regrets, I'm sure you understand, asking you to make such sudden transfers."

"Ah, a familiar event," the banker's agent said. "We know how impatient Lord Withersea can be when he seeks to advance new opportunities."

Ned concluded the transaction, carrying one hundred five-guinea coins away in a messenger's bag, with the assorted change in his pocket. He left the agent's chambers with the same feeling as the week before, lightheaded with the relief that he made it through the business without being revealed as a fraud. Yet when Ned stepped around the corner, his belly rumbled in discomfort over the risk of bearing that much gold, which bulged in his messenger's bag. In the shadows, he took off his coat and slung the bag of coins over his shoulder, enduring the pain when the bag caught on his splintered finger. Then he redonned the coat.

He made it through the streets, having to ask directions twice ("I seek the Golden Hoop Inn on Thames Street, near Pudding Lane"), then checked for landmarks along the way. He knew when he'd arrived at the Pool of London from the stink of fish as he trudged past warehouses and market stalls. The inn was where Lizzie, Aurora, and Jacob waited, with Pip. Ned arrived there at the same time as Gabriel the footman and John Coachman, who'd bought passage for the traveling party.

"A Dutch merchant ship is sailing on the afternoon tide," John said, pleased with his success.

"It's called the *Zeewolf*," Gabriel said, markedly excited about the coming journey. "It's stopping in Rotterdam, then sailing for Batavia. You cannot believe the size of this ship!"

While they stood outside the inn, John explained all he'd managed that morning. First, he'd left Ned's painting equipage at Mr. Touchstone's warehouse off Threadneedle Street.

"It was his missus what took charge," John said. "She wasn't having it when I offered her two of those Dutchmen's paintings. Thought I'd stole them. When I said your name and gave her your note, then all was cracking and bonny."

"Did she give you the price I asked in my note?"

"Aye. Proved more than enough to pay passage," John said. "Madam Touchstone is a terror, I'd say."

"*Ja,* she is." Ned guessed he'd better go round to speak with Hildegonda Touchstone before the day ended.

"Then I went to my cousin's livery," John said, "and sold the carriage. I gave him back a bit of coin to paint over the marquess's arms on each door, and to do it today."

"Good work!" Ned said, admiring John's wit and loyalty.

John said, "He has a long nose, does my cousin, with the kind of wisdom to be double sure no one finds that carriage who might come looking."

Inside the inn, they found that Gabriel had ordered bread, cheese, cold beef, and a pitcher of ale. A portion of this food had been directed to a small table where John and Gabriel sat down to tackle their breakfast.

Ned sat at a larger table beside Jacob. Aurora and Lizzie engaged in close conversation with an older man, who proved to be the innkeeper.

"All we have in our cellar is ale, my lady," the man pleaded.

"Don't like ale." Jacob fed Pip cold beef, which annoyed—nay, revolted—the innkeeper. Ned found that he now distrusted men who didn't like dogs, and he consequently felt a stab of guilt when he nabbed the last of the cold beef before Pip had it all. Since their plans had succeeded so far, Ned needed to address his belly's wamble. Jacob fed Pip a chunk of cheese when the beef plate proved empty.

"Perhaps a mild cider," Lizzie coaxed the landlord.

"I'd have to send out," the man said.

"You are so kind to do so," Aurora said. She spoke quietly with Jacob, who didn't so much complain as balk. He understood the plan and didn't like it.

"No boats, please."

If only Tom could be here now, it'd be so much better for Jacob. Ned understood the critical necessity of Tom's work in London, and likely Tom would soon be free to join Jacob and

Aurora, before they struck out on the road to Rome. Ned considered again whether he should go along as far as Amsterdam.

Despite his parentage, Ned had never enjoyed his few visits to the Low Countries, except for the time when he was thirteen and his father led him on a tour of friends' studios, where he'd met three men who'd studied under Rembrandt. Or so they claimed. Ned's father said that if every man who claimed to have worked in Rembrandt's studio had in truth done so, the line would stretch from Amsterdam to Utrecht. Ned had appreciated the paintings, but Ned found the weather, the food, and the comradeship far better in Cambridgeshire.

Yes, it'd be best for all of them if Ned stayed in England to support Tom's gambol. After all, he knew nothing about how a wealthy woman travels on the Continent. And Aurora had all the male brawn and presence she needed from her servants.

But how was Jacob to tolerate the discomfort of travel, when he couldn't even drink ale at an inn? Yet Lizzie was going along (however much that might dismay Rowland). Plus, Jacob was entirely comfortable with Gabriel and John Coachman, who both kept their eyes open for Jacob's and Aurora's well-being.

Was it selfish of Ned to wish to rejoin Perry that day, when he might be useful if he sailed with Jacob?

"Ned, do Jacob and Aurora now have enough funds to live decently in Rome?" Lizzie disturbed his thoughts just as he'd reached a conclusion not to travel.

Ned said, "Yes, with no problems. John earned enough from selling the paintings and the carriage to cover travel costs. The strong box holds the proceeds from the banker's cheque we found at Arcadia House."

Aurora said, "We'll be fine with what you've managed to gather until Tom can free my marriage portion."

Lizzie had a hand on Aurora's arm. "If you are worried about whether Tom will succeed—"

"No," Aurora said. "Not for a moment. I must, however, upbraid myself for not seeking Tom's help long before now."

"Yet you frown." Lizzie persisted.

"Because," Aurora said, "I have endured life in the marquess's house by believing that one day I'd find a way to be a noble hero. I now understand that I need all your help to escape."

"I confess," Lizzie said, "that I've learned this past week how much I need my entire family." She had a kerchief in her hand, caressing its lace edge like she did when she was distressed. "I too have given up my foolish belief in being my own hero."

"Oh, look, Jacob!" Aurora exclaimed. "The landlord found a nice cider for you. And here's a plate of sweetbreads."

"Disgusting," Jacob said dully, turning his head away.

Lizzie said, "But Pip will love it."

The dog's narrow nose sniffed its way toward the plate.

"Please move Pip off the table, dear heart. It's not good manners." Aurora set the plate on the floor by Jacob's foot.

"Yes," Jacob said. "Dish took the spoon."

Before Ned could speak, Lizzie offered the required response. "And you're the man in the moon."

After removing Pip from the table, Jacob sipped the cider, then put it aside, looking worried. "When will Tom come?"

"Soon, dear brother. But not this morning." Aurora moved the drink so it couldn't be spilled. Lizzie fished in her reticule and retrieved one of the marquess's puzzle boxes. She handed it to Jacob, which calmed his fidgets.

And which proved that Lizzie, John, and Gabriel were all Jacob needed for the brief journey to the Low Countries.

Hence, Ned kept his resolve to help in the crisis on England's side of the Channel. The side where Perry resided.

— T O M —

THE AUGUST SUN HAD barely broken the horizon. Tom did his best to appear collected while he got Tamsin out of Rowland's house and over to Mordaunt's office at Lincoln's Inn. The barrister hadn't appeared yet, but Tom gave Tamsin the satchel with the prepared papers and put her in a sedan chair.

Tamsin was barely out of sight when Tom ran to Threadneedle Street, out of breath, yet relieved that Michel Chêne waited with a hackney coach and driver. Tom hadn't caught his breath yet when he saw that Camilla and Felicity Oakes (dressed as urchins) accompanied Michel.

"My sister insisted," Michel began, but Tom waved off the explanation. The narrow timing of the day's planned events didn't allow arguments. Perhaps it was better that Michel didn't make the delivery on his own.

Mrs. Touchstone opened the warehouse door at Tom's first tap. That brought Tom up short. He'd been at pains the day before to explain to Simon Touchstone, using Ned's message and proclaiming to be the cousin Ned mentioned. Touchstone had seemed touchy at the idea of the Lely he held being stolen. Tom prepared to launch into his explanation once more, but Mrs. Touchstone would have none of it.

She demanded, "You'll remove this from our premises this moment?" The lady was a head taller than Tom, and he'd lose to her if there was a scuffle. "And save our good name?"

"You will never be mentioned today, madam." Tom asserted that as truth, quite uncomfortable with this formidable woman.

"Please sign this." She held out a long, closely written paper, then pointed to the clerk's desk near the door. He didn't read it, going against everything he'd learned at law. He signed.

She examined that paper as if it contained a mysterious code, her face a living portrait of Vexed incarnate. "I don't know what I'll tell Ned if you aren't his cousin. But at least we have that stolen Lely out of the house, and you to testify for it."

Mrs. Touchstone clapped her hands, summoning two men from within the warehouse. "They'll load Ned's paintings for you. From then, protecting the art becomes your duty."

The loading took only moments, as if the gods of Olympus were in a merciful mood. She wanted Tom to sign two copies of another long paper he didn't have time to read. Quite frankly, he was too intimidated by the tall woman to question anything.

Then he was in the carriage with his three companions and rattling down Fleet Street to St James Square while other men in London were still finishing their breakfasts. Tom asked whether everything was proceeding as planned.

"Last night, we packed up pamphlets from Chalgrove House," Michel said. "Mr. Rosewurme had a fine trunk that—"

Felicity interrupted. "It was my aunt's. It's Spanish leather and finely tooled with flowers and an iron lock."

"What matters," Michel interrupted the interruption, "is that all the anti-Catholic pamphlets fit."

"Is there room for more inside?" Tom asked.

"Aye, sir."

They paused near Charing Cross. Felicity and Camilla went to ask at an inn for bread and cheese, since Camilla declared that Tom wouldn't make it through the day, crossing London without sustenance. Meanwhile, Michel opened the trunk, lashed to the boot of the carriage.

"Help me shift these," Tom pleaded.

Near the bottom of the trunk, Tom added the "favors owed" journal, plus the letter that contained Withersea's dark news and desire for Marborne. He and Michel replaced the pamphlets on top. Atop this he added the Lely as it came wrapped from Touchstone's warehouse.

Around an opposite corner on St James Square, Tom exited the coach. He left Michel with the packet that contained the provenances for Ned's devil-drawn paintings, plus a letter of gratitude from the false Leighton Fairchild.

"I trust you to manage it all, Michel. No use taking a chance that anyone in the house might recognize me," Tom said. "I'll wait here, so we can return to Lincoln's Inn together."

Then Tom paced in the shadows of a nearby block of houses, as anxious as a mother cat who'd misplaced her kittens.

45
Sin-concealing Chaos

ROWLAND CAME WITH PERRY and Valentine Starbuck onto the plaza near the Committee's meeting chambers in Westminster, their boot heels tapping a rhythm on the cobbles amid a morning crowd of hawkers, beggars, and men on their way to work. Rosewurme followed, his nose in the air, as if unassociated with them.

Long early-morning shadows leapt out as the sun shifted between clouds on the horizon, so that Rowland kept glancing over his shoulder. He hadn't expected to be so skittish. It had never been his way to have his stomach a bundle of knots whenever he and Perry launched a gambol. But then, they'd never leaped into a gambol with two dozen of the king's closest advisors in the audience. He jumped when a voice screeched so near as to leave his ear ringing in pain.

"Is that him?"

"Nay, ye plain fool," another man answered. "That's the Marquess of Withersea."

Rowland crooked his head to catch sight of the marquess, who proved to be so near that Rowland could have reached out and touched the devil. He and the marquess both wore tall periwigs that might have come from the same street in Paris, though Rowland's wasn't nearly so fine, despite being fresh from the barber. The marquess was arrayed in golden velvet with shiny gold buttons (a warm choice for a humid August day). Rowland wore the ultramarine suit Lizzie had chosen for him. He rubbed one of his brass buttons in hopes that Lizzie's suit might bring him luck. The marquess's exquisite, scarlet-heeled shoes (also from Paris) could serve as ransom for a prince, while Rowland wore city shoes that wouldn't last till Michaelmas, however diligently Lazarus's boy Peter polished them.

In the crush of the early-morning crowd, Rowland had half a moment to take a measure of the marquess. What was it that marked the man as the prince of arrogance? The turn of his lips, and how he looked down his hawk-like nose, even if you were the same height (as Rowland was). No, too trite. It was more how the marquess looked right through you, as if you and the restless crowd didn't exist. The marquess pressed a sachet to his face, as if the smell of the crowd was too much.

Then a swarm of all the urchins in London descended. Rowland couldn't count while trying to remain upright in the rush of bodies, a few as tall as grown men, others just off their leading strings, all shouting and pushing as if they'd been promised free shillings in Westminster.

Apparently, they had been.

"Coppers by the fistful!" one stripling shouted. He brushed close by Rowland, thereby thrusting him against Valentine, who reached out one arm to steady Rowland, another to elbow aside the swarming pack.

"Silver for us!"

Two rangy cubs shouted while pushing Perry up against the gold-velvet back of the Marquess of Withersea. The marquess thrust an elbow into Perry's middle, who barely coughed from the blow. Perry recovered before the marquess had his sword-stick out, waving it to warn off the swarming plague while shouting: "To me! To me!"

Four men in livery quickly surrounded the marquess. From their matching coats and their scowls, they were meant to protect the marquess, but had failed him for the half-minute during which those urchins poured across the cobbles in front of the hall in Westminster.

A tall invader yelped, "It's King Herod come to London!"
"Swords against children!" another screeched.

"Militia, in formation!" Valentine cried, too close to Rowland's ear. "For the king's peace!" He shouted like a man in command. However, he also wore a drab suit from Rowland's new closet. Without his scarlet coat, Valentine could not demand the attention of a ragged army of Pucks, though the six men in red coats (all from last night's revelry at Xanthus House) made a line and began pushing at the ragged rioters.

"Pay us for your safety!" another tall brat called. "Better us than your cheating coves!"

While the marquess's guards swung truncheons, scattering the invading horde, Rowland stepped aside at the door of the meeting chamber to let the marquess enter first. Nothing indicated that Withersea recognized Rowland, who smiled benignly and held the door while murmuring an incorrect appellation.

"Your grace."

Letting the door close while he remained on the street, Rowland surveyed the crowd. The brats were disappearing, chased by Valentine's militiamen. Among the hundred people now milling in the plaza, he thought he recognized one of his attackers from Tuesday, but couldn't be certain. Morning sunlight danced differently on men's bearded faces than did the fading light of evening.

"Where's Tamsin?" Rowland asked Perry. "She was to be among the Knights of the Marborne Fens."

"She went with Tom to Mordaunt's chambers," Perry said. "She promised to help him fish through documents there."

"Is she safe? Did Camilla stay home, like I suggested?" Rowland's roiling gut insisted no one was safe in the middle of a gambol to snare a lofty lord.

"They promised to travel by chair and not trudge openly in the street," Perry said. "Camilla isn't here yet."

"You must have been up at dawn, Mr. Frake," Valentine said, stifling a yawn. "You are a hardy lad."

ANNIE PEARSON

Rowland blinked, seeing young faces poking up at the edge
of the crowd, mistaking one for Perry, because he'd been awake
too late the night before and up too early that morning.

Another armed escort brushed past them, surrounding Lord
Bagsham. Rowland, bowing, greeted the duke.

Without his spectacles, the duke blinked, striving to recognize
who greeted him. "Good morning, Marborne. Big day today, eh?"

Starbuck bowed. "Your grace, may I be so bold as to offer a
greeting? I'm Valentine Starbuck. Perhaps you remember when
I was assigned to your escort in Paris."

"Indeed, I do, sir. It's *Captain* Starbuck now, is it not?" The
duke shook Valentine's hand. "How is your father? I haven't
seen him since the coronation."

"He is well. But he dislikes leaving home, as you know."

"Ah, I recall," the duke said. "He's a hearth and heath man."
He laughed at his own jest, which Valentine mirrored. Perry hung
back, keeping his counsel, never being one to speak out among
dukes and such. Rosewurme bowed to the duke and had a little
finger's wave in acknowledgment.

"Ready for today's business, your grace?" Rowland asked.

"Aye." Lord Bagsham glanced at the crowd. "What dragged
the riffraff out of bed? We never draw attention here."

"Who can ever tell what riles them, your grace?" Valentine
said, to which the duke nodded in friendly agreement. However,
the correct answer was "Perry Frake."

After the duke entered the meeting chamber, Starbuck said,
"We've delivered you safely, Rollo."

"Thank you." Rowland handed over two ledger pages he'd
written the night before, aware of asking a service that reached
the bounds of their friendship, given Valentine's dedication to
his position as an officer in the king's militia. He

"You swear this relieves my pharo debts?" Valentine grinned,
showing no anxiety at what he was about to do.

"From what you now owe, and through any new debt you
incur before Michaelmas," Rowland said.

414

"I shan't incur further debt. Perry has offered to help improve my luck at cards."

~

On the way across the square to the meeting chamber, Rowland sought a glimpse of Tom in all the chaos, wanting reassurance that Tom managed to slip the proper documents into the marquess's pocket.

Or was Rosewurme supposed to do that? And who was to pick Withersea's pocket? Had that been foiled when Rowland stumbled? Ack! He feared he was losing the threads of the plot.

Worse, when Mr. Mordaunt entered the meeting chamber, Tom did not enter with him, a fracture in their plan that left Rowland even more anxious. He'd argued for more chaos, but this degree was not consoling. He slipped his gold angel from the deep cuff of his sleeve and rolled it over his knuckles, keeping his hand at his back while the coin soothed him.

"Half the alabaster in your fantastical wig shook out on Withersea's gold coat," Valentine whispered as they stepped down into the windowless meeting chamber.

"It's worth the cost of sending this wig back to the barber," Rowland said, "if it annoys the marquess."

"Aye." Valentine twitched half a smile. "But you don't shine so well in the candlelight as you did."

Rowland couldn't care about that, too busy repeating silently what Lord Bagsham had advised him.

The proper greeting for each of these lords.

The proper way to offer the traditional emoluments.

The proper toast to the king.

"I'm off now," Valentine said. "Must start the task that will relieve my debt."

Perry and Rowland headed for the back of the chamber, where Lord Bagsham had advised they should find a place, and (again, following the duke's tutelage) remained standing while the Committee members found their seats. Withersea casually took his seat before all the lords had entered. Rowland counted each lord to determine whether the required fifteen lords were present so the meeting could begin.

However, Lord Bagsham hadn't warned Rowland that every lord would have a liveried man behind him, the kind of aides Rowland and Valentine had been a decade ago in Paris. And those fellows couldn't stand still in their places, too busy carrying messages to lords on the other side of the table or running out to fetch who could tell what. Rowland made his count over again, then another flutter disturbed when a small bevy of attendants flew to the other side of the chamber and back again.

The doors to the meeting chamber banged open, and another lord entered, this one younger than most everyone in the room. The front of his wig had been combed and curled to stand high above his forehead.

"My apologies, your grace, my lords. There's a riot in the making near the bridge. Barely made my way." That lord took his seat, and his aide stepped behind that chair.

Fourteen.

The day and its plans were ruined. No business could occur. The Duke of Bagsham, as the presiding officer, was speaking solemnly but too softly. The lords bent over the table to listen as Lord Bagsham repeated his words.

"How disappointing." The words echoed back to Rowland, banging at his heart. They needed to stop Withersea that very day and no later.

His despair was interrupted by the last lord to enter, trailed by an aide who couldn't have been more than fifteen. It was Viscount Heydon, the Foxes' neighbor in Cambridgeshire. Dressed in a severe steel-grey suit and modestly bewigged, Heydon hailed several nearby lords with a handshake and a soft word, apparently a very respected man. He chose the empty chair by the duke.

The fifteenth lord made a quorum. Lord Bagsham prepared to call the meeting into order. Rowland was eating up his own insides, wondering where his cousin Tom had gotten to, fearing who might have hold of him. At the last possible moment, Tom appeared behind the barrister Mr. Mordaunt, who sat beside Mr. Rosewurme. As another relief to Rowland's ragged internals, Lord Bagsham then offered the toast.

"To the health of King James and the well-being of our own green England."

Rowland had only to hold up his glass of sickeningly sweet sherry and recite a response with the others. He held his glass high, but then tripped on his chair, tumbling over Perry, and emptying his glass down the velvet breeches of the Marquess of Withersea, who dropped his glass, which shattered on the planks of the meeting chamber's floor.

"You absolute bungling fool!" Withersea exclaimed.

Perry rushed to assist him, while claiming the fault was his and making abject apologies. He ripped off his own neckcloth and dabbed at the stained gold velvet while Withersea struggled under his hands.

"You can't sit here, my lord," Perry said. "This chair is now drenched. Perhaps..." He waved vaguely across the chamber.

After a few moments, the marquess was reinstalled in an empty seat beside Mr. Mordaunt and next to one of the stern-looking lords of the Committee. Therefore, it took a bit before Lord Bagsham could move the proceedings forward. First, he introduced every lord serving the Committee, and Rowland had to unite names with faces, then stick them in his memory. Just as an idea flitted into Rowland's thought (*It's too bad Michel Chêne isn't here to play secretary*), Perry stepped behind him and adopted the stiff posture of an aide.

Perry being behind him loosened all the bonds of anxious apprehension. Rowland knew how to do this. He thrust the angel into his pocket, where his fingers touched the black glove from the spy closet. He kept the coin in hand. In case it might be needed.

Rowland put on the masque he'd intended to present to the lords and judges, becoming the pleasantest of fellows. An open, sunny soul. The innocent, good-natured crony you like to take home for a week's holiday with your family. Perry usually commented that Rowland's masque closely resembled that of an easily duped naïf. Yet Rowland performed this sham to perfection. He should try playacting on the London stage. He often thought he might make a decent Mercutio.

"For the business at hand today," Lord Bagsham said, "We require three judges. Allow me to introduce the honorable gentlemen invited to join in this day's work."

Judges? Rowland broadened his smile, nodding to welcome each man, hiding his new trepidation. Lord Bagsham hadn't mentioned any judges.

More emoluments to be paid. Rowland might escape the day with a title, but his share of the coin earned in their last restoration would be diminished.

Perry bent near his ear. "You'll need to sign your name, my lord, to each packet I pass to you. It's the gratuities."

He slipped a folded packet into Rowland's hand, while pointing with his other hand to the quill and ink set on the table, just like every lord in the chamber had. Grateful that Perry had managed this detail, Rowland signed his name over where the traces of a seal crossed the fold. He held it in his lap while the ink dried, then handed it back to Perry and received another to sign.

He couldn't voice his thoughts (*How could I do this without you, Perry?*), because he had to smile at fifteen lords and three judges while maintaining his masked expression.

I am the jolliest, safest fellow you ever let into your ranks.

46

If the Gods Are Willing

— T A M S I N —

"WHAT ARE YOU DOING here, Mr. Foxe?" Mr. Mordaunt hissed.
"Where is Mr. Newton?"

"Your clerk Newton was waylaid on business. He gave me a satchel of letters, though. I am asked to purvey this to you."

Mordaunt took the message, his face impassive, except for flushing red, then fading to a white that matched his periwig.

The night before, Tom had agreed to the changes Tamsin proposed. "You can't be in two places at once tomorrow, Tom. Not even one of your Greek heroes could achieve that."

Tom had shrugged. "I most need to be in Mordaunt's chambers, hunting up every falsified deed and writ I can find. However, the marquess met me today. I don't want him to mistake you for me. Too dangerous."

"I'll have a moustache. Camilla can do it, since she's watched how Lizzie pasted them on me all last winter."

"You'd best wear the simple periwig Rowland loaned me," Tom said. "I'll be up to my elbows in dust, sifting through writs and letters. No need for me to be modish."

Hence, Tom had stayed behind to work, and the clerk who stood behind Mr. Mordaunt in the Committee's meeting chamber was Tamsin in Tom's Sunday suit.

While Mr. Mordaunt read the letter from Tom (which warned of dire legal peril if Mr. Mordaunt continued to support the traitorous Marquess of Withersea), Tamsin sought a focus where her eyes could rest. Not on the crinkling around Perry's amused eyes.

Rowland looked reasonably handsome in the ultramarine suit Lizzie had chosen for him, though it was already splashed with alabaster. Beyond Rowland and Perry were three dozen men, rapidly warming the dimly lit chamber.

Presiding at the head of the table was the Duke of Bagsham, who'd given Rowland a house and its servants. Astonishingly, the great man who'd threatened Rowland and Lizzie was barely as tall as the enormous carved chair where he sat. The duke was round and more than a bit elfish. Nothing about how he directed the meeting with his tiny hands indicated that he had power over all in the chamber.

Tamsin, standing behind Mr. Mordaunt, felt invisible. No one had looked her way so far; therefore, no one had seen through her masquerade. No one attended to her or any of the liveried men standing behind their lords, because all attention was on the men seated at the semi-circle of the main tables.

The Duke of Bagsham introduced each of the lords, starting with the man seated at his right, opposite Tamsin. When the candlelight shone on the man's face, it proved to be her friend, Viscount Heydon. As his gaze passed over the assembly, Heydon caught Tamsin's eye. He blinked twice, then lifted his hand in a discreet greeting.

Two blinks. Heydon assessed whether he saw Tom or Tamsin in the chamber, but she could not discern his decision from this distance. Yet she took comfort in his presence: the Foxe family had a friend in the foreboding chamber.

Lord Bagsham continued his introductions. She knew two names, but she didn't bother to learn any others, certain Rowland and Perry attended to that. Instead, she observed how the fifteen lords sat grouped in pairs, trios, a quartet, aligned by age and preferences in dress. Aside from Viscount Heydon, the lords close to the presiding duke wore extravagant velvet and silk, looking grave, apparently believing they carried forth a solemn duty. ("Like Patience on a monument." The notion came as if she heard Rowland quoting Shakespeare.)

One trio of lords who whispered with each other had all adopted a rather dissolute mode of dress: loosely tied neckcloths, less tended wigs, creased coats; one had a bit of breakfast on his cravat.

Another lordly quartet dressed as austerely as any Puritan Tamsin had ever met, rejecting periwigs in favor of powdered hair tied tightly in queues. They didn't whisper with each other, but each wrote and passed notes to the liveried men standing behind their chairs. Tamsin hoped these were dinner invitations, not an early prejudice toward Rowland.

Yet two men glared dourly at Rowland, which diminished Tamsin's bright feelings, reviving the dread she'd felt upon wakening that morning. Rowland remained untouched by such cold examination; he wore the face he'd adopted a week ago while advancing their last gambol: innocent, friendly, earnest, happy to be there. Likely as not, that hand under the table was rolling a gold coin across his knuckles.

The duke then introduced the three judges, who sat across from where Tamsin hovered behind Mr. Mordaunt. They neither regarded each other nor glanced around to greet others.

Tamsin endeavored to imitate Rowland's pleasant, mild expression. She guessed that he liked the thrill of being in jeopardy, but her heart felt the enormous weight of what they were undertaking: rescuing Tom's friend from tragedy and securing the Marborne title. She stood upright in the soldierly manner that Perry adopted, having not learned anything from examining the lords and judges, except to notice the cliques, though she had no way to tell the philosophy or alliances that bound each group.

From observing subtle gestures that Cornelius Rosewurme made, Tamsin finally understood that the Marquess of Withersea was seated beside Mr. Mordaunt, though paying no attention to the barrister. Because she stood behind Mr. Mordaunt, Tamsin had to tip her head to see beyond the marquess's extravagant wig, hoping to make out their enemy's features. When the marquess looked over his shoulder, apparently seeking his aide, she saw an ordinary man in gold velvet with a sharp nose and a complexion that signaled a life of abundant wine. He had amber eyes, rather like Rowland's, except the marquess's gleamed like a diving hawk's, as if he longed to tear his prey's flesh. He chewed off a command that sent the aide behind him scurrying, then tipped his head so his face was lost from Tamsin's view.

Mordaunt glanced up after reading Tom's message. He shifted away from where the marquess sat and examined his substitute clerk. He frowned.

"You aren't Tom Foxe. Another of the multitude of cousins?"

"Aye." She bent over his shoulder, whispering, so that even Mr. Rosewurme couldn't overhear. "Tom is in your chambers, separating sheep from goats among the writs and deeds you preserve for others. I am here to keep you safe from this day's rough business. Why, you might wonder? Because Tom likes your sons and your kindly wife. Please, do your best to stay out of that man's business." She gestured toward the marquess. When she received no answer, she added, "You have two poles in the same fish pond. Fish with the duke today. That other man's pole is about to snag in the weeds and pull you under."

"You cannot—" Mordaunt's faced burned scarlet.

"We've identified traitors and men who have cheated the Crown." Tamsin repeated the sole speech she was responsible for that day. "You, sir, do not want to be among them."

"God's fury! This is an outrage!" Mordaunt hissed at her, his face now ash white.

"Yet your wife and sons won't suffer for your past sins if you focus only on the Earl of Marborne's business today. He will best serve your future fortunes. Check the satchel of papers from your clerk. The paper at the top is what Mr. Rosewurme will be asked to read first."

There, she'd done her day's work for Tom's wholly righteous restoration. It was far too easy in comparison to Tom's work and Rowland's. When she straightened to stand impassively behind the barrister, Perry broke his soldierly calm to nod at her. An unreasonable warmth spread from her heart. Perry approved.

But when Rowland's eyes roamed over that side of the table, he smiled at the marquess and never caught Tamsin's eyes. She took a breath, then resisted touching the gold Archangel coin tucked on a chain inside her shirt, behind the neckcloth. She didn't need comfort. Because she could do no more to help, she needed only to stand patiently while a formidable array of judges and lords decided on the future of Tom's friend Jacob—and of all that she held dear.

Lord Bagsham raised his thin voice. "We shall now take up the matter of Arthur Jacob Rôche, the heir to the Cloudesley title."

The Marquess of Withersea muttered something to Mr. Mordaunt that Tamsin couldn't hear. Mordaunt, fidgeting in front of her, took the paper from the top of his satchel.

"Please pass this to Mr. Rosewurme." Mr. Mordaunt's voice sounded hollow, as if his insides had been crushed. He gave the paper to Tamsin, though Rosewurme sat right by him.

Mr. Rosewurme, she was sure of it, felt slighted.

— CORNELIUS —

TUGGING AT HIS LACE neckcloth and string tie, Cornelius found his best black suit too warm. He felt like an old-time Puritan, but it was the suit which his wife claimed best flattered his figure.

He'd enjoyed the pleasure of Lord Bagsham waving a greeting when the duke entered the meeting chamber. Then he'd endured absolute coldness when Mr. Mordaunt took a seat, leaving as much space between them as possible. However, moments before that chill, Cornelius enjoyed seeing Mr. Mordaunt greet Lord Bagsham but receive no acknowledgment. Perhaps the day might provide other pleasures. Cornelius faced across from the Earl of Marborne and his associates. The giant Mr. Frake proved to be so insolent as to raise his hand and wiggle fingers at Cornelius, like a flirting maid.

When the marquess changed places to sit beside Mr. Mordaunt, he did not glance at Cornelius. And Cornelius could not
see the marquess's face to judge his mood. However, he did see
Mr. Mordaunt's serious expression, at least until a bewigged Tom
Foxe came in and quietly passed the barrister a note.

Mr. Foxe presented a slighter figure than Cornelius remem-
bered from the day before. Perhaps it was the clerkish periwig,
Tom Foxe having been unfashionably bareheaded the day before.
More likely, Cornelius no longer felt intimidated by the Foxe
family's machinations. But he couldn't attend at that moment. Mr.
Mordaunt took all of Cornelius's attention.

Reading that note, Mordaunt appeared cadaverous. The message must have informed him of the death of someone near to
his heart. Cornelius put his hand on the barrister's forearm and
leaned in to offer condolences. "I am sorry, sir. God gives and
God takes. I have reason to know it. But heaven abides."

Mordaunt jerked his arm away, offering no response. Instead,
he whispered with Tom Foxe. And so, Cornelius turned his attention to the duke, since the proceedings were commencing.

"Now, my lords," the duke addressed the assembly, "we take
up the matter of Arthur Jacob Rôche, the heir to the Cloudesley
title. Earlier this year, God placed the rightful earl and his elder
sons in Abraham's bosom. Hence, we shall consider bestowing
the earl's title upon his surviving son."

The duke removed his spectacles and bent to examine a paper
in front of him. The man must be very blind while reading, for
he bent so close, his nose nearly touched the table. He looked up,
put his spectacles on his nose, and spoke.

"It appears the Earl of Cloudesley's surviving son is not of
age. Is the barrister here who shepherded this case through the
chancery court?"

Mr. Mordaunt sat stone still, as if he'd turned to a statue. It
was nigh on impossible to perceive the rise and fall of the barrister's shoulders, to see if the man still breathed.

The Marquess of Withersea poked the barrister, which tipped Mordaunt into Cornelius's quarter. When Mordaunt still did not respond, the marquess rose.

"My lords, I have served as guardian for young Rôche since his father's death. The honorable Mr. Mordaunt did service for young Rôche, guiding this affair through chancery court and confirming the guardian bond."

Lord Bagsham said, "Please share the young gentleman's guardian bond with all these present."

Withersea said, "I've asked a witness to the bond to read it to you." He had his hand heavily on Mordaunt's shoulder.

"Please pass this to Mr. Rosewurme." Mr. Mordaunt spoke to Tom Foxe, though Cornelius was sitting close by and could have received it directly from Mordaunt's hand.

No matter, Cornelius received it while noticing that the duke, the judges, and the fifteen lords were bored out of their wits, though the meeting had only just begun. Cornelius stood, bobbing his head to the gathered lords.

"Who is it? Oh, I see," the duke said, "it's Mr. Cornelius Rosewurme. Please proceed."

Cornelius cleared his throat to offer his best oration, as he must for the sake of his new protectors. "Your grace, I see from the date at its end that this bond was written several months after the one I signed. S'welp me, this bond names witnesses other than me."

"What?" The marquess rather croaked in surprise.

"Proceed," the duke said. "It is the bond you just now received from the honorable barrister's hand. Please continue."

Cornelius had enjoyed enough business with the duke that he perceived the man's impatience. He addressed the duke while he read and couldn't see the dangerous marquess. He cleared his throat again and began in his best hawker's voice.

Know all men by these present that I, Arthur Jacob Rôche, the lawful child of Charles Arthur Rôche of Cloudesley in

the county of Kent, my father deceased, and I being under
the age of thirty years as specified in my father's testament...

Red with fury, Withersea remonstrated in whispers with Mr.
Mordaunt, who showed empty hands and lifted his shoulders,
unable to explain. Cornelius soldiered on, lifting his voice to
heaven, the way he did whenever villagers began to drift away
from his street sermons.

> ...and therefore, incapable of recovering or receiving the
> rents issues and profits of all those messages, lands, tene-
> ments, and hereditaments situated lying and being in Clou-
> desley aforesaid given and devised unto me in and by the
> will of my said late father, and of giving a discharge for the
> same in my name, ...

Cornelius coughed. No one lord or aide so much as lifted
their head to glance his way. The entire chamber save for the red-
faced marquess might as well have been sleeping.

> I do hereby elect and make choice of Thomas Caius Foxe
> of Revelstone House in Cambridgeshire to be my curator
> or guardian to all intents and purposes in law whatsoever.

"What?" Withersea's attention turned wholly to Cornelius,
his face scarlet with anger. "No, that's wrong."

"Proceed, Mr. Rosewurme," the duke said.

Cornelius obeyed, though he feared the absolute fury in the
marquess's eyes, despite the Foxe cousins' plans. He mastered
his fear, though, and emoted as if he spoke the Word of God.

> That this my election and choice may have its due effect in
> law, I do hereby nominate and appoint a procurator of the
> Consistory Court of Canterbury to act for me and in my
> name, to appear before any competent judge and to pro-
> cure and desire this my proxy and election to be admitted
> and enacted, and the said Thomas Caius Foxe to be as-
> signed my curator and guardian...

"No!" Withersea protested, his fist striking the table.

Cornelius had his eye on the duke, but continued.

...to the purposes aforesaid, and to all other effects and purposes in law whatsoever, and to do and perform all other acts and things requisite and necessary to be done in the premises. In witness whereof I have hereunto set my hand and seal the eighth day of August in the year of our Lord one thousand six hundred and eighty-five.

Withersea stood, as if with murder on his mind. Cornelius, believing in Tom Foxe's promise of protection, took a breath to conclude his reading.

Sealed and delivered (being first Arthur Jacob Rôche, The Right Honourable the Earl of Cloudesley Duly stamped) in the presence of Eduard Wijck and Peregrine Frake.

"Outrageous!" Withersea declared, his clenched fist betraying his fury. "I know not how my barrister came to have such fiction in his possession. I am Rôche's lawful guardian."

Withersea turned an unhealthy color while protesting what had just been read, with furious glances at Mr. Mordaunt. Cornelius had read the new bond, yet he now escaped the marquess's notice. This time, Cornelius felt glad of the slight.

Perry Frake whispered in the Earl of Marborne's ear. The earl stood, nodding to those in the chamber as he spoke. "Your grace. My lords. My sergeant served the king with me. If he may be allowed to speak, he has knowledge of this bond."

"That bond is an utter falsehood," Withersea hissed. "From top to bottom."

The duke said, "Let us allow the man to speak. It's Sergeant Frake, isn't it? Were you not in the king's court last Friday, bringing the names of rebellious traitors?"

That declaration advanced Withersea's complexion to the hue of burnt brick.

"Aye, your grace." Frake remained behind the Earl of Marborne. "I signed my name as witness to the bond which was read just now. And I aver that Jacob Rôche, the Earl of Cloudesley, wrote the bond. I witnessed his hand on the pen in the writing of it. From the first words to the last."

"Nonsense!" Withersea clapped his hands in angry frustration. "The lad's a natural. He couldn't read his own name if it were writ large by God Himself."

"I can also bring you," Frake retained his uncanny calm, "the second witness who signed this bond. If you will, my lords, I can fetch him within the next three hours."

While that argument progressed, Mr. Mordaunt shrunk further into a shell of himself. He cast several looks at his clerk. Most certainly he must know, or suspect, that Tom Foxe placed the new bond in his satchel of papers. His clerk, however, stood stiff as a stone.

Withersea's protests grew more vociferous. "But my wife's brother has never met this man."

The marquess's fury washed over the giant Perry Frake as if it were a mild breeze. Frake said, "Howbeit, I aver that it is as Lord Cloudesley might say to his friends, 'Dish took your spoon. You are the man in the moon.'"

Withersea jerked back as if struck. Cornelius didn't understand Frake's nonsense or of the marquess's dramatic reaction.

Mr. Mordaunt growled in Cornelius's ear. "Mr. Rosewurme, are you part of this foolery?"

Cornelius said, "I did as you asked, reading what your clerk gave me. As the marquess instructed me to do."

Mordaunt was closer to weeping than Cornelius had seen any man in past years. "Thou hast betrayed me, like a Judas."

"Nay," Cornelius said. "No betrayal, only cleansing the crimson from my soul. I advise you to ask Tom Foxe for remedies. You can trust him."

While the lords in the chamber murmured among themselves, the three judges bent over the table, their periwigs wiggling when their foreheads nearly touched. After the three judges nodded, one wrote a note that his aide passed to the Duke of Bagsham, who held up his hand for attention.

"Your lordships, our honorable judges ask that this tangle be sent back to the Consistory Court of Canterbury. Let us take a brief recess. Then we'll turn our attention to the Marborne matter. Twenty minutes, your lordships. No more than that."

While others shuffled out of the chamber, the Marquess of Withersea towered over the confused Mr. Mordaunt, pouring his fury on the man's head.

"Get out, Mr. Mordaunt!" Lord Withersea demanded. "You ruined this day for me."

Which was unfair to the barrister. Cornelius estimated that Perry Frake and Tom Foxe had most to do with the appearance of the distressing new bond. The barrister argued that he had no knowledge of this change in Jacob Rôche's guardianship, but Withersea refused to hear it.

"Remove yourself." Withersea pointed to the door.

Mordaunt rose with as much dignity as a man might when a marquess is raging over his head. He began to weave his way through the lords rambling out for the recess.

Mordaunt's clerk leaned over Cornelius to whisper, "Thank you, Mr. Rosewurme, for playing your part so well."

That tickle of warm breath lingering, he watched as the clerk trailed after the barrister. If Cornelius had not suffered a momentary loss of pluck, he'd have noticed from the start, being a master at detecting others' fraud, that it wasn't Mr. Tom Foxe in that clerkish periwig.

47

Under the Tower's Shadow

IT WAS ALL TAKING too long. Tom would like to have gnawed on his insides while waiting for Michel to return from Withersea's London house. He calculated the timing for all to be achieved before the marquess would depart from the Committee meeting.

When Michel appeared, he claimed to be ten minutes early, not ten minutes late. Fortunately, Luke Holywell had stood ready, as agreed, at the gate to Lincoln's Inn. Tom sent Camilla and Felicity in sedan chairs to Westminster. Then Tom, Michel, and Luke walked from the hackney coach stand near the Old Bailey, each of them pretending to be calm. Luke spoke rapidly, distractedly, as anxious as the sputtering fire burning in Tom's belly.

"My Uncle Oliver—though he's not truly my uncle, only an orphaned cousin raised with my father—declined the king's invitation to join the judges in Winchester."

"What's in Winchester?" Tom asked, just to keep Luke talking, as the best cover for his anxiety. He must know about Winchester but worrying about this day's many difficulties crowded out most of what Tom knew.

"The assizes that the king called to try all the Monmouth traitors." Luke sounded impatient. Likely he'd explained this to Tom previously, but Tom's head was full of what came next, not what had already passed. "That's why Uncle Oliver was available to answer my inquiry. If you can give him any legal action that will please the king, my uncle will be as obliged as any judge we might attempt to bribe."

"We aren't bribing judges." Tom's hackles rose like a startled cat. "We are avoiding any judge who can be bribed." He'd given Michel the marquess's journal, which Ned had sent, so that it could be stored it in the fancy trunk with the pamphlets, but Tom still had the journal's list of judges who owed favors or sinecures to Withersea.

"Easy, friend," Luke said. "You asked me yesterday what judge cannot be bribed and were happy when I claimed Sir Oliver Boxworth to be an honest man. What he's worried about is, rather, that the king will dismiss him. Since King James has dismissed barrels and pecks of judges, adding on to what Charles had been doing. Here we are

A head taller than Tom, Luke had all the London polish that Tom aspired to, having not learned the posture and bearing of the loftier inhabitants of the Inns of Court. Although Tom had a wealthy-looking suit, he had again turned it with the buff taffeta side out. He hadn't met this uncle and didn't want to give the appearance of a flashy cove shopping for a judge.

"We can't keep Sir Oliver waiting," Tom said.

"As I said four times now," Luke said, his hand over his mouth to hide his laughter, "we are quite timely. I'd thump your skull for all your impatience if you hadn't explained why this action before the judge matters. But surely, we have more time than only just this morning. Your charges against the marquess are severe."

"The man's a malicious weasel," Tom said. "He's gone from his house at this moment. If we don't have a warrant before he returns home, he'll find a way to defeat what we will present to the judge."

What they were about to present was a set of truths, but truths made evident because Tom moved the proofs so that they were in physical juxtaposition. It was nothing like juggling the apostles.

Although glad to be out of the day's heat, Tom writhed in lethal fidgets. If Tamsin knew, she'd scold him for doing more in a morning than he'd done in months. He was smothering a coughing fit and reaching into his pocket for a peppermint when a clerk called them into the judge's chambers. Luke made the introductions, then began all the niceties, since the only judge Tom had ever been before was a magistrate in Cambridge, to represent mundane writs and pleas for his master.

Sir Oliver, thin as a quill, appeared to be pasted together out of the paper dust and downy bits pared from feathers to make the quills that littered the judge's table. His periwig had been cast on haphazardly, as if it were made of vanes cut away to make quills. He had milky eyes the color of robin's eggs. Yet the man's gaze bored into Tom's heart.

"Thomas Foxe of Cambridgeshire?" Sir Oliver demanded with a bark. "Not yet risen to the bar?" Before Tom could reply, the judge frowned. "Foxe? Related to Doctor Absolom Foxe of Trinity College?"

"Aye, my lord. He was my great-uncle. I was his ward."

"Ah." The judge brightened. Then frowned again. "Was?"

"Sadly, our uncle passed from us," Tom still couldn't get these words out without pausing to swallow, "last week."

"Good lord, no!" The judge looked stricken. "Grace to the living, and rest to the departed." He rubbed at his eyes. "I'm sorry for your loss. Doctor Foxe was my tutor in Latin at Trinity."

Tom disliked feeling that his grief advanced his standing with the judge. Yet Tom managed to say, "He was my first tutor, too, but in a makeshift schoolroom in our house."

"Lucky boy," Sir Oliver said, "to have begun with the best. Did Doctor Foxe approve of you going into law instead of becoming a scholar?"

"He declared a decade ago that my life's fate was to be seeking justice through the law."

"Ah." The judge smiled. "The good doctor declared that my Latin would do me for English law, but not for a scholar's life. But he declared for me the fate my own uncle preferred."

"It's my preferred fate, your lordship."

Michel Chêne, who lurked behind Luke, sneezed, then begged pardon. That interruption called the judge back to business.

"Mr. Holywell's note said that you have a difficult case to present."

"Not difficult in substance, sir." Tom laid his first paper on the judge's table. "But difficult because of the man whom we make claims against. The Earl of Cloudesley had a picture of his mother that was drawn by an artist of some fame. The drawing was taken without Cloudesley's permission and offered for sale by the Marquess of Withersea." Tom laid out his copy of Jacob's new guardian bond while the judge was still reading the writ for return of Jacob's mother's picture. "I bring this claim against the marquess as the earl's guardian, since he is not yet of age."

"You will want the drawing returned to the young earl?"

"Yes, but much more." Tom had found all the strength he needed when the judge begged grace to the living. "When I approached the art dealer who'd purchased the purloined drawing, he became alarmed and sent the sketch back to Withersea's house in London, not wanting to be drawn in disputes of provenance. He feared the reputation of his business for honest dealings."

"Then you want a warrant to enter the marquess's house, to seize the disputed drawing."

Tom held his impatience in rein, though the old-style Dutch clock on the mantle ticked away. "This young man," Tom pointed to Michel, "brought the claim to the art dealer this morning. The dealer asked him to carry the drawing to the marquess's house but sent more than that. The marquess had demanded delivery of several paintings the dealer was holding for another man."

"You are Michel Chêne? Did I remember your name?"

"Yes, my lord. I am secretary to the Earl of Marborne."

"Lord Marborne is my cousin," Tom said. "He lent me Mr. Chêne's services to retrieve the stolen drawing."

Michel said, "At the marquess's request, several paintings were delivered from the art dealer, who asked me to take them along with the drawing to be returned. When his servants unpacked them, this paper fell out." He held out the letter that "Leighton Fairchild" had promised, asking the marquess to protect certain art belonging to Danvers Duncombe from discovery by the king's men.

Tom placed the paper on the judge's table, trying not to hold his breath. Only the fictitious Mr. Fairchild had signed the paper as witness to the transaction. But Tom presented a second paper: the receipt from Withersea when he accepted the delivery of the paintings that morning.

"*Ecce!*" Sir Oliver exclaimed as he read. "This is treason. The man is withholding a traitor's possessions from the king."

"*Vero, vero,*" Tom said, with no Perry there to censure him. "But we seek to present a greater travesty perpetrated by the marquess. Mr. Chêne, can you please explain?"

Michel seemed to have ice in his veins. "My employer, Lord Marborne, was asked to serve the king by finding a printing press that had become infamous for producing anti-Catholic pamphlets. We found the press yesterday, and we also found this among the discarded papers with it."

> Received of DUX on behalf of Lord Withersea, 11s7d for ink and paper, to print the accompanying text.

That paper from Cornelius Rosewurme's box had proved immediately useful. How Rosewurme had connived to bind signatures, sums, and treasonous text together, Tom didn't know. But he'd pay a choir of angels to sing the scoundrel's praises.

Michel said, "If I might say more, your lordship?"

"Go on." Sir Oliver had drawn a blank sheet of paper before him and, quill in hand, was opening the cover on an elaborately painted inkstand. Dutch, Tom thought, like the ceaselessly ticking clock on the mantle.

Speaking with deference, yet without cowing, Michel said, "When I was in the marquess's house to make the delivery this morning, an elaborately decorated box lay open in the foyer. I am prepared to swear that the box contains the same pamphlets described in the receipt Mr. Tom Foxe just showed you."

"Young man, you are accusing a lord of treason."

"No, my lord, that's not for me to do." Michel stayed steady as a stone. "I am only swearing to what I have witnessed."

Before Sir Oliver dipped his quill, he again fixed Tom with his intense, milky stare. Then he asked the most obvious question about the farrago of accusations presented to him.

"Why have the clerk Thomas Foxe and the secretary to the Earl of Marborne been busy gathering accusations against a peer of the realm?"

"As you may know," Tom said, clinging to his belief that they'd made a sufficiently sturdy case, "my cousin Rowland Foxe played a part in uncovering the scheme by the traitor Danvers Duncombe to support the Duke of Monmouth. My cousin was sure that the Marquess of Withersea participated, too. But it wasn't in the evidence offered to the Crown when Duncombe was arrested."

Tom turned aside to cough, longing for a peppermint, refusing any weakness that might grasp hold of him here.

"Along with my new master, Mr. John Mordaunt, I heard the marquess confess in my master's chambers that he had joined Duncombe's traitorous syndic. But, of course, that would be called hearsay before the court. It's only by diligence that we've gathered this evidence. We hope—"

"That it's enough?" The judge put pen to paper. "It's enough to search his house for what Mr. Chêne has described. And it's enough to hold the marquess in the Tower, where he can be properly questioned."

That Dutch clock began to strike the hour.

"You'll have to take this to…" The judge turned to his own secretary-clerk. "Where is the closest militia quartered?"

"My lord," Tom dared to interrupt, "Captain Starbuck is housed not far from the Tower. He's the man who arrested the traitor Duncombe. Perhaps we should find him."

Sir Oliver was nodding. And Tom was smothering several forces within. One, the impatient and imperious demon that could barely tolerate the time it took to sprinkle pounce to ensure the ink dried and that the wax seal was appropriately stamped. The other, the overjoyed demon, was too ready to celebrate victory. He ignored a wave of fatigue as being an unwanted lesser demon.

If only the clock were not striking such a late hour in the morning. And if only the hackney coach Tom had paid to wait were still there when they returned.

Alas, it was not.

Tom stood, tapping a toe while Michel sought another coach. He tried to say, "Starbuck must be at Withersea's house now," but his throat, dry as the dust in the road, refused to form the words. He fished a peppermint from his pocket, tried to get it into his mouth, then looked up at the sound of an approaching coach. He missed his mouth, heard the peppermint clatter on the pavement, but then couldn't see to find either a coach or a candy.

"Blast it, Tom Foxe! You've gone too far. Help me, Mr. Chêne. He's beyond his last legs."

— NED —

IN BILLINGSGATE, THE TRAVELERS treated Ned as their leader. Aurora, Jacob, John Coachman, Gabriel the footman, each asked Ned what they should do while waiting until time to board the ship. Lizzie whispered in his ear, "Pretend you know what to do, even if you don't. I'll pretend to trust your advice."

To begin, Ned directed John Coachman to shepherd everyone through scorching streets to the ship where John had purchased Aurora's passage. However, on that earlier errand, John had walked down different lanes, so they had to ask directions of people lingering near the multitude of moored ships.

Ned walked with Jacob, who shivered like an unbroken colt and grasped Aurora's sleeve, keeping her within one step from him. Ned kept his hand on Pip's head, the only closeness Jacob tolerated, hoping to show that Ned intended to protect him.

Sailing away was the only means by which Aurora could keep Jacob safe. Yet walking by Jacob's side, encouraging him through the crowd, Ned felt as if he led the young man into torture. Jacob complained about the noise and stink of the fish markets. Yet he repeatedly let Pip jump down to follow what enticed a dog's nose, and Ned had to fetch the pup back.

"Too loud," Jacob said.

Aurora said, "It is, love."

Lizzie said, "We'll be on board soon, away from the noise."

They reached the place on the wharf from which the *Zeewolf's* sailors were loading cargo onto small barges. Across the way at the ship, other sailors winched bales onboard. Aurora's baggage had been stacked to the side, to be loaded last. John had paid two dockwallopers to watch it.

Two sailors lost hold of one bale while loading it onto a small barge. Before those below were ready to receive the bale, it tipped off the wharf's edge, upending the barge, raising a great splash. The bargemen scurried to retrieve the bale. Curses rang out.

"Devil rot thy bones, ye loiter-sack!"

"God's wounds, thou whiffle-whaffle."

"Damn your eyes, you hell-bound swingebeest!"

"Pox on ye! Tryin' ta murder me?"

Jacob stopped so abruptly that he knocked Ned's hand from Pip's head and twisted his splintered finger while pulling Aurora's cloak half off her shoulders. Jacob struggled to get his hands over his ears with Pip still in his arms. The pup whined at being clutched so tightly. Jacob keened along with Pip. And wept.

Murmuring consolations, Aurora hugged Jacob. Ned managed to get Pip out of the crush, unable to do more than hold the dog. He calmed the whining beast, but it hurt his heart that he couldn't help console Jacob. Aurora rocked Jacob, letting him weep. The bargemen's chaos settled out, leaving the wharf quiet, at least in comparison to the uproar. Jacob pointed to the closest ship.

"Makes me sick. When the wind blows."

Aurora said, "The weather is perfect today, dear heart. No whistling winds."

Lizzie asked, "Was there a storm when you last sailed?"

"Yes. Jacob was dreadfully ill."

Lizzie sat beside Jacob. "You can stand on the deck with me, Jacob. I'm never sick if I am on deck."

Jacob swiped at his eyes. He sniffed but didn't speak.

Ned fetched his sketchbook from his coat pocket. "Will you keep this, Jacob? Until Tom comes?" He flipped it open to one of the drawings of Pip, where he'd also sketched Tom.

"When is Tom coming?" Jacob stuttered the question, the quaver in his voice enough to break a bishop's heart.

"Soon," Aurora said. "But he wants you to sail away today. To be safe from anyone who might hurt you."

"You promise Tom is coming?"

Lizzie sucked in a breath, air hissing over her teeth. But she didn't say what she knew, that Tom hadn't agreed to travel to Rome. "Jacob, dear, I'll be with you and Rory. We'll be safe together. We'll have a garden where Pip can run free."

Pip perked up at the sound of his name and struggled to jump from Ned's arms to Jacob.

Jacob took his dog, lifted him to look the beast in the eye. "We'll stay on deck, Pip. You won't be sick."

"The water will be as smooth as the sky is blue," Aurora said. "No storms today."

John Coachman finally caught the attention of a ship's mate and begged information. He rejoined the travelers with news.

"It's two hours until the tide turns. They don't want passengers until all the cargo is stowed. Meanwhile, my lady, the mate recommends we beg refreshments at the chandler's shop across the way, where we can wait out of the sun."

The chandler, introduced to the marchioness and her traveling party, invited them into his wife's private sitting room. Once away from the noise and commotion of the wharf, Jacob quickly calmed. Gabriel the footman ran to the closest tavern, then returned with ale and cool water, plus a packet of biscuits. Jacob accepted the flask of water Aurora passed to him. He took off his hat and poured the water into it, then set Pip to drink.

Ned had no reason to remain. John and Gabriel could guard them. The storm of tasks and emotions was over, and it was past time for Ned to join Perry and Rowland. While Jacob was busy with Pip, the others walked to the door to say goodbye to Ned.

"Please tell Rollo," Lizzie spoke in Ned's ear, "that he knows where to find me in Amsterdam. Tell him to come soon, rather than yearning."

Ned waved farewell, most intent at that moment in finding Perry than in assuaging Rowland's yearnings.

"Hold back!" John had his arm in front of both Aurora and Lizzie. "Step away from the door."

"What is it?" Aurora asked.

"That fellow across the way." A smallish man took mincing steps up a gangway from one of the barges serving the *Zeewolf*. The dyed-purple plume in his hat swayed with the gangway, enhanced by the man's awkward steps in his high-heeled shoes. "He was at Arcadia House Tuesday. While I purchased your passage, he was haggling to ship goods on the *Zeewolf*. I struggled then to be sure he didn't see me."

"It's Caspar!" Lizzie hissed.

"Who's Caspar?" Ned asked. The man had a beaked nose like a goshawk and waved his hands like a Frenchified fop.

"Withersea's crony." Lizzie bit her lip, didn't say more.

Aurora, hidden in the shadow of John's bulk and Gabriel's slim barrier, said, "Sir Duxwold is the marquess's intermediary. The marquess never deigns to conduct business on his own."

"He's headed toward London Bridge," Lizzie said.

Ned had intended to travel in the same direction, so he finished his goodbyes and followed the knightly gentleman, content to take his time getting to Westminster, since Perry and Rowland wouldn't emerge from their meeting before noon.

By the time Sir Duxwold reached Thames Street and turned west, Ned guessed they both followed the route to Westminster. Ned kept that swaying purple plume in sight as he brushed through the crowded street, though thoughts of Perry drew Ned like a needle on a lodestone to Westminster. However, following Sir Duxwold helped Ned make his way when Thames Street ended at Puddle Docks and lanes had to be traversed until they crossed the Fleet Bridge. All through that passage, the diminutive popinjay failed to notice Ned following at every turn.

As they trod Fleet Street, Ned considered how fine he felt about his morning's successes. He had greater pride in the last few days' business than he'd had over the previous week's gambol. The world was improved from his toil, which was what Uncle Absolom insisted they must do. Perhaps, though, it wasn't proper to nurture self-pride, while everything remained in chaos. Should he pretend modesty when he related his doings to Perry?

Also, perhaps he shouldn't feel as happy as he did to be walking alone. But he'd been living in an excitable hive of activity for two days and nights. The bustle as he trod back to Thames Street felt peaceful in comparison. He let his thoughts drift deeply into how he'd report all these doings to Perry, then imagining the composition of a painting he might create of the travelers at dockside. Aurora majestic in grey. Jacob making his dog jump for a biscuit. Lizzie in glowing gold.

For a moment, that image caused Ned to halt in his tracks. He'd be the one to tell Rowland that Lizzie was sailing for the Low Countries. But then Ned was stirred to pay attention when Sir Duxwold turned off Fleet Street into Chancery Lane.

Ned had to resist the strong pull that directed his heart toward Perry in Westminster. Conquering that, he followed the purple-plumed man into the neighborhood of the Inns of Court, then to Lincoln's Inn.

Zooterkins, if it wasn't a wary, rumpled Tom who answered when Sir Duxwold knocked on a barrister's door.

48
Knights of the Marborne Fens

"WHERE'S VALENTINE?" ROWLAND ASKED as soon as Lord Bagsham declared a break in the Committee meeting.

Perry said, "You distress me, my lord. We both know it's too soon for Starbuck to do his business and return."

Perry, who never showed anxiety, left Rowland to sit alone and hide his apprehension. Circling the chamber, Perry paused beside each lord's aide to speak in his ear and shake his hand. The three judges' aides, who now stood behind empty chairs, received the same whispered greeting and handshake. Perry then went out the door and was gone for several minutes, likely to check on the Knights of the Marborne Fens.

While believing the first part of the meeting had gone as well as Tom had planned, Rowland pushed back at his uneasy sense that the next business could still go awry. As tight as every tendon felt, Rowland was steady enough to stand and greet Viscount Heydon when the man crossed the chamber.

"When we shared breakfast last week," Heydon said, "neither you nor I would have predicted that you'd appear here so quickly. My sincere congratulations."

"I'm here only due to the king's whimsy," Rowland said.

"Nonsense," Heydon said. "You, and your ancestors, performed real service to the Crown. In just a few days, you did what I couldn't manage in months of queries." Heydon, too, had worked to uncover Danvers Duncombe's nefarious ways.

"Luck, I reckon." Rowland had one hand behind his back, rolling his coin, hoping to convince his heart to calm down and beat in an ordinary way.

"Skill, I estimate," Heydon said. "It is Marborne that is lucky, to have you at its helm."

A week ago, Rowland had swallowed dark bitterness, believing that the viscount was to marry Lizzie. What a difference that gambol made, leaving the two men shaking hands among the great lords of England, as if they were friends.

"Excuse me," Heydon said. "I must greet the duke."

Perry returned. "I sent Felicity and Camilla to Tom with a message about our success so far. I'd invited my three youngest brothers to join the crowd this morning, but I signaled for them to scamper off home. Methinks I saw my other two brothers in the crowd. Yet they should still be in Knightsbridge, not London. When I looked twice, I couldn't find them again, so it must be two other lads who've grown too tall with too little sense."

"You can brag later about your heroics, how you swore to the truth of Ned's devil-writing before God and a herd of lords."

"Nay, not forgery. Ned only guided the young earl's hand. It is a true and honestly sworn bond."

That Perry took seriously their private whispers must prove that he too worried about the coming moments. Rowland diverted them both with a question. "On God's bones, tell me: did you just now pass gratuities to these lords? Those packets you had me signing earlier? Where did you find the funds?"

"From Withersea's aide's pocket," Perry said. "I swapped my purse for his on our way in. Why would I use our own funds to bribe protection from our enemy?"

"Thank you."

"There's more." Perry grinned. "In Knightsbridge, we found one of his gratuity notes." He gestured over to where the marquess was arguing with Mordaunt. "So, Ned created another set. Today, you offered each lord a five-guinea coin inside a note that says, 'God grant us good lords, good kings, and peace.'"

"What came to be in that aide's purse?"

"Shaved pound coins with messages that say—"

"Fool!" Withersea's voice rose, then dropped immediately. He still attacked Mr. Mordaunt, the marquess's fury evident in how he thumped the barrister's chest.

Perry dipped his head, speaking in Rowland's ear. "His note to the members says, 'For men among Hawkins' Heirs and Duncombe's syndic.'"

"God's bones, Perry!"

"Aren't I clever? Any man who knows what it means will feel threatened by possible exposure. The others, who can say?"

"They will be able to guess when Starbuck returns. That can't fail, can it?"

"No," Perry said. "He'll get a warrant and—"

"Don't comfort me," Rowland said. "It leaves me more anxious. I'm like a newborn colt that never saw a gambol before."

Rowland tumbled his gold angel across his knuckles, waiting with bated breath for the next act (as a hero in Shakespeare might), needing only Starbuck to return in time. He tried to rejoice that Tom, Perry, and Ned had won Jacob's case in the first act. He tried to catch Tom's eye to share a quiet celebration. His cousin stood quietly behind the barrister, holding the satchel of papers he'd brought in.

Rowland raised his hand to wave. Except—

"That's not Tom." Rowland turned to Perry.

"Once again, you distress me, my lord," Perry said. "You had me believing your Merry Andrew was only a disguise." He leaned closer. "Tom is seeking a warrant that adds every crime he can. Not just the Duncombe business."

"You didn't tell me about Tom or Tamsin."

"It was obvious, Rollo," Perry scarcely gave the words breath, "when your cousin stomped into this chamber. It's a better moustache than last week, I aver."

Rowland watched, finding the inscrutable Tamsin to be as amusing as any playacting in Drury Lane.

"Our first action worked without fault," Perry said. "Your enemy no longer has a barrister to speak for him. The Committee and judges have refused the marquess's plea about Jacob."

"We must toast Tamsin tonight for a task well done."

Withersea was pointing to the door, through which other lords were returning to the meeting chamber. Mordaunt gathered his frame up to his full height, perhaps tipping on his toes, so that he towered a full head over the marquess. Whatever he said, it wasn't more than two or three words. Then Mordaunt strode from the chamber. Withersea wrenched Tamsin by the shoulder and roughly sent her after Mordaunt.

"Poor Mr. Rosewurme," Rowland murmured. "He'll have to sit there and face Withersea's wrath alone."

"He's a brave man," Perry said, "for the sort of man he is."

— CORNELIUS —

WHILE THE MARQUESS BERATED Mr. Mordaunt at the meeting chamber's door, Cornelius stepped to the back of the room, having decided he must give the Foxes a better warning than he had so far. If he was to be protected, he had to offer in return whatever protection he could.

"Ahem. Sir. Your lordship."

It took forever for the earl and Perry Frake to break off their whispered conference and look his way, all while he checked repeatedly that the marquess didn't notice this conference.

"Please, my lord. Mr. Frake. Hear me. I fear the marquess has set your doom in motion."

"Whatever he plans to do," the earl said, "we have better to defeat him. Together with Lord Bagsham's patronage."

"But I fear…that is, I'm certain he intends the same fate for your lordship as he set for Viscount Bravewood."

"What?" Frake's whole attention, and his lordship's, turned on Cornelius.

"Canton, my lord. Or Surat. Bombay. One of those places where there's no Christians. You must be aware."

The Duke of Bagsham's voice sounded. "Let us come back to our business, my lords."

Cornelius slipped back into his chair while the lords obscured the marquess's view of him. To Cornelius's great relief, the marquess took a chair two seats away, crossing his arms and legs, and staring at the Earl of Marborne. Who paid close attention to the duke.

Letting out the breath he'd been holding, Cornelius noticed Mr. Frake still stared in his direction, arms folded from where he stood behind the earl's chair. Every other aide in the room, lordlings in waiting, dressed in brocade suits, stood a head above their lord's chair. Only the earl had a Goliath standing behind him, in buff linen, looking more like a guard than the messengers the other lords kept at their side.

When all the lords settled into their places, the Duke of Bagsham read the formal introduction to the business of the Marborne title, never once looking up until he put on his spectacles to see how the assembly responded. Which Cornelius thought made sense, given that the aged lord was now as blind as Fowlmere's ancient mother in Oxford, too blind to see how many young wights and bag snatchers were sleeping near the fire in her parlor.

Withersea coughed, exaggerating it, which broke up Cornelius's musings, bringing him back to the dark chamber, now overheated again with shuffling and snuffling lords and their minions. The duke finished reading aloud the writ before him and addressed the assembly directly.

"If your lordships will unanimously agree, then Rowland Matthew Foxe of Marborne parish in Cambridgeshire is pronounced by the king to be heir to the Marborne title and shall henceforth be known as the Honorable Earl of Marborne. What say you, Mr. Foxe?"

The Earl of Marborne rose from his chair to answer just as Withersea stood and snared all attention in the room.

"I swear that the king and each of the lords here have been duped by that scion of traitors." Withersea pointed to the earl.

"The Marborne title cannot pass. To wit, I present the Committee with a writ testifying to the perfidy of generations of the Foxes of Cambridgeshire. Mr. Rosewurme, as my agent, will you please read this writ?"

Withersea withdrew a roll of paper from his pocket and handed it to Cornelius.

Was this what they meant, when soldiers talked of facing battle and feeling their insides turn to water?

Cornelius received the paper from Withersea, fumbled while unrolling it. Dropped it. Picked it up. Unrolled it once more. He'd expected to read another of Tom Foxe's papers from Mordaunt's satchel. The marquess's disruption would destroy Tom Foxe's carefully laid plans.

"If it please you, sir." Lord Bagsham interrupted before Cornelius could begin to read aloud. "Give it to me to read."

Never again in this life would Cornelius ever choose what pleased Withersea over what his friend the duke desired. A rush of emotion clouded Cornelius's view of the chamber.

Was there a way he could stop Withersea's writ from undoing the Foxe brood's plans—and thereby undoing their promise to protect him?

Was he watching the demise of his own future before it had even one day to unfold? Such a loss could be as great as when God had gathered his blessed wife into His bosom.

Withersea snatched the paper back from Cornelius's faltering hand and carried it to the duke, who accepted it without comment. But then Withersea's aide stepped forward to whisper to the marquess, who looked startled.

He said, "I beg you to excuse me, your lordships. I have an urgent message awaiting me. I shall return in a moment."

Cornelius's sense of impending doom gave way to the kind of fear where you must stand and fight. With every muscle trembling, he stood. He glanced at the Frake giant, who smiled, as if encouraging him.

"My lords, I beg to speak."

— TAMSIN —

A LINE OF RED-COATED militiamen pressed the crowd back in the square outside the meeting chamber. Their sergeant pushed back at Mr. Mordaunt, crying that no one could pass through the line until his soldiers had quelled the crowd.

"People got their ire up today, sir." The sergeant looked out over Mordaunt's shoulder. "Don't know what's got into them. Must be the heat, for there's more interesting places to be than pushing at each other here and looking for a fight."

Mr. Mordaunt quivered with his own fury. Tamsin stood so near to him that she could feel his trembling. Since they were trapped together, and because Tom had imbued in her all his indignation over the crimes he'd uncovered, she said the most spiteful words she'd ever uttered in her life.

"I ought to feel pity for you. I ought to hope you can escape every chastisement that is due to you."

He didn't answer or act as if he'd heard her.

"But I can't," she said, "because you used the power you have as a barrister to ruin lives. Bad enough that the courts make it hard for good people to assert their inheritances, but you, sir, you helped a man like Withersea take possession from widows and other impoverished heirs."

He said, "It's *Lord* Withersea. He's not an ordinary man."

"Is that your excuse? You are missing out on seeing his machinations in that room. But I wager that the marquess will not succeed. Tom Foxe has too good a plan to prevent Withersea from ruining more lives."

Mordaunt didn't answer. The lines around his eyes were wet, either from emotion or from the hot, stagnant air in the square. She continued to scold the barrister in a way she'd never dream of indulging. But she was neither Tamsin nor Tom at that moment, just a Foxe scion playing a role in a gambol, attempting a restoration for the sake of her family and a host of innocents.

"'Vaulting ambition, which o'erleaps itself.'" She stole one of Rowland's lines from Shakespeare. "Shame, sir."

He attempted to grind his own teeth to dust. Then he said, "Every man in England must look out for his own well-being. I am looking out for my own children."

"In truth, Tom Foxe is looking out for your children. Else you might be looking out from a cell in Newgate prison."

"You think much of your—"

The metal-banded door to the Committee's meeting chambers opened. Two aides stepped out, followed by Lord Withersea. He wasn't that much taller than the men around him, but he took more space than the others. His golden velvet coat shimmered in the daylight, its gold buttons reflecting sunbeams. He stood, hands on his hips, looking down at the crowd. His gaze passed over Mordaunt, who tipped his head, looking up expectantly.

Withersea waved a hand, once more dismissing the barrister. Mordaunt turned away, disconcerted, and bumped into Felicity's Monsieur Pear Head. The militia had eased up their strong line, allowing that odd man to come close to Mordaunt. Behind that rogue were the carbuncled scarecrow and the carrot-pated man-child who'd attacked them after the theatre, but who now appeared more scared than menacing. Tamsin saw two more rogues behind them, their collars and neckcloths pulled over their faces, eyes hidden by slouch hats.

"Mr. Mordaunt," the pear-headed man said, his voice a menacing growl. "You have our pay?"

"No, Mr. Merryboy. Seek it from his lordship."

Mr. Mordaunt pointed to Lord Withersea, then pushed his way through the crowd. Tamsin attempted to follow but was hemmed in by Merryboy's followers. Merryboy approached the marquess, whipping his hat from his head and bending his knee in a rough form of submission. Only a few words passed between them, but Tamsin heard nothing. She breathed through her mouth so as not to inhale the odors of the brigands pressing against her. When she could see the marquess again, he was pointing at her.

"Have Mordaunt's clerk bring me proof if you want even a farthing of your reward."

Then Withersea was gone, returning to the chambers.

Merryboy beamed at Tamsin as the crowd writhed around them. "Now, my hearty lad. We shall be the best of friends. You'll follow me, then." A statement, not a question.

"I must join Mr. Mordaunt at his chambers." She resented having to say that much to this miscreant.

The crowd again pressed on them, and Tamsin could not wiggle away from Merryboy, stuck in that clotted knot of his brigands, the same men sent by Leighton Fairchild, and who'd run only when Camilla fired her pistol.

49
Fortune's Wheel

– T O M –

UNCLE ABSOLOM AND REVEREND Gamlingay had been united in the declaration that there was no Hell, that it was inherited from pagan myths and didn't deserve the attention of modern men.

But if there was a hell, Tom was in it, having been dumped like abandoned baggage, barely roused from that cursed bout of fainting, then left alone with no word for how well his plan progressed, not knowing if Luke and Michel had found Captain Starbuck in time. Or found any other red-coated cadre to carry out the warrant.

In Mordaunt's chambers, Tom rubbed at his eyes again, then felt he was rubbing paper dust into his burning orbs. He found a water jug and looked for his kerchief, which was wadded under more papers; he'd drenched and dirtied it the last time he rose from his work.

This time, he pulled his cravat free, doused it with water from the jug, and rubbed his eyes. Then he wiped his sticky, salty face, his neck, the stubs of hair on his pate. He washed his hands and tossed the cravat away with his kerchief, rubbing his hands on his breeches to dry them.

At least Lizzie wasn't here to scold him about ruining a respectable suit. The noble idea that possessed him at dawn, to dress as if this were a critically important day, had been defeated by dust and humidity. He sat down again and surveyed the carefully sorted piles of writs and deeds and bonds, along with the swelling pile of discarded quills that could no longer be mended. And ruined blotter paper and scraps of notes he'd tossed aside.

He made a new estimate, though a few hours earlier he'd resisted constantly assessing how far he'd come. Three quarters done? Was it too ambitious to think he'd come that far? The many piles of papers now had names, and he'd compiled all he could find for the miscarriage of property ownership for the two women his former master had tried to help in Cambridge. Tom saw how, while working for his former master, he'd failed to protect the widow in the first case his master gave him to manage on his own. How he'd failed to protect her ownership of property her ancestors had held since Henry Tudor returned to England.

Ten more hours of this and he might have mastered it all. He focused again on the next case before him. It kept him from worrying about how well Aurora fared in Knightsbridge. Or whether Rowland and Perry were succeeding before the Committee for Privileges and Conduct.

Of course they were succeeding. Rowland had insisted the night before: "We've held gambols like this a hundred times."

"More like fifteen," Perry had said, counting on his fingers. "No, only fourteen."

"We always win," Rowland said. "Because we advance our gambols as righteous, enlightened people."

"Who happen to know," Perry said, "how to trick others using their own greed. We do it better than your common man trying to trick the Crown."

No need to worry. Only to wait.

Yet he jumped when the front door of the barrister's chambers banged open. Tom left his work to find Felicity and Camilla, with two young men who were introduced as being two of Perry's five brothers. Felicity's face was flushed with heat and exercise. Camilla was bone-pale and breathless.

"Mr. Frake begged us to run and tell you," Felicity began without first offering a greeting, "that the Committee has sent your friend's guardianship and inheritance to the Con...Con... Consistory Court for review."

"Therefore, your friend Jacob is free from that evil lord," Camilla said.

Never had words sounded so sweet, so consoling. Consistory Court. And he, Tom Foxe, had done it! He'd used the law—and his cousins' help—to free Jacob from terror.

"Perfect!" Tom clapped his hands over his head, as if praising heaven, though chiefly it was Ned's careful writing. "Of all the gods, Athena is not slack to do our bidding."

"Are you Catholic?" Felicity tipped her head, as if shocked. "Which saint is Athena? Why do you pray to that idol?"

"Not a saint," Tom said. "It's a figure of speech."

Camilla slumped on the hard bench in the outer chambers. She needed succor. Where did he leave that water jug?

He said, "Miss Oakes, have Tamsin and Camilla forgiven you for deceiving them into the scheme to rob your house?"

"Yes," Camilla said. "It's all turned out for the best."

"Not yet." Felicity poked her nose close to Tom's. "Is Mr. Rosewurme going to the Tower for his crimes? Newgate prison?"

"No," Tom said, too brightly happy for the luminance to be dimmed by Felicity's pique. "He's proved too valuable to us. And he's lost everything in the world since he rose yesterday."

"That malefactor deserves God's wrath!" Felicity wrenched her hands, as if strangling a small animal. "Yet you will free him? For shame."

"You have your house again," Tom said. "Plus, your printing press and all your household goods. It's excessive to also beg divine punishment on the man."

"Please do not lecture me on the ways of righteousness." Felicity stomped her foot, if a body that slender can be said to stomp.

"It's just that under our Restorations Rules—"

"Despite the rules," Camilla spoke in a thin voice, "one can easily understand Felicity's anger. The man stole from her."

"Mr. Rosewurme did as we asked for the sake of Jacob's guardian bond," Tom said, though he only assumed so, since he hadn't been there to watch. "Now, we must hope he can do what we need in the last of the Committee's business."

"Then what?" Felicity demanded.

"We'll give Mr. Rosewurme passage to sail from England. I believe that's what he intended before we interfered."

"Interfered?" Felicity raged. "He interfered with my aunt's peace. With my safety. He tried to steal my future."

"We have rules," Tom said. "I cannot apologize. Vengeance does not have a part in our endeavors. Please be satisfied with your house and worldly goods. Now, please take Camilla to Lord Marborne's house. If you can't find your cousin Winwood, then make sure she's cared for. You've run her off her feet."

"We only did what Perry asked," Camilla said.

"And I thank you." Tom was tired of their harangue. "Now, Miss Oakes, make sure Camilla rests. I'm calling a chair."

— CORNELIUS —

"PLEASE PROCEED, MR. ROSEWURME." Lord Bagsham nodded.

"Your grace, I protest." Viscount Heydon was on his feet. "Who is this man, other than the marquess's speaking dummy? Why should we listen to him?"

"He has done service for me," the Duke of Bagsham said, "and to other lords in this room."

"Then let him swear before God," Heydon said.

Feeling Perry Frake's eyes on him, Cornelius swore the same oath he'd sworn when he served as a witness in chancery court.

"Please proceed, Mr. Rosewurme," the duke said.

Removing from inside his coat the bond that the Earl of Marborne asked him to rewrite, Cornelius had to clear his voice three times before he could ease a single word from his throat.

"'I am Cornelius Rosewurme. I am swearing that I did hear the Marquess of Withersea vow to harm Lord Marborne for the losses he suffered when Danvers Duncombe was arrested.'"

"Blooming devils!" one lord cried. Then a few minced oaths popped from around the room.

Cornelius bent his head over his paper, but caught a flash of that Goliath, nodding behind the earl. He read, grateful that he didn't have to find the words out of his own head. "'In that same meeting, the Marquess of Withersea did express great ire with the king for seizing funds held for others by the traitor Mr. Danvers Duncombe.'"

Several lords sighed, causing Cornelius to look up, but he couldn't see more than a sea of pale faces. He read more.

"'At the meeting, I witnessed with others, the marquess did confess that he participated in Mr. Duncombe's investment syndicate, to support the Duke of Monmouth's rebellion.'"

The lords' murmurs made it impossible for Cornelius to be heard until the duke again called the assembly to order. Cornelius coughed, then continued to read.

"'I testify that I heard this confession in the chambers of the barrister John Mordaunt this past Wednesday afternoon. I aver that Mr. Mordaunt also heard this confession, as did the clerk in the adjacent work room.'"

The duke held up his hand. "Sir, you swore an oath!"

"Yes, your grace." Cornelius continued, grateful to have words to read, so he didn't have to think what to say. "As my written bond says, 'In relation to my work with the Marquess of Withersea to secure certain unclaimed properties, I also helped other lords, namely—'"

"Stop, Mr. Rosewurme," the duke commanded. "Do not name any lords. It is inappropriate in this chamber. In fact, all that you just read to us is inappropriate. My lords, please disregard what you just heard. It is most irregular."

The room fell silent. No man glanced about. The lords all had their eyes on the table. Their aides shuffled quietly behind them. The duke whispered to his secretary, who circled the chamber and relieved Cornelius of his written bond.

Cornelius wished to look at the Earl of Marborne and Mr. Frake, but since he'd failed, he didn't dare. When he felt Lord Bagsham's secretary's hand on his shoulder, Cornelius handed over the bond, feeling fear jolt through his joints again.

Was there any hope that Tom Foxe's plans might yet succeed, given that the duke forbade Cornelius's confession? The earl had insisted that this confession would be crucial to their plan.

Lord Withersea burst back into the meeting chamber then, bashing the heavy door into the wall. Cornelius's thrashing, frightened heart clattered. Fear tingled in his fingertips.

The chamber remained silent as the marquess advanced upon the duke and seized back the paper he'd left moments before. Seeming to be unaware of the breathless wonder in the room, Withersea stalked to within an arm's reach of the Earl of Marborne and began to read from his paper, emoting, but not in the dramatic way Cornelius would have done.

> Let all men know, in April in the year of our Lord 1665, I did hear Samuel Foxe speak thus: 'Monarchy is against the mind of God. The execution of the late king was one of the fattest sacrifices that ever Queen Justice had.'

Withersea paused as if to judge the effect of his words. But the chamber remained quiet, except for a pair of the older lords who had coughed and hacked through most of the meeting. He continued reading.

> I did myself hear Samuel Foxe say, 'Our King is adored like a demigod, with a dissolute and haughty court about him, of vast expense and luxury, masks and revels. He has filled the court with debauchery.'

Withersea looked up from his paper, glaring at the earl. "Thus did Samuel Foxe speak."

"Bless me! I am surprised." The earl said it loudly enough that Cornelius heard. Men in the room turned their heads to the earl. "But if any of my deceased ancestors quoted John Milton, it would be my late uncle, Doctor Absolom Foxe of Trinity College. He did publish a treatise arguing against the poet Milton's ill-conceived tract. Because he was a scholar, likely my uncle quoted from it."

One of the lords sitting near the duke laughed. A viscount? Was that how he was introduced?

"Allow me to finish." The marquess spoke scornfully.

"Due to my uncle's tutelage, I am just not an enthusiast," the Earl of Marborne said. "Of Milton, I mean. I shall not be a critic of his poetics, but I question his republican views."

"This man," Withersea swept his hand, addressing the assembly, "and his entire family are traitors. I have a warrant coming. That man," Withersea pointed at Marborne, "will be arrested in the name of the king and taken to the Tower."

With the marquess's imperious command, Cornelius felt his future sail off the edge of the world. Lost. How now to escape and dissociate from these Foxes? How even to escape this room?

Cornelius judged every step to take toward the door and what to tell anyone who might stop him. But had he sufficiently warned the earl what Merryboy intended outside the door?

The Earl of Marborne stood. "If I might speak, your grace? Because it's not possible to raise the dead to speak in their own defense." The duke nodded. "Thank you. I was warned that Lord Withersea intended to bring such falsehoods to this meeting. First, if your lordships believe Samuel Foxe to have written this dissidence, then you must force John Milton to grant me the proceeds for his writings. Because that now-deceased poet published the essay from which you just heard a few lines."

Lord Bagsham said, "You offer only a facetious denial?"

"Yes, your grace." The earl swept his hand, including all the Committee in his address. "Many of you know that Samuel Foxe aided Charles Stuart's escape to France. This plagiary is as silly as if I accused one of you, saying you'd joined the marquess in Hawkins' Heirs or Danvers Duncombe's own traitorous syndic."

More minced oaths broke from the lords. *Zoonters! Adod!* Several rustled papers on the table. A coin dropped. Then another.

Silver pound coins, so shaved and nicked they didn't roll far. Two lords wadded the paper under their hands.

Cornelius couldn't guess at the uproar. The Goliath Frake, however, smiled like a cat that slinked into the buttery and got in the cream.

Lord Marborne said, "'The duke and all that know me in the city can witness with me that it is not so.'" He nodded to those who'd listened. "I offer a quote from *Comedy of Errors*, since I believe our poet Shakespeare to be greater than Milton."

"Marborne! Please refrain from humor! I must say—"

The duke began to cough. He reached for his glass on the table, missed, spilled it, and coughed more. His face began to turn the roseate color of his secretary's coat.

The Earl of Marborne leaped up, pushing past several lords who had risen from their chairs. "My grace, no!" He clamped his arms around the duke, pounding on his back. "No! Don't die!"

Viscount Heydon stood close by, holding up both men.

The secretary lunged for them, and the earl lost his hold.

His grace, the Duke of Bagsham, fell to the floor, lifeless.

As if the Devil did not already have more than his due, the chamber doors burst open, and a bevy of red-coated militia came in, two of them with bayonets fixed on their muskets, the others with pikes and blades.

"Stop that man!" the marquess cried, his finger inches from the earl's face. "Stop him before he kills the duke!"

But in a heartbeat, the earl turned the duke over, pounding on him, trying to revive him while muttering desperate words.

"Don't die! No one dies! Don't die!"

The marquess continued his harangue.

"Rowland Foxe is a traitor. The soldiers have the warrant for his arrest."

Cornelius felt his future sail off the edge of the world. Lost. How now to escape and detach from these failed Foxes? How even to escape this room?

— TAMSIN —

IT FELT LIKE HOURS passed, though only the quarter hour's tone struck from the bell tower. Tamsin folded her arms to shield against the shifting, anxious men on that side of the crowd. It took great effort not to inhale filthy odors.

The chamber's doors were again thrust open, held by two militiamen. A coterie of aides came out and lined the steps.

"What is it?" Merryboy shouted at a nearby aide that Tamsin remembered from the meeting. Which lord did he serve?

"A man with business before the Committee proved to be a traitor, accused by a loftier lord than he. It's the Tower for him."

"Ah," Merryboy said, rubbing his hands. "Pride and a haughty spirit go before a fall, as they preach in the pulpit."

That was when the prisoner emerged, closely guarded by four of the militia, so that it was hard to see the man. Except she did see the prisoner's ultramarine coat with brass buttons. And the high-crowned periwig.

The entire gambol had gone radically wrong.

She'd left the meeting only a quarter of an hour earlier with Tom's plan making great gains. And now, tragedy. She glanced around the crowd while restraining the panic throbbing behind her heart. She couldn't see any of Perry's crew. That one man might be Felicity's brother, but she'd met him for so few moments, she couldn't be sure. And where had Felicity and Camilla taken themselves off to? The Knights of the Marborne Fens were supposed to all be here.

The militiamen pushed through the crowd with their prisoner. Following, Tamsin felt for the knife in her belt, but it wasn't there; she'd left it with Tom, who'd warned her that she couldn't take a pistol or knife or her sword-stick into the meeting chamber. Now she had nothing with which to stop this.

She followed so closely that when the four militiamen reached the edge of the crowd, she was as pressed upon as the soldiers. One man stepped back, tripped on her, and fell hard on his bottom on the cobbles. Another militiaman fell on top of him. Tamsin stepped to her right to be out of the way, was jammed hard to her left, then was hustled away. Merryboy shoved her into the heart of his coterie of ragged brigands.

They had Rowland, tossed over the shoulder of the brawniest of the rowdies.

"Where are you taking him?" Tamsin shouted at Merryboy.

"To the docks at Billingsgate. Like our patron asked."

Rowland struggled in the arms of his captors, and the crush of brigands pushed closer. Then they stepped back. Rowland now hung like half-filled sack of grain.

"What did they do to him?"

"Laudanum and a good cosh on the head," Merryboy said cheerily. "You will come along now, so you can tell our patron that we've done all he asked, just the way he wants it."

He linked his arm in hers and pulled her along in a way that made it clear she had no choice but to follow.

Where was Perry? Captain Starbuck?

Was she utterly on her own?

50
No Apologies

JUST AFTER TOM HAD escorted Camilla and Felicity into sedan chairs and paid the bearers, Mr. Mordaunt exited from another chair, looking harassed and overheated and defeated. That left no time to recover from the previous visitors, but Tom squared up, prepared to get through this part of the day. He'd known this tussle was coming his way. He had to both console his new master and rile him to action.

"I understand it's you, Mr. Foxe, who has destroyed my life." The barrister didn't sound angry. More like his spirit had been punctured, like a sad puffball fallen from a mighty tree. "After this day, the world will heap ignominy on my name. Lord Withersea will make sure of it."

"Nay, sir. When you and I have finished our work today," Tom indicated the piles of papers and writs, "we shall begin to restore justice to the unfortunate. You will be seen by all as a righteous man, lifting up the honor of English law."

"You, Mr. Foxe, are a witless fool if you think any man ever escapes Lord Withersea's wrath."

Tom sat in his cubby, pointing to the other chair there, reversing the manners and custom of how a clerk deferred to his master. His elbow on the dusty work table, he leaned on his hand, thinking of how to simplify the situation for Mr. Mordaunt.

"Sir, I just learned from visitors that your creature, Mr. Rosewurme, read a correctly witnessed bond that will remove Jacob Rôche from enduring Withersea's anger. Is this true?"

"Yes, but how—"

"Let us leave the Consistory Court to settle that case. I take it that you departed from the Committee meeting before all matters were concluded."

"Lord Withersea forced me away. I have lost his patronage and gained his enmity. I shall be lucky to escape with my life."

"That's more dramatic than the King's Players undertake to entertain their audience. You left before the marquess played out his plan to stop the confirmation of the Marborne title."

"Yes, but how did you know he had such a plan?"

"I heard him declare it to you," Tom said. "I'm surprised you don't know more about how sounds carry in your chambers. Your clerks must know all your business."

"I thought we were alone."

"But you were not. The Earl of Marborne is left to deal with whatever evil the marquess invented. Before the Committee adjourns, he'll have a warrant to stop most of that evil. Then Jacob will be safe. Marborne will be safe. Even you will be safe."

The warrant must appear. Starbuck must arrive in time.

"Me, safe? What?"

"Your wife warned you," Tom said. "Which she did because her cousin the marchioness warned her. I am nearly certain that the Duke of Bagsham gave you strong hints. You ignored them all, and you'd now be swept into the marquess's maelstrom. Except..."

The warrant must arrive in time. By all the gods, it must.

"Except?"

"Except I imagine you read the note I sent before the Committee meeting. I worked to keep you out of it, for the sake of your boys and your kind wife. I must protect Jacob Rôche, but it would be wrong to do that while risking the safety of other innocents."

Astonished, Mordaunt opened his mouth, but said only, "Oh!" when someone knocked on and then opened the door, revealing the eagle-beaked man who'd come to Mordaunt's chambers with Withersea on Wednesday afternoon and later paid Tom Foxe two pounds sterling for his own murder.

Mordaunt gently elbowed Tom away from the door and handed the man a bundle. "Take this and be damned. Return it to Lord Withersea. I am discharged from handling his business."

"But his lordship wants proof," the man said.

"Be gone. I want no more of the marquess's foul business."

The barrister slammed the door on a man who was at least a knight or a baron, Tom wasn't quite sure what.

"Bravo, sir!"

"Withersea intends more than accusations." Mordaunt stood before Tom, wrapping his arms tightly around his torso, hugging himself close. "I'm not sure what. But Sir Duxwold often negotiates with the marquess's agents—"

"Mercenaries," Tom said.

"I suspect so. I know not for a surety what the marquess has planned. He left my office sounding—"

"Dire and threatening," Tom said. "I know. I heard him speak. But I'm sure Rollo and Perry Frake will stop it." *If Starbuck shows up on time.* "We can go to Westminster to be sure."

Mordaunt said, "Nothing I can say will stop whatever the marquess has planned."

"Not even if you'll swear before a judge? Say, Sir Oliver Boxworth? He took my oath. I hope his signed warrant will keep you and your family safe from the marquess's vengeance."

After another knocking on the chamber doors, a voice called, "Tom! Tom! Zooterkins, Tom! Where are you?"

Ned appeared, because of course he did. Because of course, after Tom had run around to obtain warrants and then spent lonely hours sifting through deeds and bonds, everyone would appear here at once.

"Ned? I'm happy to see you. Mr. Mordaunt, this is my cousin Eduard Wijck, the painter."

"Pleased to meet you, sir," Mordaunt said, but he didn't sound as if he were capable of being pleased by anything.

"I am honored to meet you, sir," Ned said. Tom, "I must tell Rollo that Lizzie is leaving for Holland. How best to do that?"

Tom, still cogitating on the last few words with Mr. Mordaunt, answered with impatience. "Just tell Rollo straight out. But how did Lizzie come to make such a decision? I thought she was as besotted with Rollo as he is with her."

"Besotted? My sister besotted?" Ned wrinkled his nose. "Aye, likely true. But she thinks Aurora needs a female companion. They're for Holland within the hour."

"Holland?" Tom struggled to gather all his wits to understand Ned's breathless declarations.

"Lizzie thought it the best stopping place for now. Though Aurora intends to be in Rome before winter."

"But we agreed that I'd help Aurora travel next week." Tom stood up. Too fast. He sat down again, fighting dizziness and every notion crashing about in his head.

Ned said, "The marquess came home in a rage yesterday. He wanted to move Jacob to his northern castle today. And he'll be in a blood fury, as Aurora called it, when he fails at the Committee meeting. Hence, she must leave today." He paused. "Did the marquess fail at the meeting?"

"For Jacob's sake, yes. But for Rollo—"

Mr. Mordaunt, who'd been silent, spoke up. "I was just explaining to Mr. Foxe that the marquess intends evil."

"Perry and Rollo can defend themselves," Tom said. "If Starbuck..." He grasped his aching head.

Crivens! Did Starbuck make it in time?

Ned said, "Why worry about Rollo? He has Perry with him. There's no safe place for Aurora or Jacob. Lizzie agrees that they must flee England. I agree too, and—"

"No! No! No!" Tom clapped his ears in distress.

Ned looked puzzled. "Aurora says you agreed. It's just that they must go today. For Jacob's sake."

"I didn't know then what Rollo intended to do today."

Tom felt a chill. No, not from illness. From a specter crossing his grave. Had their careful plans taken them all into a maelstrom? And what had happened to Captain Starbuck?

"What's the problem?" Ned said. "I'm the one who has to tell Rollo that Lizzie has gone to Holland."

"Starbuck has a warrant, since Rollo has proof that..." Tom glanced at Mr. Mordaunt. "Withersea invested in the Duke of Monmouth's rebellion. Didn't he, Mr. Mordaunt?"

The barrister squirmed, if such a stiff, austere man can be described as squirming.

"That's good news," Ned said. "Rollo will have the marquess in chains. That will end Jacob's torture."

"Don't you see?" Tom's heart beat as hard as it did when he'd walked into Sir Oliver's chambers. "If Aurora leaves England today, with the warrant proving Withersea is a traitor, it's as if she's guilty too. The king will seize all. She'll be a pauper. William and Mary will turn her over to the Crown."

"Then what shall we—"

"I must stop Aurora." Tom no longer cared how frantic he seemed. "Ned, you must run to warn Perry and Rollo."

"Nay, Tom," Ned said, still calm, as if not impressed by this new calamity. "I can show you to the *Zeewolf*. Let Rollo and Perry manage their own worries."

Pausing at the door, Tom turned to Mr. Mordaunt. "You'll understand what to do here, sir, from how I've arranged it. We must finish what we can tonight, so we can seek a warrant to keep these lands from being seized when Withersea is arrested."

"Arrested?"

"*Ita quidem.* That's what Sir Oliver's warrant demands. I make no apologies. Do what you can while I save my friends."

The chamber door banged shut just as Tom rounded the archway into Chancery Lane with Ned at his heels. By the time the stitch in Tom's side threatened to send him to his knees, they were in sight, sound, and smell of the Pool of London.

— LIZZIE —

AFTER LIZZIE WAVED FAREWELL to Ned, the travelers crowded into the chandler's wife's sitting room. John Coachman and Gabriel kept close watch on Jacob in the garden, where more than once Jacob tossed his dog a ball that flew too far and sent the men scrambling into the alley, scooping up the dog and cautioning Jacob to stay near his sister.

It was nearly two hours before the captain sent for the marchioness to come onboard the *Zeewolf*. First, Jacob didn't want to get into the skiff that was sent to ferry them to the ship. John Coachman and Gabriel contrived to get Jacob onto the skiff and seated. But when the skiff was halfway to the *Zeewolf*, they struggled to keep Jacob seated. He kept swiveling around to watch other skiffs and barges passing back to the wharf.

"That's Tom!" Jacob shouted, pointing at a distant skiff.

Lizzie squinted in the sun to see what Jacob did, trying to guess who in the crowded, hectic Pool might resemble Tom.

"No, Jacob. It's just a man. Tom is taller. And he doesn't have a moustache."

"When is Tom coming?"

"Not today," Aurora said for the fiftieth time. She tugged at his coat to keep him seated.

Onboard, the captain bowed to the marchioness, welcoming her. She offered effusive thanks and engaged to learn more about the coming journey. The rest of the party weren't introduced. Lizzie breathed out the last of her anxious concerns. Whatever it had been that drew Sir Duxwold to the wharf, nothing had come of it. They'd escaped the marquess and any of his picaros who might follow them.

John Coachman and Gabriel went to guide the sailors who tied down their baggage on deck. That mound seemed meager, given that Aurora was taking her brother off to the wilds of Italy. Lizzie had the same satchel she'd brought to Knightsbridge for what was supposed to have been a brief summer party. Two gowns and a nightshift would have to do until Amsterdam.

Aurora still chatted with the captain. Jacob hung close by Lizzie, who knew enough about sailing to know it involved a great deal of waiting with nothing to do.

"Jacob, shall we watch the sailors at work?" Lizzie coaxed him close to the railing, though sunburn was already blooming on Jacob's nose and cheeks. She'd be burnt umber before they reached Rotterdam. But then, the sun would set in a few hours.

"Pip is too tired," Jacob said.

"He should be, my friend. You ran him ragged today."

"He likes to play."

"Yes, but…" She unwound the shawl tied around her waist, it having been too hot to wear over her shoulders. "Let's make a bed for Pip here, so he can nap."

Jacob got busy, folding the yards of cloth this way and that, and repeating his command for Pip to sleep. Pip took the first opportunity when Jacob paused from fidgeting with the shawl to curl up, half on Jacob's feet, half on Lizzie's.

"He's a good boy," Lizzie said, having no knowledge of what that meant, since her only acquaintance in the last decade had been with snappy, ill-behaved lap dogs kept by Mary's ladies in waiting. What concerned her most: Jacob was tired and had cast his feelings onto Pip. Lizzie felt it too, after two nights with little sleep. She wanted to put her arm around him, but that was a comfort Jacob accepted only from Aurora. "Look, Jacob. They are loading that ship over there."

Boys liked that sort of thing, didn't they? But Jacob wasn't a boy. He was a grown man who saw the world differently from others. While they stood under the hot sun, she talked about winches and levers and cargos sailing to faraway places. As if she knew one thing about it. However, it kept Jacob's attention, so he only twice worried about his dog.

Then Lizzie glanced back to where they'd boarded the skiff. Sir Duxwold again loitered there, leaning against a pile of crates. Her heart beat in fear. Did Sir Duxwold wait for Withersea to arrive at the wharf after the Committee meeting? Did the presence of that despicable little man mean that all of Tom's plans had been foiled? Was the marquess coming at any moment to snatch back Jacob and Aurora?

She took several deep breaths, observing the man, knowing Duxwold to have no purpose in life other than to serve as Withersea's lackey. He seemed to watch cargo being hauled onto the wharf from barges. Was Withersea receiving a shipment? If so, then their luck had held, and the marquess had not found them.

Once she quieted the jolt of fear that the sight of Duxwold had caused, Lizzie acknowledged that it was not possible for the marquess to have found them. Only Ned knew about the *Zeewolf*, and most assuredly he had not told a soul about Aurora's journey to Rotterdam, except Tom and Rowland. And perhaps Tamsin.

Still, Lizzie wanted the ship out on the open water, escaping any possibility of encountering the marquess. How long until they sailed? Her head pounded from having frightened herself. She directed Jacob's attention to the ships coming and going in the Pool of London. She gently nudged Pip and hence Jacob, so that they both turned such that Duxwold could not recognize Jacob while they sweltered in the August sun. At diplomatic parties in Amsterdam, Lizzie had slighted his advances, not once but twice. He thereafter treated her as invisible. When she'd arrived at Arcadia House on Tuesday, he hadn't looked up when she was introduced.

Hoping her invisibility remained.

Hoping Aurora did not come to the ship's railing.

The captain approached with Aurora. Lizzie held up a hand, pointing to the sleeping Pip, hoping discreetly to keep Aurora from stepping close to the rail, so Duxwold wouldn't see her.

"Miss Foxe," Aurora said, "the captain has been kind to invite us to use his quarters on the journey to Rotterdam."

"We'll be off within the half hour," the captain said. "Allow me to show you the way."

Aurora knelt beside Jacob to coax Pip awake. The captain hovered too near for Lizzie to speak, so Lizzie also knelt, pretending to care about Pip.

"Sir Duxwold is on the wharf," Lizzie whispered. "Please don't let him see you."

"What? Why?"

Lizzie shook her head, not knowing the answer.

They had to wait, anxious to disappear from the deck, while a pair of sailors hauled a rather filthy drunk below deck. Then Jacob and the women were ensconced in the captain's quarters. John and Gabriel remained on deck, with every intention of staying there through the voyage, since neither rain nor wind threatened this voyage. Lizzie accepted only water when the captain sent his lackey in with sustenance from the captain's own stores. She'd give her tongue and toes for a flagon of wine, but circumstances argued against it.

What she did ask, for her own comfort: ink, a quill, paper.

While they waited for the *Zeewolf* to lift anchor, Jacob and Aurora became absorbed in a string game Jacob called cat's tail. Lizzie sought comfort in writing to Rowland, intending to send her letter back from Rotterdam. She wanted to console him, yet, at the same time, she waited for the ship to lift anchor, hoping for a flood-tide of relief. If only they might depart soon enough, she'd have helped rescue two innocent people, taking them beyond the reach of the marquess, safe from both his anger and his greed.

Even before the ship lifted anchor, Jacob became seasick. Lizzie did not see how she might be of help. She sharpened the quill, then found that the inkwell contained poor quality lampblacking. No matter. She wetted her quill.

Mon beau cher mouton:

I do so regret…

She scratched out those words, blotted the paper, had to begin again. She'd learned a decade ago, while first in service to Mary, to never begin with apologies.

51

Pool of London

— T A M S I N —

TAMSIN'S ENTIRE INSIDES HAD corrupted, blood boiling in the heat, eyes burning from sun and smoke in the murky London skies. Mr. Merryboy's fingers curled painfully around her arm. He didn't let her out of his grasp, which didn't matter, because she wouldn't let Rowland out of her sight.

She had nothing at hand but mother wit. She trudged on, focused on finding a chance to use her common sense and free Rowland, while telling her heart that there wasn't time for fear.

They dumped Rowland in a wherry, and Merryboy pointed to where she was to sit beside him. Coins traded hands, and they were on the way to Billingsgate. Merryboy's brigands cursed volubly and frequently, quite uncomfortable with the aged wherry and disliking the water. The day had turned humid; the river roiled, releasing a revolting stink. And her sense of desperation increased in exactly the way she'd always warned her cousins against during restorations.

During the journey, her mind seized on escaping each time the wherry came close to the riverbank, where a bevy of mud-larks crouched along steps leading down to the Thames. But she sat too far away to reach Rowland. If she leaped into the dark waters, she'd lose Rowland to his captors. Perhaps if she tipped the wherry…no, it was more barge than ship, so flat-bottomed that she could not upend it.

"What's in Billingsgate?" she asked Merryboy. "What does your patron want me to witness?"

"The *Zeewolf*. Our lordly patron wants this swingebeest gone far from London."

"Sea Wolf?"

"*Zeewolf*." He emphasized the *Zee* part. "I gather it's called *wolf* on account of them Dutch traders are tight with a coin. Or so people say."

When the wherry came to a landing, Merryboy and his men leaped out. Tamsin followed. The unconscious Rowland was once again slung over the biggest man's shoulder, and they plowed through the crowds on the wharf. Rowland's cravat had been stuck into his mouth, and the ends covered his face.

They'd traveled far enough now that she'd conquered a degree of her fear. She hoped it might be possible to appeal to the crowd to intercede. But among sailors, dockwallopers, and cart-drivers, no one glanced at the human burden that picaro carried along the wharf. Not a glimmer of concerned humanity to be seen.

On the wharf across from where the *Zeewolf* lay at anchor, Merryboy stopped so short that Tamsin collided with him.

"Lord Ducks." Merryboy growled and stuck his chin in the air, in what must be indignation. "Checking on us?"

A small man with an eagle's beak of a nose loitered beside cargo to be hauled aboard ship. *My friend Ducks.* Leighton had claimed this champion in that threatening scrap of a letter.

"I'm to ensure my lord's shipment makes it aboard. He wants the captain to sign this receipt."

Hands on hips, Merryboy said, "You are now to receive my day's pay?"

"No, dear man. My reward lies elsewhere. In fact, I have your pay." He dangled a leather purse that rattled with coins. "Take the cargo aboard, and I'll see you are paid right here."

"Isn't that what this fellow is for?" Merryboy had hold of Tamsin again. "To stand between me and your lord."

The man called Ducks held out another purse. "Here is payment for the ship's captain. And a letter to give his lordship's shipping agent in Batavia."

"I ain't going on a blood-shivering ship." Merryboy said. "You can do that yourself."

"I can do it," Tamsin said. "His lordship would approve."

She volunteered because she wasn't letting Rowland out of her sight. And this loomed as her last chance to free him.

Lord Ducks nodded and held out the second purse. "Be sure to tell the captain that his new sailor raves about injustice, thinks himself a lord. The captain must not listen to a lunatic."

With that command, the little lord took Merryboy off to a tavern across the way while Tamsin and the brawny picaro bearing Rowland were rowed out to the *Zeewolf* on a skiff. On that voyage, Tamsin fingered the purse, feeling the coins through the velvet cloth and guessing how much was to be paid to ship Rowland off to sea. While the picaro stared ahead, apparently frightened about the deep water, Tamsin slipped the greater portion of coins into the inner pockets of her waistcoat.

Onboard the ship, she was left waiting outside the captain's quarters, where Rowland had been left in a chair from which he didn't move. Tamsin could see one black silk stocking, his shoe having been lost, plus the now-tattered skirt of his new ultramarine coat with its brass buttons.

Tamsin planned a speech while cargo was slammed into the hold beneath where she stood waiting. Sailors swore and threatened each other in Dutch. Once she was admitted to the captain's quarters, she began her speech, intending to offer the cost of crimping for Rowland's release.

"Sir, I am to advise you that this man is mad as a roasted cat, that he will rave and claim to be a lord." The next part of her speech was to convince the bribed captain that Rowland was indeed a lord and to let him go. Then she spied the coshed, drugged figure lolling on the captain's chair, and spoke with great courage.

Because it was Withersea unconscious on the captain's chair. Not Rowland.

"Captain, this purse contains only the down payment for your services. This letter promises you equal payment when you reach

Batavia." Though she didn't know what that letter said. "Here's five more louis to be sure he doesn't leave the ship in Rotterdam."

The captain accepted the loose fistful of gold and answered in a heavy Dutch accent, nodding. He pocketed the sealed letter and the much-reduced leather purse of coins. He agreed to sign the receipt Tamsin presented, then took forever to sharpen a quill and uncap his inkwell. All the while, Tamsin rocked on her heels with every shift in the ship when cargo was dropped in its hold.

"When will you sail, captain?"

"Tide turns in an hour, sir."

Receipt in hand, Tamsin hastened away, her heart pounding. She leaped from the skiff as it reached the wharf, calling out, "All done as you commanded, sir."

She gave the signed receipt to the Ducks man, who snatched it, then handed the promised purse to Merryboy, who hoofed it up the road to join his rowdies, all soon lost from view.

Her lungs gulped in thick, fetid London air. With no weapon at hand, and no friend in sight, she'd just consigned a powerful enemy to the fate he'd devised for Rowland. And she'd pocketed most of the crimping funds. Would Tom declare her a hero? He was generous and might do so. Perry, however, would upbraid her for mistaking a blue coat for Rowland and for getting into a rotten pickle. They were all supposed to stick together.

She walked away from the wharf, glancing back at the first turning. The Ducks man had disappeared. She handed a penny to a pie man and asked for a pie and directions to Lincoln's Inn. The pie was gone in a few bites, then that heavy pocket of coins banged against her chest while she walked at a determined pace.

Joy washed over her, like when she ran the trails in a Marborne copse at dawn. She'd never feel fear again, not like that.

— ROLLO —

"YOUR GRACE. STAY WITH us. I beg you."

Rowland's knees scraped where he knelt on the wood floor. He struggled to get the insensible duke upright.

The duke's eyes opened.

Relieved, Rowland left it to the alarmed secretary to help with the duke's revival. When the secretary had Bagsham back in that tall wooden chair, one of the lurking redcoats came to remonstrate with the secretary.

The whole time they worried about the duke, Withersea remonstrated with the redcoats who'd come in. They protested with shakes of the head and hand gestures that they didn't know the answer to Withersea's inquiries. If Withersea expected a warrant, those militiamen didn't have it.

No one seemed to know what to do while the duke was restored to himself. A few men around him argued. Several of the lords of the Committee still stared down at the crumbled letters and coins on the table before them.

Rowland gathered his own wits to put it all back in order. Perry had handed out purloined five-pound gratuities that claimed *Parliament & Rex*. Withersea's aide had, without knowing it, passed miserable gratuities that threatened exposure to Hawkins' Heirs and Duncombe's treasonous investors. The marquess had called Foxes traitors and threatened a warrant against him.

Then the duke had died, or seemed to, anyway, and a flock of militiamen entered the chamber.

But where was Starbuck with the warrant?

Rowland had never been in battle, only roadside skirmishes with raiders. He preferred that action to this inaction. Tension in his belly threatened to eat him from the inside.

At last, the duke righted his coat and neckcloth, then spoke, though his voice didn't command as it had earlier.

"Forgive my lapse, my lords. Can we continue?"

"Your lordships." Rowland stood in the meeting chamber, determined to seize his fate. He held his hands prayerfully, nodding to each man in the assembly. "I protest the calumny and slander that the marquess spoke against my family. The king has recognized my family's right to the Marborne title."

Several lords tapped the table to indicate their agreement.

"For those who have never heard the tale from the king himself," Rowland continued, intending to hammer a nail into Withersea's undoing, "I shall tell you how Samuel Foxe helped Charles Stuart escape to France after rebels killed his father."

"They were traitors!" Withersea's voice rose, its shrill pitch echoing in the chamber. He jabbed his finger at the earl. "Your entire Foxe family are cheating, skulking vermin!"

The fifteen lords muttered with each other.

Departing from the day's plan, Cornelius Rosewurme drew more papers from his inner pocket. He stood and held them out, his hands trembling. "Here also, my lords, are original documents signed by the Marquess of Withersea, which he preserved should he need to extort...I mean to say, persuade his comrades to remain loyal to him, rather than to the king."

"Is this why," Perry spoke only to Rowland, but his voice carried in the chamber, "the marquess smashed his glass this morning instead of toasting the king?"

The Earl of Marborne nodded, which was the most he could manage, preserving his strength for the next attack.

The entire chamber went quiet, save for a few lords with persistent coughs. Rowland wanted to believe the strings of the net had been laid. The duke would close the snare. Yet the plans had been pulled together so quickly that Rowland's rabbity heart pattered as if lacking faith, while his belly clenched in rebellion, wanting him to command those in the room to believe his truths.

And where was Starbuck?

Under the cover of the table, Rowland rolled his gold angel over his knuckles, endeavoring to say no more.

The duke's secretary approached, whispering in his ear.

"We have heard enough," Lord Bagsham said. "I have just been presented a king's warrant, condemning a traitor for support of Monmouth's rebellion."

"Ha! As I told you!" The marquess crowed.

The duke's small eyes narrowed. "I'd wish to save you from humiliation here. But as you have already confessed before an officer of the court, I cannot." The duke folded his small hands on the table, just as Starbuck entered the meeting room.

Valentine! You came!

"Captain Starbuck, please ask your men to escort *Mister* Withersea to the Tower." The duke's usually soft voice broke on the word *mister.* "He is a traitor and a cheat."

Rowland wanted to cry out, to laugh with relief and delight, but he'd stopped playing Merry Andrew for that day. While the marquess repeatedly shouted his indignation, four of Valentine's militia entered. Two pinioned the marquess's elbows, another stuffed the man's cravat in his mouth to still him. The fourth stripped the marquess of his golden coat, dragging it back so that Withersea's hands and wrists were bound.

"Stop!" Rowland called. "Do not parade an English lord in the streets without so much as a coat to preserve his dignity."

A beefy corporal attempted to right the marquess's coat but instead tore it into two halves in the struggle.

"Take mine." Rowland removed the pretty blue coat Lizzie had given him. Perry and the corporal dressed the marquess.

Withersea spat out the cravat-turned-gag. "You hell-bound poltroon!" he cried. "You nick-ninny scoundrel."

If spit, curses, and foul looks were poison, Rowland would have died that day. The corporal stomped on the marquess's foot. When the man cried in pain, the corporal stuffed the cravat in the man's mouth again, deeper this time.

Rowland, his arms wide, spoke to the lords. "'The duke and all that know me in the city can witness with me that it is not so.'"

"Yes, Marborne," the duke said. "It is as you claim. Yet—"

"Your grace, I merely quote the Bard of Avon. I meant it as a mild rebuke to this man's contumely language."

"Lieutenant Foxe has bad habits, your grace," Valentine said. He opened the door and indicated for his militiamen to depart. "But he has no habits that drift beyond the fair side of the law."

As soon as Valentine's men removed the marquess from the chamber, the duke commanded everyone's attention.

Rowland kept one hand under the table, rolling his gold coin over his knuckles, draining the dregs of panic he'd felt, perhaps the greatest in his life. As if to help dull that edge, Lord Bagsham declared the next business at hand to be the lords' confirmation of the Marborne title, to be assumed by the designated heir.

"I say designated," the duke intoned, "based on a collection of missives the king received last week. His Majesty asked me to share them with your lordships for your consideration."

The duke then read, in an absolute monotone, the series of letters from Foxe uncles, great-uncles, and grandfather, then from Rowland's father, the last of them to survive the Great Plague. A chronicle of heartbreak and misery. During the reading, Rowland could not maintain the Merry Andrew mask, but disguised how he wanted to weep upon hearing his progenitors' tales of woe.

"Good lord!" Viscount Heydon murmured with other lords, who all expressed grief as the duke folded the letters.

"Allow me also to commend Rowland Foxe," the duke said, "in that he is known to the king for valiant services, the same kind as his uncles, father, and grandfather rendered to the Crown."

That led all the lords to swivel in their chairs, as if a single animal with many heads, to examine Rowland. The intelligencer part of him shriveled at being revealed before so many eyes.

"What say you, Marborne?" Lord Bagsham also turned his head to Rowland and raised his brows inquiringly. His spectacles slid down his nose and needed to be mashed up in place.

After heroically surrendering his coat to the traitor Withersea, Rowland looked out in only his shirt sleeves on the small sea of lordly faces. At least Lizzie wasn't there to see him half-dressed at the most important event in their mutual lives.

"I, Rowland Foxe, do utterly testify and declare in my conscience that the King's Highness is the only supreme governor of this realm."

He went on to repeat the entire Oath of Supremacy, hoping fervently that Perry wouldn't notice how the oath moved him, more than all oaths he'd ever repeated, save for the one he shared with his cousins. His anxious belly calmed while he recited the words that let lords under Tudor and Stuart kings keep their heads. His excitement about offering the oath—and the humbling sense that he offered it for his cousins, Uncle Absolom, and their progenitors—was dulled only by observing how it ground the lords into soul-crushing boredom. At least three of them snored before he finished.

Lord Bagsham muttered an affirmation and called for the lords to voice their approval. The judges passed a note, agreeing. Rowland Foxe was acknowledged to be the Earl of Marborne. Viscount Heydon proposed a toast to Rowland's health, which roused the other lords from their torpor.

Sherry, again. Rowland longed for decent brandy. And then lunch and a nap.

Perry toasted with other aides, then bent to whisper in Rowland's ear. "That's the easiest gambol we ever played."

"Easy? No." Rowland's voice betrayed his weary fearfulness. "Also, not a gambol. It was merely a restoration."

"Be not mifty, my lord. I merely congratulate myself for work well done," Perry said. "We've managed it all with no pain or fright to our comrades."

"I do congratulate you," Rowland said. "I also must praise Valentine for how his men took a firm hold on the glimflashy marquess. May that lord enjoy his new abode in the Tower."

"Alas, we broke one of the rules," Perry said. "And we did so after Tom made us faithfully promise. *No one dies.*"

Rowland considered the problem. "If it happens, it is not on our heads, but on Withersea for serving up treason. And on the king for advancing an abhorrent number of executions because he fears a handful of rebels. Withersea made his own bad luck."

"But it's more than luck," Perry said, "that the fire of the marquess's anger won't flash back on us. Admit it. We are cunning. And our Tom possesses a truly great cunning."

The meeting chamber door opened just then, where the lords milled about for sociability or else prepared to depart. Valentine Starbuck entered, sans Withersea.

And, from the expression on his face, sans everything.

"God blind me!" Rowland cried. "Withersea has fled!"

At least ten lords witnessed it: The new Earl of Marborne, ashen faced and in only his shirt sleeves, gripped the shoulder of his gargantuan aide, as if he needed assistance to stand.

"Colonel Ripton will have the flesh flailed from my bones." Valentine set his mouth in a grim line.

52
The Phoenix

-ଈଈ.ଈଈ-

"WE SHALL FIND THE wicked man," Perry said. "He canna hide from us anywhere in England."

"You cannot help at this moment." Starbuck, looking wretched, signaled for the redcoats in the square to join him. "I must go to my colonel to report."

Rowland, seeing that their failed gambol had ensnared his friend, said, "I'm sorry to have caught you up in this, Valentine. Let us help with the search."

"Not possible, Rollo. It's I who must stir every soldier and sailor in London to watch for Withersea."

With that, Starbuck left them, setting his redcoats to run at double-time.

Rowland turned to Perry, every bit of joy from their recent victory now up in smoke. The last few moments had come at him like a double-fisted blow to the pit of his belly. He shook his head to gather his wits. "What do we do?"

"I must sail soon for the Continent." The more than half-forgotten Rosewurme spoke as if answering Rowland's plea. Rosewurme looked as dejected and unsure as Rowland felt. He hadn't taken time in the meeting to notice, but that day the odd fellow dressed like a Puritan preaching at a crossroads. "With Withersea running free, I am in danger for helping you. You must come to my aid, your lordship. If your promise stands."

The fellow at Rowland's elbow asked fulfilment of what now seemed an ill-considered promise. *We will protect you from harm, from all quarters*. What a promise to have made. What they needed to do just then was to warn Tom that they'd failed in the quest to protect his friend Jacob from the wrathful marquess.

Perry rested his arm heavily on Rosewurme's shoulders. "You distress me, Cornelius. Never say his lordship and cousins do not stand by their word." Nudging Rowland, he indicated a path through the crowd. "We shall take Mr. Rosewurme to his reward."

"We must warn Tom," Rowland said, thinking that was the rational next step after a failed gambol.

"Right after we launch Mr. Rosewurme into his new life," Perry said. "Tom is only a stone's throw from the harbor."

"Since I'm departing for the Continent," Rosewurme said, his spirits suddenly bright as the sun, "I do want to stop by my house...ah, that is, my departed wife's house. I must recover my savings. For my travel expenses."

Rowland said, "We need to..." What? He'd failed in other gambols before, though not with others' fate at stake.

"We need to find a sailing ship soon as can be," Perry said. "Mayhap the tide will turn faster than we can travel. Best take a wherry."

"After stopping at my house," Rosewurme said.

"No time. For the sake of your own safety." Perry prodded Rosewurme along, as if he were a wayward sheep with a fixed notion to stray. The little fellow tried to remonstrate all the way to the water, where Perry shepherded both Rosewurme and Rowland from the landing stage onto a wherry with two watermen who pulled long oars.

"This board is wet." Rosewurme complained when he sat down, but then was startled by the boat's movement to grab hold of his seat.

As if he'd never heard Rosewurme's many protests, Perry spoke confidentially, but loud enough to be heard over the noise of the Thames on a hot afternoon. "Because we must hurry for the sake of your safety, Mr. Rosewurme, I shall lend you what you need to travel, from my own fortune."

"Odspitikins! That's an unlooked for kindness." Rosewurme was stunned for a moment into silence. "But how shall I repay such benevolence?"

"Tell me how to retrieve your savings," Perry said. "Then you will write to me at Xanthus House, and I shall charge a banker to forward your own funds to you in your new and safe home."

That seemed to mollify the fellow, so their rapid ride to the Pool of London passed in relative silence. Rowland, forced to sit still for that time, regained his wits, calmed his own fears, and began plotting how to spend the remaining available daylight seeking the marquess. The man would need funds, and so would surely return to his home. Where was that in London? Perhaps his banker. Who was that, besides Danvers Duncombe, now locked in the Tower? If Perry was correct, that the tide was turning, then there wasn't time for the marquess to find funds (but where?) and catch sail on the last of today's parting ships. Then departure by horse? Which must mean the marquess would go to Knightsbridge for funds. Were king's men already going there? Did this escape also put Lizzie in danger? He and Perry must find horses, then choose where…

The wherry bumped against the landing stage at their destination. Perry was helping Rosewurme out, so Rowland trailed after, noticing that the wherry's broad seat had indeed dampened Mr. Rosewurme's hind quarters. Yet the little complainer had only mentioned that discomfort once. What a champion traveler he'd proved to be.

Perry steered Rosewurme through the crowd, as if the wharf was a world he understood. Rowland followed, his hand grasping the cuff of Mr. Rosewurme's coat.

"We must find a ship headed for the Low Countries," Rosewurme said. "Not France."

Perry asked directions from a dockwalloper, then led the way to a merchant ship called the *Phoenix*. As if he'd done this before, Perry bought passage while Rowland stayed with Rosewurme, who began asking Rowland about life in the Low Countries.

"It's colder and wetter than London, yet I felt in my bones that the sun appeared more often." Rowland mused on such a memory for a heartbeat while feeling the sweltering August heat. "Though I recall the Amsterdam summer as more merciful, I confess that I'm happy to be home again in England."

"But you are blessed here," Rosewurme said.

Then Perry called out that he was turning into to a chandler's shop to purchase provisions.

Upon his return, Perry spoke most intimately with Mr. Rosewurme. "The chandler recommended these provisions for a man journeying on the *Phoenix*. There's a coat, a blanket, and a packet of food. Plus, I have added a fish supper for your first night at sea."

"S'welp me, it seems excessive." Mr. Rosewurme eyed the size of the provision pack.

"I trust the chandler. He advises that you'd best travel on to Pennsylvania, rather than remain in Massachusetts where the *Phoenix* has its home harbor. The chandler says those Quaker fellows in Penn's Wood are welcoming to folks."

"But I want to go to the Continent." Mr. Rosewurme sounded like a whining child. "Also, I need my savings to travel."

"Never distress yourself," Perry said. "Do you not preach that the Divine Creator will provide? Like birds of the field, who neither toil nor spin."

"We are grateful for your kindness," Rowland said, shaking Rosewurme's hand.

"This will tide you until you walk down the streets of gold in America." Perry tucked a purse into Rosewurme's waistcoat.

"Fare thee well, Mr. Rosewurme. We wish you only the best." Rowland offered the fellow all the coins in his pocket. Except not his gold angel, with which he'd never part.

"Not the Continent?"

"Nay," Perry said. "The safe and bountiful shores of the New World. Never say that his lordship the Earl of Marborne failed on his promise to keep you safe from long reach of the vengeful Marquess of Withersea."

Rosewurme was rather like a man who'd had the wind knocked out of him. As if breathing was too painful. Then he sighed mightily and slung the heavy pack over his shoulder, showing greater physical strength than Rowland estimated for a man with stick legs and a chicken neck. "May God make a straight path for you, your lordship. And you, Mr. Frake."

They waved all the while a skiff carried Rosewurme to the *Phoenix*, where he was lifted in a basket to board the ship. When Perry ceased waving, he rested his arm on Rowland's shoulder.

"Well done, Perry. But why the New World?"

"With Withersea free," Perry said, "the fellow is in as much danger in Holland as in England. And we can't protect him on the other side of the Channel."

"What a kind heart you have, my friend."

"Also, his enterprising nature will serve him better in a place where people speak English."

"God blind me! I almost like the little fellow," Rowland said. "I'm tempted, but then, I recall that he's a scoundrel."

"I must confess," Perry said. "He did his part to advance righteous justice, standing before those lords and speaking truth. The wee man bent to the moral side of life's balance."

"Because Tom pushed him," Rowland said. "And he merely bent but did not fall. We cannot guess how Mr. Rosewurme will resurrect himself."

Perry said. "I shall do as my mother says and leave judgment to heaven."

"Now, let's find Withersea. I have a plan."

"I had my hopes that you might gather your wits. That scene at Westminster was quite a blow."

Rowland didn't take time to acknowledge that truth. "We go to Knightsbridge on horseback. The marquess may have gone there to gather funds to flee."

"And also, you can rescue Miss Foxe from any travails or dangers there."

"No. That is, yes, but—"

"First, let's ask Ned if Lizzie is indeed in danger." He pointed down the wharf to where Ned and Tom were bent, hands on their knees, as if catching breath after a run.

— NED —

NED HEARD HIS COUSIN Tom's labored breathing and so kept begging for a moment's pause, but Tom continued to pound through crowded streets to Billingsgate. Thankfully, good fortune forced Tom to stop running.

Because, amid all of London, they met Perry and Rowland.

"Well met, Ned. Tom." Rowland greeted them, but neither Ned nor Tom could answer before catching their breath.

Perry said, "Good news, lads! We won the day! You must now call Rollo 'my lord,' because the lofty lords have declared him the honorable Earl of Marborne now."

Rowland said, "Tom, congratulations on the great success of your gambol."

Perry had eyes only for Ned. Which made Ned blush, even before Perry next said, "Also, Ned is our hero. His devil-writing saved Jacob."

"Aye, thank you, Ned." Rowland grasped his arm. "Our new friend Cornelius Rosewurme read your guardian bond to the Committee, announcing Tom as Jacob Rôche's guardian."

"Is it too late?" Ned finally had his breath to speak.

"Too late? For what?" Rowland said, as if he were dim-witted. Then he brightened. "Oh, is Withersea here? Seeking a ship?"

"Here? Isn't he in the Tower?" Tom managed those words, but he still needed more air. "Didn't Captain Starbuck arrive with the warrant?"

"The warrant worked," Rowland said. "But—"

"Then we must stop Jacob and Aurora from sailing to Holland." Tom flew from breathless to frantic again.

"This way then!" Ned urged them fifty paces further down the wharf to where he'd left his fleeing friends. "It's that ship! The *Zeewolf*. The one slipping its anchor."

Tom hailed the ship, shouting till his voice was ragged.

Ned, Rowland, and Perry added their voices.

A dockwalloper stood nearby, hands on his hips, laughing at them. "And do ye bark at the moon come night? Not a soul on that ship can hear your caterwauling."

Of course. All the noise of setting sail and the general groaning of a ship drowned their pleas. They ceased shouting.

"Gone to Holland, are they?" Perry fingered his chin. "We shall fetch them back when all else is mended here."

"No." Tom rent his hands in anguish. "If Aurora sails from England, the king will think she's guilty of treason, too."

"Aurora chose to sail today," Ned said, seeing Perry's puzzled look, "so Withersea won't find them and wreak havoc." Perry and Rowland still looked puzzled, as if not able to understand. "She didn't know that Tom had an iron-hard plan to prove the marquess is a traitor."

"The warrant worked." Perry had his hand on Tom's shoulder as if to calm him. "But the marquess escaped from the king's militia. Mayhap it's best if Aurora and Jacob hide in Holland for now."

"No," Rowland said, shaking his head. "Tom's been worrying about Jacob and Aurora all this time, and he's right to worry now. With Withersea on the fly, the king will suspect the marchioness is in league with him. How do we help her?"

"We must find a way to stop their ship from sailing." Tom paced the wharf's edge.

Rowland took to pacing beside him. "It's not so dire, Tom. We'll get a message to the king, to explain that the marchioness fled in fear of her husband. The duke is sure to help."

Tom stopped pacing, looking up at Rowland, asking to hear again what he'd said. His eyes seemed to beg for Rowland's assurance to be true, which came near to breaking Ned's heart.

Seeing Tom's passion slacken, Ned could no longer delay his mission. Time to get it over with. "Rollo, I'm to tell you, Lizzie is with Jacob and Aurora on the *Zeewolf*. To help them travel as far as the Low Countries."

"There's a breath of good news," Perry said. "Miss Ysabel Foxe possesses a fiery fight-and-be-damned warrior's heart."

Rowland closed his eyes, took a large breath, blew it out. "Yes, she does."

And that was it. All of Ned's worries about Lizzie and Rowland seemed to be for naught. For all that Tom denied his love affair, he proved to be the one they needed to worry about.

Tom straightened, pulling away from Rowland. "There's Captain Starbuck." He ran another fifty paces to meet the captain, and had already presented his worries by the time Ned, Rowland, and Perry joined them.

Starbuck was saying, "I can't leave off my task here. And the only ship faster than that merchantman is the king's cutter."

He pointed another hundred paces up the wharf. Then he saw Rowland and the others.

"I have immense sins to pay for," Starbuck said, shaking his head as if weary, "since it was my militiamen who lost Withersea. The warnings are out all over London by now. He can't sail from this port. He can't leave London by any road.

Rowland said, "Perry and I thought we'd ride to Knightsbridge, to see if the marquess went to ground there."

"I've already sent militiamen for that task," Starbuck said. "If he seeks shelter at any of his properties, the king's men are already there, waiting."

His hand on Starbuck's shoulder, Rowland was saying, "Then you've done all a man can do. Colonel Ripton can't lay it on your shoulders, since you were in the meeting room when the marquess escaped."

"Someone has to take the blame." Starbuck jabbed his chest with his thumb.

"Can you help the marchioness, Captain Starbuck?" Tom again appeared as the calm, steady fellow who'd planned this gambol, though still in the grips of his own passion, so not hearing the captain's distress. "With Withersea missing, I am certain that the marchioness's departure will look complicit."

Rowland said, "Valentine, can you use Withersea's escape as the excuse to stop that ship?"

"I'm of the king's militia, not the navy." Starbuck shook his head. "I'd have to ask my colonel to send a message up to his general, who'd send a message to one of the admirals. It'll take a day or more for an answer. The *Zeewolf* will be in Rotterdam by then."

Ned looked away, avoiding the empty unhappiness in Tom's eyes, but wishing with all his heart they could do more. Yet there they were, all miserable and helpless.

Tom folded his arms, as if to keep from shaking with fatigue. Ned had seen it before, when Tom was dire ill.

Rowland noticed, too. "Tom, you must be done in. Go home and ask Lazarus to bring you a cup of wine. Perry and I will go to Colonel Ripton, while Valentine finishes setting all of London to watch for the marquess. We can make sure that no black story is cast on the marchioness's name. Here's a chair." He had his hand up to call sedan bearers over.

"No," Tom said. "I'll stay with Captain Starbuck while he finishes his work here at the harbor. I helped lure Starbuck into this gambol." Tom still watched as the *Zeewolf* made its way out into the Thames.

Those two walked away, Starbuck with his arm over Tom's shoulder. Starbuck bent his head to hear what Tom was saying, while Tom gestured dramatically with his hands. Whatever Tom might have said, all Ned heard was Starbuck's answer.

"The worst that can happen? Colonel Ripton will have me in the stocks and whipped in front of the entire regiment."

Then Perry slung his arm around Ned's shoulder, which Ned felt as a comfort. "Let's us three go now to see Starbuck's colonel. We shall tell all that occurred in Westminster, to clear any black marks from Starbuck's name. And we'll explain the peril Aurora and Jacob see from the marquess, to confirm that she's not a traitor."

"On the way there," Ned said, "I'd like to hear all that happened at the Committee meeting."

"But didn't Tamsin tell all about what she saw?" Rowland asked. "When she returned with the barrister to his chambers?"

Perry tightened his hand on Ned's shoulder. "Did Tom send Tamsin home when you both left Mordaunt's chambers? You didn't leave her there alone with that dry-as-dust barrister?"

"Tamsin wasn't at the barrister's chambers," Ned said. "Felicity and Camilla told Tom that Tamsin was with you."

"Wait!" Rowland stopped in the street, tripping up two dockworkers and receiving a bundle of curses on his head. "Then where's Tamsin?"

53

The Zeewolf

— L I Z Z I E —

THE SHIP DIDN'T SWAY as much as it would when they reached the Channel. Lizzie ignored the disquiet of her inner workings. It wasn't seasickness that plagued her, only a longing for peace, tinged with residual fear for Jacob and Aurora. And Rowland. She blotted her borrowed paper and wrote rapidly.

Lambkin: I dream that we shall soon sit peacefully under the giant oaks outside Revelstone House, where we will debate who best understands love, your poet or mine.

Once, pretending the words were your own, not those of your Bard, you said to me, 'Of the very instant that I saw you, did my heart fly at your service.' Did I speak aloud my poet's words, confessing my desire in all honesty? 'Fall on me like a silent dew, or like those maiden showers which, by the peep of day, do strew a baptism o'er the flowers.'

What I know now, having lived through it instead of reading about it in extravagant poetry, is that you and I must be yoked together, offering service as a bonded pair, remaining together in company each day. Perhaps our two hearts will never beat as one, but the service we owe our family and the comfort we owe each other must work as one united spirit.

I am so sorry, beyond the kind of regrets a poet ever endeavors to express, that I left you on Tuesday in order to perform a service for Mary.

I have been a modest help to Tom's friends, but I was not an irreplaceable hero, like Ned was. Better that I'd stayed with you, that we'd undertaken Tom's gambol together. That I'd be there to greet you when you emerge successful, after the Committee acknowledges you as the earl destined to serve Marborne's people.

Forgive my disloyalty. My vanity.

~

While Lizzie wrote, John Coachman kept Jacob up on deck, with Aurora at his side. Through the hatch that let air into the captain's quarters, Lizzie heard John gently telling Jacob to look out at the end of the water. "See, the land is just there."

"Dear heart," Aurora's soft voice carried through the hatch, "don't squeeze Pip so tightly. You'll make him afraid. He wants to take care of you."

Their departure from England moved slowly forward. With soft words. Gagging heaves. Pip whimpering. Still, they were escaping. Lizzie returned to her missive, pondering what else she had to say, besides one promise: "*I'll return to England at first opportunity. I mean days, lambkin, not weeks.*"

"Sail ho!" A man's voice shouted. "Hail the king!"

Lizzie listened for what that meant, but when she heard the sails collapsing and sailors heaving lines, she went up to join Aurora, folding the letter and tucking it into her gown.

"The marquess found us," Aurora whispered, stricken.

"Duxwold must have seen us," Lizzie said.

"No, it's Tom!" Jacob cried, forgetting his seasick misery.

"Not Tom," Aurora said.

With nowhere to go and no way to hide, they watched as a smaller ship flying the king's banner came alongside. Its captain hailed the *Zeewolf's* captain.

"By error, you have members of English nobility aboard who travel without the king's permission. The king demands that they return to London."

They hadn't travelled far from the Billingsgate docks. The Thames was as calm as it ever was in summer. But, like watching a horrible accident progress with the slow speed of a dream, Aurora's baggage was hauled over from one ship to another. First, the men of their party were ordered to surrender to the king. Then Aurora, Jacob, and Lizzie were transferred into a ship that contained more English marines than sailors. That meant each was helped into a basket, lowered into a skiff, then rowed to the king's ship, and hauled up in another basket.

Yet Jacob, who seemed most likely to be frightened out of his wits, merely petted Pip, looking up at the king's ship, his head cocked as if listening to someone on the ship.

Lizzie emerged from the upward-hauled basket to find Jacob at his ease, waggling a finger at Pip, miming a gesture Aurora used when cautioning him. "No sailing for you, Pip."

Aurora, John Coachman, and Gabriel stood together, all ashen faced. Lizzie joined them, taking Aurora's hand in hers. Aurora was pale, frowning deeply. She said, "The gods have risen up against us."

However, the king's officer who greeted them was Captain Starbuck, the leader of the militia that had been quartered in Cambridge all summer.

"This way, my lady. Greetings, Miss Foxe." Starbuck took Lizzie's sunburned, glove-free hand. "We can provide only small comfort on the return to London, but it's a short trip. Tom says I must offer you brandy, not watered wine. But I warn you, this is fire water, likely seized from the cellars of iniquitous men. I am sure that Rollo will offer better tonight."

The mention of Rowland's name led Lizzie to seek him among all those marines. "Rollo had other business," Starbuck said, as if he knew who her eyes longed to see.

She didn't find Rowland. But Tom stood in the middle of a dozen marines. He whispered in Jacob's ear and scratched the top of Pip's head. When the two women approached him, Tom reached out to grasp Aurora's and Lizzie's hands.

"Tom saved us from sailing," Jacob said to Pip. "He's my friend. My soldier."

— TAMSIN —

FROM CHANCERY LANE, TAMSIN passed through the gates into the walled courtyard of Lincoln's Inn. She knocked at the barrister's door, surprised when Mr. Mordaunt opened it.

He was not happy to see her. "Mr. Foxe and his cousin—the one called Ned—have departed."

"Where have they gone?" Her high spirits flattened at the barrister's cold greeting. She'd longed to burst upon Tom with news of her heroic endeavors, how she'd saved them all.

"I believe they seek to save the Marchioness of Withersea from the consequences of her husband's wrath. Or perhaps to protect the Earl of Marborne."

Tamsin could honestly swear that she'd solved both problems. That knowledge kindled a warm feeling that might be called pride. She said, "The earl is now in no danger. And the marchioness need not worry about the marquess finding her."

"But the marquess—"

"Sprung his own trap and fell in. He's bound for Batavia."

Mordaunt swallowed while seeking words. "How ever did Foxe arrange that?"

"The gods of Olympus flew down." Tamsin had seen it all, but still jammed the pieces together in her mind. "The marquess came out of the Committee meeting in Rollo's coat."

"Was the earl sent to the Tower?" Mordaunt set his mouth in a grim line. "Did the marquess condemn him for a traitor?"

"I believe that to be his original idea. It's sad that you went along with such evil." She smiled at the barrister, but it felt wolfish, though she had no reason for that now.

"I did not. I cannot be blamed for that. I have quit all business with the marquess."

"Thank you for that, sir. It saves me asking how you could participate in so much evil. However, Rollo and Tom intended that the marquess should be arrested. That plan might have worked, if Withersea's rogues hadn't mistaken him for Rollo."

"How...how—"

"You pointed me out to the rogues, so they dragged me on their crimping caper. I tried to free Rollo, then saw it was the marquess caught in his own plot. Can you spare a drink of water?"

While the barrister fetched a jug and a glass, Tamsin struggled to settle the quarrel in her heart and head. She couldn't castigate a stranger, though while she stood so close to the barrister, she wanted to scold him once more, to relieve the last of the heated anger burning behind her ribs. She kept that fire tamped down, smiling as he offered her water.

"Sir, I agree with Tom, that he must not cause harm to innocents like your sons in his endeavor to rescue Jacob Rôche from the marquess's evils."

"He explained as much to me," Mordaunt said, "while also making clear the jeopardy I was in by way of my alliance with the marquess."

She noticed the ink splotches on the barrister's shirt cuffs, and how he gripped a quill as if it might save his life. "Anyone but Tom would let your family join the unfortunate widows and orphans you harmed."

"Mr. Foxe explained the righteous path I must tread. I am compelled to unravel the cases that Withersea and other lords paid me to shepherd through the chancery courts." Mordaunt's voice was hollow.

"It's better that you have the chance to correct these clerks' errors than—"

"Better than what? What could be worse?"

"Better than if Mr. Rosewurme used all his papers to extort money from those lords in exchange for his silence."

Mordaunt seemed even more pale. "That curious fellow would do just such a thing, wouldn't he?"

"I believe," Tamsin said, "he'd trade dishonor for monetary gain. Unlike Tom, who now possesses Rosewurme's papers."

"I see." He coughed. "I'd best return to my work."

"I'll help while we wait for Tom to return."

Mordaunt frowned. "What can you possibly do?"

"I can read and write Latin. I have a very fair secretary hand. And I read aloud every one of Tom's law texts while he was ill. Let me help with your work."

"Who am I addressing?"

"Thomasine Foxe." She held out her hand, then saw it was rather filthy and withdrew it.

He shrugged, then pointed to where Tom must have been at work before Ned came.

That proved to be a way to stay busy while the others rode the final waves of this gambol. However, she had to move that leather purse inside her waistcoat, since its bulge hampered her movements when she sharpened a quill and bent over the desk. She looked up each time the pendulum clock chimed the half hour, hoping that Camilla had made it safely home. But then, of course, Perry had taken care of that, since he'd promised Tom and Rowland that the Knights of the Marborne Fens were all protected. It was only Tamsin who'd slipped out from under Perry's watch. And that had turned out fine.

Though she expected Perry to scold her for it.

She mended her pen and dipped it in the ink, finding it to be the best ink she'd ever been blessed to use.

54

Magic and the Sanest Man

IT TOOK AN HOUR to find Starbuck's Colonel Ripton and discuss the Withersea affair with him. Over the thirty minutes' walk to Rowland's house, the new Earl of Marborne complained about having spent most of the past week tramping about London hungry. And, as starving men sometimes do, Rowland cited the dozen dishes he'd most like set before him.

Ned, however, mostly thought of the grand giant who walked at his side, who took multiple opportunities to touch Ned's elbow, his wrist, his shoulder. To put a cautious hand before Ned's breastbone to keep him from stepping in front of a carriage.

"Yet I'd be perfectly satisfied right now with bread and butter," Rowland said. "Wait till you taste the butter from my kitchen. What do you want, Ned?"

"A decent supper and a night's sleep," Ned said. "Then to go home come morning."

"The wonder of Xanthus House," Rowland said, pointing to the door of his new house, "guarantees at least the first two of your wishes. After years living in a barracks, I feel like a prince in a castle here. You will enjoy this, I wager."

Ned glanced up at the townhouse, counting the stories, judging the number of mullioned windows. It didn't possess the architectural magnificence of Arcadia House in Knightsbridge (this street had a whole row of identical houses), but Xanthus House was many, many steps above any kip Ned ever had in London. And here was Rowland, asking them to feel at home.

Ned stood back with Perry when Rowland, his Paris wig under his arm, put his hand up to knock on a heavy, iron-strapped oak door. But before Rowland rapped, a spectral, austerely dressed older man opened the door.

"Good evening, Lord Marborne." The man reached to take Rowland's wig, appearing to ignore that the coatless Rowland bore all the dust gathered from a run across London in shirt-sleeves. "We are happy to see you home again, my lord. I hope you will allow all of your household to felicitate you on the confirmation of your title."

"Thank you, Lazarus. You are kind to mention it." Rowland tugged Ned forward. "This is my cousin, Mr. Ned Wijck, who will be staying here with us. And you have met my partner in all business, Mr. Perry Frake. We hope we are not too late for supper. Are our other friends at table?"

"Miss Candecote has returned and brought along her friend Miss Oakes. Dr. Oakes joined them some time ago. They have dined in Miss Candecote's bedchamber. Two young gentlemen in the foyer say they were sent to await Mr. Frake."

Perry nodded to Lazarus and stepped into the walnut-paneled foyer to speak with his brothers. Ned, distracted, tried to attend to Perry's conversation with his brothers, but he only heard the exchange between Rowland and his butler.

"Is Miss Thomasine Foxe here?" Rowland asked.

"We've had no word from her, my lord," the butler said. "Nor from Mr. Tom Foxe. Will you be hosting Captain Starbuck for the night again?"

"Tom should be here soon. I'm not sure about the captain. He's out on the king's business, but may I beg for the captain to be attended if he arrives late in the evening?"

"Yes, my lord. You scarcely need to ask," Lazarus said. "We shall have supper in the dining room within the quarter hour." Glancing around, he said, "Service for seven, my lord?"

"Likely you can count better than me," Rowland said. "I cannot hide that this day has taxed my wits."

"Allow me," Lazarus said, "to show your friends to chambers where they can," he paused, "refresh themselves."

Perry returned. "Mr. Wijck will be quartering with me."

Which thrilled Ned to hear, after his exile in Knightsbridge.

"These two also," Perry pointed to his brothers, Neriah and Daniel, "if you are short of quarters for us all to kip."

Ned felt no thrill at that surprise, though Perry was still sending smiles in Ned's direction. Ned wished to be generous, since the two brothers had done good work, but what was Perry on about? Didn't he also long for a certain…ah, privacy?

Lazarus, however, declared that Xanthus House was capacious. "No need for four young gentlemen to…um…kip in the same chamber." He led the two boys to their own chamber.

Perry led Ned upstairs. The house wasn't ostentatious, like Lord Hawksmoor's in Cambridgeshire, and not full of art and antiquities, like Arcadia House. But the walnut-paneled walls, polished oak stairs, and carpets, together with the lamps and silver candle branches at every nook, announced unostentatious wealth. Could their family restore Revelstone House like this?

As if knowing Ned's thoughts, Perry said, "I should encourage Miss Thomasine to adopt such modest glory when we buckle down to work at home."

Ned closed the door behind Perry in their bedchamber. He prepared to make a claim about who they might share quarters with at home. Perry, however, began singing that tavern tune.

The shepherds' swains shall dance and sing
For thy delight each May morning.

Perry stopped singing to pour hot water from a jug into the washbowl and began to wash his face with a strip of linen, then rubbed his hands.

"I'd hoped," Ned faltered, wanting to speak delicately, "for the same freedom we enjoyed together on Tuesday afternoon."

"Aye, sweeting. You'll find that Rowland's new servants possess discreet souls." Misunderstanding Ned's meaning, Perry buried his face in toweling. When he emerged, he pointed to the

497

array on the dressing table. "See? The blessed servants have laid out a second silver brush, besides the one they left for me last night. And here's another jug of hot water for you, dearest one."

"Thank you," Ned mumbled. He got busy figuring how to wash his hands with his splintered finger, and how to again ask questions about the disposition of Perry's brothers.

"We shall struggle not to become inured of such service," Perry said. "We didn't see the like at Benson's."

Ned poured water and picked up the same toweling Perry had used to wash. It smelled of lavender, not the lye-and-ash laundry soap he was used to at Revelstone. He rubbed his hands rather than dunking that broken finger in the basin.

"Are we going home soon?" Ned dried his face and hands.

"Home." Perry came up behind Ned, wrapping his arms around him. "A delightful word. Such a change from how I have lived, even a fortnight ago."

Perry straightened his waistcoat, then tugged at Ned's collar and retied his neckcloth. Ned could happily become used to that.

"Let's go find supper," Perry said. "You cannot conceive of the manna from heaven that was laid before us last night."

They were down two flights of stairs and at the door of the dining salon when Perry said, "Don't let me forget to tell the lads that they'll be atop the coach taking Miss Thomasine and us'uns home to Revelstone. They got over-excited, thinking I'd hire horses for them to ride to Cambridge."

"They are going with us?" Ned's voice broke, so he coughed.

"If my other brothers learned I promised to let them travel on their own, they'd go running to Mother with the tale, and she would castigate me across London. It'd dampen my spirits."

Ned felt his own damp spirits darken.

~

"Shall we celebrate your title, Lord Marborne?" Perry asked when Rowland appeared, now in a clean shirt and a black coat that Ned thought fit for a parson leading a parish burial.

"Not until Lizzie can join us." Rowland took a seat at the table. Perry sat by Ned, across from the two Frake brothers. "Besides, didn't we celebrate last night with Valentine's men?"

"Merely a toast to the king's gratuity," Perry said.

Rowland said, "I must once again admire how you picked Withersea's pocket for the emoluments to offer to fifteen lords and three judges."

"I have my uses," Perry said. Likely no one else noticed, but he ran his knuckle down the lower half of Ned's spine.

Ned shivered, still collecting his thoughts. The room was painted a light blue that Touchstone called *oltramarino*. Beyond the sea. Could they afford colors like that for rooms at Revelstone House? He shook free of that thought, knowing he drifted into color and form when he couldn't manage words for the present moment.

"I owe you for the cost of Rosewurme's passage," Rowland said. "His work benefited my family."

"We'll settle that after retrieving Mr. Rosewurme's stashed wealth at Chalgrove House. And his testimony also benefited Tom's paramour," Perry said. "Though we'd best say it helped Jacob, and keep mum till we know what's in Tom's heart."

This volley of words indicated that Ned had missed much of what had passed while he was in Knightsbridge. He cogitated on Perry's surprising plan to bring Neriah and Daniel to Revelstone.

The butler and kitchen people appeared to lay out platters of food. Everyone's attention turned to the chicken fricassee, with golden chicken pieces laid atop summer vegetables in a creamy sauce. Ned had to wait to claim his share of the fricassee while each of the Frake brothers claimed triple portions. The fricassee tasted of nutmeg and wine, and went well with the small dish of cucumbers in vinegar that Lazarus set by Ned's plate. They hadn't finished the fricassee before Lazarus brought in platters of ham and ox tongue, plus a salad of sorrel with violet flowers.

Perry snagged the pitcher of small beer when his brothers reached for third helpings. Due to certain confusion at the table,

Ned had to wait until Lazarus brought another pitcher and poured a serving in Ned's cup. Yet the wait proved fortunate; the light ale came new from the cellar, its chill pleasant on a summer evening.

All the while, Ned listened to Perry and his brothers.

"Where will you find work for us?" Daniel said. "You promised Mother that you would."

"Mayhap it will be as if you'd joined the army," Perry said.

The two lads sat up straight, eager at this notion.

"Though you're a few years shy for the actual army." Perry tapped his chin, like he did when thinking. "Your new master will have stables to muck and thunder-jugs to empty. Hay to cut for fodder. Milking the cows morning and night. There's always more mowing and wood to chop. Isn't there, Ned?"

Ned, looking up from his cup, nodded. The lads had fallen despondent.

Ned's spirits dipped further. He'd missed understanding that Perry intended for the boys to live at Revelstone. When had Ned agreed? Had he done it without knowing?

"Truly, Peregrine?" Daniel beseeched him. "Milk cows?"

"Aye," Perry said, "but nowt else than you'd do in any army camp. What I'm looking for is a manservant. Now that I'm a gentleman of consequence, I must have a man to dress me, polish my shoes, keep my small clothes fresh. Which of you wants that employ?" Neither answered. "The other can serve Ned, though I warn you, he's far more demanding than I may be. You'll be washing his small clothes every morning except Sunday."

"Truly?" Neriah squeaked.

Ned wanted to squeak, too. Frake brothers living with them?

"Cease, Perry." Rowland stirred his fricassee from one side of his plate to the other. "Leave off teasing."

"As you wish, my lord." Perry sipped ale. "All Ned requires is help painting portraits. He's deft with his brushes, you know."

"How do we help?" Daniel asked.

"When Ned finishes painting the face in a portrait," Perry said, "he needs someone to wear the lush gown while the lady he's painted goes about her business. You don't suppose a rich lady sits in the same chair for days on end? It's like Shakespeare, where they find a lad to play the lady."

No, that wasn't how Ned had been picturing the future—also, it was not how he painted.

Rowland picked at his sorrel and violets. "They don't do that at the theater these days. Actresses like Felicity Oakes play the roles."

The butler hovered, awaiting Rowland's attention.

"My lord?"

"Yes, Lazarus?" Rowland looked up from where he brooded over an untouched glass of wine. Ned guessed that Lizzie going to Holland had subdued his mood. "Has word come from Captain Starbuck? Did Miss Thomasine return? Or Miss Ysabel Foxe?" A hopeful note in his voice.

Yes, Lizzie was the source of Rowland's disquiet.

"His grace the duke sent a coach to carry you to his fête. We shall keep the driver in the kitchen while he waits."

"Thank you, Lazarus. Can you help me know what best to wear to the duke's fête?"

Lazarus assented and withdrew. Then Rowland made the most ridiculous request.

"Too many adventures today made me forget the duke. Will you please come with me, Ned? I cannot go alone."

Ned offered empty hands. "I shall always do what I can for you. But I cannot dine with dukes."

"Nor I," Perry said. "Haven't the clothes for it. Howbeit, it's nice that you have a man to choose your clothes for you. I can always say I knew you when you smelled of horse and got your clothes from a *pandjesbaas* just off the Herengracht canal."

Rowland didn't answer. He looked wistful. "I wish Tamsin would return. Or Starbuck. They'd be brave enough to come."

With that, Rowland went upstairs to dress. After a quarter of an hour, he peeked into the dining salon. "Still no sign of Starbuck? What about Tamsin?"

Ned looked up. "No."

Perry didn't answer, still describing the prospects of life at Revelstone to his brothers.

"Tamsin's been missing too long," Rowland said. "Can you please rouse yourselves to find her?"

"As soon as we finish supper," Perry said. "Likely she went to Benson's for more of her baggage. She can't have gotten in too much trouble. I'm more concerned about what Tom and Captain Starbuck have got up to."

"Please look for them, too. Try Mordaunt's chambers." Then Rowland was gone, with the butler's son trailing, dressed as a page.

Ned still wasn't alone with Perry. Hence, he couldn't delve into the surprise about the two Frake brothers. He asked, being cautious, "How will it be when we are at last home?'

"Exactly as you should wish it, chucking," Perry said. "We did decide to build a house."

"What kind of a house?" Daniel asked, intruding.

"The kind of cottage as most people have in the country," Perry said. "Two rooms up, two down."

Ned searched all he remembered of Tuesday's doings. Did they imbibe so much while touring the taverns of London that he didn't hear about an entourage of brothers coming to Revelstone?

Perry said, "It shan't be much tighter quarters than you are used to, Daniel."

"You said the Foxes live in a mansion," Neriah said. "Are we not to live there?"

"Nay," Perry said. "It's not such a palace that it can quarter half a regiment of Frakes."

Though Ned knew how to swim, he felt his toes scrape the murky bottom but couldn't get a solid foothold. He couldn't break to the surface of such treacherous waters. He asked, "How are we to live in our new house as bachelors? Must poor Mrs. Bell feed us all at Revelstone?"

"Of course not," Perry said. "Who can best tend the house and kitchen but our dear Mother? Come spring, Daniel and Neriah and our other three brothers will dig the glorious garden that's only been in her heart so far in this life."

Perry said *mō-thah*. Did he mean—

"Will our cottage have a real kitchen for our mum? Or only a hearth?" Daniel said. "Our mum is a grand cook."

Neriah said, "Aye. When we find pennies for sugar and meat."

"Yet our mum can make an old hen and two turnips last for days. Better than anyone in Brick Lane," Daniel said. Neriah nodded heartily.

"There'll be no more old turnips," Perry said. "We shall eat chicken more often than only when the moon is blue."

Ned shifted uncomfortably in his chair. But then a painting appeared in that familiar corner of his mind. A landscape in an imaginary Cambridgeshire. He considered the appropriate blue for the sky, a selection of greens for oak trees and a rosehip hedge. He'd use vermillion for Perry's fancy vest, which meant the picture must be of a Sunday. A dinner under the oaks with Mr. Gamlingay, the old parish minister, at table. That way, Perry's mother wouldn't be out of place amid all the boys. Ned tallied on his knuckles, accounting for six brothers in the pastoral scene, the mother, the rector. That many figures broke the mood and tone of what could be called pastoral.

But Tom was at the door of the dining salon.

"Where's Tamsin?" Tom asked. "Isn't she here yet? And does anyone know where to find Winwood?"

Then Lizzie, Jacob, Aurora, and Captain Starbuck entered with a swarm of people, as if all of Knightsbridge had come to London. Lizzie looked especially worn, her new bright-gold gown now dingy with London filth, its lace and rosettes tattered. Fortunately, Ned had sketched that dress in Knightsbridge and created the palette so he could paint it later. All was not lost.

After quick helloes, Aurora said, "Is Dr. Oakes here? I wish he might look to Jacob, who's been much jostled today."

"If I might say," Lazarus said, "Dr. Oakes is upstairs, tending to Miss Candecote."

"And Miss Thomasine?" Tom asked.

"She has not yet arrived."

"We'll start a search for her," Perry said. "By my great good fortune, I have a pair of brothers here, prepared to run errands."

"Where's Rollo?" Lizzie said. When no answer came, she repeated sharply, "Where's Rollo?"

"Gone to the duke's fête," Ned said, sure Lizzie would hound them over Rowland instead of telling whatever great good luck had brought them back to London.

55

A Sure Uncertainty

LIZZIE RECOGNIZED VALENTINE STARBUCK when she was hauled aboard the king's ship. The men from Starbuck's militia rather gracelessly ferried the traveling party to shore.

"Captain, are we under arrest for fleeing from the Crown?" Lizzie asked when they stood on the wharf. She'd heard voices from the king's ship shout warnings to the *Zeewolf*'s captain about the king's warrant.

"That's the excuse I gave in order to commandeer the king's ship," Starbuck said. "I do indeed have a warrant to arrest the Marquess of Withersea. Tom convinced me to exaggerate the scope of my mission."

"We are free to go?" Lizzie asked, not yet certain whether luck had intervened or if they were now in deeper jeopardy.

"Yes. Tom suggests that you all go to Rollo's house in Covent Garden." Starbuck glanced at the traveling party waiting by their pile of baggage on the wharf. "Tom and I stayed there last night, as did Miss Candecote and Miss Foxe. It can accommodate you all. I'm sure that's what Rollo would wish."

By that time, Jacob was beyond his last legs. Pip's tongue lolled from its mouth. Aurora was pale as parchment. John Coachman said they should seek lodging in a good part of town.

"No, let's go to the Earl of Marborne's house." Lizzie used an imperious tone she'd never exercised in England, but someone had to act as if they knew what to do.

When the carriage drew up in front of a much finer Covent Garden house than Lizzie had expected, she stepped onto the pavement with Tom. At least, as Rowland's cousins, they had a decent basis for importuning. Tom knocked.

"Mr. Foxe, good evening." A rather gaunt butler greeted Tom by name and professed that his lordship expected them.

"This is Miss Ysabel Foxe, Lazarus," Tom said. "She's another cousin of his lordship's."

Then Tom introduced the rest of the company. The butler Lazarus was unfazed by having half of Knightsbridge descend on the house, including a marchioness and another earl.

"There is a bite of supper laid at this moment for Mr. Frake and Mr. Wijck," Lazarus said. "His lordship the earl warned us to expect additional guests. We are prepared to do all we can to make you comfortable."

Pip and Jacob had fallen asleep in the carriage and had to be roused. He came to Tom's side and looked warily around the large foyer. Coming in last, shepherding the baggage, were John Coachman and Gabriel. When Lazarus welcomed them, John immediately volunteered to do what he could to lessen the burden on the house, and Gabriel echoed the same wish.

"Is it possible," Tom asked, "that Lord Cloudesley and I can be served in the room where I slept last night? It's been too much of a day for us both."

Lazarus nodded, as if taking in how exhausted Jacob was. "Yes, sir. I will bring refreshment directly."

"Can Pip have a bone, please?" Jacob said.

The butler understood Jacob without asking him to repeat his words. "We can do better than that, your lordship."

Tom said, "And will you please ask Dr. Oakes to join us?"

With Jacob safe, Lizzie felt a weight lifted.

Perry and Ned came into the foyer to welcome Aurora and Starbuck, both eager to lead them to the dining salon.

"Here's wine," Perry said. "Two of my brothers were here earlier and destroyed the last of supper. But trust Lazarus. He'll set a feast before you in a heartbeat. Camilla and Winwood are upstairs. We ran the young woman off her legs again."

"You will have a feast such as you cannot imagine," Captain Starbuck said. "It's my second night of such glory. Can anyone dispute Rollo's good luck?"

"Where is Rollo?" Lizzie spied an empty place at the head of the table.

Rather than answer, Perry demanded the story of Starbuck's mission. Food arrived while Aurora was explaining how they came to be aboard the *Zeewolf*.

"Will you be in trouble, Captain Starbuck?" Aurora asked. "For rescuing us?"

"I shall bring Rollo when I face my colonel next. We should be able to argue the wisdom of my interdiction, given the marquess's traitorous actions."

Then they all clamored to guess the various ways the Right Honorable Earl of Marborne might come to the captain's aid, given that the Duke of Bagsham was Rowland's ally.

"But where is Rollo?" Lizzie asked once more, raising her voice to a fishwife's volume to be heard. Even though it felt like she shouted it, not one person in the crowd answered.

The butler was at her elbow. "Miss Foxe? Pardon me, but his lordship went to a fête at the Duke of Bagsham's house."

"Alone?" The idea stunned her.

"Yes, Miss Foxe. In a manner of speaking. The duke sent a carriage, and my son Peter went along as his lordship's page."

Lizzie crossed the room, collaring her brother Ned and digging her nails into Perry Frake's forearm.

"You left Rollo to go alone to the duke's fête?"

"It's not the sort of party we are fit for," Ned said, trying to wiggle from her grasp. "Rollo promised that we'd all celebrate once you'd come home."

"My dear brother, it's the sort of party you'd best get used to. I cannot believe you deserted Rollo. You left him just as the door of the lions' den opened."

"Lizzie, it's not like—"

"It's not like we all swore an oath." She seethed. "High up in our fleet of oak trees. I'd never think you, brother, would be an oath breaker." Lizzie raised her hands, as if beseeching heaven. "Is there anyone here who's not as mad as Bess of Bedlam?"

— T O M —

"WHERE'S JACOB?" AURORA ASKED when Tom answered her knock on his bedchamber door.

Tom put a finger to his lips, then pointed to the cot in the darkest corner, where Jacob and Pip slept, the dog snoring, its face pushed up against Jacob's neck. He then pointed to the other chair beside the table where he sat drinking the last of the potion Winwood prescribed. At least Winwood allowed that Tom might drink it in a hot mint tea, which almost masked the vile bitterness of the elixir.

She sat near him, so they could confer in whispers.

He said, "I've been counting all I must do in the coming days. My tally is quite high. I shall be immured in paper dust and the close air of Mr. Mordaunt's chambers."

"Since the marquess is an outlaw," she said, "I shall have to negotiate with the king to preserve what is rightfully mine."

"My work to destroy the marquess wasn't perfect. However, it shouldn't be too difficult to mend any broken bits."

"Who'd have guessed that he'd run?" Aurora said. After a moment, the flickering candle caught her eye. "This reminds me of the lamplight and the sound of the hearth fire at Trinity."

"Seeing you in the late evening's light, along with the sole candle," he pointed to the unshaded taper, "brings to mind the shadows dancing on the wall while we talked poetry and heroes."

While she mused, Tom plunged ahead with what he'd come to comprehend that day.

"I could never have joined you in Rome if you and Jacob were forced to flee there. Amid the dust and depression of today's tasks in Mr. Mordaunt's chambers, I saw what I shall do, quite happily, to meet the destiny my Uncle Absolom pronounced for me."

"Destiny?" She repeated the word, but not in the same tone as when they parried over the notion of Fate as scholars at Trinity. "Do people still have destinies?"

"I do," Tom said. "I have to unwind all the bad cases where the marquess used English law to cheat people out of their inherited lands. I intend to take on the chore like a crusading knight." He kept talking when she didn't answer. "Of course, I must take Jacob's guardianship in hand, to ensure that English law delivers justice." He sipped his medicinal tisane. "That's what I've found since Tuesday afternoon."

"I found friends." She folded her hand. "Friends who'd risk a great deal for me. I hadn't known such friendship since our days at Trinity."

"Now that you've met the charm of Foxes, you must perceive the comfort I've always known." He rubbed at the writer's bunion that was reviving itself on his right hand.

She said, "When I returned to Knightsbridge last night, I heard all the horrors and rudeness of the marquess's last visit there. The only safe action I saw was to pack and leave. But I had heroes to intercede because you gave me friends, who descended like the gods of Olympus to save us."

"Friends have a duty to help each other." He listened to Pip snore, feeling that she had more she needed to say.

"Do you perceive..." She clasped her hands more tightly. "In going to Trinity, I only dared because my Aunt Letitia urged me to do what my heart cried for. You and your cousins helped me seize the course of my own life."

"I praise your courage."

He rubbed again at his fingers. He'd bruised them with the day's scribing. It had been months since he'd raised a bunion on his finger.

"I'm accepting an invitation," she said, "to stay at my Aunt Letitia's house with my cousin Michel Chêne and his sister. You were kind to invite us to Revelstone House, but I shall have too much business that requires me to stay in London."

"A proper choice," Tom said, though he'd dreamed of Jacob running freely at Revelstone, like Tom always had. "But Jacob will be disappointed. I told him about all the generations of Pip the cat that have lived in the Marborne barns. He wants to see if Pip the dog will chase Pip the cat."

"He can visit in the autumn." She bit at her lip, as if pensive. "I trained like a Greek warrior in the past few years, teaching myself not to feel anything. When Jacob came to live with me after Easter, it upset the foolish sham of a life I was leading. Now, I feel my hopes rising again, for what my life can be."

"Hope is the life force in my entire being," Tom said. "After being ill so long, I've found my place. In the law, in London."

"My hopes are perhaps still too modest," she said. "I hope the king's men keep the marquess from finding me."

"Not hope. Rollo and I shall convince the king you are not Withersea's partner in perfidy. Though..." He wanted to break her solemn meditations; it was growing late. "I shall pretend modesty and cease congratulating myself for rescuing Jacob."

Her laughter echoed in the chamber like the soft sound of summer rain tapping the dusty earth.

"I shall never be able to adequately thank you," she said.

Tom said, "I did as I promised. And for the future, I won't be far away. For one, I'm staying in London. For another, I'm Jacob's legal guardian. I must check often on his well-being."

She squeezed his hand. "We're released from Hades, with you taking up the burden of guarding Jacob's well-being. He'll be close by in London with me."

"No!" Jacob cried out.

It sounded like he'd woken from a bad dream. Aurora went to his cot, crooning assurances.

"It's only a dream, dear heart."

But before she could kneel beside him, Jacob was on his feet. Pip barked and pawed at the blanket.

"Not dreaming. Not London." Jacob pushed her hands away.

"We must stay in London," she said. "We cannot return to Knightsbridge at the moment."

"But I'm going with Tom. He's my soldier now."

"I'm your guardian," Tom said. "I'll be in London, near you."

"Not near." Jacob was shaking his finger at his sister, the way he imitated her when he upbraided Pip. "I shall live with Tom. Like soldiers do. No girls."

"Oh!" Aurora sounded surprised, not offended.

"Right, Tom?" Jacob said, sounding sure of himself. "Here. At your house."

Tom felt it in his bones: he liked the idea of his friend in the same house. "This is my cousin Rollo's house. We shall have to ask him." Then it struck him. "I haven't yet asked him if I may live here."

"Let's go ask." Jacob sat up and began pulling on his stockings.

"Not tonight," Tom said. "Rollo isn't home. We'll ask in the morning." He sipped the last of his restorative tisane. "There's so much to do tomorrow."

56

Littlecote House

— R O L L O —

ROWLAND GREETED THE FOOTMAN he knew among the others at the duke's door. "Good evening, Isaac. Am I the last to arrive?"

"I can't say, your lordship. But the room is crowded. You may entrust your weapons with me." It wasn't just a kind offer. Isaac held out his hand for Rowland's sword-stick, then kept his hand out until Rowland handed over the knife in his boot. "It's a custom of the house when lofty persons are visiting."

By good fortune, the first person Rowland met inside was Viscount Heydon, who stuck to his side, introducing Rowland to the lords who'd been at the Committee meeting and were now here with their wives and aides. Rowland used every memory trick he had, getting names to stick in his mind.

At one point, they passed close to the entry way, where the pages nodded on a bench. Lazarus's boy Peter sat upright, apparently determined to remain awake. Yet each time Peter blinked, it took an extra heartbeat till he opened his eyes again. Rowland longed to join him.

By then, the room had heated beyond anything they'd endured in the meeting chamber that morning. And he hadn't yet found the duke to thank him for the honor of the fête. Until that happened, Rowland could not sneak away.

"I say, Marborne, you are getting on quite well," Heydon said. "You have the verve to be the man needed in a scene like this."

"My left hand is numb from holding this wine glass for an hour while I shake hands."

They stood near a table where people convened to eat and to seek more punch. The food resembled what Rowland had seen at fêtes in Amsterdam, and in his younger days in Paris, when he'd hung in the back among other diplomats' aides, never fed from the feast tables, all of it being fancy nibbles.

What might have once been a real pheasant had been taken apart and reassembled as a miniature of itself, resting in a nest made of woven biscuit and laid on a bed of caviar. A bite of cod had been pared to make it into a fish that now swam in clear jelly, capped by a tiny biscuit which resembled a cockle. The fish swam in a school of identical dozens.

Yet Rowland felt no inclination to taste even a bite of his own celebratory fête.

"Beware," Heydon whispered. "Be prepared."

"An attack is coming?" Rowland asked in jest.

"No, it's—"

"Marborne!" The duke's voice sounded by his ear. "We are happy for you tonight."

"Your grace, you are kind." Rowland slipped his wine glass onto the table behind him, hearing it tip and fall as he grasped the duke's hand with both of his own. "Please believe that I am indeed grateful."

"Say no more," the duke said.

"Aye, your grace. But tell me when I must return Xanthus House to you."

"Return it? Oh no, Marborne. It's yours. Think of it as part of my settlement for the debts between us. Or will you turn austere and philosophical like Doctor Foxe?" He chuckled. "As if it's a bribe for future adventure."

"Ha! No, duke. I'm only grateful for your notice."

Rowland had won the round on Thursday and had protected the duke from revelations about the marquess's schemes to cheat widows and orphans. He'd kept Viscount Bravewood's name off the reconstituted ledger page of Duncombe's investors. He could accept the gift of the house as a necessary evil, because he had to maintain this fraught alliance, for Marborne and his cousins. And for now, Rowland reveled at having power over a lord who'd tried to overwhelm him with threats. Likely as not, come morning he'd have to admit he was ashamed to enjoy power over the duke, because his own demand of black tribute had been heartier than the duke's.

"Follow me," the duke said. "I've come to fetch you."

Bagsham led Rowland, with Heydon trailing, to a small salon one flight of marble stairs up from the fête. A footman closed the massive doors behind them, muffling the crowd noise. Four other men were in the room, three of them standing. The seated man was not handsome (his nose was too big), and he wore a periwig that was too deep brown in color for a man his age, its locks too long and over-curled. Even in the heat of August, an ermine cloak hung at the edge of his chair. He sported an enormous lace cravat that dripped over his blue satin sash.

Heydon had warned him. This was the lofty person who occasioned the seizing of guests' weapons.

"Bless me, you look just like your father," the man said.

Rowland dropped to his knees, the way the duke taught him a decade ago, and quickly produced the required compliment. "Your majesty. My uncle, Doctor Foxe, often said your saving of London in the Fire marked you as a great man."

The king offered his ring, which Rowland kissed. Then he rose, uncomfortable, not knowing what to do with his hands, unsure about how close to stand. He simply imitated the others in the room, who seemed comfortable with the silence.

The king said, "Lord Bagsham tells me you made an adventure of today's Committee meeting, while most men struggled to merely stay awake."

"I meant no disrespect." Was this the equivalent of being called before his captain for a misadventure? "I esteem the work the peers are called upon to perform."

The king laughed, which Rowland didn't know how to interpret. Besides Perry, no one else had found one thing hilarious that day. That laughter didn't make him like the king as a man. "I refer, Marborne, to your work in bringing down that ass, Withersea." The king dabbed at his face with a kerchief. "I've had three lords complain to me about the man, with proof of nothing. Here, you come to London and uncover two rebels within a week."

"I was lucky, your majesty."

"Your luck with that devil Duncombe put a few thousand pounds into my treasury. And Bagsham says you found the printing press that's plagued me."

"Aye. A press used during the interregnum by Baroness Rôche had been commandeered. You may know the baroness's story. She used the press to help people see the benefits of our monarchy, to encourage the Restoration."

"How did it fall to rebels?"

"The marquess paid hirelings to spread anti-Catholic sentiments." Rowland had practiced telling several lies about that blasted printing press; this time, he could tell the truth.

"And now," the king smiled; he wasn't a handsome man, "you have given Sir Oliver proof that the marquess is a traitor, ridding me of an obsequious weasel."

"In fact, my cousin brought proof to Sir Oliver. And Captain Starbuck brought the warrant," Rowland said, repeating a true story. For the most part. "It was pure happenstance that the marquess escaped. Do not think—"

"That a mob can defeat four of my militiamen?" The king laughed again. "If we'd known a marquess was to be arrested today, I'm sure Starbuck's colonel would have sent more men."

"I'm happy you think so." Rowland crossed his fingers behind his back, hoping he knew the correct line to follow, given that only Heydon was there to support him. "I hope the marquess's perfidy does not bring chastisement upon the his wife. She and her brother have long suffered under the marquess's foul temper."

"Withersea always struck me as a man who'd kick his own dog. What do you recommend, Marborne?"

Startled to have his advice asked by the king, Rowland kept his sense. "Perhaps you might seize only the marquess's title? Leave the rest for his wife to live on."

"That would be overly kind." Glancing over his shoulder, the king waved two fingers at the men along the wall. "Remind me in the coming week that Lord Marborne deserves the same gratuity we awarded the former Lieutenant Foxe. After that damnable marquess goes before my assizes, give Marborne any of the marquess's lands not tied to the title."

"Your majesty, I am overwhelmed by your generosity." Rowland bowed again, not putting much store in the value of that promise. Tom's gambol had gained wealth for Marborne, though Tom would restore any such land that should belong to the marquess's victims.

The king waved a hand, no longer interested in Withersea. "I believe I met your cousin Thomas Foxe at court last week. He carried your father's tragic missive."

"Yes, your majesty." Rowland's voice strained at the king's mention of the letter read at the Committee meeting. "He's preparing to become a barrister."

"Are your cousins here tonight, Marborne?"

"Alas, no," Rowland said. "They had a complicated day."

"I'd especially like to meet Samuel Foxe's child," the king said. "He performed extraordinary services for the Crown."

Happy to be invited to speak of his beloved, Rowland said, "You likely know that Miss Ysabel Foxe has served the Princess Mary as a waiting woman for the past decade."

"Is she dark like Sam Foxe?" The king glanced past Rowland, where the duke still stood by the door. That glance left Rowland certain he was being dismissed.

"Yes, your majesty." Rowland didn't like having to answer, because the king meant nothing kind by his question. But Marborne needed James as an ally, and so its earl must hide any trace of his resentment and doubts about the king.

"Please bring her to court when next you come."

Then the king and his men were gone. The duke followed.

"Well done, Marborne," Heydon said after the door closed behind the king and his entourage.

"Except I forgot to ask—"

"For your beloved's hand?" Heydon grasped Rowland's shoulder, as if to comfort him. Rowland straightened, not knowing the viscount's intent. Heydon must have noticed. "I don't mean to tease you, Marborne. I know it matters greatly."

"How could I be such a chucklehead?"

"You aren't. We all forget what we had in mind when encountering the king by surprise. The duke interrupted us while I was in the middle of warning you."

The duke returned and stood before the chair the king had abandoned. He folded his hands over his stomach, looking stern, just as the opposite door opened and others entered.

Rowland didn't dare look around. He said, "Thank you, your grace, for the opportunity to meet the king."

"Yes, yes. The king has asked me to discover what became of the Marquess of Withersea. Can you tell me where he is? Or must I ask you to find him tomorrow for the king's sake?"

— LIZZIE —

THE BUTLER TOLD LIZZIE that her baggage had been taken up to Camilla's bedchamber. She climbed two flights of stairs, sure that she'd convinced Perry and Ned that tonight's calamity was as great as any they'd lived through in weeks. She hurried to dress with scarcely time to even wash her hands and face.

In the chamber, Camilla sat in one chair, reading.

"Oh, Lizzie! Here you are." Camilla greeted her with warm cheer. "Have you seen Tamsin?"

"No," Lizzie said. "Perry's brothers are looking for her. Camilla, can you go with me to the duke's fête for Rowland?"

"No, I'm sorry. I've had a fever again."

"Oh, you poor dear," Lizzie said, finally seeing the array of remedies and potions strewn on the table. The passion spurring her didn't allow for more bad news, yet she managed to ask, "Will you be well soon?"

"Winwood says yes, in a few days. He went searching for Tom this morning, but finally came here, just after I returned. I was able to reassure him that Tom claimed to be well."

"Tom returned here with us," Lizzie said. "He and Jacob Rôche have worn themselves to a nub."

"I supposed we should expect that of Tom."

Lizzie bent at the washstand to wipe away the grime of London. She struggled with her hair while telling Camilla what had happened that day.

Camilla said, "Your dress is destroyed, Lizzie."

"It just needs—"

A knock on the door proved to be Lazarus the butler with a fortuitous offer. "Forgive my intrusion, Miss Foxe. Miss Candecote." He nodded to Camilla. "But I understand you intend to join Lord Bagsham's fête. May I offer this gown from Xanthus House since you won't have time to prepare your own dress?"

He held out a tasteful confection of silk and embroidery. She touched it, feeling the buttery smoothness of the silk.

"Thank you, Lazarus. It's a delightful solution."

When the door closed, Lizzie shed the tattered gold gown that had brought her so much joy on Tuesday, but now needed a full day of care to rise to its former glory. While she dressed, she said, "If Tamsin appears soon, please ask her to join us at the Duke of Bagsham's fête. The butler can find a carriage for her. And tell her to wear that grey silk she bought on Tuesday."

Bringing a candle closer to the brass mirror, Lizzie tried to see if she even looked like herself.

Camilla said, "Lizzie, that dress is a bit long, even as tall as you are. Let me hitch it up at the back and tie it in place."

Lizzie agreed. "Thank you. That must be made to work."

After tying up the back of the dress, Camilla offered a pink ribbon to bind up the abundance of Lizzie's dark hair. Then she produced a small tin of carmine-colored beeswax.

Lizzie waved away the offer. "No time for cosmetics."

"I insist," Camilla said. "At least for your lips."

When Camilla touched Lizzie's lips, for just that moment, the beeswax pacified her soul.

After begging once again for Tamsin to be sent to the duke's party, Lizzie hurried away. In the foyer, Lizzie asked, "Where's Captain Starbuck?" She felt Starbuck continued to be important to the day's events.

"Gone to the duke's fête." Ned said. He fussed with Perry's neckcloth, though Perry insisted that the butler had done his best.

Perry said, "Valentine slept here last night, so Lazarus had laundered his shirt and brushed his red coat."

"Aye," Ned said. "Valentine changed and called for a horse not five minutes after you called wrath down on our heads."

"Starbuck insists," Perry said, "that he may as well be hung for his failure today as wait until tomorrow." He loosened the neckcloth, undoing most of Ned's efforts. "He won't listen to my assurance, that his colonel will blame a sergeant or a corporal for Withersea's escape, not a captain."

Lizzie counted everyone in the foyer. "Where's Aurora's cousin? What's his name? Michel Chêne? Is he not coming?"

Perry said, "While you were upstairs, he and his sister Felicity went to hire servants for Chalgrove House."

"Then let us depart now," Lizzie said.

She bossed Ned and Perry into the hired carriage. Lazarus came out with instructions for the driver to find Littlecote House. The driver called to his horses, the carriage lurched, and they were on their way. In the gloaming of a London summer evening, Lizzie hoped the light was sufficient for Ned and Perry to see that she had not forgiven their abject failure to remain at Rowland's side in the face of another challenge.

— ROLLO —

THE RELIEF ROWLAND FELT when Starbuck arrived and stood at his side made up for the past half-hour's stress with the king. He managed to keep from sighing, from betraying that he had any emotion about the day's business.

The duke fiddled in his waistcoat pocket to retrieve his spectacles. Once he'd pushed them onto his nose, he said, "Ah, Captain Starbuck. Glad you could come. I was just asking Lord Marborne how to discover where the marquess has gone. We are called to answer to the king."

Starbuck had done so much that day, and for a measly debt of four gold louis. If the Foxes' gambol led Starbuck into dire straits, Rowland was duty-bound to rescue him.

"Your grace," Starbuck said, "the king's men are watching all ships and all roads out of London. Our intelligencers are on the search for the marquess's friends and business associates."

"Dear me, that much trouble for a scoundrel." The duke lifted his brows in query, then had to mash his spectacles back in place. "What about the ruckus on the Thames this afternoon? With a king's ship chasing down a Dutch merchantman?"

"We had word that Withersea was aboard that ship." Starbuck glanced at Rowland, who touched his nose, signaling that he'd support his friend for all time. Starbuck gazed past Rowland, raising his hand as if in greeting. "But we were misinformed, perhaps by the marquess's allies."

"And Mr. Rosewurme?" Lord Bagsham asked.

"I don't know a Mr. Rosewurme," Starbuck said.

Rowland said, "We put Cornelius Rosewurme on a ship sailing for America this afternoon."

Perry appeared, as if the gods deigned to smile on Rowland Foxe. Ned was at his side. Perry said, "Mr. Rosewurme has been planning such a journey for many months."

"Ah!" The duke shook his head. "Now we shall never know more about what the fellow intended to share today."

"He left his written bond behind," Rowland said.

"I preserved it," Perry said, taking from his pocket the confession they'd guided Cornelius to write. And rewrite.

"Oh?" Lord Bagsham pushed back the paper Perry offered, even patted his hand when Perry restored the paper in his coat. "You should keep it."

It's amazing how a small gesture can tell a significant story. Rowland understood that motion: the duke didn't want Rosewurme's story made known, and he also didn't want the marquess back in England. At least, not alive.

His grace was distracted, looking repeatedly over Rowland's shoulder. Rowland felt a hand touch him, then tuck itself into the crook of his elbow.

"Your grace, thank you for inviting me." That golden voice. "My Lord Marborne, may I felicitate you on this day's events?"

Lizzie. She'd come.

Wearing that rose silk gown from the secret closet.

Rowland said, "May I introduce Miss Ysabel Foxe?"

"Miss Foxe! We met in Amsterdam five winters ago. So happy you came tonight." The duke again mashed his spectacles, this time to stare at her, his eyes open in surprise. A recognition of the rose gown? Or of the woman accused of being a spy? "Captain Starbuck was about to explain how the wife of the traitor Withersea came to be on a Dutch merchant ship."

Rowland needed to step up, though the events had tilted rather like the day he fell out of a Revelstone oak tree. Uncle Absolom and Mrs. Bell bent over him, fearing the worst, while his cousins hovered, pale, shaken—and preparing to take the blame. He again felt smashed to the ground but did not want anyone else to be blamed for it.

Before he had formulated a suitable tale, Lizzie spoke.

"Your grace, the marchioness was running for her life in fear of her husband. Captain Starbuck saved us from that voyage, though I believe his hopes were to find the marquess on that ship, rather than our little band of refugees."

57
A Fête

— T A M S I N —

TAMSIN TOOK A SEDAN chair from Mr. Mordaunt's chambers, fearing Perry's censure if she weren't cautious. Since Tom hadn't returned to the law chambers, she believed he'd be at Rowland's house with everyone else.

The journey by chair felt tedious, but it was to be the last journey of the day, so she let her thoughts turn to home. If she and Camilla found a carriage at dawn, they could be home by late tomorrow. She figured the travel time. Even if they encountered a midday shower, the summer roads must be faster than at any other time of the year. They'd only stop to change horses. But her calculations revealed that, no, they couldn't make it to Cambridge in a single day. She'd made the journey often enough to know better. And they couldn't travel on Sunday.

And Camilla still had to finish her business with Luke Holywell and Mr. Mordaunt. A week? Could they leave then?

By the time she'd set a real expectation for when she'd be home, the chair-bearers stopped outside Xanthus House, where a carriage was departing, its driver shouting at his horses.

As a complication, she couldn't offer the chair-bearers a gold louis from her crimping hoard. All they required was a few shillings. Hence, she had to beg the butler to pay the chair-bearers, with a promise to repay him the next day.

Then she learned from Lazarus that most everyone had gone to a fête the Duke of Bagsham was hosting for Rowland. "You just missed the carriage," he said.

Tom, she learned, was sequestered in his chamber with Dr. Oakes and the Earl of Cloudesley. She longed to share her adventures with Tom, but the butler didn't respond to Tamsin's hints about knocking on Tom's door.

Therefore, she ran upstairs to greet Camilla, who'd been dosed by Winwood and sent to bed for a mild fever and exhaustion. Yet Camilla excitedly related all that Tamsin had missed.

"Lizzie and Ned helped the marchioness sail for Holland to escape her husband, who's a very cruel man." Camilla barely paused for breath. "When Tom heard, he worried that the king might think she ran away with the marquess, who escaped the militiamen in Westminster. So, Tom and Captain Starbuck—"

"Captain Starbuck?"

"Yes. He had a warrant and used it to stop the marchioness from sailing. When they came here and learned Rollo had gone to the duke's fête, well, Lizzie had an absolute fit. She made Ned and Perry dress up and go to the fête with her."

"Is Captain Starbuck here?"

"No. He left for the fête. Jane, the upstairs maid, said he departed as if his hat was on fire." Camilla became solemn. "I learned pieces of this from Lizzie and Lazarus, though you can't imagine how hard it is to get a story out of Rollo's butler. It seems that Captain Starbuck thinks he may be in trouble with his colonel for stopping the *Zeewolf* and failing to find the marquess. So, he went to see the duke to—"

"The *Zeewolf*?"

"Yes, Lizzie was sailing to Holland with the marchioness, until Captain Starbuck stopped them, claiming he believed the marquess was on that ship."

"No," Tamsin said. The marchioness and Lizzie boarded the *Zeewolf*? "No. No. No."

"What's wrong?"

"Starbuck might be headed for trouble. I must go. Now."

Yet her suit—Tom's new suit—was ruined from the wherry ride. He didn't have much more than what he might be wearing, certainly not other clothes to wear to a duke's house. She entered Rowland's bedchamber, with Lazarus on her heels.

"I need to dress to go to Lord Bagsham's fête," she said.

"Yes, the other gentlemen all borrowed from his lordship's wardrobe." He examined her. "Do you prefer fancy dress? That's what most will wear at the fête."

She thought of how Rowland had dressed at Felicity's house. "No," she said. "Sober as a Puritan, please."

He presented a suit and linen for her. "You'll likely fit the late viscount's shoes better than does his lordship. Shall I find a carriage for you?"

"I haven't time. Where I can hire a horse?"

"I'll see to it...ah, sir."

Lazarus must have worked out who she was when she arrived, or did he think Rowland had yet another cousin? With no time to ponder it, she stripped and pulled on fresh linen over the same binding Camilla had tied at dawn. It had at one point been drenched in sweat when she fretted her way from Westminster to the Pool of London. But there wasn't time to redo it.

She pulled on exquisite silk stockings, then breeches, a stark waistcoat, and a wide-skirted coat, with nothing fancier than double-stitching around the buttonholes that had been made for simple tortoise-shell buttons. She'd taken care to don a wig properly that morning, so she'd look like a barrister at the Committee meeting. But now...

Good stars! Rowland had a dozen wigs in his dressing room. She chose a conservative, powder-free wig. It took more time to get her hair tucked away and the wig in place than it did to dress.

When she descended to the foyer, Lazarus stood with a young man in a servant's formal coat.

"This is Gabriel. He's footman to the marchioness and knows the way to Lord Bagsham's house."

"But I intend to ride," Tamsin said.

"I took the liberty of hiring two horses," Lazarus said. "I am sure his lordship would prefer you not ride alone across London."

Gabriel said, "If you will allow it, I'll accompany you, uh, sir."

~

The duke's house was as brightly lit as a midsummer bonfire. They stood at the dramatic entrance with massive steps and pillars, as if it were the home of ancient gods. Tamsin professed to the man at the door that she was Thomas Foxe and the Earl of Marborne's cousin. Gabriel left her side then, hanging back with pages and footmen who waited near the door.

As the second—no, third—bravest thing she'd done that day, Tamsin walked into a salon where more than a hundred people had crammed themselves close in the heat, the wide skirts of men's coats and women's panniers crushing each other.

Not a soul she recognized. Wishing she were much taller, she sorted faces in the crowd, seeking any acquaintance. Then a friend appeared, smiling.

"Hello, Tom. It's good to see you," Viscount Heydon said. Then he looked again and laughed, shaking his head. "Come with me. Rollo and your cousins are with the duke."

Heydon led her up a flight of stairs. Tamsin was struck that Heydon used Rowland's family diminutive, but before she could say anything, he pushed a door open.

"Mr. Foxe?" A voice called. "Welcome to my home. Please join your cousins."

Heydon led the way across the room to where Lizzie and Ned stood beside Rowland. She came up beside Ned, who vibrated like a top whose string had been wound too tight. When Heydon stepped aside, she spied a small round man on a wooden settle, who pushed his spectacles firmly in place and examined her through grimy lenses.

Rowland had scrubbed all emotion from his face, no longer playing Merry Andrew. "Your grace, this is my cousin, Mr. Thomas Foxe, who accompanied Mr. Mordaunt at this morning's event."

"I remember," the duke said. "Is this the same cousin who got the warrant from Sir Oliver?"

She bowed as deeply as she'd ever attempted and came back from it just short of falling. She resisted seizing her Archangel. This might be almost as great an adventure as her afternoon at the London docks, but without the pounding fear.

Tamsin said, "Your grace, I am grateful for your attention to Lord Marborne and our family." That must be the right words, though she guessed wildly.

Lord Bagsham said, "I'm happy to help set right what your uncles and fathers began so long ago. Will your sister Miss Thomasine Foxe be here?"

"N–No, your grace." Good stars! Stuttering? She'd intended to never be afraid again. But then, she'd had no idea the duke knew of her existence. "She's been ill and remains at home."

The duke said, "Starbuck was just explaining that the king can't know what happened today until the marquess is found."

Tamsin spied Starbuck standing by Lizzie. The foreboding expression on his face roused Tamsin to begin an invention, the kind she used when leading restorations on Marborne country lanes. She was confident because she knew the true story.

"I was there when the marquess ran, your grace," Tamsin said. "Shall I tell the story?"

"Please, Mr. Foxe," the duke said. "I hadn't expected such a stimulating evening."

"As you know, I assisted Mr. Mordaunt with documents at the Committee meeting. I was with him in the square at Westminster when the marquess was brought out."

"The commotion was nearly a riot," Starbuck said. "It rose while I was still in the meeting chamber."

Tamsin nodded. "A dozen rough fellows overpowered the militiamen and bore the marquess away."

"We knew that," the duke said. "Though we didn't know you witnessed the capture."

"More than witnessed it," Tamsin said. "Withersea pointed to me, knowing I worked for the barrister. And so, I was swept along with the marquess by his brigands."

"Upon my soul!" Lizzie exclaimed.

The duke said, "Is it true?"

"*Vero, vero.*" Tamsin stole Tom's words, her courage expanding again, although Rowland, Ned, Lizzie, and Starbuck must know this wasn't how Tom had spent his afternoon. And that she wasn't Tom. "They let me go my own way at the docks after the marquess boarded a ship. I was ordered to run and tell the barrister, Mr. Mordaunt, where the marquess had gone."

"Where has he gone, Mr. Foxe?" the duke asked.

"Porto Novo, your grace." Tamsin chose a place as far from England as she could recall. She felt like a fox in a tree, with no choices, heart hammering. Tom wouldn't want the marquess retrieved, and they'd all be better off if their enemy was on the far side of the world. She quickly named a different Dutch ship, recalling one she'd seen at anchor near the *Zeewolf*. "He set sail on the *Voorzichtigheid*."

Ned repeated the name, pronouncing it with a Dutch accent. "*Voorzichtigheid.* It means caution. Or merely care."

"Ah, so the Dutch have him," the duke said. "We can ask William to send him back to England."

"No," Tamsin said, awash in a flood of happy relief that came from a successful untruth. "The marquess paid for passage and protection. The ship's first stop is Tenerife."

"In the Canaries?" Starbuck said.

The duke turned to Starbuck. "Then, there's no use setting sail in pursuit."

"No, you are correct." Starbuck shook his head. "The tide has turned. It would be fruitless, your grace."

"There's nothing any of us can do," the duke said, "only be vigilant in case the marquess returns to England. There's no blame for anyone for any of this, except the traitorous Marquess of Withersea himself."

Starbuck lost his rigid, careful posture. Tamsin was happy to see his relief, yet puzzled that the duke accepted her story, which had so many gaping holes, it could be used for a fishing net.

"I must meet with my guests." The duke rose. "Marborne, I trust you'll choose to continue to be useful to the king." He emphasized the word *choose* in an exaggerated way. "Captain, Miss Foxe, good evening," he nodded to Lizzie, who curtsied. "And to you, Mr. Foxe. Thank you for such an exciting tale."

She bowed, again managing not to fall down, still trying to guess whether the duke believed her or if he knew she was lying.

As soon as the duke was out the door with his entourage, including Viscount Heydon, her friends gathered around, all looking at her as if she'd grown two heads.

"I'll tell you later," Tamsin said.

"Porto Novo?" Lizzie folded her arms across a lovely rose gown, its starched lace whispering under the crunch.

Though it was only her friends remaining, Tamsin lowered her voice. "Batavia. On the *Zeewolf.*"

"The *Zeewolf?*" Captain Starbuck exclaimed.

Lizzie said, "He paid to escape on our ship?"

"No," Tamsin said. "The marquess paid to crimp Rollo but ended up being crimped instead. And I didn't stop it."

"Thou hast done no wrong by that," Perry said.

Lizzie, shocked, said, "Captain Starbuck, a king's ship must be sent to Rotterdam, to fetch the marquess back for trial."

"Nay," Perry said. "He escaped the king's justice once already. Captain Starbuck must only ensure caution that the marquess doesn't return to England. And perhaps his colonel can warn officers in the Low Countries to be looking for the marquess in case he escapes the *Zeewolf.*"

"We need to tell Aurora that the devil cannot find her," Ned said. "At least, not any time soon."

"And," Perry said, "the evil marquess cannot send others after her since he no longer has a farthing to call his own. If he lives, mayhap it'd take him years to work his way back to England to seek revenge."

"Like a famous pirate?" Ned said. "I should like to paint that picture. I have half a mind to paint some ships."

Not replying to that flight of fancy, Lizzie said, "What kept Withersea from spying us onboard the *Zeewolf*?"

"He never saw any of you on the ship," Tamsin said. "Those rogues coshed what they thought was Rollo's head. But why was the duke so happy with my story?"

"I believe," Rowland said, "the duke and the king prefer the marquess to be on the far side of the world. Withersea knows too many men's secrets."

"Someday you'll tell me the whole story," Starbuck said. "I'd best go see my colonel now, to stop the search for the marquess. And to tell him Miss Foxe's amazing story."

"Wait!" Tamsin said. Starbuck halted as if pulled back by more than her single word. "You still must search out Sir Duckworth. He helped Withersea's plan for the crimping."

"Duxwold," Lizzie said, correcting the name. "He was lingering on the wharf near the *Zeewolf's* mooring. Aurora says he's often Withersea's agent. He lives off Holborn Road."

Tamsin said, "Duxwold carried the money for the crimping."

"Ah," Starbuck said. "That explains it. My men discovered that the marquess's banker released considerable funds today, but not to the marquess himself."

Ned coughed, then coughed again, turning away.

Tamsin once more said, "You must pursue Duxwold," while Lizzie stared at the coughing Ned. She'd have to inquire later.

"Tom was right," Starbuck said. "It's always best to do whatever Miss…his twin suggests."

"Always the better part of valor," Rowland said.

Once Starbuck was out the door, Lizzie asked, "What if the marquess convinces the captain to set him free in Rotterdam?"

"I gave the captain five extra gold coins into his own hand," Tamsin said, "to ensure that doesn't happen. I warned him about holding a madman who believes he's a lord."

"But how did you have coins to pay off the captain?"

"I kept half the bag of gold Duxwold gave me for Rollo's crimping." Tamsin shrugged. "It was a bulky bag."

Rowland said, "You must be the luckiest woman in England."

"Mayhap, upon occasion," Perry said, "recklessness and wit might unite."

"Everything that happened was pure luck," Tamsin said. "Besides, I have expected your scolding all afternoon, Mr. Frake, for becoming separated from the Knights of the Marborne Fens."

"I shall endeavor," Perry said, "to refrain until after breakfast tomorrow."

"Besides, you once again are our saving hero," Ned said. He yawned, lazily raising a hand to smother it.

"Mayhap," Perry said, "we no longer need to serve as the Earl of Marborne's entourage? Can we depart now?"

Rowland said, "All the social niceties have been done."

"Good stars!" Tamsin exclaimed. "Neither the duke nor God can expect more of us tonight. Not after a day like today."

Ned yawned. "It was yesterday."

"Aye," Perry said. "It's tomorrow already."

58
Calculations

-LIZZIE-

"MISS FOXE?" THE DUKE took his time, but eventually deigned to turn and acknowledge her.

Lizzie appreciated the extra minutes, because she hadn't yet determined how to approach him, to achieve what she wanted. Years ago, a friend at court (not Mary!) had shared all her methods: seduction, beggary, excess sentiment. In fact, when she'd first arrived, she lingered to greet Viscount Heydon, since she couldn't decide which method to choose.

"Where is the earl your cousin, madam?" He winked, which told her how to proceed: the same courtly flirtation as the duke.

"Second cousin, your grace. Rowland stopped to chat with a lord from the Committee who sought to offer advice." She offered her best, most open smile. "I want to thank you."

"Yes, madam? You are most welcome at my little fête."

He smiled, but Lizzie saw he was not used to a woman he'd just met approaching him to ask for his attention.

"Yes, duke, of course. Thank you. But I mean to thank you for your genius in seeing so quickly how Lord Marborne can best serve England." She touched the duke, rather, touched only the cuff of his extravagant sleeve. Stroking it. "Even if you had to trick him into choosing the best course of action."

"Trick, madam? Perhaps you give me unearned credit. Tonight, I'm unsure who has been tricked."

"You are too modest, duke." She leaned close. Being taller than the diminutive man, she dipped her head to ensure her

531

request was heard only by him. "I swear, you can trust Marborne to both watch and keep all your secrets. As for me, I can watch, but you must prove yourself to be trustworthy."

Astonished, the duke drew away at her last words.

"Yes? Do we agree?" she said.

The duke nodded, but didn't offer a flirtatious smile.

She decided to judge his response as genuine agreement. Rowland came up beside her. Quite close beside her. She felt him grasp a fold of her skirt.

At least Rowland knew to address the duke first. "Your grace, thank you for this night. For everything."

"It has been a good beginning," the duke said. He took Rowland's offered hand but was still looking at Lizzie. "I hope we have the chance to work together again soon."

Another lord stepped up for the duke's attention, and his grace gave the two Foxe cousins a dismissive wave farewell.

Rowland led her toward the exit. She looked back. The duke still watched her. She returned a fingertip's wave.

They weaved through the crowd and made it to the foyer, where Rowland paused near the pages drowsing on a bench.

"Why stop here?" Lizzie asked.

"For Peter." Rowland nudged a boy's boot with his toe. "He hasn't been a page before, I think."

"What, my lord?" Peter rubbed at his eyes. "Shall I fetch the carriage?" The lad ran off, not waiting for an answer.

Rowland rocked on his heels, his hands folded. "The duke sent his carriage to fetch me."

"Is it still on offer to take us home?" She couldn't tell if he wanted her to be impressed about the loaned carriage. That wasn't like Rowland, but they'd fallen into a strange world.

"You look done for." He took her hand. "If my good fortune does not hold and there's no carriage, I shall have to—"

The driver and rig appeared just then. Rowland set Peter to ride on top and commanded the driver to be off, then collapsed on the forward quarter of the carriage. He puffed as if winded.

"We got away before any of the others could cadge a ride."

"How rude." Lizzie sat stiffly on the rear quarter bench.

"No, it's because I want to be alone with you, Lizzie. I'm breathless, waiting for this moment." The small lamp the driver had lit cast a halo around his face, like an old painting of a saint, except his eyes were rimmed with exhaustion, not holiness.

"Isn't this our plan?" she asked. "To be together?"

Rowland cleared his throat. "There wasn't an opportunity to ask the king tonight. But I shall petition him next week, so we can marry. If you are ready."

"I wish I'd been with you, so you didn't have to meet the king alone. I came as soon as I could."

"Aye, I wanted you there. But Heydon says I comported myself well." Rowland swallowed, then took his sweet time to say more. "If the king grants us leave—"

"Of course, he will," Lizzie said, growing impatient with his hesitations. "Why would he not? Marborne isn't wealthy, with a grand title. He doesn't need you united with the daughter of someone he owes a favor."

"Yes, of course." This seemed to make him more hesitant. He took an enormous breath, blew it out. "Then, as a countess, you can finally return to Mary's court. You'll be free to use the Marborne title as you think best. But I must remain in England."

Lizzie said, "I owe the service that Absolom expected of me, and hence—"

"I know, I know. And you must know that I'll use the Marborne title to do whatever good I can. Though I wish I didn't have to be beholden to any Stuart ruler."

"But you can't escape being beholden to the king of England," she said. "I'm not an innocent who doesn't understand the position in which you now find yourself."

"Thank you for seeing that." He spoke so softly that she could scarcely hear over the thumping of wheels on cobbles. "If you intend to return to Mary's court, please tell me now. I need to retain my wits and stop worrying about what's next."

Lizzie said, "I have chosen. I wrote you a letter."

She rustled within her shawl to find it, then held out the letter. When he reached to take it, the warmth of his hand could be felt through her thin gloves. He held it but didn't read. She felt compelled to chatter, rather than holding her breath. "These cobbles will knock our bones to pieces."

He said, "I shall put your letter under my pillow and read it in the morning light."

"Are you teasing?"

"I want to wash and don clean clothes." He grasped her hand, mashing the letter between them. "And find where I stashed my courage. It should have been right there when you appeared and answered the duke about why the marchioness had set sail. But I think I lost all my courage just after the king said good night."

"Ah, lambkin. Let me give you a summary," Lizzie said.

"For what you'll do for Mary in Amsterdam?" He sounded crushed, his lamplit halo quivering when they crashed over the cobbles. "Will I have to cover for your...uh...work again?"

"You and I must both use our talents to help people who are lost, since the Crown has not worked hard enough to take care of many people's needs."

"I will wait, hoping, for as long as it takes." He mashed her hand again. "My poet says, 'Time is very slow for those who wait.' That is, hope cannot answer what I desire, which is—"

"Leave Shakespeare alone for a moment, please. I'm telling you, Rollo, that I shall remain in England. I asked the duke to use me as a watcher too."

"In England?"

"Together."

"As watchers?"

"Yes, my lord. I now understand that I am very much part of this family. I shall continue my work honoring the fate Absolom declared, and find happiness doing it in England. With you."

"With me? But how did you know the duke tricked me into becoming the king's watcher? I didn't tell—"

No longer able to be patient, she flew off the bench, clinging to his shoulders lest the jolting carriage topple her. She kissed his chin, his cheek, then said softly, "Forgive me. I stopped you. Will you whisper Shakespeare in my ear? So that I know this is what we both wished?"

"'Teach me, dear creature, how to think and speak.'"

Beyond that, his lips and tongue became too busy for either to learn their future. She'd never known contentment and excitement to course through her veins together.

— TOM —

TOM WAS PREPARING A punch in the dining salon with Lazarus when the crowd burst in after the duke's fête. He counted them, then said, "Good evening. Where are Lizzie and Rollo?"

"Unknown," Perry said. "They left the fête before us. Their driver must be dilatory."

"Before you tell your tales," Tom said, "Lazarus is explaining his former master's punch."

"Viscount Bravewood called this mixture 'ecclesiastical,'" Lazarus said. "I only quote him. I do not intend irreverence." He poured a bottle of dark wine into a punch bowl.

"It's spices and citrus, isn't it?" Tom said. "I use the same in my own punch."

"Only one spice. Cloves. The viscount had a special addition, orange rinds burnt on the hearth, with a pinch of muscovado sugar." Lazarus poured in more than a pinch.

"And rum from Jamaica?" Tom asked.

"Only port wine." Lazarus poured in hot water from a pitcher. "If I may beg you to let it steam, until I return in a moment."

Tom stood over the punch bowl, wafting its fumes with his hand. "Did you all save Rowland from the duke?"

"No. Rollo met the king alone, before we arrived," Ned said.

"Which put us in a pickle for a moment," Perry said. "Once the king was gone, the duke began to interrogate Rowland and Starbuck about your adventure intercepting the *Zeewolf*."

Tom coughed. "Is Starbuck in trouble?"

"Nay," Ned said. "Our Tamsin appeared just in time to spin a wonderful tale."

"It was mostly true," Tamsin said. "Tom, please tell the marchioness that Withersea is gone from England."

"Gone?" Stunned, Tom dropped the spice grater he held. Either the surprise or the spice got up his nose. He coughed again, so it was a moment before he could hear more.

Perry said, "If he finds a way to return, it will be with great difficulty. The marquess intended to abduct Rollo and send him to the far side of the world."

"But there was a confusion," Tamsin said, "and the marquess is now bound for Batavia."

"Mayhap he gets free," Perry said, "and seeks vengeance. But he has no money, and the king's men will know if he returns to England. No reason to worry about that man now."

Lazarus reappeared with platters piled high with food. "Our former master always returned from the duke's fête in need of a meal. He claimed that Lord Bagsham doesn't believe in burdening guests with succoring food. When Mrs. Flurry learned that Lord Marborne's cousins were country people, she made a custard and savory pies for sustenance after the party."

Perry's brothers once more pounced on the food, then devoured what they'd gleaned. Whenever they were too noisy, Perry cast a baleful glance their way, which quieted them but never diminished their spirits.

As soon as Lazarus departed, Tamsin repeated a fantastical story for Tom. Withersea, it seemed, paid for Rowland to be kidnapped, but was himself crimped by his own mercenaries.

"This is the happiest of news." Tom's heart and mind spun at the notion of freedom for Jacob. And Aurora too. But he paused at the idea that Tamsin had witnessed the entire affair, after being captured by the same brigands who'd pursued them all week.

Yet Tamsin seemed rather blithe about her adventure. "So, Tom. Your gambol is a success. Withersea is gone for good."

"Crimped to Bavaria!" Perry exclaimed, rubbing his hands.

"*Ja!*" Ned said. "That rat will never kick a dog or bruise a lad in England again. You are just the hero Jacob needed, Tom. And lucky to have Tamsin when you can't be there."

"Lucky indeed." Tom felt it. His mind couldn't yet encompass it all, still trying to perceive what arose from divine luck and what from planning and mad dashes across London.

Perry was accounting for whether the Restoration Rules had been ruthlessly enforced. "No one died. No innocents got caught along with the guilty. Mayhap, we must ask Rollo if all his private business with the Duke of Bagsham fits your rules."

"I'm sure Rollo has done as he knows best," Tamsin said.

"However, my finger is broken," Ned said. "Lizzie's best dress is ruined. Tom wore himself to a nib."

Perry said, "Yet Jacob and Tom's beloved are free."

"Beloved?" Tom shook his head. "No, Aurora is just a friend. If you won't believe me, you can ask her at breakfast tomorrow."

Then he began dipping punch into cups and handing them around, as if this were not the most momentous day of his life—well, of Jacob's, if Tom wanted to avoid grandiosity. After all, it had taken all his cousins and friends to restore justice.

"None for the boys," Perry said. "They're still growing."

Neriah and Daniel groaned—until Perry glanced their way.

"Just a sip," Tom said, glad that he'd never had a brother to dog him. "None of us will forget that our Knightsbridge gig would not have succeeded without them."

Tom handed Tamsin the last cup of punch, then proposed a toast. He thought to toast as men did in taverns: *Here's a health unto the king! And confusion to his enemies!* But he looked at Perry, then at the others.

He said instead, "Here's health unto England's loyal citizens. And confusion to all who cheat the innocent."

Perry lifted his brows, surprised. Then smiled and lifted his mug of punch. Tom then spoke of what had been on his mind since saying good night to Jacob.

"I do regret that we didn't come out of this richer than we began. By my calculations, we'll need another restoration to keep the parish and ourselves afloat."

"What?" Tamsin's brown eyes widened. She had her hand on that gold coin she wore as a pendant.

Tom said, "We need more income than what we earned last week. Rollo's title isn't a miraculous money tree. In this gambol, I earned only two pounds sterling by intercepting Leighton's payment to our would-be assassins. Oh, and it's six months until I earn a salary, if Mr. Mordaunt doesn't give me walking papers."

"Despite our failure to send another rebel to the Tower," Perry said, "the king promised Rollo another gratuity, for proving the marquess to be a traitor. And the king intends to give Rollo any of Withersea's lands not tied to the title."

Ned said, "Let us wait until breakfast to tell Aurora that."

"I promise you, Aurora won't care," Tom said. "Her marriage portion will provide for her living. I believe she will abandon everything to do with Withersea. Lands, title, name."

"What will become of the marquess's title?" Tamsin asked.

Tom had long guessed about that future. "The king will sell it for a large garnishment. And I don't know how much land Rollo might gain, because portions of the unentailed lands will revert to their proper inheritors when I have finished."

"In whatever way that unfolds, we earned more than two pounds sterling this week," Tamsin said. "Count it up, Tom."

Urged on, he began to tally what they'd won in his gambol, while Perry ticked each item on a finger as he liked to do.

"First, the biggest prize. Jacob can inherit his title and land as soon as his case winds through the courts."

Perry said, "You should wake every hour to celebrate, Tom. You've won a great victory."

Yet it'd take the night to wash out the thunderous waves of anxiety, the myriad of details and worry for failure points, for Tom's mind to float easy on the notion. However: *Withersea is gone for good. Jacob is free.*

"For the second prize of the day," Tamsin said, "the Marborne title is confirmed." Perry touched another finger in his tally. "Plus, I kept the greater part of Withersea's crimping fee, while making sure the marquess is gone from England."

She cited a number, and Perry ticked another finger.

"That'd be a small fortune for a poor clerk," Tom said. "It was also a large expense for a lord who sought to impoverish his brother-in-law in order to make up for lost investments."

"There's more," Ned said. "Aurora promised that I shall have the fee for Jacob's portrait. I hope to finish it next week."

"Absolom would be pleased at what you did this week," Tamsin said. Ned bowed his head over his cup of punch, likely hiding the pride Tom hoped his cousin felt.

Tom didn't add up all of what they'd called out. That was for another time, when his head wasn't floating, prepared to celebrate. He asked, "Did only Lizzie came up empty-handed from this gambol?"

"No," Ned said. "Lizzie has her share of the treasures at the World's End, which Aurora promised us."

"Like gold at the end of a rainbow?" Tamsin asked.

"A bit," Ned said. "John Coachman, Gabriel, and I removed all the marquess's artful antiques and treasures. We hired a room at the World's End Inn to store them until a calmer time." Ned then described glorious whatnots from distant parts of the world. "We'll give Jacob first choice for which trinkets he likes. I mean, if the law and his guardian will allow it."

"I'm certain about the law," Tom said. "The king cannot seize a treasure he knows nothing about."

"Shall you count farthings saved as farthings earned?" Perry asked. "Because I nabbed the marquess's purse and used his coin to pay Rollo's gratuities at the Committee meeting. Some lords didn't attend, so I used their gratuities to pay a portion of the cost to send Cornelius Rosewurme to America."

"Mr. Rosewurme is gone?" Tamsin asked. "He performed well for Jacob's sake this morning. I mean, yesterday."

"We outfitted the little man for his voyage," Perry said. "Then we shook his hand and thanked him, saw him aboard ship, and waved to send him off to the colonies."

"Massachusetts. Or perhaps Pennsylvania." Ned yawned, which proved to be a catching affliction, because most around the table yawned too.

"Must we wait up for Rollo and Lizzie?" Tamsin asked.

"It's his house." Perry also smothered a yawn. "But surely it's fair to have a kip without waiting up for them."

"I agree. Now, let's save any more stories for breakfast." Tom yawned. "Though I should say now, if Rollo will allow it, I intend to live here while I finish my clerkship with Mr. Mordaunt. And Jacob will live with me, as I am his guardian."

Tom wanted to see Tamsin's reaction. It took everything to keep from swiveling in her direction. *Please be happy for me.*

"That is very good news," she said. His heart felt free to float into the clouds. "Surely Rollo will say yes."

"And the marchioness?" Perry asked.

"She wants to be called Aurora Rôche hence forth," Tom said. "She's been invited to live with her cousins at Chalgrove House until all this chaotic business is concluded."

"I hope Rollo lets us stay while we finish our business," Ned said. "Like fetching the treasure from the World's End."

"Aye," Perry said. "It's a week or two until we're ready to return to Cambridge."

Daniel said, "Neriah and I need clothes and shoes if we are to remove to Revelstone farmland."

"Daniel. Neriah." Perry sounded stern. "Finish eating and get off to bed with you."

A motion of Ned's head, a slight jerk, caught Tom's eye. It seemed as if not all of Tom's cousins were completely jubilant.

59
Resolutions

THE SOUND OF THEIR names didn't cause Daniel and Neriah to look up from their puckish attack on the savory pies.

Ned did look up. He remained unsatisfied about having no word in this plan to install a colony of Frakes at Revelstone.

Tom said, "Aurora intends to beguile Daniel and Neriah into service here in London. Lazarus committed to helping find servants, but John Coachman agreed that it'd be good to have a few faces she and Jacob know."

At that, the boys paused from stuffing their faces. They looked to Perry, who said, "Odsme, if you lads have employment and a safe place to sleep, I suppose you both might stay in London."

"But Mother?" Neriah said. "Will you take her to the country and leave us here?"

"I'm distressed that you'd think I'd undertake such a travesty," Perry said. "I shall have to refigure our plans."

The next time Lazarus came into the room, Daniel and Neriah begged directions to their bedchamber. They followed the butler after putting the last of the savory pies in the pockets of their borrowed suits.

When Ned and Perry started up to their own bedchamber, Perry whispered, "I must thank you for helping to chaff my brothers this entire live-long night. I'd never have guessed your talent for teasing. Many's the time tonight that I'd about laughed and ruined the game, seeing your sober face. Such a tease!"

"There's no one in England so good as you," Ned said, resolving never to confess that he'd been as gullible as the two brothers.

"We've got shut of my mother's grand idea at last. Now I'm thinking, Aurora Rôche and her little cousin must need a cook."

"A grand idea."

Happiness bloomed around Ned's heart while the scheming part of his brain-pan again took up the notion of building a new house. With only Perry.

"You were magnificent each day this week," Perry said.

"Did you know," Ned said, enjoying a wave of pride for what he'd done, and all on his own, "that I pretended to be Withersea's agent in a juggle to gather funds for Aurora?"

"I perceive," Perry murmured, so close that his sweet breath tickled Ned's ears, "you will be magnificent every week hence. How shall we commence?"

"Can we go tomorrow to fetch our treasures locked up at that tavern? Likely Lazarus knows where we can hire a cart. We could also retrieve my painting kit at Touchstone's warehouse."

"Mr. Touchstone will be happy to find purchasers when you sell your pirate's stash."

"Sell?" Ned exclaimed, though he could hear Perry's teasing. "Most are priceless artifacts and antiquaries. I'd rather return to highway restorations than part with such treasures."

Perry caught Ned's sleeve, pulling it free of his coat sleeve. Glancing at the paint stain smeared there, Perry said, "Perhaps Touchstone will have more orders for a portrait painter with fine hands such as yours."

"Then I shall have all my heart has yearned for," Ned said, quietly enjoying that Perry used the same words as Absolom to describe his hands.

"I'm happy that you feel such comfort." Perry breathed on Ned's ears again. "But such a sham truth! I wager that your heart yearns after more than the treasures at the World's End."

He shut the door to their bedchamber, grabbing Ned by his shirt collar to drag him close, closer than they'd been for days.

"Aye. I must tell you, that I've yearned for," Ned was speaking right by Perry's lips, "and am comforted by your company."

"My company, eh? How comforted are you?"

"I mean, 'Come live with me and be my love.'" But then it wasn't possible to speak, to further clarify his meaning with words. He'd have to use his fine hands.

— TAMSIN —

TAMSIN AND TOM STARTED upstairs together. She said, "Mr. Mordaunt and I finished sifting your piles of papers just as the clock chimed ten. He intends to resume work after breakfast."

"You helped?" Tom cocked his head. He brightened.

"I came to Mordaunt's chambers to find you. Then had nothing to do while waiting. The barrister was working diligently, so I couldn't desert him until he dowsed the lamps and went home."

"What a lark! Who does he think you are?"

"Another Foxe cousin who can read Latin and write a fair hand. I told him as much in the Committee meeting." She stifled another yawn, tired deep in her bones.

He grasped her hand. "I can't express how indebted I am to you for all your help and kindnesses in this gambol."

"So, you are staying in London." She made it sound casual, though the notion of separating from him pierced her heart.

"Yes. Are you disappointed?" He looked way.

"No. And not surprised. It's what you've always wanted." She felt sadness lurking just out of her sight. "I'll miss you. Like I did when you went away to Trinity."

"Except I won't be walking home for Sunday dinner."

"I shall no longer worry over you like a mother hen. But, dear brother, do not undertake heroic adventures without me."

"Our restorations are better when we attack our enemies together. I'm happy to have learned that this week."

He set off down the hall, candle in hand.

"Tom?" she spoke low, not to disturb others in the house. "No more restorations, please. It's vastly fatiguing."

Inside her bedchamber, the only sound was Camilla's breathing, the only light a single candle on the washstand.

"Camilla? Are you awake?"

Tamsin kicked off her shoes, tossed aside the wretched periwig, peeled off that borrowed suit, jerked off the silk stockings, then dropped all her linen to the floor too. With extreme pleasure, she undid the bindings Camilla had tied in place at dawn.

The water in the washstand was warmer than the room. She used the soft linen cloth folded on the washstand to rinse off the fear and travail from her afternoon exercise, then another cloth to wash away paper dust wherever it had crawled under sleeves, neckcloth, and wig. The candle cast just enough light that she found a wooden comb on another table. It wasn't Camilla's, and Tamsin hadn't unpacked hers. She hesitated but found it to be new and unused. She combed out her hair, her locks springing to life after being trapped under a wig for hours upon hours.

Then Tamsin crawled into bed beside Camilla. Even with only a light linen covering, Camilla felt warmer than the room warranted. Tamsin, loathing the idea of leaving her side, rose to open a window. The latch was brass and well oiled, so the heavy window swung open easily. Back in bed, Tamsin matched her breathing with Camilla's, the cool night air drifting over her.

"No, I'm not awake," Camilla murmured. "I'm lost in a dream where you don't disappear for all day and half the night."

"I am sorry. And happy to be here now."

"Did you go to Rollo's fête? Is Starbuck in trouble for losing the marquess and only stopping Aurora?"

"Everything is fine. Starbuck is fine. Rollo too."

"And Lizzie?" Camilla asked. "She was wild for everyone to join Rollo so he wasn't alone at the fête."

"She's with Rollo. They aren't home yet."

"Do you think they are kissing?"

"Yes, I do." Tamsin considered how Lizzie and Rowland had looked at each other. She circled Camilla's ear, then whispered as she snuggled close. "I believe they've been kissing since Friday."

"Yes, lots of kissing. In private."

Camilla brushed her finger over Tamsin's lips. Tamsin shivered, despite the warmth of the room.

"When are we going back to Revelstone?" Camilla's words brushed Tamsin's neck, together with the summer zephyr coming through the window.

"You have legal business to finish on Monday. We'll know from that meeting when we're free to return home."

"Tuesday, perhaps?"

"Ah, my sweet nutting. You say the most pleasing things." Tamsin turned to lie on her side. She put her arm around the curve of Camilla's waist, despite the low heat glowing from her friend. "We shan't hurry to do anything until you're well again."

"Tell me what it will be like. Tell me how we shall be together, spending every ordinary day at Revelstone. Without adventures."

Tamsin closed her eyes, remembering what she'd been imagining in private moments. "We shall rise refreshed each morning, our sleep not troubled by dreams or filled with worries." Because they were no longer poor. Because she'd promised not to worry over Camilla and Tom. "We'll cast off our nightshifts and—"

"Soft wool in the winter," Camilla breathed softly. "Linen in the summer. I shall embroider a new shift for you once we are home together."

Home together. Tamsin drew a breath, filled with gratitude. Joy. They'd live peaceful, ordinary lives. Together.

"We'll dress for a working day, and eat bread hot from the ovens at breakfast, with cold butter and honey from the hives."

"In the quiet of the day," Camilla said, "I'll embroider by the light of the windows, while you read one of Absolom's books."

"I shall carry new books home with us. In Portugal Street, one shop has an edition of *Paradise Regained and Samson Agonistes.* Uncle Absolom had me read from it in his last days, but he'd borrowed it from Mr. Gamlingay, and so I've returned it. But now, it'd be a comfort to ponder the words that had entranced Absolom in his last days."

Camilla didn't answer, having returned to sleep. Which she mostly likely would any time that Tamsin read aloud on quiet afternoons at Revelstone. Else, Camilla would beg for a comedy, saying, "If you make me choose, then let it be *As You Like It*." Tamsin would always comply.

"I yielded, and unlocked her all my heart."

That was the last line she'd read to Absolom. What she'd read then was the opposite of the story which had unfolded this week. Yet that one line from the poem fit how she felt, listening to Camilla breathe in the dark. Yielding. Unlocked.

— ROLLO —

ROWLAND HAD LOST HIMSELF, his mind swamped in the rocking carriage, adrift in an eddy of images and sounds: waves dashing on sand, a wind high in the trees, the swirl of tall grass. All while learning what her tongue and lips were capable of while his thumb stroked her jaw.

During the extended shuffle inside the carriage, he heard the distinct sound of stitches tearing through silk.

"Alackaday!" Rowland sat up, startled. It was hard to speak, with his lips swollen and numb. "Are you hurt?"

"No," she whispered. "It's likely the skirt. Though there's no telling in the dark."

When had that carriage lamp been extinguished?

"Perhaps this is where it tore," she said, guiding his hand to find the slippery places where he'd repeatedly fingered her skirts. "The silk is now so creased, I'm afraid I've ruined this gown. If I can't repair it, I must reimburse your butler for the use of it."

"No fear." Rowland's lips still brushed near her ear. Her pins and ribbon had fallen from her hair. He had to navigate a great deal of hair to reach her ear. "It's my gown."

"Then it's you that I owe for ruining this gown?"

"No. I mean that it's from my new house. Both the duke and the butler assure me that the contents of the house are wholly mine to use." He pulled her closer and whispered in her ear. "I am in possession of a closet of well-made suits and another closet of gowns and shawls and daggers. If you intend to join me in spying for the king, I have all the accoutrements."

"You aren't teasing, are you, my lord?"

"You know me well enough to hear that I mean it. The duke entrapped me into doing what I swore that I no longer want to do. Then I found that it might suit me."

"I'm sure we can endure an arrangement with the duke."

"Then you meant it? You asked to serve as a watcher?"

"My arrangement began differently than it did with you," she said. "The duke thinks I'm extorting him, holding secrets over him. But shouldn't you and I do what we know best?"

"To serve as the king's watchers?"

"No, my lord. To serve as watchers to help people, like Tom did. The king and your duke can think we serve them. But you and I know in our hearts that Absolom formed us to serve people, not royal figureheads."

"I don't know how we shall play this, Lizzie." He brushed her swollen lips with his thumb, then kissed her again.

"I like the idea of staying in London," Lizzie said. "I didn't enjoy last winter at Revelstone. Do not tell Tamsin, but Cambridge country life does not suit me."

"I'm sure she knows. You can live at my house. I believe the household staff will accept anything I ask."

"No, not until we're married. I'll stay at Chalgrove House."

"I intend to ask the king to give us leave to marry, as our ancestors promised earlier kings that we would."

"I wish you'd forego that custom," Lizzie said. "James has been a slavemonger most of his life. I don't want to be beholden to him."

"I'm beholden to him for the Marborne title."

"I prefer it be nothing more than that." She brushed his lips and changed the subject. "'I long for the day when you and I fight for justice and endure danger together.'"

"Which poet wrote such glorious lines?" He kissed her again, so it was several moments before she replied.

"Me. I wrote them. But, Rollo, I'm not a zealot for King James. I don't care for him enough to risk danger."

"Did Absolom teach you lessons different from those I was taught? We don't undertake service for a particular man." He stroked the lace that crossed the embroidered stomacher over the rose gown, which didn't help him with rational thought.

"What then, Rollo?"

"We want peace in England. No sham trials, no deposed leaders, no burned priests of any kind, no bloody civil wars that starve people and destroy their lives and villages."

"Oh." She relaxed into his arms, rubbing her fingers at the smooth bone buttons that closed his shirt, finding he wore silk, not linen. "Fine reasons to risk danger."

"'I do love nothing in the world so well as you.'"

— CORNELIUS —

CORNELIUS LEANED ON THE ship's railing long after he'd lost sight of his new friends, whom he'd quickly made and just as quickly lost. He took several deep breaths, controlling how he longed to weep. Then he regretted those deep breaths: He'd never liked the stink of the wharves, being an Oxford boy from a different part of the river.

His heart felt as if it had been sliced open and emptied, as if finding one's purse cut and purloined. He had, after all, lost everything he'd worked for these many years.

The silver he'd spent years collecting and preserving, coin honestly earned from his divinely inspired elixirs.

His pamphlet business, which had done so much to raise up penurious boys like he'd once been.

The vast efforts he'd made as a humble servant to lords who sought more equitable distribution of land, so that the king's greed did not control all land in England.

Worse, he'd lost his beloved wife, with no time to recover from that grief before he lost her house, the shelter that had consoled him with moment-by-moment reminders of her grace, her love of beauty, the elegance of her sweet soul.

Now he had to give up two consoling dreams. First, because he'd made the wrong alliances in recent years, he'd never be made a Knight Bachelor. They didn't have those in the colonies, did they? Second, he had to give up the dream of leaving England for civilized life on the Continent. Again, a dream lost because of the bad alliances he'd made.

He had to find new dreams now. The New World, many said, was where people with a sense for business could manifest what the Divine Creator intended to show the world: that busy disciples are always shown divine grace. And what had old Fowlmere taught him? A sense for business.

Eons ago, Cornelius had claimed to be headed for the New World. He and Merryboy begged as motherless half-orphans for fare to find their father in the Americas. When the constable asked, Cornelius claimed their father was in Virginia, but Merryboy said Maryland, which everyone knows is peopled by Catholics. That constable set them running out of Oxford.

No use standing here on the ship's deck and weeping for his losses, observed by half-naked deck hands. He grasped the rail as the ship plowed through the Thames, pushing his past life into the growing distance. Then, as the ship made its way to the center of the river, sailing to the east and escaping the foul city, he inhaled a sweet breath of the wild Thames in summer.

"Do you think we shall ever see England again?" asked the woman beside him. Tears at the edge of her eyelashes showed her also to be deep in the emotions provoked by departure.

"Doesn't every soul ask that when sailing to the colonies?" Cornelius answered, in his best comforter's voice. "Only a hedgebird flying from sin could say farewell without tears."

"You speak wisely, sir. I'm Pleasance Green, from Sussex."

"I am Cornelius...um..." He coughed. "Knatchgull of Oxfordshire. Is it Miss Green? Or mistress?"

"I was Mistress Green for most of my life, but my dear mister is in the Burwash churchyard now."

"You have my deepest condolences, madam."

"You are kind to say so, Mr. Knatchgull. Though it's two years now this Christmas. I should be done with tears."

"I too lost my beloved not so long ago. I do not begrudge that our Creator holds her in His arms. It's just so—"

"Lonely," she said. "So I'm joining my son in Virginia."

"You are lucky to have a son, madam."

"Yes, I am. But he's been a sickling his entire life. I never should have agreed to him going to the New World with my brother." Her voice trembled. "Now my brother is in the ground in a far-off place. I am sailing to settle his affairs and take possession of his farm, while praying that my son is well."

"How brave you are," Cornelius said. "I will keep you and your son in my prayers."

"What do you sail to the colonies to find?"

"I intend Virginia, too," he said. "Several from my village have found a new life there, and they write that they have too few men who can help with the curing of souls."

"You are a man of God?" she asked. "For the Church of England? You won't look askance at me, I hope, but since I lost my man, I've come to follow the Dissenters."

"How now, madam! What a curious coincidence. That's what many in England call me. And other men like me, we who look only to God and not a host of wealthy bishops to guide our souls along the path to heaven."

"I am blessed to have met you here, while we sail away from England. How will you serve in the colonies?"

"To tell you the truth…ach!" He chuckled. "Of course, I am bound to God to speak only truth. I searched my soul, and begged guidance from our Heavenly Father. I feel called to succor souls in the New World."

The evening was fading, the lights of London now behind them. A sailor lit a lamp high on the mast. Cornelius held out his elbow, offering her an escort, the way that good women like. "May I help you to your quarters?"

"It's only steerage," she said. "Where blankets and baggage make our walls."

"I chose steerage," Cornelius said, "because the chandler insisted that anything else only enriches the captain without furthering comfort. May I invite you to share the fish supper my friends gave me for the first night at sea?"

Day 5, Saturday:
Out of this Nettle

If I were a woman, I would kiss as many
of you as had beards that pleased me,
complexions that liked me,
and breaths that I defied not...
— William Shakespeare, *As You Like It*

—

Out of this nettle, danger,
we pluck this flower, safety.
— William Shakespeare, *Henry IV, Part I*

60

Let Me Hear Thee Going

— TAMSIN —

COME SATURDAY MORNING, TAMSIN and Camilla walked together to Cheapside, seeking a goldsmith. They had the name from Felicity, whose aunt sent her with a brooch to this man for cleaning, "because he was the best in London." They had Rowland's page, Peter, along with them. Lazarus had somehow impressed upon them that they shouldn't go on the streets without a page or maidservant, for Lord Marborne's sake.

"How can I help you, ladies?" The goldsmith was a chubby, affable person. Tamsin and Camilla introduced themselves.

"We are seeking a set of mourning rings," Tamsin said. "I…my cousins recently lost a cherished uncle. I'd like to create a memorial for him."

"I am so sorry for your loss," the man said. "Let me show you what you might like."

He showed several rings while chatting politely. "It's a wise choice, though only just coming into style in England."

Most were too ornate for Absolom. And too expensive, especially given how shy Tamsin felt about spending her new money in this way. At last, though, she chose a design with faceted rock crystal over Absolom Caius Foxe's initials: A.C.F. Each ring was to be gold with an enameled black vine twining it.

"Do you wish an engraving?" the goldsmith asked, then explained what that extra cost would be.

"Yes," Tamsin said. "It should be, 'Keep his memory.' Shall I write it for you, so there is no mistake?"

"Indeed, madam." The goldsmith handed over a quill, ink, and paper. "How many rings do you desire?"

Tamsin had a hand behind her back, counting off everyone's name. Rollo, Tom, Ned, Lizzie, of course. And Camilla and Winwood had sat beside Absolom throughout his illness. Perry had never met their uncle, but had risked everything the previous week, seeking justice for Absolom. Also, Reverend Gamlingay, who'd been Absolom's closest friend. Mrs. Bell, who'd managed Revelstone House for three decades. And one for her own.

"Ten," Tamsin said.

The goldsmith wrote out the order. Restraining her surprise at the total cost, Tamsin wrote a banker's draft for half the cost, the rest to be paid upon delivery.

"Send them to my cousin's house. The butler will have your final payment." Tamsin wrote Rowland's name and address.

"Please allow me ten days," the goldsmith said, then offered a warm farewell.

Tamsin walked with Camilla to Covent Garden, saying, "We won't be the first to see them, because we'll be at Revelstone."

— NED —

PERRY HAD THEM BOTH up at what felt to be an ungodly hour.

"I haven't slept an entire night since…" Ned paused to think. "Monday. I've been running over half of England for Tom's sake, or waiting for Rowland to do all the things it takes to be a lord."

"I'd rather kip until noon myself," Perry said. "But I promised John Coachman a look at servants for Aurora. Do you suppose in London we should call her Lady Withersea, like we have good manners?"

"I rather think she never wants to hear 'Withersea' again."

They hauled the two Frake brothers up from the servants' quarters, then met with John and Gabriel at a handsome dwelling in Covent Garden called Chalgrove House. Their destination, as it turned out, lay on the same street they'd taken on Tuesday, that is, to Perry's mother's house.

Perry dragged his brothers inside but made the other three men wait on the curb. "A woman does not want to be taken by surprise over her breakfast."

Once Perry was gone, John said, "You've met her, Mr. Wijck. What is Mother Frake like? Will she do for the marchioness?"

"The Frake boys are good fellows," Gabriel said. "I'd take them into the house in a heartbeat."

"Too bad it's only boys in that house," John said. "Our new house and kitchen need at least two maids. And the marchioness needs a lady's maid. She says not, but it's different in the city than the country life she's used to."

"What about Miss Foxe?" Gabriel asked. "She's to live there as our lady's companion. Does she need a lady's maid?"

Ned could confess that he'd never once in his life given the idea a moment's consideration. He settled for the convenient, "I suppose you'll have to ask Miss Foxe."

Though it had better be after Ned could ask Lizzie when she'd decided to take up housekeeping with Aurora.

Mother Frake waved at them with her apron. She had three younger sons lurking curiously behind her. Her massive oldest son embraced the diminutive woman who barely reached Perry's waist. Ned was struck by her quick, bird-like motions and bright eyes. Feathery white locks framed her face. "Come in. I just took scones off the hearth. And I have a bit of butter from how generous Peregrine has been with his shillings."

They ate scones. They drank an infusion that, for all Ned knew, was harvested from the tiny garden in back.

This day, Mother Frake wasn't stern with Perry at all, not begging him to take up his lot for the family. John Coachman liked her and engaged her to consider Perry's suggestion.

"I'm a baker, not a true cook. And I've got boys to care for."

"I believe, madam, that they will all take employment too."

"Ach, no," Perry said, putting Ned again on guard. "Neriah is to serve the Earl of Cloudesley at Xanthus House. Rowland must keep him on. He hasn't got enough staff for all of us there."

"Take more of this honey for your scone, Mr. Coachman." She pushed the small jar to him.

It was quite a small jar in a very small house, which indicated scant honey in the cupboard. John seemed to notice, and he took another dollop of honey with a sleight of hand, no real honey added to his scone. He said, "If the terms are to your liking, we shall arrange for your removal to Chalgrove House."

The terms were to Ned's liking. Mother Frake and her sons were to be well provided for, with an excellent employer. In London. Not Revelstone.

"We shan't have to milk cows and muck stables," Daniel was saying as they left Mother Frake's cottage.

"We'll be safer in the city," Neriah said. "Away from wild animals and brigands."

"The country isn't dangerous," Perry said, still teasing his brothers. "I've a mind to choose one of you as a manservant. I'll need such, with all the worldly wealth I have risen to."

But Ned recognized brotherly mischief, not an argument. He had no care in that business and was instead sketching in his mind's eyes the homely scene before Mother Frake's hearth with its rough-hewn table and chunky stools.

Perry and his two older brothers made the journey with Ned to the World's End, where they packed up the bounties of the week's restoration. The next stop was Touchstone's, where Ned fetched his trappings and that unfinished canvas with Jacob and Pip. He'd already found the room with the best light in Rowland's house. It was right up under the eaves, where Rowland had stashed that odd Mr. Rosewurme for a night.

Good light. Out of the way. That garret under the eaves offered all he lacked for happiness in London. He felt like singing, like that swarm of men had been singing in The Rose on Tuesday.

> Come live with me and be my love,
> And we will all the pleasures prove

"Well done, Mr. Wijck." Perry clapped a hand on his shoulder, pulled him close to his side. "We'll make a singer of you yet. Just let the song swell within your heart-cage, then it will burst forth into the world."

— LIZZIE —

LIZZIE WAYLAID MICHEL WHEN he returned to the house and explained the proposal.

"It's straightforward," Lizzie said. "We hire a carriage directly, go to Knightsbridge, and fetch back what we can of Aurora's clothes and books. If we go now, we can do it before the king's men seize everything."

As quick as they were at starting out (slowed down because Aurora insisted on joining them), they found red-coated militiamen loading wagons when they arrived.

Unlike her usual self, Aurora wanted to pass by, giving up the endeavor rather than engaging with the king's men. Lizzie, however, recognized Captain Starbuck and alighted from the carriage, boldly approaching him with a cheery good morning. "Well met," she said. "It appears you have a task similar to our own."

"To search and seize?" Starbuck returned her bright smile. "And seal it under the king's command?"

"Similar, but not the same. If I might importune—"

"Like Rollo did yesterday? And then Tom?" He shook his head. "Unlike Rollo, I intend to keep my commission."

"And yet."

When Lizzie said it, Starbuck looked to heaven, sighing. "My men are loading wagons to carry evidence to the Exchequer. It's better, Miss Foxe, that we not speak, if I'm ever called to swear to how faithfully I've performed this task."

"It's only a philosophical question I have," Lizzie said. "Do women's gowns and small clothes or an armful of Greek texts add to the king's wealth? Or his sense of safety from rebels? May I persuade you that we can assist with resolving these philosophical questions?"

He again shook his head. "I am writing the inventory. Please point to what should be loaded onto any particular wagon."

"Or carriage?"

He didn't answer, busy upbraiding a militiaman, instructing him to repack a crate of crystalware, while Lizzie was motioning for Aurora and Michel to join her.

It was, therefore a quietly busy morning. Lizzie enjoyed her first foray into leading a restoration that, coincidentally, saved the king from bothering to seize a few items that the exchequer would not find valuable.

Later, Aurora proposed inviting Captain Starbuck to Sunday dinner, but Lizzie argued that it might be too easily misconstrued as an attempt to corrupt the king's officer.

They went home then, to meet the staff that John Coachman had found to revive Baroness Rôche's house. After introductions were done, Lizzie faded from the household crowd and had Gabriel call a chair so that she might see Rowland, regretting the six hours since she last saw him.

— ROLLO —

INTENDING INDOLENCE, ROWLAND STAYED in bed with nothing to do until he met Lizzie at midday. He'd read her letter; in fact, he'd fallen asleep clutching it in his hand.

Lazing in soft linen sheets, he considered, rather idly, the questions that had remained unanswered the previous night. Tom had found a magistrate to give him a warrant, who'd hoped to ingratiate himself with the king, since he'd declined to participate in the assizes that the king called to deal with the traitors who supported Monmouth. The king loved his new assizes, yet the duke and the king obviously didn't want the betraying marquess sent to the same assizes. What secrets did the marquess hold which that lofty pair didn't want revealed?

Perhaps those secrets didn't matter, since the marquess was permanently gone from England. Yet it provoked Rowland's curiosity. It could be worthwhile for a watcher to learn such secrets. With no answers, he let his thoughts drift instead to whether he'd done all he'd set out to do when he first came to this house. Some had been resolved in Tom's chaotic gambol. What still lay ahead: taking up burdens for Marborne by becoming a reaper of justice on a grand scale. Tom had led him into the first such act. Now, as the king's watcher, he could discover great sinners in England.

Days ago, Rowland's key worry had been whether Bagsham would drag him into the kind of corruption that Absolom had helped him avoid. Since then, he'd learned to make compromises while gaining what his family and Marborne most needed.

And by fortuitous coincidence, he'd avoided being snatched by rogues and sent to distant and foreign climes.

Rowland sat up suddenly, sending Lizzie's letter falling to the floor. What had the Rosewurme fellow said, just before the marquess released chaos in the Committee meeting? *He intends the same fate for your lordship as he set for Viscount Bravewood... Canton. Or Surat. Bombay...Places where there's no Christians.*

Why hadn't he remembered when Tamsin told her story? The rush of yesterday's excitement was no excuse. What to do now? Neither Withersea nor Rosewurme were available to ask if Bravewood was alive. The duke? Rowland couldn't ask the man without revealing Tamsin's falsehoods.

Lazarus knocked on the door, entering with a tray. Hot rolls. Chocolate in cream, Paris style. A glimmering apple galette.

Rowland managed a greeting before he blurted, "Was Lord Bravewood recovered from the Sedgemoor field after the battle?"

"Aye, my lord. He was buried with his forebearers at the Bravewood estate."

"Was his grace the duke there?"

"Indeed. And he gave us all a free day to attend. A great kindness. We appreciated our service under the viscount."

Rowland couldn't ask more of Lazarus. *Who saw Bravewood in the casket? Who knows for sure?*

"Would you care for assistance, my lord, with shaving?"

"After breakfast, if it's no bother."

He noticed immediately that he'd embarrassed Lazarus. That wasn't what he was supposed to say. He had to learn to confine his responses to yes and no. When Lazarus departed, Rowland sat at the table to sip chocolate and cream, finding a note on the tray, folded and letterlocked.

Your lordship: My brother Michel is staying in London. He says that you need a secretary and I need protection. He has also persuaded our cousin Aurora to abide in my house, though he didn't ask me first. However, it will be a blessing to the memory of our aunt.

Cousin Aurora thinks the king will be watching her, so Michel says it's best, and I must agree, that we place in your hands our *objet de guerre*. That way, my house will never be suspect. And who would suspect you?

We shall visit when it's needed for our familial duties. Perhaps you can teach some of Mr. Frake's too many brothers to work it. They most certainly cannot all stay here. The house has already become a circus, like the New Spring Gardens on a holiday. —Felicity Oakes

"Lazarus!"

Rowland leaped into a shirt and breeches, stepped over last night's stockings and shoes, and bounded down the stairs. He found Lazarus in the servants' quarters below, where the four roustabouts from the theatre were reassembling the printing press in an empty servant's room.

"God blind me!" Dismay racketed through Rowland as far as his toes. "I'm sorry, Lazarus, for the disruption." He tapped one of the giants on the shoulder. "Stop what you're doing. This can't remain here. You'll have to take it away."

"It's not a bother to the house," Lazarus said. "There's adequate space here, my lord, as long as you don't call the grooms and horses back from the country estate."

"Our maestro forbids it from being kept in the theatre's warehouse," one of the giants said. "Wanted it out before the noon bells strike."

"Leave it." Rowland threw up his hands. "I'll..."

But the roustabouts were already up the stairs and on their way out of the house.

I'll learn to compromise, I suppose.

Lazarus said, "I was on my way to inform you, my lord, that there's a man waiting in the rose salon who has an eleven o'clock appointment."

"How? No one knows I'm here except the duke, and he—"

"He came from Lord Bagsham's staff, on an engagement you formed Wednesday, to come today for lessons in swordplay."

There, Rowland had done it to himself. He had put off to another day that which he didn't want to do at all.

"Where shall we—" He stopped, feeling overwhelmed by the notion of being stuck as Lord Bagsham's spying creature.

Lazarus said, "I warrant the unused laundry gallery at the top of the house will do for such exercise. We keep the steel and practice blades there."

Rowland stood unshaved and unshod in a knot of curious servants, his bare feet stuck to the freezing cellar tiles, his shirt open, his breeches unfastened, his hair uncombed and hanging down his shoulders like a debauched fuddle-cap. And he'd just been philosophizing on his plan to be Marborne's reaper of justice.

"I'd best fetch my shoes." He started up the stairs. "Oh, Lazarus. Miss Foxe is coming for luncheon. Might we have a private meal together?"

"I'll set luncheon in the blue salon. No need to have a care for that." Lazarus gestured and the onlookers scattered.

Mrs. Flurry remained, though. "Your pardon, my lord, but have you had sufficient sustenance to undertake such travail? Won't you step into the kitchen for a cat's whisker of time, so I can be sure you're fortified?"

"Thank you, Mrs. Flurry. I..."

"I have good honey bread with Holland carraway just from the oven. And I advise a pair of hen's eggs. You look to be in need of fortifying victuals, if you don't mind my saying so. This kitchen is happy to have the care of you, my lord. Do you like a coddled egg? That's quickest."

He hadn't had anyone offer to take care of him since...time out of mind. "Perhaps I'd best be guided by you, Mrs. Flurry."

— T O M —

TOM ROSE EARLY ON Saturday and went to his new place of work, where he met the barrister who was master of the chambers. They worked side by side for a good twelve hours, occasionally calling out for assistance to the other clerks, who seldom saw Mr. Mordaunt on a Saturday.

"You've put us all on the right with King James," Mordaunt said at one point, looking up from a sea of documents.

"That wasn't a goal," Tom said. "But it's good for Marborne."

"Your family are royalists?"

"My forefathers were, before and after the wars. Life here in England could be better, but Cromwell proved there's worse ways to rule a nation. I suspect that sometime not far into the future, history will find better."

Beside such small exchanges, the two men enjoyed only one interruption of their work. A trio of militiamen appeared, calling for Tom. His heart thumped, though he considered himself free of any criminal activity that could be identified under English law.

It proved all they wanted to do was restore that Lely sketch to the Earl of Cloudesley, because it was excluded in the warrant for the Marquess of Withersea's London house. Tom signed the receipt as Jacob's guardian.

After that interval, they sent Mr. Newton out to bring midday sustenance, then continued their work while munching manchet bread and Cheshire cheese.

At one point, Mr. Mordaunt said, "Do you have plans for the list of investors Withersea called Hawkins' Heirs. I so regret being beguiled into that scheme."

"We'll wind up that business with the rest of his syndicates."

"You won't," Mordaunt paused, "expose the members?"

"I have no plans for it now," Tom said. "Rowland did what he wanted with it. Can you dissolve the legal contract?"

"The investors will want their money back."

"They'll have to beg the king," Tom said. "He'll be holding all of Withersea's funds."

"I doubt that any will choose to be so bold." The quill in Mordaunt's hand quivered. "I would not dare it."

When they put their papers aside at the end of the day, Tom said, "Farewell until Monday? Or shall I come with my cousins to take the sermon in your church on Sunday? I should like to see your sons again. Perhaps I can introduce the Earl of Cloudesley."

"I...I...ah, yes, Mr. Foxe." Mordaunt didn't like being boxed in by such a request. Then he shrugged. "That would be grand."

Tom walked to Xanthus House, bearing a new red ball he'd bought from a stall on Fleet Street. He and Jacob tossed the ball to Pip and each other in the garden until the gloaming dimmed and it became so dark that Neriah brought a lantern to guide them inside. It had been decided, some time the night before, that Neriah would stay at Xanthus House as Jacob's valet.

Under candlelight in the rose salon, Tom unrolled the Lely sketch. After Jacob studied it and chose where it should hang in his bedchamber, he drank the warm milk that Neriah brought.

Jacob said, "Neriah says my bed is safe."

"Is it?" Tom said.

Neriah said, "We both looked under Jacob's bed to be sure there's nothing to fear."

"It's a good house. No one shouts," Jacob said.

After the warm milk, Neriah walked with Jacob and Pip up to his new bedchamber, promising to sleep in a trundle bed there, so that Pip wouldn't be frightened in the new house.

When the house seemed quiet, Tom slipped and walked to Chalgrove House, intent on reassuring Aurora about Jacob's well-being. They traded news, including the day's adventure to retrieve Jacob's and Aurora's clothes and books. They enjoyed a glass of wine—only one glass, since Tom had promised to observe Winwood's strictures, though Winwood now lived at his cousins' house, instead of being lodged every day with Tom.

"You have been heroic," Aurora said. "You deserve a hero's reward. Laurels. Accolades."

"I'm happy with Jacob's safety and his friendship."

"That's too modest, Tom. Consider all you've done."

"I've done what I should." He counted each item, in terms of Absolom's rules. "I kept my promises, to Jacob and my family. I used my talents to help others. The world is improved, at least in a modest way, from my toil."

He omitted any claim to observing the last rule. *I never fool an honest man.* He hadn't, after all, been thoroughly frank when he begged Sir Oliver for those warrants.

"I've been musing all day on my own changes," Aurora said. "This is the first week since Trinity, that I haven't felt a bell of loneliness tolling deep inside."

"Perhaps I feel the same. Though I have no business indulging any sense of loneliness. I have my family and good friends."

"It's probably a character fault," she said, "to carry a sense of loneliness with people all around."

She came near him, whispering in Greek. He thought it meant, "I'm so happy we are friends."

He reached to touch her shoulder, the kind of reassurance friends share, but in the dim light, he instead touched her neck. Just when she touched his. Sharing that touch, he came fully alive, sensations ravaging his exhausted body: His nose overwhelmed by scents of lavender and angelica and mint; his soul thrilled by the silky feel of almond oil at his fingertips; his ears buzzing with the sounds of a most precious being, breathless in the dark. The taste of mint in her mouth and scent of lavender in her hair overcame the last of any bitterness lingering after so much time supping from his restorative elixir.

He knew exactly what came next, because, like Odysseus the Cunning, he'd sailed home.

— E N D —

A Casual Glossary for the Curious

altitudes (in the): Drunk.

amanuensis: A skilled assistant who copies manuscripts, takes dictation, or writes letters.

anticks: Old stone images, like those collected by an antiquary who dotes on ancient relics.

arrack: A rum-like liquor, distilled from rice and, often, molasses. Not the more modern licorice-flavored liquor.

arsworm: A diminutive person (and an insult, obviously).

Aspirat primo fortuna labori: Fortune smiles on this first effort.

baldric: An over-the-shoulder belt to carry a knife or a sword.

barrister: A lawyer who advocates for patrons in higher courts.

berk: A doltish fellow.

Bess of Bedlam: From a Henry Purcell song, popular and widely printed from about 1683.

Billingsgate: 1) Adjective: Vulgar language; called after the habits of merchants in a London fish market. 2) Noun: Docks that grew in east London when merchant ships became too large to pass under London Bridge.

black tribute: An archaic term for what's now called blackmail.

blether: Talk nonsense.

blockish: Stupid.

bodkins: A minced oath; God's body.

bog-eyed: Half asleep.

"Bold knaves thrive without one grain of sense…": From John Dryden, *Epilogue to Constantine the Great* (a play).

bon sang: Good grief.

borachio: A drunkard.

bram cove: A strong rogue.

branleur: Wanker.

bubukles: A pimple.

bugbear: A dog.

buttery: A cellar or other cool space for storing provisions.

by Gemini: An oath first recorded in William Congreve's work, but for imagination's sake, let us say it was rattling around the theatre before he wrote it down.

ça me fait chier: That pisses me off.

ça me saoûle: That annoys me (literally, "it gets me drunk").

cacafuego: A fiery fellow.

cadger: A fellow who gets that which he is not strictly entitled to.

Canary sack: Sherry from the Canary Islands.

Captain Sharp: An enormous cheater.

Captain Hackum: An eager fighting fellow.

carissime: My dearest friend (Latin).

carl: A man of low birth.

carrot-pated: A redhead.

c'est naze: It sucks.

ceteris paribus: All things being the same.

chafe: Fret.

chancery courts: In earlier English court systems, these courts (presided over by the Lord Chancellor) had authority over trusts, land law, lunatics' estates, and guardianship.

charm of foxes: A collective noun.

Charybdis and Scylla: Sea monsters who beset a narrow strait where Odysseus sailed.

chittifaced: A puny child.

chuck; chucking: Dialect for chick, as a term of endearment.

chuffing: Boorish; a churl.

churl: An archaic term for a person of low birth.

clodpate: A dull fellow.

cobweb cheat: Easily found out.

coleus: Bollocks.

compeer: A companion or close associate.

contumely: Insulting language.

Covent Garden Theatre; the King's Theatre: Called the Theatre Royal in later decades.

cow-handed: Awkward.

crimp: To trap into sea service.
crimping fellow: A sneak.
crinkum-crankum: Elaborate decoration or detail.
Crivens: A minced oath; Christ in heaven.
crop sick: Sick in the stomach.
crowbait: An old horse.
cully: A friend.
dab: An expert at roguery.
dearworthy: Dearly loved.
deft fellow: Someone who's tidy, neat.
dégage: Clear off (a command).
devil drawer: A painter of forgeries.
Dick Whittington: A fourteenth century mayor of London. Folklore (and then plays, ballads, and fiction) tells a rags-to-riches story of a poor man who grew wealthy by selling his cat as a rat catcher.
dockwalloper: A casual laborer.
donna con donna: Woman with woman.
dot: A dowry from which the husband can draw only an annual income. The principal remains the wife's property.
ebullition: A bubbling eruption of emotion.
factor: A business agent.
"Fall on me like a silent dew...": Robert Herrick, *To Music, to becalm his Fever.*
farrago: A muddle.
faugh: An interjection, indicating disgust.
fauntkin: "Little child," an endearment.
fibble-fabble: Nonsense; obsolete, but may be precursor for "fib."
fillip: A nickname for a liquor-and-citrus punch.
fizgig: A silly or flirtatious woman.
flux: Diarrhea or dysentery.
footpad: A highwayman without a horse.
forfend: Avert or prevent something evil or unpleasant.
fuddle-cap: A drunkard.
Game of Cupid: A board game, from Spain; a bit like Snakes and Ladders. On a sixteenth century Flemish game board, the rules included these notes: "Love guised as a snake sneaks into the heart of those who possess it, and poisons them with its venom, and

for several other attractive reasons, which the lack of space on this piece of paper does not allow to explain here."

Ganymede: Seventeenth century cant for homosexual; after the myth of a Trojan youth so beautiful that Zeus carried him off to be the cupbearer on Olympus.

genever: A Dutch liqueur; originally a medicine with juniper berries to mask the taste.

"Giddy Fortune's furious fickle wheel": From Shakespeare's *Henry V*.

gilflurt: A vain, posh woman.

gingamobs: Testicles.

glimflashy: In a passion.

God's hooks: A minced oath, a precursor to gadzooks; the nails on the Cross.

good lack: An interjection, like "oh my."

goose-cap: Fool.

gutfoundered: Starving hungry.

hackbut: An archaic firearm with a long barrel; from the Dutch, harquebus.

Hawkins' Heirs: A fictional syndicate in this story; the Elizabethan Admiral Sir John Hawkins of Plymouth is often deemed to be "the pioneer of the English slave trade."

hedge-bird: A scoundrel.

heigh: An interjection indicating surprise.

hell-bound: Profligate.

hen-hearted: Coward.

"Her white arms round him pressed as though forever": From Robert Fitzgerald's translation of *The Odyssey*.

herbary: An herb garden.

hobbledygee: A pace between a walk and run, a trot.

hoddy doddy: A small clumsy fellow.

howbeit: Nevertheless.

hoy: An exclamation to attract attention; similar to "hey."

"I have lived long enough": Lines from Shakespeare's *Macbeth*, from a scene just before the final battle.

inamorata: A female lover.

infelicitas: Misfortune.

ita quidem: Yes indeed.

"I yielded, and unlocked her all my heart": From John Milton's *Samson Agonistes* (when Samson reveals how he lost his power).

ja: Yes.

John Chump: blockhead.

justacorps: A knee-length men's coat with wide skirts, worn with a long waistcoat; a French fashion made popular by Charles II and widely worn until the frock coat overtook men's fashion in the mid-eighteenth century.

kinder: Children.

king's touch: A laying on of hands practiced by French and English monarchs, who touched their subjects to cure them of various diseases, most often the form of tuberculous called scrofula.

Knight Bachelor: The lowest rank of knighthood in the British system.

knights of the post: A mercenary.

la foudre de Dieu: God's lightning.

lambkin: A term of endearment.

larcener: Thief.

leading strings: Straps of fabric attached to a child's clothing, to keep the child from straying or falling while learning to walk.

leech: A doctor (because they used leeches to bleed their patients).

letterlock: Folding and securing a written letter without an envelope.

lief: As happily; as gladly.

linsey-woolsey: A coarse fabric with a linen warp and woolen weft.

lob-cock: A heavy, dull man.

loiter-sack: A lazy, worthless idler.

long-headed: A person of good judgment.

mad as a roasted cat: Insane.

majolica: Anglicized spelling for tin-glazed pottery, typically from Spain or Majorca.

malapert: Impudent; presumptuous.

maneuvering the apostles: Robbing St Peter to pay St Paul.

mantelet: A short sleeveless coat or shawl.

marchpane: A marzipan-like sweet of ground almonds and sugar, usually including rosewater.

marquess; marchioness: A marquis and his wife; in British nobility, above an earl and below a duke in status.

Martin Mar-All: A spoilsport, after the title character in a John Dryden comedy.

martinet: A taskmaster who insists on strict discipline.

mayhap: Perhaps.

Merry Andrew: "A buffoon; a zany; a jack-pudding" (per Samuel Johnson's dictionary).

Michaelmas: September 29; Feast of Michael and All Angels.

mifty: Inclined to be out of humor.

milk a pigeon: Try and do the impossible.

minium: An oxide mineral, also known as red lead, used in paintings until replaced by cheaper New World sources for red pigment.

mirabile dictu: Wonderful to tell.

mithering: Annoying.

mudlarks: Scavengers on the Thames tide flats.

muff pistol: A small flintlock pistol, so called because a woman could conceal it in her hand muff.

natural: A person born with intellectual disabilities.

New Spring Gardens: Later, Vauxhall Gardens.

nick-ninny: A simpleton.

nowt: Nothing.

odds bodkins: A minced oath; God's body.

odsme: A minced oath; God smite me.

odspitikins: A minced oath; God's pity.

Original: An eccentric individualist.

"Pains of love be sweeter far": From John Dryden's poem, "Ah, How Sweet It Is to Love!"

pandjesbaas: Pawnbroker.

paysan: A peasant (from the French).

pensioner (at Cambridge): Undergraduates whose wealthy families paid tuition and board, and who often used the university more like a finishing school, avoiding their inferiors among sizars and scholars.

perambulation: To walk around in a leisurely way.

peregrinate: To travel or wander from place to place.

peterman: A thief.

phanatic: A dissenter from the Church of England.

pharo: Early term for a card game that rose as pharaon in Paris in the late seventeenth century, then swept England as faro in the eighteenth century.

physick: A medical or drug treatment.

picaro, picaroon: A scoundrel, a rogue.

plumbago: Graphite. Pencils don't contain actual lead, even in the seventeenth century.

poacher's cheese: A hard cow's milk cheese.

Portugal Street: Named after the homeland of Henrietta Maria, wife of Charles II. Now, Piccadilly.

potation: A beverage.

pounce: A fine powder used to keep ink from spreading on paper.

prithee: please

progress: A tour. Cornelius is alluding to the tours, called progresses, that Elizabeth I took of her country.

prorogate [Parliament]: To discontinue meetings without dissolving the body.

pudding-headed fellow: A total idiot.

punk, punk box: Crumbly, decayed wood used as tinder, plus the box in which it is stored.

Qu'est-ce que tu fais à Hadès ici: What in Hades are you doing here?

rampallian: A scoundrel; an ad hominin that Falstaff uses in Shakespeare's *Henry IV, Part 2.*

rara avis: A rare bird; an oddity.

Ravenscroft's crystal: A lead glass, created by George Ravenscroft, that was less breakable than Murano *cristallo.*

reave: An archaic terms for carrying out a plundering raid.

rover: A pirate.

running smobble: A snatch-and-grab raid on a store or hawker.

sabot: When used as an insult, a dull-witted person, called after a French wooden shoe.

sanguinary: Involving or causing much bloodshed.

sarding: Medieval precursor to the phrase "sod off."

scarlatina: Scarlet fever, a formerly virulent upper respiratory bacterial infection, now treated with antibiotics.

scholar (at Cambridge): A student usually chosen from among the sizars; freed from serving chores; most obtained degrees.

scrag: Neck.

settle: A high-backed wooden bench with arms.

sexton's spade: In this era, the sexton was often the gravedigger.

shiver-the-wink: A rascal.

sizar (at Cambridge): A poor university student who does chores for Fellows and Masters for the chance to study for a degree.

skulk: A group of foxes or any animal considered vermin.

sluice [one's] gob: To take a big swig of a drink.

sly boots: A mischievous, engaging person.

snicket: An alleyway.

sooth: Actually; "in sooth."

stomacher: A decorative piece of cloth worn over a woman's chest, to close the gown and present an elongated waist.

swede-and-gammon: Rutabagas and ham.

s'welp me: A minced oath; "so help me God."

swingebeest: A swaggering fellow.

swiving: Archaic term for copulation.

taffety tart: A dainty version of an apple tart.

tatterdemallion: A man with his clothes in tatters.

"There's nowt so queer as folk": People do the strangest things.

"The scum that still rise upmost...": From *Don Sebastian* by John Dryden.

three-card loo: A variation of lanterloo, a trick-taking card game popular in the seventeenth century.

trespass: A sin or offence.

troth: Loyalty solemnly pledged.

turn [one] adrift: Keep from doing me harm.

understrapper: An inferior.

up in the boughs: In a ferment.

vero, vero: True, true.

videant semper: They always will.

villein: A feudal tenant who pays dues and owes service to a lord in return for land.

visitant: An archaic term for a visitor.

Walloon sword: A double-edged sword about thirty-six inches long, from francophone Belgians living in the Netherlands.

wamble: Sound of stomach rumbling.

watcher: An intelligencer.

whapper: A large person.

wherry: A light barge or a light rowboat that ferries passengers.

whiffle-whaffle: A time-wasting fellow.

whipperginnie: Cheeky young person.

wigeon: A kind of duck.

walloper: Short for dockwalloper; a casual laborer.

withal: Nevertheless.

wont: Accustomed.

Zeus Apemios: A name for Zeus as the healer of ills.

zooterkins: A minced oath; likely from "God's wounds."

Author's Notes

History versus Fiction

This is not a supplement to the history of the Restoration era. It's fiction about imaginary individuals. If you are in the U.S., it will not help you pass AP European History. If your secondary education was in the U.S. (and even if you passed AP World History), it's unlikely you read more than three pages about this period, most of which focused on the Great Fire, Samuel Pepys, and the extravagances of Charles II after everyone had had their fill of Oliver Cromwell and his Commonwealth. Some key historic events match "Milestones: The Foxes of Marborne Parish":

1642–51   Civil wars in England

1649   Execution of Charles I, the second Stuart king; Commonwealth and Interregnum

1660   Restoration of Charles II

1665   London plague and Great Fire

1673   Test Act, enforced on all persons holding office, "preventing dangers...from popish recusants"

1677   Marriage of Mary Stuart, presumed royal heir, to William of Orange, of the Low Countries

1685   Death of Charles II; Coronation of James II, third Stuart king; Monmouth Rebellion, led by James Fitzroy, Duke of Monmouth, Pretender to the Crown

Find a bit more through popular history sources such as:

Peter Ackroyd: *Rebellion: The History of England from James I to the Glorious Revolution.*

Ian Mortimer: *The Time Traveler's Guide to Restoration Britain*, who notes that the kingdom was not "Great Britain" until 1707.

Bibliographies in those references will lead you to deeper details about the Restoration and related historical periods.

—

People, Places, Things

Marborne parish is fictional. The Foxe and Rôche families are fictional, as are all the titled persons in this story.

Chancery Courts: Over most of its history, the Lord Chancellor sold offices of the chancery courts as sinecures for significant sums. Clerks and other officials did not receive wages. Instead, they levied fees to advance court cases; hence, the huge cost of bringing a case to the chancery courts. See, for example: genguide.co.uk/source/land-and-property-records-including-title-deeds/35/

Edward Whalley, William Goffe, and John Dixwell: Men condemned as regicides for signing the death warrant for Charles I, they fled to New England, escaping capture for years.

Estimating Costs and the Foxes' Wealth: From *Two Tracts*, by Gregory King. See: york.ac.uk/depts/maths/histstat/king.htm

Green Ribbon Club: An association of men hostile to Charles II, who met in coffeehouses and wore green badges to recognize each other in street brawls. See: "Green Ribbon Club" at wikisource.org/wiki/1911_Encyclopædia_Britannica

Guardian Bond: The document naming Tom as Jacob's guardian closely follows the example from "Guardianship Bonds in England and Wales" at: familysearch.org/wiki/en/

World's End: Samuel Pepys notes a visit to a Knightsbridge inn. It is not the tavern Edgar Wright and Simon Pegg made famous.

—

Literary References

Ajax—Aias Mastigophoros: In *The Iliad* and in Sophocles' play, Ajax is offended when Odysseus is given Achilles' armor. Athena intervenes to stop him from killing Odysseus. Humiliated, Ajax throws himself on his own sword. See:
archive.org/details/ajaxsoph00soph

Chapman's Translations: This story uses Chapman's texts because that is what Tom would have read in Absolom's chambers. Recent translations of *The Iliad* and *The Odyssey* are more accurate, and better all around.

"Come live with me and be my love": Perry's song lines, learned in a tavern, are from Christopher Marlowe.

"Our King is adored like a demigod...": Withersea plagiarized lines from an essay by John Milton. See:
google.com/books/edition/The_Works_Historical_Political_and
_Misce/4jlnaaaacaaj

"Monarchy, no creature of God's making...": Withersea also plagiarized from a pamphlet by John Cook. See:
quod.lib.umich.edu/e/eebo/A34420.0001.001

William Shakespeare: Rowland endeavors to quote lines from plays and sonnets with precision, but feels free to alter the Bard's lines when he must.

—

Acknowledgments

My profound thanks to Jacyn Stewart, Susan Urban, Laurie Cropp, Carol Buchmiller, and Martin Fossum for critical and editorial reading. Special thanks to Jane Dow for copyediting and to Ajax Bell for close developmental reading.

All the errors here? I made those without any assistance from others.

From Jugum Press